Praise for Alexey Pehov:

'An exciting take on classical themes . . . the story is engrossing, the characters intriguing and dynamic; there are mysteries galore and the very real sense as we set out that far creepier things are waiting down the road. In short, a book I didn't want to put down.'
    Chris Claremont, bestselling writer of the X-Men and Wolverine

'Toothy, gritty, and relentless. Alexey Pehov sneaks up on you and fascinates with the wry voice of a young Moorcock. Clear space on your shelf – you'll want the whole series.'
    E.E. Knight, bestselling author of the Vampire Earth series

'Shadow Prowler is a fresh, exuberant take on territory that will be familiar to all fans of classic high fantasy. Alexey Pehov introduces a cast of charming, quirky, unsavory, even loathesome characters in a fast-paced, entertaining adventure.'
    Kevin J. Anderson, co-author of the bestselling Dune books

'It's not too often debut novels come with a legacy, but in this case it's a pretty impressive one . . . If this were an English novel, we'd be reaching for the rest of the trilogy right now'
    SFX Magazine

'Shadow Prowler reminded me of why I fell in love with fantasy in the first place'
    Book Thing

About the Author

Alexey Pehov is the award-winning author of The Chronicles of Siala, a
bestselling series in his native Russia. His novel *Under the Sign of the
Mantikor* was named 'Book of the Year' and 'Best Fantasy Novel' in 2004 by
Russia's largest fantasy magazine, World of Fantasy.

Shadow Blizzard

TOR BOOKS BY ALEXEY PEHOV

Shadow Prowler
Shadow Chaser
Shadow Blizzard

Shadow Blizzard

ALEXEY PEHOV

TRANSLATION BY ANDREW BROMFIELD

**SIMON &
SCHUSTER**

London · New York · Sydney · Toronto · New Delhi

A CBS COMPANY

First published in Great Britain by Simon & Schuster, 2012
A division of Simon & Schuster UK Ltd
A CBS company

1 3 5 7 9 10 8 6 4 2

Simon & Schuster UK Ltd
1st Floor
222 Gray's Inn Road
London WC1X 8HB

www.simonandschuster.co.uk

Simon & Schuster Australia
Sydney

A CIP catalogue record for this book is available from the British Library

ISBN: 978-1-84737-565-0

Printed and bound in Great Britain by
CPI Group (UK) Ltd, Croydon, CR0 4YY

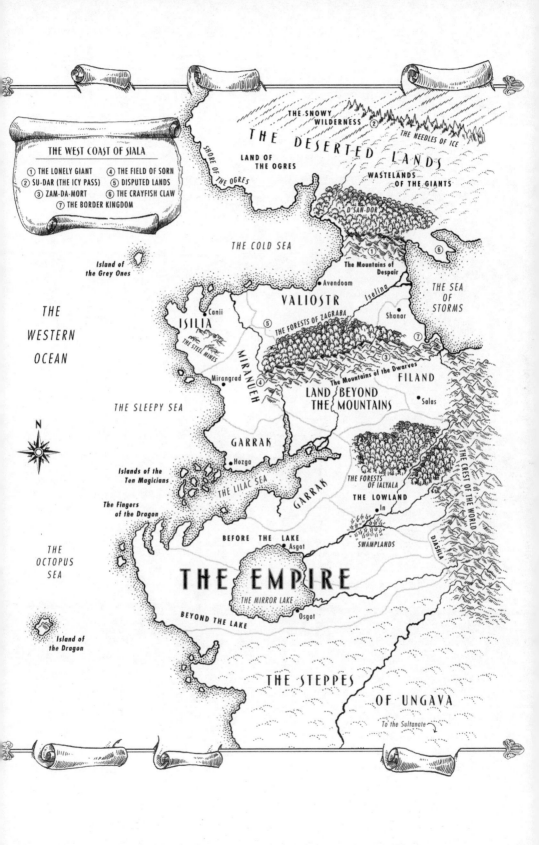

THE WEST COAST OF SIALA

1. THE LONELY GIANT
2. SU-DAR (THE ICY PASS)
3. ZAM-DA-MORT
4. THE FIELD OF SORN
5. DISPUTED LANDS
6. THE CRAYFISH CLAW
7. THE BORDER KINGDOM

THE DESERTED LANDS

THE SNOWY WILDERNESS

THE NEEDLES OF ICE

LAND OF THE OGRES

WASTELANDS OF THE GIANTS

SHORE OF THE OGRES

D'SAN-DOR

THE COLD SEA

Island of the Grey Ones

The Mountains of Despair

Avendoom

Iselina

THE SEA OF STORMS

VALIOSTR

THE WESTERN OCEAN

Canji

ISILIA

THE STEEL MINES

THE FORESTS OF ZAGRABA

Shanar

FILAND

MIRANUEH

Mirangrad

The Mountains of the Dwarves

LAND BEYOND THE MOUNTAINS

Salas

THE SLEEPY SEA

GARRAK

Hozga

THE FORESTS OF IALYALA

Islands of the Ten Magicians

THE LILAC SEA

GARRAK

THE LOWLAND

In

The Fingers of the Dragon

THE OCTOPUS SEA

BEFORE THE LAKE

Asgot

SWAMPLANDS

DIASHLA

THE CREST OF THE WORLD

THE EMPIRE

THE MIRROR LAKE

Island of the Dragon

BEYOND THE LAKE

Osgot

THE STEPPES

OF UNGAVA

To the Sultanate

Shadow Blizzard

1

THE GOLDEN FOREST

The little green goblin reacted rather sensitively when I criticized the Forests of Zagraba. "So what were you expecting, Harold? A fanfare?" Kli-Kli asked, waxing indignant. If I expressed dissatisfaction with anything, even some withered little flower, the royal jester launched into a passionate tirade in defense of his home country.

"No, I just thought Zagraba was a bit different from this," I relied peaceably, already regretting that I'd started this conversation.

"So what do you think it ought to be like?" Kli-Kli asked me.

"Well, I don't know . . . ," I drawled thoughtfully, trying to get the tedious goblin off my back.

"If you don't know, then why are you talking nonsense?" The blue-eyed fool kicked a tussock of grass that was unfortunate enough to be in front of his foot. "He doesn't like this! He doesn't like that! What did you hope your naïve and innocent gaze would behold? Majestic trees ninety yards high? Or streams flowing with blood and oburs under every bush? I'm sorry, we don't have that here. Zagraba's a real forest, not a collection of children's stories!"

"I realize that," I said with a placid nod.

"He realizes, hah!"

"Kli-Kli, don't make so much noise," Eel said without turning round. He was walking in front of us.

The surly titch gave the tall swarthy Garrakian a resentful look, pouted, and stopped talking, and for the next two hours it was impossible to drag a word out of him.

This was our fifth day of walking through Zagraba. Yes, yes, that didn't seem to make sense. Nine crazy characters, including two dark elves, one goblin, one broad-shouldered dwarf, one cantankerous bearded gnome, one gloomy knight, two warriors, and a fairly young, rather shifty-looking guy, striding along between the pine trees and bawling at the tops of their voices.

Why were they bawling? Because they were all crackpots.

Why were they crackpots? Because no normal person would stick his nose into the Land of Forests for any kind of money, and especially not into the territory of the orcs, who were famous throughout Siala for the warm welcome they give to strangers.

But in actual fact we weren't all that crazy (speaking for myself, at least). It's just that we were forced to stick our noses into Zagraba by a certain circumstance that went by the name of the Rainbow Horn.

What in the name of darkness did we want that damned tin whistle for anyway? Well, if it was up to me, I wouldn't go to Hrad Spein to get the Horn for love or money. But I wasn't a free man; I had a Commission hanging over my head, and by midwinter, I had to bring the Horn back to the Order of Magicians in the glorious city of Avendoom, otherwise we could say good-bye to the kingdom.

The Rainbow Horn, stupidly hidden by magicians of the past in the very depths of the Palaces of Bone, was the only thing holding back the Nameless One, who had borne a grudge against our kingdom for the last five hundred years or so. And the power of the Horn was weakening, and next May we could expect the sorcerer to come visiting, together with all the forces of the entire Desolate Lands. Naturally, nobody was exactly waiting to greet the Nameless One with open arms, and the Order of Magicians was desperate to get hold of the Horn in order to drive the enemy back into the icy wilderness.

So that was what we were doing in Zagraba. We were collecting the Horn, saving the world, and getting up to all sorts of other useless and foolish nonsense.

Stupid? Well, maybe. I woke up every morning with that idea in my head, but for some reason no one wanted to listen to me. Miralissa didn't—and Alistan Markauz most certainly didn't.

But it was my own fault—I accepted a Commission that couldn't just be torn up. So I had to puff and pant, run and shout as I struggled to clamber out of a heap of . . . problems.

But then, the Commission did have its good points, too. When the work was done, I'd get fifty thousand gold pieces and a royal pardon . . . it's just that I'd never heard of dead men being in any need of money or a pardon. What corpses usually require is a deep grave and a headstone.

Why would I say all this? Because everything that happened to our group on the way from Avendoom to Zagraba was a mere afternoon stroll in the park. But in Zagraba, and especially in Hrad Spein, things were going to get really tough. I didn't have any illusions (well, maybe just the tiniest little one) about the success of our mission.

"Harold, are you playing the fool again?" Kli-Kli's voice distracted me from my gloomy thoughts.

"Playing the fool is your job. I'm a thief, not a royal jester," I told the little swine morosely.

"That's your bad luck. If you were a jester, you wouldn't have got caught out with this Commission from the king. You'd be sitting at home, swigging beer. . . ."

I suddenly felt an irresistible desire to give the little green wretch a good kick, but he evidently read my thoughts and went darting after Eel, so I had to postpone my reprisal for another time.

From the very moment we set foot in Zagraba, Miralissa had set a frantic pace for the group, and at the end of the first day I almost died. We stopped for the night in a forest clearing, and I felt like I wouldn't be able to get up next morning. If everyone else liked tramping through the forest so much, then that was their right, but I'd rather lie on the grass and take a rest. If they liked, they could take turns carrying me piggyback, because I was willing to swear by Sagot that I didn't have any strength left for strolling through the woods.

And the next morning really was tough. I had to force myself to get up, grit my teeth, and tramp, tramp, tramp. But by lunchtime I'd more or less got into the rapid rhythm, and the next day I almost stopped feeling tired. In fact, I began to suspect the elfess was adding some of her magical supplies to the cooking pot to make our daily marches easier to bear.

Since we entered Zagraba, all the fires had been lit by Egrassa. And amazingly enough, a fire lit by Miralissa's cousin gave almost no smoke. The first night I was a little bit nervous that the flames might attract unwelcome attention, but the cautious elf didn't seem too worried, and that meant there was no point in me getting agitated, either.

Despite my skeptical attitude to Zagraba, during the five days we had been walking through the forest, we had seen many wonderful things. We followed animal tracks that appeared and then disappeared again in the tangled ferns and prickly brambles. We walked through dense copses of black Zagraban oak, pine groves, forest clearings, and small meadows flooded with sunlight and overgrown with forest flowers. We jumped across babbling brooks with crystal-clear water. The forest stretched on and on: leagues and leagues of groves and copses, impenetrable tracts of fallen timber that we had to skirt round, losing precious time in the process, dozens of meadows and boggy hollows in places where streams dammed by unknown creatures had overflowed.

And not a sign of orcs.

Only the squirrels greeted us with their furious chatter and followed the group, jumping from branch to branch and tree to tree. The day before yesterday, after clambering through trees felled by a spring storm, we came out into a beautiful forest meadow covered by flowers in colors so bright they seemed to ripple in front of my eyes. But the moment Egrassa stepped into the meadow, the flowers exploded into a brilliant rainbow and went soaring up into the sky, turning into thousands of butterflies of every possible size and color. With his natural curiosity, Kli-Kli tried to catch one of them, but he wound up stuck up to his ears down someone's burrow. We wasted a lot of time getting the goblin out of there and he caught it hot from Miralissa and Count Markauz. From then on Kli-Kli tried to keep out of their sight and strode along in the company of your humble servant.

Beside a copse of oaks, where there was a jolly babbling stream carrying along the fallen leaves like little boats, we came across a wild boar. He was a mature tusker—two men could easily have sat on his back at the same time. If a beast like that ended up on the dinner table, two companies of ravenous soldiers would have had a hard time finishing him off.

Deler, as the most intelligent and agile, was up a tree in a moment. And that despite the fact that the beech had no branches near the ground, which any self-respecting dwarf would have needed for climbing up. The tusker gazed at us with his small, black, malicious eyes, grunted furiously, and came for us.

But Miralissa only had to flash her yellow eyes and hold out her hand for the boar to stop dead and then just walk away, grunting apologetically.

Deler looked down at the elfess with sincere admiration from the height of his refuge and then climbed back down. We moved through the forest in single file, following Egrassa's lead, with the rear of our little column brought up by Alistan Markauz. The count's hand never left the hilt of his beloved sword, but the triangular oak shield hung behind his shoulder.

The elf said that moving in this way had already saved our lives three times. With true gnomish stubbornness, Hallas objected rebelliously that that was absolute nonsense, and he definitely didn't like seeing a dwarf's backside right under his nose. Egrassa simply laughed at that.

"As soon as I get the chance, I'll be glad to demonstrate the surprises of Zagraba to the respected master gnome," he said.

His chance came soon enough. Egrassa jabbed at the ground ahead of him with a stick that he had picked up, and it collapsed, revealing to our gaze a deep wolf pit, with its bottom set as thick with spikes as a hedgehog's back.

"Just think, gnome, what would have happened if you weren't walking behind me," the elf said merrily, flashing his fangs to emphasize the point.

Hallas grunted in bewilderment, took his helmet off, and scratched the back of his head, but he only took his words back after the elf had disarmed another two traps in front of his very eyes—a bow rigged with a tripwire, hidden in the bushes, and a huge heavy log hanging high up in the leaves of an oak right above the path. If that had come tumbling down, someone would have been crushed.

"But who set up these traps?" Lamplighter asked, shifting his terrible two-handed sword from his left shoulder to his right.

"Who knows?" said the elf with a cunning smile, looking down at the short man. "There are too many paths to follow every one."

"But you know where to find a trap like that!" said Mumr, determined to get an answer to his question.

"Just a little magic—that's all there is to it," said the swarthy elf, adjusting the s'kash behind his shoulder.

Egrassa was clearly not prepared to share the secrets of his people with outsiders.

Once, after Kli-Kli sank up to his chest in a swamp (when he got the bright idea of wandering away from the path) an elk came out onto the path in front of us. It was a king of the elk, with horns more than three yards across. The beast sniffed at the air, glanced at us indifferently with its huge velvet eyes, and trotted off briskly into the young fir trees. Hallas grunted in annoyance and regretted he hadn't thought of felling the massive beast.

"What a feed of meat we'd have had then."

Deler laughed merrily and said that all the gnome's brains must have gone onto his beard, or he'd realize what a bad idea it was to tackle a huge monster like that.

All day long birds chirped and twittered and sang in the branches of the trees. When we lay down for the night the oak trees whispered a forest lullaby to us and the owls hooted soothingly in the silence of the night. On the fourth day of our journey Miralissa said that we had to pick up the pace, and from now on our group would travel at night, too. Someone groaned quietly (I think it might have been me) but, naturally, no one took the slightest notice.

The full moon appeared in the sky, so there was plenty of light in the forest, and in any case the elves seemed to see in the dark as well as cats. Now we walked for most of the night and lay down to sleep in the hours before dawn, in order to continue on our way to Hrad Spein after midday.

It was at night that I learned about the magic of Zagraba. During the hours of darkness the forest was transformed into a world that was wild, alien, and mysterious, but very beautiful in its own way.

The dark branches of the oaks and maples were like arms, and there was a mysterious murmuring in the crowns of the trees—either the leaves rustling or some mysterious creatures talking to each other. We could hear low whispering and squeaking and faint laughter from the trees, the bushes, and the tall grass. And sometimes we were followed by the bright sparks of tiny eyes. Green, yellow, and red. The nocturnal denizens of the forest observed and exchanged opinions, but they were in no hurry to come out of their little hidey-holes and meet us.

"Who's that?" I asked Kli-Kli in a whisper.

"You mean those little chatterers? My people call them the forest spirits. Every tree, bush, forest clearing, and stream has its own forest spirit. Take no notice of them, they're perfectly harmless."

"They're small fry," said Deler, testing one of the blades of his poleax with his thumb. "You should see the kind of forest spirits we have in the Slumbering Forest! You never know what to expect from them, but these just sit there and don't bother anyone, they just . . ."

"They just watch," Hallas concluded for Deler.

"That's right," said the dwarf, agreeing with the gnome for once.

But the spirits weren't the only things in the Zagraban night. Once we saw the air in the forest burning. There were thousands of fireflies soaring between the trees, flashing with emerald, turquoise, and scarlet fire. Kli-Kli caught a dozen or so of these harmless creatures and put them on his shoulders, and for a few minutes the goblin shone like a holy character from the priests' stories, then the glowworms got tired of riding on the royal jester and flitted off to join their brothers in the living kaleidoscope.

Night was the time of the owls, who drifted silently above the meadows in the moonlight. The birds were looking for food, listening to the sounds coming from the grass.

Night was the time of the wolves—we heard them howling in the distance several times. Night was the time of creatures whose names I didn't even know. The cries of the night birds sounded like a madman's laughter; there was roaring, hooting, chattering, growling. All sorts of different creatures lived in the night, and they weren't always welcoming to uninvited guests.

Four times Egrassa and Miralissa led us off the path and we hid and waited for danger to pass. The elves didn't condescend to explain what we were hiding from in the bushes alongside the track. But at moments like that even the fidgety goblin and the argumentative gnome fell silent and obeyed all the elves' instructions.

At night Zagraba became multicolored. The colors were bright and lush—fresh, pure emerald, delicate turquoise, icy blue, sweet fiery red, and poisonous green. Flaming auroras of cold fire filled the forest with a magical, enchanting life. The glowworms glimmered with all the colors of the rainbow, a gigantic spider's web glinted bright blue, and the body of the spider that owned it shimmered with purple (the beast was at least the size of a good pumpkin), rotting tree stumps glowed bright green, and the veins on the emerald caps of the huge mushrooms—big enough for a grown man to shelter under during a shower—pulsed blue and orange. Pink fire wandering through the branches of willows by a lake was reflected in the water.

The cold fire of wandering lights, the bright blue sparks in the crowns of the trees, the glimmering of the forest spirits' eyes, the scent of the forest, the grass, the damp earth, the half-rotten leaves, the fir tree needles, the resin of the pines, oak leaves, and the freshness of a stream. Whatever I might say to Kli-Kli during the daytime, I was completely overwhelmed by the incomparable, wild beauty of the Zagraban night. Although most of the time at night Zagraba was almost black, and then we had to walk by the pale silver light of the moon.

In the evening of the fifth day the narrow track winding between moss-covered larches finally led us to the Golden Forest.

"The gods be praised!" exclaimed Lamplighter, dropping his sack on the ground. "It looks like we've arrived!"

"You're right," Miralissa confirmed. "It's only one and a half days' march from here to Hrad Spein."

For some strange reason, when she said that I got an unpleasant prickly feeling in my stomach. So this was it! We were almost there! What had seemed so distant that it was almost out of reach only two hours earlier was now less than two days' journey away.

"Just an ordinary forest," said Hallas, squinting contemptuously at the trees with the golden leaves. "The Firstborn are always making themselves out to be some kind of chosen people! Anybody would think their shit was solid gold, too!"

"I hope you won't get a chance to ask them, Hallas," Eel said with an ominous laugh. "The orcs are not in the habit of answering questions like that."

"Come on, we have to keep going." Milord Alistan took off one of his boots, shook out a stone, and pulled it back onto his foot.

The Golden Forest was called such because, as well as all the ordinary trees, the golden-leafs grew here, too. They were majestic giants with dark orange trunks and broad leaves that looked as if they were cast out of pure gold. The golden-leafs only grew here, in the Golden Forest, and their timber was highly valued throughout the Northern Lands, not to mention both of the Empires and the Sultanate. If the orcs found a woodcutter felling a golden-leaf, first they chopped his arms off with his own ax, and then they did things to him that are too horrible even to mention.

"Harold, you should see how beautiful the golden-leafs are in the fall!" Kli-Kli gushed.

"Have you been here before?" Deler asked the jester.

Kli-Kli glared at the dwarf with theatrical disdain.

"For those who don't know—the Golden Forest is my homeland. It reaches all the way to the Mountains of the Dwarves—and that's all of eastern Zagraba, so it's not really surprising that I know what it looks like in the fall."

"It's the fall already, as a matter of fact," I said, just to provoke the goblin.

"Early September," the jester exclaimed with a contemptuous sniff. "Just you wait till October comes. . . ."

"I'd like to be long gone from Zagraba before October comes."

"Is your home very far from here?" asked Lamplighter, absentmindedly fingering the fresh scar on his forehead (a memento left by an orcish yataghan).

"Do you want to visit?" Kli-Kli chuckled merrily. "Then you'll have to walk for about another three weeks until you reach the center of the orcs' territory. Then another two weeks from there to the densest thickets in the forest, and then you have to trust in luck. Maybe you'll be able to find some goblins; of course, if they want to be found. The orcs have taught us to be wary, and in the past you humans used to hunt us with those wonderful dogs of yours."

Kli-Kli was right there—in olden times the goblins had been treated very badly by men, who had decided that the little green creatures were terrible monsters. Before they finally realized what was what, there were only a few tribes left of what had once been a large population.

"But the history of this forest is really interesting. Is it true that this is the place where elves and orcs both first appeared?"

"Yes." Kli-Kli giggled. "And then they went straight for each other's throats. I think the elves even have a song about it. 'The Tale of the Gold,' it's called."

"'The Legend of the Soft Gold,' Kli-Kli. You've got it all mixed up," said Egrassa, who had overheard our conversation.

"Ah, what's the difference!" Kli-Kli said with a careless wave of his hand. "Tale, legend . . . there still won't be peace in Zagraba as long as there's a single orc still alive."

"Egrassa," Mumr said to the elf. "Could you tell us this legend?"

"It has to be sung, not just told. I'll sing it for you. At the next halt."

"So you've decided to sing forbidden songs, cousin," Miralissa chuckled, plucking a reddish-golden leaf from the nearest tree and crumpling it in her fingers.

"But why is it forbidden?" Kli-Kli immediately asked Miralissa.

"It's not exactly forbidden, it's just singing it in decent elfin company is regarded as the height of disrespect. But it is sung—mostly by rebellious youths, and mostly in secret, in dark corners, in order not to disgrace the honor of their ancestors."

"What's so bad about it?" asked Eel, raising one eyebrow.

"It doesn't show the elves in the best of lights, Eel," put in Milord Alistan Markauz, who had been silent so far, "and the orcs are shown as pure white lambs. I'd bet half my land that the song was made up by men."

"Milord is mistaken, the song was composed by an elf. A very long time ago. Have you heard it?" Egrassa asked in surprise.

"Yes, in my young days. One of your light elf brothers sang it."

"Yes, they could do that," said the dark elf, adjusting the silver coronet on his head. "Our relatives rejected the magic of our ancestors, so it's not surprising that they sing such things to strangers."

"But you promised to sing it to us!" Kli-Kli teased Egrassa.

"That's a different matter!" the elf snapped haughtily.

Whatever the dark elves might say to anyone, relations between them and their light brethren were not problem-free.

We marched for another three hours before the elf ordered a halt. The group stopped in a meadow overgrown with small forest daisies, and the white flowers made it look as if snow had fallen. The autumn had no power over the Land of Forests. At least, not yet. We still came across butterflies and summer flowers.

There was a small stream gurgling through the roots of a broad-trunked hornbeam at the edge of the meadow, so we were well provided with water.

"We'll stay here tonight," Miralissa said decisively.

Alistan nodded. From the moment we entered the forest he had completely surrendered his command to Miralissa and Egrassa, and he obeyed all their instructions. One thing you couldn't accuse Milord Rat of was a lack of brains. The count understood perfectly well that the elves knew far more about the forest than he did and he should take whatever they suggested seriously. That is, drop the reins of command when necessary.

"Egrassa, you promised us a song," Kli-Kli reminded the elf after supper.

"Let's get some sleep instead," Hallas said with a yawn. "It's the middle of the night."

The gnome only liked the songs of his own people. Like the "The Hammer on the Ax" or "The Song of the Crazy Miners." He had absolutely no interest in anything else.

"Not on your life!" the goblin protested desperately.

"Hallas, you're on watch tonight," Eel reminded the gnome. "So don't start settling down, you won't be getting a good night's sleep anyway."

"Oh, no! The first watch is yours and Lamplighter's. Deler and me only come on for the second half of the night, so I'll have plenty of time."

Hallas turned over on his side, ignoring everyone else, and immediately started snoring.

"So, are we going to hear the song?" asked Mumr, who had just had the stitches taken out of his wound by Miralissa.

Thanks to the elfess's shamanic skills, instead of an ugly scar, all Lamplighter had as a reminder of his terrible wound was a faint pink line running across his forehead.

"Yes, just as I promised," Egrassa replied. "But it requires music."

"So what's the problem? I've got my whistle with me," said Lamplighter, reaching into his pocket.

"I'm afraid we need music that's rather more gentle," said the elf, declining Mumr's offer. "Your whistle makes too much noise. I'll just be a moment."

Egrassa rose lightly off the grass, walked over to his bag, and took out a small board about the size of an open hand. There were thin silvery strings, barely visible in the moonlight, stretched across the board.

"What's that?" Deler asked curiously.

"A g'dal," Miralissa answered. "Egrassa likes to play it when he has the time."

Egrassa likes to play music? Well, now, I'd never have guessed. At least, I'd never seen the elf doing anything of the kind in all the time we'd been traveling together.

The dark elf's rough fingers ran across the fine strings with surprising agility and the strange instrument sang in a quiet voice. Egrassa kept plucking at the strings and the sleeping meadow was filled with the melody.

"Don't forget that the legend should really be sung in orcic. It won't sound as beautiful in human language," Egrassa warned us, and started to sing.

Arrows of bronze are used by orcs,
The elves make theirs of gold.
The Golden Forest and the Black—
The song of the branches is cold.

Led by their King, the elves arrived,
The orcs were led by their Hand.
Facing each other eye to eye
Argad and the King did stand.

"This forest is ours," said the King,
"Turn back, my friends, and go.
What use to an orc is a bleeding skin
Pierced by arrows of gold?"

"Your words will not serve you for soldiers,"
Came the answer from the Hand.
"I have two thousand bold warriors
And you but a small fighting band.

"We will take back our forest as booty,
Fortune favors the hardest blades,
Gold is the softest of metals,
And our bronze will rule the day."

For long minutes King Eldionessa
Replied not a single word.
Then he took out an empty quiver
And smiled at his enemies' lord.

"No arrows?" asked Argad in wonder.
"Then this is surrender, it seems."
The King laughed: "Hand, you are dreaming,
Woe unto you and your dreams.

"Argad, your time is approaching!
Do you hear the war horns sound?
Those are men in armor arriving,
Their boots are tramping the ground.

"Indeed bronze is strong, I know.
You were right to say that, Hand. . . .
But I changed our golden arrows
For a fighting force of men."

The orcs closed their ranks together
And stood with their shields raised high,
The Hand he frowned and glowered.
The King had a glint in his eye.

"Foolish elf!" Argad's harsh words
Struck like a mighty sword blow.
"Do you think, when they finish with us,
The men will just turn and go?"

Then metal on metal sounded
As blade struck hard against blade. . . .
Argad fell, twelve times wounded,
And could not rise again.

"Hand, why are you now so silent?"
Asked the elf, leaning down over him.
"Gold is the softest of metals,
To lie here is good, oh King.

"Death will sharpen the meaning
Of these few words that I speak.
Fight for your home with your own strength,
Though your forces may be weak."

Thus saying, he opened his eyes
And death stopped the breath of the Hand.
"What was it you said?" asked the Elf-King.
"How am I to understand?"

"A hard battle," the weary man panted,
"And dearly indeed has it cost.
Orcs are stubborn and bronze is hard,
Many good men have I lost."

Said the King: "We are most thankful.
This service will not be forgot."
The man asked: "Are we mere servants?
Surely, my friend, we are not!

"A hired soldier is a fine thing
When he fights on distant ground,
But at home greater honor is given
To the lowly hunting hound."

"Now what is it you seek?
You were paid! And we fought too!
You know we are not mean!
Yet more pay? Here, will this do?"

"No more pay," proclaimed the man-soldier,
Addressing the elf with a grin.
"Gold is the softest of metals,
And we shall just take everything."

Egrassa sang well, and the song flowed quietly and beautifully. The rousing words were like a furious battle in the distance and the strings wept when the Hand of the orcs died after giving his final words of advice to his kinsman and bitter enemy.

The elf's g'dal sang its final plaintive chord and an oppressive silence descended on the meadow.

"A beautiful legend," Deler eventually said with a sigh.

"It's hardly surprising that the elves are not very fond of that song. Milord Alistan is right: It doesn't show your race in the best possible light," Mumr commented.

"And the orcs are so very noble," Miralissa replied with a contemptuous expression.

"Not the best possible light . . . so very noble . . . ," Kli-Kli drawled. "It's nothing but a stupid song, and nothing like that ever really happened!"

"How do you know it didn't?" asked Deler, stretching out on his horse blanket and yawning widely.

"Because it's nothing but a legend. Without a single shred of truth in it. When the elves appeared in the Golden Forest, there weren't any negotiations. The orcs went straight into battle. And definitely nobody called each other 'friend.'"

"But Eldionessa did exist. The first and last king who ruled our entire people," said Miralissa, pouring cold water on Kli-Kli's belligerent passion. "His children created the houses of the elves."

"And Argad lived eight hundred years later, and he almost reached Green Leaves; you barely managed to stop his army at the edge of the Black Forest," the goblin said disdainfully. "And men appeared in Siala one thousand seven hundred years after the events described, so Eldionessa, Argad, and the man couldn't possibly all have met each other. And the elves are certainly not such idiots as to make their arrowheads out of gold. And the orcs are not so stupid as to forge their yataghans out of bronze. It's nothing but a legend, Tresh Miralissa."

"But you must admit it's beautiful, Kli-Kli," I said.

"It's beautiful," the little jester said with an amicable nod. "And very instructive, too."

"Instructive? What lesson does it teach, goblin?" asked Alistan Markauz, stirring the fire with a stick.

"That you shouldn't rely on men or trust them, otherwise you can lose your home forever," the goblin replied.

Nobody tried to argue or object. This time the king's fool was absolutely right: Give us a chance, and we'll finish off all our enemies, then our friends, and then each other.

That night my nightmares came back, and at one point when my head was filled with incomprehensible hodgepodge, I opened my eyes.

Morning had already come, but everyone was still asleep, apart from Lamplighter. Hallas and Deler were dozing, having laid their own responsibilities on the shoulders of reliable Mumr. The soldier nodded without speaking when he noticed that I was awake. I lay there for a while, feeling surprised that Miralissa was not in any hurry to get up and wake the others. Perhaps the elfess had decided to let the group have a rest before the final dash for Hrad Spein?

That was probably it.

I heard Kli-Kli crooning gently somewhere at the edge of the meadow. The goblin was wandering along the line of the trees, singing a simple little song. So I wasn't the only one who couldn't sleep.

"What are you singing?" I asked, going up to him. "You'll wake everyone up."

"I'm being quiet. Want some strawberries?" Kli-Kli held out a hat, filled to the brim with fine strawberries.

The berries were giving off an amazing smell, and I simply couldn't resist.

"You were groaning in your sleep again, Dancer. Bad dreams?"

"Probably," I said with a casual shrug. "Fortunately I hardly remember them."

"I don't like the sound of that," the goblin said with a frown. "Someone doesn't want you to see them."

"And just who is this someone?"

"The Master, for instance. Or his servant—Lafresa."

"You certainly know how to keep your friends' spirits up," I told Kli-Kli. "Come on, let's get a fire going while everyone's asleep."

"You go on. I'll just finish off the strawberries and take Deler's hat back."

"Hmmm . . . Kli-Kli, surely you can see the inside is all stained with juice? You squashed half the strawberries!"

"Really? I never thought about that," said the goblin, thoughtfully contemplating what he had done. "It's just that I think squashed strawberries taste a little bit better than ordinary ones. Maybe I should wash the hat in the stream?"

"Please don't, you'll only make it worse," I told him, and set off back.

Kli-Kli was like a little child; he didn't seem to realize that now Deler would be yelling the whole day long about how his hat had been ruined!

And the jester had made that unwelcome comment about the Master and Lafresa, too.

The Master was the nasty piece of work who had been making our lives a misery since the very beginning of our journey, but we still hadn't found out who he was. The bastard was virtually omnipotent and vindictive, and his powers rivaled any of the gods'. But the lad obviously didn't want to simply swat us like flies, so he just mocked and battered us, and when we ruined his latest tricky plan, it didn't upset him at all, he simply came up with a new one even more elegant and dangerous in no time at all. The Master, like the Nameless One, was not very keen on the idea of us retrieving the Rainbow Horn from the burial chambers. But while it was a matter of life and death for the Nameless One, it was just one more whimsical fancy for the Master.

Lafresa was a servant of the Master, and although she looked like a twenty-year-old, she was several hundred years old—at least that was according to one of my dreams. (Yes, indeed, imagine that—I happened to have acquired the remarkable gift of prophetic dreams!) And Lafresa was also the most powerful shamaness (or should that be shawoman?) that I had ever seen in my life. The Master's servant possessed the forbidden magic of Kronk-a-Mor, and she had managed to kill two of us with it after we stole the Key and left her with egg on her face. And to be quite honest . . .

"Watch where you're treading, beanpole!" someone barked in a deep bass voice under my feet.

I was so startled I almost sprouted wings and flew away. I certainly jumped a serious distance up into the air.

"I've seen all sorts of things in my time, but I've never seen a beanpole jump like that before! Hey! Where are you looking, idiot? Look down! Down!"

Sitting there on the ground was a creature that looked like a strange mixture of a grasshopper, a dragonfly, and a goat. That's right. This little creature had the legs of a grasshopper, the head and body of a goat, and the transparent, segmented wings had been inherited from a large dragonfly. Its entire body was covered with yellow and black stripes. In other words, sitting there at my feet was an actual legendary dragoatfly. The little beast was no larger than the palm of a man's hand.

"Well, how much longer are you going to go on gawping at me?" the same voice asked.

It was only then I saw there was a tiny man, the size of my little finger, sitting on the dragoatfly's neck. Curly golden hair, a tearful-looking face, a little suit of velvet lilac, a small bow, and a quiver. *This* creature was looking at me with an expression of high dudgeon.

"A flinny," I gasped.

"How very perceptive, may the forest spirits drink my blood! Are you always so bright, or is it just in the mornings? Take me to elfess, quick!"

"What elfess?" I asked, staggered by the little minnow's cheek.

The dragoatfly shot up into the air and hovered in front of my nose, fluttering its wings. The flinny on its neck gave me a hostile look. "Are all beanpoles this stupid, or did they dig you out especially for me? Tresh Miralissa of the house of the Black Moon. Ever heard of her?"

"Yes . . ."

"Then wake up and take me to her, you idiot!" the little man yelled.

"What's the noise?" asked Kli-Kli, who had joined us unnoticed. "Ah, a flinny's shown up!"

"I'll give you 'shown up,' greeny," the midget fumed.

"Greeny, you say?" Kli-Kli asked ominously. "You just shut your mouth, you golden-haired half pint, or it'll be worse for you!"

"All right, all right, keep your hair on," said the flinny, backing down immediately. "I was just introducing myself."

"Well, now you have. So what have you *shown up* here for?" asked Kli-Kli, deliberately emphasizing the two words "shown up," but the flinny pretended not to hear the insult and he sang out: "A message. Information. News."

"Well, go and pass it on. The elves have already got up—look!"

"I have to be introduced, you know yourself, it's the custom," said the flinny, making a face as if someone had stuffed sour gooseberries into his mouth.

"I know," Kli-Kli sighed, "your kind are all full of dragoatfly's milk! Come on, then."

The dragoatfly's wings hummed as it flew alongside the goblin's shoulder. I walked behind them as a guard of honor.

"Lady Miralissa, permit me to present the flinny. . . . What's that your name is, titch?"

"Aarroo g'naa Shpok of the Branch of the Crystal Dew, you blockhead," the flinny hissed, stretching his lips out into a smile.

"Aarroo g'naa Shpok of the Branch of the Crystal Dew."

"I am glad to greet my brother of the little people at my campfire. What brings you here, Aarroo g'naa Shpok of the Branch of the Crystal Dew?" Miralissa asked with a nod of greeting.

"A message. Information. News," Aarroo answered with his ceremonial phrase, and set the dragoatfly down on the ground.

"Have you sought me out especially, or is your knowledge for any of the dark elves?"

"I have sought you out. The head of the House of the Black Moon sent several of my brothers to look for you, Tresh Miralissa, but I am the only one fortunate enough to have found you. And that is all because I can think."

"Luck serves the worthy," the elfess replied seriously to the little braggart. "Would you care to taste our food and drink our wine?"

"Gladly," Aarroo shouted, rubbing his little hands together in anticipation of the forthcoming banquet.

Egrassa had already brought the food, and the delighted flinny was presented with a tiny little golden plate of gruel cooked by Hallas and a tiny little goblet of fragrant wine. The elf obviously carried these miniature items around with him especially for little loudmouths who rode around on dragoatflies.

I touched Kli-Kli's elbow and led him aside to make sure that the flinny couldn't—Sagot forbid—overhear our conversation.

"Why are they making such a fuss of that little squirt? Wouldn't it be easier to first find out why he came to us, and then feed him?"

"Oh, Harold," the goblin said, clicking his tongue in disappointment. "Of course it wouldn't be easier. He's a flinny. You should never forgive their rudeness, or those flying nosey parkers will hound you to death, but you can't just dispense with the ancient rituals, either. If it was something urgent or dangerous, he would have told us already, but since it can wait a bit, it's best to stick to their silly rules. He'll eat up his gruel and tell us everything. You should just be thankful that he was *sent* to us with a message, otherwise we wouldn't have got away with just food. Freelance flinnies usually take something more substantial than a full stomach for their information. Let's go back, I want to hear what the little gasbag has to say."

The flinny had almost finished his meal. The little fellow ate with the speed of a ravenous giant, while the dragoatfly peered over its master's shoulder at the plate and mewed gently, making a sound like the squeaking of a drowning mouse. Aarroo whatever-his-name-was shoved the dragonfly-goat's face aside yet again.

"Have you got anything left in that great big cooking pot? Flolidal won't leave us in peace until he gets fed," the flinny said peevishly, taking a swig from his goblet.

Egrassa took a wooden spoon and scraped it round the pot, and the dragonfly-goat fell on the spoon with its wings humming, like a hungry vulture attacking a chicken.

Meanwhile Hallas woke up. The gnome yawned, then he spotted the flinny eating breakfast; he slammed his mouth shut so hard that his teeth clattered, and rubbed his eyes furiously. After this slapdash procedure Hallas took another look at Aarroo but, as was only to be expected, the flinny was still there, and he carried on chewing and gave the astonished Hallas a dour look.

"Strange," the gnome declared thoughtfully, nudging the sleeping Deler in the back with his elbow. "Hey, hathead! I don't remember us drinking anything yesterday. So why in blazes am I seeing little men?"

Deler woke up, took a look at Aarroo and said, "That's a flinny, you bearded woodpecker!"

"In the name of the Nameless One, what do you mean, a flinny? Deler, flinnies only exist in children's stories, and they don't eat the gruel that I cooked!"

"Gnomes are even worse than people," Aarroo declared in annoyance, apparently addressing everyone in the meadow at the same time. "As for the gruel, dear sir, it's only my respect for Tresh Miralissa that prevents me from throwing this swill into your beard. I've never tasted such disgusting muck in my life!"

The gnome almost choked on this insolence and couldn't come up with an answer.

"Well, then," the flinny said with a sigh, pushing his plate away. "All the laws have been observed."

Aarroo whistled to summon his dragoatfly, climbed onto its neck, circled round above us, then hovered in the air and announced in a singsong voice:

"A message. Tresh Eddanrassa, the head of the House of the Black Moon, sends his daughter Miralissa greetings and a mournful message. Tresh Elontassa has been killed in a skirmish with the Clan of the Bloody Axes. Tresh Epevlassa was killed at the same spot. Tresh Miralissa is now the third in line for the leafy crown, after only Tresh Melenassa and Tresh Epilorssa. Tresh Eddanrassa asks his daughter to abandon other business and return home as speedily as possible. The message is concluded. Do you wish to send a reply?"

"How did this happen?" Miralissa asked abruptly.

"The message is concluded. Do you wish to send a reply?" the flinny repeated stubbornly.

"The reply is: Until the business entrusted to me last year by the united council of the houses is completed, I shall not return home."

"It has been heard," the flinny said, nodding solemnly, and the dragoatfly flew another circle above us.

"Just like a dragonfly," Mumr said with an envious whistle, following the flight of the magical creature.

"Information. Unpaid," the flinny chanted, and made a wry face. He clearly didn't like doing anything without pay. "In the Red Spinney, which lies beyond the city of Chu, all the birds have disappeared. And also the wild boar, the elk, the bears, the wolves, and almost all the forest spirits."

"Why?" Egrassa asked curtly.

"If I knew, the information would not be unpaid," Aarroo replied irritably. "I was told about it by the spirit of a large tree stump, who lives three leagues' journey away from this spot. He didn't know anything himself, but in recent times the small inhabitants of the forest have tried to keep as far away as possible from that area. And they keep their mouths tight shut about it, too."

"Stupid information!" said Hallas, tugging on his beard in annoyance.

"The information is every bit as good as the porridge," the flinny said furiously, and his dragoatfly buzzed angrily. "If the gnome wishes to taunt, then get your news from someone else! Let beard-face here tell you about it!"

"Shut up, Hallas," Eel said immediately.

"Please forgive my servant, honorable Aarroo g'naa Shpok of the Branch of the Crystal Dew," Miralissa said in a conciliatory tone of voice.

"Servant?" the gnome asked with a silent movement of his lips.

Deler waved his fist at Hallas. The gnome turned redder than a red-hot sheet of metal in a blacksmith's forge, but he didn't say a word.

"That's a bit better," the flinny said with a satisfied grin, and the dragoatfly made yet another circle in the air above our heads.

"Will we be passing through this Spinney, Lady Miralissa?" Alistan Markauz asked while this was happening.

"Unfortunately, yes. It's the shortest route."

"But there are others?" the count inquired, emphasizing every word.

"Yes, but if we go through the Red Spinney, we shall be at the Palaces of

Bone tomorrow evening. By taking a detour we shall lose five or six days. And the path will lie right along the edge of the orcs' inhabited lands. It is far too dangerous."

"No more dangerous than a place from which all the forest spirits have disappeared," Egrassa contradicted his cousin.

"We'll take the risk," said the elfess with a flash of her eyes.

"You are the senior in our line, it is for you to decide," said the elf, raising his hands in the air to indicate that he did not intend to argue with her.

"News," said the flinny, after waiting for the end of the conversation. Then he sang out: "Three pieces of news. The price of the first is a dance by that obstinate gnome."

"What?" Hallas bellowed. "Gnomes never dance for anything!"

"Then I am doubly fortunate!" the flinny laughed mischievously. "If you wish to know the first piece of news, the gnome has to dance. If you do not wish to know it, I shall fly. I have already completed the assignment I was given and am only talking to you out of simple politeness."

"Ah, you little . . . ," said the gnome, jumping up and clenching his fists.

"He will dance," Alistan Markauz said firmly.

"What? Why, may I be—"

"That is an order, soldier! Dance!" said the captain of the guard in a voice with a steely ring to it.

"Dance, my friend," said Deler, putting a reassuring hand on the gnome's shoulder. "It's only a dance for a flinny, after all. Imagine you're dancing for me."

That settled the matter. The gnome snorted disdainfully. "A gnome dancing for a dwarf! I'd rather dance for a flinny."

And he did dance. It looked like some kind of gnomish military dance. At least, Hallas performed it with his battle-mattock in his hands, and it resembled a fight more than a dance of celebration. The Golden Forest had probably never seen a performance like it before. Lamplighter played along, helping the gnome out with his whistle. Kli-Kli clapped his hands merrily. Deler almost burst his sides laughing.

"That's all!" the panting gnome declared.

"You gnomes dance even worse than you cook," the flinny declared.

Deler managed to grab Hallas by the arm just in time and drag him out of harm's way.

"Now, how about the news?" said Miralissa, trying to be polite despite everything.

"News. People have been seen in the Golden Forest. They are two days ahead of you. More than twenty men. All armed. One woman. I saw no crests on their clothing."

"Which way were they headed?"

"They were moving toward the Red Spinney. Two days ago it was still calm there."

"I'd wager my soul that's Balistan Pargaid and his men," Milord Alistan said with a frown.

"And Lafresa. They'll be at the entrance a lot sooner than us," Kli-Kli sniffed.

"After their blunder with the Key, do you think they've decided to arrange an ambush for us at the entrance?"

"Perhaps, Harold, or perhaps not." There was an anxious glint in the elfess's eyes. "They might take the risk of trying to grab the tastiest morsel of all."

"The Horn?"

"Yes. If you tell anyone about our conversation, I shall find you," the elfess said, turning to the flinny.

"I understand that it is best not to interfere in elves' secrets. I shall be as silent as the grave," the flinny muttered discontentedly.

"Were any of the men wounded?" I asked him.

"One of them was missing his left hand."

"It's them."

Well, if his hand was missing, it was definitely Paleface. That rat had been hunting me for ages, and during his last attempt to dispatch me into the light, Hallas had cut off his left hand. Paleface worked for Influential, or Player, as the Master's servants called him. Player was some bigwig in Avendoom and it was thanks to his loving care and attention that I had almost lost my life. And for the time being Paleface was a member of Balistan Pargaid's retinue.

Count Balistan Pargaid, for those who don't know him, was a servant of the Master, and it was from his house in Ranneng that I stole the Key that we hoped to use to reach the very heart of Hrad Spein. Lafresa was supposed to deliver the Key to the Master in person, but I stole the Key, and then Balistan Pargaid and Lafresa set off after us in hot pursuit.

So far we had somehow managed to get the better of them, and not even a trial by combat had done them any good. Mumr had carved up his lord-ship's prize warrior, and then everything had suddenly gone quiet. Balistan Pargaid and his retinue had disappeared. We had been wondering where he could have gotten to. Lafresa had already disappeared sometime during the trial by combat, and now it seemed likely that she had set out for Hrad Spein, and the count had caught up with her along the way. It was clear enough why Lafresa wasn't afraid of entering Zagraba—she hoped that her shamanic skills would keep her safe. And she had no other choice any-way: The artifact had been lost, and the Messenger, who had instructed her to deliver the Key, would be very upset, not to mention the Master himself.

"What is the second piece of news?" Egrassa asked, looking at the flinny.

"The price of the second piece of news is a pinch of sugar."

"We don't have any sugar," Hallas said spitefully. "We're not confection-ers, you know. Maybe I should do another dance for you?"

The gnome's words sounded like a challenge.

"Oh, no! My heart couldn't stand another spectacle like that! What do you have instead?"

We looked at each other. Darkness only knew what might interest this dealer in news.

"I have a sweet!" Kli-Kli suddenly announced.

"Show me it," said Aarroo, leaning forward.

Kli-Kli hastily rummaged through the many pockets of his outfit and took out a battered-looking sweet, still wrapped in its bright golden paper. He must have been saving it since Avendoom.

The flinny studied it closely and then, with a bored expression on his face, as if he was doing us a humongous favor, declared, "Garbage, of course, but it'll do. Throw it on the ground."

I thought it was all an act, and the flinny actually liked the sweet. He lowered his dragoatfly right onto the sweet and started tying it to the belly of his mount.

"News. A man has been seen in the Golden Forest. Wearing a gray cloak, his face was not visible. Armed with a spear. Walking quickly, almost with-out stopping at all. Four hours' flying away from you. Coming straight here. Seems like the Golden Forest has been smeared with honey; I haven't seen so many outsiders in a long time. Ah, yes! I advise you not to interfere with him—the forest spirits say he's a warrior."

"We're not exactly cobblers," Deler protested.

"When the forest spirits say that someone's a warrior, we usually take notice, but that's up to you. The price of the third piece of news is the ring of that beanpole over there with the long mustache," said the flinny, with a nod toward Alistan Markauz.

"Which one?" the count asked.

"Well, certainly not the silver one with your crest," the little extortionist quipped. "You people are too sensitive about those little family knickknacks. It's stupid to ask for them—you won't give them up anyway. I like that one, with the red ruby."

Alistan took the ring off his finger without the slightest objection and put it on the ground. The flinny smiled contentedly and the ring joined the sweet under his dragoatfly's belly.

"Is your news worth it?" I asked.

"That's for you to decide, not me. News. There are orcs nearby."

"Where?" asked Egrassa, reaching for his bow.

"In the ruins of the city of Chu. Six of them. Ordinary scouts. They're not waiting for you. They'll stay there for another five days."

"How do you know that?"

"I heard," the flinny said with a grin. "One of them fell into a trap and broke his leg, and now he's delirious, so only five of them are fit to fight. You can finish them off, or you can just avoid them."

"We shall take note of your information. Is that all?"

"Yes. There is no more news, good-bye."

The dragoatfly hummed as it rose up into the air and flew off toward the forest with its belly touching the tops of the daisies. The little beast was well loaded, and I was surprised it could get off the ground at all carrying that weight.

"Flinnies are very fond of all sorts of rings," Kli-Kli enlightened me.

"I'll remember that."

"Rotten skunk!" Hallas exclaimed, watching with anger in his eyes as the flinny flew away.

"What can you expect from a flinny?" Kli-Kli asked with mock surprise. "They earn their living by peddling the news."

"So won't he sell us to that group of orcs? I think the Firstborn could find something to pay for information on our whereabouts. I don't trust those little runts."

"He would do that, if the Firstborn would bother to talk to him. But they have no respect for flinnies, and the flinnies are too proud to put up with that kind of treatment."

"Pack up your things!" said Egrassa, getting up off the ground. "We have the whole day until it gets dark, and then the night in reserve. We have to cover as much distance as possible today."

"What are we going to do about the orcs?"

This was no idle question from Mumr—there were Firstborn up ahead, even if they weren't expecting us.

"We'll kill them," said Egrassa, glancing at Miralissa, who nodded. "We could just avoid them, of course, but it's never a good idea to leave enemies behind you."

"And what do we do about this fellow who's coming up behind us? Why don't Deler and I stay behind and ask him a few questions?"

"Hallas, you have no brains and no imagination!" said Deler—the dwarf never pulled any punches talking to his partner. "All you ever want to do is to wave that mattock about. The flinny told us this fellow is dangerous and we should stay well clear of him! And even if we beat him, then how are we going to find the group afterward, have you thought about that? Or since this morning have gnomes learned how to wander through forests without getting lost?"

"It's no more difficult than walking through the mine galleries," Hallas muttered.

"But I don't want to get lost in the forest and then one fine day discover that I've wandered into an orcs' nest," Deler snapped.

"No one's staying here," said Milord Alistan, putting a swift end to the argument between the gnome and the dwarf. "If that man wants to follow us, let him. If he catches up and attacks us, then we'll fight him. I'm more concerned about Pargaid and his dogs waiting for us up ahead, and this Spinney."

"We'll deal with Pargaid when we reach him, milord," said Eel, who had already packed his sack.

"There's no reason to be so concerned about the Spinney, either," said Miralissa, throwing her s'kash behind her shoulder. "The forest spirits could have left it for a hundred different reasons. We'll hope for the best."

"And expect the worst," I muttered quietly, but I think the elfess heard me anyway.

"Kli-Kli." The dwarf's voice was very soft, but it sounded rather ominous for the goblin. "What did you do with my hat?"

The goblin decided the best thing to do was hide behind my back. That's always the way—he plays his pranks and Harold's left holding the baby.

2

THE RED SPINNEY

What used to be here before, Kli-Kli?"

"Can't you see for yourself, from the ruins? A city, of course!"

The goblin and I were lying on a heap of gray stones with a thick covering of moss. Standing beside us was a tall fluted column of the same stone, also overgrown with dark, dense moss, like the entire city of Chu.

The ruins of the ancient city stood in between the trunks of golden-leafs and larches. A column here, a wall there, a little farther off an arch beside some wolfberry bushes, and beyond that, a huge building with a dome that had collapsed. And so on in the same way for as far as the eye could see. The ruins rose straight out of the soft carpet of moss, they were drowning in it, choking in the undergrowth of ferns and thistles, crushed beneath the roots of the mighty golden-leafs. This city had probably been great and beautiful once, and now there was nothing left of its past glory but phantoms. Now it was nothing more than dead stone, eaten away by the hungry moths of time.

"I can see it wasn't a country village. Who used to live here?"

"How should I know?" the jester asked with a shrug. "These ruins can remember the retreat of the ogres into the Desolate Lands and the arrival of orcs and elves in Siala. There's no way I could know who lived here in those days. But believe me, Chu is very beautiful. Or it was very beautiful."

"Have you been here before, too?"

"Of course not. It's just that Chu isn't the only abandoned city in Zagraba. There's another one, a lot like this, near the area where my tribe lives. We used to call it Bu. It's a lot better preserved than Chu."

The evening was drawing in as the sun sank behind the horizon, and only a few of its bright rays could penetrate the branches of the trees. Twilight was advancing in the forest. I moved my miniature crossbow closer and checked for the hundredth time that it was loaded.

To my great joy and Kli-Kli's intense annoyance, Alistan Markauz had left us here while the others went to deal with the orcs.

Well, it was the right thing to do! A thief and a jester aren't made for waging war and doing battle. The goblin, of course, thought differently, but after grumbling for a while he had finally decided to stay with me.

Cra-a-a! Cra-a-a! Cur-a-a-a!

The bird's call soared above the ruins like a mournful ghost, echoing off walls and shattering the peace of this deserted spot. For a brief instant the top of the tall skewed column and the trunks of the trees glinted with the blue flash of a spell worked about two hundred yards away. Then the usual calm of the dead city returned.

"It's started," said Kli-Kli, sitting up. "That's Miralissa at work."

"I can't hear anything."

"So much the better. It means no one else can hear anything, either. Let's wait."

So we waited. The minutes seemed to drag on for an eternity.

The thick carpet of moss deadened our footsteps, and we first saw the runner when he was just ten yards away. Kli-Kli pinched me very painfully on the arm and nodded toward the column. At first I thought the runner was Egrassa. But then why was the elf holding a yataghan instead of his usual s'kash?

Of course, it wasn't an elf, but an orc. The two races were too much alike for me to be able to tell the difference in the first few seconds. Sagot be praised, at least we were lying behind the stones and the orc couldn't see us.

"What are you waiting for? He'll get away!" Kli-Kli hissed, taking the first pair of throwing knives off his belt.

The fool was right. If the orc managed to get away alive, he would warn his tribe, and we would pay with our heads. The enemy was so close to me I would have had to try really hard to miss.

Twang!

The bolt easily pierced the light chain mail and stuck in the orc's back. He stumbled and fell facedown in the moss. I didn't feel any pangs of conscience about shooting a running enemy from behind. If he'd had a chance, he wouldn't have thought twice about trying to finish off me and Kli-Kli.

"Did you kill him?" Kli-Kli asked, pressing himself against me in fright.

"Looks like I did," I said uncertainly, keeping the crossbow out for the time being.

"That's just the point—it looks like you did. Maybe he's got enough wits to play dead!" said the goblin, also in no great hurry to go near the body.

"Kli-Kli, he's got a bolt stuck in his back almost right up to the flight. How could he possibly be alive?"

"I still wouldn't go anywhere near him," the jester warned me.

Fear and doubt are always infectious. I started watching the motionless orc apprehensively. What if the goblin was right and the Firstborn was only pretending to be a corpse? In any case, he was still clutching the yataghan in his hand.

"All right," I sighed. "Just remember, I'm only doing this for your peace of mind."

I had to walk a few steps closer to the body to put another bolt in the orc's back. But the lad didn't even twitch in response to this act of sadism.

"Well, now are you convinced he's as dead as stone?"

"Almost." The jester walked cautiously up to the body and prodded the dead orc with the toe of his boot. "The gods be praised, you finished him."

"They're not so very frightening, and they die just like men."

"If you take them by surprise."

I swung round sharply at the sound of Egrassa's voice and raised the crossbow.

"Harold, if it had been an orc in my place, you'd be dead already. And anyway, your crossbow's not loaded. What happened here?"

"An orc, one of the Firstborn you were supposed to kill. Harold shot him, but I spotted him first," Kli-Kli babbled, determined not to let me take the credit for his victory.

"No, Kli-Kli, he's not one of ours." The elf tugged the body onto its back and leaned down over the orc, studying his face dispassionately. "Miralissa bound them with the Net of Immobility and we finished them all off, they never even saw it coming. Four sitting round a campfire, another one nearby with the wounded soldier, six altogether. We killed them all."

"Then where did this one come from? Or is this orc just the product of my morbid imagination?" the goblin muttered peevishly.

"It's just that your lousy flinny didn't bother to tell us about the seventh one," said Hallas, appearing from behind a wall. "From the very beginning I said we shouldn't trust that little flying bastard."

"Where there was a seventh, there could be an eighth," Egrassa said thoughtfully.

"Or even a ninth and a tenth," said the goblin, deliberately rubbing salt into the wound.

"Let's go and join the others, then decide what to do."

We set off after the elf, with Hallas panting along behind us. Egrassa confidently led us through the labyrinth of overgrown buildings. There was ruin and decay on all sides, but at the same time the place was . . . well, beautiful. With the strange, mysterious beauty of thousands of years of time.

Columns soaring up to the height of the golden-leafs or lying on the ground, broken and overgrown with moss. A statue on a pediment, so ancient that it was impossible to tell who you were looking at—a man, an orc, or someone else who lived in Siala before the start of the Gray Age.

The four orcs lying beside the fire that was barely glowing had more arrows than necessary sticking out of them. Miralissa and Egrassa had really made sure of things. There were two more bodies lying a little distance away, under an old larch tree.

Egrassa told Milord Alistan briefly about the orc I had killed.

"The flinny might not have seen the Firstborn if he was in some secret hiding place," said Miralissa, fingering the sleeve of her dark green jacket thoughtfully.

"He just didn't want to see, milady," said Hallas, still unable to forget the dance he had performed for the little news peddler.

"Hallas, Deler, Mumr, Eel! Divide up into pairs and find where that seventh orc was hiding," said Alistan Markauz.

Eel nodded for them all, and the Wild Hearts disappeared into the ruins.

"It will be completely dark in an hour," said Milord Alistan, narrowing his eyes and looking up at the sky. "Shall we stay here or carry on?"

"That depends on what our soldiers find," Miralissa replied wearily, "but I'm in favor of moving on. There's a full moon now, and plenty of light; we can easily walk until the morning and rest—and then we'll be at Hrad Spein."

"I don't think we should stay here, either, cousin. We can rest once we get past the Red Spinney."

"Harold, let's take a look at the bodies," Kli-Kli called to me.

"I'm not interested in corpses."

"Well, you should be."

While the goblin wandered around, looking at the bodies, I loaded up the crossbow with two new bolts.

"Skillfully done, Lady Miralissa. In the finest traditions of the Green Platoon! I definitely approve," Kli-Kli told the elfess when he came back.

"Well, if even you approve of my work . . ." She laughed.

"No, I'm serious. We cast the Net of Immobility, then we have five seconds to stick arrows into them. I think that even when the net broke the last two had no idea what was going on and they were easily killed. Who finished off the wounded one?"

"Deler," replied Alistan Markauz. "So how do you know about the methods of the elves' commando groups?"

"I'm a polyglot in general," Kli-Kli answered irrelevantly.

"Well, you can command your pooglits later," said Deler, who had only heard the fool's final words. "We have to get going, Milord Alistan. We missed one."

"He got away. There were two of them. Over that way there's something like a well shaft. That's where they were hiding. One was unfortunate enough to run into Harold, the other made off to the southwest. Unharmed, milord. I tried to overtake him, but the moss doesn't really hold tracks," Eel said with a grim expression. "And anyway, I'm no tracker. The man we need here is Tomcat, may he dwell in the light. . . ."

"What were they doing in the well?" Alistan Markauz asked, and Mumr held out a scrap of cloth to him without saying a word.

"A man?"

"Yes, milord, he's dead, and his face is cut to ribbons, but I recognized him from his clothes," Lamplighter said with a nod. "He was with Balistan Pargaid's men at the duel."

"Are you planning to hide from them in the Palaces of Bone, milady?"

"That won't be necessary. In the first place, they're no fools. Since the evil awoke on the lower levels of the burial chambers, they don't come within a league of that place. Nothing, not even the presence of elves, would make the orcs do something as stupid as approaching the Eastern Gates of the Palaces of Bone."

"Then we won't delay," said Markauz, nodding to Egrassa for him to go on ahead and show us the way.

Our group walked on into the night.

In the forest at night, darkness comes quickly and yet somehow imperceptibly. The faint, narrow path ran out from under your feet, and then the night hid it completely.

The trees, branches, and bushes dissolved into the all-enveloping blanket of darkness, leaving nothing but memories (there was a pine tree there, and there was an old maple growing there, in that patch of inky blackness) and you had to raise your eyes to the sky in order to see the silhouettes of the interwoven branches that fenced off the stars sprinkled across the heavens.

For a few long, exhausting moments, you staggered along, straining so hard to see in the pitch blackness that your eyes hurt. And then the full moon came rolling reluctantly out from behind the dark veil of night.

It looked like a thick, dark yellow disk of Isilina cheese and, just like the cheese, its broad surface was covered with holes and wrinkles. The moon brought light into the world and gave it to the night below, and the beams of the moon's gift flooded the sleeping forest, playing over the branches and trunks of the dreaming golden-leafs, creating the moon-mother's reflection in a slowly murmuring stream, dancing on the fields of night mist rising from the moss in white wisps and reaching upward into the air. The moonlight made the forest as beautiful and magical as a fairy tale. And the moon transformed the ruins of the ancient city of Chu.

Falling on the faces of nameless idols, gnawed away by the teeth of time, the moonlight made them look alive, firing our imaginations.

Oo-oo-hoo-hoo-oo! The hoot of an owl, or some other bird, spread in thick ripples through the beams of moonlight, echoing off the larches and golden-leafs and the walls of the dead buildings.

The whole world and the whole of Zagraba breathed gently, snared by the silver threads streaming from the spindle of the full moon. It was as light as day, and only the stars were displeased by the moon's awakening. They all dimmed their light and crept farther away from the earth to avoid falling under the spell of the radiant lamp of night.

The group was walking briskly, and the idols of the city of Chu, who had watched us go with reproachful eyes, had been left far behind. The track wound this way and that, appearing and disappearing in the thickets of bushes. And after another hour, it disappeared completely, and we had to force our way through close-growing young fir trees.

The shaggy, prickly arms lashed at us, and we had to protect our faces with our hands and double over. While I was scrambling through these prickly, unwelcoming thickets I cursed the entire world. Mumr, who was walking in front of me now, swore viciously when Eel let go of a branch too quickly, and the fir tree's hand slapped him across the face. I don't think I was the only one who sighed in relief when the path reappeared among the fir trees. It ran downhill now, and the firs were soon replaced by deciduous forest. We tramped across low hills overgrown with maples and bushes of blossoming redbrow. In the sunlight the small red flowers on the bushes probably looked like drops of blood, but now, like the rest of the forest, they were painted silver by the moon.

We walked along the edge of a lake with the moon and stars reflected in its black water, climbed yet another hill and walked down again, jumping across a small stream hurrying about its urgent business. There was a lot more redbrow here than beside the lake. It was growing everywhere I looked, squeezing out the other bushes and even the trees.

"Look, there's one left at least," Kli-Kli muttered behind my back.

"What are you talking about?" I asked him.

"Look, over there, there's a forest spirit among the branches. Do you see the little eyes glowing? The flinny said they'd all left the Red Spinney."

"You mean we're already walking through the Red Spinney?"

"Well, where do you think we are? On the Street of the Sparks?" Kli-Kli asked acidly. "It's obvious this is the Red Spinney."

"It doesn't look all that red to me; you've got something mixed up again, Kli-Kli," Lamplighter said with a dubious chuckle.

"Open your eyes, Mumr. It's night now! But in the daytime, and especially in early September, everything here is covered with redbrow flowers."

"But the place doesn't look anything like a spinney," I said, supporting Lamplighter.

"Fools!" the jester said sulkily, and stopped talking to us.

That night the goblin was in a bad mood. But I think he was just feeling nervous.

I wasn't feeling anything of the kind, and Valder wasn't saying anything. But of course, he hadn't said anything since I had that dream about the Master's prison. Maybe the dead archmagician had finally left me in peace and gone his own way? Ha! There wasn't much hope of that happening.

Who was Valder? I thought I'd already told you that. Valder was a magician who had unfortunately been killed because of the Rainbow Horn a few hundred years earlier, but had now moved into my head. . . . All right, it's a long story, maybe someday I'll write my memoirs, and then you'll know all the details.

The grassy path rustled under our feet and Lamplighter's back loomed close in front of my eyes. How many hundreds of steps had I taken since we left the ruins of the city of Chu?

It was already long past the middle of the night, the stars were floating across the sky, and the moon was getting brighter and brighter. The entire forest had been taken over by redbrow—it was growing under almost every golden-leaf. I thought there would never be an end to these accursed bushes. But what really annoyed me was the sour smell the blossoming bushes gave off. It worked its way up my nose, and after about an hour and a half of it, my head was splitting, and I had this monstrous urge to sneeze.

The deeper we went into the Red Spinney, the tenser the silence became. I couldn't hear the usual whisper of the wind or rustling of the branches anymore, or the calls of the night birds or the buzzing of the nocturnal insects. Not a single glowworm . . . and there was no more sign of any forest spirits. Nothing but the quiet rustling of our footsteps drifting into the night.

All the life of the forest seemed to have died. The silence was oppressive and it made me feel vaguely anxious. Even the moonlight looked dead now, draped across the landscape like a pale shroud.

Behind me I heard the quiet rustle of a weapon being drawn from its scabbard. I looked back. Milord Alistan was walking with his naked sword in his hand, and the count's face looked gloomy and anxious.

"I do-on't li-ike this si-ilence," Kli-Kli muttered, drawing out each word.

"It's never killed anyone yet."

"Oh, don't say that, Harold. It has, it definitely has," our little know-it-all replied.

For the next half hour we didn't say a single word to each other. Everyone was listening to the silence that enveloped everything, hoping to catch at least some kind of sound apart from the rustle of our own steps.

That's always the way of it. You never took any notice of the sounds around you, just took them for granted. A bird chirped on one side, a cricket chirred on the other, leaves rustled somewhere else. But as soon as the sounds your ear was used to disappeared, you realized how much you missed all this outside chattering and nattering that could sometimes be so very annoying.

"We're here," Hallas hissed through clenched teeth, tightening his grip on his battle-mattock.

The path ran onto a bridge that looked as old as Chu. I wouldn't have been surprised in the least if it was the work of the same builders. But unlike the city, the bridge was still intact.

It was made of stone, thirty yards long and two yards wide. Two men could easily walk across it together. Running along the sides, taking the place of railings, were stone barriers, rising up to half the height of a man. Every few yards a column rose up out of the barriers to twice the height of a man. They had probably once supported a roof (which no longer existed). Or perhaps there never had been any roof, and the columns had been put there simply as decoration.

The bridge connected the two sides of a ravine or gorge—I don't know what it was called, but the steep sides descended almost vertically into darkness filled with a silvery mist rising from an invisible bottom.

"This is the heart of the Spinney," Kli-Kli informed us.

"We have to cross that? Somehow it doesn't inspire me with confidence."

"Don't worry, Milord Alistan, the bridge is stronger than a cliff and has stood here for thousands of years," Miralissa reassured the captain of the royal guard. "So let us not delay."

"Wait," said Eel, raising one hand and peering keenly at the far bank of the Spinney. "Lady Miralissa, Egrassa, you take your bows, and Deler and I will cross to the other side."

"Eel's right, if there's an ambush over there, they'll pick us all off on the bridge like plump partridges," said the dwarf, changing his beloved hat for his helmet.

"All right," Alistan Markauz said curtly, and nodded. "Go."

The dwarf ran ahead with the blade of his battle-ax glimmering ominously in the moonlight. Egrassa and Miralissa stood with their bows bent, ready to fire. The two warriors ran across the bridge and disappeared into the bushes of redbrow.

I started counting to myself. When I reached sixteen, Eel appeared and beckoned to us with his hand. It was our turn now. Very soon the only ones left on the first side were Egrassa, with his bow still bent, and Lamplighter, covering the elf against any possible danger from the rear.

"Is it a long way down?" I asked the goblin halfway across the bridge.

"I've never been here before, just like you."

"It's just that you seem to know all these places so very well. . . ."

"To know places, you don't have to have been there before, Harold. How do the gnomes and the dwarves find their way through their underground labyrinths? They're children of the mountains, and they don't have to ask every time which way is east and which way is west. The goblins, dryads, elves, and orcs are the children of Zagraba and we never get lost in it. We always know where we are, no matter which part of the forest we happen to be in. That's something you men can't understand."

We carried on along our way. The redbrow started to thin out. The fir trees and larches gradually edged the bushes aside and the cursed smell of those flowers almost disappeared, but the silence still hadn't gone away. Our group was still in the Spinney.

We walked on and on and on. The light sack gradually began pulling me down toward the ground, the chain mail chafed my shoulders and weighed heavy on my back, my legs were tight knots of pain and fatigue. It was well past time for us to call a halt, we'd been tramping along for hours, but Egrassa only stepped up the pace, trying to get us out of the Spinney as soon as possible.

Kli-Kli was the first to sense that something was wrong. He stumbled, looked back, and drew in a sharp breath of the night air.

"Kli-Kli, please don't stop," Hallas said to the goblin.

"Something's not right," the goblin said anxiously.

"What?"

"I don't know," the fool muttered, and hurried on.

Then Egrassa stopped and raised his hand to tell us to make less noise. The elf listened carefully to the gloomy darkness of the nighttime forest and then said something to Miralissa in their guttural orcic tongue.

She replied in the same language, and Egrassa led us on again. The elves kept looking back. I couldn't help myself and looked back, too, but there was nothing behind us except a narrow path silvered by moonlight and dark walls of fir trees rising up on both sides of it.

"What's happening?" asked Alistan Markauz.

"Nothing yet, milord, just don't fall behind," said the elf, almost switching into a run.

Miralissa was muttering something to herself and occasionally fluttering her hands. I realized with horror that she was preparing some spell as we walked along. May the darkness drink me—could they tell us what was going on or not?

Kli-Kli was skipping along ahead of me, with his sack bouncing up and down on his back—it wasn't easy for the little goblin to keep up with the pace set for us by Egrassa.

The goblin was whining quietly. At first I thought he was just breathing like that from the effort, but then I realized: Kli-Kli was whining in fear. And that was when I got frightened.

Very frightened.

"Kli-Kli!" I growled at him. "Give me your sack, it won't be so hard for you keep up!"

The jester looked at me. His blue eyes were full of primal animal terror. I had to repeat what I'd said before he understood what I wanted him to do. The goblin didn't argue, and immediately handed me the little sack with his bits and pieces in it.

"What's going on?" I said, repeating the question I'd already asked.

"A flute!" the jester squeaked.

"In the name of darkness, what flute?"

"Just keep moving quickly, all right?"

That was all I could get out of him.

And then I heard *it*. And when I heard it, for the first second I couldn't even believe it was possible. The silence was broken by a pure crystal trilling sound. It was barely even audible—the unknown flautist who was drunk enough to play in the forest at night was quite a long distance away. The flute broke the silence of the night so unexpectedly that I stopped dead on the spot and Deler crashed into me.

"Move, Harold, if you want to stay alive! I don't know what that thing behind us is, but I'm sure it doesn't mean us any good."

Egrassa broke into a run. There was another trill of the flute, much closer than before, and then I realized what it was that was gaining on us. Only one creature made sounds that resembled a trilling flute so closely. And the orcs had named this monster the terrible flute, or h'san'kor.

"Sagot save us all," I blurted out.

"That's not very likely! Just run, Harold!"

And we ran. Each time the trilling sounded closer and closer. And those flute sounds urged us on better than any bull whip could have done. Whatever this beast that was used to frighten us in our distant childhoods might be, it was running very fast, a lot faster than us.

"I . . . thought . . . they . . . all . . . died out . . . long . . . ago . . . or they . . . were . . . just . . . a . . . fairy . . . story," Lamplighter gasped.

He threw away his sack; the weight of his bidenhander was enough for him now. But Alistan was the one having the hardest time. The captain of the guard eventually had to give up: He threw away his helmet, then his shield, and then came the turn for his small mace. The only weapons the count was left with were his sword and dagger.

"As you see . . . not all of them," Kli-Kli wheezed. "This one's definitely alive . . . and hungry. He's no fairy story. . . ."

"Why are we running?" I panted. "Three more minutes of this and I'll die."

"So he . . . won't eat us . . . you fool! We're waiting . . . for Miralissa . . . to work a spell!"

I wish she'd get a move on, I thought. Sagot, if you can hear me, please hurry her on a bit.

The trees fused into a single flickering blur. The world shrank to a narrow path, Kli-Kli's back, the wheezing in my chest, Miralissa's muttering, and the howls of a h'san'kor on the hunt. The sweat smothered my eyes, my hair was glued to my forehead. I wanted to stop, fall to the ground, and die right there. But everyone was running, and I had no choice but to keep running with them.

"Drop . . . both . . . the sacks," Kli-Kli advised me in a squeak.

I gratefully tossed his sack away and dropped my own off my shoulders; then it was a lot easier to run. If only I could have dumped the chain mail— but for that I would have had to stop, and stopping now was the shortest way into the belly of the beast.

A flute trilled . . . and a second later another replied.

"There are two of them!" Kli-Kli squealed.

At that very moment Miralissa finished muttering, and the bushes on the right of the path parted to form a passage.

"That way!" the elfess gasped.

We didn't need to be told twice. As soon as we left the path, the bushes closed together behind us and the trampled grass sprang back up as if our feet had never touched it. Our group was in a grove of fir trees, surrounded by pitch blackness. There was a strange blink and a cold tremor ran over my body.

"We're invisible now, but lie down just in case!" Miralissa ordered. "Kli-Kli, your people know defensive spells. The magic of the elves has almost no effect on a h'san'kor. You help!"

"I don't know anything," the frightened goblin whinged. "Only the little bit my granddad taught me!"

"Do what you can!" the elfess hissed furiously, sprinkling some powder through the air.

Kli-Kli nodded and started spinning like a top. After ten long seconds the goblin collapsed on the ground and for a brief instant the world around us flared pink. I didn't know what it was, but Miralissa nodded approvingly.

"Good, now don't move, don't even breathe. Now you're nothing but tree roots for the flute. For a minute at least . . ."

She murmured the last words very, very quietly.

We really were in the mother of all fixes.

Almost nothing was known about the h'san'kor, which was only natural, since those who had encountered one didn't usually tell anyone about it, because of their sudden death. So all our knowledge of terrible flutes amounted to no more than terrible legends from the elves and goblins about these mysterious monsters of the forest and a few engravings of bodies of flutes (I personally had no idea at all of what the beast looked like).

Two bodies of h'san'kors that were found by particularly brave trappers who wandered into the Golden Forest were sold for huge amounts of money (one went to the Order of Magicians, the other was bought by some collector). And also, about three hundred years earlier, a certain very brave and stupid baron from the Borderland had organized a h'san'kor hunt. Half of his men lost their lives, but they did manage to capture one of the monsters alive. The magicians of the Order, drooling at the mouth, were hurrying to the baron's castle, but the flute decided not to wait. It smashed apart the cage in which it had foolishly been detained and killed everyone in the castle and the neighboring village. Then it waited for the magicians and finished off almost all of them. It turned out that battle magic had no effect at all on the beast, and so three adepts and seven acolytes were lost. It was a stroke of luck that the members of the Order included an archmagician, who killed the monster by dropping a nearby windmill on its head.

But these were tales of times long past. We didn't happen to have an inventive archmagician or spare windmill with us. We just lay there on the ground, not moving and barely breathing. The trill of a flute sounded again. O, so close, the darkness take me! The first flute was immediately answered by a second.

"I'm a log, I'm invisible," I whispered quietly. The hair on my head stood up in terror.

Kli-Kli gave me a very painful kick and put one finger to his lips. I blinked at him to say: I understand, not a sound.

Our refuge had a magnificent view of the path. The silence of the night was broken occasionally by trilling flutes, and the only thing I could do was pray to Sagot that we wouldn't be noticed.

"They're chasing someone!" Mumr whispered, earning himself a painful dig from Eel.

What I saw a moment later is etched in my memory forever.

A man came running along the path. Not even running, but flying, putting all his strength into it. The stranger's feet were barely even touching the ground, he was moving in immense leaps to get away from the monsters pursuing him. His boot touched the ground, pushed off, and the man flew a good three yards, another touch of the ground, another long leap. I'd gladly have bet that if the lad really wanted, he could have matched the speed of a horse. A gray cloak fluttered out behind his shoulders like a night bird's wings, his face was hidden by a hood. In his hands the man was holding a spear with a black shaft and a very broad leaf-shaped blade.

In the space of four seconds the man appeared, ran past us, and disappeared behind the trees.

And then they came.

A flute sang again, and a creature leapt out from round the corner. It ran past so quickly that I couldn't even see it clearly—it was a blur of red, black, and green with absurdly long arms and legs. The h'san'kor was gone in an instant. The beast was too intent on pursuing its quarry to take any notice of us, and anyway, thanks to Miralissa and Kli-Kli, we had become invisible to its eyes for a while.

Another flute sounded to say that it was getting close, and the h'san'kor that had run past us replied.

The second beast burst out onto the track, unexpectedly stumbled, and stopped exactly opposite our hiding place. Its eyes, blazing with purple fire, looked in our direction. I pressed myself down into the ground. Now I could get a very good view of the creature.

The tall figure, three times the height of a man, seemed absurdly thin. It had immensely long arms and legs and the neck supporting the head was as skinny as the body. The h'san'kor's head looked like some bizarre frog's skull with skin tightly stretched over it.

I couldn't see any fur or scales on the beast, its skin was entirely covered in red, black, and green stripes. The nose was a black hollow; the huge eyes filled with purple flame covered half the face; there were short, curled horns on the head; and the mouth . . . For some reason I'd thought it would be filled with teeth, but when the beast parted its lips and grinned, I saw it had no more than five crooked, yellow stumps in its jaws. No armor or clothing, but one clawed hand was clutching something like a spiked club, and in its left hand it was holding the sack I had abandoned only five minutes earlier.

I felt icy worms stir in my stomach. It had to see us now! But it mustn't see us!

The beast raised the sack to its nose, sniffed at it, snorted, and tossed it away.

Somewhere in the distance a flute played a triumphant melody—evidently the first beast had finally overtaken the man. Distracted, the h'san'kor lowered its head to one side and started listening to its comrade's call. The triumphant trill suddenly changed to a bellow of pain, and once again the nighttime forest was filled with deafening silence.

Lamplighter was lying next to me and I could hear his heart pounding. But the question hammering through my mind was: Why had the beast bellowed so loudly? Obviously I was not the only one worried about this. The h'san'kor took several uncertain steps along the path in the direction that the bellow had come from. . . .

Suddenly the world flashed pink again, the prickly shivers running across my body disappeared, Miralissa and Kli-Kli's spells vanished, and . . . the monster saw us. With a menacing growl the beast moved toward us, parting the bushes.

"Scatter!" shouted Miralissa, already on her feet. "Attack from all sides, all together!"

I was scared absolutely witless. The elfess was chanting a spell, the soldiers fell back, drawing the h'san'kor on, and I watched as the beast advanced on us, like death come to life. The lilac flame in the flute's eyes was burning with a hungry glow.

Egrassa's arrow whistled through the air and I recovered my senses.

"Shoot, Harold!" he shouted to me.

I shot on target, the bolts slammed precisely into the forest monster's chest, and I started reloading the crossbow, but this time with ice bolts, because the ordinary ones had no effect, just like the elf's arrows—there were already at least six stuck in the monster, but it didn't seem to be bothered in the least.

A green wall flared up in front of the h'san'kor (just like the one that Miralissa had created at the lair of the Nameless One's servants). The monster stopped and roared so loudly that my ears popped, and slammed its club down on the magical barrier. It was obviously some special kind of club, because the wall shuddered visibly.

"I can't hold it for long!" the elfess shouted. "Egrassa, Harold, go for the eyes! Put out its eyes!"

By this time, the elf had stuck the h'san'kor with arrows all the way up to the top of its head. The monster took a step back and then attacked the wall again. The elfess groaned with the strain of trying to maintain the barrier. I unloaded the crossbow into the beast and the ice bolts exploded without causing our enemy the slightest harm.

"Battle magic doesn't work on it!" cried Kli-Kli, flinging his first pair of throwing knives. "Ordinary bolts! Go for the eyes!"

"I'm out of arrows!" shouted Egrassa.

Another roar, a blow, a flash of green from the wall, and a muffled groan from Miralissa.

"Take mine!" the elfess shouted, and started desperately whispering a new spell.

Egrassa dashed across to her. Kli-Kli parted with another knife. . . . The h'san'kor seemed to understand human speech perfectly well. It saw me aiming at its most vulnerable spot, stopped storming the wall between us, and, at the very moment when I pressed both triggers, it put one hand over its eyes.

Smack! Smack! Both bolts stuck in its hand. The beast gave me a malicious glance that promised a thousand years of torment when it got its hands on me, and smashed its club down on the wall again. The wall moaned pitifully, but still stood firm.

Twang! Twang! The elf's bowstring sang out again. One arrow went into the beast's mouth, the other stuck in its head, by some miracle just missing its eye. The next arrow loosed by Egrassa burned up in the air before it even reached its target. And the same fate overtook my bolt.

So this vile monster could use magic, too?

"It's useless!" cried the elf, baring his s'kash.

Kli-Kli howled and spun like a top, working a spell. Miralissa finished her own magic, and by the light of the moon and a small fire lit by the gnome, all the grass around rose up into the air, gathered together in the form of a huge knife blade, and struck at the flute's chest.

It didn't work. The knife fell and scattered into harmless tiny scraps of green. Alistan Markauz swore; the monster chuckled triumphantly and smashed its club down on the wall that was barely holding up.

Bang-bang! Two shots from a pistol fused into one, distracting Kli-Kli from his spell.

Hallas was wreathed in vile-smelling gunpowder smoke. Our enemy's left eye burst and went blank, and the h'san'kor roared in pain and fury. The second ball hit a little lower, passing through the h'san'kor's neck. Its body was already black from the blood oozing from dozens of wounds, and now the life started pulsing out of its neck in sharp spurts. Good old Hallas—he had realized that the flute's spell might work on arrows and crossbow bolts, but balls—or bullets, as he called them—could pierce the magical barrier. And they had.

Bang!

The gnome was a skilled master of his weapon, and this time the monster's right eye went blank. But I was astounded to see the h'san'kor still standing firmly on its feet. Blinded, and howling like a hundred sinners roasting on a skillet, it flung itself at the wall.

The wall flared up brightly for the final time, and shattered into a thousand bright green shards. I thought my head would explode from the terrible ringing sound. Three fir trees standing close to the demolished wall burst into green flame, burning from the ground right up to the top of their crowns and illuminating the forest with a green light.

Deler was howling and rolling around on the ground—his jacket had caught fire. Eel dashed over to the dwarf and started beating out the flames on his back. The fire roared as it devoured the trees. The h'san'kor shrieked piercingly and flailed blindly in front of itself with its club, hoping to catch one of us.

"Everybody back! Over here, quick!" Hallas yelled.

Eel helped Deler to his feet and they ran into the forest. Alistan and Egrassa picked up Miralissa, who was lying on the ground, and carried her away from the monster. I went running after them—this was no time to hang about, the gnome might have another surprise up his sleeve.

"Get down!" Hallas shouted, and we all dropped to the ground.

"This way, you ugly brute! Come to me!" Beside the howling h'san'kor the gnome looked like some little bug.

The beast smashed its club blindly against the ground and walked toward the voice.

"Well? Here I am! Catch me, you horned bastard!"

The h'san'kor growled something, and its weapon reduced the nearest young fir tree to a million tiny chips of wood. When the flute drew level with the little fire that Hallas had lit, the gnome tossed something into the flames and ran with all the speed his little legs could muster.

A brilliant flash lit up the forest and for a moment I was completely blinded. Then there was a deafening bang, flames went soaring right up to the sky, and I definitely felt the earth shake.

When the bright spots cleared from in front of my eyes I saw before me the scene of destruction caused by Hallas's unknown weapon. The fir trees were still burning and there was more than enough light to make out what was happening all around us. The gnome was standing on all fours, shaking his head furiously. The victor's face was covered in blood and his eyebrows were singed. A hole had appeared in the ground at the spot where the fire had been burning a few moments earlier. The h'san'kor was lying beside it. The blast had torn off both its legs, but the monster was still trying to reach for its club.

"That beast's hard to kill!" exclaimed Mumr, adjusting his grip on the hilt of his sword.

"Cut its head off!" Egrassa shouted from somewhere behind him.

"Harold, you help Hallas!" Deler told me, picking up his battle-ax.

Eel, Deler, Alistan Markauz, and Lamplighter all dashed to the h'san'kor.

"Are you all right?" I asked, helping the gnome get up.

"I can't hear a damn thing, Harold!" the gnome roared, and shook his head. "Not a damn thing!"

Meanwhile Milord Alistan bounded up to the monster and plunged his sword into its chest with all his strength. The monster roared and swung its hand blindly. The blow caught the count on his chest plate and knocked him off his feet.

Mumr swung his sword and halted the hand that was raised to strike at Milord again. The bidenhander sliced through the h'san'kor's wrist, leaving the hand dangling by a scrap of skin. Eel thrust his "brother" and "sister" into the beast's other hand, pinning it to the ground, and Deler took a wide swing and buried the crescent-shaped blade of his battle-ax in the h'san'kor's forehead.

The beast howled and shrieked, waving the stump of its arm, with blood pouring out of it. Mumr darted over to the hand that Eel had pinned to the ground, and hacked the arm off at the shoulder with three stout blows.

"Die! Die! Die, will you, you bastard!" said the dwarf, raining down blows on the h'san'kor's head.

The heavy weapon pulped flesh and crushed bone. The flute twitched . . . but it was still alive. Breathy gasps and incomprehensible fragments of phrases came out of the monster's mouth. I suspected it was about to treat us to another spell. And I wasn't the only one who thought so.

"Cut its damn head off at last, will you!" Kli-Kli shrieked.

"Harold, where's my mattock?" asked Hallas, pressing his left hand to his split eyebrow and trying to push me away with his right.

"Calm down, they'll manage!"

"Oh, sure they will. Get its head off, you idiots!"

"Deler, you go right!" Mumr barked, swinging the bidenhander back above his head. "Eel, milord! Cut off its stump, so that it can't jerk about! Here we go! *Hey-yah!*"

The bidenhander smashed down on the monster's neck. Then the battle-ax. Then the two-handed sword again. The dwarf and the man started hacking away like lumberjacks. When Deler brought down his battle-ax for the third time, the h'san'kor fell silent. This time, forever.

Deler swore in the gnomic language and wiped the sweat off his forehead with his sleeve. "That was hot work! Hallas, how are you?"

"What? Alive! And how's your back?"

"My jacket's ruined," the dwarf said, making a wry face, and set his battle-ax on his shoulder.

The fir trees were still burning, but the magical green flames had already given way to ordinary ones.

"Tell me, my friend Hallas, what was that you threw into the fire?" Kli-Kli asked the gnome thoughtfully as he studied the hole blasted into the ground.

"Speak louder!"

"What did you fling in the fire?"

"Wouldn't you like to know!" the gnome snapped. "The powder horn, that's what! Thanks to that brute all I've got left is one loaded pistol! But never mind. . . . Damn the pistol, the important thing is that everyone's still alive. When I tell the lads back in the Giant I felled a h'san'kor, they'll never believe me!"

"You felled it? If Lamplighter and me hadn't lopped its head off, you'd have more to worry about than a singed beard!" Deler didn't intend to miss out on the credit for a heroic feat like this.

"Have you not forgotten about the first monster, milord?" I asked Alistan Markauz. "Somewhere up ahead there's another one just like this, only that one's alive!"

"I don't think we need worry about that flute, Harold," Egrassa said in a quiet voice. "If the h'san'kor were alive, all the noise we made would have brought it here."

"Could that man really have killed it?" Hallas simply couldn't believe the idea.

"Apparently so."

"Then he's even more dangerous than a flute," Eel declared. "How is Lady Miralissa?"

The Garrakian's question hung in the air and everyone looked at the dark elf, who had stayed with the elfess all this time.

"She's all right now," Egrassa replied, hanging his s'kash behind his shoulder.

3

AT THE GATES

It took us an hour to build the funeral pyre. There were plenty of trees all around; Deler's battle-ax worked away without a pause, and all the others kept up well with the dwarf. The pile of timber on which we set Miralissa rivaled the size of the pyre we had built when Ell died. The elfess's s'kash and bow lay beside her and Egrassa kept only the quiver.

When the elf first led us to Miralissa, no one could believe that she was dead. She seemed to be sleeping or resting with her eyes closed. There were no wounds, and her bluish chain mail was undamaged. Only when we picked the young elfess up to carry her to the fire, a single drop of blood flowed out of her right ear.

Miralissa had been killed by her own shamanism. At the moment when the magical wall burst and shattered under the furious pressure of the h'san'kor's attack, the thread of the elfess's life had also snapped. The princess of the House of the Black Moon had put all her strength into the magic and she had no chance of surviving the powerful backlash from her own spell.

When the magical flame of the pyre was transformed into a wild roaring dragon that threatened to consume the moon and the stars, and Miralissa had disappeared forever behind the red tongues of flame, Egrassa sang the funeral song.

The flames roared furiously as they accepted Miralissa's soul and escorted it to the light, but the elf's voice could be heard even above their roar. The bright glow of the fire flickered on the faces of the warriors silently observing the raging flames.

Hallas and Deler looked like brothers now—both silent, with gloomy faces. Alistan Markauz gritted his teeth and clenched his fists. Eel was as impassive as ever; there was not a trace of emotion in his face, only weariness dancing in his eyes the color of steel. Lamplighter leaned on his bidenhander with his eyes narrowed, peering into the fire. Kli-Kli was crying his eyes out and wiping the streaming tears off his face. And I . . .

How was I?

I suppose . . . desolated . . . and very tired. I felt that now there was absolutely nothing that I wanted.

"Kli-Kli, stop crying," Egrassa said when he finished the song.

"I'm not crying," the goblin whined miserably.

"Do you think I'm blind?"

"If I say I'm not crying, then I'm not crying!"

"She knew what she was doing. Take comfort in the fact that if my cousin had not maintained the wall for so long, we would all be dead."

"But . . ."

"She was a true daughter of the House of the Black Moon—she did it so that we could finish what we came here to do. We elves have a completely different attitude toward death. She did not die in vain, and there is nothing more to say."

The goblin nodded hastily and blew his nose into a huge handkerchief.

We moved on when there was nothing left of the pyre but a heap of glowing embers.

There was no more than two hours left until dawn and Egrassa led us on without making any allowances for our tiredness.

I still couldn't believe we had lost Miralissa. Anyone else, but not her. Somehow I'd been sure that she would be with us right to the very end. But as they say, man proposes and the gods dispose. The elfess with the ash-gray hair and mysterious yellow eyes, and that polite half smile constantly playing on her blue-black lips, had left us now, disappeared into the fire.

Now as we made our way through the forest, we were completely dependent on the elf's knowledge, and, to a lesser degree, the goblin's. If they hadn't been with us, the group would have lost its way in the trees and never found the burial chambers, even if they were only a hundred yards away from us.

Miralissa's death was an irreplaceable loss in another way, too—we had effectively been left without any magical defenses. Yes, Egrassa knew how to do a few things, but they were limited to the superficial knowledge possessed by every member of the ruling family of a house of dark elves. The elfess wasn't a fully fledged shaman, either, but her knowledge was far deeper than Egrassa's.

Of course, there was still Kli-Kli—the one-time student of his shaman grandfather—but you couldn't afford to trust him in serious business like this, or you might end up getting the soles of your feet roasted at the most inconvenient moment. There had been precedents already, when the goblin's knowledge of magic had almost dispatched our group to a meeting with the gods. I personally didn't feel like taking any more risks.

As we prepared to leave the site of the funeral pyre, the goblin pulled his throwing knives out of the h'san'kor's dismembered body and gave the severed head a final kick of farewell. I picked up the sack the monster had dropped.

Kli-Kli was still sniffing as he trudged along in front of me.

"How are you?" I asked the goblin sympathetically.

"Fine," he said through his nose, furtively wiping away his tears. "Absolutely fine."

"I'm sorry she was killed, too."

"Why do things like that happen, Harold?"

"I don't know, my friend. I don't make a very good comforter. Everything is decided by the will of the gods."

"The gods? That gang of bandits only exists because some Dancer allowed them to move in when he created this world!" He sighed. "All right, let's not talk about that."

A Dancer . . .

That's my curse. According to the goblin, I'm a Dancer in the Shadows, too. At least, that's what the goblin shamans' famous *Book of Prophecies* says. I don't know how Kli-Kli figured out that I'm a Dancer (the first one for ten thousand years), but if a goblin says you're a sheep, proving to him that you're not is about as easy as making the sun run backward—one thing is as impossible as the other. So sometimes the jester called me Dancer in the Shadows. I tried for two weeks to shake out of him exactly who this Dancer was and what he was supposed to do, and eventually the infernal little blackguard gave way and fed me his half-witted tribe's old campfire yarn.

Apparently there used to be a world of Chaos, the first and only world in the Universe, and people lived there. Some of these people possessed the strange power of being able to create new worlds. And to do this they required any shadow from the world of Chaos.

So these special people were called Dancers in the Shadows. They created thousands of worlds and eventually made so many of them that the world of Chaos had almost no more miraculous living shadows left, and Chaos died. But that's not the point. If the goblin's theory is right, then our world was created by one of the Dancers in the Shadows. And the lad was obviously a little crazy—otherwise would our world have turned out to be such a rotten, lousy place?

And as for me, I didn't feel like any kind of Dancer, no matter how much Kli-Kli harped on about it. Although it would be fun all right, to create a world of my own, where mountains of gold would just appear, and there wouldn't be any rotten skunks of guards or municipal watchmen. But anyway, there's nothing I can do about that, because to create new worlds, you need shadows from Chaos.

Ah, darkness! Who can make any sense of these goblin superstitions?

Egrassa suddenly threw his arm up in the air as a signal for us to stop. Another slight gesture—and everyone reached for their weapons. With an arrow already on his bowstring, the elf took a step forward and one to the side in order to let the warriors past him.

The track had led us to a small forest clearing with two bodies in it—a h'san'kor, slit open from the neck to the groin, and a man in a gray cloak who had been torn to pieces. His legs and the lower half of his trunk were lying beside the h'san'kor, and his upper half had been tossed a few dozen yards away.

"Both dead," Alistan Markauz declared, thrusting his sword back into its scabbard.

"What a stench its innards give off!" Hallas said, making a face and covering his mouth and nose with the sleeve of his shirt.

The gnome was right, the dead h'san'kor stank worse than a hundred corpses decomposing in the heat.

"We-ell now," Lamplighter drawled, "this lad gutted the beast very neatly. Putting paid to a h'san'kor single-handed sounds like a very tall tale, in fact. . . ."

"A legend," put in Eel, who was carefully examining the spot where the fight had taken place. "He put paid to it all right . . . but look at the signs here. . . . Egrassa?"

"Yes, he slit its belly open with this." The elf was holding the stranger's black spear. "But that still didn't save him. The mortally wounded monster was still dangerous. Even as it was dying, it was able to tear the man in half. . . ."

"A blow for a blow," Eel muttered, studying the flattened grass.

"What do you mean?" asked Milord Alistan.

"They each struck only one blow, milord. You see these marks here on the grass? I'm not Tomcat, but I can read them quite clearly. It was over very quickly. The man stepped forward, struck upward, and spilled out all the flute's innards."

"He must have been very agile to do that. He'd have to move as fast as the h'san'kor," said Deler, refusing to believe what Eel had said. "Men aren't capable of that."

"Did you see how fast this man in gray ran past us? And you see what he did to the monster? What more proof do you want, in the name of darkness," Hallas asked Deler.

"I don't know," the dwarf muttered reluctantly. "I just can't believe it."

"But it's true," Eel continued. "The lad killed the beast all right, but it was the first time he'd come across a h'san'kor, and his ignorance of the monster's ways was what killed him. He thought he'd struck a fatal blow and he let his guard down. Before the flute died, it had one second to tear its killer in half."

"Come on, Deler, chop the horns off its head," said Hallas, thoughtfully stroking the handle of his beloved mattock as he looked at the dead beast.

"What?" asked the dwarf.

"You heard! Is that a battle-ax or a stick in your hands! Chop the horns off the head!"

"Why should I, may the darkness take me?"

"Because! Do you know what a h'san'kor's horns are worth?"

"No, I've never sold any to anyone."

"There, you see! You've never sold any! They're priceless! Just think how many gold pieces the Order, may it burn in the abyss, will shell out for a wonder like this! Imagine it, we'll buy a hundred barrels of the finest elfin wine, that Amber Tears, for example."

"You'll burst, Hallas," said Lamplighter, teasing the gnome.

"No, I won't. I won't buy it just for myself! We'll take it to the Lonely Giant, it's high time we fill our cellars up with some good wine."

"Wine for the Giant, you say? Well then, let's give it a try!" Deler spat on his hands and picked up his battle-ax.

"Ah!" Hallas exclaimed regretfully. "We should have grubbed out the first beast's horns, too!"

"Harold!" Kli-Kli called, indicating the man's body with his eyes.

"What?" I asked, knowing what the goblin had in mind.

"I want to see his face. Eel, coming with us?"

"Let's go," Eel replied curtly.

The man was lying facedown with his arms flung out.

"Harold," Kli-Kli said warily, "you turn him over."

"Turn him over yourself."

"Hey, Mumr," Eel barked. "Light a torch and get over here!"

"Coming!"

"Harold, the body won't turn over just because you're standing there," said Kli-Kli, shifting impatiently from one foot to the other, as if he had a sudden urge to visit the bushes.

"Let Eel turn him over," I said, trying to get out of it again.

"I won't do it, I'm not interested. But at least it's obvious he's the same lad the flinny told us about," said Eel.

Just as soon as there's any dirty work to be done (say, going down into Hrad Spein to collect the Rainbow Horn, or turning over a dead body) everyone suddenly remembered Harold. Now, why would that be?

I sighed and did as I'd been asked, and just at that moment Lamplighter arrived with the torch.

"What's all this, never seen a dead man before?" he growled ill-humoredly.

"Bring the torch closer," Kli-Kli said instead of answering. "Pull back his hood, Harold."

I did as the goblin said and saw the dead man's face. This was the last thing I'd been expecting—the warrior was no more than a boy. There was no way he could have been any older than eighteen.

A pale bloodless face, thin bluish lips, chestnut hair sticking to his forehead. A torn gray cloak, a coarse shirt of undyed wool. A thick silver chain hanging down across his chest. And hanging on the chain—a long, smoky-gray crystal.

I leaned down over the dead man, trying to get a closer look at the mysterious stone.

"Kli-Kli, get Egrassa over here, quickly!" Eel suddenly blurted out.

"What for?" the goblin asked in amazement.

"I don't like this—he was torn in half, but there isn't a drop of blood anywhere."

And then the dead man, who only had the top half of his body left, opened his eyes. His hand darted out as fast as a striking snake and grabbed the collar of my jacket.

"You must not . . . take the Horn . . . the balance could be . . . disrupted!"

I tried to break free, but his hand had a strong grip. The gray eyes were looking straight at me, and the young guy's pupils were no larger than pinheads.

The dead man had come to life! But that wasn't what really frightened me. The man (and it was a man lying in front of us) had four long, thin white fangs glittering in his mouth.

"Don't take it . . . do you hear? The balance . . . ," he wheezed.

Someone pulled me back hard by the shoulders and the stranger's hand released its grip.

Kli-Kli yelled for Alistan and Egrassa.

"Are you all right, Harold?" asked Eel.

"Yes," I said, trying not to let my voice tremble.

The elf came running up.

"What's happened here?"

"He came to life and grabbed Harold!" Kli-Kli babbled, nodding at the man with a frightened expression.

"Don't talk bunk, fool," Milord Alistan said with a frown. "He was torn in half, how could he grab anyone?"

"It's true, milord," I said, confirming what Kli-Kli had said, and earning myself a suspicious look from the captain of the guard.

"It's not so very strange; they're telling the truth," said Egrassa, going down on his knees beside the body.

"Careful!" Lamplighter warned him.

"Don't worry, he's dead," said the elf, staring impassively into the stranger's eyes.

Egrassa was right, the veil of death had clouded the warrior's eyes and they had a glassy sheen.

"How could he have stayed alive for so long?" asked Alistan Markauz, still unable to believe it.

"That's easy to explain, look," said Egrassa.

Without the slightest sign of squeamishness, the elf raised the man's upper lip. I hadn't imagined it—the lad really did have thin fangs, like needles.

"That's incredible," Milord Alistan exclaimed, stunned.

"But it's a fact. "

"In a single night we encounter a h'san'kor and . . ." Markauz hesitated.

"Why are you so shocked? A vampire, milord. A genuine vampire."

"Vampires don't exist!" Hallas snorted contemptuously, twirling one of the flute's severed horns in his hands. "That's just a story, like . . ."

The gnome glanced at the horn and stopped in confusion.

"A story? Then who was it that grabbed hold of me? A ghost?" I asked. My heart was still pounding away furiously.

"Vampires do exist, and if you haven't seen them, that doesn't prove anything. That's why he was able to make such short work of the flute and stay alive until we got here," said Egrassa, cautiously feeling at the vampire's fangs.

"Harold, he didn't bite you, did he?" the dwarf suddenly asked out of the blue.

I automatically raised my hand to my neck.

"No. I'm all right."

"Milord Alistan, perhaps we ought to . . . put a stake through this . . . vampire . . . to make sure he stays quiet?"

"He's dead, don't talk nonsense," Eel replied instead of Alistan.

"He's dead now, but what if he suddenly jumps up and starts drinking our blood?"

"Hallas, you've heard too many horror stories. Vampires are almost like people, they're just faster and stronger, and they drink blood. You can kill them with plain ordinary steel, but not with aspen stakes, silver, garlic, or sunlight. All that's just absolute nonsense, like the idea that a vampire can turn into mist or a bat. All right! Now, what's this?"

Egrassa had spotted the crystal. He took it off the body and showed it to us.

"Milord?"

"Now this is getting absolutely absurd," said Alistan, shaking his head.

"What is that thing?" Lamplighter asked, looking at the smoky crystal as if it were a poisonous snake.

"It is the badge of the Order of the Gray Ones," Eel answered his comrade.

Hallas grunted in shock and amazement. Deler whistled, took off his helmet, and scratched the back of his head.

The Order of the Gray Ones.

I didn't know much about them. But then, neither did anyone else there. All my knowledge came from hushed conversations in taverns, unconfirmed rumors, and a book that belonged to my teacher For, which devoted one brief passage to the Order of the Gray Ones.

Far away in the Cold Sea there is an island that is known to the common folk as the Island of the Gray Ones. It is protected by magic and no ship can land there if the island's masters don't want it to. This little scrap of land got its name because it is where the Order of the Gray Ones made its home.

They say they are great warriors, invincible. They are trained from early childhood, and rumor has it that a single Gray One can take on fifteen experienced soldiers and dispatch them all to the darkness with ease. Of course, every tavern has its own bright spark who has met one of these mysterious warriors in person, and if you pour this bright spark a brimming glass, then he'll tell you a colorful tale of how the Gray One killed a hundred knights and then defeated a dragon into the bargain.

I don't know just how much truth there is in all these rumors. But even the most stupid rumor and the most fantastic story are based on at least a tiny grain of truth.

They also say that the Gray Ones are the guardians of equilibrium—the balance—in Siala. They only leave their island when the world is threatened by some really serious danger that could tip the balance in one direction or the other. To put it in simple terms (although this is not quite right), it doesn't matter to the Gray Ones which way the world is tilting—into good or evil, toward the white side or the dark side.

They maintain the balance and in any particular situation they join the weaker side. When good is winning, they're on the side of evil; when evil is winning, they're on the side of good. It's a matter of indifference to them what goals or ideals you pursue and what it is you want—peace throughout the world or evil throughout the Universe. If you threaten the balance, they will try to persuade you to stop. If persuasion doesn't work, then . . . The Gray Ones have a reputation as dangerous warriors and superb magicians, and they will find other ways of changing your mind. The order of mysterious warriors has no ambitions of its own and stands above all sides. It is not white, it is not black.

It is Gray.

"Are you sure this is an absolutely genuine Gray One?" Hallas asked in amazement.

Hallas got up off his knees and tossed the crystal to the gnome.

"Look for yourself. The Order of the Gray Ones gives a chain like that to all its warriors. At least, that is what it says in our chronicles. I've never met one of this brotherhood before in my entire life."

"So the Gray Ones are vampires?" Kli-Kli squeaked, giving the motionless body a wary sideways glance.

"Probably not. Their order is said to include men, and elves, and even orcs. So why not a vampire?" Egrassa said with a shrug. "But what concerns me is what this young lad was doing here in the forest."

"The flinny told us about him," Eel said again. "The vampire was following us."

"I know, but that doesn't answer the question. What did he want from us? The last time these warriors left their island was during the Spring War."

"He said something to Harold," Kli-Kli blurted out.

Everyone turned to look at me.

"What did he say, thief?"

"That we mustn't take the Horn, or the balance could be disrupted," I answered quite candidly, remembering the stranger's whisper.

Silence fell in the clearing.

"Mmm, yes," Kli-Kli murmured thoughtfully, and scratched his hooked nose.

"How did he find us? How does the Order of the Gray Ones know that we're trying to retrieve the Rainbow Horn?" Deler asked.

The dark elf laughed. "They have their own ways of discovering secrets."

"We were fortunate that he was alone," Alistan Markauz murmured.

"What if he isn't?"

"He was alone, Harold," Lamplighter reassured me. "The flinny said so."

Hallas snorted loudly to indicate his opinion of anything Aarroo might have said.

"The Gray Ones must have known that we want to take the Horn out of the burial chambers in order to stop the Nameless One," Kli-Kli insisted. "Why do they think that if Harold gets it, the balance will be disrupted?"

"Perhaps they know something that we don't, Kli-Kli?" I said, remembering the living dream I'd had about how the Forbidden Territory appeared in Avendoom because of the Rainbow. "After all, the magicians of the Order must have had some reason for hiding the Horn in the Palaces of Bone."

"But if the Gray Ones are so afraid of the Horn's return to the world . . . if it's that dangerous . . . maybe we shouldn't try to retrieve it," Lamplighter said uncertainly, forcing out the words.

"We've come too far to stop now," Milord Alistan objected. "And the Order of the Gray Ones might be mistaken. It's just half a day's journey to Hrad Spein, surely we're not going to stop when we're at the very gates?"

"Milord, don't think that I'm a coward, it's just that if that's the way things are and they really did send this mysterious killer after us —"

"Nobody thinks you're a coward, Lamplighter," the captain of the royal guard interrupted him. "You know as well as I do how badly we need that Horn. Egrassa, it's been a hard night and everyone's tired. It's time to make a halt and get some sleep."

The little campfire lit by the elf crackled cheerfully and threw sparks up into the sky. I couldn't get to sleep and just lay there, watching the cold twinkling of the stars. The Archer, the Crayfish Tail, the Swineherd, Sagra's Dogs . . . dozens of constellations gazed down on me through the branches of the trees. The Crown of the North, stretching halfway across the sky, glimmered on the horizon like the coals in the fire.

When an elf dies, a new star lights up in the sky. Perhaps Egrassa was right and it was a foolish superstition, but I strained my eyes until they ached, gazing up at the night sky and trying to make out the star that should have appeared when Miralissa died.

Hopeless.

Even if a star had appeared, I couldn't see with all these trees around us.

A falling star whooshed silently across the night sky. It hurtled past above my head, blinking one last time as it disappeared behind the trees. Usually, when people see a falling star, they make a wish.

What did I want to wish for?

Those who had died on the journey could never be brought back again. Tomcat had been left behind forever in Hargan's Wasteland, beside the old ravine. Loudmouth, who had turned out to be a traitor, never left that cellar near Ranneng. Arnkh and Uncle were at the bottom of the Iselina, thanks to Lafresa's magic. Marmot was buried in the ground of the Border King-dom, Ell's ashes had become part of the river, and Miralissa had found her resting place under the shade of the fir trees. They had all been left behind us. They had done everything they could to get to Zagraba, they had faced deadly danger, caring nothing for their own lives . . . So I had to get my hands on that cursed Horn so the Order could stop the Nameless One. And . . . let no more of those sleeping round this fire be killed on our journey.

Another cold flash in the sky—and another fiery trail streaked between the stars. The orcs called September Por Za'rallo—the Month of Falling Stars.

One more star.

If you looked at the sky for a long, long time, you could see dozens of falling stars that could become our wishes, even if those wishes will probably never come true.

I turned my head and saw Deler. The dwarf couldn't sleep, either. He was sitting huddled up by the fire, staring intently at the flames. Hallas was snoring quietly beside him.

I got up, carefully stepped over Lamplighter, and walked across to Deler. "Can't sleep?"

He broke off from contemplating the dancing flames and looked at me. "You should sleep while you have the chance; I've got to stand watch for another hour until beard-face gets up."

"I can't get to sleep," I said, sitting down beside him.

"I can understand that. After all this . . ."

He paused for a moment and then said reluctantly, "It's so stupid . . . an absurd way to die . . . killed by your own magic . . ."

I didn't say anything, and no words were needed anyway. Everyone was mourning for Miralissa, although they tried not to show it. It was just . . . just that that was the way things were with the Wild Hearts: When a friend dies, don't give way to your tears; find the enemy and take revenge.

Deler grunted as he turned round, picked up a small log off the ground, and threw it into the fire. The flames recoiled and then cautiously licked at the offering, getting the taste of it, and finally fed themselves on the fresh food voraciously.

"You know, a Gray One came to the Mountains of the Dwarves once," Deler said unexpectedly. "It was a long, long time ago, in the very last year of the Purple Years, when we'd almost defeated the gnomes. The final victory was very close, we had our relatives pinned back against the Gates of Grankhel, and he turned up. Well, we dwarves are no fools; we welcomed

our guest with every possible honor and courtesy, took him to the Council . . .
And then the Gray One told us it was in our own best interests to make
peace with the gnomes, and the sooner the better, otherwise in hundreds of
years the balance would shift. He warned us that if the gnomes left the
mountains and moved away, sooner or later they would come back. Some
hothead immediately said: 'Let them come back, we have enough battle-
axes for all of them.' Do you know what the Gray One's answer was? That
we'd sing a different song when the gnomes came to the mountain with
the gunpowder, pistols, and cannons that they would invent because we
drove them out. And he said that someday the gnomes' inventions would be
seized by men, and sooner or later the dwarves and the gnomes would both
be left weeping bitter tears. He told us all that and then he went away. He
didn't even wait for our answer—but then the answer was obvious even to a
Doralissian."

"He just went away?" I asked, unable to believe it.

"Yes, imagine that, Harold. He just went away. He didn't try to persuade
us, he didn't hack us to pieces. . . . He just went on his way. The Council
thought about that, and then decided that even if everything he'd said was
true, there were still hundreds of years before the balance shifted. The Gray
Ones had decided to wait. . . . We won that war, the beard-faces left the
mountain and went to the Steel Mines of Isilia, and for the time being everything more or less settled down. One generation followed another and this
story was almost forgotten. . . . Until the moment came when the gnomes
invented that darkness-damned powder. And then the cannons. And then
our wise old heads remembered the old story, and when they remembered,
it set them thinking. It turned out that the Order of the Gray Ones had told
us the truth. It all happened—the powder and the cannons . . . only no one
had heard anything yet about those strange pistols. But now I've seen Hallas
holding one of them in his hands. And that means the day's not far off when
the gnomes will decide to return to their old home. . . . And then you'll grab
their weapons, and then we'll all be in a bad way. . . ."

"Why are you telling me all this?"

The dwarf looked at me thoughtfully.

"Darkness only knows, Harold. It's just that this story shows the Gray
Ones don't often make mistakes, and if that vampire told you that when we
fish the Horn out of Hrad Spein the balance will be disrupted, then that's
probably exactly what will happen."

"He said it *could* be disrupted."

"Do you understand the old gnomes' fable? You're sitting on a keg of gunpowder and the fuse is burning. And your only hope is that it will start to rain and put out the fuse. Do you understand what I'm getting at?"

"Perfectly," I chuckled.

"That Horn was created by the ogres to protect them against their own magic, right?"

"That's what the Order says."

"Well then, I don't have to explain to you how dangerous things that were made in the Dark Era are."

"So you think like Mumr, that the artifact should be left where it is now? In Grok's grave?"

"I don't know, Harold. The Rainbow Horn neutralizes the magic of the Nameless One. If the Horn is in Avendoom, the sorcerer will be forced to retreat forever. Without his magic, he's nothing. . . . So, we need the Horn. On the other hand, that phrase 'could be' . . . Perhaps we'll be bringing something even more terrible into the world? There must be a reason why it was so well hidden, mustn't there?"

"More terrible than the Nameless One?"

"Yes."

"There's nothing we can do but trust in the gods, Deler."

The dwarf chuckled quietly and stirred the embers with a stick, frightening up a cloud of sparks.

"I shouldn't have started this conversation. Now you'll have doubts. Get that thrice-cursed Horn, and then we'll figure out what's what. . . . Go and sleep."

"In a moment," I said.

"Did you see the spear that Gray One had?" the gnome asked.

"The one that Egrassa took?"

"Our elf knows a good thing when he sees it." Deler laughed. "Yes, that's the one."

"A spear like any other," I said with a gentle shrug. "Just a bit strange."

"Ah, you men. . . . You're always boasting about how superior you are, but in so many things you're just like little children," Deler grumbled. "When you say 'strange,' do you mean the shape or something else?"

"The shape," I replied, although I knew it was the wrong answer.

"That's what I thought," the dwarf sighed. "It's not really a spear, it's a krasta, a kind of pike. You can slash with it and stab with it. You don't come across them very often, especially in the Northern Lands. It was invented in Mambara, a country way beyond the Sultanate. But that's not important right now. None of you men took any notice of the handle and the metal of the blade. But Egrassa and I spotted it straightaway. And Hallas probably did, too, although the dratted beard-face isn't saying anything."

"What about the handle and the metal?"

"There are ancient runes on the handle. You can barely even see them, but it's the first language of the gnomes. The language of the time of the great ones Grahel and Chigzan—the first dwarf and the first gnome. Don't ask me what it says, I'm a warrior, not a Master, and I could only recognize a few runes. With a spear like that you can strike through any magical shield."

"Oho!"

"Yes indeed, 'oho.' And as for the metal that was used for the blade, in the old days, back in the Age of Achievements, it used to be known as Smoky Steel. Ever heard of it?"

"No."

"That's not surprising. We forgot a lot of things during the Purple Years. The secret of smelting . . . it has been lost—forever, I'm afraid. But there was a time . . . there was a time when gnomes and dwarves worked together. Some prospected for ore and made steel, others gave it the required form and invoked the magic. Ruby Blood can never compare with Smoky Steel. It cut through everything. Anything the blade fell on—a silk handkerchief, stone, or the finest armor."

"How much did it cost?" I blurted out.

"A lot," Deler chuckled. "So much that only a king . . . or the Gray Ones . . . could afford a blade made out of it. Imagine you're facing a front-line knight-at-arms. Heavy armor, a full-length shield. Like a tortoise in a shell. You could sweat yourself to death trying to get at him with a sword. But you just take a blade of Smoky Steel and hit him across the helmet, and it will slice through the man like a knife through butter, split him into two neat halves. And his helmet, armor, and shield, too."

"So it's very valuable?"

That earned me a suspicious glance from the dwarf.

"Valuable? It's priceless! Give it to the king and you can ask for a duke-dom and a hundred ships and a summer palace, and anything else you might fancy."

Deler tossed more wood into the fire.

"Come on, Harold, get some sleep. It's a hard day tomorrow. Or are you trying to follow the elf's example?"

"Where is he, by the way?"

"Over that way, not very far."

"I'll take a stroll that way," I said, getting up off the log.

Deler just waved his hand: Okay, take a stroll.

The night was coming to an end; the stars had faded and the full moon was already turning pale. The elf was a dark silhouette against the pale background of a golden-leaf's trunk. He was sitting on the ground, with his hands on his knees, and his eyes were closed.

The grass rustled under my feet. Egrassa made a movement too fast for me to follow, and there was an arrow pointing straight at me, already poised on his bowstring. I froze to let the elf take a good look at me.

"What are you doing here?" Egrassa asked in a surly voice, but he put the bow away.

"Deler said you were here."

"So what?"

I hesitated. Yes, so what? What in the name of darkness had brought me this way? Those yellow eyes were watching me closely.

"I'm very sorry about what happened to Miralissa, too."

Silence.

"She has a daughter, doesn't she?"

"How do you know that?"

"She told me."

"She told you. . . . She trusted you people so much . . . she respected you, she didn't think you were really that bad. She should never have left the House of the Black Moon. None of us should have."

"I . . ."

"Just get that Horn, Harold. Just get it. Prove to me and my kinsmen that Miralissa was not mistaken. Now go, you're bothering me."

That was it. Who can ever tell what's going inside these elves?

"Harold!" he called to me.

"Yes?"

"Will you get it?"

"Yes, I'll get it."

"No doubt or hesitation?"

"No doubt or hesitation," I answered, after a pause.

He seemed satisfied with my answer; at least, he didn't say another word about it.

"We don't have to worry about the Firstborn any longer," said the elf, leaning on his new weapon.

"But we do have to worry about Balistan Pargaid and his men; there are more than twenty of them," said Milord Alistan, checking to make sure that his sword left the scabbard smoothly.

"And Lafresa," Kli-Kli reminded him. "She's worth twenty warriors."

The fool was right: Lafresa was dangerous, especially now, when we didn't have Miralissa with us.

"Let's go, but quietly, it's not very far to the gates now," the dark elf warned us, and set off along the track.

We walked through a grove that consisted of nothing but golden-leafs, trees beyond compare with anything we'd seen before. The huge, ancient trunks were more than fifteen yards around, the crowns of the trees soared so high that they seemed to prop up the very sky. Here and there orange roots protruded from the ground, each of them four times as thick as a grown man's thigh. The sun's rays pierced the golden crowns like arrows, flying down through the morning mist that had still not dispersed and striking the ground. This was how I had pictured Zagraba in my imagination— majestically beautiful.

D-r-r-r-r . . . d-r-r-r-r-r . . .

"That woodpecker's working hard," Deler croaked admiringly.

"Quiet!" Egrassa hissed, listening to the sounds of the forest.

The wind quietly rustled the murmuring crowns of the golden-leafs, and the woodpecker continued with his tireless search for food, setting the forest ringing with his *dr-r-r-rr-r*. Little birds chirped and insects buzzed in the grass; the forest was as alive and busy as if it was midsummer, not early autumn.

"There are men . . . nearby."

The elf leaned the krasta against a tree, set a new string on his bow, and took an arrow out of his quiver.

"I'll go to check . . . if you hear any noise, be ready. . . ."

"Eel, go with him," Alistan Markauz ordered.

"Yes, milord. Harold, will you lend me your crossbow?"

"It's loaded," I said, handing the Garrakian the weapon and two extra bolts.

"If everything's all right, I'll whistle," said Egrassa.

The elf and the man disappeared into the dense undergrowth of gorse. For a long time we heard nothing apart from the sounds of the forest, and everyone listened to the trilling of the birds and the rustling of the branches. Eventually we heard a faint whistle in the distance.

"Forward!" ordered Alistan Markauz. "Kli-Kli, don't get under our feet."

"When do I ever get in the way?" Kli-Kli grumbled. "That's what Harold does."

I laughed, but didn't say anything and picked up the elf's spear.

Egrassa and Eel were waiting for us in a shady meadow surrounded by a neat circle of golden-leafs . . . with three men lying at their feet. Two of them were dead. The elf's arrow had easily pierced the chain mail of one of Balistan Pargaid's soldiers and stuck in his heart. The other, who was still clutching a small ax, had taken an arrow in the eye. The third man was alive—squirming on the ground with a crossbow bolt in his leg.

"Who have we got here?"

"That's what we're trying to find out, milord," Eel said, clearing his throat and handing me the crossbow. "Egrassa killed the first one straight-away, the second one grabbed an ax and got shot in the eye. The third one tried to run; I had to shoot him in the leg."

"Who are you and what are you doing here?" Alistan Markauz asked sharply, turning to the prisoner.

The man just wailed and clutched at his wounded leg.

"Why do you ask, milord, as if you didn't know?" Kli-Kli asked in surprise. "These are Balistan Pargaid's dogs, you can tell from their faces!"

"He'll tell me everything he knows," said the elf. He stepped on the man's injured leg and the man howled and lost consciousness.

Hallas took out a flask of water and splashed some in the man's face. No response. He had to slap the man hard on the cheek. The man shuddered and opened his eyes.

"And now we'll have a talk," said Egrassa, holding his crooked dagger to the man's chest. "How many of you are there?"

"What?" said the man, licking his lips.

"How many of you are there?" Egrassa repeated, pricking the man with his dagger.

That worked.

"Three, there were only three of us! Don't kill me, milord! I'll tell you everything!" the man babbled, staring wide-eyed at the dark elf and obviously taking him for an orc.

"Where are the others?"

"They all . . . went away."

"You're lying," said Egrassa, pressing in the dagger.

The man squealed and yelled.

"I'm telling the truth, they all went and left us here on guard! I haven't done anything, honestly! Don't kill me!"

"Perhaps this goon really doesn't know anything?" Deler boomed.

"Of course he does! Egrassa, you leave him to me and I'll soon shake him out of his trance!" Hallas suggested, rolling his eyes furiously.

"Where did they go?" asked Egrassa, ignoring the gnome.

"Into the burial chambers, they all went into those burial chambers cursed by the darkness, milord orc!"

"When?"

"Two days ago."

"How many men went down there?"

"Ten."

"He's lying," said Kli-Kli, performing simple calculations in his head.

"That's not important. . . . Did the count go with them?"

"Yes, milord."

"And the woman?" I blurted out.

"The witch? She's with them, too. It was all her idea! She was the one who decided to go down there!"

"Why did they go?"

"They didn't tell us. Me and the others were just supposed to stay here and wait for the rest of them to come back. That's all. I don't know anything else."

"That's a shame," said the elf, plunging the dagger into the man's chest up to the hilt.

The prisoner shuddered and went limp. Without showing any sign of emotion, Egrassa pulled the dagger out and wiped it on the dead man's clothes.

"Deler! Hallas!" Alistan Markauz called to the dwarf and the gnome. "Bury these three. There's no point in us hanging about any longer."

And that was the end of the matter, except for the dwarf and the gnome muttering discontentedly that they were soldiers, not gravediggers.

"Well, how do you like it, Harold?" Eel asked me when I walked away to one side.

"Elves," I said with a shrug, thinking he was asking how I felt about the recent killing.

"That's not what I meant," Eel said with a frown. "I meant the entrance to Hrad Spein."

"Why, where is it?" I gasped.

Kli-Kli heaved a tragic sigh. "Harold, you're hopeless! What do you think that is, if not the entrance?"

"A hill?" I asked in amazement.

"A hill!" Kli-Kli teased me, pulling a silly face. "Open your eyes, will you! What kind of hill, may you choke on a bone, is that? Go on, walk round it!"

"All right! All right! Just stop yammering," I said, trying to calm the goblin down. "I've got a splitting headache from that squeal of yours."

It really was the entrance to Hrad Spein, or at least, on closer examination the hill turned out to be artificial. It was hardly surprising that I hadn't realized—the structure was so old (from the start of the Dark Era, after all!) that the back of it was all overgrown with grass and bushes. When I walked round it to the other side, though, I realized I'd got the era wrong.

Of course the gates weren't from the Dark Era at all (although that was when unknown beings had founded the first and deepest levels of Hrad Spein). The gates had appeared much, much later, during the period when the orcs and the elves were in their heyday. It was just that after the ancient evil awoke in the Palaces of Bone and elves and orcs (and, after them, men) left the burial chambers to be demolished by the centuries, the gates fell into decay and were overgrown by the forest.

After all, Zagraba, and especially the Golden Forest, hadn't always been here. The trees had been advancing for thousands of years. And they advanced until they swallowed up the gates and concealed them from prying eyes.

From this side the hill looked as if it had been sliced vertically with a knife. And instead of grass and bushes there was a gaping square entrance four times the height of a man. The rays of sunlight slanted into it and fell on a stone floor.

I shuddered.

"Well, how do you like it, Harold?" the Garrakian asked again.

"Are we really here, then?" I still didn't believe it.

"The corridor stretches for a thousand yards, gradually sloping down. It's a long tramp from here to the first level," said Kli-Kli, waving his hand jauntily.

"You're a real expert on the subject, jester. So can you tell me what's written over the entrance and what those statues are at the sides?"

"I don't know orcic, Harold, ask Egrassa what that scribble says. And as for the statues, they were carved out of the solid rock, see? And they're so badly decayed, there's no way to tell who they once depicted."

"Hey, you historians!" shouted Hallas. "Let's go and get the camp laid out, you'll have time enough to feast your eyes on that!"

"And so," Alistan Markauz began when everyone was gathered together (apart from Lamplighter and Eel, who had been sent to stand guard at the entrance to Hrad Spein), "Balistan Pargaid and his men are already down below."

"May something down there gobble them up!" was the kind-hearted goblin's sincere wish for our enemies.

"They're two days ahead of us, thief. You have maps of the Palaces of Bone. Where do you think they could be now?"

"Anywhere at all, milord," I answered the count, after a moment's thought. "It's a genuine maze starting from the very first level, if they don't have maps. . . ."

Everyone understood what I had in mind. In Hrad Spein without maps you were a dead man for sure. Fortunately, I did have maps; I'd made a special excursion into the Forbidden Territory in Avendoom to get them. So I would find the way to the eighth level, where the Rainbow Horn was. That is, I'd be able to find the way, but would I actually get there?

"I think we should start out straightaway," said Alistan Markauz, tugging on his mustache.

"It will be night soon, milord. Let's wait until morning," Hallas began cautiously. "I don't like the idea of climbing down that hole in the dark."

"Night, day . . . what's the difference? Down below it's always night anyway. Pargaid and that woman want to steal a march on us and take the Horn, in order to take it to the Master."

"They won't be able to steal a march on us, milord," I said, chuckling sardonically. "They don't have the Key, and the Doors on the third level can't be opened without it. If they don't have a map, and Lafresa decides to make a detour . . . Well, that will take them a couple of months."

"A couple of months?" the dwarf asked incredulously.

"This is Hrad Spein below us," said Egrassa, stamping on the ground. "I hate to shatter your rosy illusions, Deler, but the Palaces of Bone are a lot bigger than all your underground cities in the Mountains of the Dwarves. Hrad Spein is like a gigantic layer cake, it's dozens of leagues deep and wide. It was worked on by ogres, orcs, men, and others we don't even know about. So Harold is right. If you don't go through the Doors, you can lose a great deal of time searching for ways round them."

"And run into some very big problems," Kli-Kli bleated.

"So do you suggest we should wait until morning, too," the captain of the guard asked the elf, ignoring the goblin.

"Best go down well rested."

Milord Rat pursed his lips and nodded reluctantly.

"All right. That's what we'll do. Then let's decide who's going with Harold, and who's staying up here."

"I think that's for Harold to decide," said Egrassa, and looked at me.

"The thief should decide?" Alistan Markauz said in amazement.

"Certainly. He knows best who should go with him and who should stay."

"All right," the count hissed. "What do you say, thief?"

I took a deep breath and said, "No one's going with me."

"What? Have you gone completely insane?"

I was afraid Alistan Markauz was about to have a stroke.

"No, milord." I decided to say exactly what I thought about our crazy excursion to Hrad Spein. "When you led us out of Avendoom, I didn't interfere and I did what you said. And when we were walking through Zagraba, you did what Egrassa told you. I don't need anyone else to go into the Palaces of Bone with me. You'd only be a burden to me."

"We're soldiers, Harold, not a burden," Deler said resentfully. "Who's going to save you from those zombies?"

"That's just the point," I sighed. "On my own, I'll slip past a corpse unnoticed or simply run away, but with you I'll get into a fight every time. I won't be able to look out for you in there, too."

"We can look out for ourselves, thief." Alistan Markauz didn't like what I'd said very much. "How am I going to protect you if I stay up here?"

"You have led us to Hrad Spein and performed your duty, milord. And in addition, they say the lower levels are flooded and I'll have to swim, and you're wearing too much heavy metal."

"Then I'll take off my armor."

"Milord, I'll move fast, but with you . . . Just don't interfere with me carrying out the Commission."

"What about Balistan Pargaid's men?"

"The chances of meeting them in a maze like this are not very high."

It took me an entire hour to persuade the captain of the guard that it was easier for me to go alone. He ground his teeth and frowned, but in the end, he gave up.

"All right, thief, have it your own way. But I'm not very happy with my own decision."

"Do you have the maps of Hrad Spein?" Kli-Kli asked.

"Yes," I sighed.

Since first thing in the morning the goblin had been getting on my nerves worse than a crowd of priests chanting their sacred rubbish.

"What about torches?"

"I've got two."

"Are you joking?" the fool inquired acidly.

"Certainly not. Two torches will be more than enough to reach the first level."

"And after that are you going to grope your way along?"

"You told me yourself that there's plenty of light in the underground palaces."

"If the magic's still working, but what if it isn't? And not all of Hrad Spein is palaces. . . ."

"I have my lights, too."

"Why didn't you tell me that straightaway? Instead of treating me like an idiot!" he said, genuinely furious. "All right. What about food?"

"Kli-Kli, are you deliberately to trying to get my goat? You've asked me that twice already!" I groaned. "I've got plenty of magic biscuits. I don't have to worry about food for two weeks."

"Warm clothes?"

"Uh-huh."

Darkness only knew what it was like down in the depths. I'd taken Eel's double-knitted wool sweater—it was the kind that Wild Hearts wear in winter on patrol in the Slumbering Forest. Wearing it was as good as sitting in front of a hot stove. And its greatest advantage was that it could be rolled up into a slim little bundle that fitted easily into the half-empty canvas sack hanging over my shoulder.

"And have you . . ."

"No more!" I implored him. "You and your questions will drive me into my grave! Take a break for half an hour at least."

"In half an hour you'll be beyond my reach," Kli-Kli objected, and carried on mercilessly. "Do you remember the poem?"

"Which one?"

"He still has to ask!" the goblin exclaimed, appealing tragically to the heavens. "Have you forgotten the scroll you showed us at the meeting with the king?"

"Ah! You mean the verse riddle? I remember it perfectly."

"Repeat it."

"Kli-Kli, believe me, I remember it perfectly."

"Then repeat it. Don't you understand that it's the key to everything? It mentions things that aren't in the maps."

"Darkness take you." It was easier to recite it than to argue with the detestable little goblin. "From the very beginning?"

"You can leave out the flowery bits."

"All right," I growled. "But if you don't leave me alone after this, I'll strangle you with my bare hands."

So I strained my memory and recited the verse riddle for Kli-Kli.

I came across the poem purely by chance. It was scratched on a small scrap of paper lost in among the maps and papers about Hrad Spein that I found in the abandoned Tower of the Order. The poem was written by a magician who took the Rainbow Horn to the Palaces of Bone. And it was thanks to this work of literature that I'd been able to see my future route as I looked through the maps of Hrad Spein during our group's evening halts.

"That'll do," the pestiferous goblin said with a satisfied nod when I finished declaiming the final quatrain. "Don't forget it. And, by the way, remember that one section has been changed, I already told you about it. In the *Book of Prophecies* . . ."

"I remember," I interrupted him hastily. Believe it or not, but by this time I couldn't wait to dash into Hrad Spein so I wouldn't have to hear any more good advice.

"You're rotten, Harold," said Kli-Kli, offended. "I'm trying my best for you! All right, damn you, someday you'll remember this goblin's kindness, but it'll be too late. Bend down."

"What?" I asked, puzzled.

"Bend down toward me, I tell you! I can't reach up to you, I'm too short!"

I had to do as the jester asked, although I was expecting some farewell trick from him. Kli-Kli stood on tiptoe and hung a drop-shaped medallion round my neck—the one he found on the sorceress's grave in Hargan's Wasteland. The medallion had one invaluable quality—it could neutralize shamanic battle spells directed specifically at the wearer.

"In olden times the elves and orcs filled the palaces with magical traps. And this bauble can keep you safe from at least some of them."

"Thank you," I said, genuinely moved by his unexpected generosity.

"You bring it back to me," the goblin said peevishly. "And bring yourself along with it, preferably with that Horn."

I gave a brief chuckle.

"Well then, thief, it's time," Milord Alistan said.

"Yes, milord." I ran through my equipment in my mind for the tenth time to check that I hadn't left anything out, and then slung the crossbow over my shoulder. "Expect me in two weeks."

"We'll wait for three."

"All right. If I'm not back by then, leave."

"If you're not back by then, someone else will go in. I won't go back to the king without the Horn."

I nodded. Milord Rat was a stubborn man and he wouldn't give up until he got what he wanted.

"Here, Harold," said Egrassa, holding out a bracelet of red copper, "put this on your arm."

It looked just like an ordinary bracelet, although it was very old, and it had badly worn orcic runes on it.

"What is it?"

"It will let me know that you're alive and where you are. And it will get you past the Kaiyu guards safely."

I gaped at the elf in amazement, but he just shrugged and smiled.

"They say that it protects against them, that's what it was made for, but don't rely on it too much. I haven't tried it myself."

I nodded gratefully and put the bracelet on my left arm. Sagot had obviously decided this was Harold's day for collecting trinkets. Well, I didn't mind, the verse riddle mentioned the Kaiyu guards, and if the elf believed this artifact could save me from the blind guardians of the elfin burial chambers, I should definitely accept his gift with gratitude.

"May the gods be with you," the elf told me as we said good-bye.

"Don't let your king and his kingdom down, Harold," Milord Alistan declared pompously, calling me by my own name for once.

"Good luck!" said Eel, shaking me firmly by the hand.

Deler, Hallas, and Mumr did the same.

"Good luck, Dancer in the Shadows," the jester said with a sniff.

"Expect me in two weeks," I reminded them again, then swung round and walked toward the black hole that led to the heart of the ancient burial chambers.

4

THE ROAD TO THE DOORS

The torch hissed and spat furiously. It obviously didn't like the idea of being carried down into the murky gloom of the world underground.

I stopped twice to look back. The first time was when I'd only walked a hundred and fifty paces along the corridor. I just wanted to take one last look at the sunlight.

A long, long way behind me, I could see a tiny bright rectangle.

The way out.

There it was, left behind now, the world of sunlight, the world of the living, and below my feet lay the world of darkness and the dead. When I looked back for the second time, the light had disappeared and there was nothing but the darkness all around.

My huge black shadow slid along the wall, dancing in time to the flames. After a while pictures and inscriptions in orcic appeared on the walls. At first they were faint and I could barely make them out (despite the constant darkness in this place, the colors used for the paintings and writing had faded very badly), but after I walked another two hundred yards, I could distinguish the images and letters.

I didn't look very closely at the pictures, and I didn't understand the writing. I only stopped once, when the torch picked out of the darkness a huge painting of an epic battle between ogres and some other beings, who were the spitting image of the creatures shown on the casket where Balistan Pargaid used to keep the Key.

The creatures—half birds, half bears—were fighting the ogres between the trunks of stylized trees. There was a squiggly inscription below the scene, but what it meant was a total mystery to me.

I walked for quite a long time. The corridor had no branches, and it bit deeper and deeper into the earth. I didn't know exactly how deep I'd gone, but I took the opportunity to thank Sagot that I wasn't afraid of underground places.

My steps echoed hollowly off the floor, bounced off the walls, and died away under the high ceiling. The torch started to fade and I had to stop to light a new one. I hadn't even noticed the time passing. How long had I been tramping along this corridor?

The surprising thing was that it didn't feel cold in here at all. Dry warm air blew into my face as it rose up toward the way out. I didn't bother wondering where a breeze could come from at that depth. It could have been ventilation shafts, magic, or something else. Darkness only knew. All I knew was that there was a draft. And the most important thing was that it wasn't chilly.

The flights of steps began. At first only three or four steps at a time, then they got longer and longer. Corridor, then steps, another hundred yards of corridor and then another stairway. Getting deeper and darker all the time.

I decided to make a halt and stopped. Leaning back against the wall, I arranged the torch so that it wouldn't go out, stretched out my legs, and took a swallow of water from my flask. I'd tramped all this way and still had not reached the first level yet! I took the piece of drokr out of my bag, unfolded it, and took out the maps of Hrad Spein. I didn't know exactly where I was at the moment, but soon the corridor would start twisting round into a spiral. Six huge turns leading down into the abyss, toward the first level of the Palaces of Bone. But I had to go on farther than that—to the eighth level. That was where the grave of General Grok was, and the Rainbow Horn was lying on his gravestone.

Long weary days of travel lay ahead before I could reach the eighth level. At least a week, even if I was lucky. A week to reach the eighth level—then how long would it take to get to the forty-eighth? Or even deeper, to where the levels had no names, where no living creatures had set foot for nine thousand years?

The corridor took a twist, and then another. I started winding round and round, getting deeper and deeper all the time.

The light picked another inscription out of the darkness and I stopped dead—it was written in human language.

I moved the torch close to the wall. Just as I'd thought—the letters were dark red. They were written in blood. Someone had patiently traced out just

three words in large letters: DON'T GO DOWN! I stood there for a moment, looking at this warning, then walked on a few more paces and came
across another two words: GET OUT!

After another eternity of time, after the sixth wide turn of the spiral, it
started getting brighter in the corridor. At first I thought it was my eyes
playing tricks, but the darkness retreated, giving way to a thick twilight.
After another ten paces I was surrounded by a pale gray light that seemed to
flow out of the walls. I could see perfectly well, and I had to struggle to stop
myself putting the torch out.

The floor under my feet began sloping down even more sharply, until it
was like a steep hill. I had to walk very slowly and carefully in order not to
miss my step and go slithering down on my backside. The light was still
there and, after hesitating for a moment, I tossed the torch away. The hill
came to a sudden end, the floor leveled out, the corridor turned a corner,
and I saw what I'd already despaired of seeing—the entrance to the first
level of the Palaces of Bone.

Well, when I call it an entrance, that's a slight exaggeration. There was
nothing left of it. The stairway connecting the Threshold of Hrad Spein
with the first level had collapsed, and the upper part that remained led
down into a gaping hole.

I cautiously walked up to the edge of the hole and looked down.

Four steps, and then empty space. The path continued about eight yards
away from me and the fragments of the stairway lay in a heap. It was all
very strange . . . Very strange . . . What lousy skunk could have smashed it
like that?

Oh yes, it had been smashed, all right, otherwise why would the surviving steps be so thickly covered in soot and even melted in places? Someone
used a spell on the stairway before I got there. And there was no doubt that
this someone was Lafresa.

But I couldn't quite understand the logic. In the first place, how were she
and Balistan Pargaid and his men planning to get back out now? And in the
second place, it was rather strange, to say the least, for her to think that I
wouldn't be able to get down. No, of course, jumping from that height was
a sure way to shatter all your bones into tiny little pieces, but there are other
ways of getting down from high spots apart from jumping. For instance, an
elfin cobweb rope that sticks to any surface and naturally lifts its owner to
any height he wants.

Lafresa was no fool, and she must have known I could get down. That meant things weren't as simple as they looked and there was a warm welcome in store for me, complete with royal orchestra and heralds. It was better to check a hundred times over that there was no danger before I jumped down the demon's throat.

I had to lie on the floor and hang over the hole to study the spot where I would land as painstakingly as possible.

Mmm, yes.

A magnificently lit corridor with burning torches on the walls and a heap of stones, splinters, and fine dust on the floor. The torches were no surprise, they'd been blazing away here for thousands of years, and they'd keep burning for at least as long—the shamanic magic wouldn't let the flames go out.

It was time to reach into my bag and take out a vial of a certain magical substance. I lay down on my stomach again and poured a few drops straight down onto the heap of rubble.

What I saw exceeded my wildest expectations. In fact, to be honest, I was so surprised I almost tumbled over the edge. Because there was a creature sitting on the rubble heap. The beast had been hidden by a spell that made it invisible until I splashed the magical liquid on it.

Anyway, it was sprawling right underneath the hole with its jaws wide open, waiting patiently for supper to drop in. This monster must have been born in the charming but definitely insane head of my friend Lafresa. There couldn't be any natural beast in the world that consisted of nothing but jaws and row upon row upon row of blinding-white, dagger-sharp teeth! With a bit of an effort, an entire knight on horseback could have been forced down the throat of that hungry monster.

What a devious snake Lafresa was; what a magnificent trap she had set for me! I imagined how astonished I would have been to climb down the rope and find myself in the belly of this ravenous beast. What an inglorious way to go, and at the very first level of the Palaces of Bone!

I felt like shooting a crossbow bolt straight down the monster's throat, but what I needed for that was a ballista, not a crossbow. An ordinary bolt wouldn't even touch it. And Kli-Kli's medallion probably wouldn't be any use against a nightmare like this.

I furiously felt around on the floor, picked up a fragment of stone a bit larger than my fist, and tossed it right into the middle of those gaping jaws. The trap worked perfectly. When the stone landed, the toothy mouth slammed shut.

Snap!

I hope that gives you indigestion!

The stone wasn't to the monster's liking, and it disappeared, with a deafening *pop*.

What in the name of . . . A trap that only works once and then isn't needed again!

But I'm far too suspicious by nature to fall for the sudden disappearance trick. So I used a few more drops of the liquid that revealed any hidden magical traps. Nothing. The jaws really were gone.

Even so, I felt a bit apprehensive as I climbed down the rope. So for my own peace of mind, when there were only two yards left to the floor, I took one hand off the rope, reached into my bag, and dropped a stone I'd brought along. It clattered on the floor, no one was waiting underneath me. I climbed down and mentally ordered the cobweb rope to release its grip, then coiled it up and attached it to my belt.

Time to be moving on.

Now I was in a large empty hall with eight lighted torches. There was an opening in each wall, and it took me a few seconds to get my bearings from the maps. At that depth it was absolutely impossible to tell which way was north and which way was south, but fortunately for me the Hall of Arrival, as it was called in the maps, had a very clear sign for anyone foolish enough to visit the Palaces of Bone. To discover which way was which, you just had to raise your head and look up at the ceiling, on which someone's skillful hands had marked out a huge arrow to tell the traveler which way was north. And according to the arrow, I had to go through the opening on the far right.

Naturally, the universal law of Harold's good luck determined that this opening led into the darkest and narrowest corridor. And unlike the other three, which were wider and brighter, this one ran upward instead of down. I stopped at the entrance and listened carefully.

Not a murmur. Not a sound. Just a single torch burning about forty paces ahead of me. Was this really my way? I had to reach into my bag and check the maps again. Yes, it looked right. I cast another wistful look at the more inviting corridors, but there was nothing to be done, I had to trust the map.

The passage to the halls that followed was so narrow that my shoulders touched the walls and I had to walk half-sideways, like a crab. And I felt so frightened by the stories about the reawakened evil of the ogre's bones that I kept stopping to listen to the silence.

Fortunately for me, the silence remained just that, silence, and I didn't hear any strange or inexplicable sounds. I walked past the first torch, then a second, and a third. The corridor kept rising gently upward and I started getting more and more worried that I was going the wrong way, even though this was definitely the way shown on the map. As far as I understood things, the eighth level ought to be below the first, not above it. Up there above me was Zagraba, not a complex of the burial chambers. I stopped at the seventh torch and tried to take it out of its bracket. It was a waste of time—the torch was set absolutely solid and it wouldn't budge.

The slow climb came to an end, the corridor took a sharp right-angled turn and led me out into a small space with two passages branching off it. Here it was as bright as in the first hall, and there was no need to check the map. I remembered which way I had to go.

It took me six hours to reach the stairway leading to the second level. Not so very long, if you think about it. To be quite honest, I must say I wasn't really very impressed by the first level. It would be a lie to say I was actually disappointed, but the rumors about Hrad Spein seemed to have been seriously exaggerated.

And I was hoping the rest of my journey would be just as tedious and boring. In fact, though, I shouldn't really have expected anything else on the first level. Not even men had ever buried anyone here; it was more of a general entrance. The levels of the ogres were very far away, and the Doors on the third level protected everything above them against the evil of the depths. The human burial sites started on the second level, and there were some on the third level, too (where the dead had been buried off to the sides of the Doors). And on the sixth level, too, of course, where the bones of the heroic warriors lay. Grok's grave, down on the eighth level, was something of an exception to the rule.

The entire first level had turned out to be a tangled network of halls, corridors, and rooms. Twice I lost my way, checked the map, and had to retrace my steps, looking for the right passage. Everywhere I found dreary walls of gray basalt with no decorations of any kind, and sometimes the surfaces were crudely worked. Three times I came across stairways leading down into darkness, but I prudently avoided going down them. Who could tell how far they might take me out of my way—and they weren't shown on the maps, anyway. Four times I stopped to rest. The dreariness and semi-darkness in this place were terribly depressing, my eyes and my head and my legs all ached unmercifully, and when I finally reached the stairway I needed I heaved a sigh of something very much like relief.

The silence of the mute halls weighed heavy on my ears and I felt like howling, just to hear some kind of living sound. Surprisingly enough, even at that depth it wasn't cold; in fact, if anything it was actually warm. And best of all, there were no drafts, not even a breath of wind, and the flames of the torches burned steadily without trembling and setting the shadows dancing across the walls. At the same time the air in the halls was as fresh and clean as if I was strolling through Zagraba, not wandering through the catacombs. There must have been some magic involved in that, too.

Anyway, the impressions I took away from the first level made up a rather blurred picture. Fortunately for me, the quatrain from the verse riddle hadn't come true. Which quatrain was that? This one:

> If you are artful and brave, bold and quick,
> If your step is light and your thought is keen,
> You will avoid the tricks that we have set there,
> But be wary of earth and water and fire.

So far, Sagot be praised, none of this had happened. And I was hoping that none of the other verses in that stupid little poem from the magicians of the Order would come true, either.

But even though I hadn't run into anyone, I was still desperately tired. Maybe because, out of old habit, I had stuck close to the walls, running from half-shadow to shadow, trying to avoid the brightly lit spots and stopping every two minutes to listen to the silence. So I was mentally tired as well as physically.

I found a comfortable place for a rest, in the far corner of the hall, where the walls were hung with thick shade. The journey had left me ravenously hungry, and I wolfed down another half biscuit without the slightest hesitation. The magical biscuit was a thin slab no larger than my hand. After eating half of one I felt as full as if I'd dined at a king's feast and worked my way through a hundred and one different dishes. It was filling all right, but not very tasty. At best its taste could be compared to bread, and at worst to moldy straw. You could eat it, but you couldn't really enjoy it. Unless, of course, you happened to be a horse.

When I finished chewing the biscuit, I washed it down with water from the flask and settled down for the night. I needed at least a short rest to re-store my strength. I set the crossbow down beside me and fell asleep.

I can't say that I slept like a baby. Hrad Spein isn't exactly the best place for sweet dreams. I hovered in the boundary zone between sleeping and waking, sometimes sinking deeper into sleep, sometimes rising to the sur-face. It was a very nervous kind of sleep, and I opened my eyes about six times and grabbed the crossbow, but there was no danger and the hall was as empty as ever, with just the torch twinkling on the far wall.

The sleep did me a world of good. At least, I woke feeling refreshed and—most surprising of all—safe and sound. No one had tried to bite off my leg or my head while I was sleeping, for which I immediately rendered thanks to Sagot.

I paused for a short while at the broad stone stairway that swept down into darkness. I didn't know what might be hidden down there in the gloom, and I didn't feel like testing my skin against the sharpness of some ugly monster's teeth. But no matter how long I stood there, the Rainbow Horn wouldn't come crawling up to meet me. I sighed, took out a light, gave it a shake to make it flare into life, and put my foot on the first step of the stairway leading to the second level.

It was absolutely pitch black on the stairway, and if not for my cold magical light, it would have taken me at least an hour to get down.

The steps kept going down. They didn't curl round into a spiral, they didn't dance about like a drunken viper, they just stretched on and on, leading me deeper and deeper, and the feeble light of my magical lamp barely even reached the ceiling.

Before I reached the second level, I counted 1,244 steps. It will always remain a mystery who built this monstrously long stairway, carving the steps straight into the body of the earth, but in my mind I cursed them roundly, especially when I thought about climbing back up again.

I was surprised by how different the second level was from the first.

In the first place, the ceilings here were all vaulted, not flat. In the second place, the walls didn't look bare and lifeless. In one hall after another there were images on the walls, and even inscriptions. Some of them were in hu-man language, although the ancient letters were very elaborate. And most of them were signs indicating the way to the various sections, and saying which burial place was where.

In the second place, there were lots of stone gargoyles, one planted almost every hundred paces, in fact. The statues all seemed absolutely different; at least while I walked along, I didn't see two that were the same. The unknown sculptors had created gargoyles of every possible size and set them in the most incredible poses. Many of the statues were so hideous that just looking at them was enough to set your knees trembling.

Water was running out of one gargoyle's mouth in a jingling, silvery thread and falling into a shallow chalice that the statue was holding in its hands. I tasted the water gingerly. It didn't seem to be poisoned, so I took the opportunity to drink my fill and top up my flask.

In the third place, on the second level there were no torches. Fire only flickered in the open palms of the gargoyles or in small cages up under the ceiling. But for the most part there were no flames at all, and the light flowed straight out of the ceiling. In some places it only glowed very faintly, and then the hall was flooded with a dense, obscure twilight.

The reputation of the Palaces of Bone as the most gigantic graveyard in the world was well deserved. In addition to the architecture, pictures on the walls, and gargoyles by the dozen, the Palaces were also the resting place of thousands and thousands who had departed to the light.

There were two sarcophagi waiting to greet me at the very entrance to the second level. Stone boxes with massive lids that were obviously tremendously heavy. Out of simple curiosity I went up to one and read the man's name and date of death on the plaque. He had been buried more than seven hundred years earlier. I walked on, occasionally stopping at one coffin or another out of curiosity, to learn the name of the departed. But my curiosity was soon exhausted; there were far too many sarcophagi—if I'd read the names of all the dead, I'd have been stuck there for ten years—and I had to keep looking around desperately to make sure, Sagot forbid, that I didn't turn off into the wrong corridor.

Sometimes the stone boxes were piled up on top of each other, reaching right up to the ceiling, or hidden away in niches in the walls, which started to look like the honeycomb in a bees' nest. And very often there was a carved likeness of the dead man on the lid of his sarcophagus. More often than that, especially in the halls farther away from the stairway, the dead had been buried in the walls, and the niches closed off, or in the floor, with a gravestone left on the spot as a memento.

I thought there would never be an end to all those halls, corridors, galleries, passages, rooms, and stairways. And everywhere I went I was greeted by the silence of the graveyard, graves beyond count, and gargoyles, who followed the visitor to this place with their sightless stone eyes.

I came across my first body after wandering through the second level for a long time, on my way ignoring several stairways that led down to the third level. (The only way I wanted to get into the third level was through the Doors; that was what I had the Key for, after all. And any detour around the Doors made about as much sense as plunging headfirst into a whirlpool or running naked into a burning house.)

The body was lying on the floor with its arms and legs flung out, and the man must have been dead for a few months at least, because his clothes were well rotted and there was no flesh left on his bones.

To be quite frank, this is exactly the kind of dead body I prefer, because they cause the least trouble. Only I didn't like the look of his clothes, because they were gray and blue. And any brainless sparrow could have seen that this wasn't a civilian outfit, but a military uniform. The uniform of a member of the royal guard. The broken sword lying beside the man's remains also confirmed that he had been a soldier.

The lad could have been a member of the first expedition, the one that had been sent to get the Rainbow Horn in the late winter or early spring. That time no one had returned to the surface, and Alistan Markauz had lost more than forty of his men in the Palaces of Bone. This warrior was one of them. Or perhaps I was mistaken, and the dead man was a member of the second expedition who had found his final resting place in the gloomy depths of these catacombs.

His skull had been crushed thoroughly and I wondered what could have killed him. I leaned down to study the body more closely and my eye was caught by a black bag lying underneath it.

Without any squeamishness (bones are just bones), I moved the skeleton aside and picked the bag up off the floor. The cloth had been turned stiff and dark by blood that had soaked into it. There was a book in the bag but, unfortunately, I couldn't make out what was written in it—it was almost entirely blotted out by the blood. I tried turning the pages, but they were stuck together, and only a few of them yielded to my insistent efforts. Darkness! It was impossible to read anything, although I could see that the book had been used for writing in the margins.

    . . . *a* . . . *ch* . . . *6*
    . . . *fe* . . . *int* . . . *t* . . . *ap* . . .

Mmm, yes, I can't make out a thing. Maybe it would be easier on the later pages?

As I leafed through the book, I came across one inscription that I could just barely make out.

. . . arch 28
D ors locke . . .   going to look for a wa   rou   . . . Blue
1   t brings d   ath!

Aha! So the expedition had reached the Doors leading into the third level. What was "Blue 1 t"? Perhaps light?

On the last page there wasn't a single drop of blood, but the only piece of writing was almost illegible and I had to struggle to make out the scribble. Whoever wrote it seemed to have been in a great hurry.

April 2
The lieutenant is dead, the beast squashed him as flat as a
pancake. Siart and Shu have gone to the steps.

Poor fellow. . . . What was it that crept up out of the depths and crushed his head?

I cast a wary glance round the empty hall and the entrance to the next one. But whatever it was that had killed the poor man, it had gone away a long time ago, so I walked on without making any attempt to hide.

There were no tombs here, just tall square columns set on broad bases. They seemed to go on forever. The ceiling glowed faintly and that made the hall seem obscure and endless. I began sticking close to the columns. Darkness only knew what came over me, but suddenly I didn't like this place at all. I was about a quarter of the way across it when the trouble started.

The entire hall was suddenly filled with an appalling rasping sound and I froze, taken completely by surprise. After eight seconds of deafening silence, the rasping was repeated and two columns ahead of me, three long, deep scratches appeared in the wall. As if a set of powerful, invisible talons had scraped furrows into the stone. I was dumbfounded and my teeth started chattering. Then a new set of scratches appeared on the next column, and I heard the same terrifying rasping sound.

The piercing noise set all my teeth on edge.

I didn't waste any time trying to figure out what was happening; I just took off at top speed in the opposite direction. The column behind me exploded in a cloud of grit and splinters. Something struck me a painful blow on the right shoulder and almost knocked me off my feet.

Boo-oom! Boo-oom!

The heavy footsteps and rasping noises were right behind me, but I kept hurtling along as fast as I could and didn't look back (in the Palaces of Bone, the penalty for excessive curiosity was death). The columns flickered past on the right and the left, but the way out of the hall suddenly seemed an impossible distance away. As ill luck would have it, the cobweb-rope I thought I had attached so securely slipped off my belt and fell to the floor. There was no question of stopping to pick it up—my life was more important to me than all the magical rope in the world.

Whatever it was that was chasing me, it wasn't going to give up, and another three columns snapped behind me, spraying out crumbs of stone, as if some enraged giant was pummelling them with his fists. But what kind of strength did it take to smash a stone column as thick as a hundred-year-old oak?

I darted into the hall where the dead guardsman was lying, skipped over his body, ran the whole length of the room, and stopped at the far doorway. Whatever the beast might be, the exit from the hall of columns was too narrow for it. The footsteps came closer, but I swear by Sagot that I couldn't see anyone!

I heard that terrible rasping sound again, and then a large section of the wall beside the entrance to the hall of columns groaned as if it were alive, and collapsed in a heap of rubble.

Boo-oom! Boo-oom!

The invisible monster stepped on the guardsman's skeleton, reducing it to fine dust, and then came in my direction, with the obvious intention of doing the same to good old Harold.

I believe I actually squealed before I turned and ran without thinking about which way I should turn or worrying about getting lost. I just wanted to save my skin. I could still hear that terrible booming noise and the rumble of collapsing walls behind me. I dashed into a corridor, turned left, then right, then left again. . . .

Long after the monster's rumbling faded away in the distance, I was still too frightened to stop running. I only realized I was lost when I didn't have any more strength left to run.

Cursing the world and everything in it, I sat down on the floor and leaned back against a sarcophagus. Come what may, but Harold wasn't going to run anymore. The longer I spent dashing through the dim corridors, the less chance there was that I would ever find my way back. The shoulder that had been hit by a fragment of the column was aching painfully. I was obviously going to have a massive bruise there. What I ought to do right now was take a rest, catch my breath, and think about where exactly I was.

What had really happened was that everything had begun just as calmly and innocently as on the first level, and I had committed the unforgivable sin of relaxing too much because I wasn't expecting any trouble. Apart from losing my way, I'd lost the rope as well. And without the cobweb I couldn't get back out, because Milady Lafresa had smashed the staircase and there was no way I could get across that eight-meter gap. The odds on croaking in Hrad Spein had suddenly shortened dramatically. There was no point in trying to retrieve the rope—I wasn't certain I could find the way back and I didn't really feel like sticking my nose into the Wall Smasher's lair again.

So, the way back into the sunshine was closed off. I had no doubt at all that there were other ways out of the Palaces of Bone. At the very least, there were four main entrances. The west entrance was somewhere in the middle of Zagraba, but that was hundreds of leagues away. There were another two entrances near spurs of the Mountains of the Dwarves, but after the evil awoke in the burial chambers, the dwarves had blocked off the entrances closest to their kingdom just to be on the safe side. So I could forget about the main entrances. But apart from them, there had to be less-important entrances as well. There had to be, but would I be able to find them?

Wandering aimlessly round the second level and clinging to the elusive shadow of a hope wasn't going to get me anywhere, so I took the maps out of my bag and started poring over them in the dim light. It took me more than half an hour to find an old stairway leading up to the surface from the first level. According to my calculations, provided that the stairway had survived all these thousands of years, to get to it from the Doors I would have to walk two leagues on the second level and five on the first. A long, long way, but it could have been worse.

Well then, after (that is, *if*) I got the Horn, I would have a chance of getting out of the burial chambers, although I would be a huge distance away from the place where our group was waiting. But I'd still rather be stuck in some unfamiliar stretch of forest than starve to death in these dreary stone halls. (Just who was the rat who first invented the story that it was incredibly beautiful down here?)

The most important problem I had to face now was that I had no idea which part of the second level I was in. In my panic-stricken race against the Wall Smasher, I had completely lost my sense of direction, and now only the maps could help me find the right way to go. I had to find some distinctive and unusual hall, then locate it on the map and take my bearings.

An easy enough little task at first sight, but in practice it turned out to be very far from simple. In this sector all the halls and corridors were very similar. Half-light, graves, and hundreds of gargoyles. The longer I wandered through the stone labyrinth of this vast mausoleum, the more desperate I became.

Hall, corridor, room, intersection, hall, hall, corridor, half-light, and gargoyles. Those cursed monsters with the ghoulish faces affected my nerves far more badly than a hundred goblin jesters high on charm-weed. My legs were aching, I had to take another break and have a bite to eat. I was still somewhere on the level of men, but there wasn't a single sign or mark anywhere on the walls. I had been staggering around Hrad Spein for a day and a half now, but I still hadn't reached the Doors. And Lafresa was still on the loose somewhere, with the Master's servants. It would be highly unpleasant to bump into them just at the wrong moment.

Finally, when I was just about ready to start howling out loud, I came out into a huge hall where all the sarcophaguses were arranged in the form of an immense eight-pointed star. On closer inspection, the hall also proved to be star-shaped, only it had five points.

I had to get the maps out again. I found the star hall fairly quickly—I'd have had to be blind not to spot it. But when I traced the route from there to the Doors I gave a low whistle—I'd really gone a long, long way off track. So now I had a long walk ahead of me. And this route looked far more dangerous than the one the magicians of the Order had marked on the map—there was nothing to show the locations of the traps or any other pleasant surprises that might be in store for me. Everything that I'd been giving such a wide berth could turn up right under my very nose now. There was no point in retracing my steps—I was so far astray that the walk back and the onward journey to the third level would be far longer than the route from here to the Doors. And not for a moment did I forget about the monster that had almost flattened me into the floor. I didn't want to end up anywhere near those feet again!

I set off, every now and then cursing the damned magicians who had hidden the Rainbow Horn so far down, the builders of the Palaces of Bone who had created this endless maze, monsters that wouldn't sit still in their corners, and myself, for tying the cobweb rope on my belt so badly.

After walking through forty-three more halls, I ran into a trap, but fortunately it had already been activated. A short section of corridor with a hole where the floor ought to have been. A pit about three yards deep, with sharp steel spikes set thickly across its bottom. And lying on the bottom was a skeleton with spikes sticking up through its ribs like young saplings. The poor fellow had failed to notice the trap and paid with his life.

The problem here was that Harold, unfortunately, was not a flea. Even if I took a good run up, I wouldn't be able to jump across a gap of more than fifteen yards. The harsh reality was that I would tumble into the pit halfway across.

A dead end.

There was no way around it, I had to get across that pit or waste another day going back and looking for another route to the Doors.

A close study of the gap where the floor had been revealed that there were long, wide slots in the wall that could easily hold the flagstones that had disappeared. Did that mean there was some kind of concealed mechanism and, if it could be activated, the stones would move back into place over the pit, giving me a chance to carry on?

It seemed likely.

After further investigation of the scene I noticed a rectangular block of stone protruding from the ceiling. There was the answer to the riddle. Only it was so far away from me that it might as well have been on the moon, especially if you took into account the fact that the cobweb-rope was irretrievably lost.

But I still had my crossbow. I took aim and pressed the trigger. The bolt struck a spark from the ceiling beside the block and bounced off, falling down into the pit. All right, so we'd have to try a different approach. I lay down on my back so that the projecting section of the ceiling was right above my head and held my weapon with both hands.

Clang!

The block sank back smoothly and silently into the stone, until it was invisible. Something in the wall started humming quietly, and then the slabs of stone slid out of their recesses and started moving very slowly toward each other. I didn't wait for them to come together and form an uninterrupted surface—it was far too likely that the trap would be rearmed.

I jumped onto the moving slab on the left and hurried across, being careful not to tumble into the pit. I managed to step onto the normal surface before the slabs came together with a dull *crump*.

After another two halls, there was another corridor with long slits in the walls, only this time they were at the level of my hips. Another nice little surprise, may the darkness take it!

I walked over to a broken sarcophagus. I had no idea who it was that had tried to shatter the lid of the grave, but now the remains could easily be reached. A yellow skull grinned out at me. I picked it up and tossed it onto the floor of the corridor.

Semicircular blades sprang out of the far ends of the slits and flew through the air with a whine until they reached the entrance, then stopped. So that was it. I could easily have been sliced into two Harolds. While the blades were withdrawing into the wall and the trap was being rearmed for the next unwary traveler, I slipped past and hurried on.

So far all the traps had been fairly crude devices, but that only meant that they had been made by human hands. I expected the elves and orcs to be far more inventive in their methods for dispatching undesirable visitors to the sacred Palaces into the light.

Quite a lot of time had gone by, and I felt very tired. This time I chose the site for my nest in the hands of a large, repulsive gargoyle. It cost me quite an effort to scramble up into the stone hands that were folded together to form a cup, but once I was up there, I felt as cozy as if I were nestling in Sagot's pocket. I ate half a biscuit, took my boots off, laid my head on my bag, and my hand on my loaded crossbow, and slept like a baby.

I don't know how long I slept—time passes imperceptibly in the catacombs, with no sun and no stars. I had to rely on hunger and fatigue to guide me, and since my fatigue had disappeared without a trace, it seemed quite possible that I'd been asleep for a long time. In any case, there was an urgent rumbling in my stomach, and I had to wolf down another half portion of my magical rations to keep it quiet.

My body was numb from lying on stone for so long, and it was an effort to stand up, stretch, and pull on my boots. It was time to be moving on, there were no more than ten halls left before I reached the Doors.

"Walk, walk, walk, and we still don't get anywhere! Do you realize we're lost in all these damned corridors!"

I instinctively ducked down at the unexpected sound of a voice, but no one would have seen me, even standing fully upright. The gargoyle's cupped hands made a magnificent hiding place.

"And it's all your fault!" said a second voice.

"My fault?"

"Who was it suddenly needed to take a leak? It's your fault everyone went on ahead and we couldn't find them! What a fool I was to stay with you!"

"Don't panic. Milord Balistan Pargaid doesn't abandon his men."

"Sure, he's been searching real hard for us for the last eight hours," the second man snorted.

The voices started moving away, and I decided I could jump up, grab the edge of the cup, and pull myself up to take a look. Two soldiers dressed in chain mail and carrying swords were slowly tramping in the direction that I'd just come from.

The poor souls were lost. And serve them right. After another two halls they'd reach the trap that would reduce them to bloody pulp. And I certainly wasn't going to try to stop them.

So Balistan Pargaid and Lafresa had reached the second level. That was bad news. I just hoped they'd lost plenty of men on the way.

I waited until the two men disappeared into the distant corridor, then jumped down and went on. The route from here was as straight as Parade Street, and I could go as far as the next intersection without worrying about a thing. The two lost sheep who had just tramped past would have activated any traps, and since they were still alive, I could assume that there were no traps on the path ahead. I ran through the next six halls (just in case the lost men might suddenly decide to come back).

In the seventh hall, where the walls were riddled with the black openings of corridors leading in every possible direction, I paused and rummaged through my papers, then stepped into the fourth corridor on the right. It was a little strange, to say the least—seven paces and then a sharp turn to the left, another seven paces and another turn to the left, then to the right, and so on for quite a long way, a kind of crooked-snake toy put together by a drunken child.

I gave thanks to Sagot when I found myself facing a stairway. There were two stone sculptures waiting for me there—those familiar beasts, half bird and half bear. I wondered whose sick mind could have come up with the idea of such ugly monsters. It certainly couldn't have been a man's. When the stairway ended I found myself in a hall. A huge hall. And pitch dark, I couldn't see a thing. I was just about to reach into the bag for my lights when the floor started glowing and a brightly lit path appeared, running out into the distance from under my feet.

More magic, but at least this time it didn't threaten instant death. The path ran on and on, showing me the way, until it stopped at the far wall, and at that point a bright rectangle blazed up at that. It was so far away that I didn't realize what it was at first, but when I did . . . When I did, I gave thanks to Sagot.

It was the Doors.

5

THROUGH THE SLUMBERING GLOOM

My footsteps echoed off the white marble slabs of the floor and multiplied as they bounced about under the ceiling, fluttering like bats startled by the light of the torches.

I felt a desperate urge to walk off the path into the surrounding gloom, where I would be less conspicuous but, darkness take me, the lighted path had been created especially for anyone coming this way to walk along, and Sagot only knew what was in store for me if I left it.

About twenty marble slabs right in front of the Doors were lit up in a rough semicircle, forming a kind of platform about twenty yards across. From that point two corridors ran off to the right and left of the Doors. There were little light blue lamps on the high ceilings of the corridors, flooding the entrances with a pale bluish light and filling the corridors with a bluish haze. I didn't know where the corridors led to—there was no mention of them in the papers from the old Tower of the Order.

But the Nameless One take the mysterious corridors! I certainly wasn't going to waste any time exploring them. Just at that moment there was nothing in the world apart from those Doors towering up seventeen yards above my head.

I took my glove off one hand and gingerly pressed my palm against the surface of the Doors. They felt warm, as if there was a gentle flame burning somewhere inside them, and at the same time icy cold, as if they'd been carved out of a single block of dark ice. And they were very smooth. I didn't even try to guess what material they were made from, but it looked very much like black glass. I would have wagered the income from my next hundred Commissions that an entire regiment of giants or an army of magicians of every possible hue could never even have made this barrier tremble.

The elves had created something magnificent, and only someone who possessed the Key could pass this way. (I imagined how furious the orcs must have been when they discovered that the easiest and quickest route to the tombs of their ancestors had been closed off by the elves.)

I stood at one edge of these magnificent Doors, set one hand on their surface, and walked the ten yards from one edge to the other. Nothing at all. An absolutely smooth surface, entirely unbroken, if you didn't count the elaborate images worked into it by the dark and light elves' master sculptors, images that told the story of their people's battles with the Firstborn.

The pictures were incredibly beautiful and the attention to fine detail was astonishing. Here was an elf armed with a s'kash setting his foot on the body of his prostrate enemy. The figures seemed to be alive and I could see every hair, every ring of chain mail, every wrinkle in the corners of the middle-aged elf's eyes.

And here was a gigantic oak tree. I could see every single leaf, every crevice in the thick bark. Orcs hung from the tree head-down, their eyes filled with absolute terror. Elves stood below them. Many elves. From what I knew of the race of the Secondborn, I'd say the lads were preparing the appalling Green Leaf torture for the orcs.

Of course, all this was very impressive, but the Doors didn't have what was most important to me—a keyhole that the Key I had brought could fit into. I almost went blind staring at that surface as I walked from one corner to the other, but I didn't find even the tiniest opening. As if it wasn't enough that the surrounding gloom and the blue haze of the two corridors were beginning to set my nerves on edge, there was something not quite right about the Doors, too. But I just couldn't understand exactly what it was that had been bothering me since the moment I walked up to them.

Calm down, Harold, calm down. I had the Key, and it was created to open the Doors. So it must open them, and all I had to do to find the keyhole was exercise my imagination.

I tried coming at the question from every possible angle, but I got nowhere. Maybe it was some kind of elfin joke—to make Doors that didn't open? But then, why in the name of darkness had they gone to all the trouble of bringing in the dwarves to make the Key? Not just for the fun of it, surely?

But eventually I found the answer. It was concealed in the figures on the Doors, or rather, in one of them. In the lower left corner there was a figure of a tall elf. He was holding his right hand out, palm upward, and it was hollow. The color of the glass made the hollow almost invisible, in fact it was barely even a hollow, just a slight irregularity that was lost among the dozens of figures embossed into the Doors. But the size of the hollow was exactly right for the Key to be set into it.

I pulled the chain with the Key on it out from under my shirt and set the slim, elegant, icy-crystal artifact in the elf's hand. The crystal flashed with a purple light and for a moment the elf's entire figure lit up. The transparent Key turned exactly the same color as the Doors and fused into a single whole with them.

And then a glowing purple line ran from the bottom to the top of the huge Doors, right at their very center, and they started slowly opening toward me without a sound. I had to step back so that they wouldn't catch me. I felt something snap gently in my chest, and I realized that the bonds with which Miralissa had tied the Key to me had broken. Which was hardly surprising: I'd opened the Doors and the bonds were no longer needed. The artifact had done its job.

"The bonds are strong," the Key purred. "Run!"

Run? But the Doors had only just opened!

"Run away! The smell of the enemy!" the Key whispered in farewell, and fell silent.

The smell of the enemy? What did that mean?

I sniffed the air and caught a faint scent of strawberries. Lafresa!

"Kill him!" a man's voice barked in the darkness.

Maybe sometimes I'm not all that bright, maybe I'm as dense as a cork, maybe I don't know how to use a sword, but there's one thing that can't be denied—in a really tight spot I think with the speed of lightning and run even faster.

When Count Balistan Pargaid roared his command, I was already far away from the Doors and flying along the corridor on the left as fast as I could go. In the distance someone yelled that I had to be caught, others shouted for me to stop immediately or it would be worse for me. Naturally, I had no intention of stopping. Fortunately, the group that had been waiting for me to open the Doors hadn't brought any crossbows along, otherwise I would have been dispatched into the light already. There was only one thing they could do now—try to catch up and put a few holes in me. I had one slight advantage over the Master's jackals—I started running a lot sooner than they did, and running in chain mail with swords is a lot harder than running without them.

I hurtled along the endless corridor flooded with blue light, praying to Sagot for an intersection so that I could confuse the chase. But it was just my luck, there wasn't a single branch off the corridor—its walls just moved farther apart, its ceiling rose even higher, and every second blue lamp went out.

That made the place even gloomier—the murk was so thick, it felt like I was running through a phantom world, wallowing in a syrupy bluish haze. The blue light made everything that was happening seem unreal.

Whoo-osh . . . Whoo-oosh . . . Whoo-oosh . . .

The lights on the ceiling were blurred spots rushing past above my head. The floor was laid with slabs of white marble with gold veins, just like in the Hall of the Doors, but fortunately it didn't glow. On the other hand, I could hear the tramping feet and menacing roars of my pursuers very clearly. The idiots still hadn't realized that yelling your head off in places like Hrad Spein can be bad for your health. I had a good lead, so I could afford to look round to see what my chances of surviving today's race looked like.

The thick blue haze filled the corridor, so I could only see about a hundred paces. But I'd opened up a much bigger lead than that, so there was nothing in my field of vision yet. There was no time to think things over—Balistan Pargaid's dogs would be there at any moment, and then only a miracle would save me.

There were broad decorative friezes running along the walls of the corridor, with stone gargoyles, each twice the height of a man, grinning down at me. The sculptor had created a set of brutes who were absolutely identical—they all had heads in the form of human skulls and unnaturally long hands with three fingers. The gargoyles were leaning over the corridor, looking for all the world as if one of them would come to life and jump down. I suddenly had an idea that just might work.

I leapt up onto the frieze, flung one leg over a gargoyle's thigh, heaved myself up, grabbed the statue's neck, and hid between its back and the wall of the corridor.

A magnificent spot. In the first place, the men chasing me were not likely to look up. In the second place, they couldn't see me, and, in the third place, I had a fine view of everything.

For a second I thought the gargoyle's stone back trembled slightly. It was absolute nonsense, of course—in that blue murk you could imagine seeing anything. I took the crossbow out from behind my back and waited for my guests.

After about ten long, but far from tedious seconds my pursuers appeared. Count Balistan Pargaid had sent four soldiers after me and these lads didn't look any different from the other two who had got lost in the maze of the second level. Just as I expected, the lads didn't even bother to look round. They were putting all their energy into yelling and waving their swords about. The four of them ran past my hiding place, howling triumphantly, and disappeared into the blue haze. Well, I thought I'd sit there for a while and wait until they got tired of running and then clear off.

How brilliantly Lafresa had fooled me! But it was my own fault for under-estimating a dangerous enemy. After all, I knew how important she was to the Master's intrigues, and you'd be hard put to find another sorceress to match her anywhere. No wonder the woman had managed to find the way to the Doors and avoid the traps and also prepare a pleasant welcome for me. I couldn't imagine how she'd guessed I would reach the Doors, too, but the Master's servant had certainly made the right decision.

Without the Key, Lafresa wasn't able to open the Doors, so the only thing she could do was wait until the blockhead who was bound to the ar-tifact opened them for her. I'd done exactly what she expected, and then Balistan Pargaid's men had swung into action, thirsting for my blood. Yes, there was a faint scent of strawberries in the air near the Doors, that was what had been bothering me, but I hadn't taken any notice, and if not for the magical Key . . .

A long, appalling howl of pain and terror rang down the corridor and I hiccupped in surprise. A hesitant moment of silence, and then another choking scream. And another. The hair on my head stirred and stood up on end. I pressed myself against the gargoyle's back as hard as I could and tried to dissolve into thin air.

"Save me, Sagra! Save me, Sagra! A-a-agh! Save me, Sagra!"

A man came dashing out of the haze, screaming—one out of the four who had just been chasing me.

The man tossed his sword away and went dashing back toward the Hall of the Doors, calling on Sagra to help him. As usually happens, the goddess of war didn't heed his call. But someone else did. A gargoyle on the wall opposite me turned its head toward the soldier's howls.

At first I thought my eyes were playing tricks on me in the strange light, but then the fingers on the long hands moved, the shoulders twitched, and, just as the man was running past the gargoyle, the stone monster leapt down nimbly off the frieze, landing on the man with all its weight.

Crunch!

The lad never even knew what hit him. The monster picked the body up by the legs with its long hands, swung hard, and smacked the dead man's head against the frieze. There was a sound like a nut cracking and a dark spot appeared on the stone. The gargoyle went back to its usual place and froze in the same position as before, suddenly transformed into lifeless stone again. As if the terrible scene I had just witnessed had never even happened.

I tried to calm my wildly pounding heart, but that was more than I could manage. May Sagot save me, I couldn't take my eyes off the monster that had just killed a man! But the beast was absolutely still now; it gave no signs of life at all.

Ah, but you won't fool me like that anymore!

The back of the gargoyle I was hiding behind trembled slightly again. But no, I imagined it. . . . Or did I? I stopped breathing. The head on the stone neck slowly started moving. . . .

I jumped down and ran as hard as I could for the Hall of the Doors, and somewhere behind me there was a gargoyle awakening from a long sleep. Of course, I hadn't bothered to wait for the unpleasant moment when the stone monster would be fully awake. I just ran for it before it could grab me.

Whoo-oosh . . . Whoo-oosh . . . Whoo-oosh . . .

The little blue lamps turned into long blurred streaks. I was running in the opposite direction now. Darkness take Lafresa and Balistan Pargaid and his men! I'd break through one way or another! In the Hall of the Doors at least I had some kind of chance, with just a little bit of luck and the factor of surprise, but if I ran the other way, I was a dead certainty for the light. And another foolish idea came to mind, too—if I could just get to the Doors, the gargoyle could easily turn his precious attention to one of Pargaid's men and forget about me.

The rasping of stone talons rang along the corridor. There was something big and very unfriendly chasing me. I stepped up the pace to avoid ending up in its stony embrace.

A gargoyle standing ahead of me stretched and clambered down off the frieze, but I had already gone flying past before this latest animated spawn of darkness could gather its wits. The end of the corridor was close now, but my way was blocked by a third stone monster, standing straight ahead of me, with blazing blue coals for eyes. To stop now would have been quite unforgivably stupid, so I dropped to the floor like a stone and slid across the marble slabs on my stomach, skidding between the ugly beast's legs. I don't think it even realized what was happening.

I jumped up and ran for it, and heard a terrible crash behind me as the monster who was chasing me smashed straight into his friend—the one I had slid under so smartly.

The glowing floor in front of the Doors. The dark depths of the hall. And nobody there. Just as I thought: Balistan Pargaid hadn't bothered to wait for his men to finish me off. He'd gone on to the third level, since a certain idiot had kindly opened the Doors for him.

I heard a stifled wail of frustration from the corridor and turned round.

Several statues that had come to life were standing on the threshold between the corridor and the Hall of Doors. They stared at me in helpless fury for a second, then turned and tramped away.

I grunted in relief and tried to catch my breath. No wonder the dead guardsman's book had said that blue light brought death.

Kli-Kli had warned me; in fact, he had often made fun of me, saying that if I survived the Palaces of Bone, my best memories would be of running. First from one beast. Then from another. And another.

I missed the moment when the Doors started to close. It happened without a sound, and when I did look at the magical gates, they had already moved a quarter of the way together.

I certainly couldn't hang around any longer. I went dashing toward the barrier, feverishly trying to spot the figure of the elf in whose hand I had left the Key. The Doors carried on implacably closing.

Darkness! I needed the Key! Egrassa would tear my head off if I came back without the elfin relic!

Darkness! Darkness! Darkness! Darkness! May a demon of the abyss eat my brains!

The elf's hand was absolutely empty! That infernal Lafresa had taken the artifact!

But this was no time to hurl curses at the heavens—there was only a narrow gap left between the Doors, and I had to make a dash for it. Otherwise I'd have to gnaw a hole through the Doors with my teeth.

I made it.

The danger of being crushed by the closing Doors sharpened my wits and I slipped through and out the other side like a cork out of a bottle of sparkling wine.

The gates came together soundlessly behind me, putting an end to any chance of going back. Now I would have to take the Key from Lafresa (which was unlikely) or make my way through the abyss of horror and find another way out (which was even less likely). There was only one way I could go now—forward. And I had to keep on going in the hope that some kind soul would deal with the witch and take the Key off her body.

I leaned back against the smooth black surface and gazed into darkness. Right in front of the Doors there was still a faint glimmer of light, but beyond that . . .

Thirty paces away I couldn't see a thing. Just dense, velvety darkness. I was standing on a faintly lit granite platform that was slightly wider than the Doors and about fifteen paces across.

The entire platform was littered with bones. On the left and the right the floor merged into the walls of a cave that receded into impenetrable gloom. I couldn't see any ceiling, it was too high, monstrously high, and completely invisible without any bright light. The platform broke off at jagged edges with an empty void beyond. It looked as if the Doors had released me into some unbelievably huge natural cave that the builders of Hrad Spein had discovered many thousands of years before.

The third level was a lot lower than the spot where I was standing, and the way to it ran across a stone bridge that began at the magical doors and ended somewhere *out there*. I had to walk through the cave across the bridge.

Not a very encouraging prospect, especially bearing in mind that the bridge was only four paces wide and it didn't have railings. And if I was careless enough to fall off, I could keep on falling until I died of hunger.

An untimely fit of curiosity made me pick up something that used to be someone's arm bone and toss it into the abyss. I immediately regretted this fleeting impulse—who knew what creatures I might disturb? But even though I regretted it, I didn't forget to count; at least I could find out how deep this bottomless cave really was. I gave up at ninety-three, realizing that I wouldn't hear anything anyway, even if the bone landed. It was already too far away for the sound to reach my ears.

It was more than fifteen minutes since the Doors had closed. I had to get

moving and for the time being abandon all thoughts about how I would get
back out.

All I was doing right now was just spinning things out, trying to put off
setting foot on that bridge. I would have bet a gold piece that it was longer
than an ogre's life, but I couldn't see any supports underneath it. What was
holding all that weight up? What magic had transformed the stone into a
path?

And then again, the servants of the Master could still be quite close,
and running into them on a platform only four paces wide could be fatal.
Lafresa, Balistan Pargaid, Paleface, and a dozen men into the bargain. I
thought how delighted they would be to see me. But then, if I let them get
away, lost sight of them in the maze of palaces and halls, I could forget all
about the Key. And any chance of ever getting out of here and back up into
the sunshine. No thinking was needed! I had to act! How did that verse
riddle go on?

> And then, carry on! The twin doors stand open
> To the peace of the halls of the Slumbering Whisper.
> Where the brains of man and elf and orc alike
> Dissolve in unreason. . . . And so shall yours.

An encouraging prospect, especially bearing in mind that the Doors
were anything but open, and to reach the Halls of the Slumbering Whisper
I still had to travel for days across a thin thread of stone stretched between
the darkness and the abyss.

I cast hesitation aside, lit one of my lights, stepped onto the bridge, and
walked on.

Trying to walk along the center and not look down, I held the little magical lamp at arm's length and hoped that the light in the darkness would not
attract unwelcome attention from unfriendly individuals who might happen
to inhabit this place.

The road was as straight as a bowstring and easy to walk along; I just had
to forget about where I was and keep away from the edge.

Silence and darkness. Darkness and silence. How could you ever describe
the Palaces of Bone, if the words "darkness" and "silence" and "half-light"
were thrown out of the language?

You couldn't. Because Hrad Spein *is* the darkness of subterranean catacombs, the silence of ancient tombs, and the half-light in the gloomy halls that are sometimes lit in mysterious ways.

My little light struggled to keep the gloom at bay, illuminating the bridge for seven paces ahead and seven paces behind. But there wasn't enough light, and I felt like a little bug stuck in a demon's pocket. The bridge had a very slight incline, and I gradually moved lower and lower.

Far, far ahead of me a series of dense white flashes flared up in rapid succession. From where I was they looked like the blinking of a white-hot grain of sand. But that was quite enough to make me stop and put both hands round the magical light to make quite sure that it wouldn't be seen.

Another sequence of whitish sparks—they were more than a thousand yards away. I gazed into the gloom for three long, weary minutes, but no more flashes came. Whatever Lafresa had been up to over there (I was certain this was one of her tricks), it was all over now.

I sat down with my legs crossed and waited for another ten minutes just to be on the safe side. A perfectly reasonable precaution—I didn't want the Master's servants to suspect anything; let them think I was still stuck on the other side of the Doors.

After that I wasn't at all afraid the men would see the light—the distance between me and Balistan Pargaid's brigade was too great, and my little light and Lafresa's magical flashes, were like a glowing ember and a forest fire.

After walking for about twenty minutes, I started hearing a low, regular drone. The kind of sound that alarmed bees make in their hive, or water makes when it falls from a great height. The straight bridge, which held up so mysteriously under the pressure of time, sloped down almost imperceptibly, so that now I was about three hundred yards lower than the Doors. And the longer I walked, the louder the obscure drone became.

The droning gradually became a rumble, the rumbling became a bellow, and the bellowing became a roar. The air was filled with a feeling of freshness and fine droplets of water that I could hardly see. Now I knew what was there up ahead.

A waterfall. Just then I didn't have the time or the desire to figure out how it could have got there. It started getting noticeably brighter. Walls appeared out of the phantasmagorical darkness, glowing faintly with a dead, pale green light. They came together somewhere way up high where the uneven ceiling sparkled.

The roaring became indescribable and the walls moved in, until they were only forty yards away from the bridge. The moisture hanging in the air settled on my clothes like dew and chilled my skin. I thought the rumbling of the falling water would split my head in half. The bridge became wet, and the stone glittered in the light of my little magical lamp. Thank Sagot it wasn't slippery, or I would have gone tumbling into the abyss at the first careless step.

Another two hundred yards, and there they were—a waterfall on the right and a waterfall on the left. Huge heads, thirty yards high, appeared on the walls. They were grotesque, half bird and half bear, their beak-mouths were wide open, and the torrents of water were roaring out of them. The black water, barely visible in the pale green light of the cave, roared and raged and it went hurtling downward.

Sagot! As I walked past the waterfalls roaring like a hundred thousand demons of the abyss, I was afraid I would go deaf forever (I forgot all about the earplugs I'd brought along) or that the torrent of water would sweep me away. I felt as if I could reach out my hand and touch one of them. And those familiar half bird, half bear heads looked as if they could strike a stranger down, or at least give him such a scare that he wet his pants. But my pants were already wet anyway, like all the rest of my clothes.

The waterfalls of the underground river were behind me now, their roar was fading away. The walls parted again and their pale green light died, inviting the gloom back in.

Darkness take me, but I was monstrously tired, and I settled down right there on the bridge for a bite to eat. I had to take my soaking clothes off and wring them out, too—I was shivering and shuddering after my involuntary bath in the spray of the waterfalls. After I'd got my outfit into more or less decent condition, I turned to the needs of my stomach and took out a soaking biscuit. My light blinked one last time and went out. I swore and lit up a new one. How long had I been staggering across this bridge? By my calculations, almost three days had passed since I first entered Hrad Spein, and I was still only somewhere between the second and third levels.

After a short rest I had to start moving again. By this stage the bridge was no longer straight; it had twisted into a spiral, increasing the speed of my descent. After what seemed like an eternity the walls moved in again, the bridge took a final turn, and there before me was the way out, or rather, the way in to the third level.

———

A hall.

I can't even find the words to describe what the light showed me. I only had to give the right command, and the circle of light expanded to forty paces (then I could see everything really well, but the life of the magical lantern was shortened by several hours). Nothing I'd seen in Hrad Spein so far could compare with the first hall of the third level.

I was entering the level of the elves and the orcs, which had been created without any involvement by men. Cracked stones, basalt and granite, all the crude statues and coffins of roughly dressed stone had been left behind above me, and here . . . Here the scene before me was one of absolutely astounding, incomparable beauty.

The color scheme of the hall was black and bright scarlet. A very beautiful combination if you looked closely. Black walls with red veins and flecks, elegant black semi-arches with red ornamentation that looked like orcic letters, a ceiling where the red lines and strokes merged to form the image of a huge cobweb. A floor laid with matte black slabs, with the same red veins as on the ceiling, with a fine seam of red between each slab. The light of my little lamp set the hall sparkling and gave the place a truly magical, fairy-tale appearance.

Now I really was in the Palaces—once they were famous throughout all Siala, and even gnomes and dwarves came to Hrad Spein to gaze at the beauty of the burial halls. But those times are long gone now, together with the Age of Achievements.

Hrad Spein became unsafe, the road to it was abandoned, and those who decided to come here were few and far between. But elves and orcs, dwarves and gnomes, men and goblins—they all remember what lies hidden beneath the green crowns of the Forests of Zagraba, they all tell their grandsons legends, fables, and myths about the former magnificence of the underground palaces. After the evil of the bones of the ogres and others unknown awoke on the lower levels, the place was left deserted and dead.

For some reason the third level was pitch dark. There was none of the magic of glowing walls that I'd become used to, and if not for my lights I would have had to grope my way along. My steps could hardly be heard, but I made myself walk carefully and reduced the power of the light to its normal level. No point in shining like the sun—Balistan Pargaid's lads could be somewhere nearby.

The black-and-red hall was followed by another just like it, from which three openings led into another three exactly like the first. And from each of those there were openings to another three. And so on to infinity. The maze was as complex as anything on the upper levels. In every space one or another small part of this frozen black-and-scarlet beauty was picked out by the light of my little lamp and then disappeared again, shrouding itself in the night. A frozen column here, an elegant arch there.

How many halls had I seen in all these hours? If I hadn't had the papers from the abandoned Tower of the Order, I would have lost my way long ago in the cunningly contorted labyrinths. Probably that was what had happened to the servants of the Master, who were now an hour and a half ahead of me. If not for Lafresa, I would have written all the lads off as candidates for the darkness. But the blue-eyed woman had some kind of inner instinct, and even without a map she was able to find the right way through the labyrinth of the Palaces of Bone.

Every hall on the third level was an immense tomb. The latest burial sites of the elves and the orcs were on this level. Tombs first appeared here in the final years of the Dead Truce, which both races had observed for many thousands of years—but everything comes to an end. Blood was spilled, and the truce collapsed. The elves erected the Doors, shutting the orcs (and themselves) out from the easy route to the graves of their ancestors.

Unlike men, the older races didn't put up memorial gravestones, they simply built the dead (or their ashes) into the walls, and the structures of the graves were not visible, so anyone who didn't know would never have guessed that the bones of orcs and elves who had died hundreds or even thousands of years ago lay behind a skillful piece of molding or a picture or a column.

The third level, and then the fourth.

And all of this in absolute pitch blackness. I had been in Hrad Spein for six days. I ate, slept, and went on my way. Walking through halls, corridors, and galleries. Ever onward and downward, deeper and deeper. . . . Not a single sign of the presence of man or any other creature.

But on the fourth level I came across something different from everything I had seen for the last two days. The undisturbed peace was missing here; this place had a distinct smell of death. The walls of the hall were covered with a material like the bark of oak trees, the ceiling was a tangle of stone branches, and the floor was grass frozen in marble. A freakish combination of smells—roses, cinnamon, cardamom, ginger, dog-roses, and decomposition.

The dead.

Many of them, more than thirty. Skeletons covered with yellow parchment skin, wearing steel armor shimmering with the blue of the heavens and with crooked swords—s'kashes.

Elves. The bodies were especially numerous in the center of the hall. My little light picked out a coffin of black Zagraban oak with its bottom turned toward me.

I walked closer, trying not to disturb the bones of the dead elves. Probably, when the elves were attacked and taken by surprise, the ones carrying the coffin had dropped it and when it hit the floor it split open.

The elves had fought to defend their dead, but lost their own lives. Most men would say that dying for someone who is dead already is stupid, but Egrassa's relatives took a very different view. The word "house" and the word "kin" meant more than their own lives to these creatures with fangs.

The lid of the coffin had been thrown a yard away, and the dead elf had tumbled halfway out of his final refuge. I wondered if his spirit had seen how the elves who brought him here died?

The elf in the coffin was wearing a crown. A circle of platinum with black diamonds, alternating with expertly crafted roses of tarnished silver. I was looking at the ruler of one of the dark elfin houses.

Sagot only knows what came over me, but I did something that was very stupid (even by my standards). I went over to the king's remains, put them back in the coffin, and with a great strain turned the surprisingly heavy box back upright.

During these maneuvers the crown that had stayed on the dead king's head for more than forty years fell off and hit the floor with a repulsive clang. I picked it up and in the light of my magical lamp the black diamonds suddenly came to life, sparkling more brightly than ever.

I couldn't help exclaiming out loud in delight and admiration. Sagot! That subtle, shimmering play of light was so beautiful. I imagined what would happen if the stones were shown to the sunlight. The crown on the second level that had been melted by the pink ray from the ceiling simply couldn't compare with the crown of the head of the House of the Black Rose. Well, how could horse dung possibly compare with the nectar of the gods?

I froze for a few seconds, struggling with myself. A part of me wanted to take this priceless thing; after all, the dead elf had no more use for it, and it would bring me an immense fortune. But another part of me appealed shrilly to my wisdom and prudence, pointing out that no one had ever managed to rob an elf from a ruling house, regardless of whether he was alive or dead.

This time the greed heaved a sigh of disappointment and gave way. Darkness take the diamonds, in the name of Sagot! Elves are vengeful even after they're dead. Without the slightest regret, I cautiously set the black crown back on the dead elf's head. Rest in peace, king, and forget that I unintentionally disturbed you.

My glance fell on a s'kash with a jade handle that was lying at my feet. I bent down and picked up the weapon, and the rippled pattern of the metal glowed dully in the light of my magical lamp. A blade worthy of the ruler of a house. As I laid the curved sword on the elf's chest, my nose caught a faint scent of dog-roses. I folded the bony hands over the hilt.

First the left hand, then the right. The dead king's right wrist suddenly flexed, setting his hand on top of mine, and I felt a sudden chilly sensation on my skin. The elf's hand fell back onto the sword before I even thought of pulling my hand away.

Frightened, I held the hand against myself, unable to believe that I'd got away so lightly. The dead elf had only held me for a fraction of a second, but I could still feel that sudden searing chill on my palm. I staggered fearfully back from the coffin, realizing in some corner of my mind that I had instinctively closed my hand into a fist because the elf had somehow managed to put something in it. I opened my fingers fearfully, as if there was a vicious scorpion with a fiery sting hiding in them.

The fleeting flash of a falling star.

I just had time to see that it was black. The star fell to the floor with a faint tinkling sound. I bent down and picked up the beautiful thing—it was warm now, not cold. I couldn't stop myself exclaiming out loud again.

Lying there on my palm was a ring every bit as beautiful as the crown of the lord of the House of the Black Rose. The body of the ring was made of interwoven threads of black silver and platinum, and its heart was a black diamond. It wouldn't be surprising if the ring had magical properties, too—by the light of my lamp its facets shimmered with all the colors of the rainbow. Of course, the ring wasn't as valuable as the crown, but even this black diamond was enough for eight years of the good life in my own little palace.

I walked up to the coffin and looked hard at the dead elf. The play of light and shade made his face look almost alive, almost animated, but very old. A faint odor of roses tickled my nostrils. With a final glance at the king, I walked away, clutching the ring tightly in my fist, realizing that it was a gift. An unexpected gesture from the race of elves, but it was true. I took the glove off my right hand, put the ring on my finger, and gazed at the facets of the stone.

A gold spark was suddenly born in the depths of the diamond. It flared up and went out, and then flared up again. Flash. Darkness. Flash. The spark pulsed slowly, languidly, regularly, as if there was a real heart hidden inside the diamond.

Enlightenment always comes unexpectedly. My heart was beating with exactly the same rhythm as the stone. Or rather, the stone was glimmering in time to the beating of my heart. I didn't know what kind of ring I had on my hand and what the consequences of wearing it would be, but I did understand, or rather, I felt, that I was bound to it in exactly the same way as I had been bound to the Key. I could feel myself in the stone and the stone in me.

It was a kind of tickling sensation that only lasted for about three seconds, then the glimmering of the stone faded and it became an ordinary diamond again. I put my glove back on, concealing the precious thing, cast a final glance round the tree hall, pulled the hood of my black jacket up over my head, and went on my way, leaving the elf still unburied in the dense gloom.

Dead silence, broken only by the sound of my steps. I don't have the words to describe all the beauty of the underground Palaces. Black and red, orange and gold, blue and aquamarine, intense purple and dull ochre, the cold of blue marble and the heat of fiery granite.

Walls sparkled with mica and magnificent columns of pure amber, reaching up to immense heights. Entrancingly beautiful statues of orcs and elves, pools with their bottoms covered in fanciful patterns of turquoise and flowing water. Ethereal stairways with slim banisters that seemed to have been carved by some master craftsman out of a single block of green mountain crystal, and balconies woven out of fine threads of some unfamiliar metal, running round the upper stories of the halls.

Shimmering walls and ceilings of black silver, the beauty of the faded autumn in the gestures and poses of every statue. A faint, barely audible *hmmmm*—the song of halls that guard the peace of the dead. Not even the faintest breath of wind, no drafts, and no sounds apart from the song of the halls, not a single whisper, not a single ray of light. Whatever magic once lit up these places, it died when the elves and the orcs left Hrad Spein.

I kept on going, deeper and deeper under the ground. I didn't even want to think about how many leagues of stone there were above my head. Who could have created all this frozen beauty at depths so incomprehensible to the mind of man? What miraculous means could they have used? And this was only the fourth level, there were forty-eight of them, plus those that had no names, where even the ogres never ventured when their race was at the height of its power. Whoever created Hrad Spein at the dawn of time must have been equal to the gods, or superior to them.

The gloom slumbered, the dead slept their eternal sleep in the niches of the ancient tombs, and I was the only one who knew no rest. No longer paying attention to the beauty of the underground Palaces, I tramped on and on, and every second, every step brought me closer to my goal, my Commission—the Rainbow Horn.

It was the second day of my journey across the fourth level and my seventh day in Hrad Spein. A week had gone by, and I was amazed that I hadn't been driven crazy by the oppressive sense of loneliness.

A week. A whole week, spent Sagot only knew where. But I was halfway through the journey, with only four levels left.

Ha! Only! I still hadn't got to the places mentioned in the verse guide. A week had flashed past like a confused nightmare that I could hardly even remember. There wasn't much chance that I would get back on time now, and it would be just like Milord Alistan to come down here himself.

I had about half of my original supply of biscuits and lights left, and I was beginning to feel a bit concerned that soon I'd have to ration myself more strictly, tighten my belt and learn to walk in total darkness. And what's more, there was no water in this part of the level and I had to be brutally economical with the small amount still splashing about in the bottom of my flask. My face was itching desperately, too—the effect of a week's worth of unshaven stubble.

I should have reached the stairway to the fifth level a long time ago, but there was no sign of it. I was starting to worry that I must have turned into the wrong hall by mistake and got lost.

The map was almost no help to me. I could tell where the way out was, but there was no way I could tell exactly where I was myself. All the halls in this sector were the same—indigo and ochre walls, mother-of-pearl columns, and turquoise floors (a diabolical combination for the eyes).

I was looking for just one hall. One with an entrance to a long, absolutely straight gallery that ought to lead me to the stairway I needed. But I had been searching for more than three hours, and still had not found it.

Then I had a sudden stroke of luck (if you can really call it luck).

This place wasn't like all the ones before it. A small room with a closed iron door in the far wall and a narrow little manhole in the floor, covered with a steel grille. I walked up to the door, wondering feverishly why anyone would have wanted to put up a barrier here, especially since I hadn't exactly seen a lot of doors in Hrad Spein. Realizing that I must have missed a turn somewhere, I turned to walk out of the room, but halfway across it I got a very big surprise. The wall closed up, as if it were alive, blocking off the way out and locking me in.

"I don't get it," I told the darkness rather stupidly.

The answer was a rumble from the ceiling. I hastily told the light to shine at full brightness and uttered a phrase that was rather offensive to the ears of the gods.

The ceiling was moving toward me, threatening to skewer Harold on two-yard-long spikes that would have been the envy of every hedgehog in Siala.

When I recovered from my stupor, I ran to the iron door and hastily inspected it again. A keyhole. . . . There it is! My hands were shaking a little as the ceiling slowly and implacably moved lower.

The lock pick slid into the keyhole and broke off with an apologetic *ping*. I gaped stupidly at the stub left in my hand. Would you believe it! I flung it aside in a fury, struck the door hard with my shoulder, and hissed in pain. There was no way it was ever going to shift!

My eye fell on the manhole in the floor. I grabbed the grille with both hands and pulled with all my might, straining so hard I almost snapped in half. But, as I ought to have expected, the grille didn't budge an inch.

I had to do something, and quick! The unknown builders who had built this manhole for some strange reason had given me a chance to avoid being killed, and I didn't intend to waste it.

I scooped a handful of vials out of my bag, chose one that had a skull in flames drawn on it, and put the others back. I flung the magical vial at the grille and the glass clinked as it broke. I darted off to a safe distance—as far as I could get.

A bright flash of flame!

I crawled to the manhole on all fours, praying to Sagot that everything had worked properly. The spikes on the ceiling were almost scraping my back. The grille covering the manhole in the floor had disappeared. I dived into the hole, without even thinking about the consequences. I fell for a second, hit a stone floor, and hissed at the pain.

A grating sound from somewhere up above told me that the ceiling spikes had made contact with the floor. The light flared up to its previous brightness in a gesture of farewell, and died.

Magnificent! The space I'd fallen into was so narrow, I had to perform miracles of agility just to reach the bag at my waist. I hooked a new magical lamp out of one of the pockets with two fingers, squeezed my eyes shut, lit it, waited for a few seconds, and then started inspecting my new refuge.

A small square room with a narrow stone tunnel leading out of it.

Twisting myself into an impossible position, I looked up. There was the square manhole I had come through, and the ceiling, grinning at me with its spikes. I twisted myself even farther out of shape, almost lying down, and shone the light into the stone tunnel. I could only see five yards; after that it was pitch black.

Of course, I could have just died there, like a rat in a trap, but somehow I didn't really want to depart for the light so soon. So I would have to crawl through the narrow passage and just hope it didn't narrow all the way down to the eye of a needle. Sagra be praised, it didn't, and eventually I could see the end of the tunnel.

The hole leading out into the hall was no more than two yards above the floor. First all the things I had been pushing along went flying down, and then I followed. I had to twist pretty sharply to land on my feet instead of my head, but I managed this little task successfully and found myself standing in a brightly lit space.

There was no time for looking around, and I quickly gathered up my things that were lying on the floor. I put one bag over my shoulder, the other on my belt, set the knife on my thigh and pulled the straps tight, slung the crossbow behind my shoulder. That seemed to be everything. Now I could take a look at the place, since this was the first time on this level that I'd come across a hall that was brightly lit.

The architecture was rather inelegant for elves or orcs—too coarse, simple, and plain. There was a large stone head of one of those half bird, half bears on each wall. As usual, the faces in these sculptures were hostile and the eyes blazed brightly in the light of the magical lamps—lamps that were like my own little lights, but much larger.

The blazing eyes caught my attention. Caught it and held it. In the first head they were green; in the second, fiery red; in the third, intense yellow; and in the fourth, the deep color of the sky just before a thunderstorm. The palms of my hands immediately started sweating, because those eyes were actually precious stones, and each one was just a little bit smaller than my fist.

If I could collect all those stones, I'd never have to work again. They'd make me rich for a hundred years, and the price of the Commission—the fifty thousand that Stalkon had promised me if I dragged back the Rainbow Horn for him—would seem laughable. Why, the dwarves would sell me half their mountains for a single stone like that!

This time I didn't hesitate. I took out my knife and went over to the nearest face, the one with green eyes. I stuck the knife between the gem and the ordinary stone and started using it like a lever, working the gigantic emerald loose.

The green jewel yielded with surprising ease and I caught it in my hand. Then a torrent of green cascaded out of the empty eye socket onto the floor. I even forgot to open my mouth. In ten seconds an entire fortune in small emeralds (small, that is, after the emerald eye) spilled out.

They scattered across the smooth floor like grains of millet, sparkling bright green in the light of the lamps. I stuck the large eye-emerald in my bag and started gathering up its smaller brothers with trembling hands, obsessed with the feverish thought that once I emptied all the treasure out of the eye sockets, I'd be far richer than any king.

There was a stairway that started beside the head with the yellow eyes and led straight up to the ceiling, where there was a hatch. That was my way out.

I was distracted from gathering up the emeralds by a shadow that appeared from behind my back. From my hands and knees I flung myself sideways in a most inelegant manner, and a yataghan came down hard on the spot where I had just been, clanging loudly against the marble floor.

When I swung round and saw the creature that had almost killed me, I was stupefied. Standing there just three yards away from me was a skeleton. Not a human skeleton—the bones were too broad and heavy. Most likely it was an orc's; at least the fangs were the right size.

A yataghan in its right hand, a small round shield in its left, and eye sockets filled with myriads of crimson sparks—the sign of reawakened magic. Darkness only knows how its bones held together, but the creature threw itself at me.

I'd never have thought that skeletons were so nimble. This lad was just as fast as I was, and his yataghan turned into a blur of steel. He almost drove me into a corner but, fortunately for me, the stairway was close by and I started scrambling up it as fast as I could. I forgot all about the precious stones—now I had to save my own skin. When I'd covered a quarter of the eleven yards that separated the ceiling from the floor, I felt the stairs shudder.

After a quick glance down, I started moving my arms and legs twice as fast. The skeleton wasn't planning on stopping halfway. Throwing the shield away and grasping the yataghan in its teeth (what a sight that was!), the dead orc came scrambling nimbly up after me. I must say, he climbed a lot better than I did, and he caught up with me at a height of about nine yards.

There was nothing else for it; I had to take desperate measures. I grabbed hold of the banister rail with both hands, waited until there was almost no distance at all between my enemy and me, then slammed both boots into the yellow skull with all my might.

My enemy went crashing down onto the floor and was smashed to smithereens.

I didn't really feel like going back down again. What if there was another surprise waiting for me? For always used to tell me to be content with a little and never make money more important than my own life. As usual, the old thief and priest of Sagot was right. I'd better follow his advice and be happy with what I already had in my bag.

A minute later I was back in the familiar purple and silver halls of the fourth level and I had to use another light. I looked round to see where I was, and chuckled. Whatever happens is always for the best. The gallery leading to the stairway down to the fifth level started from the hall that I was in.

I certainly hadn't been hoping that somehow, completely out of the blue, I would end up in the Halls of the Slumbering Whisper, which turned out not to be halls at all, but the gallery that led to the fifth level. Naturally, no one had warned me where I was, and there were no indications at all on the maps.

The gallery was lined completely with black marble with white flecks. Marble floor, marble walls, marble columns on the right of the balcony. I walked up to the edge and looked down. There was only just enough light for me to see the floor of the hall down below.

I thought I heard something. . . .

Sh-sh-sh-sh . . .

I stopped and listened. Yes, my ears hadn't deceived me, there was definitely a hissing sound. I looked around, but couldn't see the source of the sound anywhere nearby. It seemed to be coming from inside my own head. I marked the unexpected sound down to an overactive imagination, stopped thinking about it, and carried on.

About a hundred paces farther on I thought I could hear vague, indistinguishable words starting to take shape through the hissing, but no matter how hard I strained my ears, I couldn't make out what they meant.

I found the dead man about twenty paces later. All that was left of him was a heap of bones. Ah, but wait, men don't have fangs growing out of their lower jaws. Like the skeleton that had almost chopped me into stewing steak, this was either an elf or an orc, but I could thank my lucky stars that this skeleton wasn't going to attack me.

By this point the hissing had changed to a totally incomprehensible muttering, as if the speaker had stuffed his mouth full of hot porridge. Twenty yards farther on there was another corpse waiting for me, and in the next five minutes I counted twenty-six skeletons. But there was no way of telling what they had died of or how they had gotten there.

The muttering was hammering away insistently at the door of my mind now, as if some bastard had stuffed an entire hive of angry bees who could talk into my head. I could only pick out occasional words from the ragged droning—"blood," "die," "brain," and the like.

Well, let's just say the words I heard weren't exactly the kind that would cheer my heart. I could feel the muttering in my head, and the corpses that kept turning up with increasing regularity set my nerves on edge, so I started singing a simple little tune to crowd out the voices, but it didn't really do much good.

The next corpse was a great surprise. This was no heap of old bones, but a perfectly fresh body. I would have wagered my soul that only a few hours earlier this lad was still alive and well, and not planning to die.

I'd seen him at Mole Castle with Balistan Pargaid—from which I could draw the conclusion that Lafresa and her companions had already walked through the gallery and gained a few hours on me. What a cunning bitch!

But at least things were a bit clearer with this corpse. Even a thick-witted Doralissian could tell what the lad had died of. He'd stuck a yard of iron into his own chest a few times—in other words, he'd committed suicide.

His hand was still clutching the handle of the dagger sticking out of his chest.

The muttering was pulsing in my head like a dull ache now. I frowned and ground my teeth, but I couldn't understand just what foul plague could have affected me like this.

Five steps farther on the whisper suddenly broke into a howling chorus of triumph in my head, making me drop to my knees and squeeze my head in my hands. I was swamped by a wave of universal revulsion and horror.

I didn't just hear words. There was everything here—visions of unbelievable horror, the smell of decomposing corpses, the taste of death-worms on my tongue, the sensation of rummaging through a corpse's belly. The voices were insistent, calling me to them, chanting a song that set me howling in horror and excruciating pain. My senses were completely confused, but absolutely everything was clamoring for and craving my death, urging me to take out my knife and thrust it into my throat.

The song rumbled on, massaging my mind insistently with its soft, slippery fingers. Every word, every chord of the voices brought new horrors that crept into my ears, blinded my eyes, smothered my tongue. . . .

That was when I realized that I'd found my way into the Halls of the Slumbering Whisper, but there was nothing I could do about it now. The voices were stronger than me, and I was slowly, inexorably going out of my mind. I wanted to take a few steps and throw myself off the edge of the balcony, or beat my brains out against the wall, or turn my knife on myself.

I had to do something, anything, to stop THIS! Against the will of my faintly glimmering mind, my hand reached out to the handle of my knife. As Sagot is my witness, I tried to fight it, but the struggle was like trying to smash a massive boulder with a twig. The voices INSISTED that I had to die, and it was impossible not to submit.

Just as he did in Hargan's Wasteland, Valder spoke in a barely audible whisper:

"I'll help!"

The voices howled in unison with the irresistible torrent of the song and retreated to the very boundaries of hearing. My hand obeyed my will once again.

"Quick, Harold, I can only give you a minute! At this moment that's as much as I can do!" said the dead archmagician.

I jumped to my feet and dashed back toward the place where the voices still had no power over me. My hands were shaking, but I managed to fish

the cotton earplugs out of my bag and stick them into my ears. The muttering came closer again, so that I could almost make out the words. It took
me another ten precious seconds to take out the vial with the liquid that
neutralized any hostile magic for a couple of minutes. I tore the seal open
with my teeth and poured the contents into my mouth. The bitter taste
flooded over my tongue and my stomach protested and shuddered, almost
turning me inside out. I had to make an effort to hold the foul muck down.

"That's it, I can't do any more!" Valder declared, and the dam he had
created burst and collapsed.

The voices came back, but now they were just voices, mouthing abomina-
tions without any visions to support them. The bitter liquid was working—but
for how long? Casting aside all doubt and hesitation, I rushed forward, hoping to get through the gallery before the defensive magic weakened enough
for the whispering voices to take control again.

"Kill yourself! Go to the darkness! Die! Die! Die! Blood! Kill!" the voices
whispered in powerless fury. "Stop! Wait! Die, it's so easy!"

I ignored the whispers, gritted my teeth, and kept dashing on as fast as I
could, constantly leaping over the bones that lay in my way.

I came across another two of Balistan Pargaid's men, but where were the
others? Had Lafresa managed to fight off the whispers?

The voices sensed a moment of weakness and moved in, whispering and
threatening every possible kind of nightmare and all the pain in the world.
It was really hard for me not to stop, and to keep on running. The bitter
taste on my tongue was gradually fading, and the whispering was coming
back.

I covered the last five yards of the gallery in three huge bounds, without
any magical protection. The voices howled in triumph, thrusting their talons into my brain, but I was already covering the final yard and it was too
late for the whispering to bind my reason with the nets of insanity.

I flew out of the gallery and the hall, and suddenly everything went
quiet. Kli-Kli's medallion scalded my skin with a cold flame and, before I
could even understand what had happened to me, I went crashing headlong
into Count Balistan Pargaid.

I had to lie there for a little while, gasping for breath and waiting for the
sparks in front of my eyes to fade away. The collision had completely winded
me and knocked me to the ground. Damn Balistan Pargaid, for getting
under my feet at just the wrong moment.

His Grace and one of his soldiers were standing there, transformed into frozen statues. They looked as if they had been carved out of cloudy ice and then sprinkled generously with hoarfrost.

I walked up to them and carefully touched a hand. The cold fingers scalded my palm. It really was ice. Some kind-hearted soul had turned the servants of the Master into statues of ice just for the fun of it. A ludicrous, but entirely appropriate end for one of the most powerful lords of Valiostr and servants of the Master.

Following the encounter with Balistan, it took me a few moments to spot the spiral stairway leading down through the floor toward the fifth level. Well, then, that was one more landmark passed.

6

THE MASTERS OF GLOOM

Counting steps in Hrad Spein had become a habit. It helped distract me from my gloomy thoughts. Only this time the counting wasn't really helping much. At 573 all the black thoughts came down on me so hard that I lost count and gave up.

Lafresa was still ahead of me in the race for the Rainbow Horn, and she still had the Key—I'd never get out of the Palaces without that. She found her way unerringly through the labyrinth of dead halls, moving on as if she was strolling along Parade Street, taking no notice of the menaces lurking on every side, and paying for her safe passage with the late Balistan Parga-id's men.

By my calculation there were no more than twelve of them left. Probably not even that many. Who knew which path the blue-eyed witch had led her little detachment along and how many bodies I hadn't noticed? In fact it was quite likely that now the Master's woman-servant was continuing on her way alone.

The first of the main dangers—the Halls of the Slumbering Whisper foretold in the verse riddle—was behind me now, but the fun was only just beginning. How did it go on in the scroll . . .

> Through the halls of the Slumbering Echo and Darkness
> Past the blind, unseeing Kaiyu guards,

'Neath the gaze of Giants who burn all to ash,
To the graves of the Great Ones who died in battle . . .

Encouraging lines, weren't they?

I woke from a nightmare, although I couldn't remember what horrors I'd been dreaming of. All that was left of the dream was a stabbing pain in my chest and an immense weariness, as if I hadn't slept at all.

The rest I had allowed myself on the final turn of the staircase hadn't brought the relief I'd been hoping for, and I set off in a depressed mood.

The fatigue of the last week weighed on my shoulders like a heavy burden, pressing me down. I was only just starting to realize that the journey through Hrad Spein wasn't as easy as I'd thought. The constant tension, the constant anticipation of danger, were having an even worse effect on my health than all the distance I'd tramped from the entrance of the Palaces to the entrance to the fifth level.

I got up with a groan (unfortunately, stone steps are not the most comfortable place to sleep) and stretched my numb arms and legs. Hundreds of tiny needles started wandering over my body, pricking me first in one place, then another. But strangely enough, this minor discomfort pepped me up better than anything else could have done, and I reached the fifth level in a perfectly cheerful state of mind.

The fifth level. The very first hall—and once again an unexpected change in the decor. Where was the gold, where was the subtle elegance, where was the charm of the statues and the delightful visual beauty of the walls? All of that had been left behind on the third and fourth levels of the underground Palaces. Here there were only monotonous stone walls with mediocre paintings, and the floor was made of flagstones about two square yards in size, carelessly aligned with each other.

I noticed that all the slabs on the floor had different colors and markings, and not all of them would have met with aesthetic approval from a decent artist. Most likely someone had laid the slabs out in a huge mosaic, but because it was so immense, there was no way I could see what it showed. Every hall had its own mosaic, its own set of colors on the floor, but by the meager light of my little magical lamp it was impossible for me to make out the overall picture.

I didn't know why these halls were called the Halls of the Slumbering

Darkness; as far as I could tell, this honorary title could easily have been awarded to any of the unlit spaces from the third level on.

I tramped through the underground labyrinth for half a day, only occasionally checking the maps and starting a new light—the number of those was dwindling rapidly. I tried not to think about the time when I would have to grope my way along by touch.

It was a lot cooler down here than on the upper levels. Essentially I was wandering through huge natural caves with graves in the roughly worked walls, mosaic floors, and stalactites and stalagmites that had grown together to form fantastical fairy-tale columns.

The fifth level seemed to go on forever, and the cave-halls seemed boundless. The farther I walked, the more I felt enveloped in the dead cobweb of decline from the former majesty of the Palaces of Bone.

The columns were covered in lumps and bulges and in some places water dripped from the ceiling and the first signs of future columns had appeared on the mosaic floor. I couldn't see the walls, they were a very long way off, and I tramped on and on, taking my bearings from the path laid out in red slabs.

Sometimes it branched into two, three, four, or even eight new paths, and I had to leaf through the papers for a long time, straining my eyes and my brain as I tried to compare the orcish squiggles on the maps and on the flagstones of the floor.

The constant darkness was enough to drive anyone crazy! I would have sold my soul for a helping of well-roasted meat, a pint of beer, and a ray of sunshine. The gods be praised, at least I wasn't short of water. There was more than enough of that here. Once I even crossed a little hump-backed bridge over a small lake of black water as smooth as a mirror.

The underground caves came to an end and the gloomy halls of the Palaces of Bone began again. It got warmer, water stopped dripping down the walls, and the smell of damp disappeared, giving way to a faint smell of decomposition.

I didn't like that smell at all. Why was there still a stink, if the age of the burial sites on this level was measured in centuries and everything that could rot ought to have rotted away, leaving mostly bones? That aroma of old death made me feel vaguely anxious, but a smell is just a smell, and so far nothing worse had happened.

There was a light breeze blowing in the Halls of the Slumbering Darkness. It sang somewhere up under the ceiling, making a constant eerie *hmmmmmm*.

When I first heard the sound, I thought it was the terrible whispering coming back, but after what seemed like an age drenched in cold sweat, with my knees trembling, I realized that it was only the wind.

I walked on until I came up against a wall. It was slightly concave for some reason, and I was surprised by this, so I allowed myself the luxury of ordering the light to burn at full brightness.

The magical light picked an immense column out of the darkness—it was so big that it would have taken forty men holding hands to put their arms round it (assuming they joined hands first, of course). Mmm, yes . . . many of the trees in Zagraba could have envied the thickness and height of this stone monster. And there were hundreds of these columns in the hall. I walked past the stone giants, feeling like a pitiful little bug. The morose gray monsters soared upward out of the light, hanging silently over the un-invited guest and threatening to drop the distant vault of the ceiling on his head.

A vague sense of alarm stayed with me all the way through this place, with its constantly howling wind—*hmmmmm*—dismal grayness, and faint smell of decomposition. . . . At one point, when cold shivers suddenly started running down my back for the hundredth time, I decided, for some reason that I didn't understand, that I ought to look round as quickly as possible. I don't know if it was my impulse or Valder's. A single fleeting glance was enough to make me hide the light under my jacket and order it to go out.

Far, far away, at the very beginning of the columned hall, there was a faint sprinkling of orange dots. There could be no doubt that they were torches. I could see several dozen of the bright blinking points. They would disappear behind a column and then reappear again, advancing slowly but surely in my direction.

I would have wagered my soul that the torch-bearers couldn't be Balistan Pargaid's men. There couldn't be many left from the group that had come down into the Palaces of Bone with Lafresa. . . . But this group numbered fifty or sixty. So it was someone else parading through the hall.

Hoping that I'd managed to hide the light in time and the strangers hadn't noticed it, I darted behind a column close to the wall and as far as possible from the center of the hall. Were the strangers actually looking for me or was this their regular daily stroll around the local sights? Just to be on the safe side I got the crossbow ready, pulled my hood up over my head, and pressed my-self back against the wall.

Hmmmmmmm.

The wind of the ancient halls sang a lullaby to the slumbering gloom of eternity. The sound of the wind was a faint dreary note in my ears and the only thing I could hear above it was the desperate pounding of my heart. For a long time there was no other sound but my heartbeat and the lullaby of the wind. And then the Halls of the Slumbering Darkness shuddered and the night awoke.

The steps came closer and closer. . . . First an orange glow appeared on the distant columns, and then I could hear the strangers' heavy snuffling as they breathed. On the one hand that was good—if they snuffled, it meant they were alive. But on the other hand . . .

I didn't finish what I was thinking, because at last I saw *them,* and I immediately wanted to be ten leagues away. It's not every day you get to see the images on walls come to life. Somehow I hadn't been expecting to see living examples of the creatures that the makers of the Palaces of Bone had depicted with such obsessive accuracy in their statues, paintings, and mosaics.

Half birds, half bears that even the Order didn't know about (I was sure of that!). The creatures walked past me—tall, about the same height as an ogre, massively built, almost square, with thick arms and legs and bare clawed feet. Large, elongated heads rather like a bear's, with little ears, round birdlike eyes, and small curved beaks that gleamed like steel in the light of the torches.

These strange, in fact absurd creatures were dressed in loose violet robes. The shapeless tunics almost completely covered their bodies, leaving only the hands, feet, and heads exposed to view, all covered with reddish fur. Or perhaps it wasn't fur, but feathers. From that distance it was hard for me to tell.

No jewelry and no weapons. I could sense that the creatures were strong, confident, and . . . old. Not even old, but ancient—their age could rival eternity itself.

"They are the world," Valder suddenly whispered. "They came to Siala at the moment of its birth. The firstborn were not the ogres and certainly not the orcs. . . . These beings lived at the very beginning of the Dark Era. A race that was once mighty, and alien even to the ogres, now condemned to live here. Quite different from us. Absolutely alien . . . Look, Harold, there they are—the firstborn of this world."

I didn't know how the archmagician knew about the half bird, half bears, but I literally gaped wide-eyed at the beasts.

They were walking past, only fifteen yards away from me. Walking in single file, snuffling loudly, and waddling from one foot to the other. Every third one was carrying what at first I had taken for torches. In fact they were knobbly black wooden staffs, polished until they shone, and set on the top of every one was a skull. Skulls of elves, orcs, men, and even ogres— they gave out an orange light very similar to the light of an ordinary flame.

One figure followed another until it seemed the procession would never end. The sound of snuffling, footsteps, claws scraping on the stone slabs of the floor. They drifted past me, these ships of ancient, bygone glory that had sunk to the bottom of the centuries, and their huge shadows slid ominously across the bodies of the columns. Finally the last of them, the eighty-sixth wayfarer, walked past me, and darkness fell.

Where had these creatures come from, what obscure depths of the Palaces of Bone had they lived in for all the millennia of Siala's existence, what did they want, what did they aspire to? I didn't know if they were dangerous, but, Sagot be praised, they had missed me. Darkness only knew how the firstborn (the genuine firstborn!) would react to an uninvited guest. Perhaps they'd greet him with open arms and lead him along a safe route straight to Grok's grave and the Rainbow Horn, or perhaps they'd simply turn my skull into a new lamp without thinking twice about it. Something told me the second alternative was far more likely than the first.

But even so, I couldn't just stay where I was. The column of creatures was moving in the direction I had to go in, and so I set out very quietly, scarcely even breathing, after the Ancient Ones.

I kept my distance so that—Sagot forbid—I wouldn't be heard or, even worse, get caught in the circle of light from the skull-lamps. I crossed the entire gigantic hall, running from column to column. The string of lights ahead of me trembled and divided into three parts that flowed off into the labyrinthine corridors, and the hall went dark.

In all this time I didn't hear a single word from the creatures. Where had the bird-bears gone, what goals were they pursuing, what did they want? Naturally, I didn't go chasing after them to ask stupid questions. Wherever the creatures had gone, they weren't going my way. In the literal or the figurative sense. My path led into a barely noticeable narrow corridor that began between the last two columns of the hall, but the three bands of Ancient Ones had taken other roads.

I felt a strong temptation to take out the maps and see where these creatures could be heading, but I ruthlessly suppressed this impulse of treacherous curiosity. The less you know, the better you sleep. I had no doubt that the bird-bears who had just walked through the columned hall had come to it from the depths of the levels without names, where no one had dared to go for the last seven thousand years.

"What do they want, Valder?" I blurted out.

Surprisingly enough, this time the archmagician condescended to answer me.

"They're waiting, Harold."

"Waiting? What for?"

He said nothing for a long time. A very long time. I thought I was never going to get an answer.

"A chance. A chance to come back to our world. They are a mistake of the gods, or perhaps of the one they call the Dancer in the Shadows. They were created as . . . as an experiment, as the first creatures, and they almost destroyed Siala, and were punished for it. . . . They are waiting for someone to smash the fetters that hold them in the bowels of the earth. Waiting and dreaming of *their* world being as it used to be. With no orcs, ogres, elves, and, of course, no men. They are waiting for the Holders of the Chain, those we are used to calling the Gray Ones, to bungle things, and the thread of equilibrium to snap, as it almost did on a fierce winter night many years ago."

The dead archmagician's words struck me like a physical blow.

I realized what he was hinting at.

"The Rainbow Horn?"

"Most likely. They were the ones who awoke the evil that was sleeping here. Their own evil. They can sense that the time is near. . . ."

"But how do you know all this?"

No reply. Valder disappeared, leaving me to my questions and doubts.

A meager supper, sleep that brought almost no relief, and back to the journey. The corridor led me into a cave where at last I could stop wasting lights and banging my nose against the wall.

It was every bit as large as the hall with the columns. Reddish orange walls, a ceiling with light beaming down from it and lighting up the whole place magnificently. And I could have sworn it wasn't magical light, but absolutely genuine sunlight.

For the first two minutes my eyes, which had grown completely unused to anything like this, simply couldn't see a thing. I squinted and tried to blink away the involuntary tears. But it cost me a lot of pain before I finally got used to it and could look at the world normally.

The light streaming from the ceiling more than sixty yards above my head was like the light of the evening sun shining through the leaves of a dense forest. It was something warm, gentle, not too bright, and, of course (after the gloom of the catacombs), unbelievably beautiful. This was probably the first time in a week of strolling through the Palaces of Bone that I felt grateful to the architects and magicians who had created such a miracle in one of the deep caverns.

The cave was so large that someone had even built a little fortress in it.

Yes, yes! An absolutely genuine fortress!

Walls about twelve yards high, gates torn off their posts and shattered. Four ethereally elegant towers with spires as sharp as spears. (Correction—three with spires; the fourth seemed to have been flattened by a magical fist: all that was left of it was a stump.)

Another tower set right at the very center, with the same architecture as the other four, but incomparably larger. If someone suddenly got the urge to move in there and set up defenses, even professional soldiers would have a hard time trying to storm the fortifications (in my ignorant view as a thief).

The reason I hadn't noticed the citadel straightaway was that its walls were almost the same color as the walls of the cave. I had to walk a long way before I reached this bastion that was sited so mysteriously, tramping along the reddish path that wound its way between the tall outcrops of stone sprouting up all over the floor like fingers. The path was littered with fine fragments of stone and every now and then one of them crunched under the soles of my boots.

When I got closer, I realized there was no way to go round the fortress. Its walls ran into the walls of the cave, and without the lost cobweb-rope, there was no way I could storm a barrier that was twelve yards high.

The only way to get to the other side was to walk through that yawning gap and hope there were gates on the other side of the fortifications, too.

I wasn't exactly happy with the idea of going inside. There were far too many bones outside the entrance.

They were fearfully old . . . many of the dead had arrows stuck between their ribs. The archers defending the place had reaped a rich harvest. There were plenty of weapons, but they were so old and rusty that the touch of a boot was enough to make them crumble into dust.

Shields, helmets, bows with their strings rotted away, armor with barely visible engravings of a Black Rose, a Black Flame, a Black Stone, a White Leaf, or White Water. Elves from the dark and light houses, who had fought shoulder to shoulder, attacking the fortress.

And I knew the only enemy the elfin houses could reunite against. It had to be their eternal and most important enemy, their closest relatives—the orcs. There was a battering ram lying beside the smashed gates.

I stood there weighing up my chances, then sighed and took out the crossbow. I removed one of the ordinary bolts and replaced it with an ice bolt. There was nothing else for it; I had to go back or go on into the fortress.

Surprisingly enough, nothing grabbed me, either in the gateway or the narrow corridor with loopholes for firing arrows at uninvited guests. Now there were old bones crunching under my feet instead of small stones. The elves had been given a warm reception in here, too. The corridor smelled of mold and damp from the old wooden ceilings and of bitter almonds. A strange aroma for a place like this, to say the least.

I walked out into the courtyard and the red column of the central tower was directly opposite me. The entire space was littered with bones, like the area in front of the gates.

A serious battle. The skeletons of orcs and elves were sometimes intertwined in the most incredible poses. The rusty crescents of s'kashes and yataghans were scattered around under my feet. In many places the ground, the walls, and the bones were covered with soot, or even fused and melted. In the western part of the yard there were heaps of red blocks and fragments of stone from the ruined tower. Magic had been used, as well as arrows and swords.

Many elves had laid down their lives, very many, but I had no doubt about who had been victorious. The bodies of eight orcs were embedded in the wall of the central tower at a height of about ten yards above the ground. I wouldn't be at all surprised if the orcs had suffered for a very, very long time, even after the elfin shamans and magicians had finished the execution. It was surprising that time didn't seem to have touched the dead orcs; for some reason it had spared them. I had the impression that they could have died only a minute earlier.

Their flesh hadn't melted away like the wax of a candle or rotten meat, and it hadn't dried up like a salty plum from over the sea. After traveling round the Border Kingdom, mixing with Algert Dalli's men, and fighting that battle at Crossroads, I knew a little bit about the badges of the most famous clans of orcs. The defenders of the fortress had badges that were white and black, almost completely faded. I'd never come across clan insignia like that before. If I ever got out of Hrad Spein, I'd have to ask Egrassa what clan of orcs wore black and white.

There was a large old tree growing right in front of the tower. It looked a bit like a dwarf warrior resting after a long journey: short, stocky, and sturdy. And as old as the red fortress that now enshrined the bones of the fallen warriors. But unlike the dead fortress that had been abandoned for so very long, the absurd old plant was still alive. All the branches of this long-lived tree were covered with small white flowers and it seemed to be nestling under a fluffy blanket of snow.

The flowers had a scent of almonds, and I could even taste the bitter aroma in my mouth. The smell was beginning to give me a headache, so I moved on in a hurry. I couldn't afford to stay any longer than necessary.

I took long, careful strides, trying not to step on any bones. Stupid really, but I couldn't help myself—something told me it was best not to disturb the remains of the elves and orcs without good reason. But I wasn't always able to avoid the yellowish bones encased in rusty armor. There were too many skeletons and sometimes my foot had no choice but to press the bones down into the crumbly sand of the fortress's courtyard. Then I misjudged the distance and stepped on a skull.

CRUNCH!

It burst with a deafening sound, as if it was an overripe Garrakian melon under my foot, not a skull. I winced squeamishly and looked up from the bones for a moment at the tree.

My heart performed a crazy somersault in my chest, soared up into the sky, then fell back and got tangled up in my guts.

The flowers on the tree weren't white anymore—they were red! Bloodred! The blood built up into huge drops on the petals and then fell down, sprinkling onto the bones and the sand. Like rain in some madman's nightmare, the heavy drops fell from the branches and oozed out of every pore of the tree's trunk. In a few seconds a small pool had already formed under the tree. The pool grew wider and wider, consuming the bones lying on the sand like some eerie predator.

A tormented, endless, spine-chilling howl of pain rang out from somewhere above me, making me stoop down and pull my head into my shoulders. I raised my eyes to look up, expecting to see a gryphon-dragon-manticoreharpy-Messenger-of-the-Master-or-the-Nameless-One swooping down on me, but . . . there wasn't anyone.

It was one of the orcs fused into the wall of the tower, screaming continuously in agony. His face was contorted in incredible pain. That was more than I could take.

I ran for it, without even looking to see where I was going, scattering bones. The orc screeched like a pig under the knife of a clumsy butcher. I dashed to the other side of the courtyard and jumped over the stones from the ruined tower that littered the ground, lost my footing and fell, almost tumbling into the blood flowing across the courtyard, rolled away, jumped up, pressed my hands to my ears, and set off again at a run.

I realized I'd dropped the crossbow, went back, flung aside somebody's ribs, grabbed the weapon, and ran for it. . . . The howling of that creature in torment was driving me insane, stirring up icy rafts of terror from the bottom of my mind.

My memory of the courtyard as I ran through it is a blur of the red column of the tower, the bitter smell of almonds, the bleeding tree, and the scream of an orc doomed to eternal agony.

Fear made me whimper as I ran. It took over almost all my mind; it was a miracle that I managed to leap out through a hole broken in the wall on the opposite side from the gates. The orc's screams pushed me along from behind, forcing me to run faster and faster along the red path. I fell twice, skinning and bruising my knees, but I jumped up again and ran on.

I only stopped after the howling of that eternally living and eternally dying creature had faded away into the distance.

I leaned my hands on my knees and tried to get my breath back. Ah, darkness, all I ever seemed to do was run. Where would I ever get the strength to survive the Palaces of Bone like this?

I looked back at the derelict fortress. From that distance it looked just like one of those little caskets that some dull-witted individuals use to keep their brain-rotting weed in.

The sunlight that had been shining down on the orange cave throughout this part of my journey was gradually fading, losing its brightness and vitality. Looking up all the time at the darkening ceiling, I set off along the red path toward the distant wall of the cave. The small slivers of stone squeaked under my feet like a crust of frozen snow or fragments of ancient bones.

When I reached the wall of the cave, the sparse rays of sunlight were too weak to light up the entire space. But just when I was about to use another little magical lamp, a miracle happened. All the stone-finger columns that the path had wound through suddenly flashed, then flared up and started glowing with a cold, pale blue light.

There were exactly the same kind of stone fingers, only smaller, growing straight out of the wall, and in their bright glow I spotted a path that I hadn't noticed before, which led upward in a whimsical, winding spiral.

What else could I do—the path ought to lead me to the way out, and it looked like the only one, unless I wanted to walk along the wall, hoping to find another way out of there. But why waste time on that kind of nonsense, if the cave wasn't even marked on the maps? And what if there was no other way out?

Even though I was walking uphill, it was quite easy, and after nine tight twists and turns I reached quite a height. The path was narrow and I had to lean back against the wall in order to feel reasonably secure. If I lost concentration or stepped awkwardly on a stone, I would have gone tumbling down over the edge.

Of course, the drop beside my feet wasn't an abyss of a hundred yards, but if I had fallen, I would have smashed every bone in my body. I tried not to look down until the winding path that was carved straight into the sheer cliff face finally led to the way out.

It was time for a rest. I made myself comfortable, took out a biscuit, shook my flask to check how much water I had left, and clicked my tongue in disappointment when I realized there was no more than three or four mouthfuls. I had to find a spring or a pond quickly to replenish my scant resources.

As always, the biscuit was as tough and tasteless as the sole of an old army boot (but—thanks be to Sagot—it didn't smell the same way). As I chewed on my ration, I admired the vista before my eyes. From where I was it was only about six yards to the ceiling, and about fifty to the floor. I could see the whole cave laid out in front of me. The entire expanse was lit up by the bright points of hundreds of columns blazing with a steady magical light like cold, bright glowworms. The floor and the walls were covered in circles of bright blue light radiating from the columns, and the light columns farthest away fused into a single bright line. These islets of blue light transformed the cave into a fairy-tale dream. Not even the lights in Zagraba at night could come anywhere close to this beautiful sight.

I could have sat there enjoying the view forever, but if I did, I'd never get the Rainbow Horn. I got to my feet regretfully, shook the crumbs off my hands, put away the flask, and walked into a spacious corridor with its walls marked by soot from torches.

I scraped it with a fingernail, and it was fresh. I was sure it was Lafresa. She must have conjured up wings for herself and now she was increasing her lead on me all the time.

Warm, sunny amber walls and a few magical torches, just barely keeping the shadows of the halls at bay.

Endless patterns on the walls, weaving together into carelessly drawn pictures—something like a chronicle. The story of every more or less significant event in the history of Siala, for the Nameless One only knew how many thousands of years, unfolded before me. But I had no time and no desire to examine all these artistic efforts by the orcs and the elves. I didn't have a million years to spare.

The floor, made of the same red mineral as the walls, was polished as bright as a mirror, and so now two Harolds walked through the halls together, only one of them was up here and the other was down there, in the reflecting floor. For some reason or other the flagstones were slippery. Giving way to a childish impulse, I took a run up and then slid along, as if it was genuine ice under my feet.

After about an hour's travel through the Amber Sector (the name I had decided to give this place), I realized where I was when I came out at two four-yard-high statues standing beside the entrance to the next hall. On the right an orc, and on the left, an elf. Both dressed in equally loose robes belted with chains, both with untypical double-handed swords with wavy-edged blades. The elf and the orc had their hands over their ears. There was some kind of inscription on the floor in orcish, but I ignored the incomprehensible squiggles, just as I had done before.

A warning? A wish for a safe journey? Sagot only knew what it was! Why in the name of darkness should I rack my brains and worry about it, if I couldn't understand anything anyway?

So without thinking too much, I walked past the frozen sculptures into the next hall. Although I must admit that since those gargoyles had come to life, I naturally regarded statues with a certain suspicion.

. . . *bang! Boom! BOOM! BangBOOM! BaBANG-ng-ng!*

Now that really was a surprise! I was almost deafened by the thundering echo of my own footsteps. It got louder and louder, until it turned into the roar of a deluging torrent, a waterfall, resounding like the thunder of the gods and then disappearing without a trace, leaving nothing but a ringing in my ears.

"Quiet," I whispered, and the echo immediately took up the word and seemed to spread it to every corner of Hrad Spein.

Quiet! quiET! QuiET! QUIET! QuiET! QUIET! ET-et!

I winced as if I had a toothache. The best way of informing the entire world of your existence is to yell in the Halls of the Slumbering Echo. The slightest sound roused an echo that should have made the dead leap out of their graves a league away from the place.

I tried taking a couple of steps, making as little noise as possible. Useless. Even walking carefully produced the same magically amplified echo.

I had to take off my boots and walk barefoot. Surprisingly enough, this actually helped, and the echo was hardly awoken at all, so I was able to carry on without worrying about being heard on the next level of Hrad Spein. But that damned mirror-polished floor was very cold on the feet.

After a while, when my toes had simply stopped feeling anything at all, the path brought me to an underground river imprisoned in banks of marble. The black ribbon of placid water flowed out of a hole in an amber wall, divided the hall into two halves, and disappeared into an identical hole in the opposite wall.

As it ran across the hall, the underground river cut off my path. There had been a bridge over it once, but now all that was left was a stone stump about a quarter of a yard long. The water was only half a yard below the marble bank, so I could reach it with my hand, and I took advantage of the opportunity to fill my flask.

The canal was about three or three and a half yards wide, so it was quite possible to take a run up and jump across it, and that's what I did, after putting my shoes on first. The floor was still as slippery as ever, and the jump turned out rather awkward. My heart skipped a beat when I thought I was going to fall short and land in the water, but a second later my feet touched the opposite bank. The floor promptly slid away from under me and I collapsed and slid at least ten yards on my side. Just like I said—it was exactly like ice in January! But least I didn't break anything.

"Ah, darkness!" I swore, and suddenly realized that the echo hadn't repeated my words.

I was past the Halls of the Slumbering Echo.

———

I walked on and found myself just two paces away from the edge of a precipice. There was a final torch burning beside the door, and that was what
stopped me from stepping into the abyss. I was on a small platform about
six paces across. The wall was smooth and it ran straight up into the darkness and the platform merged into a narrow track, carved straight into the
wall. A step to the left, and my shoulder struck the cold basalt of the wall, a
step to the right and . . . nothing.

Empty space. An abyss.

The path looked as if someone had gnawed it into the cliff with his teeth.
It was crude, careless, slapdash work. The surface was uneven and there
were protruding rocks, so I had to press myself tight against the wall and
creep along like a tortoise. Every now and then I came across dark openings
leading into the cliff and I tried to get past as quickly as possible. Darkness
only knew what might come leaping out of them.

The path narrowed to a quarter of a pace. Now I could just barely set my
foot on it, and the danger of tumbling off the cliff was much greater. I had
to cling on to the basalt with my nails in order to stay up there.

Ahead of me and a little to the right a string of six lights appeared. The
path ended right beside them, at a small platform in front of an opening.
There was no point in clambering into the hole—I needed to go in the other
direction. I turned toward the lights and something that the map showed as
a thin line barely visible on the yellowed paper. It was called Nirena's Thread.

It was just a bridge, but it was no wider than the last few yards of the
path. And what's more, it was rounded! A genuine hair, with barely even
enough space to set my foot on it, and it stretched for thirty yards and more.

I'm not afraid of heights, but this miracle of architectural design was
more than I could manage. I wouldn't have been able to take more than ten
teeny-weeny steps before the inevitable moment came and I fell. There were
six large magical lamps, trembling and winking, suspended in the air above
the bridge.

Well, gazing at the bridge wasn't going to make it any wider or get me
any closer to the other side. I decided not to try anything too fancy and to
cross the bridge in the simplest way possible—I simply lay down on Nirena's Thread, wound my legs round it, and started pulling with my hands.

I crawled along about as fast as a caterpillar. But I moved! And it was
better to move slowly but surely, without any fear of falling. Well . . . almost
without any fear. I tried not to look down; below me there was nothing but
blackness.

When I'd covered a quarter of the distance, I decided I deserved a little break and I stopped, hugging the bridge with my arms and legs as if it was the most precious thing in my life. Faint currents of warm air rose up from somewhere below me, bringing the aroma of a cesspit, and the stench made my eyes water.

I crawled forward, holding my breath until finally, I reached the opposite bank.

I gave another wide yawn and splashed water on my face from the flask in an attempt to drive away sleep. It didn't help. But that was hardly surprising. More than twenty hours on my feet, virtually without any rest at all. My fatigue was making itself felt, remorselessly demanding rest and refusing to back down.

I closed my eyes, but told myself I wouldn't sleep . . . not for anything. . . .

7

THE DANCE OF THE SUNLIGHT

I don't know how much time went by, but I woke up suddenly, as if someone had jabbed their elbow into my side.

The maps called the place I had reached the Eighty-Sixth Northeastern Hall of Stairways. It was a hall of onyx, and the black stone greedily devoured the light of the magic lamp, so that visibility was lousy. I couldn't risk increasing the brightness; at this stage I had to be careful with every new light and make it last for as long as possible, so that I'd be able to reach the way out.

I tried not to think about the fix I was in. Up on the outside, in the old life, I used to think that going down into Hrad Spein would make me part of the greatest and most dangerous adventure of the century. Only now I realized it was something far more serious than that. I couldn't find the words to describe the way I felt about the present situation.

Alone. Completely alone. In almost pitch darkness, going deeper and deeper, with my remaining supplies vanishing at catastrophic speed, without the Key, without any hope of getting back out through the Doors.

What was I hoping for? Probably nothing more or less than a miracle. A Great Big Divine Miracle. Of course, the gods were just desperate to save a certain Harold; they were queuing up for the chance.

My mood could hardly have been worse.

Dozens of black staircases running upward or winding downward like corkscrews. No difference between the staircases at all, as if the architects had followed some strict system that I didn't understand.

I walked past them for a long, long time, sometimes touching the cold stone with my fingers and listening to the silence. The onyx devoured every sound. At least, that's what I thought until I heard the scream. Although I didn't really hear it so much as feel it. The scream didn't last long, it broke off a second after I heard it, and it was very far away.

I stopped and listened. Silence. After walking right through the Hall of Stairways and tramping through a few small vestibules, I reached the entrance to a hall where there was light, and quickly put out my little magical lamp.

The entrance was every bit as tall and wide as the Doors, and once again there were two statues waiting to greet me, just like at the Hall of the Slumbering Echo. An orc on the right, an elf on the left. The orc's double-handed sword was broken, and the Firstborn was using a stiletto to poke out his own right eye with an impassive look on his face. There was already a gaping socket where his left eye should have been. I shuddered—the huge statue, five times the height of a man, seemed alive. The sculptor had certainly been granted talent from the gods.

The elf's sword was still in one piece, but the weapon was lying on the floor, with its handle toward me. I chuckled—it wasn't every day you could see an elf voluntarily discarding his weapon. But the elf had decided to keep his eyes and not stick any sharp objects into them. He had simply covered them with his hands.

How could I possibly understand what the builders had tried to say with these statues! There was writing on the floor. I was about to walk on past, but the letters impressed into the stone slabs flared up with a gray pearly light, forcing me to take notice of them.

At first they were orcish squiggles, then they trembled, diffused, and gathered back together as the squares, circles, and triangles used for writing by the gnomes and dwarves. A few moments later in some incredible way the gnomish scrawl rearranged itself into human letters that froze, glinting like pearls.

Here lie the sixty-nine rulers of the House of the White Leaf, sleeping their eternal sleep. If you are a gnome, a dwarf, a man, or the child of another race and you can read these lines, we adjure you not to disturb those who guard the peace of the dead and to seek another path.

But if you are a contemptible orc or are stubborn and refuse to listen to the voice of reason, or simply ignorant and cannot read—enter and accept the fate predetermined for you by the gods, and do not complain that you were not warned.

The letters gleamed for a few seconds, then re-formed into orcish squiggles and faded. This was probably the first moment in Hrad Spein that I thought about just giving up and trying to find another way to the sixth level.

I'm one of those people who usually listen to the inner voice of reason. And after all, the elves wouldn't go and warn a traveler about danger for no particular reason, especially if you bore in mind that there hadn't been any warning notices before any of the other traps I'd met. It would be better to err on the side of caution and not go blundering into a nest of vipers.

To reach the main route leading to the descent to the sixth level I only had to go through a few more halls, walking straight ahead without turning off (if the maps were telling the truth, of course).

A detour would cost me an extra day and a half of wandering through stairways, corridors, and halls, and I simply didn't have a day and a half to spare. I was far enough behind schedule already, and the time estimates I'd given Milord Alistan weren't worth a demon's belch anymore.

My stay in the Palaces of Bone really was having a very bad effect on my brain. I'd started rating the value of time above my own life. Anyway, the result was a kind of momentary blackout inside my head, and I only came round when I'd already taken twenty paces across the hall that I'd been categorically advised not to enter.

That's the way the most stupid mistakes in the universe are made. I didn't do it, I didn't want to, it just happened.

The fear was churning inside me like the geysers on Dragon Island. And it was about to spill over at any moment.

"Calm down, don't panic!" an inner voice whispered to me. "Nothing terrible has happened, you can still go back. Try to keep calm. Look around!"

At long last Valder had given me a piece of useful advice! I took several deep breaths, trying to control my breathing and the thundering drums of my heart. It was true, I had already taken twenty paces across the forbidden hall and I was still alive and well, despite the ominous warnings at the entrance. Had the elves just been trying to give me a fright? I should just take a look around and decide whether to go back or go forward.

The hall wasn't large (for Hrad Spein). Only the size of a jousting field. The walls were made of huge blocks of stone, each the size of a smallish carriage. The architecture was rather basic, especially bearing in mind that there were sixty-nine rulers of one of the light elves' houses lying here.

This hall couldn't compare with the beauty I'd seen on the earlier levels. It was strange. Were elfin kings really buried here, or was that just another fairy tale for the gullible? There was no way to check now—the niches between the stone blocks had been walled over ages ago, and there was no way to tell just from the bones if someone was a member of a royal house or some plain, boorish peasant.

The arrangement of the columns was totally chaotic. Three here, one there, and eight over that way. They were eight-sided, tall, and very slim— you couldn't really hide behind one of them. But the strangest thing was the patches of light slowly wandering chaotically around the floor. As if there were rays of sunlight falling from the ceiling; but, naturally, there weren't any rays and there wasn't any sun, either.

This was a rather strange sight, and somehow ominous, too. The hall was in semidarkness, lit only by the pale light radiating from the walls, but every column threw a dense, inky shadow, and creeping around entirely at random were about forty patches of sunlight, each one a good yard and a half across. There weren't any bright patches to be seen where I was standing, but up ahead . . .

You could call it an assembly, or a swarm. I turned toward the way out. Eight patches of sunlight had appeared out of nowhere and were blocking my way: If I wanted to leave the hall now, I would have to walk straight through them.

I didn't have the slightest desire to tread on something when I didn't even know what it was, and the only thing left for me to do now was jump through them—fortunately for me there were small black areas of floor between the patches that had lined up in front of me. As if they could read my thoughts, the patches started moving and fused together into a single large blob.

"Bastards!" I exclaimed.

There was something about these patches of sunlight and the way they wandered about that bothered me. I even shot a crossbow bolt at one, but it just clanged against the floor and nothing happened.

"I won't walk on you, and that's it. Slit my throat, but I won't do it," I muttered, and turned away from the door.

I'd have to get across the hall. There had to be some pathway through!

I stopped right at the edge of the patches and stood there. There had to be some system to this aimless wandering, some principle behind this movement, but I just couldn't grasp it.

They crept around with all the speed of a paralyzed mammoth. Whatever they were, they were in no hurry and they moved at their own leisure.

Some patches decided it would be a good idea to go right, others decided to go left, some followed a diagonal from corner to corner, some went round in circles or spirals, and some followed jagged lines that only they could understand. Sometimes they crawled onto each other and for a moment fused into one big patch, then they separated again and went their own ways. But there were always fairly large gaps left between them, so if I was agile enough, I could simply run around these sluggish creepers. Here at the edge of the hall there weren't very many of them, but the closer to the center, the more of them there were. And there was an especially large number beside some kind of heap lying about eighty yards ahead of me.

I strained my eyes hard, but I couldn't make out what it was lying on the floor. And then I saw something I hadn't noticed before—the places where the patches absolutely refused to crawl.

The shadows from the columns! They lay across the floor in long dark lines, and not a single bright patch dared to cross them.

The shadows were little islands in the pattern of movement that covered the floor. So I had a good chance of getting through the hall if I followed them and avoided the patches of light.

I stepped in just as soon as the next patch of light had crept past me. A long leap! Then another, and another! A halt. Two patches started moving toward me and I jumped back, almost stepping on a third one. Jump left! Jump right! Straight ahead! In three leaps I covered the distance between me and the first shadow and, once I was safe, I sighed in relief and caught my breath. Basically, it wasn't all that complicated, the main thing was to keep your wits about you and make sure you didn't step on a patch of light by accident.

The eight yards of space between me and the next shadow were empty.

Forward! I ran like a hare, hoping to confuse my pursuers and avoid a long chase. Sometimes I had to stop to let a patch go by, jump over two patches at once, or run in the opposite direction. My arm began to throb with pain; I couldn't understand why.

Either the patches realized I was skipping around between them like a drunken Doralissian, or they simply decided to have a bit of fun, but they started creeping a lot faster and more randomly, so I reached the fifth island of shadow puffing and panting. And apart from that, three times I almost blundered and only avoided stepping on a patch of "sunlight" by some miracle.

The pain in my left arm had started systematically gnawing into my bones. I had to lean back against a column, sit down on the floor, and rummage in my little bag to find the appropriate magical elixir. During the game of leapfrog across the hall everything in the section of the bag where I kept the vials had got jumbled up.

I swore and started sorting out the confusion. I had to stuff several unimportant vials in the pockets of my jacket—they could lie there until I found a free slot for them. It took me about two minutes to put everything back in order, and all that time the patches kept on stepping up the pace.

The patches seemed to have gone wild, and in one place my way was blocked by an unbroken stream of them. The pain in my arm was becoming unbearable now and I had to grit my teeth. My improvised route had come to an end. From here to the middle of the hall it was only ten yards at the most, but the next haven of shadow was thirty yards away. And the space between me and it was filled with creeping patches, so many of them that I could see virtually no black areas between them. This was a real challenge! How could I get across a space like that without touching a patch of "sunlight"?

Then I finally paid some attention to the heap lying about fifteen paces away from me. What I hadn't been able to make out from a distance, turned out close up to be nothing other than a pile of human bodies. Balistan Pargaid's men.

Of course, Lafresa and Paleface didn't happen to be among the dead. There were seven corpses lying on the floor in poses that no normal person could possibly have imagined. "Grotesque" and "unnatural" are probably the most respectful words to describe what I saw. It looked as if the dead men had all been born without any bones in their bodies. One's neck was twisted so that the back of his head looked forward and his face looked backward.

And as well as that, his elbows and knees were bent in completely the wrong directions, not at all the way that Mother Nature intended, so that he looked like a strange parody of a spider. Another dead man had simply been tied in a knot and a third had his legs woven together in a way that looked very frightening. Lots of bloody streaks across the floor indicated that death had overtaken the unfortunate fellows at different points in the hall, and then the bodies had been dragged into a single heap.

This was bad. Very bad. As usual, Harold had got involved with something very, very nasty. The main thing now was to find out what this nasty thing was before it snipped my head off. Any information at all about the enemy would be a step toward victory.

And then it hit me . . .

"Why, you thickhead, brother Harold!" I swore, smacking myself on the forehead in annoyance.

That was the secret of it! May the darkness crush me—those words at the entrance: "Do not disturb those who guard the peace of the dead," meant exactly what they said. And the statues weren't watching, they were pretending to be eyeless or blind. Blind guards, eternally watching over the peace of the elfin lords! The rhyme riddle had a line about it, but I'd managed to forget it at just the wrong moment. And it was no accident that my arm was hurting, either—I was wearing the red copper bracelet that Egrassa had given me! It was protecting me against the guards of this hall, even if the protection was painful.

All these thoughts went rushing through my head like a storm wind. But now I didn't know what to do—feel afraid of what might happen or feel happy that I was still alive.

I glanced sideways at the bodies of the unfortunate men (which did nothing to raise my spirits or inspire me with optimism). Eventually I plucked up my courage, consigned the world and its mother to the Nameless One, and went dashing through the middle of the hall without even a glance at the dead bodies. I flew off to the side to avoid a patch creeping up silently from behind me, and performed a mind-boggling somersault as I tried to avoid three patches that were advancing on me at once. The shadow stretching across the floor was only five paces away now, and I was just figuring out how to move on from there, when . . . When I finally I failed to spot one patch of "sunlight" and stepped on it with the very edge of the sole of my boot.

To say that I was on a safe island in a single heartbeat is to say nothing at all. What heartbeat, may a h'san'kor take me. It was five, ten, a hundred times faster than that!

The crossbow jumped into my hands of its own accord, the pain from the copper bracelet started smarting really badly, but I never even thought of taking off the dark elves' amulet. It was my only defense now, the only thing that could save me from the guards watching over the remains of the dead lying in this hall. The patches of light all over the floor stopped moving, and then little golden sparks started appearing above the patch that I'd stepped into so clumsily. First one, then a dozen, then a hundred . . .

The sparks appeared, hanging in the air, flashed for an instant with a blinding golden light, and then started to pulse in time with the beating of my heart! There were more and more of them, until I could already make out a vague silhouette. An instant later and there standing in front of me was a creature of gleaming gold, made up of millions of tiny little sparks.

A Kaiyu.

One of the elves' greatest myths, one of the orcs' greatest horrors.

Two thousand years earlier, when the elves went for the orcs' throats in the Palaces of Bone and the blood of the feuding relatives flowed like a river in the burial chambers, something happened that should never have happened.

The orcs took their revenge by despoiling the graves of the elves, and they chose the graves of only the very noblest houses of the Black Forest, scattering the remains of the dead across the halls and leaving their bones to be mocked by the darkness. The Firstborn attacked the thing that was most important to any elf—the honor of his house and the memory of his ancestors. The elves tried to fight back by leaving guards beside the graves, they set traps and whispered spells. . . . But there's an effective response to every attack, every guard gets tired sometimes, any trap can be disarmed, and any spell can be overcome with another spell.

The despoliation of the burial sites continued, and then one of the elfin houses decided to summon these Kaiyu from another world to defend the graves against violation by the Firstborn. What happened after that can be read in the legends that the orcs and the elves tell on especially dark nights. But none of the Firstborn ever dared to ravage the elfin tombs again.

And there, standing just five yards away from me, was one of these incorruptible, blind guards who couldn't be killed. The Kaiyu seemed to be made of thousands of glittering sparks. It was impossible to look at the creature for long—the bright golden gleam made my eyes start to water, and the figure of the soulless guard blurred and trembled like a mirage at noon on a hot summer day. I could only make out the silhouette.

The creature was a head taller than me. Two arms, two legs, a head. No tails or horns or teeth. How could this creature have teeth? It didn't even have a mouth! And where the eyes ought to have been there were two empty, gaping holes. The creature was completely blind.

Well now, blind or not, it seemed to have a very definite and accurate idea of where I was. At least, it came toward me, and without hurrying, as if it was quite confident that I couldn't get away from it.

I panicked and shot a bolt at it. It flew through the creature's body without causing any damage and clattered against the far wall in the darkness. The beast was suddenly only one pace away from me and it raised its hand. I roared in fright, realizing that this was the end, but the Kaiyu's hand simply swept through the air beside my ear and the guard moved past me and stopped, giving me a good view of its back.

I don't know which of us was more surprised. The Kaiyu stood there for a brief moment, obviously trying to figure out why I was still alive, and then it had another try. With the same result. As if some force had erected a barrier between us. The guard could see me (strange as that may sound), but he couldn't harm me. Thanks to Egrassa and his bracelet.

Meanwhile the Kaiyu stepped on the nearest patch of light and the sparks making up his body showered down onto the floor in a golden rain. All the patches in the hall started moving again. What was I to make of that? Did it mean they had decided to let me go?

The bracelet was scorching my arm more and more painfully, and the moment was rapidly approaching when the pain would become so unbearable, I would have to take it off (if I wasn't going to lose consciousness). I had to risk it and try to reach the way out before it was too late.

Taking no more notice of the patches of light, I set out toward the exit. As soon as my foot touched the first patch, another Kaiyu appeared. This time the golden sparks assembled into the body of the guard a lot faster. But the beast didn't even try to attack me. I stepped on another patch, and then another. . . .

Not every patch threw up a Kaiyu; if that had happened, the entire hall would have been crowded with them. Five guards appeared, formed up into a semicircle, and followed me. A fantastically beautiful and at the same time terrifying sight.

The five golden creatures "looked" in my direction, then crumbled into a shower of sparks that were drawn into a patch of "sunlight," disappeared for a fraction of a second, and then reappeared, but now outside the patch that I had just stepped on. And we walked across the hall like that.

Once I left the hall the Kaiyu stopped following me. The patches on the floor started moving about and waiting for their next visitor, who would arrive in darkness only knew how many hundreds of years. The pain in my arm gradually eased as the amulet protecting me relaxed and became a perfectly ordinary copper bracelet again.

I had passed through the Kaiyu Hall and lived. That was worth celebrating, which was exactly what I did straightaway. Of course, instead of wine I had to make do with ordinary water from a subterranean river, and instead of quail I had to chew on half a dry biscuit.

Forty paces farther on, the first side tunnel appeared, and I started counting the intersections to make sure I wouldn't miss the turn I needed. At the eighteenth intersection I stopped and turned to the right, leaving the central vestibule.

Up ahead of me the vestibule led to a stairway down to the sixth level, and I was absolutely certain that was the way Lafresa and the rest of Balistan Pargaid's men had gone. I was going to be more cunning and turn off the main highway. There were many routes leading to the sixth level, and the one mentioned in the verse riddle was a lot shorter than the route chosen by the Master's woman servant.

I would reduce the distance by three quarters and go straight to the very heart of the sector I needed on the sixth level, while dearest Lafresa would have to tramp across the sixth level from its very beginning and lose almost two whole days. That would leave me well ahead of my rivals. And what if I managed to prepare for the encounter and take back the Key? Almost all (or perhaps all) of Lafresa's companions had been killed in the Palaces of Bone, and my chances of victory had improved enormously. The important thing was to keep enough lights and food for the journey back.

I spotted the statues of the giants "whose gaze burns all to ash" immediately. They were standing facing each other, clutching stone hammers in their gnarled, knotty hands.

The giants had an air of antiquity and hidden menace. Whose chisel could have carved these huge colossi out of stone? How had they been brought down to this depth and what for? Instead of faces the statues had the smooth surfaces of closed helmets with tall crests and narrow eye-slits. Both of them were looking down at the ground in front of their feet. Between them there was something that looked like a pool or a basin, but from where I was I couldn't see any water.

> 'Neath the gaze of Giants who burn all to ash,
> To the graves of the Great Ones who died in battle . . .

Perhaps that "basin" was the way down to the Sector of Heroes on the sixth level? That was exactly where I needed to go, but that phrase about the apparent ease with which the giants' gaze reduced anyone who came too close to ashes made me feel a bit cautious.

Once I was in the hall, I didn't try to hurry; I leaned back against the wall and started looking for the answer. There had to be an answer, no fool would ever build an entrance especially so that no one could ever use it. So, if I was going to get to the basin, the giants had to close their eyes for a while.

But how could I make them do that? They were statues, after all. Some kind of mechanism? I couldn't see anything of the kind. I must admit I thought long and hard over this puzzle. But no clever ideas came to mind. The statues looked monolithic and immovable.

Deciding to test their fiery gaze, I put my hand into my bag and took out the very smallest of the emeralds. It was the only thing I wouldn't be sorry to part with. I put the stone on the smooth floor and gave it a smart kick. It slid along the surface, flashing in farewell to me like a little green star, moved into range of the giants' gaze, and disappeared in a blinding flash.

"Oho!"

I had to go back to work on the essential problem of how to get down to the sixth level. I rummaged through all the papers I'd taken from the Forbidden Territory, paying especially close attention to the parts I'd thought were unnecessary. A heap of incomprehensible drawings, showing the architecture of several halls, a meaningless sequence of symbols, and some other obscure rubbish . . . Mmm, yes. Damn all in the papers. It was a rotten idea. But the answer had to be somewhere close! I could feel it in my gut.

I approached the giants cautiously, almost turning myself cross-eyed. With one eye I tried to watch the statues' heads and draw the line limiting the effect of their fiery gaze across the floor. With the other I tried to spot some kind of clue to the answer. Eventually I had to stop or risk being roasted and then incinerated.

The giants were close now, and from where I was standing I could see quite clearly that the statues were not so very perfect and the craftsman's chisel had worked the stone rather crudely. And I also noticed something else, something that made it worthwhile almost going cross-eyed. The giants were both standing on rather tall round plinths. Well, what was so special about that—a plinth's a plinth, isn't it? But I would have offered up an eyetooth if those plinths didn't rotate (together with the giants, of course), if you just knew how to make them to do it. The seasoned eye of an experienced man will always spot a concealed mechanism. All I had to do now was find out how the mechanism was activated and the job was as good as done.

The hall with the giants was subjected to another intense inspection. I was looking for something like a lever or a protruding block of stone, but there didn't seem to be anything of the kind there. Then my gaze fell on the floor, slid over the smooth claret-colored slabs, and stopped on the signs of an alphabet that I didn't know.

I'd seen squiggles like that somewhere before. Why, of course! In the "unnecessary" part of the papers! In among the drawings and incomprehensible sketches there was a piece of paper with a sequence of symbols like those. I took the bundle wrapped in drokr out of my bag again, opened it, and started rummaging through the manuscripts.

There it was! My memory hadn't deceived me. There on the paper were the same symbols as on the floor. Some kind soul had noted down the key, but forgotten to mention when and where it should be used.

I leaned down, found the symbol that was shown first on the sheet of paper, and pressed the appropriate little slab. It moved an inch. Everything turned out to be outrageously simple (if you happened to have the answer on a piece of paper, that is). All I had to do was to press fourteen of the seventy or so symbols shown here in the right order. As soon as the last of the blocks slid in, the hall was filled with a quiet humming sound, as if counterweights and pulleys had started moving somewhere under the floor, and the giants started slowly turning their backs to me and their fiery gaze toward the far wall.

I gave a whoop of triumph, as if I'd found the entire treasure of the Stalkon dynasty under my bed.

The way was clear, the menacing giants were no longer looking at the basin, and I set out in the appropriate direction.

The humming started again, the plinths trembled and started slowly turning in the opposite direction. I broke into a run, trying to cover the distance to the basin before the giants' gaze became a deadly threat again, and jumped into the black hole without thinking.

"Aaaaaaaaagh!" I howled in fright, realizing that my feet wouldn't be touching the floor again in the immediate future.

The hole turned out to be very deep. I fell the first twenty yards like a stone, and I'd already said good-bye to life, but just then the air thickened, I started falling more slowly, and the descent became smooth and gentle.

I had enough wits and courage to stop yelling and light up one of my magical lamps. I was falling slowly down a narrow shaft. Its walls drifted past me and disappeared upward. If I'd wanted to, I could easily have reached out and touched them with my hand. It was only through some caprice of the gods that I hadn't smashed my head against the wall when I first started falling. About two hundred yards farther down I slowed down even further and found myself in one of the halls on the sixth level, in the very heart of the Sector of Heroes.

8

PLAYING TAG WITH THE DEAD

The sixth level is the deepest limit for men. Even during the centuries when the evil of the ogres' bones and the evil of the bird-bears had awoken and roamed freely around the Palaces of Bone, it was a rare human being who was bold enough to descend below the sixth level.

There were rumors of crazy men who wandered even as deep as the twelfth level, but no one had ever seen the lunatics alive afterward.

The Sector of Heroes, located on the sixth level, was the only proof of a human presence at this depth. For some reason, neither the elves nor the orcs had ever been in any hurry to bury anyone at this level, and men jumped in to exploit this oversight by the older races. When the Firstborn and the elves moved out of Hrad Spein, the Palaces of Bone were left entirely in the custody of men, and they immediately started "planting" the empty sector with their most prestigious corpses (prestigious during their lives, that is).

For five and a half centuries they put coffins and tombs in the Sector of

Heroes. Only great and famous people were granted the honor of being buried in the sixth level: generals, warriors who had distinguished themselves in battle, the higher nobility, kings.

Then they started putting everybody down there indiscriminately and in the end the sector was so crammed full with bones that some people even started thinking they ought to clean out the old graves and put new corpses in instead of the old ones. But then they got too lazy to take the bodies down there, and the burials continued on the upper levels. There was only one human burial site below the sixth level—Grok's grave, which was where I happened to be headed.

Men only realized why the elves and the orcs had not been in any hurry to bury their dead in the Sector of Heroes when the evil awoke in Hrad Spein. For some reason this was the level affected most palpably by the Breath of the Abyss—the ominous name given by the big brains of the Order to whatever it was that had risen up from the levels without names and was playing games with the dead.

For no obvious reason, old bones that had been lying in their coffins for centuries suddenly started growing new flesh and then wandering about. Eventually there were more living dead in the Sector of Heroes than cockroaches in a dirty kitchen.

At least they didn't come out onto the surface, they just stayed in one place as if they were glued there, feeding on the emanations of evil rising up from the depths. But those in the Order used to say that what was happening on the sixth level was mere child's play, and what was rising from the depths wasn't the Breath of the Abyss at all, but merely its distant echo. Unlike a certain Hallas (who starts trembling in fury at the very mention of the word "Order"), I am inclined to trust the magicians of the Order, in the same way as I trust manuscripts in the Royal Library. And to judge from all of this, there could be some very, very nasty things waiting for me, problems I wouldn't be able to solve that easily.

I started trembling nervously, and tried to reassure myself with the thought that I only had to tramp across the sixth level for a pitiful three hours, and that was nothing at all in comparison with the fourth level, where I'd lost heaps of time. And the idea that Lafresa and her group would have to walk through the entire sector from start to finish gave me hope and warmed my heart—I hoped my enemies would run into an entire regiment of dead men, so that they could learn for themselves how I felt when I was wandering around the Forbidden Territory.

I walked very carefully, almost as carefully as at the beginning of my visit to the Palaces of Bone. I kept stopping and listening to the oppressive silence. It was dark here, with twenty or thirty paces between every hissing magical torch, and the torches barely kept the darkness at bay. There was plenty of shadow and murk, places where I could hide (I knew how to do that) and where others could hide, too (I hoped that they didn't know how). In any case, I darted through the lighted areas, shuddering at the prospect of falling into the tenacious embrace of a dead man.

Reddish granite walls, low ceilings (sometimes I almost had to double over as I walked along), narrow passages, an abundance of coffins that looked no different from the vaults on the first and second levels. After about forty minutes of nonstop walking, the narrow, barely lit corridors started alternating with gigantic (but also poorly lit) halls.

Sometimes the silence was broken by the sound of falling drops of water. There was a smell hovering in the air. . . . It wasn't exactly unpleasant, let's just say it wasn't very encouraging. Mustiness, old sweat, and a very faint aroma of rotten meat.

I came across the first "bad" coffin after I'd just checked for the hundredth time to make sure I had the light crystals and vials of cat's saliva in my bag. There was a jagged gaping hole in the stone lid, big enough for a man to climb through—whether he happened to be alive or dead.

I recoiled from the coffin and looked around. I couldn't see anything out of the ordinary—if the corpse had decided to take a stroll before his eternal rest, he must have gone quite a long way.

The farther I went, the worse things got. Soon in every hall I could count from one to a dozen smashed coffins alongside the intact tombs.

I ran into my first dead person quite unexpectedly. (Isn't that always the way?) I simply failed to notice her in the semidarkness of the hall—the corpse was a woman, and she was lying facedown, dressed in beautifully preserved, antique clothes.

The ash-colored skin of her hands was pocked with the ulcers of the earliest stages of decomposition, her long and once-beautiful hair was tangled and matted. This lady didn't smell like a corpse at all. She had been buried here quite a long time ago, and there ought to have been nothing left of her but bones, and certainly not any flesh almost untouched by time. These were the kind of jokes that Kronk-a-Mor played.

She started coming toward me clumsily and I had time to gather my wits. First of all I jumped well out of reach of her hands, then I took a small glass pea with cat's saliva in it out of my bag and tossed it at the dead woman's feet. Everyone knows the dead who turn into zombies can't tolerate sunlight or cat's saliva.

The wheezing corpse collapsed on the floor. The saliva had destroyed the magic of the Kronk-a-Mor that was holding it in this world. Now the flesh came away from the bones in huge slabs and melted, giving off a horrifying stench. It broke down almost exactly the same way a lump of sugar melts when it's thrown into hot water. The sight of instantaneous decomposition and the smell that filled the hall was sickening. I covered my nose and mouth with the sleeve of my jacket and turned away. When I recovered a bit and looked to see what had happened to the corpse, all I saw were separate fragments of bones and a clump of hair, floating in a puddle of what had once been a human being. The bones were gradually dissolving away, as if someone had poured an entire barrel of acid over the dead woman.

I walked out of the hall, upset that the stench had eaten deep into my clothes and I'd never be able to wash it out. I stopped in the next corridor and did something I should have done much sooner—I changed the ordinary bolts in my crossbow for one fire bolt and one ice bolt.

Alas and alack, my encounters with the walking dead were only just beginning. A little farther along the corridor I met another one. I heard him moaning and wheezing long before I could see his dark, clumsy silhouette. I quickly stepped back, away from the torch, and hid behind one of the stone tombs, clutching a light crystal in my hand. The zombie shuffled past without noticing me and turned into one of the side corridors. I waited for a minute before carrying on, to make quite sure I wouldn't run into the shambling corpse again.

There was a quite incredible number of walking dead. In some halls I came across up to twenty corpses in various stages of decay. Some shuffled from corner to corner like the dwarves' wind-up toys, others stood without moving. The whole stinking, wheezing, croaking, growling mass was a hideous sight.

The rest of my journey was like a game of hide-and-seek. I hid and they tried to find me. Or rather, they wandered about without—fortunately for me—even suspecting who they should be looking for and where to find him. The worst places were the narrow corridors, when a half-rotten corpse blocked my way. I had to go back in the opposite direction and pray that I wouldn't run into another shambler at the other end of the corridor.

But apart from the narrow corridors, there was another place where the danger was very great—halls that were too well lit. It wasn't all that easy to slip through those unnoticed. Some sharp-eyed stinker was always likely to notice me. So far Sagot had been kind, but things couldn't go on like that forever. The laws of universal meanness always apply in the end.

Just what I was expecting to happen, did happen. I was noticed twice and they tried to eat me. The first time I simply ran into the dead man, mistaking him in the semidarkness for some kind of fanciful statue that someone had left beside the coffins. By the time I realized he wasn't a statue, it was too late. I'd been spotted. The foul creature came shuffling toward me, holding out its grappling-hook hands. The bones were sticking out of the dead man's body, and the rotted muscles could barely shift. I was amazed that he could walk at all.

"Where do you think you're dashing off to?" I laughed and was gone.

The corpse decided to join in the race, but fell hopelessly behind in the web of corridors and ended up with nothing for all his pains. Hah! If anyone wanted to catch Harold, he had to be a bit quicker on his feet than that!

Then I was spotted in a hall with coffins attached directly to the walls. It was my own foolish carelessness—I tried to slip past a torch and, naturally, a chunk of rotting flesh wandering about took a fancy to dining on my liver, even though the corpse concerned had no lower jaw at all. I was almost nabbed before I knew what was happening. The lad was still fresh, too—he looked as if he'd only died yesterday. I had to run for it and plant an ice bolt in my pursuer's chest.

He froze instantly, but the melodic ringing sound brought all the corpses in the neighborhood running; that is, all six and a half of them (including the upper half of a corpse that moved about on its hands). Naturally, they were delighted to discover the unexpected arrival of my own humble personage, and I had to use two light crystals and one vial of cat's saliva to calm them down and get them to understand that molesting peaceful passersby led to unpleasant consequences. I had to withdraw from that hall with unseemly haste.

The sheer number of coffins and tombs set my head spinning. The cramped corridors had been left behind, now there were just spacious halls with identical columns and narrow stairways.

Unfortunately, all the stairways led up, not down, so I took no notice of them. Hiding from the dead was easier now—I just hid behind a column, and I was invisible. Sometimes zombies crept past only two paces away from me and still didn't notice anything. Fortunately for me, the walking clothes-hangers' noses could only smell one thing—and that one thing was blood.

After that there were empty halls, as if the walking dead had all suddenly decided to disappear. I was in high spirits as I walked through a huge area of underground burial chambers without meeting anyone.

Then came more narrow corridors with low ceilings. Sometimes wandering lights, each about the size of a man's fist, flew slowly and majestically between the gloomy columns and the gray stone tombs. All this was very inconvenient for me, since it was getting harder and harder to hide from the walking dead, who had appeared again, and I had to use up my precious crystals and crossbow bolts.

Usually, when one of the creatures noticed me I simply ran away from the clumsy, stupid monster, but I couldn't always manage it. One of the corpses pursued me for twenty minutes, drawing others after him. Eventually, when I had a string of fourteen of these creatures in various stages of decomposition chasing after me, reason triumphed and I sacrificed a precious crystal to finish off my jolly companions.

Just after I'd finished off my string of pursuers and clambered up onto a crossbeam to let a nimble zombie pass by below me, the floor shuddered and swayed, and the walls started shivering. The column I was clinging to struggled to stay upright and fine cracks ran across it. A few coffins from right up under the ceiling tumbled down onto the floor and split open, flinging the remains of the dead across the hall. Even the water in the canal rose up in waves and splashed onto the bank. Then I heard a muffled rumble in the distance and the sudden earthquake subsided.

I looked up anxiously at the ceiling. The gods be praised, it hadn't collapsed and I wasn't buried under massive lumps of stone. And thanks be to Sagot, I hadn't been walking along the wall, or one of the coffins could easily have flattened me.

I walked on cautiously, gazing in amazement at the destruction caused by the earthquake. In one hall twenty columns had collapsed and I could easily have broken a leg as I scrambled across the rubble of shattered coffins, overturned gravestones, and collapsed bridges over canals. I had three more halls to get through before I reached the stairway.

Well, of course, in the last hall but one, there was a nice surprise waiting for me in the form of sixty or more corpses! How had they all managed to squeeze in there?

They were lined up like soldiers, as if they were waiting for orders. I quickly dodged back into the darkness of the corridor before these hostilely inclined individuals could notice me. We-ell now . . . It would be hard for a mosquito to slip past a gathering like that, let alone a man. I put a second light bolt into the empty slot of the crossbow and walked out into the hall.

Surprisingly enough, they took absolutely no notice of me. Every last one of the walking dead was gazing in the opposite direction. What could be holding their attention?

Overcome by a sudden insane urge to play the hero, I blurted out loud enough for the entire hall to hear, "Can I please have your attention just for a moment?"

The sound of my own voice was frightening. The frozen sea of the dead stirred into movement, wheezing in excitement. One of them turned round, then another, then another ten, another twenty, until the entire hall was looking at me. Faces eaten away by the leprosy of decay, skin that was tinged yellow, black, gray, or green . . . ulcers and holes. Some had no nose, some had no eyes. Some had lost a jaw or an entire arm. White bones gleamed through the decomposing flesh and gray scraps of what had once been burial clothes. Skulls grinned at me and hissed, they reached their hands out. . . . Then, as if a command had been given, the sea of corpses started moving toward me. I shot the first bolt straight into the crowd. Light, groans, stench . . .

The second time I fired at the ceiling, and the light poured down on the zombies like genuine sunshine. Then I flung two vials of cat's saliva and beat a hasty retreat to get as far away as possible from the hall, speedily loading the crossbow with two new bolts as I went.

I came back. The smell was so bad, I almost died. The floor was a seething gurgling mess of melting flesh and disintegrating bones. Of all the corpses who had been in the hall only five were showing any feeble signs of life (blasphemous as that might sound). The creatures were still twitching and wheezing. Without wasting any time, I shot another light bolt at the ceiling and withdrew into the corridor again.

I loitered out there for a good twenty minutes, waiting for the stench in the hall to ease off a bit. To be quite honest, I felt too disgusted to walk through the thin soup that had recently been human flesh. But there was nothing to be done; I had to walk through it. I asked Sagot to give me strength, tore off a piece of the lining of my jacket, wrapped it round my face, and walked through the hall.

A winding, crooked corridor, eight steps down, a corridor, a turn, a corridor. A hall.

"May you all rot in the darkness!" I yelled.

There was no more stairway to the seventh level.

If I'd walked faster, I could have got here before that fateful earthquake. But now it was too late. The jolt that hit the Sector of Heroes had collapsed the columns holding up the ceiling, and now my way was blocked by a massive heap of stone blocks and small debris. The dust hadn't settled yet, but the stairway had been blocked off securely by the rock pile, and it would take years to shift it.

What could I do? As Kli-Kli liked to say in situations like this—drop your pants and run. The dust swirling in the hall made it hard to breathe, and I had to go back out. I sat down under a torch and studied the maps and papers for the hundred thousand millionth time.

The results of my research were not encouraging. This stairway was the only one in the Sector of Heroes, and in order to get down now, I'd have to go back to the spot where I first entered the sixth level. And from there . . . From there I'd have to tramp such a huge distance that it was easier just to lay down and die. The Sector of Heroes is a pretty large place, and I was sure to meet plenty of the walking dead before I could reach a stairway. And I didn't have unlimited supplies of crystals and magic bolts—they were already running out.

I was desperately tired, but sleeping there would have been suicidal. So I had to walk on a bit farther while I still had the strength, and then we'd see whether I could get some sleep or not. . . .

I lost my way in the tangled network of winding corridors and halls in the Sector of Heroes. I walked on and on and on, and after three hours of walking and a brief doze on a tomb up on the "second story," I still hadn't come across a single rotten zombie. It was as if they'd never existed. But the shattered tombs suggested that wasn't really true, so I stayed on the alert until I reached the "quiet" area (that is, where the coffins were still intact and there was no stink of corpses). But that was a big mistake—I mean letting my guard down like that. And my punishment came swiftly, with a perverse sense of humor.

Something leapt out of the darkness at me. It was so agile that I barely managed to dodge to one side, but the taloned hand missed me and caught the bag with the magical bits and pieces hanging on my right side . . . the strap holding it on my belt snapped.

All my magical supplies, crossbow bolts, and everything else that was important and useful fell to the floor. There was no time to pick them up— thank Sagot, at least I was still alive! While the corpse (and it was a corpse, only a very agile one) mauled my things, I leaped back and fired an ice bolt into him.

There was a tinkling sound, an icy-cold blast knocked me off my feet, and heavenly bells started chiming in my ears. When I got up, the sight presented to my eyes was an entire brigade of corpses jostling together on the spot where my broken bag was lying. The vile creatures came straight for me.

They moved much faster than ordinary zombies—in fact, they moved every bit as fast as living men. But I had no time to think about that. There was no way I was going to get the bag back, so I fired the second bolt into the crowd, slung the crossbow behind my back, and ran. Right now I had to save my own life—I could cry over the lost bag later.

I'd never have believed that desiccated and mummified bodies could have so much pep in them. I dived into side corridors and hurtled across halls, trying to lose my pursuers, but none of it did any good. They stuck with me all the way, and that lent me wings, but, I must admit, I was starting to feel tired. Eventually I found myself in a dark vestibule, shrank back against the wall, took my knife out, and prepared for the inevitable.

They didn't notice me. A dozen dead men went rushing past and, without thinking twice about it, I ran back in the opposite direction. I turned into the tangle of narrow corridors, trying to confuse the pursuit and at the same time get back to the hall where I'd left my bag. With no weapons, maps, food, or other supplies, I was a dead man for sure. It didn't work, though—the sound of wheezing breath told me the lads were on my trail again.

I cursed and ran. What else could I do? I wasn't ready to take on the corpses with nothing but a knife.

The corridor started turning smoothly to the right. I ran on, past the opening of a passage even narrower than this one. I ran. Turned. Ran. Turned.

Ran . . . and came face-to-face with a crowd of creatures just like the ones running after me. There was a moment's confusion—they were as surprised as I was by this unexpected encounter.

Recovering my wits an instant before they did, I swung round and went dashing back toward the first posse. The second group also set off in pursuit, and I could hear them wheezing and croaking behind me. I stepped up the pace until I was running as fast as I could possibly go—I had to reach the intersection before the hunt ahead of me. Dark angular figures, barely visible in the light of the solitary torch, appeared right in my path.

But I made it in time. I reached the opening of the other corridor a split second before they did. The bony grappling-hook hands grabbed at the empty air as I ducked into the passage, and then the second brigade of zombies went crashing into the first. In the scramble that followed, I managed to beat it with my skin still intact.

More wheezing behind my back. Those lads were sticking to me like leeches! Forward. Left. Forward. Left. Right. Right. Right. Forward. Jump over a canal. Forward. Forward. Right. Forward. Left. Round a coffin lying in the way. Forward. Left. Dead end. Back. Right. Forward. Right. Left.

I flew out into a corridor and gazed in bewilderment at the backs of a crowd of zombies. The same ones who had been galloping after me less than fifteen minutes ago. They were standing, sniffing at the air. Then one of the corpses turned round and "looked" at me with the black hollows of his eye sockets. . . .

I was running. Again. I went flying into a hall with just a few of the ordinary walking dead shambling about. One shuffled toward me and blocked my path. I smashed straight into him at top speed. A foul stench in my nostrils. We both fell. I did a forward roll and jumped back up, cursing the ugly brute for getting in my way.

I heard wheezing behind me. All I could do was run.

So I ran.

9

THE DEAL

I went flying into another hall. It was quite small, with a pool of water splashing against one of the walls. There were two ways out. And eight torches. Urged on by the sound of wheezing, I started running across the hall, when suddenly corpses started pouring in through both exits. And the ones chasing me came flying in behind. I only had a few seconds. I leapt across the three yards of water in the pool in a single bound, found myself standing on someone's tomb, scrambled up the wall using lumps and projections that were almost invisible, and clambered onto the second-story coffin.

I caught my breath. Looked around. The view from up here was remarkable. Five yards of empty space below me, and straight ahead of me—a hall crammed full of corpses. The dead had gathered together from almost the entire Sector of Heroes. They stood staring in silence.

If I went down, I'd be eaten. I could never break through and escape. But if I sat up here, I'd die of hunger—somehow I didn't think anyone was planning to feed me. All I could do was hope for rescue and play "stare" with the walking dead. But I soon got fed up with that—my guards' faces were absolutely repulsive, and they didn't exactly make me feel like playing games.

The first thing I did, of course, was try to get my breath back and recover a bit. Running huge distances takes all your strength. When my breathing was back to normal and my heart had stopped trying to jump out of my chest, I took a look around. A stone box three yards long and a yard wide— plenty of space to accommodate an uninvited guest. A massive lid with an inscription on it: *The favorite cupbearer of the Sixth Count of Patia.* For some strange reason, they'd forgotten to inscribe the cupbearer's name on the stone. And the date of his death, too. But someone very creative had left a moss-covered bottle on his coffin.

I inspected this surprise with a skeptical eye. The name and numbers molded into the glass told me it was wine and it was at least four hundred years old. I had nothing else to do, so I took out my knife and cut the seal off the cork. Since I didn't have a corkscrew, I pushed the cork into the bottle. I took a sniff. Tried it. And gasped in approval. This wine was worth real money.

I was still hoping to get out of there alive, but an hour later I realized the repulsive creatures had absolutely no intention of going away, and I abandoned all hope of a happy ending. Either I went down and they ate me, or I died of hunger. But then, even if the zombies did back off, I'd wandered too far astray while I was running and now I could never find the way back to my bag with the maps of Hrad Spein. And without the maps . . . Without the maps, I'd never get to the eighth level, let alone find my way out of this place. In other words, I was as good as dead. All I had left was the canvas bag on my back with the sweater and the emeralds and the one vial I'd put in there, but there were no maps or food in it. . . .

The outcome of all this was that I polished off the wine, and I felt just fine, without a care in the world. Until I awoke with a hangover. . . .

By the end of the second day my stomach had stopped rumbling in fury, but the hunger pains hadn't gone away. Nothing had changed. The corpses hadn't gone away, either.

"Well, what are looking at, you brutes?"

Naturally, I didn't get any answer. Nobody even hissed. I was simply ignored in the most insolent manner you could possibly imagine. I would have fired my crossbow at the vile creatures, but I didn't have any more bolts. The only thing I could do was fling the empty bottle at the crowd. It somersaulted in the air a few times and smashed into one of the dead men, demolishing half of his rotten head. The dead man wasn't bothered in the least by this strange circumstance and he just stood there.

"Having fun?"

The voice that rang out in the hall came as such a shock that I jumped.

He was standing in the shadow of a column and I could only see the vague outline of the dark silhouette with massive wings. The golden eyes were watching me with veiled mockery. The Messenger wasn't paying any attention to the walking dead, and they were ignoring him.

"Something of the kind."

I tried hard to sound calm, but the treacherous squeak in my voice gave me away.

The servant of the Master! The Messenger! Here! In the hall! Right in front of me!

My mouth went dry, my palms started to sweat, and my spine dissolved. Now I knew beyond any doubt who had herded the corpses in here and why.

"I have a proposition for you," said the Messenger.

"What is it?" I asked, finding enough courage not to faint.

"You've come a long way through the Palaces of Bone, thief. Not many can boast of that. How annoying to end up trapped, and by these stupid monsters. Tell me, are you planning to stay long?"

"Until I get bored."

I didn't know what the Messenger and his Master had cooked up, but they weren't going to frighten me. There was no way I could be any more frightened than I already was.

"Mmmm? I think you're already bored. Or am I wrong?"

I didn't answer, and I thought I saw the Messenger smile.

"All right, Harold. Let's stop playing games and get down to business."

"What business is that, Messenger?"

"Oh! I see you know my name!" he said, and chuckled again. "Did you just guess, or were you eavesdropping when you were wandering round my Master's property? How is your wound, by the way? You took off to the Primordial World—I see they still heal people as well as ever there!"

Once again I didn't answer, and once again he pretended not to notice.

"I've been sent by the Master. Sent to offer you a way out of this trap. Are you interested, or should I leave?"

"I'm interested."

"Good. Abandon the Commission, forget about the Rainbow Horn, and you will be rewarded."

"How? Are you going to rip my belly open again?"

"Oh, don't be so touchy! If I wanted to, I'd have killed you by now. How much did the king offer you? Fifty thousand? How would you like an offer of, say, three hundred thousand? Not enough? Perhaps you prefer the sound of eight hundred thousand? Name your price, thief."

Uh-huh, sure. I might get the gold, but only if he left it on my coffin. So I wasn't going for any deals that came from lads like him.

"I'm perfectly happy with the price offered by the king. A Commission . . ."

The Messenger snorted loudly to express his contempt.

"A Commission? What are you, some kind of nobleman? Since when do thieves keep their word?"

Why did everyone take such a liking to the word "thief"? First those shadows in the world of Chaos, and now *him*! I had my own professional principles. And I wasn't insane, so I had no intention of violating a Commission. It was more than my life was worth.

"Ah . . . so you're afraid of violating the Commission and upsetting your beloved Sagot?" he said, apparently reading my thoughts. "You men are too much in awe of those you call the gods. Don't worry, thief. The gods are nothing but a gang of good-for-nothing layabouts, and they are all subservient to the Master. There's no need to be afraid, no one will punish you for violating the Commission. The Master will make sure of that, as soon as you agree."

The gods were subservient to the Master? Well, that was news!

"I don't need money," I muttered. "You can't stop hunger with gold."

"I forgot to mention that if you accept the proposition, you will be taken anywhere you please. Or perhaps you simply don't need money at all? You have enough emeralds in your bag to buy a small country, and the title to go with it. What else could you want? Or perhaps you do want something else? Tell me, and if it lies within the Master's power, you shall have it. You must agree that's a fair price. You can have anything you like, all you have to do is forget about the Rainbow Horn."

"Immortality?" I blurted out at random.

"Immortality? Perhaps . . ." He gave me a suspicious glance.

"Who is the Master? Why doesn't he want the Rainbow Horn to leave Hrad Spein?" I asked, deciding to stop beating about the bush and get down to basics.

"All right, we have plenty of time and the Master said I could answer a few questions. Not in a hurry to get anywhere, are you?"

The golden eyes glittered, but I didn't bother to answer.

"My lord is the Master of this world. He created Siala from a shadow of the Primordial World, he is—"

"A Dancer in the Shadows!" I blurted out.

"Now I see that your question about immortality really was just a test. You have found out a great deal. . . . Unfortunately."

A test? But I hadn't been trying to test him. I'd just said it.

"Correct, thief. A very long time ago the Master was a Dancer in the Shadows and he created this world. I see you already know much more than we assumed. But that's not surprising; after all, you're a Dancer in the Shadows, too."

I started.

"Don't try to deny it, thief. You are a Dancer, otherwise I wouldn't give you the time of day."

"I don't deny it."

Well, I was no fool. Why would I put my head in the noose? If it was to my advantage to be a Dancer, then I'd be one. If he called me an ass, I wouldn't have objected.

"All right then. You're a Dancer, and that's the only reason why you're being offered a choice. There's no point in killing you anyway: Until you reach one of the Great Houses, you're immortal anyway. You've seen them, haven't you?"

"Who?"

"The Master's first children. The Fallen Ones."

I realized he was talking about the bird-bears and I nodded.

"They were the firstborn, and the Master gave them powers almost equal to his own. They took this gift and tried to become the new Masters of the world. They decided to play the Game. So then the Fallen Ones were cast down and imprisoned in the heart of the Palaces of Bone."

"I still haven't heard what the Rainbow Horn has to do with all this."

The Messenger sighed.

"The Master couldn't destroy his firstborn, and he simply plunged them into sleep. But one not so very fine day the Second Race, those you are accustomed to calling ogres, accidentally awoke the evil slumbering in Hrad Spein. And that was when the ogres created the Rainbow Horn. It was created a lot earlier than is usually thought. The artifact restrained the Fallen Ones, it prevented them from escaping and taking possession of the primordial power of this world. All they could do then was wait for the chains to break. The Rainbow Horn was not made just to neutralize the Kronk-a-Mor, the primary magic: Its other purpose—not to let the Fallen Ones into Siala—was far more important. The ogres paid dearly for their curiosity. They created an artifact and saved the world, but the price was the death of their own race. That is why the creatures you call ogres are no more than animals now. In saving the world, they lost their reason and fell under the power of the primary magic. As long as the Rainbow Horn remains here, the Fallen Ones will not be able to escape into the world of Siala."

"The Rainbow Horn hasn't been in Hrad Spein for all that long. Not for all the thousands of years you've been talking about."

"True. While it was with the elves, everything was well, and if not for a certain party opposed to the Master, nothing would have happened. But I'm not going to tell you everything. Just remember what happened when the Order tried to use the artifact to stop the Nameless One."

"I remember that very well, the renegade magician said he was told what to do by the Master!"

"Are you blind, Harold? The Master has nothing to do with it. At least, not the Master of Siala."

I was left with my jaw hanging open again.

"Surprised? Every world has its own Master, and the Dancers constantly play the Game. While one tries to save his own world, another tries to change it for the worse. The Game is the struggle to test a world's right to life."

"And whose plaything is the Nameless One?"

"It's not good to know too much. So, what is your answer?"

"Your Master serves evil, Messenger!"

And that was when he laughed. It was jolly, genuine laughter. He laughed and he laughed, on and on without stopping. He laughed until the very echo was weary of repeating his laughter.

"What is evil, thief? Enlighten me! What is good? Who can determine what either of them is? Where is the elusive boundary between good and evil?"

"Your Master tried to kill me and my friends!"

"And that is evil?" he asked with a mocking chuckle. "So evil is different for everyone? If a man wants to kill you, that is evil. If the same man gives you a gold piece, saves your life, and kills someone else, is that good? Answer me, thief."

I didn't say anything, but he wasn't really expecting an answer.

"An orc kills a woodcutter and, of course, from the viewpoint of the man's family, a terrible evil has been committed. But from the viewpoint of the orc, his act was one of great goodness; he has saved the sacred trees from the depredations of man. You see, thief, evil becomes good and good becomes evil, as soon as you look at them from the opposite bank of the river of Life! They tried to kill you, but you were lucky, as lucky as the darkness! The Master started wondering who you really were after our dear Lafresa's spell failed. And after you found your way into his house, survived my blow, and prevented the bonds of the Key from being broken, everything fell into place. A Dancer in the Shadows does not kill another Dancer."

"Lafresa and her people seem to have forgotten about that, though."

"She acts on her own responsibility. The Master did not have time to warn her."

Or he didn't want to. In any case, I didn't believe a single word of the story about the Rainbow Horn.

"We've settled the matter of the attempts on your life. What else can you call evil?"

"The Master released the demons from the darkness."

"What of it? You have no understanding of the Game; you cannot understand why the demons were needed. Or what part they will play in this story."

"Then explain it to me!"

"Oh no, Harold! I promise that you will have good reason to remember the demons, and you will understand why the Master was right to release them and to bring the Horse of Shadows to Avendoom."

"If he brought it, then why did he try to take it back in such a hurry?"

"The Horse had done its job, and another Master—"

"Are you trying to tell me there's a whole crowd of Masters wandering around Siala?" I exclaimed, without realizing that I'd interrupted him.

"Oh come now! There is only one Master, but there is also the one who plays the Game."

"Why does he do that?"

"Why? Such is the Game."

"The Game?" I echoed.

"What are you so surprised about? Life is boring for those who create worlds, and sometimes they play Games. That's all there is to it. And it's not for you to go complaining about demons. As I recall, if not for a certain unknown scroll discovered by chance, they would still be scampering around Avendoom. You see, you also have taken part in the Game. And now it is continuing, and the Rainbow Horn is the trump card. The Master is trying to prevent its return to the world."

"So this is all just a stupid game to them?"

"Stupid? It is the Game that keeps the world alive."

"I don't believe you!"

"You don't have to. I am only talking to you because I was ordered to."

"All right!" I said, getting more and more furious. "Surely you won't try to deny that the Nameless One appeared thanks to your Master?"

"I will not," the Messenger replied calmly.

"And you won't deny that the Nameless One is evil?"

Once again the hall echoed to the Messenger's laughter.

"Evil? I thought we had finished with that subject, Dancer! For you, per-haps, he is evil. . . . After all, he wishes to overthrow your king and destroy the kingdom. . . . History is written by the victors, thief! That's the way it has always been. Somehow everyone seems to have forgotten one small detail—that Stalkon's dynasty wiped out the entire family of the person they now call the Nameless One! All of them! Is that not evil? And is his desire to take revenge not good?"

"It is not good. It is vengeance."

"Perhaps so," he admitted. "Perhaps so. But this world needs the Name-less One. He holds you in check, stops you getting out of hand, getting above yourselves."

"What do you mean?"

"When the Fallen Ones and the ogres lived in Siala, and the Game had not yet begun, the Master tried not to interfere in the affairs of the world, but later the younger races appeared, including you men. Everything changed. You are worse than little children. You have to be directed, given a goal to achieve. Otherwise, left to your own devices, you would make such a mess of things that the Game would come to an end without having unfolded. Without a goal to pursue, you wreck everything your eye falls on. The day will come when you destroy this world. And the Master would not like that to happen, so he gives you many goals. The Nameless One, for instance."

"I don't understand."

"You are a Dancer only in the blood. In order to understand, you have to become one in the spirit, you have to pass through the Great Houses, but for you, that is all still to come. What would happen if the Nameless One did not threaten Valiostr from the north?"

"Everybody would have a happy life," I muttered.

"I doubt it. Perhaps that might have been possible six hundred years ago, when the kingdom was not yet so strong, but now, when your army is the most powerful in all the Northern Lands, I doubt it very much. Without a constant threat from the north, you would turn your attention to the south. War with Miranueh. How many thousands of dead would be left on the battlefields? And then the orcs. They have always been a thorn in your side, and you would wipe them out. Thousands of thousands of lives lost yet again. And what do we get as a result, Harold? If not for the Nameless One, who is like a sword suspended over Valiostr, the whole north of Siala would have drowned in blood. And the Nameless One is not the only force restraining men."

"Leave all that verbiage to the philosophers, Messenger!" I said, getting angry. "Once the sorcerer reaches Valiostr, everything will happen just as you said, only after the fall of the kingdom, it will be the orcs who do it."

"You do not understand the purpose of the Game, Dancer."

"I couldn't give a damn for these games! How can someone decide everything for everyone else?"

"It is his world, do not forget that."

"So if it's his world, he's allowed to destroy the alliance between the dark and light elves in order to save the orcs?" I objected, remembering my recent dream.

"This world needs the orcs, and the Master does not want them to disappear because of your whim."

"Another restraining force?"

"Not only," the Messenger replied evasively, and asked, "So what answer will you give me? Do you agree to forget about the Rainbow Horn?"

I said nothing, thinking very hard, then came out with: "And what will happen if I don't agree?"

"Why, nothing!"

"Nothing?" I couldn't believe my ears.

"What did you expect? That I would try to frighten you? Nothing will happen! You will sit there until you die of hunger. Of course, you will be reborn in the House of Love . . after a while, when everybody has forgotten all about the Horn. Do you think that artifact is so very important to the Master? Everything you see around you, all your friends, the entire world—it is all just one big Game that you will never understand. If the Horn stays here, the Master will win. If you take the Horn, the master will still win anyway, although it may be ten times more difficult. Even if the Gray Ones do nothing, even if the balance is disrupted, even if the Fallen Ones break out and destroy Siala, the Game will simply move on to the next turn of the spiral. Nothing depends on you. It is simpler if the Horn remains untouched. It is easier to win the Game, that is all there is to it."

I didn't like anything about our conversation, all these stories about the Fallen Ones, other Masters, some stupid Game. I didn't believe the Messenger.

"Why don't these Fallen Ones take what's lying under their very noses?"

"Question time is over now, I need your answer."

"Since nothing depends on me, my answer is no."

The golden eyes studied me closely. Eventually, after a long silence, the Messenger said, "Well, the Master knew that would be your answer. That is a pity, thief. But in that case I would like to make a deal with you."

"What sort of deal?" I asked cautiously, suspecting a trick.

"I will offer you two ways of getting out of this trap, and for that you will carry out a Commission for the Master."

"What sort of Commission?"

"Who knows what might need to be stolen for the Master in the near future? All I need now is your word."

I didn't say anything.

"So you agree?" he asked with a note of annoyance in his voice. "If the Horn is destined to reappear in the world, let it be by the hand of another Dancer. We'll liven up the Game."

What risk was I taking? The Master obviously had some kind of plan, otherwise he wouldn't allow me to take the Horn, even if I was a Dancer in the Shadows three times over. But I couldn't give a damn for the games of the gods, or whoever it was that controlled the world.

"I agree."

"Wonderful! The first way of getting out of here is to kill yourself. Do you have a knife? You are a Dancer, and you are immortal. As soon as you die, you will find yourself in the House of Love."

"That option doesn't suit."

Of course, it's delightful to learn that you're immortal (although I didn't believe it), but the last thing I was planning on doing was to slit my throat from ear to ear.

"Then you will prefer the second option. Below you there is a pool. If you dive into it and swim, you will come to the Level Between Levels. From there you can reach any place in the Palaces of Bone. Look for a door with a red triangle on it. Walk through it, and you will find yourself on the eighth level, very close to Grok's grave. Keep straight on without turning off the path and you will reach your goal. Until we meet again, thief, I leave you in pleasant and trustworthy company."

"Wait! Who is Player?"

"You'll find out in good time. Do you have any more questions?"

"If you're here, why don't you take the Horn yourself?"

"If I could, this conversation would never have taken place."

"How long do I have to swim underwater?"

"Oh, not very long! Six minutes at the most."

An instant later, he was gone.

And that was when I started getting the shakes. I still couldn't believe I'd been talking to the Messenger, I still couldn't believe he hadn't laid a finger on me. I still couldn't believe I knew who the Master was and what he wanted.

Six minutes without air! I sent a curse after the yellow-eyed beast, hoping that it would catch up with him. For another hour I couldn't bring myself to do anything.

In the first place, I didn't trust the Master, who was always scheming and intriguing, and now had suddenly decided to help me. If he wanted me to get the artifact now, why not send me straight to him?

In the second place, I was afraid of what might be hiding in the black water. And I wasn't at all confident that I could stay underwater for so long. But I couldn't just do nothing, could I? The walking dead were still waiting for me to come down to them, and they seemed to be showing signs of impatience. I didn't want them to climb up to me. . . .

I'd have to dive in my boots. Yes, swimming like that would be awkward, but it would be even more awkward wandering round the Palaces of Bone barefoot. I'd have to sacrifice something for the sake of the boots. In order to make it a bit easier to swim. Of course, my jacket! I took it off, and I was left in just my white shirt. I took out the vials with spells that had got into the pockets of my jacket when I was sorting out my things in the Hall of the Kaiyu.

Three items. Two "frighteners"—the same kind I'd used in Ranneng, when the Nameless One's gang was chasing us. The third one . . . the third one had black liquid in it, and Honchel had thrown it in free of charge (which was strange, to say the least, for a tight-fisted dwarf). Until now I'd thought I'd never have any use for it—the vial was intended to let you breathe freely underwater. But it would be very useful to me today, even if its effect did only last for a minute.

After the jacket, it was the crossbow's turn. My hands touched my faithful friend for the last time and then, without the slightest regret, I put it down on the sarcophagus. Without bolts it was useless anyway, and I didn't need any extra weight underwater.

What next? The knife? Probably not; parting with all my weapons would be the ultimate stupidity. I took my trusty razor out of my boot and put it beside the crossbow. It was the canvas bag's turn next. I'd have to take it with me. If I made it to the Horn, I'd have something to carry it in. I ought to keep the tightly folded sweater and the drokr, too. As for the emeralds— away with them! Not all of them, of course. I kept the "eye" and just a quar- ter of the small stones. They didn't weigh all that much. And I was delighted when my eye fell on the one and only light that had survived by some mir- acle in the bottom of the bag.

What else should I keep? There wasn't really anything else. Kli-Kli's medallion, Egrassa's bracelet, and the elf-king's ring weighed next to noth- ing, and I certainly couldn't say the magical trinkets were unnecessary.

Well, that was it. I hoped that someday somebody would find the things lying here and they would help him.

It was time.

I stood on the edge of the coffin with my face to the wall and my back to the hall, went into a handstand, holding onto the edge of the tomb of the duke's favorite cupbearer, opened my fingers, and fell five yards through the air, down into the pool.

10

THE LEVEL BETWEEN LEVELS

Ninety-eight. Ninety-nine. A hundred!

I surfaced, gulped in the air, and coughed. The evening sun was slowly sinking behind the horizon and there was no warmth in it at all. After an hour spent in the water, I was trembling and the only thing I wanted to do was to get out of the River of the Crystal Dream, dry off, and have a drink of something hot. Mulled wine, for instance.

"How long?" For's voice asked, distracting me from my daydreams.

"A hundred forty-seven!" I lied, without batting an eyelid.

"Lies, you weren't under the water for more than a minute."

I gave my teacher a sulky look. For was squinting at the setting sun through half-closed eyes, like a cat, and gnawing on a little green apple.

"A minute's a long time," I protested, refusing to back down.

"Not long enough!" objected my teacher.

"It's cold," I said, trying to play on his pity. Uh-huh, some chance! It was easier to coax a gold piece out of a dwarf than to soften For's heart during a lesson!

"What do you mean, it's cold? It's an exceptionally fine day."

"Just try climbing in the water with me, and I'll see how fine you think it is," I muttered peevishly to myself, but For heard me.

"You're a fourteen-year-old ignoramus, and you talk too much," he remarked good-naturedly, and threw his apple core, which hit me right in the middle of the forehead.

"Why am I wasting my time on this nonsense, but Bass isn't?"

"Because Bass will never make a decent thief."

"And I will?"

"If you didn't lie and argue so much, you might just manage it."

"I don't lie all that much!" I exclaimed indignantly.

"And you don't argue much, either, I suppose?"

I had enough wits not to answer that.

"Come on, kid, carry on. You've still got time for another couple of dives before it's time to go home."

"All right, teacher," I sighed miserably. "But what good is all this to me? I'm not a fish!"

"Being able to hold your breath is very important. Every second improves the chances of saving your life."

"Why's that?"

"Well, if you get into a house and a trap with poisonous gas goes off, and you have to avoid breathing until you get out of the danger zone. Or if some sly fellow throws you off the pier. Tied up. And you need a little time to untie yourself. Or you have to dive under the water and sit there, so that no one can stick an arrow in you. See how many reasons there are to stop whinging and get on with your studies!"

"I'm not whinging! How long do I have to keep on ducking like this?"

"Until it's no problem for you to sit there for at least two minutes."

"Two minutes!" I gasped, horrified.

"But three's better," said For ruthlessly, to drive the message home.

"Three minutes!"

"Listen, Harold!" said the master thief, looking at me closely. "Did you decide to be my apprentice or not?"

"Yes, I did."

"If you're my apprentice, then dive! Time's wasting."

Uh-huh. That was exactly what I was after. The longer I could keep For talking, the less time I would have to sit under the water. The sun was almost hidden behind the sea that the River of the Crystal Dream ran into.

"I won't be able to stay under for three minutes today, anyway," I gloated.

"No, and not tomorrow, either. But don't worry about it, kid, we've got all summer to practice, and when the cold weather comes, I'll fill a barrel, and you can practice at home."

A blow below the belt. I could see that my mentor would never leave me in peace until I sprouted gills and sat under the water for those damned three minutes. I looked at For resentfully, took a deep breath, and dived.

Ah, dear old For! Did my teacher know then that sitting in a barrel of water for hours at a time would actually save my life someday?

Because of the dim lighting, the water in the Palaces of Bone had always looked black to me. But as soon as I slipped under the surface I could see it was as clear as a teardrop. The light, attached to my left forearm with strips of cloth ripped off my abandoned jacket, lit up the vertical shaft I was falling down excellently. The shaft ended at a depth of four yards.

There was a round entrance in one of the walls. That way. And now a horizontal corridor. I didn't need the magical lamp here, because the walls radiated a pale green light.

I swam in relaxed style, using powerful strokes of my arms and helping myself along with my legs. Forward, ever forward. One minute.

The round passage suddenly turned upward and ended. I shot out of it with the speed of a pike darting out of its burrow and found myself right under the ceiling of a hall that was completely flooded. The water was so transparent, and the walls were glowing so brightly that I could see every detail of the floor nine yards below me. Down to the smallest slab of marble, down to the images on the lids of the coffins. All this drifted slowly past below me. Here was the wall. I had to dive a bit to get through the opening into the next hall.

Two minutes.

Everything was the same in here. Dark spectres of tombs, statues, and walls. Elfin beauty. And I remembered very clearly that there was nothing of the kind on the maps. I swam on, keeping just under the ceiling, and spotted a new "burrow." My chest was gradually filling up with lead and everything was starting to go dark in front of my eyes. I was already close to my limit. I dived into the "burrow" and left the hall behind. My lungs were on fire. I uncorked the vial, and the thick black liquid mingled slowly with the water. For a second nothing happened, and I started to panic.

Three minutes.

I opened my mouth in fright and . . . I breathed. The black liquid had dissolved in the water and now I was surrounded by a kind of large bubble with invisible walls. The water passing freely through the bubble could be breathed tolerably well. I had a little more than a minute.

I swam on, redoubling my efforts. The corridor seemed to be endless. An intersection. Three directions. Which one? The one in the middle! Straight ahead! That way, it had to be that way!

The magical bubble burst, giving me just enough time to fill my lungs. Another dead end ahead, and the passage turned down vertically. Three yards down the shaft, and I emerged from the gaping jaws of a gargoyle. Into a hall. There were thousands of little bubbles rising up to the ceiling, and I could hardly see a thing.

One minute.

I swam blind, unable to see the opposite wall. I tried to go down to the floor, but I couldn't. I could feel hundreds of prickly bubbles pushing me upward. I didn't even try to resist. There was no time for that. I swam on. The pain in my chest was getting worse.

Two minutes.

I'd already been underwater for nearly six minutes, but there was no sign of the way out I needed so desperately. Either the Messenger had lied, or I'd taken a wrong corridor. The wall! At last. I floundered from side to side like a tadpole in a boiling cauldron. No way out. And I didn't have another magical vial! I struggled my way up to the ceiling.

Yes!

The bubbles were crowding cheerfully out through a ragged opening above me. I followed them and found myself in a vertical shaft again, but this time it ran upward. And there was something subtly beautiful shimmering up ahead of me.

I worked away with my legs. There was a dark mist in front of my eyes, and I was thinking it was about time to learn to breathe underwater or to pack my things for the journey into the light. The silvery shimmering was very close now; it looked like a thin membrane stretched across from one wall to the other. The bubbles passed through it easily. That meant I could, too. I touched the membrane. There were little needles dancing all over my body . . . I was flying. . . . And I wasn't in the narrow corridor anymore, I was somewhere. . . .

I was sitting on the bank of a huge underground lake. Or perhaps it wasn't all that huge, but the light of the magical lamp wasn't bright enough to reach the other shore.

I was trembling. While I was swimming, the water had seemed very warm, but once I climbed out onto the shore, I suddenly started shivering. I would have lit a fire to warm myself up, but there wasn't any wood. I immediately peeled off all my clothes and took the sweater wrapped in drokr out of the soaking-wet bag. Thanks to the elfin fabric, it was as dry as if it had never been in the water at all. Once I had the heavy sweater on, I felt better straightaway. I jumped up and down and waved my arms and legs about, which usually helped me recover after a long time in the water.

I didn't know how I'd got to the lake, I didn't know where it was—in a cave or in a hall—but the messenger hadn't lied to me. This had to be the Level Between the Levels. Because there was certainly nothing like it in the Sector of Heroes.

But darkness! It was still cold! I wrung out my clothes, but without any sun, Sagot only knew how long they would take to dry.

I only had the one light with me, and its power was already fading. It was getting dark all around, and I had to hurry if I didn't want to stick my nose against the wall like a mole and grope my way along. I tried not to think about what would happen after the light went out, and just kept running along the perfectly straight corridor with walls that were the color of dried blood in the light of the magical lamp.

I'd felt as if I had a blunt needle stuck in my side for ages, and I was forced to slow to a walk. I was very tired and very, very hungry. Two days of enforced fasting and filling my belly with water at the lake (even though after my underwater journey the very thought of water made me feel sick) had not left my stomach in a very calm state. I'd have given my right eye (or my left one) for a piece of bread.

The painful moment finally arrived. First the light of the little magical lantern faded away, then it blinked uncertainly and went out. It flared up again and fluttered in fright as it tried to glow more brightly, then flashed, lighting up the corridor for at least twenty yards, and finally went out forever, leaving me blind. Now I was as helpless as a newborn kitten.

I flung the small stick away in annoyance. Now I was in a mess. For always warned me that sitting in a cell in the Gray Stones was better than wandering through the darkness like this, not knowing what lousy trick to expect at any moment from someone you couldn't even see.

After I'd enjoyed myself with enough whinging, I put my left hand against the wall and shuffled on (yes, that's exactly what I did). And what followed reminded me very much of my tour of the Master's prison. I walked in exactly the same way then. Keeping my hand on the wall and staring hard into the darkness.

I won't lie and say I know how much time went by. I stopped three times to rest for a while, and once I tried to doze, but the hunger pains wouldn't let me sleep.

Lift my foot, put my foot down. Hold on to the wall. Don't stop. Keep going. I tried not to think about the fact that all my efforts would probably come to nothing. I tried to drive the bad thoughts out of my head, but they just kept coming back stronger than ever.

There was a faint crunch from under the soles of my boots, and I stopped. I bent down and rummaged around with my hand near my feet. My fingers touched some small objects, with sharp, jagged edges. They felt like fragments of bone. Someone else had tried to walk this way before me, but they'd never got out of here.

Crunch, crunch. Crunch, crunch.

After about fifty yards the bones stopped crunching under my feet. I strode out, walking faster, and I spotted a faint spark of light trembling somewhere up ahead. It looked as if I was going to escape from the darkness after all.

I took heart and walked on toward the yellow spark. A small point of light separated from it, trembled, and disappeared from view. I suddenly realized that what I could see was certainly not the light of torches or lanterns.

The fact that one of the lights moved worried me. I recalled the bird-bears and their lamps made out of skulls. This place was very much in their style. But the spark that the little light had separated off from still didn't move and, after taking a moment to calm my long-suffering nerves, I carried on.

The accursed corridor was behind me now, and I was in . . . well, it was probably a cave. I simply couldn't judge its real size. There was a real wind blowing here. And there was a smell of earth, fresh spring grass, and mushrooms.

The caps of the mushrooms looked like huge cathedral domes and they gave off a steady yellow light that lit up the area for twenty yards around them, and I could clearly see the grass growing in the cave and a path that led off somewhere into the gloom. I could also see four . . . hmm, I suppose you could have called them ants, bustling around.

At least, the creatures looked more like ants than anything else, although you're not likely to see ants the length of a man's arm anywhere else in the world, and completely white, as if they had been rolled in flour. Six legs, eagerly twitching feelers on long heads, massive mandibles, and nothing at all that looked like eyes.

They took no notice of me and it didn't look as if they meant to attack, which was very cheering for my own peaceable and by no means aggressive personage. I walked round the brigade of oversized ants and set off toward the strange mushrooms. An ant was sitting on one of the mushroom caps and I stopped, uncertain whether to go any closer. Sagot only knew what kind of tricks the insect might pull if it was distracted from what it was doing and caught my scent.

Meanwhile the ant cut a piece out of the mushroom's cap, which had already suffered plenty of damage, and clambered down the mushroom's stalk, clutching the trophy in its jaws. I waited until the ant and its edible lantern were out of sight and then walked toward the mushroom. Why was I any worse than an ant? I ought to cut off a small lantern for my own needs as well.

No chance. An ant appeared out of nowhere and blocked my way. And this wasn't a worker, he was a soldier, I could tell that from his size (a cubit longer than his brothers) and his massive mandibles (they could easily cut through your leg). I waved my hand, trying to attract his attention, but it had no effect, except that his feelers twitched. I took a step toward the ant and he clattered his mandibles irritably in response. Clear enough. I wasn't going to be allowed anywhere near the mushroom.

"If I had my crossbow, you'd be a bit more polite."

The guard didn't respond to that, either. Why bother talking to me, if I didn't have the crossbow?

Well, now we could try a different approach. I walked back a bit and waited for the ant to leave. Eventually, he did.

I then approached the mushroom, cut off a piece the size of my fist, and set off along the path.

The mushroom gave off even more light than my magical lanterns and, after the long dreary corridor between the hall and the underground lake, it was a gift from the gods.

The path was like a convolution in a Doralissian's brain. No intersections, no branches.

What about food? May Sagot have mercy! I could have wolfed down an entire bull, stuffed with three sheep, and they had to be stuffed with wood grouse or whatever it was such dishes are supposed to be stuffed with. I was desperately hungry. The piece of mushroom I was holding gave off a divine aroma, and every so often I had to gulp down my saliva to avoid choking on it and dying the death of the bold and the brave. Or the death of the hungry. But I still hadn't gone completely insane from hunger, and my reason refused to let me try the mushroom. In the first place, I wasn't a goblin shaman, going around guzzling raw mushrooms and writing crazy books of prophecies. In the second place, I didn't want to end up writhing on the grass in my death agony if the mushroom turned out to be a poisonous toadstool.

The cluster of mushrooms I'd come across when I left the corridor wasn't the only one in the cave. From time to time my gaze fell on new islets of light. Naturally, every mushroom had already been claimed and had one or even two soldier ants guarding it.

The deeper I went into the cave, the more ants I met. Most of them were workers dashing about their business, but sometimes I met guards. They took no notice of me, as long as I didn't make any sudden movements or go too close to them. The workers were obviously busily maintaining the welfare of their own anthill. I reined in my curiosity and didn't bother the insects. Why provoke the local inhabitants, especially since I'd never get away from them if they decided to tear me to pieces? No weapon could save you against numbers like that.

But later I broke my vow and came into very close contact with the ants' property. It happened when the number of insects dropped pretty sharply, to no more than two or three insects a minute, instead of fifty.

By the light of the mushroom I saw the following picture: Low thorny bushes growing alongside the path with a couple of worker ants crawling around them. The lads were plucking small green fruits about the size of an apple off the bushes. I waited until they'd eaten their fill and gone on their way, then I looked around and, since I didn't notice any guards, I started picking the fruit and stuffing it into my bag, on the reasonable assumption that if it didn't kill the insects, it wouldn't kill me . . . probably. The huge thorns on the branches pricked my hands even through my gloves and I winced, but didn't stop until my bag was crammed with fruit. As soon as it was, I got out of there as quickly as I could, before the ants could catch me at the scene of the crime.

But actually tasting the fruit still required great courage. It was covered with a thick skin and I had to use my knife on it. My nostrils were tickled by the aroma of plums and raspberries. My stomach started gurgling insistently. I took one bite and only came to my senses again after I'd wolfed down four of the fruits. Amazingly enough, my hunger disappeared as if I'd devoured an entire roasted goose. If the fruits turned out to be poisonous after all, at least I was going to die feeling satisfied.

Things looked better immediately. I cheered up a bit and the road ahead no longer seemed weary and endless. About forty minutes later I'd left the Cave of the Ants—as I'd decided to call the place—behind me and walked up a broad stairway into the next cave. The columns here reminded me of dragon's teeth, and I felt as if I was somewhere in the mouth of a huge monster.

The mushroom was still shining away, and the path wasn't showing any signs of disappearing, so Harold arrived at the final goal of his present journey without any problems or sudden surprises.

The teeth-columns parted to reveal the entrance to a rather small room. The path divided into eight branches, leading into eight corridors. But they weren't for me—if what the Messenger had said could be believed, my journey through the Level Between Levels would end here.

The walls were covered with doors cast from bronze that had turned dark green with the passage of time. They had massive handles of the same metal, and there was no sign of any locks or bolts.

I stepped off the path and walked over the grass to the nearest door. After a spot of difficulty, I found what I was looking for. A small blue circle in the bottom corner. Now all I had to do was find a door with a red triangle, pray to Sagot, and walk into the eighth level. I set off along the doors, looking for the right mark.

A green circle, a yellow square, a red square, a black rhomboid, a purple circle, and a triangle—but it was orange. I walked past doors marked with circles, squares, and rhomboids of every possible color. But there wasn't a single red triangle. Eventually I reached the last door on my tour. There was a green line on it.

Could I possibly have missed the sign I needed? Or maybe no such sign existed? Maybe this was one of the Messenger's jolly jokes? I'd have to check the marks carefully again. I suppose I could simply have missed it.

The first door. There was a red circle on it.

What was going on? I remembered clearly that there was a blue circle there before. The next door—and now, instead of a yellow circle there was a white rhomboid. The next door—and instead of a yellow square there was a brown triangle. Once I went all the way round, all the signs changed.

Keep calm, Harold! I inspected all the doors again and still didn't find what I needed. Every single shape and color imaginable, like the Great Market in Ranneng, but there was no little red triangle to be seen anywhere.

Round the circle a third time. The first door. A green square. How much longer could this go on?

I accidentally touched a cold bronze surface and recoiled sharply—the door had turned transparent for a moment. I'd seen what was on the other side! My curiosity was too powerful to resist, and I pressed my palm against the cold surface again. For a couple of seconds nothing happened, then fine ripples started running across the surface and the door turned transparent and I saw the Doors to the third level in front of me.

I went up to the next door and put my hand on it, too.

A huge, brightly lit hall filled with heaps of diamonds. I didn't know where in the Palaces of Bone this wonder was, but anyone who could get to it was an incredibly lucky man. He'd be rich until the end of time.

I moved on, looking through the doors and not forgetting to search for the red triangle at the same time. Dozens of faceless halls on all levels. But after the Doors, I didn't see a single place that was even vaguely familiar. In the time I spent walking round those doors, so many pictures of Hrad Spein appeared that my head was filled with a total muddle. The only thing I remembered was a skeleton striding from corner to corner in some vestibule and crimson sparks in some large hall. Imagine the smooth black velvet curtain of night, with crimson sparks scattering across it in the distance, looking very much like the fiery snowflakes of the world of Chaos. I had no doubt that this door led to one of the deepest levels of the Palaces of Bone.

Another door. I put my hand on it and gasped out loud in surprise. It was a night scene. The light of the slim moon was barely enough to light up the

clearing surrounded by majestic golden-leafs. There was a small fire glowing close to the entrance to Hrad Spein. Its timid flickering awoke a strange
yearning in my heart. There were soldiers sleeping beside the fire. There was
just a still figure of the sentry standing on the boundary line between the
firelight and the night. The sentry stirred and I recognized Eel.

This was my chance! I could escape from Hrad Spein this very moment!
All I had to do was open the door and step through it, and I would be free!
No more cursed stone walls, coffins, catacombs, fear, weariness, endless night-
mares, and lack of sleep, no more hunger, no more running.

I could send the quest for the Rainbow Horn to all the demons of darkness, send the Commission even farther, and forget these last few days, as if
they were nothing but a terrible dream. My hand reached out for the door
handle against my will, and the door opened very easily.

A breath of the fresh autumn night and campfire smoke blew into my
face. I breathed the aroma in like a gift from the gods. One step, and the
nightmare would be over. Just one step, that was all. I opened the door a
little wider and the hinges creaked gently. The sound was enough to alert
Eel and make him start walking toward me. I didn't know if he'd seen anything or was simply following the sound, but I wanted very much to shout
out and attract his attention.

"Look to the right, Harold," Valder whispered to me.

His voice broke the spell, and I looked. In the lower corner of the door to
my right, there was a triangle. A red one.

Cursing all the gods and the Master, and fickle fate into the bargain. I
slammed shut the door to freedom, lifted my hand off the handle, and took
a step back. I was trembling convulsively, and no wonder! I'd almost ruined
everything. Almost burned my bridges. Curses! What on earth had come
over me?

"Thank you, Valder."

"I just thought you might not like to walk through all eight levels again,"
he said with a gloomy chuckle.

"You thought right," I replied, still unable to gather my wits. "Thanks again."

"Don't thank me too much, I have my own interest in this business."

"And what's that?"

"My non-death started with the Rainbow Horn, when . . . well, you know
what I mean."

I certainly did. That was the very first dream vision I'd had.

"I console myself with the hope that—" He paused, as if afraid of extinguishing this timidly flickering flame of hope. "—that when I'm somewhere near the Horn again, I shall be able to leave this world and find peace."

"Let's hope you're right, Valder, and the artifact does help you."

"I hope so," he sighed.

"Did you hear my conversation with the Messenger?"

"Yes."

"Is he telling the truth?"

A long pause, and then . . .

"Yes, the Rainbow Horn is the force that can disrupt the balance."

"What about the Master? Is what the Messenger says about him and those other beings, and about me, true?"

"I don't know."

"But if the Horn is capable of disrupting the balance, perhaps we shouldn't . . ."

"The balance can be disrupted whether you take the Horn or not. It doesn't depend on the Horn any longer."

"But what should I do?"

"Fulfill the Commission and pray to Sagot," Valder said, and stopped talking.

Fulfill the Commission and don't think about a thing. . . . Hah! I walked up to the door with the red triangle on it, took a deep breath, opened it wide, and walked into the eighth level of the Palaces of Bone.

11

THE RAINBOW HORN

I found myself in a small room that smelled of age, dust, and candles. Whatever else might be lacking, there were certainly plenty of candles—the entire room was crammed with candlesticks.

A hefty metal table piled high with books and scrolls, heavy drapes of dark claret velvet on the walls, a faded Sultanate carpet on the floor—it almost came unraveled under my feet. In the far corner, beside the way out, a small cupboard with shelves packed with jars and flasks. A picture in a heavy, ornate, gilded frame on one of the walls. It was impossible now to tell what the unknown artist had originally painted—all the colors had faded. Two bronze-bound chests standing beside the table.

I looked back, but the door I had come through to enter the room was gone. There was no way I could get back to the Level Between Levels now.

I walked over to the table and lifted the lid of the nearest chest out of curiosity. No, there wasn't any treasure inside. The trunk was filled right up to the top with fine quality wheat. A very strange choice. Who on earth could have got the idea of bringing something so useless down from the first level? The second trunk was filled halfway up with wheat berries.

I slammed the lid down in annoyance and turned my attention to the table, with its books and yellowed scrolls, covered with an immensely thick layer of dust. I had no intention of touching them, but for some reason Valder decided to say something.

"Wait. Go back to them."

I walked back to the table and picked up the first book that came to hand.

"I can't read these squiggles," I said, looking at the book without the slightest interest.

"I can. It's old orcish. A magical book. It's priceless."

Well, maybe it was priceless, but I wasn't going to lug it back up to the surface. The book was as heavy as Kli-Kli after a binge on cherries.

"Pick up that one, with the yellow cover."

I raked aside the scrolls, raising a thick cloud of dust, and fished out the book that Valder wanted. It was a bit larger than my palm and about two fingers thick. There was gnomish writing on the cover.

"*The Little Book of Gnomish Spells.*"

Was that a note of awe I heard in Valder's voice? Well, I supposed that wasn't so very surprising. All the gnomes' books were hidden away in the Zam-da-Mort and neither the gnomes nor the dwarves could get at them. The dwarves wouldn't let their closest relatives within a cannon-shot of their mountains, but they couldn't figure out how to open the magical depository without them.

That was why what I was holding in my hands was immensely valuable to both the races. I twirled the book this way and that, then carefully put it back in its place. I certainly wasn't going to take it with me, or even tell Hallas and Deler about my find. There was no point. The little book in the yellow cover could easily ignite a conflagration that would end in a new

Battle of the Field of Sorna. I certainly wasn't going to be the one who unleashed another round of slaughter between the dwarves and the gnomes.

"Is there anything else that interests you, Valder?"

No reply.

I shrugged and walked toward the door. It was time to grab the Rainbow Horn and get out of this inhospitable place . . . fast.

Now that was talking big! "Grab the Rainbow Horn"! I had to get to the lousy tin whistle first! And getting to it turned out not to be so simple.

When I stepped out of the library room, I stepped into a wide corridor or hall. It was shrouded in shadows and semidarkness, just like the sixth level. Wax torches spluttered in an attempt to illuminate the underground Palaces, but unfortunately they didn't have the power for it. Everything seemed to be quiet, but I stayed alert and kept stopping to listen. Thank Sagot, there was nothing terrible or mysterious. The eighth level was cold, though, and the constant drafts blowing out of the side corridors cut straight through me.

I didn't have any maps, but, remembering what the Messenger said, I kept walking straight on without turning off. Of course, it was stupid to trust a servant of the Master, but so far everything he said had been true, and I thought that improvising was probably not the best way out of the difficult situation I was in.

After I'd walked for half an hour, the torches on the walls were spaced wider apart and I had to take my mushroom lamp out again. Then came a series of halls with rows of massive, squat columns along the walls, vaulted ceilings, and buttresses. The architectural style was quite crude and careless, very hasty, although I was certain that the halls had been created by orcs and elves. This was the slapdash way all the Young Races had done things when they were desperate to get out of here. But, strictly speaking, that was a perfectly sane desire for any rational being—although I only started to understand what the reason was forty minutes after I left the last torch behind me.

The light of my mushroom lamp picked a rather interesting picture out of the darkness of the immense hall. Something that not even a madman from the Hospital of the Ten Martyrs could have drawn—he could never even have imagined that such a thing could exist.

I admit quite honestly that cold shivers ran down my spine, my throat went dry, and my tongue stuck to the roof of my mouth. It's not every day I have the "good luck" to see a scene from the play that the priests used to frighten us so often (I mean the story of the arrival of the darkness in Siala and similar fairy tales). Anyway, right there in front of me was a wall nine yards high. Nothing so very special about that, except that in this case, instead of bricks, the builders had used human skulls.

Thousands of thousands of them staring out at me with the dark holes of their eye sockets, thousands of thousands of them grinning at me sardonically with their bare teeth, thousands of thousands of them gleaming blinding white.

Thousands of thousands? More than that! How many skulls had it taken to make a wall like this? It was an appalling and yet fascinating scene. A scene of unreal and macabre beauty. Who had created this and how? What for? And where had they got such a massive number of human skulls? And was my own head likely to end up as one more brick in this terrible wall?

The wall completely blocked off my path. I walked along it, but ran up against the wall of the hall. I set off in the opposite direction and discovered a way through in the form of an archway with its vault made of ribs. I slipped through the archway and . . .

Yes indeed, and . . . Now I was certain that the Palaces of Bone had got their name thanks to this place. There before me lay a depository, a collection, a veritable treasurehouse of bones and remains that had once been people.

Nobody could ever have dreamed this, even in their most terrible nightmare. The walls of the hall were faced with skulls, the ceiling was covered with crossed ribs and shoulder blades, the huge chandeliers were made of yards and yards of spinal columns, rib cages, and skulls with magical lamps burning inside them and lighting up the Halls of Bone.

As I walked past these remains, I glanced at the bones and shuddered. It wasn't very pleasant walking through a gigantic open warehouse of human death. The breath of dread and horror was palpable. It was as if the souls of everyone who had not been properly buried in all the centuries gone by were staring out at me through those dark eye sockets.

In these vast deposits of bones there wasn't a single complete skeleton. Whoever put together this huge, macabre museum had taken the time to pull the skeletons apart and sort out the bones. There were heaps of different kinds of bones clustering, crowding, towering up along the wall. The vertebrae were in one place, the ribs in another, there were pelvises, lower jaws, large and small shinbones, upper arm bones, ulnas and radiuses, finger bones and toe bones, there were even piles of teeth.

Winding through the hills of bones (some of them were over six yards high) was a perfectly decent path. I walked along, trying to keep my wits about me and especially not to look at the skulls. The stares of thousands of thousands of eye sockets drilled straight through me. I felt a childish terror seething inside me. Walking through mountains of human remains silently contemplating eternity and all living things—this is truly cosmic horror.

And then the pyramids started. As was only to be expected, the skulls of the unfortunate dead had been used in their construction, too. Every one of these structures rose up to a height of more than ten yards. The skulls were laid with geometrical precision and fitted perfectly against each other. I think several thousand dead men's heads must have been used in each pyramid. And in every pyramid there was a dark triangular opening or niche. I didn't know why in the name of darkness they were put there, but I certainly was never going to climb into them.

I heard the ringing sounds in the distance soon after I passed the eighth pyramid.

Clink, clink. Clink, clink.

The sound was coming closer, and I started looking for a place to hide. I ought to have known—you should never say never. Sagot had obviously heard me and decided to have a joke, because the only place where I *could* hide now was in a niche in a pyramid. There was no time to think about it, the unknown Chimer would be with me any moment now, and then darkness only knew what might happen. I only had a knife—and not too much confidence in my ability to fight whatever it might be.

The niche proved to be quite roomy, and I fitted into it without any difficulty. I had to put the mushroom away in my bag, or the light would have given me away. The world around me was plunged into darkness.

Clink, clink—the steps were getting closer. Suddenly the walls of the pyramid directly opposite me emerged from the darkness. The unknown Chimer was carrying a torch. And then I saw the lad himself. Every step it took produced a ringing sound. The Chimer turned out to be a member of the numerous tribe of the restless dead. At least, its face was mummified, as dry and wrinkled as a raisin, it had no nose at all, its cheeks were ripped open, and the teeth were visible through the holes. The eyes were as black as agate and dead. Like Bass's eyes.

The creature was wearing a court jester's cap, with little miniature skulls on it instead of bells. In its left hand the creature was holding a torch, and in its right—a stick with an iron ball on a chain. The Chimer's appearance was terrifying and impossibly absurd at the same time.

I sat in my refuge, as quiet as a mouse. The Chimer walked through the territory entrusted to its care and disappeared into the darkness. I waited until its steps faded away and climbed out of the pyramid. I had to get through the Halls of Bone as quickly as possible, or I could be in for trouble. A knife isn't the most effective weapon against a ball and chain.

When I heard the ringing sound again, I dived into the next pyramid without thinking twice, and once again the dead man didn't notice me. I had to hide another four times from the creatures patrolling the Halls of Bones.

The bones piled up in heaps along the walls somehow didn't bother or frighten me anymore. Right then, Shadow Harold had only one thing on his mind—making sure he didn't run into any Chimers.

The pyramids of bone parted and I found myself in . . . Well, probably you could call it a square. An entirely open space without a trace of bones. The mushroom lamp wasn't giving much light, so I just had to walk forward, hoping there was no one anywhere nearby. Standing right in the center of the square was a statue.

I beheld the figure of Death. She seemed to be carved out of a single piece of bone with a texture and blinding pearly whiteness that were reminiscent of a mammoth's tusk.

Death was sitting on a massive throne built of human bones with her bare feet resting on a huge skull that was an integral part of this monumental sculpture.

Death was wearing a plain sleeveless dress, more appropriate for a simple peasant woman on her way to the local harvest fair than the Queen of Lives and Fates. She was wearing a skull half-mask, so all that could be seen of her face were the plump lips (pressed tightly together) and her perfectly formed chin. Her luxuriant white hair tumbled down onto her naked shoulders.

The sculptor's skill was beyond all doubt. The hair seemed real, the figure was almost alive. In the shrines, Sagra's servant Death is always shown with a weapon (a scythe, or a sickle on a long staff), but there was nothing like that here. The woman had a bouquet in her hands. Her long elegant fingers held the flowers carefully—white narcissi, the symbol of death and oblivion. But what struck me most of all were her eyes, or rather, the lack of them (everyone knows that Death is blind, but she never errs in her choice).

The two dark gaps in the skull-mask seemed to be fixed on me, as if they were telling me that the time was not far off when my sorted bones would also be lying in the halls of the eighth level. I can't say that I really felt afraid. Death never frightens those she comes for. Why would she? Ultimately we will all be her prize, in any case. No matter how long we live, the end is the same for all of us—she comes. With narcissi or a scythe—that's not so very important. Even the immortals, even the gods, will be hers in the end, it's only a matter of time, and Death knows how to wait.

Oh, those eye sockets! I didn't know who had dared to create this statue, who had managed to make her look so alive, but it must have been one of the very greatest Masters of Siala. The black gaps in the skull really were all-seeing. Whichever way I moved, I could feel them watching me. Not in menace, but with a certain restrained curiosity.

I heard the ringing footsteps approaching again and, with a farewell glance at Death, I dashed away, hoping very much that my path and the path of the Mistress of Lives would not cross soon, that we would meet at the final crossroads.

The Mistress of Lives? The final crossroads? Where did I know those phrases from? Was this Valder's memory playing tricks, or was it the knowledge of a Dancer in the Shadows?

I plodded on until I came to a wall of skulls, found an archway, ducked through it, and I was back in the usual underground burial halls.

The dream is flooded as full of nightmares as an Isilian loaf is stuffed with raisins. I am dreaming. In the dream Death stands over me, with the wind of Chaos fluttering her white hair and her linen dress, as if it wants to tear it off. In the dream she leans down, preparing to lay a bouquet of pale narcissi at my feet, as if to say that I belong only to her. In the dream a blizzard wind—a fiery vortex of blazing crimson snowflakes—grabs the flowers out of the hands of Death and bears them away, then tears the skull half-mask off her face. But she covers her face with her hands and turns away before I can glimpse her face.

"It's not time yet," the wind of Chaos whispers, fluttering her incomparably beautiful flowing hair.

"It's not time yet," murmur the fiery snowflakes, swirling around Death in a sparkling dance.

"Go, our world needs him," the scarlet flame that has appeared out of nowhere tells the intransigent Queen.

"Everything has its price. Do you agree?" Her voice is extraordinarily young and clear.

"He is ours," the three shadows reply in chorus. "We will pay."

She nods and steps aside to let the shadows pass, then disappears. Death is patient. She knows how to wait.

I woke up and stared into the darkness for a long time, looking toward my feet, afraid of seeing a bunch of pale narcissi flattened by a stormy wind. Afraid of hearing the roar of the crimson flame and the wind of the world of Chaos. Terrified of meeting the shadows.

A dream. It was only a dream, a sequence of meaningless nightmare images. But, by Sagot, how real it was! I got up, stuffing one of the fruits from the Cave of the Ants into my mouth. I took two steps and then froze, with icy shivers dancing a jolly jig up and down my spine.

Lying there on the floor, glittering forlornly in the light of the mushroom lamp, was a tiny little golden skull. A bell from a Chimer's cap. While I was asleep, the creature had stood only two paces away from me, but he hadn't killed me. Why would he have left this elegant little trinket on the floor? A hint? A warning that Death had not forgotten me? That the dream was not just a dream, and everything I had seen in my latest nightmare was nothing but the simple truth?

A h'san'kor only knows! I couldn't even imagine why the skull had been left for me, but I certainly wasn't going to pick it up. I skirted round the trinket lying on the floor and walked on into the tangled halls of the eighth level.

I traveled for three and a half hours, still following the Messenger's advice and walking straight on along the central vestibule of the level, without turning left or right. Soon torches appeared in the halls again and there was no need for the mushroom lamp, so I put it away in my bag.

The architecture of the halls on the eighth level changed fundamentally once again. The crude, careless granite gave way to the amazing elegance and precision of silver and the gloomy tranquillity of black marble. Every hall was a treasure house, there was enough silver here to make five castles.

Beautiful silver inserts in the black marble of the columns, incredibly elegant brackets for the torches, balconies built from thin slabs of marble entwined with silver threads, doors from one hall to the next standing open, made of the finest timber in Siala—Zagraban oak and golden-leaf—with massive hinges of precious metal and elegant handles in the forms of animals that I didn't recognize. Pictures in silver paint on every door, for the most part depicting trees and also—rather strangely for the culture of the orcs and the elves—the gods. But these gods looked very much like people and didn't inspire the reverential awe that some philistines feel when they visit the shrines or the Cathedral in Avendoom.

The Silver Halls were probably every bit as beautiful as the scarlet-and-black Palaces of the fourth level.

The central vestibule took a right-angled turn to the left. That wasn't really so very alarming, except that the Messenger had told me to keep going straight on without turning left or right.

Following simple logic, I ought to go on along the corridor and not get any other silly ideas into my head, but if I did as I had done so far, then . . . then I ought to go through that little silver door over there, hidden between those two projecting blocks of marble.

I couldn't see any keyholes or other similar human nonsense. If the door had a secret lock and it had been made by elves and orcs, I'd be struggling with it for a long time—without much hope of ever actually opening it.

I examined it from a safe distance. Never fiddle with anything that makes you feel vaguely anxious—that's one of the most important rules of a master thief. Study the situation thoroughly before you go jumping feet-first into the gnome's fiery furnace.

I spotted a gap no thicker than a hair between the marble wall and the door. In short, I only had to push the door with my finger and it promptly opened.

Immediately behind it was a narrow corridor with a low ceiling. The flames in the small lamps standing in equally small niches in the wall fluttered like wounded moths. I had to walk along hunched over, with the ceiling just above my head. And I had the impression that this passage must have been made for short dwarves, gnomes, and goblins, not for men, orcs, and elves.

Fortunately for me, the corridor wasn't too long, and after walking a few dozen paces I came to another silver door. This one wasn't locked, either. I opened it, forgetting all about caution, walked through, and froze.

What was it the verse guide said?

> In serried ranks, embracing the shadows,
> The long-deceased knights stand in silence.
> And only one man will not die 'neath their swords,
> He who is the shadows' own twin brother.

Well, those four lines were a pretty good description of what I saw in the hall. The orcs and elves stood facing each other in broken ranks, pressing back against the walls in the shadows cast by the square columns. But Kli-Kli claimed that the lines had been changed and in the famous *Book of Prophecies,* the *Bruk-Gruk,* they went like this:

> Tormented by thirst and cursed by darkness,
> The undead sinners bear their punishment
> And only one will not die in their fangs,
> He who dances with the shadows like a brother.

I didn't know which of the gentlemen verse-mongers was right and whose verse was more accurate. In any case, the first and the second versions both warned quite openly that if you forgot to be cautious here, you could say good-bye to your ears.

The orcs and the elves stood along the walls and glared at each other. I ventured into the hall and started studying the figures from a safe distance. They turned out to be sculptures of warriors. Life-size figures, all in armor and all with weapons. I had the impression that any second now the statues would come to life and throw themselves at each other.

The columns running through the center of the hall gave out a silvery light, but there were thick shadows along the walls, and that gave most of the shadows an ominous look. Remembering that in Hrad Spein things sometimes came to life when they really shouldn't, I walked through the hall very cautiously indeed.

There were several thousand statues in the immense hall. Some overzealous individual had managed to put together an entire army. And do I even have to mention that the statues were not identical, in fact, they were all completely different?

Every elf had his own face and bearing, his own armor and weapon. At first I thought the sculptures were standing about at random, and it took me a while to realize that this was a formation. A complex and highly effective formation.

At the front were elves in heavy armor, with very broad s'kashes set on long poles; behind them came bowmen in light chain mail; and behind the bowmen were three rows of swordsmen, standing with spaces between them, so that the bowmen would be able to pull back.

The orcs were frozen facing the elves. Their spears were raised and they were protecting their bodies with long, heavy shields. They also had bowmen, swordsmen, and some lads with mighty two-handed axes. Like I said—an entire army.

I walked past the ranks of this stone army and into the next hall. . . . I stopped and caught my breath.

It looked as if the gods had clapped their hands and stopped time right in the middle of a furious battle. The jagged formation had fallen apart, and now the statues of the orcs and the elves were all jumbled together. There were Firstborn and Secondborn fighting all the way across the hall, and the sculptural composition was simply breathtaking.

Most of the elves and orcs were lying on the floor. Some with arrows stuck in the eye slots of their helmets or the joints of their armor. Some with their chain mail hacked apart, some with spears stuck into their stomachs, some were missing arms that had been chopped off, some had lost their heads.

Right in front of me an orc was frozen in the act of thrusting a spear into an elf who was trying to get up off the ground. A little farther on, the yataghans and s'kashes of dozens of irreconcilable enemies were locked in bloody combat. I walked past the frozen battle, looking at the warriors as I skirted round them.

There was a grinning orc protecting a fallen comrade with his shield, but he hadn't noticed the elf armed with an orcish ax standing behind him. There was a Secondborn struggling to stay in the saddle, and a Firstborn had grabbed his horse's bridle and was just about to hack off the elf's leg with his yataghan. There were an elf and an orc, twined together in a knot of death, each struggling to hold back the other's arm and at the same time reach him with his dagger.

I forgot all about being cautious and looked at the statues as if I was spellbound. Waiting for frozen time to thaw out again, for the underground hall to resound with the clash of weapons and roaring of the warriors.

There, at the very center of the hall, was a small brigade of Firstborn with spears, drawn up into a circle to form a round "hedgehog" and trying to hold off elves on horseback. Over there a group of elves had fired arrows into ten orcs who were attacking them, and now they were reaching to take more deaths out of their quivers. Six Firstborn were already lying on the floor, despite their chain mail, but the other four—one of them was wounded in the leg—were still running toward their enemies. I wondered whether, if this was a real battle, they would manage to reach the Secondborn before the bowmen could fire another volley.

I walked on.

There was an elf desperately trying to protect himself with his arm against an ax that was being swung down on him by a brutal orc wearing the clan badges of the Grun Ear-Cutters.

I walked on.

An elf with his arms raised, and his open palms upward. But he wasn't thinking of surrendering. There were heaps of orcs lying around the elf, like trees felled by a fierce hurricane. The elfin shaman had swept away a whole detachment of Firstborn, like a vicious dog that has come across a litter of blind kittens.

I walked on.

An orc was protecting himself with a shield that had a picture of some mythical bird as he tried to repulse an attack from three very young and very eager elves. Four of the Secondborn had already lost their lives, and a fifth was grimacing in pain as he tried to bind up the stump of his right arm.

I walked on.

An elf sinking his fangs into an orc's throat.

Farther . . .

An elf trying to hold in the entrails tumbling out of his gashed stomach.

Farther . . .

An orc smashing an elf's head with a spiked club.

Farther . . .

An elf firing an arrow at point-blank range into an orc who was looking the wrong way.

A new scene . . .

The commanders of the Firstborn and the Secondborn have launched into a duel with spears; orcs and elves have forgotten their own mutual hostility and are standing around together, watching the fight.

An elf holding a Firstborn by his braid and raising his s'kash to hack off his enemy's head.

An elf lying crushed under his own horse, with his arm twisted at an unnatural angle.

An orc standing alone in the shadow, aiming his bow at the commander of one of the elfin detachments.

I walked on.

Like a weightless shadow, I slipped between the figures, under the spears poised to thrust and swords suspended in the air.

I looked at the elves and the orcs trying to deal with an ogre that had appeared out of nowhere, clutching a stone hammer.

My gaze fell on an orcess. It was the first time I'd seen a woman from the race of the Firstborn. She looked a lot like Miralissa, except that her hair wasn't gathered into a braid, but a long tail. The orcess was armed with two crooked swords and the sculptor had caught her as she was spinning round. One crooked sword had slit an elf's throat and the other was thrusting forward toward another enemy.

I walked right up to the orcess and gazed into that smooth face with its imprint of wild beauty and desperation. I couldn't resist touching her cheek with my finger. For a second nothing happened, and then a series of thin, winding cracks ran across the statue's cheek. The cracks ran across the entire face, branching and spreading, and small pieces of stone started to fall away, revealing the true face of this female warrior.

Staring out at me through empty eye sockets was a skull bearing the remains of rotted flesh. The orcess's wild beauty had disappeared in an instant.

And then I realized that it wasn't stone, but only a thin glaze, covering bodies that had once been alive. I realized that the figures in the halls were not statues, but orcs and elves who had once been alive and had been frozen instantly in eternal sleep. Someone had played a vicious joke, forcing the dead soldiers to continue with a never-ending war that had been going on for thousands of years now. I stopped admiring the battle and tried to get out of the halls of "toy soldiers" as quickly as possible. I made my way through the ranks of elves, trying not to touch anyone, in order not to break the dead warriors' covering.

But I still wondered if there really had been a battle here. If there had, then what power and what magic could have instantly transformed all the soldiers into statues that had stood there for thousands of years? Of course, I couldn't come up with an answer to that question, so I simply walked faster, quite reasonably assuming that the foulest surprises happen at the most unexpected moments, and I could easily get caught by some nasty magical trap, too. It wasn't very pleasant to think of somebody seeing me in a thousand years' time as a statue entitled *Harold, who tried to reach the Rainbow Horn but never got there.*

The Halls of the Warriors ended as suddenly they had started. There were no more statues ahead. Well now, it was the first time I could remember when not a single line of a verse had come true. Nobody had tried to stick a knife or a pair of fangs into me. And I didn't understand those phrases "tormented by thirst" and "undead sinners," either. I wasn't particularly upset that nothing genuinely unpleasant had happened, but . . . the verses had never been wrong before, and then suddenly here was this surprising discrepancy between the word and the fact. Maybe I'd just walked through at a safe time?

"More likely someone walked through before you and made the path safe," Valder whispered, and I shuddered in surprise.

"Valder!" I whispered. "You want to stay inside my head for a bit longer, don't you? Then please don't frighten me like that again, or I'll die of a heart attack, and you'll have to look for a new refuge!"

No reply.

It was only then that I realized what the archmagician had been talking about. . . . Who could have walked through ahead of me and made the path safe? The answer was obvious.

"How would I know?" the archmagician said, and fell silent.

Well, that was the worst possible news. The very last thing I needed was that sorceress right in front of me! Even if the Messenger did say that the Master had abandoned his grudge against me, I wasn't stupid. I didn't want to come face-to-face with a witch who had risked entering Hrad Spein to get the Key from me. And, of course, there was no reason to believe that Lady Iena felt any particular love for me, so I really ought to keep as far away from her as possible.

A sequence of faceless, dimly lit halls with stairways leading down into the depths of the Palaces of Bone. I walked through a gallery, then came to another hall. As I walked into it I quietly flipped my lid, as Kli-Kli would have said. A round hall about sixteen yards across. Mirror walls, a mirror ceiling, a floor concealed from my eyes by a thin layer of dense white mist. Strange. Very strange.

The world blinked and I felt the pressure of the air against my eyes. An instant later, the strange sensations had disappeared. And so had the way out. Where it had been there was an unbroken mirror wall. I turned round. The way in had gone, too. Someone had decided to seal me in the round hall.

Trying not to panic, I walked over to the place where the way out had been, put my hand on the mirror, and tried in vain to push it aside and open up the passage to freedom. On closer inspection it turned out that the walls of the hall weren't made of mirrors, but of silver.

They were built of massive slabs of pure silver that had been polished for a long, long time with river sand so they gleamed like a mirror. But the most interesting thing was that the ideal mirrors of the walls reflected everything else in the hall, but for some reason they had forgotten to show my own thievish personage.

I moved along the wall, walking round the circle and trying to guess the hall's secret, trying to find the way out. One full circle. Two. Three. No clues. Something in the hall had changed, but I couldn't understand what. Then I noticed that the mist had disappeared, and now the floor was covered with the small pieces of a red and yellow mosaic.

I walked on round like a man under a spell. After another circle, the mosaic was yellow and blue. Another round—and it was black and white.

What sort of nonsense was this? Either the floor had decided to change color, or . . . Oh no, that was nonsense! Although . . . although it could be the right answer—by walking on and on round the circle in the little mirror hall of Hrad Spein, I was also moving forward. Did that mean I could reach the way out like this? I had nothing better to do.

A few more times round the circle, and a man appeared out of thin air in front of me. I grabbed my knife, because my walking had led me to Paleface. The Master's hired killer and running dog wasn't moving, and his attention was focused entirely on the mirror he was facing. I called his name. No response. But what if my dear old friend Rolio, who had been hunting my carcass ever since Avendoom, was only pretending and waiting for his chance? No, it didn't look that way.

Holding the knife at the ready, I walked up to my sworn enemy. I was right beside him, but he didn't move. I only had to reach out my hand, and Paleface was a dead man. I'd been wanting to do it for so long, but I didn't hurry, I just stared at his face in amazement.

He was gazing into the mirror, mesmerized. Out of curiosity, I tried doing the same thing, but I didn't see anything special. Just Paleface and the hall. Still no reflection of me. A strange mirror in one more strange and mysterious place in Hrad Spein.

Rolio's clothes were tattered and torn in places, and he had several bruises on his face. The only weapons he had were a dagger and a few throwing stars on his belt. After thinking for a moment, I took the stars for myself. I wasn't very familiar with this kind of weapon, but if your pockets were empty, it was a sin to complain when you found a copper coin. I clicked my tongue in disappointment when I saw the assassin didn't have any food or personal belongings on him.

I didn't kill him. I don't know what stopped me, but . . . I just couldn't do it! Rolio was absolutely no threat now. His mind was wandering somewhere far, far away, and I'd never been trained to slit a defenseless man's throat. So I just left Paleface there in his world of dreams with the mirror. But, naturally, I didn't turn my back as I walked away from him.

When I finally did turn away from the assassin and walked on for another three steps, I suddenly heard someone gurgling and wheezing. Paleface was lying on the floor and scarlet blood was gushing out of his mouth. Reason had returned to Rolio's eyes, together with horror at the realization that death was near. He noticed me, tried to twist his lips into that eternal sneer of his, and died.

His eyes glazed over and rolled up, the blood stopped pouring out of his mouth onto his clothes and the floor. I looked calmly at the body of the man who had been trying to dispatch me into the darkness, and walked on.

As was only to be expected, on the next circuit, Rolio and his blood had simply disappeared. I cast a glance of annoyance at the mirror and froze in absolute amazement. This was the very last thing I was expecting the mirror to show me. . . .

A familiar room. A massive table, chairs with ornate backs, and a deep armchair by a window covered with a fancy wooden grille. A picture on some spiritual theme painted onto the nearest wall. The table was groaning under plates of food and bottles of wine. The man sitting there was gobbling a whole chicken. He looked up from his plate, reached out a huge, fat hand for his glass of wine, and noticed me.

"Hey kid! What's been taking so long?" asked For with a friendly wave. "Come on in, before the food gets cold, don't just stand in the doorway!"

I stared at him in astonishment.

"Well, how are you, Harold? How did it all go? Don't just stand there, I wanted to tell you it seems like our little deal is going to be quite profitable, and we ought to—"

I leapt back from the mirror as if it was a man with the copper plague. I was shaking. A h'san'kor! I'd really been taken in! Almost fallen for it completely! But that really was For! My old teacher! Only he wasn't in Avendoom any longer. He'd taken off to Garrak just as soon as I left with my group. It was a lot safer in Garrak than in our capital city. I looked hard into the mirror, but I couldn't see the room or For in it anymore. The mirage had disappeared, and once again the silver reflected nothing but the hall.

I walked on.

The sunset on a clear summer evening is always beautiful, especially when you're up on top of a high hill, and you can see the area all around. There was a broad river running past below, and the rays of the setting sun had turned its water the color of molten copper. On the opposite bank there was a settlement—either a big village or a small town. The gentle evening breeze was blowing in my face, bringing with it a scent of water, clover, and the smoke of a small campfire. I could hear a herd of cows lowing in the distance as the cowherd drove them home.

There was a large tree with spreading branches growing on the hill. The campfire was burning under the tree, and there was a cooking pot in it, bubbling away merrily and giving off an incredible aroma of fish soup. There were three men sitting round the fire. The oldest, who had a thick gray beard that looked like matted sheep's wool, was solemnly stirring the food with a wooden spoon. The other two—a tall, bald soldier with a scar right across his forehead and a small plump man with a funny mustache—were playing dice and swearing at each other good-naturedly. A fourth man appeared from behind the tree. He had a net in one hand and a pike in the other.

"A fine catch, Marmot," Arnkh said with a nod of approval as he tossed the dice.

"Ah, Sagra! You win again!" Tomcat exclaimed, shaking his head in disappointment. "What rotten lousy luck! Uncle, when are we going to eat?"

"When everyone's here," the sergeant of the Wild Hearts growled into his beard.

"A-a-ah, that's no good!" Marmot drawled, dropping the pike and the net on the grass. "We'll be waiting forever!"

"Look, Harold's already here," Arnkh announced, getting up off the grass. "Are you here to stay or just dropping by?"

"Just dropping by," I mumbled stupidly.

"Like some fish soup, Harold?" asked Uncle, trying the broth with his spoon and grunting in delight as he took the pot off the fire.

"But you're all dead," I said stupidly.

"Really?" Marmot and Tomcat glanced at each other in surprise.

"I'm more alive than all the living, and I'm very hungry," Tomcat eventually replied. "Are you joining us?"

I shook my head and backed away from the fire.

"Well then, if you're not hungry, we'll get started, and you go down to the water to get the others; we can't wait for them forever!"

I nodded, but kept on backing away. This wasn't where I belonged! This was only a dream! It was a different world! A different reality! Where my friends were still alive and had no intention of dying.

"Hey, Harold! Tell Hallas I wasn't supposed to be cooking today!" Uncle's shout reached me just as the picture in the mirror started to disappear.

I walked on and saw Lafresa. She was staring into the mirror about ten yards ahead of me.

Lafresa tore her gaze away from the mirror, noticed me, and narrowed her eyes. Then she took a step away from me and froze in front of the mirror wall. I followed her example and found myself . . .

A forest meadow, surrounded by a stockade of tall fir trees. The grass was completely covered with the bodies of elves. Only two of them were still alive, standing there without speaking, looking at the prostrate body of a h'san'kor. I couldn't make out who these two were, I could only see that they were an elf and an elfess. Then I understood. . . .

I involuntarily took a step toward them. They both heard the rustling of the grass and turned round. The elf drew his bow, and the arrow pointed straight into my face. The elf's one golden eye carefully followed every movement I made. The other eye was missing—an old injury from an orcish arrow.

Ell.

"What do you want here, man?" Miralissa asked in a hoarse voice.

"I . . ."

"Get out, this is our forest!" said the k'lissang, and his one eye glinted brightly.

"Why have you come here?" asked Miralissa, wiping away the blood streaming out of her ear.

"For the Rainbow Horn."

"The Rainbow Horn?" she asked, shaking her head sadly. "Too late. The Firstborn have the Horn now, and even we can do nothing. The elves lost the battle, and Greenwood is destroyed. This is no place for you."

"Very well," I said, and stepped back.

The elves in front of me were not the ones I had known. They were quite different. Alien.

Ell kept his one eye firmly fixed on me and said something in orcish. His words sounded like a question.

"*Dulleh*," Miralissa answered, and turned away, no longer interested in me.

Dulleh. I thought I'd heard that word before. I jumped at the very same moment as the elf shot his arrow at me. . . .

I fell on the floor and looked at the empty mirror in horror. In orcish *dulleh* means "shoot." If I hadn't remembered the word that Miralissa once said to Egrassa, I would have been lying dead with an arrow in my head. I walked on, hurrying after Lafresa, who always managed to be ahead of me, waiting to see what surprises the mirrors had in store. . . .

The mirrors called to me with offers, requests, entreaties, demands, and threats, trying to draw me into themselves forever. Faces passed before me in a series of bright pictures—the faces of those I had known, the faces of those I would know in the future, the faces of those I would never see.

"Harold! Come here!"

"Die!"

"Why can't you just stop?"

"Come in, you're one of us now."

"Hey, Harold, can you see me?"

"Please, kind gentleman, please!"

I took no notice of them, I just pushed them away and tried to break free of the mirrors' sticky cobweb, now that I'd learned to tell reality from illusion. I didn't always manage to do it straightaway, sometimes the pictures were so bright and powerful that it cost me a great effort to reject the hallucination.

Lafresa was walking on ahead of me, and she was having difficulty. Sometimes I started to catch up, and then I fell behind again when I froze in front of one of the mirrors. And then Lafresa would disappear, and I was left completely alone. A step, another step, another . . .

"Hey, Harold!" Loudmouth called to me with his monstrously gnawed face. "Come here, let's talk!"

I just shook my head and walked past the mirror.

"In the name of the king, thief!" Baron Frago Lanten and ten guardsmen tried to block my way. "Come here, or it's the Gray Stones for you!"

I took no notice of them at all.

"Do you want gold, Harold?" asked Markun, shaking a whole sack of gold under my nose. "All you have to do is stop!"

I just laughed, and he shouted shrill obscenities at my back.

"Who's going to pay for my inn?" asked Gozmo, wringing his hands in despair.

I shrugged.

"Hey, Harold!" a familiar voice called to me. "Come here!"

I stopped, stared at the reflection for a long time, and took a step toward the mirror. . . .

I looked at him, and he looked at me. We had time to study each other. We had an entire eternity of time in our hands; there was no need to hurry.

"Well, how do you like the look of me?" he asked, genuinely curious.

"To be honest, not very much."

"That's not surprising, I had a bad example to follow." He grinned, and his grin turned out ugly and repulsive. Was my grin really like that, too?

I carried on looking at my double—a perfect copy of the master thief, Shadow Harold. A pale face; black circles under tired, sunken eyes; a back stubbly beard; clothes that were dirty, crumpled, and torn. A fine sight. Some dead men, not to mention beggars, looked better.

"Who are you?"

A rather timely question, wasn't it?

"I'm just me. Or you. It all depends what side you look at us from and what you really want to see in the end."

"You called me, didn't you? So tell me what you want, I've got plenty of my own business to deal with, without making conversation with my own reflection."

"Which of us is the reflection, that's the question, Harold," he said, and his eyes narrowed maliciously.

"Are we going to have a battle of words, double?"

"Do you have something against battles of words, double?"

"Yes."

"That's the first difference between us; you're not very fond of talking, Harold."

"What do you want?" His face (my face) was beginning to infuriate me.

"Come on, take it easy!" he said, with a glint of mockery in his eyes. "Take a more cheerful view of the world, reflection! There are lots of fine and beautiful things in it; you just don't know how to take advantage of them."

I said nothing, waiting.

"Well, all right," he said with a sigh. "What do you want all this for?"

"All what?"

"You don't understand?"

"No," I told him quite sincerely.

"All this stress and strain trying to save someone or something, all these friends, all these moral complexes and other unprofitable garbage. Why did you get involved in this crazy adventure? You were never like this before. You used to be more like me."

"I'm glad we have nothing in common any longer."

"Oh, come off it, Harold! All this scurrying about has turned you into a namby-pamby, a wimp who depends on other people. Remember the golden days when there was just you and the night, when you relied on no one but yourself and didn't drag all these friends, obligations, and rules around with you? Didn't we have good times then? Remember the times when you used to break into some fat-assed goon's house just for fun and completely clean him out! Remember the times when you used to plant a crossbow bolt in anyone who got in your way without thinking twice. You used to kill easily, you wouldn't have left Paleface alive before."

"I never killed anyone who simply got in my way, reflection! That way I'd have put half of Avendoom in the graveyard. I always defended myself to save my own life. Don't confuse me with you. I don't take any pleasure in killing! If this is just a friendly chat about old times, I'd better be going. This conversation's not going to get us anywhere."

I stepped back and ran into the cold silver surface of a mirror. He laughed, and I didn't like the sound of it. He and I were not at all alike now, we were completely different people.

"You can only leave here with me, Harold."

"Who are you?" I asked him again.

"I already told you who I am."

"You didn't call me over just for idle conversation, did you? You're always looking for your own advantage, aren't you, double?"

"Advantage? Well, you're not completely hopeless, reflection." A faint gleam of interest appeared in his eyes. "Yes, there's a very profitable deal in the offing, and for old friendship's sake, I want to offer you a share in this little business."

I decided to play by his rules.

"A little business means small profits," I said with a grin, trying to copy his leer.

He laughed again.

"Good old Harold! And I thought I'd lost you completely! Don't worry, there's a great big profit to be made from this paltry little business."

"What do we have to do?"

"We? I swear by the darkness, but I like that! Strictly speaking, nothing. How do you like those odds? A heap of gold for doing nothing at all?"

"I'm always ready to take part in that kind of difficult business." This time it was much easier to copy his leer.

"Excellent! All you have to do is not drag that cursed tin whistle out of the Palaces of Bone, and we'll collect a whole sackful of gold."

"A whole sackful?" I asked, making a surprised and doubtful face. "Are you sure about that?"

"Don't worry, my old friend, I've already agreed to everything."

"And who's the client?"

"Let's just say, an outside observer. His name wouldn't mean anything to you."

"I've got nothing against it in principle, but there's just the previous Commission. . . ."

"Oh drop that. I don't believe in stupid signs and the wrath of the gods. Well then, do you agree?"

"I think so," I said with a nod, and the reflection relaxed. "But I do have just one small thing to add to what I said before."

"What's that?" he asked, moving closer to me.

"Remember I said I didn't take any pleasure in killing?"

"Well?" my double asked, with a puzzled look in his eyes.

"I lied," I said, pulling out my knife and stabbing at my reflection's chest. He either knew what was coming or he sensed something and managed to jump out of the way. I only tore his clothes. And an instant later there was a knife in his hand, too.

"Fool!" he spat out, and flung himself on me.

It's very difficult fighting yourself. I always knew where I was going to strike, and if I knew, then he knew, too. We were equally good with our knives, and after a minute circling between the mirrors we only had a few shallow cuts each.

Now he was going to strike at my throat, and when I stepped forward and to the left, he would try to get me on the shoulder with the backswing.

He struck at my throat, I stepped forward and to the left, and the reflection immediately tried to strike me in the right shoulder. I knew it was coming and parried his knife with mine. Then I moved straight into the attack, aiming for his face, grabbed him by the chest with my free hand, pulled him toward me, and immediately got a knee in the belly. I jumped back and ducked to avoid a slashing blow, put some distance between us, and tried to get my breath back.

"You're getting old," he chuckled, blowing a tuft of hair from my head off the blade of his knife.

I didn't say anything, and he came at me again. Whirling and spinning, knife clanging against knife, hissing through teeth when one of us got another scratch. Neither of us could win; all my efforts to reach my double ran up against my own (or his?) defense. Finally we stopped, facing each other and breathing heavily.

"It's tough fighting someone who can read your mind, isn't it, reflection?" he asked, licking his bloody wrist.

"It's easy," I said, and threw the handful of the metal stars I'd taken from Paleface at my double.

Of course, he read what I was going to do and tried to dodge out of the way, but this time he couldn't. I threw the stars without aiming, and with my left hand, and he didn't know which way to jump. After I flung them, each of the five stars followed its own absolutely random trajectory (I told you already that I'm not much of a thrower).

Three missed, but two struck home. The first hit my double precisely on his right wrist and he dropped his knife and jerked out of the way of another two stars flying at him, but ran into a third that stuck in his left leg. My double cursed and collapsed on the floor. In two bounds I was there beside him, then I moved behind his back and held my knife against his throat.

"What a stupid way to get caught," my reflection said in a wooden voice. "I don't think you'll do this."

"Why not?"

"It's rather hard to kill yourself. Did you know there's a superstition that if you kill your double, you follow him into the darkness?"

A single drop of sweat slid down his temple.

"Wasn't it you who said you don't believe in stupid signs?" I asked the reflection, and slit his throat.

The mirrors around me broke and I was back in the hall, only now there was a door where one of the mirrors had been. The body of my double trembled and spread across the floor as white mist.

I'd passed the test of my own self, and now the way ahead was open. I stepped out of the mirror hall.

At first I didn't even know where I'd got to. It was a perfectly ordinary, entirely undistinguished space without any exit. I walked forward uncertainly, not understanding where I had gone wrong, and what could have brought me into a dead end. And then it happened. The hall changed.

It gave me such a fright I almost wet myself. At least, my stomach dove down into my boots, and I thought I was falling off a precipice. A perfectly understandable reaction from anyone who suddenly found himself suspended somewhere between heaven and earth. I had to try really hard not to panic, and understand that I was still standing on the floor and not dangling darkness only knew where.

I don't know if it was magic or some other kind of secret, but it was as if the walls, the floor, and the ceiling didn't exist anymore. I had the impression that I was somewhere up in the night sky.

There were stars twinkling all around me. Thousands and thousands of bright stars. An enchanting fairy-tale spectacle. The stars were on the walls, on the floor, and on the ceiling, and the pale circle of a moon was shining steadily in the center of the hall. The purple moon by the name of Selena. And if Selena was here, then the Rainbow Horn couldn't be far away.

As I walked toward the moon, my heart was pounding hollowly. I'd almost done it! Done what I didn't believe I could do until today!

Roo-oo-oo-oo-oo-oo-aa-aa-aa-aa!

The pure, deep, melancholy call spread out across the stars. Somewhere up there above me, the wind was blowing in Grok's grave, and the Rainbow Horn was echoing its eternal call.

Roo-oo-oo-oo-oo-oo-aa-aa-aa-aa! Oo-oo-oo-oo-aa-aa-aa-rr-rr-rr-oo-oo-oo-oo!

The sound sent shivers running up and down my spine. It was calling. The melancholy song of the wind and the Horn cut me to the quick.

But I never reached Selena. A blinding bolt of lightning struck the floor under my feet and I jumped aside and squeezed my eyes shut, desperately trying to recover my vision after the bright flash.

There was a smell of thunder and magic in the air.

When I was able to see again, I saw Lafresa in the starry sky on the other side of Selena. She wasn't trying to attack me again, just waiting until I recovered my wits.

Even now she could have been at a ball somewhere, and not in the heart of the Palaces of Bone. At least, the young woman didn't look at all like someone who had spent two whole weeks in the catacombs. Her traveling clothes were perfectly clean and not even crumpled, she still had the silver earrings in the form of spiders and a broad-bladed dagger on her belt. Lady Iena hadn't changed at all since the first time I'd seen her at Balistan Pargaid's reception.

Average height, light brown hair gathered into a short ponytail, with the purple light of the moon playing on her broad cheekbones. Her blue eyes were no longer thoughtful, but wary, she was watching every gesture I made, every movement. There was a small crimson sphere glittering on her open palm. I knew what it was, and it cost me a great effort to tear my eyes away from it and look Lafresa in the eyes again.

"Lady Iena."

"I'm glad to see you remember me, thief."

Her plump lips twisted into a wry smile. The woman's voice was in sharp contrast with her appearance. It was tired, very tired.

"You are planning to live to a ripe old age, I suppose," she asked out of the blue.

"I was certainly thinking of it."

"Then I advise you to move away from Selena and not get in my way, otherwise I shall have to stop you."

"I thought your Master had told you not to touch me."

"If you don't get under my feet. You don't want to end up feeding the worms, do you?"

"But the Messenger gave me some hope of being immortal."

I was just playing for time.

"All who belong to the houses are immortal. Except, that is, in the houses themselves. This hall is an antechamber to the House of Pain and you and I are both mortal here. So step aside, thief!"

"As you say, Lady Iena."

I'd heard everything I needed to hear, so I started slowly moving toward the wall. I'm not stupid enough to fight with one of the most powerful sorceresses alive.

She watched every movement I made. And I prayed to Sagot that everything would work out and Lady Iena wasn't planning to fling a ball of crimson fire at me against the wishes of the Master.

Lafresa waited until I had my back against the wall, and only then started moving toward Selena. She still seemed to be wary of the Dancer in the Shadows. (That's just me flattering myself.) Just before she reached the purple moon she hesitated for a moment, and then she stepped onto Selena. Lady Iena was immediately enfolded in a gentle velvety glow. And then, surrounded by the light of the moon, she began slowly rising off the floor toward the stars.

She laughed; her exultant, sincere, childish laughter wound around the stars, and they replied to Lafresa as they swirled around the violet radiance in a merry dance. I must admit it was all very beautiful.

Lady Iena had completely forgotten about me, but I didn't move from the spot. I watched her rise up to the stars and waited. Of course, I would have liked to say that she laughed in my face in farewell or said something like "Now the Rainbow Horn is mine!"—but nothing of the kind happened.

The stars and the column of light growing straight up out of Selena carried Lady Iena to the Rainbow Horn, which was calling to her: *Oo-oo-oo-oo-aa-aa-aa-aa.*

Then what I was waiting for happened.

Selena's color turned from purple to black and her light died. The stars dancing with Lafresa flashed into crimson streaks and started falling from the sky, leaving sparkling trails behind them, but not one reached the floor, they all melted away in the air. With no light to support her, the Master's servant fell, without making a sound, into the very center of the moon.

A fall from a height of darkness only knows how many yards is always fatal, and in this case it was fatal in a double sense. Death in one of the Great Houses is final even for those who used to be immortal and have been reborn in the House of Love.

Lafresa herself had told me where we were and, remembering Sagot's warning not to stand on Selena, I felt no compunction about letting her try out one of the traps of the Palaces of Bone. The gods be praised, everything had gone well. The gold piece paid for the old beggar's advice had been well spent. If that scrounger who answered to the name of Sagot hadn't warned me not to step on Selena, there was no telling how things would have ended.

I watched as a dark patch of blood spread out under the body that was twisted and broken by the fall. Until the very last moment I still hadn't believed that I could outwit the woman who had once been called Lia.

Oo-oo-oo-oo-aa-aa-aa-aa! The melancholy song of the Horn from somewhere up above me brought me back to reality.

I looked up at the ceiling, trying to spot where the Horn was lying but, of course, I couldn't see anything. It was too high.

While I was vainly gazing upward, Lafresa's body started slowly sinking into Selena, as if it wasn't a firm floor, but some kind of sticky slime or mud. A few seconds later Lady Iena, who had caused our group so much trouble, disappeared forever into the dark moon, and a moment after that Selena turned purple again, and thousands of stars and constellations sprang to life in the "sky." It was just as if nothing had happened.

Something glinted brightly in the center of Selena. I screwed up my eyes, trying to make out what it was, but unfortunately I couldn't. After Lady Iena's death I didn't feel too keen to approach that dangerous spot, but on the reasonable assumption that I wasn't in any danger until I actually stood on the magical moon, I walked right up to it—and there was the Key lying in the middle. Either the magic of the dwarves and the Kronk-a-Mor were inimical to the magic used to create this hall, or I was simply lucky, but the artifact was there, I could simply reach out and take it. At least now Egrassa wouldn't wring my neck for losing the elfin relic. I hung the Key round my neck, since Lafresa hadn't taken it off the chain.

R-r-oo-oo-oo-aa-aa-aa!

It was time to be going. There had to be another way up. At least, that was what Sagot had said, and he had advised me to use my legs. I just had to find the path.

I strode across the starry sky, looking for a stairway leading upward.

R-r-r-oo-oo-oo-too-doo-oo-oo!

"I hear you, I hear you," I muttered, walking along the wall.

I couldn't really call *that* a stairway. It was nothing but a series of square stone steps set into the sky between the masses of stars. And very awkward steps, too. Climbing them would be sweaty work. But there was nothing to be done about that; the Rainbow Horn wasn't going to come down to me.

I stood on the first step, jumped, grabbed hold of the second, and pulled myself up. I stood up again, jumped, and pulled myself up. The world blinked and the magic of the starry sky disappeared. The space below me was once again a perfectly ordinary, unremarkable eighth-level hall, brightly illuminated by the light streaming from its walls.

I had to climb for a long time and I was puffing and panting. Balancing on narrow steps where there was barely enough space to set my feet was very difficult. I tried not to look down. I'd climbed so high now that if—Sagot forbid—I started feeling dizzy, I would fall just like Lafresa. When my arms were just about ready to fall off, I found metal brackets hammered into the wall. That made climbing a lot easier, and after a while I reached a wide stone platform.

There was quite a substantial wind blowing up there.

Oo-oo-oo-oo-aa-aa-aa-aa!

At this level the call of the Horn sounded a lot deeper and clearer. That damned tin whistle was somewhere close now. The world blinked again, and once again I seemed to be in the center of a starry sky. Somewhere below me I could just make out the purple spark of Selena, barely visible among the scattered stars. I hadn't realized just how high I'd climbed.

Right. Which way now? There were no more brackets. The wall above me was smooth, and I could barely even see it because of the magical stars. The ladder leading upward turned out to be where I was least expecting to see it—it was hanging in midair three yards away from the platform I was standing on. And for the thousandth time during my tour of the Palaces of Bone I regretted having lost the cobweb rope.

Now I had just one try at it, a single chance to make the leap.

I studied the stairway leading up into the starry sky carefully again. I could certainly give it a try—and I had no other option in any case. Sagot preserve me!

The stars flickered past below my feet, the ladder grew larger and seemed to go rushing upward, and I just managed to grab hold of the very bottom rung. It turned out to be terribly slippery and it was only by the will of the gods that my fingers held their grip and I wasn't launched into my final flight to a meeting with Selena.

I jerked my arms, wriggling like a grass snake and gritting my teeth, pulled myself up, threw my left arm over the next rung, then heaved myself up again, swung my feet onto the bottom rung, and started climbing.

Oo–oo–oo–oo–aa–aa–aa–aa!

The wind started getting frisky and the Horn was singing all the time now, filling the Hall of Stars with its mighty battle roar. I tumbled into a brightly lit corridor, leaving the stars behind me.

Oo–oo–oo–oo–aa–aa–aa–aa–r–aa!

The Horn's roaring made the floor tremble, but I was in no hurry now. Nothing would happen to it, it could wait for me to get my breath back. After twenty yards of corridor, a new starry sky spread its canopy out over my head. Hanging among the lights of the stars was a pearly bridge. I walked across it and came to Grok's grave.

It was a beautiful structure of amethyst. Something between a summer arbor and a memorial chapel. Four slim, elegant columns supported a dome of delicate blue. Below the dome was a gravestone with the following words carved into it: *To Grok, the great warrior, from a grateful country.*

"I made it," I sighed, still not able to believe that I had reached my goal.

I was standing at the grave of the famous military leader and the brother of the Nameless One. But I felt no sacramental tremor, or anything of the kind. So he was a great general, a legend, and he saved the country from the orcs during the Spring War.

So what?

I'd almost saved the country, too, and from the patchy information I had, Grok wasn't such a great hero, since he was responsible for the appearance of the Nameless One.

The goal of my quest was lying in full view on the grave. The Rainbow

Horn. It hadn't changed at all since the first time I saw it in my waking dream in the Forbidden Territory. A large twisting horn gleaming with a shimmer of bronze, encrusted with mother-of-pearl and bluish ogre bone. A beautiful, skillfully made object. A genuine battle horn that any king would be proud to own.

"May I?" There was a note of pleading in Valder's voice.

"Go ahead," I said, opening up and giving him complete freedom.

And now I saw a completely different Horn, surrounded with a rainbow halo that glimmered faintly in the power emanating from the artifact. The power that held the Nameless One in the Desolate Lands. The power that held the Fallen Ones in the depths of Hrad Spein and prevented them from returning to Siala. The power created by the ogres. The power that had destroyed that race and saved others.

It was failing, disappearing, like water draining away into sand. The hours of the magic that filled the Horn were numbered.

"Can you bring back its magic?" I asked the archmagician, keeping my eyes fixed on the treasure.

"No, that would require the power of the entire Council. I'm sorry."

"Never mind," I said, although in my heart I had been nursing a vague hope that Valder could do it and I wouldn't have to carry this dangerous toy with me. "Can you leave now?"

"No. . . . It's too weak. Perhaps later, when they fill it with power. I'm sorry."

"Don't apologize. Your company's beginning to grow on me. It's better than talking to myself."

The reply was a quiet little laugh. And then:

"Take it, Harold, and let's go home."

Valder was right, there was no time to waste on thinking things over. I licked my lips, which had suddenly gone dry, and approached the grave with my heart pounding in my chest.

There it was. Lying right in front of me. The salvation and the destruction of this world. The trump card in the stupid games of the Masters. What would happen if I dared to carry it out of Hrad Spein? Would that save anyone, or just cause more grief and woe? What should I do? The choice was such a terrible one! To decide the fate of the world and hold power in your own hands. To know that what you do could tip the scales completely and everything could go straight down the ogre's throat.

Should I really take this thing? Was it worth the lads from our group giving their lives for it?

I stood there, not knowing what I ought to do. I was in some kind of stupor. I couldn't move a hand or a foot, as if I was spellbound. I stood there looking at the artifact, and it lay there, waiting for the man who had come to Grok's grave to make up his mind.

"With no doubt or hesitation," I said, repeating the promise I'd made to Egrassa as if it was an incantation, then I sent the world and its brother to the darkness, stepped forward, and picked the Horn up off the grave.

The last thing I remembered was the sky flashing and weeping a fiery rain of falling stars for the second time that day.

12

THE MOTH

Sleep is always a relief. It's like a waterfall that washes away the traveler's accumulated fatigue. Everyone needs sleep, but sometimes sleep brings nightmares with it. They are its eternal companions, never far away. Waiting for you to drop your guard and give them free rein—and that's when the nightmares that have been building up their strength really come into their own, bursting into your mind like a tornado and fastening onto your resting brain like ticks.

Every nightmare has its own purpose. One creeps up to frighten and to drink its fill from the well of its victim's fear, another is no more than an echo of your own conscience, yet another will tear open old wounds, and another will awaken doubt and uncertainty. There are nightmares that will drive you insane and make you want to commit suicide, and there are some . . .

Bright. Blinding. Radiant. Unreal. Astounding. Glittering. Sparkling snow.

Lying on the streets of Avendoom in a thick blanket, luxuriating in the rays of the good-natured winter sun. The snow crunches as a myriad beautiful, perfectly formed snowflakes break under the soles of my boots. I walk through the empty streets, listening to this crunching. Trying to hear some other sound in the city, but the city is either asleep or lying low in anticipation of what is coming, and it doesn't wish to make any noise.

There is no one in the Inner City of Avendoom, either, not even the guards who watch over the peace of the rich men in this district and are always so eager for a gold coin or two. The blanket of snow looks absolutely untouched, as if no one has dared to walk across for an entire week.

I make a few turns and walk away from the central street, through two neighborhoods where the snow is banked up against the houses, and they are just as empty as the city streets and squares. Three hundred yards ahead of me the beautiful Tower of the Order rises up majestically into the air. In the winter, the tower looks as if it is carved out of a single massive block of light blue ice. Another one of the Order's many tricks that make the stones of the tower look like ice, or wood, or fire, according to the season.

Standing between me and the tower is a figure wearing a gray cloak. The stranger pulls back his hood and I recognize him. I have had the pleasure of making this man's acquaintance.

Man? No. Vampire.

A pale, bloodless face, thin lips blue with cold, chestnut hair. A gray cloak that's torn, a coarse shirt of undyed wool. A thick chain on his chest, with a long, smoky-gray crystal hanging on it, sparkling in the sun as brightly as any diamond or dragon's tear. The vampire is holding a krasta carelessly in his hands. He is not threatening me, there's no need for that, and the tip of his bizarre weapon is pointing up at the sky.

I stop and look into the Gray One's impassive eyes. We say nothing. I don't know how much time goes by, but neither of us wants to speak first.

The face of the sun is suddenly hidden behind a thin veil of gray, and a few seconds later the blue sky has been replaced by low gray clouds. Something white and pitifully small falls to the ground between us.

A snowflake. Others follow the first down from the sky, falling through the completely still air in absolute silence. The world darkens and the winter twilight captures the city with the speed of light cavalry.

"You know why I'm here." He isn't asking, he's telling me.

"I can guess," I say reluctantly, and pull a wry face.

"You have all taken things too far. The chains restraining the Fallen Ones could snap at any moment, and the world will tremble. Give it to me, before the balance of the scales is finally overthrown."

It's not even worth thinking of trying to fight this warrior. I know what will happen if I refuse and don't give him the treasure—the krasta will slice me in half in the twinkling of an eye, and the Gray One will take the Rainbow Horn anyway. This lad's far too good for me. It's painful to lose the prize I struggled to get for all those months when I'm only a few steps away from completing the Commission. Without saying a word, I take the canvas bag off my shoulder and hold it out to the vampire.

"Is it in here?"

"Yes."

He takes one step, reaches out his hand, and takes the thing that is the goal of my life.

The sparse snowflakes have given way to a thick blizzard and a wind has sprung up, swirling powdery snow across the square. The snow turns the Gray One's chestnut hair white, but he doesn't seem to notice. The bright winter day that held the city in its power only a few seconds ago is replaced by a deep, impenetrable night that has crept up unseen.

One more heartbeat, and fiery stars are born in the night sky. They appear on the horizon, move closer, and fall onto the square. Almost all of them fall in the snow, hiss angrily, and go out. One almost hits me, just missing my foot.

It's an arrow with red and green flights. The Gray One is less fortunate than me; four blazing arrows strike him in the chest at once, as if the bowmen know what their target is.

The warrior sways and goes down on his knees, but he doesn't let go of the krasta and the bag with the Horn. The first volley of "stars" is followed by a second, far more numerous and in tighter formation. But this time the arrows don't reach the square, they fall on the roofs of houses in the distance.

A third wave immediately descends on Avendoom, but this time instead of arrows there are huge balls of flame fired from catapults. They smash through the roofs of the houses and explode with a loud *whoo-oosh!* splashing out tongues of flame and setting buildings on fire. I spot a ball of fire that's falling into the square and dash away as fast as I can, forgetting all about the Gray One and the Rainbow Horn.

Behind me a giant sighs, a soft hot hand pushes me in the back, and I realize that against all the laws of nature, I've learned how to fly. I fly . . . for a second . . . an instant . . . for one heartbeat I soar above the square like an eagle, then I crash at full speed into a snowdrift that has sprung up along the wall of one of the houses.

Whoo-oosh! the giant sighs belatedly.

I crawl out of the snowdrift into islands of snow and fire. The wind rages, driving the herd of snowflakes this way and that, tossing the unfortunates into the fire, where they die in their thousands, but still can't extinguish the rampant flames.

The Gray One is still on his knees, he isn't even trying to get up, and I realize that no more than ten seconds has gone by since the first volley of arrows. The vampire and I are separated by flames, but I can see a way through, marked out in little white islands of snow. It's now or never! I take out my crossbow, and by some miracle it is already loaded with two ice bolts. I have to risk it. I take my first step toward the vampire.

The silence bursts like a soap bubble, and from somewhere in the distance I hear the sound of battle horns calling the inhabitants of Avendoom to arms. The bell of the Cathedral sounds the alarm.

Alarm! Alarm! Get up! Get up!

About thirty soldiers go running past. Holding spears, swords, halberds, and crossbows. Some have blue and gray bands on their arms—the royal guard; some have black and orange bands—the municipal guard. Taking no notice of me, the guards form up at the entrance to the square and block off the narrow street. The front row goes down on one knee and holds out its spears, the second row is made up of men with halberds and men with crossbows. The crossbowmen fire a volley from behind their comrades' backs. Some of the soldiers start reloading their weapons, some fling the crossbows aside and take out swords. A flood of soldiers appears through the veil of snow with a roar. They have red and green plumes waving on their helmets. Darkness! The soldiers of the Crayfish Dukedom are in the city! How did that happen?

The battle starts. The crossbowmen fire another volley and several of the enemy fall. And then the hand-to-hand fighting starts. Red and green soldiers die on the spears and halberds, but Avendoom has too few defenders, and the enemies keep on pouring out from behind the curtain of snow in an endless torrent. In a minute or two the "crayfish" will break through into the square.

I have to take the Horn and carry it into the tower, before it's too late. I spin round and run toward the Gray One. The vampire is leaning on his krasta, trying to get up. I run as hard as I can, but someone gets there before me. . . .

The figure emerges from the tower of the Order . . . is it a phantom? I can see the silhouette of a figure. I know it's a living man, but I can only make out a blurred patch. He skims across the fire and the snow until he is beside the Gray One. . . . Despite his wounds, the vampire is quick, quicker

than any man, his krasta explodes into a blur, howling like a scalded cat, but
the man veers to one side, ends up behind the Gray One's back, and attacks.

The crimson sphere tears the vampire warrior in two and the man, who
has already completely forgotten about his enemy, leans down nimbly and
picks my bag up off the ground.

The unruly wind blows snowflakes straight into my eyes. I can't hear the
bell, or the battle horns, or the battle. Everything has disappeared. He and
I are the only ones left in all the world. The stranger looks at me. It's only a
fleeting glance, but I realize that the Gray One's killer has given victory to
one of the Masters. I blink to clear the detestable snowflakes off my eye-
lashes, and the man takes his chance to disappear. I pluck up my courage
and approach the Gray One lying on the snow. As I expected, the vampire
is still alive.

"The Master's Player has gone over to the other side . . . and taken possession . . . of the chain. . . . You shouldn't have . . . taken the Horn . . .
now the balance . . . has been disrupted. . . ."

I look at him, puzzled, and can't understand a thing. The Player has refused to serve the Master of Siala? Could the Gray Ones' prophecy really
have come true? Could the Dancer in the Shadows who created Siala really
have lost? And then the world stops. The snowflakes stand still. The tongues
of flame freeze in the square and in the skeletons of the blazing houses, the
fiery arrows hang in the air, the warriors pause, with their swords and spears
held still. A moment of nothingness that consumes everything.

And then the world trembles. The world explodes. The world dies.

I see, or someone sees, the laws of magic collapse, the chains of the millennia snap, I see the world slither back to its first primordial day, when
nothing of what we now call Siala existed yet.

Seas roused to fury annihilate countries, volcanoes spring to life, stars
fall from the sky consuming entire cities with their heat, the gates of other
worlds open wide and Siala is entered by demons and creatures who are
even worse. The entire world swirls around in its final dying dance, its death
agony, a blizzard of awoken shadows of ancient times. Conflagrations, insanity, epidemics, famine, wars, and the creatures of darkness destroy the
world and clear the way for those who have been waiting so long for this
sweet moment—the moment when the balance is disrupted. They emerge
from Hrad Spein in a black wave, a black flood, treading on the bones and
the ashes of dead races—those the Gray One called Fallen Ones, that I
called bird-bears.

I scream. I scream until I go hoarse; the world shatters like a crooked mirror and I awake. . . .

I woke up in darkness. It was hot, so hot that it was hard to breathe. Every breath threatened to scorch my lungs, my eyes felt as if they were about to pop, and I was genuinely amazed by the miraculous fact that my clothes and hair hadn't burst into flames. I covered my face with my sleeve, but that didn't give me any relief, it was still difficult to breathe.

"Thousands of demons!" I muttered. "Where have I ended up this time?"

"Where you've been twice before, and now you're back again. Was it not we who told you that those who have discovered the way to the Primordial World always come back?"

In some incomprehensible fashion I had found my way to the world of Chaos, and been met once again by the last three shadows. It was so dark that I couldn't even see them, only hear their voices.

"Yes, it was you who told me, my ladies."

"We are glad that you have not forgotten us. Hello, Dancer."

"My respects to you. It's hot."

"Our world is dying, and what you have brought here is only hastening its final agony."

I automatically reached out one hand and felt the bag with the Horn in it.

"A dream," I muttered in relief, recalling the vision in which Siala had died.

One of the shadows laughed bitterly.

"A dream? Perhaps you saw the future? Or the past?"

"Or what will never happen now?" one of her sister shadows put in.

"I don't know."

"We don't know, either, what visions a Dancer might have and where these visions might lead. The pans of the balance are already trembling, and you should hurry."

"Where to?" I asked the darkness rather stupidly.

"To the final throw of the dice. The place where this round of the Game will finish. It can still be won, even though the Horn has emerged once again from the subterranean halls of the Prison of the Fallen Ones."

"Go away, Dancer. The presence of the artifact is hastening the death of our house."

Three rectangles of bright light sprang out of the darkness and I screwed my eyes up in pain. When I opened them again, I saw three exits in front of me, leading out somewhere into a white light.

"What's this?" I asked, turning to the shadows, who were visible now.

"This? It is your way out of our world."

"But there are three doors here!"

"We know," said a shadow—the second one, I think—and laughed. "You will have to choose one of them."

I sensed some kind of trick.

"There is no trap in this, Dancer. These are simply the doors of Destiny. All subsequent events depend on which door you choose to leave through."

A fine prospect, no two ways about it!

"What's behind them?"

"Nobody knows. Choose with your heart and go. Farewell," said the third shadow.

"Farewell, Dancer."

"Farewell," the first shadow repeated like an echo.

Darkness take me! What difference did it make which door I went out of? Everything would turn out badly anyway, I was absolutely sure of that. I stepped toward the door closest to me, the one on the right.

I stopped halfway there. The odd little thought had just come into my head that this time the shadows had shown me the way out of the world of Chaos without being asked. That was probably because of the Rainbow Horn, which was poisoning the Primordial World and threatening it with total collapse. The last time they had asked me to stay, asked me to help them to bring life back to their world, which had turned into a nightmare thanks to the Dancers in the Shadows. This time I hadn't heard a single word about help from them.

I looked round and saw they had been watching me in silence.

"What will happen to it?"

They understood what I meant.

"The world of Chaos will die. If not today, then tomorrow. It has been clinging to life for too long, but everything comes to an end eventually."

"And everything must be paid for," said the third shadow, and I immediately recalled Death saying those words.

The shadows had paid for my life with the death of their world.

"And what will happen to you, ladies?"

No answer. I waited, and eventually the third shadow replied: "This is our world. We are the last and we shall stay here until the end."

I know it's absolutely stupid, but I just can't help it. I don't like being obliged to anyone, and if there's a way I can pay back a debt . . . I turned my back on the exits from the Primordial World, and they were immediately veiled in darkness. But this time the shadows didn't merge into the gloom, and I could see their silhouettes very clearly.

"You realize you can't get out of here now?" I could distinctly hear fear in the first shadow's voice.

"I'll get out through the fire, like before."

"The fire has already died, Dancer!"

"Shall we dance, ladies?" I asked, ignoring what they had just said.

When I left that world, it wasn't under any kind of threat. The crimson primordial flame was roaring, and the fiery snowflakes were swirling round me in a slow, entrancing dance. Between the eternal void and the insanity of the fire there was a little island, overgrown with tall silvery grass. In the middle of the island a small lake had appeared, with water as smooth as a mirror, reflecting the flashes of flame and crimson snowflakes.

Towering over the lake was a young chestnut tree with leaves of ice and fire, covered in a froth of white blossom. Its fruit would soon ripen and give life to hundreds of scraps of land. But for the time being this island was the first brick in the rebirth of the world of Chaos. For the time being I could leave the Primordial World and get on with my own business. That world would live. Together with the three shadows it would wait for me or another Dancer. I paid my debt to the shadows in full. . . .

I awoke, cautiously sat up, and looked around to try and figure out where I was. Everything suggested that this time I'd ended up in Zagraba. At least, this spot wasn't anything like Hrad Spein. Fir trees, golden-leafs, yellow grass, a blue sky above my head. By some miracle I had been transported out of the Palaces of Bone to the surface. Some prank of the Rainbow Horn's, no doubt.

The Horn! I felt all around myself in panic. Sagot be praised, the artifact was lying beside me, under the carpet of fallen leaves. I immediately put the relic away in my bag.

I turned over on my back and looked up at the sky through the half-naked branches of the golden-leafs.

Ah, Sagot bless me, how good this was! After those dark gloomy labyrinths with that musty smell of dead time, the sight of an ordinary sky filled me with childish delight. I didn't have a blind clue how I'd gotten back to Zagraba from Hrad Spein, but it was a good thing, even if I didn't know which part of the forest I was in, and how far away I was from the entrance where my friends were waiting for me.

Zagraba was good. A lot better than the Palaces of Bone. I could find some way to feed myself here, and the chances of running into serious trouble were incomparably smaller than underground. And to be quite honest, if I'd stayed in Hrad Spein, there would have been one more dead man in the catacombs, because I couldn't have coped with the return journey, especially without any maps. And so may all the gods be praised!

On the other hand, it was worth giving a little thought to where I actually was. I was in the Golden Forest in Zagraba, but where exactly, and how long would it take me to reach the group? But then, what was I saying? Reach the group . . . I didn't know where the gates of Hrad Spein were now, and wandering around Zagraba without knowing where you were going was like . . . well, wandering round Zagraba without knowing where you were going.

A stupid waste of time. And in addition, bearing in mind that I'd tramped darkness only knew how many leagues through the Palaces of Bone, and then been thrown out into Zagraba right above Grok's tomb, I would be walking to the gates of Hrad Spein for quite a long time. I had only one chance—to go northward and hope that I would emerge from the Golden Forest and find myself in more familiar territory, perhaps even somewhere inhabited. And then I could figure out what was what. And, of course, I could put my trust in Egrassa's amulet. It had saved me from the Kaiyu, and I could hope it would tell the elf where to look for me.

A large golden leaf traced a golden arc across the sky and landed precisely on my face. I removed the pestiferous object and flung it away. The leaves were falling. May the most revolting member of the family of demons devour me! It was only now I realized that while I was underground, September had come to an end. So it was only natural that the leaves were falling and the sky had turned that bottomless pale violet color.

Of course, this wasn't Avendoom, where it was already quite cold and there was torrential rain at the end of September, but even in Zagraba there was a faint breath of autumn in the air. I had to get out of the forest before the real rain and cold weather came, with the frosts to follow. With no cloak and just a sweater to keep me warm, sooner or later the cold would kill me.

Fortunately for me, although I was a city dweller, For had taught me all sorts of useful things, and I could tell which way was north. I ought to find a small animal track—walking along that would be a lot easier than forcing my way through the brush and dried grass. I was also a little concerned about the chances of coming across some swamp or running into a pack of wolves.

Zagraba was beautiful, as always.

The forest was dressed in its astoundingly brilliant autumn colours, reveling in the colors of decay—gold and fiery red. Bright yellow groves of redbrow that had already lost its blossom merged smoothly into golden groves of golden-leafs, and they gave way to fiery red splashes of Zagraban rowan and aspen. The blue leaves of tears-of-woe were like fantastic fairy-tale islands in autumn's golden kingdom. Only the gloomy, severe fir trees, with their dirty green color, rebelled against ubiquitous autumn and refused to join in the September festival. The ground was completely covered with a thick, undisturbed layer of fallen leaves. The air in the forest was still and quiet as the giant started falling asleep on the threshold of winter. I seemed to be completely alone in Zagraba.

I walked until nightfall and—miracle of miracles—didn't feel tired at all. I didn't find any track, but the walking was relatively easy. No fallen trees, no gorges, no swamps. Only one small stream cut across my path, winding through the massive roots of the golden-leafs.

It got dark quickly in the forest, and I barely had enough time to find myself a place to rest by the broken trunk of an old alder. Dim twilight descended and then in a single moment it was replaced by impenetrable darkness. The sky turned hazy, without a single star, and only the small copper coin of the full moon peeped through the haze, like a pale imitation of the moon that had shone in the sky in the middle of summer.

Although I was thoroughly sick of them, I had a snack of the fruits from the Cave of the Ants. I didn't feel like sleeping and I just sat there, gazing into the darkness of the forest at night. After a while, little colored lights started appearing on the trees nearby. The forest spirits were starting to wake up. It wasn't so lonely with the forest spirits for company, and I watched their blinking eyes until I was overcome by sleep.

———

I opened my eyes, stood up, and shivered. It was cool that morning. It had been worse at night. By the middle of it I was thoroughly chilled, and it was a miracle that I managed to get back to sleep again. If things went on like that, some night soon I'd freeze to death or catch a serious cold, as sure as eggs.

Judging from the mist clinging to the roots, it was early morning and the sun had only just risen. And I didn't much like the look of the sky—I hoped there wouldn't be any rain. Autumn rain is one of the vilest "pleasures" known to the traveling man.

Sagot be praised, there wasn't any rain all day long, and I covered quite a substantial stretch of the route through Zagraba. Toward evening I came across an animal track and my speed increased significantly. Neither Valder nor the Rainbow Horn gave any signs of life. It was funny really, there I was with one of the most powerful artifacts in the world, and it was no use to me at all. No warm clothing, no trusty crossbow, no food. It could at least have sent me straight to Avendoom and not made me trudge through the autumn undergrowth!

The path dove into tangled thickets of bushes that looked suspiciously like briars, and I stupidly decided to push my way straight through them, with the result that the whole of Zagraba must have heard me swearing. But when the undergrowth came to an end, the track led me out onto the shore of a small forest lake, with dried rushes growing all around and rusty brown water with small ripples running across it.

There was about an hour left before darkness fell, so I had time to find a more comfortable place to spend the night than the shore of the lake. On summer nights and mornings, water gives off a pleasant coolness, but in autumn it makes the air cold, and I certainly didn't want to get any colder than circumstances absolutely required. Unfortunately, there weren't any tracks leading away from the lake and I had to trudge on as best I could, with Sagot's help.

When I'd left the lake and a small bare ravine behind me, quite large bald spots began to appear in the forest, overgrown with low young pine trees. I walked through these as if I was out strolling along Parade Street, and I would have liked to spend the night in that spot. But my nose sounded the alarm—I caught the very faintest aroma of smoke mingling with the smell of autumn.

"Either it's a forest fire, or someone's lit a campfire," I muttered, backing against the trunk of the nearest pine tree and pulling out my knife.

Anyone else lost in the great Forests of Zagraba would have acted differently—he would have gone dashing toward the fire with whoops of joy, to meet the rational beings who had lit it, but I knew better. I wasn't going to make that mistake. The company of rational beings can be a lot more dangerous than being alone. There was no point in looking for trouble. First I had to reconnoiter properly, and then I could try shouting out: "Here I am, brothers!"

It could quite easily be a patrol of orc scouts or even worse—elf patrols that had infiltrated the orcs' territory. The Firstborn and the Secondborn were fond of a bit of quiet slaughter on each other's land. But at least I ought to find out who it was.

I had to advance, guided by a smell of smoke so faint that I could barely sense it. The bald spots came to an end and the forest around me was once again taken over by the majestic golden-leafs, together with low aspens and birches.

That meant I could see less, and now it was hard to make out what might be hidden behind the red and gold wall of leaves and the stockade of tree trunks. Add to the list of difficulties the onset of twilight, threatening to give way to another pitch-dark night at any moment, and things weren't looking very good. But the smell of smoke was growing stronger, and that told me I was going in the right direction.

A twig cracked treacherously under my foot. The crunch could hardly be heard, but I froze. Ah, that was bad timing! I could thank my thief's luck that I was still too far from the fire and I couldn't have been heard.

You ought to be more careful, Harold, I thought for the hundredth time, shifting the knife from my right hand to my left and wiping away the sweat that had suddenly appeared on my palm. It was a long time since I'd felt so nervous. I was just like a novice, preparing to rob his first passerby!

Finally the flames of a campfire blinked between the trunks of the trees. I darted over to the nearest golden-leaf, pressed myself back against the trunk, and started staring into the thickening twilight. The fire blinked again, trembled, disappeared, and then reappeared.

"Careful, Harold! Careful! Make haste slowly!"

Twilight had given way to night. The smell of food cooking, the smell of meat, which I hadn't tasted for a hundred years, tormented my mind and set my stomach gurgling. The fire lured me toward it, and I approached it cautiously, getting closer and closer. Quietly, inconspicuously.

When the fire was still about fifty yards away, I stopped, hiding behind another tree trunk. I tried hard to make out who was sitting round the fire, but I couldn't. The view from my cover wasn't very good, and I couldn't see anything but gleaming reflections of firelight.

I took a step forward and the sky immediately fell in on me, crashing down with all its weight on my back and burying my nose in the leaves. I jerked and tried to strike out blindly with my knife, but some excessively nimble individual was impolite enough to step on my hand.

I howled and unclenched my fingers. They were more precious to me than the knife. I tried to turn over, but I couldn't. There was no point in kicking out—the person who had dropped on me out of the tree was perched precisely on my shoulder blades, and I couldn't reach him with my feet. And I couldn't throw him off, either—the lousy skunk was really heavy.

I only stopped flapping about when a second enemy sat on my legs and twisted my left arm behind my back. I howled—the lad had almost twisted my arm out of its socket. Then it was my right arm's turn, but I'd already wised up and stopped resisting, so this time the procedure wasn't quite so painful.

Whoever it was sitting on my back didn't say anything, he just kept his huge paw on the back of my neck, making me breathe the smell of moldy leaves and damp earth. Meanwhile, the second one tied my wrists securely with rope. It was all done quickly and without a single word being spoken.

Wonderful! Eventually the one who was sitting on my legs got up, but his comrade grabbed me by the hair, jerked my head up, and then put something sharp and horribly cold against my throat. I thought it wisest to stare up at the sky and say nothing.

"Well, well, well," said the one who was standing. "It looks like a foolish moth has come fluttering to the flame. . . . Who have the forest spirits sent to our fire?"

"A little monkey, I think," said the one who was holding me by the hair.

"Turn him over."

I was turned over rather offhandedly, but just to make sure I didn't start thrashing about, a foot was prudently placed on my chest so that I could hardly draw breath.

I couldn't make out who was standing over me. They were just dark silhouettes. Either men, or elves, or orcs.

"It really is a monkey," chuckled the one who had turned me over. *"Karadr drag su'in tar?"*[Shall we dispatch him to the darkness?]

"Kro! Alle bar natish, kita'l u Bagard." [No! Let's take him to the fire. Bagard can get to the bottom of this.]

Darkness only knew what the lads were bantering about, but that language was definitely orcish. On the rational assumption that men were unlikely to chat in such a disgusting language, I struck them off the list. That only left elves and orcs. Meanwhile the two of them kept on yakking to each other, and one of them kept saying *"kro"* all the time, while the other kept mentioning some *"tara"* or other. The lads didn't seem able to agree about something. I tried to weigh in with my own sound opinion, and moved a little. The lad standing with his foot on me immediately pressed it down a bit harder and I gave a disappointed croak and shut up. Eventually the one who kept saying *"tara"* gave in.

"All right, what's one more or less? We'll take him." These words were spoken for my ears.

I was jerked to my feet.

"If you so much as twitch, little moth, you'll never reach the fire. We'll singe your wings for you right here. Is that clear, or do I have to hit you?"

"I understand."

"That's just great." I was pushed in the back rather impolitely. *"Misat'u no alddi Olag."* [Keep an eye on the moth, Olag.]

"Misat'a." [I'll keep an eye on him.]

What a fool. Somehow it hadn't even occurred to me that there could be listening posts and sentries around the fire.

Well, my captors were right—I had fluttered to the flame like a moth, and I'd got my wings singed.

13

IN CAPTIVITY

My companions were not distinguished by refined manners, and while the one who had been sitting on my legs merely hurried me along, the other one kept pushing me in the back so that I almost fell. Eventually we came out into the large forest clearing where the fire was burning. There were about ten men (or not men) sitting round the fire. A few more were standing or lying some distance away, and I simply wasn't able to count them. A large group.

"Ghei Bagard! Masat'u ner ashpa tut Olag'e perega!" [Hey, Bagard! Look who me and Olag have caught!] Hefty shouted.

The figures round the fire stirred and got to their feet. I was shoved closer to the fire. The lads who had captured me had dark skin, yellow eyes, black lips, fangs, and ash-gray hair.

"Elves!" I thought delightedly, and then I took a closer look and felt very, very disappointed. My fears had been justified. Of the two possible evils, I'd ended up with the worse one. Elves never gathered their hair into ponytails, elves weren't so heavily built, and elves never carried yataghans.

Firstborn! I'd fallen into the hands of the orcs! But I had been just a little bit lucky; the badges on the yellowish brown clothes of the Firstborn belonged to the clan of Walkers Along the Stream, and that was a lot better than running into the Grun Ear-Cutters. At least they wouldn't kill me straightaway.

"Where did you find this?" asked a short orc.

"He was wandering round the fire, Bagard," said Hefty's friend, switching into human language.

"Was the little monkey alone?"

"Yes. Before we took him, we checked the whole area. He was alone. Olag can confirm that."

Hefty's friend nodded. The orcs switched back into their own language, talking fast. I stood there like a sheep, waiting to see what would come of all this rigmarole. Bagard seemed to be in charge of this detachment; he spoke a few abrupt phrases and six Firstborn disappeared into the dark undergrowth.

"Weapons?" Bagard asked, switching back to human language.

Olag handed the commander my knife. Bagard twirled it in his hands impassively and handed it to one of the orcs standing beside him.

"Is that all, Fagred?" The Firstborn seemed a little surprised.

"Yes," said Hefty, nodding.

"Have you searched him?"

"Kro."

"He doesn't look much like a warrior," said one of the orcs.

"We'll soon find out, bring him over to the fire!"

Fagred and Olag grabbed me by the arms and dragged me to the fire. Naturally enough, I thought they were going to roast the soles of my feet,

and I started to resist, but the orc who had taken my knife hit me hard under the ribs and I suddenly didn't feel like resisting anymore. The only concern I had now was trying to breathe. They sat me down by the fire and
Fagred started asking questions.

"Who are you? How many of you are there? What are you doing in our
forest?"

The orc backed up each question with a resounding slap to my face.
Bearing in mind the size of his mitts—and the orc was every bit as big as
Honeycomb—I felt justified in worrying whether my head could take the
strain. Unfortunately, I didn't get a chance to answer, because the slaps
rained down on me as fast as the questions. And the questions followed one
another at a very brisk rate indeed. When Fagred started asking them for
the fifth time, growing more and more enraged at my silence, Bagard's
voice interrupted.

"That's enough!"

Fagred muttered discontentedly and walked away.

"Search him."

They stood me on my feet again, took my bag, and rummaged adroitly
through my clothes.

"*Nedl kro.*" [Nothing there.]

"I told you he didn't look like a warrior," one of the orcs muttered, and
threw some fir-tree branches into the fire.

By this time the six warriors sent to reconnoiter by Bagard had come
back. One of the Firstborn shook his head and put an arrow back in his
quiver.

"If he doesn't look like a warrior . . ." Bagard's yellow eyes studied me
intently. "Shokren, check this monkey!"

An orc walked out of the shadow, and I turned cold—the lad was wearing a strange headdress that looked far too much like a shaman's cap. And a
shaman was just what I needed to make my day complete! Shokren resembled Bagard in some elusive way; they must have been relatives. The shaman
came over and ran his open palm over me without touching me.

"His neck," Shokren murmured, and someone's deft hands relieved me of
Kli-Kli's drop-shaped medallion. The shaman nodded contentedly. "The
left arm."

Egrassa's bracelet joined Kli-Kli's medallion on the ground.

Shokren took his hand down to the level of my boots and said, "That's
all, he's clean."

"What are these trinkets?" asked Olag, twirling the bracelet of red copper in his hands.

"That's a long story," said Shokren, putting the droplet medallion away in his bag. Then he took the bracelet out of Olag's hands.

He held it for a while, studying it closely, then threw it on the grass and said, "Everybody get back!"

The orcs obediently stepped away and Olag took it on himself to take care of me and dragged me with him. Meanwhile the shaman muttered something, formed the fingers of his left hand into a complicated sign, and Egrassa's bracelet melted, turning into a small puddle on the ground.

"They won't find you now, little monkey," the shaman sneered.

"A leash?" Bagard asked Shokren with a knowing air.

"Yes."

"The inferior ones?

"Probably."

The inferior ones? Unless I was mistaken, that was what the Firstborn called the elves. Anyway, now it would be rather difficult for Egrassa to find me.

"So our moth is mixed up with that bunch, is he?" Fagred said with an ominous leer.

"Give me his bag," the shaman suddenly said.

One of the Firstborn immediately handed my bag to Shokren. Do I need to say what happened when the shaman took the Rainbow Horn out of it? Naturally, the ordinary orcs didn't understand a thing, but Shokren, Bagard, and Olag exchanged pointed glances. And the shaman's hands were actually shaking.

"What is it?" asked Fagred, craning his neck.

"It's something that will help the Hand in his battle with the inferior ones," Bagard said reverently. "Remember this day, warriors."

"Well done, moth!" Olag said with a crooked sneer. "What other treasures have you brought for us?"

Shokren carefully set the Horn down on a cloak that one of the warriors had spread out, and turned his attention back to my bag. The handful of fruit was flung aside disdainfully, and then the Key emerged from the bag. The dragon's tear glinted in the light of the campfire and the Firstborn all gasped as one in wonder and delight. They seemed to know what the shaman was clutching in his hand. He took the relic between his finger and thumb, as if he was afraid it might simply disappear.

"The Key to the Doors!" one of the warriors gasped.

"Correct. But how did a man come to have the inferior ones' relic?" said Shokren, looking at me. "Have you been in Hrad Spein?"

"Yes." I couldn't see any point in lying.

"Is that from there?" the shaman asked, nodding at the Horn.

"Yes."

"All right." The shaman seemed to be quite satisfied with my monosyllabic answers.

"Has the moth brought us any more presents?" Fagred inquired.

The shaman turned my bag upside down without saying anything, and an emerald rain cascaded down onto the orcish cloak. One of the Firstborn cleared his throat quietly.

"What shall we do with him, Bagard?" Fagred asked.

The commander of the detachment shrugged indifferently.

"We don't need any extra mouths."

The huge orc gave a knowing chuckle and put his hand on his knife.

"Wait, Bagard," said Shokren, unhurriedly putting all the treasures back into the bag. "This little monkey's not as simple as he seems. When we have time, I'll have a talk with him, and I think the Hand will, too."

"The Hand is far away," Bagard said with a frown.

For some reason the orcs didn't seem to want to talk their own language.

"I'll send him a message by raven, he can decide what to do with all these things. In any case, the moth will make a good wager at the mid-autumn festival. Put the little monkey with the others."

"All right," Bagard agreed, and started speaking in orcish.

The Firstborn seemed to have lost all interest in me; they talked excitedly, and started rearranging themselves round the fire. The shaman hung my bag over his shoulder, and I thought that now he wouldn't part with it even if he was attacked by all the dark elves in the Black Forest.

Curses! Now the orcs had the Rainbow Horn and the Key! If Egrassa found out, he'd be devastated; he'd have an apoplectic fit. The orcs didn't seem to be paying any attention to me, and I decided to risk it and take off. Running around Zagraba with my hands tied behind my back would be better than staying in the company of the Firstborn.

Well, of course, every stupid mistake has to be paid for, and I paid for mine. Fagred had kept his eye on me all the time, and I only got six yards. That lousy yellow-eyed skunk overtook me, knocked me off my feet, and smashed his fist into the back of my head so hard that five moons flared up in front of my eyes and I passed out.

"Leave him, none of us is going to live very long anyway."

"That's my business. Get me some water, man."

I felt something cold and incredibly pleasant on my forehead. It seemed like a good idea to open my eyes.

"Welcome back."

I stared at the speaker in amazement. I didn't think I was dreaming, but I was still having visions. Or was it a dream after all?

"Kli-Kli, is that you?" I wheezed, trying to sit up.

I shouldn't have done that. The ground and the trees started spinning around, and I collapsed on the bed of fir branches with a groan.

"You're mistaken, son," the goblin chuckled, and took the wet cloth off my forehead.

Yes, I could see for myself now that it wasn't Kli-Kli. This goblin was much older than my royal jester. His green skin was duller and a lighter green, he had bushy eyebrows and a hooked nose, half his teeth were missing, and his eyes weren't light blue but violet. In general he looked like a wrinkled little green monkey.

"I . . ."

"It was rather stupid of you to try to escape from the Firstborn. I'm absolutely amazed that huge brute didn't kill you. How are you?"

"My head hurts," I said, wincing, and made a second attempt to get up. This time I managed it, and the ground didn't even spin.

"Don't worry, they'll lop your head off soon, and then nothing'll hurt," someone beside me said, coughing.

I made the effort to squint sideways and saw the speaker. He was a huge man with a black beard growing right up to his eyes. He returned my gaze defiantly and started coughing again.

"That's Kior," the goblin explained, and I didn't hear any love for this shaggy natural wonder in his voice. "And this is Mis."

There was a skinny man about forty-five years old sitting beside Kior. Bald, with brown eyes and a mustache. His right shoulder was bandaged up in a slapdash fashion. He gave me a friendly nod.

"Welcome to our unfortunate little group, lad."

"A warrior?" I asked, finding the strength from somewhere to nod back.

"Yes," Mis replied, and closed his eyes.

How had a warrior from the Border Kingdom ended up out here in the wild?

"Do you have a name?" the goblin asked me.

"Harold."

"And I'm Glo-Glo," the goblin said with a grin. "Pleased to meet you."

Morning was waking over Zagraba, but there wasn't much light because the sky was blanketed with clouds, and it was about to start raining at any moment. How long had I been out, then? All night? That Fagred had a heavy hand, all right! There was a dull throbbing pain in the back of my head and I winced as I put my left hand to it. That was when I realized my hands weren't tied anymore.

"There's no need," the goblin said as if he was reading my thoughts. "Where can you run to? Look over there."

I looked in the direction the goblin had indicated. And saw a man suspended by the legs dangling from a branch of the nearest tree.

"That's Kior's partner," Glo-Glo explained cheerily. "Yesterday he got it into his head to run off, so they hung him up there to teach the rest of us a lesson. And they slit his belly open for good measure."

"Why don't you shut up and keep quiet, greeny!" said Kior, and his eyes flashed angrily.

"I've kept quiet long enough, no more!" The goblin sat down beside me and started whispering in my ear.

"Take no notice of him, Harold. Kior's a poacher, he hunts golden cats in the orcs' territory, and the Firstborn caught him. Actually, they caught him yesterday, about three hours before you turned up."

"I see," I muttered.

"But how do you come to be in Zagraba?"

"I was just taking a stroll," I chuckled.

Glo-Glo sighed. "You can tell Kior you were out for a stroll. Do you think I didn't see what the Firstborn took out of your bag?"

"How do you know what those things were?" I asked curiously.

"I just happen to be a shaman."

I cleared my throat doubtfully.

"Shamans don't get caught by the orcs that easily."

"As long as they stay alert, that is," Glo-Glo sighed regretfully. "I really am a shaman, though."

"Then what are you doing here?"

I figured that if the goblin was a shaman, he ought to have been able to find some way to do a vanishing act.

"The same as you. Look." The goblin showed me his hands, and they were covered with mittens.

Strange mittens they were, too, I must say. At least, each one had a restraining chain and a lock, so they looked a bit like manacles. Taking them off would be pretty hard. Although they were rubbishy locks, and I thought I could have picked them if I really tried. The mittens had runes drawn on them, too.

"What are they for?"

"So I can't work any spells," the shaman groaned miserably. "The mittens restrict the movements of my fingers, and the runes prevent magic from working, so spells are out of the question. I can try, but the forest spirits only know what will actually happen."

"And some people still claim that shamanism is better than wizardry!" I muttered.

"Just give me time. I'll get my hands free, and then they'll be dancing to my tune!" the goblin hissed, narrowing his eyes and peering at the orcs.

"If they don't cut your hands off first," Mis said encouragingly.

"They won't do that," the goblin said, waving one hand blithely in the air. "I don't have anything to worry about until the mid-autumn festival."

"And then what happens?" I asked.

"You'll see," snapped Glo-Glo.

Meanwhile it had started to rain, and that's never the most pleasant start to a morning. The camp was gradually waking up. Despite the rain, the orcs relit the fire. The Firstborn went about their business, and we sat in the rain and got soaked. An idyllic scene. Two hours went by like that, and despite the continuous drizzle, I somehow managed to doze off. I was woken by Glo-Glo poking me violently in the ribs.

"It's started," said Mis, and added a foul oath.

"What's started?" I asked, confused, but none of my comrades in misfortune saw fit to answer me.

They were all staring at the center of the clearing. Since I hadn't been given any explanations, I started watching the orcs bustling about, too. Some were dousing the campfire, some were hastily packing up their things. Two of them dragged a huge tree stump out of the forest—what on earth was that for?

"How many of them are there?"

"How many of who?" Mis was kind enough to reply.

"The orcs."

"Nineteen. They're an advance detachment, they were pursuing dark ones."

"Dark ones?" I asked.

"Dark elves. A detachment of elves was running riot in the orcs' territory and Bagard's unit set off in pursuit. In the end they caught the elves and all of us as well," Glo-Glo said, and spat.

"They caught elves?" I was definitely very slow on the uptake today. But then that quite often happens when someone applies something heavy to my head.

"Well, not all of them . . ." Glo-Glo drawled, watching Fagred set the stump in the center of the clearing. "Only those who were unfortunate enough not to be killed in the fight. And there they are."

Eight orcs pushed four elves out from behind the tree that one of the prisoners was hanging on. They were too far away for me to make out the prisoners' faces and the crests of their houses, but one of them was definitely a woman. The elves weren't a very pretty sight; they looked as if they'd spent the night in a room crammed full of deranged cats. The Secondborn were bruised and battered, they'd been worked over really well. One of the elves could hardly walk, and two of his comrades had to support him. The dark ones were led out into the middle of the clearing, where all the orcs were gathered together, and Bagard gave a brisk nod.

"What are they going to do with them?" I asked, although I already knew the answer.

The executions were bloody and swift. The orcs didn't bother with subtle tortures. The Firstborn simply set each of the elves on the improvised block by turn and the huge Fagred chopped their dark heads off with his ax. The orcs watched the executions impassively, and when it was all over, they dragged the bodies across to the dead man hanging on the tree.

"Well, that's over," said the goblin, clearing his throat.

"Not quite, I think," Mis hissed.

I followed his glance and my stomach turned to ice. Bagard was directing some of the Firstborn to our hushed little group. Three warriors separated off from the detachment.

"I won't let them take me that easily," the Border Kingdom warrior muttered. "They can find themselves another sheep to slaughter."

Mis was clutching a short pointed stick in his hand. I had no idea where he'd got it from, but it could easily be used to strike at an eye or a neck. The question was, would the orcs give him a chance to do it?

Two of the warriors came over to us, and I pulled in my feet in case Mis decided to try something and I had to kick the nearest orc. But the First-born took no notice of me or Mis, they just grabbed Kior and dragged him off toward the block. The trapper kept yelling and trying to break free until the third orc smashed the shaft of his spear into his stomach.

"Why him?" I asked in a hoarse voice.

"He's a poacher," Glo-Glo said reluctantly. "When they caught him, they found several gold cat skins. And to the orcs a poacher is as bad as a wood-cutter."

They dragged Kior, howling, to the block, but they didn't put him on it, just stretched him out on the grass as if they were going to quarter him, and Fagred raised his terrible ax. Two quick blows—and the poacher's howls were reduced to a wheeze.

"Sagot save us," I muttered, and turned away.

The orc had cut off both of the man's arms at the shoulder.

"Sagot won't be much help here," said Mis. "What's needed is twenty of our lads from the Forest Cats brigade, with their bows. . . ."

Kior had gone quiet. None of the orcs even thought about binding up the appalling wounds, and the poacher bled to death very quickly—and if the gods were merciful, he lost consciousness immediately. Meanwhile the orcs had hung the elves' headless bodies up beside Kior's friend, and now they were setting the dark ones' heads on spears stuck into the ground.

Olag walked across, looked intently at all three of us, and said: "Take a look at the hanging meat and remember: The same thing will happen to you if even one of you tries to get away. Do you understand me, little monkeys?"

"Don't think we're more stupid than you are, orc," Glo-Glo said, cough-ing. "We're not stupid, we understand."

The shaman didn't seem to be at all worried that the Firstborn would hurt him. Olag chuckled and looked at the goblin as if he was seeing him for the first time.

"Well, since you understand everything, greeny, get the monkeys ready to leave, we're moving on."

And he walked away.

"Where are we moving on to?" I asked, shuddering in the cursed drizzle pouring down from the sky.

"Somewhere else," the goblin muttered vaguely, and wrapped himself up in his cloak.

Any thought of escape was absolutely out of the question. The three of us were put in the center of the line, which made running off without being seen a pretty difficult proposition. And then, how could I forget that Olag was striding along behind us, crooning a little song to himself, and Fagred was there, too, with his ax. He made me feel distinctly nervous, because every time our eyes met, the orc smiled wistfully and stroked his terrible weapon.

It was clear enough what the lad had on his mind. He wouldn't be happy until he could chop my head off. I had to try to put off the time when he could have that pleasure for as long as possible.

Fortunately, the rain stopped, but I still wasn't warm and dry enough to feel comfortable. My teeth chattered and I shuddered and prayed to the gods to drive away the clouds and let us have some sunshine. I knew I had to keep going, keep myself alive—I wouldn't have Miralissa's sacrifice be in vain . . . I wouldn't let that happen. Little Glo-Glo ambled along in front of me, coughing, grunting, and swearing quietly to himself. The orcs seemed to find this amusing.

"Hey, lad!" Mis called to me.

"What?" I asked without turning round—no point in attracting unnecessary attention from the Firstborn.

"You mentioned Sagot. Are you a thief, then?"

"Bull's-eye," I said, stepping over a thick branch lying on the animal track.

"How did you end up here?"

"No talking, monkeys!" Fagred roared. "You can talk as much as you like at the halt!"

I shut up—I already knew that Fagred had no sense of humor and Olag wasn't the most patient orc in the world.

Bagard led the detachment to the south, into the heart of Zagraba. I couldn't exactly say we strolled through the forest, but we certainly weren't in any great hurry. Even Glo-Glo, with his short legs, was able to keep up with the pace set by the orcs.

But to give Bagard his due, he wasn't careless at all, and there were always several orcs walking ahead of us, scouting out the territory for any possible problems like elfin bowmen or a h'san'kor taking a doze. Shokren tramped past, hurrying up to the head of our little column. The shaman had a huge raven perched on his shoulder. I gazed longingly at my bag dangling at the orc's side. Shokren noticed my interest and frowned. I saw the shaman over-take Bagard and say something to him, pointing to me. Bagard nodded thoughtfully and stopped, waiting for me to hobble up to him.

When I drew level with him, he said, "My brother told me we ought to give you a jacket."

I must admit, I didn't know what to make of that.

"I'd be very grateful," I said cautiously.

"I don't need any monkey's gratitude," the orc snapped. "You're inferior beings, and the most amusing thing is that you don't even realize it. *Fagred, skell drago s'i llost!*" [Fagred, give him your jacket!]

Darkness only knew what Bagard had barked, but Fagred moaned dis-contentedly behind me: *"Prza? Shedo t'na gkhonu!"* [What for? He's going to croak anyway.]

"Not yet. The Hand might have some use for him, or do you want the monkey to freeze to death on the way?"

The huge orc immediately stopped arguing and a minute later he handed me a leather jacket with a hood that he had fished out of his shoulder bag. It turned out to have a fur lining as well. This was a day full of surprises! Of course, the jacket was a bit bigger than necessary, but, naturally enough, I didn't complain. I started feeling warmer straightaway. But the expression in Fagred's eyes somehow didn't suggest that he was overjoyed about sacrificing his jacket.

We made three halts to rest. Once they actually fed us, and then drove us back onto the track. By the time evening came we'd covered quite a dis-tance, and when Bagrad halted the detachment for the night, I collapsed on the ground.

"It's not sleeping time yet, little monkey!" said Fagred, planting a painful kick in my side. "First you have to make up your bed."

I had to get up, grinding my teeth in anger at the orc, and scrape the fallen leaves together into a heap. Then Mis and I were told to break branches off the fir trees, and after that the orcs left me alone. Shokren showed up, made a few passes with his hands, and cleared off again.

"What was that?"

"A kind of alarm," Glo-Glo explained reluctantly. "If you step outside the circle, there'll be a loud noise, and all the orcs will come running."

Darkness fell. The orcs lit a campfire and seemed to forget about us. And why shouldn't they? Shokren's magic did all their work for them. Then the Firstborn started cooking supper, and I started drooling. But surprisingly enough, when the food was ready, Olag and another orc came over, and they left us a decent serving of meat and a flask of water. So, the Firstborn certainly weren't planning to starve us to death.

We got talking as we ate. Glo-Glo started pestering me about the Rainbow Horn, and I had to give the pushy little goblin the short, edited version of the adventure. The old shaman seemed satisfied with my story and he left me in peace.

"And how did you get here, Mis?" I asked the Border Kingdom warrior when we finished our food.

"Well, these . . . ," the elderly warrior began reluctantly, nodding toward the Firstborn. "Do you know what a long-distance raid is?"

"I have a good idea," I answered. "Isn't it something like that game the Wild Hearts play when they march all the way to the Needles of Ice?"

"That's it," Mis agreed morosely. "The very thing. But for us a long-distance raid is an outing to the Golden Forest to see if the orcs are behaving themselves or if they're thinking of getting up to some of their tricks. Well, anyway, me and the lads got into a fine mess. This lot dropped down on us out of the trees like overripe pears and finished everyone off like sitting ducks before we even had time to say boo. But that sorcerer of theirs tied me in a knot. Just for the fun of it."

"I see," I said sympathetically. "Glo-Glo, you still haven't told me why they want us alive and where they're taking us."

"Why they need you alive is obvious enough. They're going to have a serious talk with you. But they want us alive to amuse themselves with, though I think you'll probably suffer the same fate," the goblin replied, lounging back on the fir-tree branches.

"What do you mean?"

"As if you couldn't guess!" Glo-Glo cackled merrily.

"Believe it or not, but I don't understand a thing."

"They're taking us to the Labyrinth. The Labyrinth, lad! Have you heard of it?"

"Yes, I have," I said, frightened out of my wits.

"He has," the goblin teased me. "These yellow-eyed rats have their midautumn festival soon. And what kind of festival would it be without a goblin in the Labyrinth? Do you think they're kind-hearted, just because they haven't killed us all yet? They're saving me for their shitty Labyrinth, that's why they'll put up with any crap I throw at them."

"Hey you! Monkeys! Have you eaten? Then sleep, we're marching again tomorrow!" one of the sentries growled.

It was the middle of the night, and I still couldn't get to sleep—that was obviously the effect of the news that they were going to stick us in the Labyrinth.

The Rainbow Horn was in the hands of the orcs, I was a prisoner, the somber prospect of the Labyrinth was looming on the horizon, and my friends and brothers-in-arms couldn't come to my rescue because the shaman had melted my bracelet. Trying to escape was impossible, at least as long as Shokren and Fagred were around. And where would I run to anyway? There was thick forest on every side, and the orcs were at home here, they'd find me in no time, and then it would be good-bye, Harold. And the shaman would still have the Horn. . . . What did that leave? All I could do was wait for my chance and hope that fortune would smile on me. I fell asleep, still trying to console myself with this pale illusion of hope.

The next day was no different from the one before. The lousy drizzle was still falling, but I was feeling quite comfortable, because Fagred's jacket protected me against the whimsies of the autumn weather. We tramped on through the yellow and red forest that still hadn't fully woken from its slumber.

"I hope there's going to be a halt soon," said Mis, who was walking behind me. He spat, earning himself a dig from Fagred.

"Tired, little monkeys?" the orc inquired. "Just let me know and I'll put an end to your suffering. Forever."

Naturally, no one thought of answering him. No one wanted another clout from that massive brute.

"It'll be dark in half an hour," Mis muttered.

"We're almost there," said the goblin, rubbing his aching back. "You'll see for yourselves in a moment."

Less than ten minutes later, the bushes gave way to red maples, then they gave way to mighty oaks. The rocks stopped looking like rocks and started looking like ruins. And a few minutes after that I was walking through a city, although that city was in a far worse state than Chu.

All that was left on the ground were the skeletal outlines of the old foundations of buildings and massive blocks and slabs of stone scattered around among the trees. I didn't see a single complete building. I only saw a fallen column once, more than half buried in the ground. We reached a point with oaks growing so close it was like a solid wall, and I had to squeeze through between the trunks to get into the center of the ring formed by the trees.

Another of nature's jokes, or had these trees been planted by someone's caring hands? This place reminded me very much of the ring of golden-leafs at the entrance to Hrad Spein. If I'd been wandering around here on my own, without the orcs keeping a keen eye on me, I'd never have guessed anything could be hiding behind the trees.

Right in the center the wide clearing that was overgrown with young oak saplings, there was a round raised stone platform, with a tall, brilliant-white, needle-like obelisk growing up out of it. It seemed to absorb the light from all around, and even against the background of majestic oaks it looked absolutely perfect.

"The only thing that has survived in this city," said Glo-Glo, nodding indifferently toward the building, with no sign of the admiration that Mis and I felt at the sheer beauty of the place. "Time has reduced everything else to rubble."

"Is this the city of Bu?" I asked the old goblin, remembering what Kli-Kli had once told me.

"No, this is the Nameless City," Glo-Glo replied. "But how do you know about the city of Bu?"

"A goblin I know enlightened me."

"Ah, yes, some people have goblin friends. What did you say his name was? Kli-Kli?"

"Yes."

"And where is he now?"

"Somewhere near the entrance to the Palaces of Bone."

Glo-Glo frowned discontentedly, but he didn't say anything.

We prisoners had been seated right at the edge of the circle of oaks, and Shokren had traced out his magical circle again so that we wouldn't—may the gods forbid—slink off. Nobody intended to let the monkeys go near the obelisk. A pity. I really wanted to touch that strange stone. I could physically feel the warmth radiating from it.

"Glo-Glo, do you know who built this wonder?" I asked the goblin, who was already settling down for the night.

"Those who were here before the orcs and the ogres," the shaman answered. "Let's sleep, I don't think they're going to feed us today."

Glo-Glo was wrong. Exactly an hour later they brought us food and—may the gods of Siala save me—wine! Genuine orcish wine, which not many men have ever tried.

So when it got dark, we had a real little feast. Olag was even kind enough to bring a torch on a long pole and set it up beside our prison with no walls or bars.

"The Firstborn have even decided to give us light for our meal," said Glo-Glo as he chomped on the food (he'd woken up in an instant when it arrived).

"Wait!" snorted Mis, sniffing at the wine in the flask. "This is to make it easier to keep an eye on us!"

"The man's no fool!" Glo-Glo chuckled, stuffing a huge piece of meat into his mouth.

"Why are they so generous all of a sudden?" I asked, looking at the obelisk glowing in the darkness.

That was a real sight, let me tell you!

"We're valuable prisoners. And tomorrow we don't have to walk. We'll probably hang about here for at least six days. We can relax."

"But how do you know all that, greeny?" asked Mis, handing me the flask. I nodded in thanks.

"I'm a shaman, after all," the goblin said resentfully. "Two hours ago, just after the swamp, a raven arrived with a message for Shokren."

"Can you read at a distance, too?" I asked in amazement.

"Of course not!" Glo-Glo retorted. "But we goblins have good hearing. Much better than you hulking brutes. I heard Shokren telling Bagard about it. Basically, the instructions were to lead the detachment into the Nameless City and wait at the Obelisk of the Ancients for another detachment to arrive. And that detachment is still at Bald Hills, so they have to walk for at least six days to get here."

"By the way, you don't happen to know how far it is from here to the Eastern Gates of Hrad Spein, do you?" I asked the shaman, trying to sound casual.

Glo-Glo shot a quick glance at me from under his knitted brows and answered, "If you mean in your leagues, I don't know; I don't understand your distances. But in days . . . well, you'd be tramping for two full weeks or more, but I'd get there in a week and a half, if I really wanted to. And the orcs and elves could do it in a week, if they were desperate. Do you think your friends are still waiting for you?"

I shrugged. "Even if they are, they think I'm still underground."

"Or dead," Glo-Glo said to cheer me up. "Your bracelet's been destroyed, and the one who gave it to you might think you're deceased."

"Couldn't you get a message to them?" I asked the goblin, hoping the shaman would work a miracle for me on the spot.

"How? Ask a little bird, or a moth? Things like that only happen in fairy tales. Come on, let's get some sleep. We can talk as much as we want tomorrow. It's almost midnight."

Nightmares are the bane of my life. And after Hrad Spein there wasn't a night that passed without some beastly horror descending on me. That night I dreamed I was back in the room with the ceiling moving down, only this time there was no hole in the floor, and all I could do was run from one corner to the other, waiting to be flattened.

I woke up. Judging from the moon, there were still about three hours to go until dawn. The torch left by Olag had gone out, and no one had thought to replace it with a new one. Four campfires were blazing away merrily in the clearing, and the obelisk was giving off quite enough light for me to see the orcs lying around here and there. The only one not sleeping was the one tending the fires.

Everyone was asleep, and it would have been a magnificent chance to escape, if not for Shokren's cursed magical circle. I wondered if Glo-Glo could have broken the orc shaman's magic, if he didn't have the mittens on his hands. I'd been pondering a crazy idea for two days, thinking about freeing the old goblin from his magical shackles. Unfortunately, on closer inspection, the locks holding the mittens on the goblin's hands had proved to be pretty tricky, and there was no way I could ever get them open with an ordinary sliver of wood. I needed some thin piece of metal, and neither I nor Mis nor Glo-Glo happened to have a little trinket like that. There was nothing I could do but wait for a stroke of luck that would allow me to open the miniature locks.

Purely by chance, I happened to glance at the remains of our meal, and my jaw dropped open. Sitting there on a piece of fried salmon was a dragoatfly. And nearby there was a flinny, struggling to open the tightly closed top of the flask of wine. My heart started pounding furiously. Whatever I did, I mustn't frighten him off!

I cautiously propped myself up my elbow and whispered, "Hey, flinny!"

He jumped and swung round, pulling out his miniature dagger. The dragoatfly also abandoned its meal and flew across to its master, trembling slightly. Unfortunately, this flinny was a stranger and he didn't look anything at all like Aarroo g'naa Shpok. Even the little fellow's curly hair was black, not gold.

"Push off, beanpole!" the flinny said, waving his ridiculous little weapon menacingly.

"I didn't think flinnies were thieves."

"I'm no thief!" the lad exclaimed resentfully. "This food doesn't belong to anyone!"

I clicked my tongue reproachfully. "It belongs to me, and you know that perfectly well."

"Oh, all right!" the flinny growled irritably, mounting his dragoatfly.

"Wait!" I whispered hurriedly.

"What do you want?" he asked rather impolitely, but the dragoatfly stopped and hovered in the air.

I struggled desperately to find the right words. "I want you to take a message for me."

"No way!" the little squirt snorted. "I don't want anything to do with your lot!"

"I'll pay!"

"No way! What could a prisoner have that's worth anything, when the orcs search him five times a day?"

But the little rotter was still in no hurry to fly off. He waited. Just in case I might suddenly manage to find something. . . . And I did find something. Shokren had missed the gift from the dead elfin king. Perhaps he hadn't sensed it, or perhaps the ring didn't have any magical powers, and the heartbeat in the black diamond was just some kind of trick. Whatever the reason, the ring had been on my hand all the time, hidden under my glove. But now I would have to part with it.

It was a shame to let the precious thing go when I'd had it for such a short time, but at least now I could put the dead king's gift to good use. I remembered Kli-Kli saying that flinnies were crazy about all sorts of rings. I took the glove off my hand and even now, in the light of the white obelisk and the cold moon, the little light was still flickering in the depths of the stone, following the crazy rhythm of my heart.

"Oo-oo-ooh!" the flinny exclaimed in a surprisingly shrill voice.

The little creature couldn't take his eyes off the ring. I sat down, and the dragoatfly landed at my feet. I took the ring off my finger and rolled it in my hand, allowing the black diamond to catch the sparse rays of moonlight and transform them into a spectacular display of icy flame. I think the flinny was in a state of absolute ecstasy.

"Is that valuable enough for you to do a simple little job?"

The lad pulled himself together enough to nod, but he didn't take his eyes off the prize.

"I am Iirroo z'maa Olok of the Branch of the Lake Butterfly. What do I have to do for this?"

"Can you free us and lead us away without the orcs noticing anything?"

"No," he said with a sigh of regret. "Perhaps there is something else I can do for you?"

The flinny was politeness itself.

"I will give you the ring, if you will deliver a message."

"Agreed! What is it, who is it for, and where are they?" the little news peddler rattled off.

"Fly to the Eastern Gates of Hrad Spein, find Egrassa of the House of the Black Moon or Milord Alistan Markauz, and tell them that that Harold is alive, and a prisoner of the Firstborn. The orcs also have the Horn, and they are taking me to the Labyrinth. And also tell them where you met me. Is that clear?"

The flinny repeated every single word like a parrot. I nodded and put the ring down on the ground. The dragoatfly immediately landed on the precious item, and the flinny, hurrying in case I changed my mind, tied the ring to the belly of his little flying mount.

I watched all the details and, to be quite honest, I felt a bit nervous. The doubts gnawing at my heart were perfectly understandable—the lad had been paid in advance, but would he do the job or just fly straight home, and then laugh with his relatives at how smartly he'd diddled one of the beanpoles?

Something must have shown in my face, because the flinny cast a quick glance at me and chuckled sympathetically.

"Relax, man. We always do the job, that's professional etiquette."

What damn fancy words he knew! Well, if it was "professional etiquette," I definitely could relax.

"They might not be at the gate."

"It wouldn't be the first time," the flinny said with a nonchalant shrug. "I'll look around for them. How long ago could they have left?"

I reckoned it up.

"Three or four days."

"Excellent! Good health, man!"

"When will you reach the entrance to Hrad Spein?"

"At noon today," the flinny replied. Seeing my look of amazement, he chuckled. "We have our own little secrets when it comes traveling round Zagraba, otherwise the news we carry would be too old to have any value."

"Hurry, flinny."

"Don't teach a cock to crow, man! What you have given me is priceless, so, out of simple politeness, after I find your friends, I'll warn the right people. Forward, Lozirel!"

Before I could even ask who the flinny had decided to warn, the dragoatfly had disappeared into the night sky, bearing away the tiny little rider and my great big hope.

"Let's hope the flinny will find your friends and they can get us out of this in time," said a voice behind me. I started and swung round.

Glo-Glo was gazing at me with a mocking smile. The old goblin had been awake all the time I was talking to the flinny.

In the thieves' profession, one of the indisputable virtues is being able to wait. On the roof of a building, in a dark, dusty cubbyhole, up to your throat in shit—it doesn't matter where you are or who you're waiting for, but if you're patient, you'll always be lucky. So after the flinny flew off, I tried to put him out of my mind, otherwise the time would have dragged catastrophically slowly.

Four days went by, and the orcs still weren't thinking of leaving. The Firstborn didn't pay any attention to us, except for Olag checking to make sure we weren't getting up to anything, and Fagred casting dark glances in our direction. It's no secret that all our knowledge of orcs is based on idle fantasy and legend. Not many of the authors of scholarly works on the race of the Firstborn have actually seen any Firstborn in the flesh. And so in my mind (especially after my brief encounter with orcs in the cabbage field and in certain waking dreams), the Firstborn were cruel, coarse, unrefined creatures, and all in all . . .

All in all, their personalities were so much like elves' that sometimes I was absolutely amazed. But then, what was so very astonishing? They were close relatives, the darkness take them! The only difference was that the orcs couldn't bear even the smell of outsiders and thought all other races were greatly inferior to themselves.

I personally had been expecting them to keep us on starvation rations, give us a thrashing every day, stick red-hot needles under our fingernails, and commit other similar atrocities. But that wasn't the way things were at all—no one had any intention of touching us (a couple of pokes from Fagred didn't really count), they fed us remarkably well, and our food was exactly the same as what they ate, although we didn't get us any more wine.

The weather improved, the wind carried the clouds away to the south, toward the Mountains of the Dwarves, and once again the sky had that astounding autumn blueness that harmonized so well with the yellow leaves of the trees. And it got a bit warmer, too. It was probably the last, or perhaps second-to-last, more or less warm week in the year.

Ravens arrived for Shokren twice, but we could only guess at what was in the messages that were delivered. Glo-Glo spent all day huddled up under his old patched cloak, replying sarcastically to our questions or making meaningless remarks about my conversations with Mis. The old shaman's main occupation was mumbling to himself. Either the old goblin had gone completely gaga, or he was preparing some kind of spell, despite the mittens. The second assumption was probably the right one, since Glo-Glo shut up the moment any of the orcs appeared, and when Shokren's face hove into sight on the horizon, the old shaman pretended to be asleep.

At first Mis wasn't much inclined to make heart-to-heart conversation, but after a while the man from the Borderland proved to be a fine conversation partner. The warrior's wound was gradually closing up and the orcs paid him absolutely unheard-of attention by giving him a clean rag and some kind of ointment to help it heal. Glo-Glo stuck his nose in the ointment, seemed satisfied with the result, and advised Mis to change the bandage as often as possible, then he went back to playing his whispering games.

On the fifth day Olag came over with Fagred, who was smiling and had a coil of rope in his hands. The unpleasant thought immediately sprang to mind that someone was going to get eliminated.

"Get up, moth!" Olag told me.

As you've probably already guessed, this suggestion distressed me so much that I stayed sitting on the ground.

"Where are you taking him?" the goblin interceded for me.

"None of your business, greenie!" Fagred growled.

"Get up, moth! Shokren doesn't like to be kept waiting! Or do I have to get you up?" Olag asked.

Sensibly accepting the fact that Shokren was not the gallows, I got up, and Fagred immediately put a noose round my neck and wound the other end of the rope round his hand. I was led off to the shaman on this improvised lead.

Shokren was talking to Bagard about something, but when he saw they'd already brought me, he cut the conversation short.

"Pero at za nuk na tenshi," [Lead it after me.] the shaman said, and set off toward the obelisk.

There are times when I really regret not knowing orcish.

Fagred tugged on the rope, almost breaking my neck, and dragged me off after Shokren. Olag walked alongside and gave me an occasional push in the back. They led me along just like a sheep to the market fair! Naturally, I didn't wax indignant, because being stubborn was a very good way to get a poke in the teeth from Fagred.

They brought me to the edge of the forest, and Shokren sat down on the ground and fixed his thoughtful gaze on me. Of course, no one suggested that Harold could sit, so I had to stand there with that stupid lead round my neck and act like a bored idiot. The shaman seemed a bit upset that his hard-stare treatment hadn't produced the desired result. He frowned and said, "I need to clarify a few details of the way you appeared in our forest and find out how you managed to get the Horn. Will you answer me, or shall I tell Fagred to hang you up for a little while?"

"I'll answer," I blurted out hastily.

"Sa'ruum," [Shaman] hissed Olag, who was standing behind me.

"I'll answer, sa'ruum," I repeated obediently.

"Good. If I sense that you're lying to me, Fagred will hang you up."

I squinted at the huge orc's happy face. The bastard was just dreaming of Shokren catching me out in a lie.

Then the questions came thick and fast. Naturally, despite the orc's threats, I had no intention of blabbing about the Commission. Four days of idleness had been quite enough time to invent a plausible cover story, go over all the moves, and modify a couple of them, so that in the end not even my inestimable acquaintance, the head of the Order of Valiostr, Artsivus, could have told the truth from the lies, let alone some orc shaman. And so Shokren and my two guards were treated to the heartrending story of an old and very rich count who commissioned this thief to get a Horn I had never heard of for his collection.

I was given heaps of gold, helped to get to Hrad Spein, and after that it was in the hands of the gods. I took the Horn, collected the emeralds along the way, and then somehow found myself in Zagraba. How had I got there? I had no idea at all, not a clue. Some sort of magic, tricks of the darkness. How had I got hold of the Key? That was very simple, Mr. Sa'ruum, sir. It was already in that count's collection, the elves must have sold it to him.

At that Olag snorted loudly, letting the entire forest know what he thought of the idea of elves selling their own relics to men, but Shokren told the warrior to be quiet and started asking me his endless questions again. How had I got to Hrad Spein? With what kind of group? Were there any elves in the group? Sure, if I told you there were elves, you'd mark me down as one of the elves' cronies.

"There weren't any elves," I blurted out, and immediately regretted it.

Fagred's face suddenly had a really, really pleased expression.

"That's a lie," Shokren answered me in a bleak voice. "In the city of Chu you and your monkey friends killed some of our warriors. Fagred was the only one who managed to get away. Hang him up!"

"You killed my brother! He was wounded!" Fagred yelled, and tugged on the rope so hard that I fell to my knees, scrabbling at the tightening noose.

What a shame we didn't finish you off, too! I thought. Darkness, what a stupid way to get caught out! Talking to the shaman was as hard as talking to Vukhdjaaz. I had to improvise again.

"There were elves! There were!" I squealed as I saw Olag throwing the rope over a branch of the nearest tree. "Only they weren't real elves."

Shokren held his hand up to tell the warriors to delay the torture for a moment.

"What nonsense is this, little monkey! What do you mean, not real elves?"

What was that I used to say? If you tell a lie, make it a really big one!

"They were bastards!"

"We know without you that all elves are bastards!" Fagred said, and he tugged on the rope again.

"No! I mean their fathers were men, and their mothers were elfesses!"

The more incredible a falsehood is, the more like the truth it sounds. I didn't know if what I'd just made up was even possible (I hadn't heard of anything of the sort anywhere), but the orcs swallowed the bait—hook, line, and sinker. The Firstborn didn't have a very high opinion of elves in any case, and when they heard something like that, they believed it was true straightaway. I think Olag cursed, and the very sight of Fagred was frightening, but absurd at the same time: I thought he was going to be sick. Shokren rubbed his chin thoughtfully.

"I knew they were sadists, but to do . . . that . . . with monkeys . . ." Olag didn't even bother to say it in orcish.

"All right, bring it back. I have a few more questions for it," Shokren snapped.

Realizing that the hanging was postponed for the time being, I cheered up a bit. The "few questions" went on for a good hour, but in all fairness, I must say that I never got confused even once, although the shaman was pushing me really hard. Eventually he got up and said, "Take it away, I've found out all I wanted to know."

So saying, the orc set off toward the obelisk, and I was led back to Mis and Glo-Glo, who were at the other side of the clearing. Halfway across Fagred decided he wanted to play games—he started jerking on the rope and chuckling, and asking me if I wanted to play doggy.

"Come on, now, moth, say 'woof'! That's not too hard for you, is it? Oh, come on! Say 'woof'!"

Every phrase was accompanied by a tug on the rope. I maintained a stoic silence.

"Bad dog! Bad dog! Say 'woof'!"

"That's enough, Fagred," his comrade warned him. "This one might still be useful."

"Shokren found out everything he wanted from him. Say 'woof,' moth, or I'll have to punish you!"

"And when the time comes, who are you going to bet on?" Olag suddenly asked. "A greeny or a wounded monkey?"

Fagred frowned, thought for a while, and then nodded.

"Okay, you're right, Olag. You don't have to bark right now, moth. But your time will come soon. Ah, the eternal forest! That's Bagard calling. Keep an eye on the monkey, I'll be back in a moment."

Fagred handed the rope to Olag and trudged off toward the commander of the orcs.

"Sit down," Olag ordered, and set me an example by sitting on the yellow leaves that covered the ground.

I had to sit down. In theory, at this point I might have been able to handle the orc, one to one, but two things stopped me—the dagger that Olag took out as soon as his partner left, and the fact that we were in open view. They'd simply stick me full of arrows while I was running for the trees. So I had to sit beside the Firstborn and wait for Fagred to come back.

"You're a silly little monkey," Olag said unexpectedly. "Why couldn't you have just played along with Fagred?"

"I don't think of myself as a silly little monkey and I don't want to amuse your friend."

When I was talking to Olag I could get away with things I would never have said when I was talking to Fagred.

"Not a monkey?" the orc said, and a faint spark of curiosity lit up in his eyes. "Then who are you?"

"Me? Certainly not a monkey."

"All men are monkeys!" Olag declared. "You're worse than animals, you're inferior beings, you're a mistake of the gods, like the elves who appeared straight after us. This world should belong to us! We were its only masters until the inferior beings appeared. Yes, you can talk, but give me two months, and I'll teach a raven to talk. Just because you can talk, it doesn't mean you can think! All of you who have appeared on our land, you, who fell our forests and keep us out of our own land, you're no better than stinking monkeys who've learned to talk and make weapons! A herd of crude beasts! If you weren't here, Siala would be a much better place. We orcs are the first children of the gods. The superior race! Why should we share Siala with elves, who came to Zagraba when all the work had already been done, when we'd already run the last ogres out of here, losing thousands of orcs in the process? That was very convenient for the elves, wasn't it? They're cruel and cunning, they've made my brothers' lives a misery, but sooner or later we'll crush them. And as for men . . . You were the very last to appear; even the Doralissians, those brainless oafs with goats for mothers, arrived before you did! You appeared in our world, and we didn't realize what a threat you were. We were fools. While we were fighting the elves and trying to drive the dwarves and the gnomes out of the accursed mountains, you spread all round the world, and then it was too late. All you can do is kill and destroy everything beautiful that there is in our world! Men are stupid little monkeys, and you won't stop until you tear Siala into a thousand pieces, you'll never have enough blood and wine to satisfy you!"

He paused for breath.

"It's our duty to do everything we possibly can to stop you, to wipe the human race off the face of Siala, so that there isn't even a trace of you left behind! And when the last of your children drowns in the ocean, we'll come back and settle our accounts with the elves, and all the others who are your friends. If we overthrow you, then we can crush the others, too! What we failed to achieve in the War of Shame, we shall achieve now. While I'm talking to you, little monkey, the Hand is leading my brothers in arms out of our cities and soon, very soon, we'll march out of Zagraba and we'll march as far as Avendoom and Shamar, and then it will be the turn of the other lairs of men. We won't leave a single stone standing, because there's no place in our world for anyone like you. And what you brought here will help us in the battle!"

I listened carefully without speaking. A heartfelt speech from a true fanatic, but then, they were all fanatics. The orc's eyes blazed with golden fire and he kept clenching the dagger, clearly preparing to use it, if I raised any objections. The Firstborn, the Firstborn. I wondered what he'd say if he knew about the Fallen Ones.

"And you animals, who have no sense of honor, demand admiration from us, you demand an alliance! You say we have to give you our forest, which belongs by right to the Firstborn, the first to come to Siala! How can you demand anything at all from us? How are you any better than animals? How? The elves deserve to die, although at least they know the meaning of honor and pride, but cattle like you simply deserve to die. Even your king's own eldest son is insane!"

"Leave him, Olag," Fagred said in a surprisingly gentle voice. He'd walked up while I was listening. "He won't understand anything anyway."

"No, he won't," Olag sighed, and tucked the dagger behind his belt. "Get up, moth, and remember—if you dare to open your mouth again before we reach your pen, I'll cut your tongue out."

But I wasn't thinking of making conversation. I was alarmed by the very bad news the orc had let slip while he was talking. I was afraid that this autumn the Firstborn had decided to feel out the boundaries of the kingdom and launch a new Spring War.

14

THE LABYRINTH

Glo-Glo was wrong—the detachment of orcs we had been waiting for all this time didn't arrive on the sixth day, but on the seventh, and only when evening was already drawing in.

With nothing to do, I was quietly going out of my mind, and I tried either to sleep (until Fagred's boot drove sleep away), or to watch what the orcs were doing and observe their habits, until some fang-mouthed brute advised me (in the most polite manner possible, I hasten to add) that it was time to sleep. I couldn't get what Olag had said out of my head—that after all these centuries of peace the orcs had decided to tickle the bellies of Valiostr and the Border Kingdom.

Well, the Border Kingdom might hold up, but the southern borders of my native Valiostr (with its slack garrisons, where the men didn't know how to properly hold a sword) would falter and break, and the Firstborn would drive our army all the way back to the Iselina. It would be at least a week before the armchair generals gathered their wits and moved forces down from the north and Miranueh, and that was enough time for the orcs to cause catastrophic damage. And would we hold out, even if the army did arrive in time? Our only hope were the barons, like Oro Gabsbarg—and the towns like Maiding and Moitsig, which lay right beside Zagraba. Their walls could hold back the army of orcs for a little while. At least, I hoped so, I really hoped so. . . .

I hadn't forgotten about the little flinny, either: If he had carried out my assignment and found my group, then help should already be hurrying on its way. The question was—would they get here in time?

Well then, about the detachment of orcs that arrived. In the early evening a bird called somewhere in the trees. The orcs sitting round the campfire and beside the obelisk pricked up their ears, and one of the Firstborn shouted in reply. A few moments later the orcs spilled out into the clearing. They just kept on coming, and when the last orc emerged from the trees, I had counted seventy-six of them. And they had prisoners, too.

Most of the prisoners were elves, but there were also four men, and they were all Border Kingdom warriors. When Mis saw them, he started in surprise.

"I know them! They're lads from the garrison at Drunken Brook. How did they manage to get here? Maybe you're right, Harold, and these subhuman monsters are already on the march."

"I don't think so," said Glo-Glo. "If they were, there would be a lot more prisoners. They probably came barging into the Golden Forest and ran into trouble, the same way you did."

"I suppose that's possible," Mis sighed.

"Now it'll start again."

"What do you mean, Glo-Glo?"

"The usual thing, Harold. They'll chop a few elves' heads off!"

The goblin was right, but not completely. They only executed two elves, and not in the clearing, they took them off into the forest. The others were led to the obelisk under double guard and Shokren's wary eye and left there with the men until their time came.

"Maybe they won't cut their heads off," Glo-Glo said thoughtfully. "Maybe this time they've decided to make an exception and put the dark ones into the Labyrinth."

"Can you see what badges they're wearing?" I asked the goblin.

"The same as the others—Walkers Along the Stream. A middling sort of clan, not very strong."

"No, that's not what I meant! I was asking about the elves!"

"A-a-ah . . . I think it's the House of Black Water. They're really vicious, the Dark House closest to the Golden Forest, they make the orcs weep tears of blood, but it looks as if it's the elves' turn to cry now."

That inseparable pair, Olag and Fagred, were heading toward us.

"Get ready, monkeys, we're moving out in five minutes. I hope you haven't got any ideas about escaping? If you have, just let us know. Better to lose your head straightaway than end up dangling from a tree, gutted like a fish."

Naturally, none of us was planning to escape, or if anybody was, he certainly wasn't thinking of letting the Firstborn know about it. Olag nodded contentedly, adjusted his yataghan, and tramped off toward the obelisk. Fagred was about to follow him, but he stopped, bared his teeth in a grin, grabbed hold of my hair, and whispered in my ear, "Yesterday a raven arrived for Shokren, moth. You're not needed anymore, so get ready to run 'round the Labyrinth."

Then, feeling very pleased with himself, he went hurrying after Olag.

"I'm sorry, my boy," said Glo-Glo, giving me a comforting pat on the back.

"I'm not really all that upset," I answered quite sincerely. "Sooner or later . . ."

"Ah, we're not done with this fight yet!" the goblin told me with a cunning wink.

Well, naturally, I hoped that if we really did start fighting, the orcs would remember us for centuries to come, because where could you possibly find any finer warriors than a slightly crazy old shaman and a thief stupid enough to come calling on the Firstborn?

"That Olag was telling the truth," said Glo-Glo, plumping up a genuine straw mattress. "The orcs have gone. All the villages are empty—nothing but women, children, and the minimum number of warriors. The Firstborn have moved their forces to the north. Oho, now there'll be fun and games."

"Isn't that stupid?" asked Mis, who was lying with his hands behind his head, staring up at the low ceiling. "While they're busy with us, the dark elves will take their homes. . . ."

"No, I don't think so. . . . I'm sure they've moved large forces to the west as well, and now there's a band of orc garrisons between the Golden and Black forests."

Maybe the goblin was right, who could tell? In any case, during the five days we'd spent tramping through Zagraba, all the orcs had talked about was the great march. We had swerved farther and farther to the south, moving into the very heartland of the orcs' forests. Along the way, every now and then we came across little villages. In fact, I'm not even sure I would call them villages. They were well fortified and camouflaged settlements. The forest itself protected their inhabitants against attack by enemies. There were just enough warriors in these fortresses to hold out against a sudden attack. The houses of the civilians looked substantial and prosperous, built of stone and wood, and there were also little houses with two, or even three stories in the trees.

Light, airy bridges had been stretched between the trees, making it possible to move quite freely from one tree to another—provided, of course, that you didn't have any fear of great heights. These bridges and houses were ideal sites for archers if the enemy managed to break through the lines of defense and flood into the settlement. While the adversary was running around down below, the archers would make him pay a heavy price, and enemy warriors who tried to scale the massively thick trunks of the majestic trees would have no cover against the arrows and be killed in droves.

We'd spent the last two nights in villages like this. The three of us were kept separately from the other prisoners—Glo-Glo said we were Bagard's property, we were his racehorses for the mid-autumn festival. We were fed, treated well, and given a place to sleep in some shack that even had straw mattresses. But we were guarded in grand style, too—as well as Shokren's circle, there was a sentry posted at the door.

The weather had hardly changed at all while we were traveling. Every day was bright and sunny, although it was rather cool. There wasn't even a hint of rain, although autumn was already almost half over.

"Tomorrow afternoon we'll reach the Labyrinth," Glo-Glo informed us casually.

I felt a nasty stabbing sensation in my belly.

"And the day after tomorrow is the orcs' lousy festival, so get ready."

The goblin started muttering to himself again, as if we weren't even there. May the Nameless One take me—did all goblins like to ruin other people's mood at bedtime? Or was it just my luck to meet the feeble-minded representatives of the green tribe?

The old goblin was right again! The next day we reached a low, half-ruined cliff, overgrown with a forest of fiery-red maples, and the Labyrinth was only a stone's throw away. At least, that was what the goblin said. Speaking for myself, I couldn't see any sign of a labyrinth. We were surrounded by forest, low cliffs that looked more like hills, and the silence of autumn. And then there was a little orc village without any sign of walls or fortifications.

"Is this the Labyrinth?" I asked. I'd never felt so disappointed in my life.

"Of course not," the goblin said with a shrug. "The Labyrinth is farther on, Harold."

"Shut up there, you lousy beasts!" an orc growled, waving his spear at us threateningly.

We had to postpone the conversation for a while. They put the three of us in a deep pit at the very edge of the village. And just to be on the safe side, they closed it off with a steel grille.

"Great," Mis grunted. "We can't reach it, even if we jump. If it rains, we'll get soaked."

"As long as we don't drown—getting soaked's not so terrible," Glo-Glo replied. "Now, what was I saying? Ah! The Labyrinth! Right . . . It's just beyond that spinney that we passed on our right. Ten minutes' walk from here."

"You mean there's a city only ten minutes away from the village?"

"Who said that?" he asked, gaping at me in amazement.

"You did."

"I didn't say anything about a city," the old shaman objected. "I was talking about the Labyrinth."

"Well, isn't the Labyrinth a city—something like the elves' Greenwood?"

The shaman gave me a very leery kind of look, but when he saw I wasn't joking, he snorted disdainfully.

"Greenwood and the Labyrinth are nothing like each other! Greenwood is the city of the Black Flame, the biggest city on Zagraba and, as it happens, the former capital of the elves, before the light ones and the dark ones fell out with each other. But as for the Labyrinth . . . Your "experts" have got something confused there. It's not a city, it's a structure. Just a labyrinth, in fact. The orcs don't live there; the Firstborn come here once a year for the mid-autumn festival, to enjoy themselves and watch a few goblins run."

"Ah, so that's it . . . ," Mis drawled.

"Only don't expect packed grandstands. This won't be a good year for applause. The orcs are going to war, so I don't think there'll be many Firstborn here."

"Never mind that. . . . But I thought Shokren was going to meet the Hand here and give him the Horn."

"Oh no, Harold. The Horn's not that urgent, the Hand doesn't need it yet. What would he do with it? Until the Firstborn come face-to-face with the Nameless One, who they've nominally acknowledged as their lord, they have no use for the Horn. And unless I'm mistaken, Shokren won't be able to monkey about with it on his own; that will take a powerful group of sorcerers. So first Shokren will enjoy himself watching the runners in the Labyrinth, before moving north with all the detachments. At least, that's what I think."

"Is he the only shaman here?"

"How would I know? I'm not a clairvoyant. I hope he's the only one, and I really hope he's not as strong as they think he is, otherwise my magic isn't worth a copper coin."

"Take your mittens off first, before you try working any magic," Mis chuckled.

"We've got a hard day tomorrow," said the goblin, avoiding an argument. "We'll need all our strength, may the gods help us."

Of course, I was hoping for help from the gods, too, but usually when I'm in a really tight spot, all the gods are somewhere very, very far away, and I have to cope with the cunning wiles of fate on my own. So I could only rely on myself—and my comrades, who should have been here a long time ago.

"Eat, Harold," Glo-Glo said with his mouth full, holding out the food that the orcs had lowered into our pit early in the morning. "You mustn't go hungry today."

"No thanks, I don't feel like it," I muttered.

I couldn't eat a scrap, even though I'd slept remarkably well. The goblin and Mis ate breakfast until it was coming out of their ears, but I couldn't stop listening to the roaring. The orcs, may the darkness take them, had started their entertainment first thing in the morning and they'd already put someone in the Labyrinth. Perhaps elves, or perhaps the captured warriors from the Borderland, perhaps someone else, I didn't know. The roar of the crowd died away and then grew louder again, reminding me of the rumble of distant thunder.

"They're enjoying themselves, the lousy scum," Mis hissed through his teeth as he listened to the shouts of the crowd.

No one answered him. I was too tense, and Glo-Glo was still mumbling those goblin tongue-twisters to himself. Eventually our turn to take part in the performance arrived. The grille moved aside and Fagred's face appeared against the background of the cloudy sky. With the help of an orc we didn't know, he lowered a ladder into the pit and barked, "Hey, bald monkey! Time to join the show!"

Mis got up without hurrying and stretched.

"What about us?" I asked quietly.

"We'll be in the next round," Glo-Glo answered just as quietly.

"Remember me kindly," Mis said in farewell, and set off up the ladder.

He clambered out of the pit and the orcs set the grille back in place.

"Listen to me very carefully, lad," Glo-Glo suddenly whispered. "I didn't say anything before, because I wasn't sure who I would be tied to, and speaking too soon would have meant losing the one tiny chance that we still have. But since the forest spirits have chosen you to be my companion . . . listen and remember. I won't have time to tell you this again. I've already run round the Labyrinth, a long time ago, more than thirty years ago, in fact. That time I managed to get away from the Firstborn unharmed, so I know what I'm talking about. They always put the prisoners in the Labyrinth six at a time—in three pairs. Each pair is fettered with a single chain. And they fetter them in completely different ways—however the forest spirits happen to whisper. The easiest way is hand-to-hand. But there are others: hand-to-foot, foot-to-foot. Or even worse: foot-to-neck or hand-to-neck. We can't manage the last two—if they put the chain on your neck and my foot, we won't run very far, so let's just pray that's not what happens. When they take us to the Labyrinth, don't forget to limp. . . ."

"Why should I do that?" I interrupted.

"Listen, will you!" the goblin said furiously. "Limp, but make sure it's convincing. Sometimes the Firstborn get the idea that their prisoners can run too fast, and that's not good. To slow some of them down, they cut a tendon in their leg. You don't want to crawl round the Labyrinth, I suppose? I should hope not. When they let us go, we have to run to the center of the Labyrinth. At the center there's a stone, and all we have to do to win is stand on it. But that's not so easy; in fact, it's almost impossible. Only one pair in fifty ever gets there. If we run along the path that leads to the stone, we're doomed, but there is another way round. I came across it last time, when I was stupid enough to run in the wrong direction. The path is guarded by 'pillars,' and if we can get past them we can slip through a narrow passage to the stone. It's not much of a chance, but it's better than running like everyone else."

"What's in store for us in the Labyrinth, what are the dangers?"

"Firstly, the Hunters. Four orcs. Their job is to get our heads, but we're allowed to kill the Hunters, too, and none of the Firstborn watching this stupid show will touch us if we do. I don't know how the Hunters will try to catch us—working separately or together. Secondly, the traps. Ordinary traps and magical ones. I think I can handle the second kind. Thirdly, the beasts. They're created by the orcs' magic and there are different kinds, but the most dangerous of them are the 'pillars.' They can all be killed, you just have to know how, but let's hope we won't have to go that far. Remember the most important thing—do what I tell you to do, no matter how strange it seems. Is that clear?"

"Perfectly. But do the orcs know about this secret passage of yours?"

"They do, but they don't think they need to block it up. It adds a pleasant edge of uncertainty to their bets. The forest spirits be praised, they have no idea I've already had the dubious pleasure of taking a stroll around their Labyrinth."

"This information could have saved Mis's life."

"What can I say to that, Harold?" Glo-Glo sighed, without trying to make excuses. "Perhaps you're right, and it would have saved him, or perhaps you're wrong and he would just have lost his way in the winding corridors and never found the right place. All I know is that if I'd told him, my chance of survival would have been immeasurably reduced. The orcs will never allow more than one prisoner a day to squeeze through that passage and reach the stone. That's just the way life is."

I didn't say anything to the goblin. Probably he was right. But maybe he wasn't. Who could tell? There was no way I could judge.

I listened to the distant roar, trying to guess when our turn would come. We had to wait a long time before anyone came for us. More than two hours. I was shivering a little, or rather, shuddering. Those damned nervous shudders really unsettled me, and I was longing for just one thing—for the cursed waiting to be over.

The metal grille moved aside, the ladder was lowered, and Fagred's face appeared again.

"Your friend has departed for the next world. Out you come, monkeys! It's your turn now."

So Mis had failed. May he dwell in the light!

As soon as I clambered out of the pit, I was knocked down and my hands were tied, and then they did the same to Glo-Glo.

"Follow me, keep quiet, and listen. Do you understand?" asked one of the orcs.

"We understand," Glo-Glo replied.

"Pick those feet up, moth," said Fagred, shoving me forward, but this time the shove wasn't rough at all. He was treating his racehorses gently, the lousy snake.

Anyway, I hadn't forgotten the old shaman's instructions and as I walked I limped picturesquely on my right foot.

"What's wrong with your leg?" Fagred immediately asked.

"I turned my ankle climbing down into the pit," I lied. Fagred frowned anxiously, but he didn't say anything.

"Before you go into the Labyrinth, they'll tie you together with a chain," said the orc, beginning our instructions. "In the Labyrinth, you have to find a triangular stone lying on the ground. Stand on it, and the game's over.

Four Hunters will come after you—trying to kill them isn't against the rules. You have the right to choose any of the weapons offered. There's no limit to the time you can spend in the Labyrinth. That's all. Do you understand?"

"We understand everything," Glo-Glo answered again.

The cries of the crowd grew clearer as we left the village behind and the maples parted to reveal a valley squeezed between the forest-covered cliffs. I had the impression that magic had been used on this place sometime in the past. In any case, about fifty yards away from us the valley ended in a gigantic steep-sided pit that stretched on between the overhanging cliffs for as far as the eye could see. Observation platforms had been cut into the cliffs. Many of the platforms were empty, but I could see orcs on others. Glo-Glo's calculations weren't exactly right—there were more than three hundred Firstborn. I reckoned there were thousands of orcs on the hillsides, watching the action unfold in the pit. Not everyone had set off on the march to the north.

"We'll wait here," Fagred growled after they led us to the very edge of the pit.

I had a unique opportunity to look down. The pit was about twenty-five yards deep. It was divided up by walls set in a haphazard, hit-or-miss fashion, and this chaotic disorder created the so-called Labyrinth. I was a bit disappointed. I never expected the orcs' grandiose structure to be just an ordinary hole—even if it was deep—in the ground, with a few partitions set up in it. The partitions were made of some kind of wild creeping plant that was still green, even in the middle of October. At least, that was what it looked like to me.

"Glo-Glo, what are those plants down there?" I asked in a quiet whisper.

"I advise you to keep as far away from the walls as possible," the goblin hissed back. "Those are yellow eyes, and they eat absolutely anything, apart from happening to be poisonous."

"Thanks, that's really cheered me up."

Just then Olag came up and led us along the edge of the pit toward a stairway leading down into it. At the bottom we found ourselves in a pen fenced off from the main part of the Labyrinth by a heavy grille. As well as Glo-Glo and me, and the five orcs who had followed us (including Olag and Fagred, who were making sure no one did any premature damage to us), there were at least ten other Firstborn, as well as two men and two elves. The elves were dirty and had been beaten very badly, but they maintained a proud bearing, as if the orcs were their prisoners and the entire Labyrinth belonged to them.

"The final group?" an orc in a leather apron asked Olag.

"Yes."

"Let's get started."

"Hand-to-hand," he said, jabbing a finger at the elves.

"Foot-to-foot." That was for the two men.

Two Firstborn started carefully chaining the runners together for the Labyrinth. Leather Apron came over to us, thought for a moment, and announced:

"Neck-to-foot."

Glo-Glo gave a dull groan, but then Fagred stepped up, grabbed Leather Apron by the sleeve, and dragged him aside. I noticed one of my emeralds disappear into Leather Jacket's hand. The orc came back to us for a moment and announced:

"Hand-to-hand."

They put a heavy bracelet on my left wrist. The bracelet at the other hand of a yard of heavy chain was fastened on the goblin's right wrist.

"Don't let me down, moth," Fagred whispered menacingly into my ear. "We've wagered too much on you."

"How fast can you run?" Leather Apron asked me.

"Can't you see he's lame?" the goblin answered for me, and immediately collected a slap to the back of his head from Fagred.

But luckily enough, Leather Apron left me alone after that.

"How fast can you run?" he asked one of the two human warriors.

"Very fast," the man replied gloomily. "Too fast for you to catch me."

"That's good," Leather Apron said with a serious nod, and moved away. "Choose your weapons, but don't try anything stupid!"

No one was going to try anything stupid—not even the proud, taciturn elves. How far could you get with a sword, if six bowmen had you in their sights?

There was a whole heap of steel lying on two large tables right beside the railings. And the same amount lying along the walls. Nothing for throwing or firing, of course. No bows, no crossbows, no javelins, no throwing knives, not even a sling. The clever orcs didn't want any of the prisoners to try killing the spectators. So we had to choose from an assortment of cutting and stabbing weapons.

While the goblin and I wandered round the tables, the elves each chose themselves a s'kash, and the two men settled for a sword and a single-handed ax. Of course, I would have taken something like a spear or a pike—with a weapon like that you can keep any enemy at a distance, or almost any. But for that you had to have both hands free. And you couldn't do much running with a spear. So after hesitating briefly, I chose a short sword with a broad blade, the kind that armored infantry use. It was about the same length as my knife, although it was wider and heavier. And it had a scabbard, so I didn't have to carry the weapon in my hands.

The goblin inspected the hardware and snorted in disappointment, but then he rummaged for a while in the very last heap and pulled out a Sultanate dagger with a blade shaped like a flame. He tried waving the weapon through the air a few times and then stuck it behind his belt.

"That's it, out you go!" Leather Apron ordered, and on his sign the orcs started raising the heavy grille.

Without waiting until the grille was raised, the dark elves leapt forward into the Labyrinth and then ran off as fast as they could go. The lads obviously also had some kind of plan. At least they certainly weren't planning to face the Labyrinth together with us.

Then it was the men's turn. Glo-Glo didn't waste any time, either; he dragged me forward and jumped out into the Labyrinth. The grille started slowly descending behind us, creaking so terribly that I barely heard Leather Apron shout, "Hey, runner!"

We all turned at the same time, and one of the orc bowmen put an arrow into the leg of the man who'd said he could run very fast.

"Now try running fast, little monkey!"

The orcs roared with laughter.

"And you told me they cut the tendons," I muttered, setting off toward the fallen man.

"Times have cha— Look out!"

Glo-Glo leapt aside and dragged me after him. The goblin might have been small, but he had plenty of strength, and I had to struggle to keep my balance. Two creatures came darting out of the passage the two elves had just run into. They looked pretty much like ordinary human skeletons, but they were a bit taller and had four arms instead of two. And the creatures were exactly the same dark green color as the walls of the Labyrinth—they seemed to be made out of plants, not meat or bones. The orcs' roar of delight thundered along the cliffs. The show had begun.

"Run!" the goblin yelled. "There's nothing you can do to help them!"

Cursing all the gods and the damned goblin into the bargain, I dashed after him, forgetting about the creatures advancing on the two warriors. Following my companion, I dived into a narrow passage with high walls. The little shaman was incredibly agile, and I could hardly keep up with him.

"Left . . . past three corridors on the left . . . right . . . straight on . . . left again . . . ," the goblin muttered, leading me along the route that only he knew.

I glanced back anxiously, but the green creatures apparently weren't following us.

"Who were they?" I asked Glo-Glo.

"Creations of orcish shamanism, not really dangerous, unless you get under their feet. A petty nuisance."

"They why did you beat it so promptly?"

"Don't distract me! I think we go right now. . . . Yes! This way!"

And the goblin set off again at a run, dragging me behind him. In the last three minutes I'd completely lost my bearings in the green labyrinth and I ran after the goblin like an obedient dog. Eventually Glo-Glo turned sharp left and we found ourselves at a dead end.

"That does it!" I panted, and the hills replied with a rumble of joy.

Tell me, if you please. How could the orcs see us? But they could, may the demons of darkness take them!

"Now where have you brought me, Glo-Glo?"

"Keep quiet for a moment and let me think! It's thirty years since the last time I was here, and my memory's not what it used to be. Ri-i-ight now, where could I have gone wrong?"

"Maybe . . ."

"Shut up!"

I had to do as the goblin said and wait for him to be struck by another brilliant idea. I really regretted ever having anything to do with goblins. Scatterbrains, every one of them; they always did everything back to front.

While the goblin was thinking, I shifted impatiently from one foot to the other, casting anxious glances along the green corridor. Sagot be praised, everything was quiet (that is, if you didn't count the yelling of the orcs and the goblin's furious argument with himself).

Now I could take a proper look at the Labyrinth. The thickets of green towered up ten yards into the air, and it was pointless even to think of trying to climb over the wall. Apart from being so appallingly high, all these bushes were so dense and thorny that it was frightening just to look at them.

I was very surprised by the floor of the Labyrinth—it was completely paved with small gray tiles, set tightly against each other. And there wasn't a spot of dirt anywhere, as if the place was cleaned every day.

"I didn't spot a single trap."

"No, you won't," the goblin growled. "They're all on the central pathways, and usually nobody's stupid enough to run that way."

"Apart from us, perhaps," I sniped.

"Uh-huh. Let's go, know-it-all, I have a short cut!"

Glo-Glo led me back the way we'd come. When he was sure he was going in the right direction, the goblin started running. We plunged back into the green abyss of the Labyrinth and dashed along between the walls until a creature that looked like the twin brother of the ones that had attacked us near the entrance appeared ahead of us. But some zealous individual had hacked off one of its four arms. Spying outsiders, the green skeleton started trotting briskly toward us.

"Ah, darkness!" I swore, and took out my sword.

Glo-Glo had obviously lost it completely, because he went running straight toward our death—he even growled in outrage when I tried to stop him. There was nothing I could do but run after him and hope he knew the right thing to do. The goblin suddenly stopped, held out his hand, swung round on his axis, swinging me round with him, said something in a rapid whisper, and wiggled the fingers in his mitten. At first nothing happened, and then the creature hurrying toward us stopped and lots of little yellow flowers started sprouting all over it. The same thing was happening to the nearest section of the wall, too.

"Let's get as far away as possible," Glo-Glo said in a perfectly calm voice. "Just in case it hasn't worked properly."

We retreated.

"It won't work a second time; I had that spell ready since before they put the mittens on me," Glo-Glo declared smugly.

Meanwhile the little yellow flowers completely covered the wall and the creature that had attacked us. Then they burst, and the creature fell apart into something that looked very much like dry hay. The same thing happened to the section of the wall. It simply collapsed, opening up a way through into the next corridor.

As bad luck would have it, an astounded orc walked out through the gap. The Firstborn was armed with a long spear with a broad head, which I was not glad to see. The orc spotted us and promptly got down to work.

Neither I nor Glo-Glo had any intention of letting some Hunter have our heads just like that. So we went dashing off in the opposite direction. Unfortunately for us, the orc was rather quick on the uptake, and he came dashing after us, shaking his spear. The orc spectators started baying.

I took my lead from Glo-Glo again and simply followed him. The goblin ran to an intersection and took a couple of turns, and we found ourselves in a corridor running parallel to the one where we met the orc.

"That Firstborn thinks he's smarter than I am," the old shaman suddenly said with a giggle.

He'd definitely flipped! What kind of time was this to gloat!

The secret of the goblin's happy mood was revealed a few seconds later. There was the huge hole that had appeared in the wall thanks to the goblin's shamanism; we dived through it, and were back in the corridor we'd just been forced to run out of.

"Now straight . . . right . . . straight, past four intersections . . . that's it . . . three . . . four . . . fifth on the left . . ."

I was amazed that the goblin, who had only been here once, could be carrying such a precise route in his head. We came out into a fairly large round space with six passages leading off it and started dashing across.

"Third on the right!"

But we stopped short of the passage we needed, because Glo-Glo hissed: "Freeze and don't move a muscle!"

I squinted sideways at the shaman, who had turned into a very convincing statue. What was wrong with him? Then my eyes moved from the goblin to the center of the open space, where something green had appeared out of nowhere. It looked like a cross between an immense soap bubble and a spider, except that instead of legs it had human arms—either six or eight of them. I couldn't see any head, or eyes, or mouth. The creature just sat there with its arm-legs folded up under it, gurgling quietly.

"Harold, don't move, and keep quiet," said the goblin, keeping his eyes fixed on the spider. "It won't touch us as long as we don't move."

"What is it?" I whispered anxiously.

The goblin decided not to favor me with an answer. Then a very smug-looking orc came dashing out into the space with his spear held at the ready. When he spotted the spider, the Hunter's face suddenly fell and he stopped dead, too. The spider jumped to its feet (or rather, its hands), gurgled a couple of yards toward the orc, and then sat back down on the ground—it had clearly lost view of its motionless quarry.

The Firstborn glared at us furiously with his yellow eyes, and even though the situation was so dire (at least, judging from the way the orc and the goblin looked), I couldn't resist winking at the Hunter. The orc seemed to find this gesture quite unbearably annoying, and he started growling. The spider promptly moved another two yards closer to the orc, who was forced to shut up.

Glo-Glo started muttering to himself again and then he made a sound as if he'd snapped his fingers, even though he was still wearing those idiotic mittens. The orc howled in surprise and jumped a yard into the air, as if someone had stuck a red-hot needle in his backside.

The spider leapt forward nimbly and grabbed the howling Firstborn with all eight of its arms. I didn't see what happened after that, because I was dashing like grim death after Glo-Glo. But I don't think the orc was to be envied. Well then, we'd got rid of one of the Hunters; that just left the other three. Eventually Glo-Glo decided that after such a long run it would be a good idea to get our breath back, and we stopped at an intersection.

"What . . . was . . . that?" I wheezed, gasping for air.

"That? It's a monster that appeared . . . in the thickets of the forest after the elves and the orcs experimented with battle shamanism. That's what the experiments produced. In principle, it's perfectly harmless."

"I thought you said the same about those things with four arms?"

"No, it really is harmless. The important thing is not to disturb it. A bubblebelly is just very protective of its territory and thinks everyone who enters it is an enemy. You just have to stay still and wait for it to crawl away. It doesn't even eat anybody, just chews them up into mush and spits them out again."

"That's a very encouraging thought—being chewed into mush. By the way, that was a clever trick with the orc."

For some reason Glo-Glo seemed a bit flustered by that and he muttered, "Actually, my magic was supposed to strike the bubblebelly with lightning, but thanks to the mittens, it made the orc jump."

Mmm, yes. The gods be praised it wasn't us who jumped!

"And by the way, what are you doing with lightning? I didn't know goblins had any battle magic. You only have defensive shamanism."

"Who says so?"

"Well, I thought you said—"

"We told you men that so we wouldn't have these Orders of yours wandering around in our forest! Why should we want to share our secrets with your magicians? Shall we go?"

"Is it far now?"

"About the same distance again," the goblin told me after a moment's thought.

I groaned.

Left, left, right, right, straight on, left again, then right, then straight on, then back at full speed to get away from another of those skeletons with four arms. Those beasts were agile, all right, but they turned out to be pretty stupid. We ran into a dead end, waited until the creature made its final leap, and simply dropped to the ground. The creature went flying over our heads like a huge grasshopper and smashed into the wall. The wall immediately came to life, wound its branches round the green creature, and sucked it in.

"Ugh!" was all I could say at the sight of this wonder.

"Nothing surprising about that," said Glo-Glo, dusting off his cloak. "Those things were created by the same spell as the wall, so if they touch each other, they just merge together."

"The things you know!"

"I'm a shaman, my boy, not some marketplace charlatan! And a shaman has to know all sorts of things, otherwise his tribe won't last very long. Come on, get those hooves moving, there's not far left to go now."

And we didn't go very far, because at the next intersection we came across another Hunter. Fortunately, he was standing with his back to us and gazing off into the distance, holding an arrow ready on his bowstring. Was he lying in ambush for someone?

The Hunter was no more than seven yards away from us. No distance at all but, speaking for myself, I wasn't too sure that if I tried to attack him, I wouldn't end up with an arrow in me. Glo-Glo and I looked at each other, and he pointed to my sword with his eyes. I sighed and started slowly pulling the sword out of its scabbard. Fortunately for me, the orc never turned round. But then, as bad luck would have it, our chain clanked.

There was no time to think, and I flung the short, heavy weapon at the orc with all my might. And something impossible happened. Luck must have been on my side that day, because the sword turned a few somersaults in the air and buried itself in the Firstborn's chest before he had time to shoot. It hit him so hard that he went flying backward and smashed into the wall.

"Well, may the forest spirits take me!" Glo-Glo exclaimed, shaking his head in delight. "I had no idea you could do that."

"Neither did I," I told the goblin, watching ruefully as the orc's body disappeared into the thick green barrier, taking my sword with it.

"Come on, Harold, only two more intersections to go and we're there. Orcs! We'll diddle the lot of them." And Glo-Glo stomped on, paying no attention to where the orc's body had disappeared and my lost sword.

"Are you sure that in the last thirty years the orcs haven't blocked off your little passage?"

"No, but we have to hope for the best."

Two intersections after that the goblin grabbed hold of my arm and said, "Look."

We were facing an open space exactly like the one where we met the bubblebelly. But there weren't any exits leading off this one, and there were three tall green columns standing in it. Two of them were just plain columns, but the third one had two arms growing out of it, and they looked very much like the jaws of a praying mantis.

"What are we in for this time?" I groaned.

"These are the pillars I told you about," the goblin muttered. "The ones without claws are sleeping, and that one's on guard. They're terribly quick, but if we can slip past them, we'll be right beside the passage."

"But where is the passage?" I asked. The pillars didn't seem to be taking any notice of us, and I relaxed a bit.

"There it is, look!" the goblin said, as cool as a cucumber, pointing to the other side of the open space.

I had to strain my eyes to make out the goblin's passage.

"Are you kidding?" I roared almost at the top of my voice. "A pregnant mouse would have a hard time trying to get through there."

"Let's not forget that last time I got through without any problem," the goblin replied peevishly.

"But I'm not you! I'm not climbing in there!"

"Oh yes you are!"

"Why in the name of darkness did I ever listen to you?" I groaned.

"Because there's a very good chance that thanks to me, you might survive." Nothing could embarrass the goblin. "Believe me, my boy, the passage is a lot bigger than it looks. All right, if we waste any more time, one of the other Hunters or some other beast will find us. Just sprint for the passage as fast as you can and don't get in the way of that pillar's claws."

"What about the others?"

"The others will take half a minute to wake up. Ready?"

I gulped hard and nodded.

"Run for it!"

Before we'd covered even a quarter of the distance, the pillar started moving toward us very fast, without making a sound.

In a single heartbeat, it was already towering up over us, and it took every last drop of agility I had to avoid a descending claw. I avoided it, but the pillar immediately struck again, after swinging its arm back round in some incredible fashion. I jumped one way, Glo-Glo jumped the other, and the claw hit the chain fettering us together close to the goblin's arm.

The chain snapped, and Glo-Glo was left with just a bracelet, while I had all the rest. Setting the Labyrinth ringing with choice obscenities, I launched into a run, winding the chain onto my arm as I tried to catch up with the goblin.

The pillar was treading on my heels, so I dived into the narrow entrance after Glo-Glo like a fish. Somewhere behind me, claws clattered on the stone slabs, and I started working desperately with arms and legs, hauling myself as far away as possible from the rather agitated pillar. Fortunately for me and the goblin, the rotten beast didn't try to storm the wall, and gave up on us.

"Glo-Glo, may you . . . ," I growled at the goblin crawling along in front of me. "Go slower, I can't keep up."

The goblin obligingly stopped and waited for me to catch up with him.

"Well, we pulled that off neatly, eh?"

"If you ignore the fact that your pillar very nearly nailed us and your passage is narrower than the space under a tight-fisted merchant's bed, then yes . . . it was very neat."

"Don't worry, you'll fit through here just fine!" Glo-Glo was much too pleased with himself to take any notice of my whinging. "Only don't lift your head up, or you'll end up in the wall!"

He didn't have to remind me! I already knew that one twitch to the left or the right, and I'd touch the green walls of the patch.

"How far do we have to crawl?"

The shaman didn't risk turning his face toward me. One wrong move in this place could lead to a grotesque death. It would be like escaping from the Gray Stones, tripping over your own feet, and breaking your neck. The law of universal swinishness in action, so to speak.

"Can you manage a hundred and fifty yards?"

I ground my teeth and said, "What choice do I have? I'll manage it. Just as long as it doesn't get any narrower."

"It won't. Keep crawling."

We crawled on. The only place I'd ever "enjoyed" myself so much was in Hrad Spein, when I crawled through that long, narrow stone tunnel. When I reckoned we'd already covered most of the distance, Glo-Glo suddenly stopped moving, stopped panting, and announced: "Er, Harold . . . we've got a little problem here."

"What kind of problem?" I asked in a trembling voice, already imagining that the goblin had come nose to nose with some other monster of the Labyrinth.

"There's a skeleton lying across the path."

"So what's the problem?"

"The problem is that he's lying right across our path," he repeated patiently. "I might be able to crawl over him, but I doubt very much if you can."

"Just don't tell me we have to crawl back," I hissed angrily.

"Absolutely not! I'll take him apart."

"What do you mean?"

"Bone by bone. Wait."

I had to lie there, listening to the goblin snuffling. Eventually even my patience ran out and I hissed like a grass snake with a cold: "Well, how much longer?"

"It's done. I hope the deceased isn't offended with us. Right, I'll just get the skull out of the way. . . . Why, you! There . . . that's it. Crawl!"

I didn't know how the goblin had managed it, but all I found on the path were a few bones pressed into the earth (there weren't any stone slabs in the passage). Glo-Glo had fed everything else to the wall. The rest of the journey to safety passed off uneventfully, and when the shaman and I emerged from the passage, we were greeted by a roar from the stands.

We were in another round space, with a massive triangular gray stone lying in the middle of it. And standing between the slab of stone and us was the third Hunter. When he caught sight of us, he smiled and bowed (which was surprising enough in itself) and drew his yataghan.

The Firstborn was in no hurry to attack. He was clearly waiting for us to try to get through to the stone. I looked at his yataghan, and regretted the untimely loss of my sword.

"Now what do we do?" I hissed through my teeth without moving my lips. "This snake's just dreaming of slicing you and me to ribbons."

"I have a dagger," said Glo-Glo, taking the Eastern trinket out from behind his belt.

"Are you counting on this lad laughing himself to death when he sees your toothpick?" I asked, keeping my eyes fixed on the smiling orc.

"What if you throw the dagger at the Hunter? Like the sword."

"Two miracles in one day would be too much. It won't work. But how's your magic doing?"

"Out of the question. In the mittens it could go very wrong. Better not to try."

The orc was clearly starting to get impatient, and he beckoned to us with his finger, keeping that smile fixed on his face.

"Come on, Glo-Glo, go all the way round him," I suggested. "He won't get two of us at once."

"Nonsense."

"That way at least someone will reach the stone."

The shaman didn't argue, and started running round the orc in a wide circle. The Firstborn hadn't been expecting such an original move from the monkeys and he stopped smiling and dashed to intercept the goblin.

Glo-Glo stepped up the pace even more. I dashed toward the stone, and the orc immediately forgot about the goblin and started for me. I hurtled toward him, twirling the chain round above my head—a full yard of it.

The smart shaman did what I'd told him to do and didn't get involved in the fight. He hopped up onto the stone and instantly disappeared.

The orc was blocking my way. I flung the chain forward, trying to hit him in the face. He dodged to one side as smoothly as if he was dancing and slashed with his yataghan. I dropped to the ground rather clumsily, rolled, and swung the chain. The warrior obviously wasn't trying to kill me straightaway, he'd decided to entertain the crowd. Now I was between the orc and the stone, and I wasn't about to let an opportunity like that slip. I dashed for the stone, leaving my opponent with his mouth hanging open.

Had that cretin really been expecting me to tempt fate and take on a yataghan with a pitiful length of broken chain? The Firstborn really did underestimate men far too much! Maybe we were monkeys, unworthy of living in Siala, but we certainly weren't fools!

"Stop, you coward! Fight!" I heard him roar behind me, but it was too late, I'd already hopped up on the stone.

Bang! I was back in Leather Apron's pen. And there was Glo-Glo, grinning. Some of the orcs were rubbing their hands in delight, and some were swearing blue murder. For an instant Olag and Fagred's leering mugs actually looked like those of friends and family. No doubt they, their commander, and the shaman had won a whole heap of valuables, or whatever it is orcs use for wagers.

"Hold your hands out, monkeys!" Leather Apron growled. "I'll take your chains off."

"Congratulations, Harold!" Glo-Glo chuckled. "Now you can count yourself one of the few who've been through the Labyrinth and lived."

"Don't be in such a hurry, greeny," Leather Apron rumbled. "We'll see how you run tomorrow, when they close that passage off."

I just stood there with my jaw hanging open until Olag and Fagred took me and the goblin back up the steps.

"You didn't tell me anything about a second run in the Labyrinth!" I told Glo-Glo angrily, after we'd been sent back to our pit.

"I didn't want to upset you before I had to," the goblin began cautiously.

"Glo-Glo," I began, speaking from the heart, "when *were* you going to tell me?"

"This evening," he replied promptly.

"So how many times altogether do I have to go down into that darkness-damned Labyrinth?"

The goblin hesitated and tried not to look at me.

"So, how many?" I asked, determined to be pitiless.

"The festival starts in mid-autumn and lasts for eight days."

"Eight days?" I repeated after the shaman, like an echo.

So we had to entertain the Firstborn and risk our skins another seven times.

"Well, if I'd told you about it this morning, just think what a state you'd have been in when we entered the Labyrinth!"

"Eight days?" I still couldn't believe in such an absolutely swinish twist of fate.

"There, you see?" the goblin sighed. "That's exactly what I'm talking about."

"So tell me, has anyone ever managed to last that long?" Naturally, I asked the question rhetorically.

"Actually, no," the shaman replied reluctantly. "No one ever has. The longest is three days."

"Then what are we hoping for?"

"Maybe I'll be able to think of something."

"How did you manage to avoid the troublesome attention of the orcs during your first visit to the Labyrinth?"

"A-a-a-ah . . . ," said the goblin, with a smug grin. "That time I escaped straight after the first run. There weren't any pits back then, and the orcs did a poor job of guarding us. And bearing in mind that the orcs got truly plastered in honor of the festival, then in the distant halcyon days of my youth it was fairly easy to escape. Not like now."

"But that means the orcs will have more than a few drinks tonight, too. . . ."

"Yes, but you and I can't soar up into the air, and even if we could, that grille wouldn't let us out."

At that very moment the grille slid to one side and Olag and Fagred looked down on us.

"You run well, little monkeys. Bagard and Shokren are very pleased with you."

The orcs lowered a bag full of food and two flasks down to us.

"Eat and build up your strength. You have to run again tomorrow."

The grille slid back into place, but Fagred still felt he had to remind us that he was keeping his eye on us.

That evening we had a real feast. They'd given us heaps of food, all sorts of things. One flask was full of water, the other was full of wine.

The orcs weren't just sitting about doing nothing, either, and every now and then we heard singing and drum rolls. The rotten snakes were making merry and, basically, they had every right to. They weren't the ones sitting a damn lousy pit!

"Pssst! Psssst! Hey! Harold, are you there?"

Through my dream I could hear the hissing of a frantic skillet. I decided to take no notice of this extraneous noise and sleep a bit longer, but it was hopeless! The hissing carried on, and then it was joined by pokes in the ribs. That was Glo-Glo. I had no choice but to wake up.

"What?" I asked the goblin.

"There's someone up there!"

I looked up, but the clouds had hidden the stars and moon, and the night was dark, so there was no point in trying to make anything out. I heard that squeaky sound above me again.

"Pssssst! Harold, are you there?"

"Who's tha— Kli-Kli, is that you?"

"Well, at last!" the royal jester jabbered in delight. "I was beginning to think that flinny had lied!"

"Are you alone?"

"No, with Egrassa."

"Can you shift the grille?"

I never thought I could ever feel so delighted. I almost launched into a dance!

"No, Harold," Egrassa replied. "There's a lock on it. If we break it off, the orcs will hear. Do you know who has the key?"

"Wait a moment! If I get your mittens off, can you shift the grille quietly?" I asked Glo-Glo, who hadn't said a word all this time.

"Yes."

"We don't need a key. Have you got anything thin and sharp?"

"I do! A nail!" Kli-Kli informed me.

"Throw it to me!" I said happily, trying not to think about what the goblin would want a nail for on the march and whose boot he was planning to put it in when the time came.

The nail was very, very small and very, very thin. It could have been made to order.

"Have you found it?" a voice asked from above.

"Yes, now wait."

"Get a move on! The orcs could turn up at any moment."

"Don't rush me!" I hissed, and started desperately fiddling with the lock on Glo-Glo's left mitten.

The shaman waited patiently.

"How much time is there before it starts getting light?" I asked him in a quiet voice.

"About two hours . . . ," he replied just as quietly. "Maybe a bit more. It will start to rain in about ten minutes."

"How do you know that?"

"Shamans have to know when it's going to rain."

"Like frogs?" I asked with a stupid giggle.

Was it my imagination, or was the goblin really smiling in the darkness?

Just at that moment the lock gave a gentle click and the shaman took the mitten off. I started on the other lock.

"If it starts to rain and the alarm hasn't been raised, we have an excellent chance of covering our tracks."

"And if that doesn't work?"

"Imagine what the Firstborn will do to us for ruining their festival after they sober up."

I gave an involuntary shudder, but then the second lock clicked. Now Glo-Glo was free of his mittens.

"That's great," he muttered. "Get back against the wall and tell your friends to move away from the grille."

"Egrassa! Kli-Kli!"

"Yes? How did it go?"

"Fantastic! Get away from the grille. About ten yards! There's going to be a bit of conjuring!"

"But you . . ."

"Kli-Kli, for once just don't argue!"

"But . . ."

"We're moving," said Egrassa.

The elf probably just grabbed Kli-Kli by the scruff of the neck and dragged him away. In the darkness I couldn't see what the goblin was doing, but a wind suddenly started humming in the pit, then it darted upward, and the grille went flying off and up into the sky without making a single sound.

"That's all," Glo-Glo sighed. "Call your friends and get them to hoist our backsides out of here."

"Won't it fall back down on our heads?" I asked. I must admit, I thought the demonstration the old man had given was marvelous.

"Don't worry, my boy."

Then the ladder was lowered down into our pit, and I clambered out first. At the top I was grabbed by a pair of strong hands and there it was—the surface of the earth. There was much more light up here than down below, and I could make out the contented faces of Kli-Kli, Alistan Markauz, and Egrassa.

"Alive, thief?"

"Yes, milord."

"That was some conjuring trick you just did!" Kli-Kli jabbered. "Whoosh, and it went flying up into the sky! I couldn't believe my eyes!"

"I'm not alone," I warned my rescuers, and just then Glo-Glo appeared. "This is the venerable Glo-Glo, a shaman."

"Oi!" Kli-Kli squeaked when he saw my friend, and for some reason or other, he hid behind the elf.

"Pleased to meet you," Milord Rat said with a nod. "And now, if nobody has any objections, let's get away from here before the orcs turn up."

"They've got the Horn," I announced.

"Not anymore," Egrassa contradicted me, and handed me my bag.

"But how?" I asked, unable to believe my own eyes.

"The flinnies made a special effort. For that ring you gave them they're indebted to us to the grave," the elf explained.

"And Shokren?"

"What Shokren?"

"The shaman who had my bag," I explained.

"He got an arrow in the throat," Milord Alistan said, and I felt delighted. "So we'd better get away from here before they raise the alarm."

I didn't ask them how they'd managed to steal into the heart of an orc village, then kill the shaman and take the bag with the Horn, all without being noticed. And I also tried not to think about the fact that they'd saved the Horn first, and then me.

"Follow me, but quietly," Egrassa warned us, and set off.

I followed straight behind the elf, but Kli-Kli overtook me and installed himself in front of me. Glo-Glo and Alistan brought up the rear. We could see fires burning somewhere on the edge of the village and hear singing. Eel rose up out of the tall dry grass like a phantom. He noticed me and gave a sight nod, then looked Glo-Glo up and down in surprise, but didn't say anything until Alistan Markauz asked him, "All quiet?"

"Yes, but these two were going toward the pit, so I had to deal with them."

I saw the two dead bodies now, and I couldn't resist going closer. I was right. Olag and Fagred. Both killed with throwing knives borrowed from Kli-Kli.

"Was there any noise?" Milord Alistan asked anxiously.

"They never knew what happened," Eel said with a chuckle.

Glo-Glo spat juicily on Fagred's body.

"Everyone into the trees!"

We crossed the clearing at a run and took shelter under the sleeping maples. Two short figures detached themselves from tree trunks.

"I told you they'd do it, beard-face!"

"And if we hadn't been stuck here in the forest, it would have been done even better, hat-head! Cheers, Harold! I haven't seen you for ages! Ugh! You've grown yourself a beard, just like me! And who's this with you?"

"Looks like a goblin," said Deler, moving closer.

"I couldn't stand another jester!" Hallas groaned, but Egrassa promptly told them both to shut up.

Something rustled through the leaves of the maples and the first drops of rain fell on my face.

"We need to get away, honorable sirs, and get away quickly!" said Glo-Glo, taking the initiative.

"So now a goblin's going to tell us what to do!" Hallas grumbled.

"We should go east now," the old shaman continued as if he hadn't heard. "As soon as we get past the cliffs, we can walk along the stream, and I can try to confuse our tracks."

"Agreed!" said Egrassa—for some reason he trusted the goblin straightaway. "Will you show us the way?"

"Yes, let's go."

We moved deeper into the wet forest. The rain whispered a lullaby to the leaves. It was wet, cold, and very dark. I was walking behind Hallas, so I didn't notice when Mumr joined the group. He simply appeared beside me, gave me a friendly punch on the shoulder, and hurried on ahead to report to Alistan.

"Eel," I called to the Garrakian walking behind me. "Didn't the orcs set any sentries for the night?"

"We took out five of them round the perimeter, but otherwise things were quiet," Eel replied. "What would they be afraid of in their own home, and at the start of the festival? I think without it we wouldn't have got you out of there so easily, never mind the Horn."

"The flinnies told us everything," said Kli-Kli, appearing beside me. "About the Horn and about you."

"Is that ring worth so much to them?"

"Yes. And by the way, we had to hurry to get here in time. Galloped all the way to rescue you, and you haven't even said thank you!"

"Thank you, Kli-Kli."

"Don't mention it," the jester replied magnanimously. "I'm very glad you survived, Dancer in the Shadows. Wordofonner."

"Me, too."

"By the way, how did you come to meet him?" the goblin asked, nodding toward Glo-Glo, who was walking at the front.

"We ran through the Labyrinth together."

"Aaaaah," the goblin drawled in surprise, and left me in peace for a while.

After that we walked on without speaking. Glo-Glo kept pushing up the pace, and sometimes we had to run after him. The rain kept falling, getting stronger all the time, and I wrapped myself tighter in the jacket of the newly deceased Fagred, may a h'san'kor devour his bones! We walked for an hour without any rest, and I imagined what it must have been like for the warriors who had rushed halfway across Zagraba to help me, and were now running away from the orcs with me. Just as it started to get light, we left the area of the old cliffs and found ourselves beside a very wide stream that babbled merrily. Our path now lay along its banks. About twenty minutes later Egrassa asked Glo-Glo to stop and raised his hand to ask for silence.

"What's going on?" I asked Kli-Kli.

"Shhh," he hissed at me.

Like everyone else, I started listening to the morning silence and the sound of the rain. And eventually I heard that other sound, too. It almost merged into the rain, so I didn't realize what it was at first.

Boo-oom! Boo-oom! Booo-oom!

Very faint, barely distinguishable—the rumble of the orcs' war drums, sounding the alarm.

"So they have noticed the pit's empty and the shaman's turned his toes up!" Hallas said, and spat.

"We have to hurry."

"How can we hurry any more, Harold?" Deler grumbled.

"Go in under the trees, I've got to do a bit of work here," said Glo-Glo.

Milord Alistan was about to object, but Egrassa shook his head. The count frowned in annoyance, but decided to follow the elf's advice.

By this time the rain had changed to a fine drizzle, which made things a bit more pleasant, and the trees at least offered some sort of protection. Everyone walked away from the old goblin and started watching as he twirled like a top, waving his arms about and stirring up the leaves. All this went on for quite a long time, and Milord Alistan started getting a bit nervous—and so did all the others.

"How long are we going to watch the old crackpot prancing about?" Lamplighter asked when he couldn't take any more.

"He's not an old crackpot," Kli-Kli snapped. "He's Glo-Glo, one of the very greatest shamans of our time!"

"So how do you know?" Hallas sneered.

"I just know, that's all!" Kli-Kli said sulkily, and stared down at his boots. "And by the way, he happens to be the keeper of the great shaman Tre-Tre's *Book of Prophecies*."

Boo-oom! Boo-oom! Boo-oom! The orcs' drums sang faintly in the distance.

"We have to be sure they don't overtake us, milord!" Now it was the patient Eel whose nerves were feeling the strain.

"Oi!" Kli-Kli squealed and put his hands over his eyes.

Lamplighter swore. Everybody stared at what Glo-Glo had done. And there was something to stare at! The goblin finished casting his spell, and for as far as we could see, all the leaves fell off all the trees and hung in the air. Then they were joined by the leaves that had been lying quietly on the ground.

And what came after that was really strange—I had the impression that thousands of hands started tearing up the poor leaves and didn't stop until every leaf had been reduced to a hundred little pieces. In another instant they were transformed into thousands and thousands of winged creatures. A thick, dark cloud rose up and hung, trembling, above the forest. And then every part of this vast cloud started to grow, and grew until it reached the size of a large fist.

"May the gods save us!" Hallas exclaimed, trying to shout above the droning roar.

"They won't!" Eel shouted.

And then the goblin waved his hand in the direction of the rumbling drums and the cloud of magical hornets went darting away. There were thousands and thousands of them, and it really was frightening. One of the hornets broke away from the cloud and flew to us. I got a very clear look at its impassive, glowing silver eyes, its shaggy black and yellow belly, and fearsome purple sting.

We only moved again when the drone of hornets' wings had faded into the distance.

"Well, what kind of leaves do you call those?" Hallas blurted out, looking at Glo-Glo warily.

"I'm glad you liked it, gnome," said the shaman, scowling wearily as he walked over to us. "I spent a week preparing that spell, so I was curious to see how it would work out, myself. Now I have to rest for half an hour. You don't need to hurry anymore. The Firstborn will be too far busy to think about you. Gnome, do you have any water?"

Hallas hastily held his flask out to Glo-Glo, who took a mouthful, handed the flask back, and said, "Everyone take a stroll in the rain for half an hour, and I'll sit here under a tree and recover my strength."

Egrassa agreed with the goblin again, and we walked off, leaving the shaman alone. Without its leaves the forest was naked, and it seemed colder.

"Did you see that?" Deler asked Lamplighter in amazement.

"Did you? I wouldn't change places with the orcs for all the vessels of Sagra."

"I told you he was the great Glo-Glo!" said Kli-Kli, with his eyes staring wildly. "Be thankful he didn't turn you into worms!"

Hallas gave the goblin a frightened glance. Glo-Glo was sitting with his eyes closed. He looked as if he was asleep.

"He is a very powerful shaman. The most powerful I have ever seen. To work the Hornets of Vengeance would have taken five of our First Ten sorcerers," the elf told Milord Alistan in a low voice.

As usual, the count nodded without speaking, and sat down under the nearest maple.

"I don't think we'll lose anything by waiting for him to recover."

"Have you noticed the drums have stopped?" the jester yapped from under his hood. We listened. He was right. Zagraba was totally silent, not a sound apart from the cautious babbling of the stream trying not to attract the great shaman's attention. A very interesting little thought was gradually taking shape in my mind. Supposing that . . .

"Oh, Harold!" Kli-Kli's voice shattered my reverie. "Of course, you didn't hear a thing I just said to you, did you?"

"Ah? Sorry, Kli-Kli. I was thinking."

The jester sighed and asked me again: "Where's your crossbow? Did the orcs take it?"

"No, I left it in Hrad Spein."

"Will you tell me what happened there?"

"Not now. Some time later, maybe."

"I understand," Kli-Kli sighed, and stopped pestering me with questions.

"Did you have a hard time?" Hallas asked sympathetically.

"Yes."

"But you still did what the king told you to do. Well done. I'm glad I was wrong about you," the captain of the royal guard put in unexpectedly.

"Thank you, Milord Alistan."

I pulled my hood off and raised my face to the streaming rain, which had grown stronger again. Kli-Kli gave a quiet gasp.

"What happened to your hair?" asked Eel.

"What's wrong with it?"

Kli-Kli hastily fished a little mirror out of one of his pockets and handed it to me. In the mirror I saw that my temples were completely gray.

15

THE SHAMAN AND THE JESTER

Fortunately, no one bombarded me with questions and I hung about beside the stream for about ten minutes completely on my own. I needed to settle my nerves a bit and have a think. A touch of gray at the temples was nothing to worry about; the important thing was that my head was still on my shoulders. Then, when the idea that had been eluding me all this time finally took shape, I walked away from the stream, straight toward Glo-Glo, who was sitting under a tree. Hallas watched me go, but he didn't say anything; neither did any of the others. I walked up to the goblin and squatted down beside him. The old shaman didn't even open his eyes. Was he asleep?

"Was there something you wanted to ask, my boy?" Glo-Glo said suddenly.

"Yes."

"I'm listening."

"I was wondering how, with spells as powerful as that, the goblins perished under the swords of men and the yataghans of the orcs."

"Surely you do not think your historians would tell you the truth?" the goblin asked with a crooked smile. "We are not sheep, Harold. We died, but we took many of our enemies with us."

"You mean . . ."

"I mean, do not believe all those tales about the goblins being a defenseless race. Yes, we are short in stature, but our shamanism is much closer to the Kronk-a-Mor, and we sold our lives for a high price. Do you know why men started hunting us all of a sudden?"

"Well . . . ," I started, and hesitated.

"No, not because we have ugly faces—I won't even mention what kind of faces you have. And not because you thought we were allies of the orcs. We possess a magic that is almost primordial, and from early times your Order was obsessed with our magic, or to be more precise, our battle magic, and so they went to any lengths to get their hands on our shamanism and our books. Naturally, we did not wish to share—this knowledge is not for men—but the Order pursued us until it almost exterminated us. Or, to be more precise, until more than a hundred thousand men were lost in our forests. Do not be surprised that you have never heard about any of this. Nobody has. It happened in times long past, and the Order will never speak of its defeats."

The goblin chuckled again and opened his eyes.

"But . . ."

"But this is no secret to the goblins. We are always glad of a chance to remind you of how we gave your magicians and soldiers a bloody nose. No one bothers us any longer, and we have no great wish to leave our forests. We have our work to do, and you have yours. Have I answered your question?"

"Arising out of what you just told me, I have another one."

"Ask."

"I'll never believe that a shaman with such great power as you have could have fallen into Bagard's hands so easily."

"You're a smart one, Dancer," the goblin chuckled, and I started in surprise.

"How do you—"

"I just know. Didn't I just tell you that the goblins have their purpose in this world? I won't bore you with a long lecture on the balance and the Great Houses, I think you know quite a lot about that already. In recent times my greatest concern has been, just as it was my father's and my father's father's—"

"I understand," I said, interrupting the goblin hastily. I suspected the listing of all the old shaman's ancestors could go on for so long that I'd forget what my question was.

"He understands . . . ," Glo-Glo said, peering at me in annoyance. "Did no one ever tell you that it's rude to interrupt your elders? Now, where was I? Ah, yes . . . The primary concern of my ancestors, who trace their line back to great insane shaman Tre-Tre, has always been waiting for the Dancer in the Shadows. That is, for you."

"Nice to meet you," I chuckled skeptically.

"Don't try to be clever. We had to wait until a Dancer came to our world, as Tre-Tre foretold in his great book, the *Bruk-Gruk*. And when the Dancer arrived, we were supposed to teach him how to reach the Primordial World and give it life once again."

"Oh!" That was all I could think of to say.

"But I can see you've managed all that without any help from me," the goblin declared in a disappointed voice. "Don't try to deny it, I can see the glitter of the primordial flame in your eyes, and that hoarfrost on your temples. . . . It speaks volumes to one who knows."

"You still haven't answered my question."

"Haven't I?" Glo-Glo asked, putting on a surprised face. "I have been unlucky. I am the last of the male line in Tre-Tre's clan, and you appeared too late. When the stars pointed to you, I was already too old, and the responsibilities I bore were too great for me to leave Zagraba. I had to find other ways to act, hoping that others would be able to do what I could not. You bear a mark, my boy, a mark that any goblin of my line can see. Not even see, but sense a hundred leagues away. So I knew when you escaped from Hrad Spein, I knew what was going to happen next, and I didn't like it one little bit. I had to improvise, and after that all I could do was wait until you fell into their hands and play the role of a half-witted shaman. So that is what I did."

"But things didn't turn out the way you wanted, did they?"

"No, indeed. I hadn't anticipated that there would be a shaman in the detachment, that I would be identified and deprived of my powers. If I hadn't been wearing those mittens, we would have escaped the first night we met."

"Wouldn't it have been easier not to get yourself captured by the orcs, but simply to warn me not to go near the orcs?"

"No, it wouldn't!" the old shaman snapped. "I knew what was going to happen, but I didn't know where to find you. You Dancers are tricky lads. Hard to locate using search magic. I had to make use of the orcs."

"And were you really in the Labyrinth before?"

"Yes. Everything I said about the Labyrinth is absolutely true. But I hadn't been counting on going back there again after thirty years."

"You took a risk."

"The risk was entirely justified. If your friends hadn't come, I would have used the aces I had up my sleeve."

"And what are they?"

"That's not important now. Well then, it's time to be going, before the Firstborn can gather their wits."

"One more question."

"Ah! You really are quite excessively curious. What else?"

"What makes a Dancer so important to you?"

"The balance! I want my descendants to carry on living in Siala for thousands of thousands of years, and a fellow like you can send the balance way off kilter with a snap of your fingers."

"And the Horn?"

"Forget about that silly tin whistle! The Horn is just the Horn. You and the Horn are like a candle flame and a moth. That's enough, no more questions!"

"You said that others would do what you weren't able to do. Who did you mean by that?"

I asked the question and immediately found the answer, standing quite nearby and gazing at us apprehensively from under his hood with his bright blue eyes.

"If you understand everything, why do you ask?" the shaman laughed. "I couldn't go myself, I had to send . . . my apprentice. Kli-Kli, come here!"

The royal jester approached us warily.

"Apprentice?" I echoed stupidly.

"What's so surprising about that?" Glo-Glo chuckled. "There wasn't anybody else I could send. The *Bruk-Gruk* said you would meet the king of Valiostr, so to make sure of running into you, my apprentice had to become a jester."

"Kli-Kli?" I said, turning to the sullen, silent goblin for an explanation.

"Yes?" he squeaked from under his hood. "It's all true, Harold. I'm terribly sorry if I caused you any inconvenience, but it had to be done."

"Why don't you tell him where I told you to stay all the time?" Glo-Glo suggested, knitting his brows menacingly.

"With Harold," the jester muttered.

"Louder! I can't hear you!"

"With Harold!"

"Then why did he go into the Palaces of Bone alone, and why did I have to abandon all the affairs of the tribe and come dashing to his rescue, while you were busy—"

"But grandfather!" Kli-Kli interrupted.

"Grandfather?" I said, gaping at him wide-eyed.

"Why are you so surprised, Harold? It's only natural for me to take my own flesh and blood as an apprentice."

"Granddad!" Kli-Kli squeaked, and gave me a frightened look.

"It's just that Kli-Kli mentioned several times that his grandfather used to be a shaman, and I thought that meant you were dead."

"So you buried me as well?" said Glo-Glo, rolling his eyes furiously. "Well, thank you!"

"But I—"

"Who on earth do you take after? You've shamed your ancestors again!"

Kli-Kli tried to make excuses, and Glo-Glo gave him the tongue-lashing of all time, saying a granddaughter like that must have been a gift from the forest spirits. I listened, and I was puzzled. The intensity of the shaman's feelings seemed to be confusing his tongue.

"Kli-Kli!" I put in, when Glo-Glo decided to take a break to catch his breath. "Why is he talking to you as if you were a girl?"

The goblin looked as if he wanted the ground to open up and swallow him. At least, that was my impression.

"The man's a fool!" said Glo-Glo, throwing his hands up in the air. "I told you in plain human language that I'm the last in the male line of the great shaman Tre-Tre! Kli-Kli is my granddaughter."

"Kli-Kli! You're . . . you're a SHE? You're a girl?"

The goblin (gobliness?) had the good grace not to look me in the eye, and she muttered something under her breath. All I made out was "yes."

I stood there open-mouthed, and then sat down. I must say, this was quite a blow! Life had never treated me to such an unexpected surprise before! It was inconceivable. Kli-Kli was *she*. A female goblin! A girl! The jester's little oddities suddenly made sense to me and didn't seem so odd anymore.

I must have been a fine sight. Glo-Glo chuckled sympathetically, while Kli-Kli didn't know where to put herself. When I more or less recovered, I thought the best thing to do was laugh.

"You're . . . you're not angry?" she asked me fearfully.

"No, Kli-Kli!" I exclaimed, shaking my head. "If I'm angry, it's only with myself, for not realizing straightaway."

"You couldn't have," she told me with a superior note in her voice. "All goblins look the same to men."

"But why, in the name of a h'san'kor, why?"

"It was simpler that way, Harold," she said with a faint shrug. "It opened lots of doors to me, including the door of the royal palace. And things were much simpler with all of you, too. If Milord Alistan had known who I really was, he probably wouldn't have let me go on the journey. And if that had happened, I couldn't have taken care of you."

"I don't think he would have done anything. After all, you brought a letter from the king, giving you permission to take part in the expedition."

"The letter was a forgery," Kli-Kli chuckled. "Do you really think the king would have sent his jester on business like this?"

"Was it hard playing a male part, apprentice?" Glo-Glo put in.

"I got used to it, Granddad. It was harder being a jester and a fool. Although . . . when you're a jester and you're out in open view, nobody notices you, nobody takes you seriously or thinks of you as a threat, and you can do things that others aren't allowed to do."

"Did nobody guess who you really were, Kli-Kli?"

"I told you, Harold, we all look the same to people."

Ah, darkness! I just couldn't get used to it! She was right! How often did we see goblins in Valiostr? Not very. How often did we see female goblins? Even less often than male ones. Or, rather, we'd never seen any. It was rumored that the goblin women never left Zagraba. I'd never trust rumors again.

"Aaaaah . . . ," I said, shaking my head, still unable to believe what had happened.

"Well, it is true . . ."—she wrinkled up her forehead—"it is true that Miralissa knew. I had to tell her. She helped me guide you and save you."

"Guide? Save?"

"How many times did I save your life? And there were so many times you'll never even know about!"

I didn't say anything.

"That's gratitude for you! Do you think it was easy to squeeze you through into the Primordial World the first time? Miralissa and I almost made ourselves sick doing it. And as for guiding you . . . Hah! There were so many times I can't remember them all," she said, gesturing with her hand.

There was nothing I could do but listen to her revelations and feel amazed. Good going, Kli-Kli!

"So, apart from Miralissa—may she dwell in the light—and you, no one knows. Oh, and I told Honeycomb before we left."

The goblin girl chuckled. So that was why Honeycomb had laughed so loud and long when Kli-Kli whispered in his ear!

"So what now?" I asked.

"What now, my boy?" Glo-Glo replied. "If we're talking about long-term plans, then you need to get to Avendoom as quickly as possible and hand the Horn over to that Order of yours. You turned out to be a lot stronger than I expected. . . . In a good sense, of course. So there's no need to be too worried about the balance just yet. No, don't tell me about the Horn, the Fallen Ones, and the Great Game of the Masters. I know all about that. Compared with what you could have got up to, what might be coming—and that, please note, is a possible shift in the balance—is no more than a minor inconvenience."

"And what could I have got up to?"

"There's no point in talking about that now," said Glo-Glo. "You've been through the Mirror of Choice and chosen your path. My mind is easy, so there's no need for you to worry. You don't have to know the entire background of the prophecy at this stage. You'll find out in good time, you virtually have an eternity in your hands—in the literal and the figurative sense. The only important thing at this moment is the Horn; everything else is secondary."

"Master Goblin!" Egrassa called to Glo-Glo. "Have you rested?"

"I'm coming!" the shaman replied. "Resting's all very well, but now I won't be able to work any magic more complicated than a fireball for a week. Harold, do I need to tell you there's no need to spread the word about our conversation?"

"No, you don't."

"Well then, that's just wonderful. Now help an old man get up. Creating that damned spell of mine has swallowed up all my strength."

I gave the goblin my hand and helped him get to his feet.

"Thank you, my boy. I'll go and have a word with the elf and your marshal with the mustache."

Glo-Glo plodded off toward the warriors, who were waiting for him impatiently. I was about to follow him, but Kli-Kli called to me.

"Hey, Harold!"

"Yes?"

"Are you really not angry with me? You know, for . . . You know what I mean."

I paused for a moment, trying to find the right words, and she kept her cautious glance fixed on me all the time.

"I'm really not angry, Kli-Kli," I said eventually. "It's impossible to stay angry with you for long."

Did I imagine it, or did I catch a glimpse of relief in her eyes?

"Wordofonner?"

"On the noble word of honor of a master thief, Kli-Kli."

"Okie-dokie!" she said, more cheerful now. "Only don't tell anyone, or they'll all start worrying about me. Trying to take care of me, make sure nothing happens to me. Deler's worse than a broody hen, if he found out the truth. . . ."

My lips curved into an impish smile as I imagined Deler's face when he learned that Kli-Kli was not he, but she. And Hallas would probably be so surprised, he'd swallow his own beard. Kli-Kli obviously read my thoughts, and she gave me a good-natured poke in the ribs. Life is never boring when there's a goblin around—boy or girl.

The rain didn't stop until the next morning. In that time we'd tramped darkness only knows how far and built up a pretty good lead over any possible pursuit. At least we hadn't heard the rumbling of the orcs' drums again. We stopped to rest for the night beside some huge boulders that gave us some protection against the rain. The halt was appallingly brief. I felt as if I'd only just closed my eyes, and there was Lamplighter shaking me awake.

Milord Alistan finally deigned to notice that I had no more weapons than a nun of Silna. Mumr immediately presented me with his dagger, and Deler attempted to give me the small ax that always hung behind his back, with his shield, but I refused. That's not my weapon.

"Can you handle a battle staff, Harold?" Egrassa asked unexpectedly.

"No," I said, rather surprised by the question. "A walking staff, maybe, but only a little bit."

"It's all the same. In that case, you'll be able to manage the spear." The elf handed me the Gray One's krasta. "The s'kash and the bow are enough for me, but this will suit you better. At least you can hold your enemies off for a while."

"Thank you," I said, taking the weapon.

"Only, if you're going to swing it, don't forget that one end's weighted. I wouldn't like to see it go flying out of your hands at just the wrong moment," Egrassa warned me, and after that the question of the weapon never came up again.

With the gray vampire's legacy in my hands, I felt more confident. And the chain mail that had been left in Mumr's safekeeping while I took my trip round

Hrad Spein inspired me with some hope, too. We had to eat on the march, whatever the gods provided. And that day the gods weren't very well disposed toward us, or you could say my stomach was never anywhere near full. Kli-Kli ambled along up at the front, behind Glo-Glo, and I kept catching myself thinking I couldn't get used to the idea that the goblin was really a gobliness.

The group was in fairly high spirits, which was understandable enough—the orcs didn't seem to be planning to chase us. In his joy, Hallas even started crooning "The Song of the Crazy Miners."

To build his dam across the stream
The beaver gnaws the bark
The badger digs to build his set
And we carve out the rock!

In arrogance that does not speak
The haughty mountains stand.
Behold our fury surge and seethe
As our mattocks pound and pound.

Who fears the mountains' arrogance,
With beer himself consoles,
But we drink fury for our strength
And the laughter in our souls.

The granite trembles as we swing
And we hack and hack away.
Beneath the mountains in our mines
No god could last a day.

We are the mountains' only Kings,
The depths defer to the gnome.
Be wary, then, of entering
The vastness of our home.

We level mountains to the ground,
Make rivers seethe and surge,
And death and blood can only feed
The fury of our rage!

The fire and flood we both do scorn
For the distant battle's story.
We are the true Bones of the earth—
Behold the Miners' fury!

"Well, well," Deler muttered good-naturedly after listening to the song all the way through. "Lucky's started his crowing again."

"You're just envious because your race doesn't have any songs like that, even in the Zam-da-Mort," Hallas chuckled in anticipation of an old familiar quarrel.

"You can find all sorts of things in the Castle of Death, and you know that perfectly well," the dwarf said, avoiding an argument with the gnome.

"So I've heard," said Hallas, suddenly serious, and he didn't sing any more songs.

By lunchtime the sun peeped out, which made the walking much more pleasant. Glo-Glo suddenly started veering farther and farther left, and the stream that had been our companion for so long was left behind among the trees. Now we were not walking south, but west. Milord Alistan seemed rather unhappy with this circumstance, and Glo-Glo had to explain that there was an orc city nearby, and we had to make a detour. Unless, of course, we wanted to enjoy the hospitality of the Firstborn.

After trudging a fair distance through the forest undergrowth, by evening we were back beside our old friend, the stream, and while it was still light, we reached a dense grove of fir trees that held the stream tight in its shaggy, prickly embrace. We spent the night there, safely concealed from prying eyes by the huge fir trees. Egrassa forbade us to make a fire—there were orcs nearby—and we had to spend the whole night without any warmth. Twilight fell in the forest suddenly—but then, it always does in autumn.

Halas and Deler went to sleep straightaway (they were on sentry duty for the second half of the night). I started settling down to sleep, too, but as soon as I lay down and snuggled up tight in my warm blanket, someone shook me by the shoulder. Mumr.

"Yes?"

"Show me it, eh?" he asked in a plaintive voice.

"What?" I asked, puzzled.

"The Horn. We never had a chance to get a decent look at it back at the Labyrinth. I'm really curious to see what we've done all this for."

"But it's dark! Egrassa said we can't light a fire. The Firstborn might smell the smoke."

"I've got a way out," Egrassa said unexpectedly, and a small glow appeared between the palms of his hands. "I don't know much shamanism, but I can give you three minutes of light."

The magical light lasted just long enough for us to take a good look at each other's faces. Apart from Deler and Hallas, nobody was even thinking of sleeping. Everybody was waiting for Harold to show them the Horn. I had to get up and open the bag that never left my side.

"So that's it . . . ," Eel murmured, examining the artifact with an amazed expression.

"May I . . . ," Milord Alistan inquired timidly.

I gladly handed him the Rainbow Horn. As far as I was concerned, he could have it. He could keep the tin whistle safe for his beloved king.

The old shaman was standing closest to the captain of the guard, and the Horn ended up in his hands. He closed his eyes, held the artifact against his forehead, made a face as if he'd eaten a whole plateful of sour gooseberries, and delivered his verdict:

"It is weak. Very weak. The power has almost left it; it will only hold out for a few more weeks, and then . . ." Glo-Glo didn't finish what he was saying, but everybody knew what would happen then.

"So we need to press on," said Alistan Markauz.

"We still have masses of time, milord. In early November the S'u-dar is already snowbound, and it will be very difficult for the Nameless One to leave his lair. And then it's a long journey from the Needles of Ice to the Lonely Giant. The sorcerer's army won't reach the fortress before mid-January," Lamplighter reassured the count.

"Mumr's right, milord. A winter campaign is too difficult. The Desolate Lands are completely snowbound. In winter the Slumbering Forest is a dangerous place, even for servants of the Nameless One. The Crayfish Dukedom will take another two months to start moving," said Eel, shaking his head thoughtfully. "The enemy will wait until spring, when the passes will be free of snow."

"And what if he doesn't?" Egrassa asked.

"If he doesn't wait, then this winter campaign will cost him a quarter of his army, Tresh Egrassa."

The warriors argued and discussed the various possibilities for an attack by the enemy. Kli-Kli yawned frantically, covering her mouth with her hand, and to be honest, I must confess that I was struggling to stay awake, too. But the others seemed just fine. Were they made of iron, or what? Before going to sleep, I put the Rainbow Horn back in the bag and checked on the other things, too. The Key was there all right, but the emeralds I had carried so diligently halfway across the Palaces of Bone had disappeared without trace. I would have laughed, but I was far too sleepy. Those cursed orcs had stolen what was rightfully mine, may the darkness take them.

I was the last to wake up; all the others were already on their feet. Hallas was handing out the meager ration. When he noticed me, the gnome winked and thrust a piece of stale bread and a slice of dried meat into my hand. That was all there was for breakfast.

"What time is it?" I moaned.

"Darkness only knows, Harold," Deler answered, sharpening the blade of his beloved poleax with a whetstone. "The mist's incredibly thick, so I can't really say, but dawn was no more than fifteen minutes ago."

"We're moving out, Harold, roll up your blanket," said Alistan Markauz. He didn't intend to wait until I was wide awake.

We walked slowly now. Who knew what might be hidden in the mist, and running into an orc outpost would be the easiest thing in the world. So we had to be on the lookout as we advanced. It was absolutely silent all around. The shroud of mist swallowed up all the sounds, and even the babbling of the stream sounded strangely subdued and ominous. Kli-Kli shuddered and kept turning her head warily this way and that. When she caught me looking at her, she said, "I hate the mist. It makes us all blind."

"Don't be afraid, Kli-Kli," Hallas said to cheer her up. "If there was anything here, we'd have run into trouble a long time ago."

"I know," she muttered. "But even so, I've got a bad feeling. Something's going to happen. I can smell it."

"Please don't start spreading panic, Jester," Eel implored her. But despite his skeptical tone of voice, he still checked to make sure his "brother" and "sister" came out of their scabbards easily.

Forty minutes later we remembered her warning. It was already quite light, but the mist was showing no sign of disappearing, and so we couldn't make the sound out clearly at first.

Boo-oom! Boo-oom! Boo-oom!

The mist swallowed up the sounds, and we felt the rumble of the drums more with our skin than with our ears.

"Orcs!" Deler hissed, grabbing his poleax.

"They caught up after all!"

Hallas uttered a long, florid curse combining human and gnomish. His brief oration included a mention of the orcs appearing in Siala through some misunderstanding, and that was followed by a listing of the kinds of intercourse orcs indulged in when they weren't banging on their drums.

"Hallas, shut up!" Milord Alistan growled.

The gnome stopped in the middle of an especially florid turn of phrase, and Egrassa lay down on the ground, parted the leaves, said a few words in his guttural language, and started to listen. The drums carried on.

"They're an hour and a half away. Moving very quickly."

"How many of them are there, Tresh Egrassa?" the count asked, gripping the hilt of his sword and straining to see something through the wall of fog.

"I don't know, milord. I'm no master at weaving these spells. I can only say that there are many of them."

"Your little bees didn't do us much good, shaman!" Hallas told Glo-Glo in a frankly spiteful tone. "Now what are you going to do?"

"Take you by the legs and give the orcs' army a good hammering with your head!" Glo-Glo replied furiously. "If it wasn't for my spell, they'd be roasting the soles of your feet already!"

"Can you help us, most venerable sir?" asked Milord Alistan, taking the bull by the horns.

"If milord has in mind delightful little bees or some kind of thunder and lightning, then my answer is no. I won't be able to work any real impressive magic for a long time. Just a few small things."

"What about Kli-Kli?" I blurted out.

"Not advanced enough, Harold," said Glo-Glo, shaking his head. "He still has far too much to learn."

"A jester working spells is all I need now! Is there anything you can do?"

"Yes, I can draw the pursuit away from you, at least for a while. And take this." Glo-Glo handed Milord Alistan something that looked like a lump of soil.

"What's that?" Lamplighter asked.

"Your salvation," said Glo-Glo, wiping his hands on his cloak. "If you really have your backs against the wall, crush this lump in your fist, and those who are pursuing you will follow the one who crushes it."

"How do you mean?" Eel asked.

"The idea is that the one who activates the spell runs away from the group, and the orcs will follow him, thinking that they are chasing all of you. The trouble is that the solitary individual will probably be killed, the orcs will not lose the trail, and sooner or later they will catch up again. So milord, decide for yourselves which of you will run if it should come to that. I can lead away those who are following us now, and lead them a long way off—the forest spirits be praised, I have enough strength for that—so beware, not of those who are behind, but those who are ahead. Since they have survived, our pursuers have probably informed their kinsmen about the fugitives, and there are two large orc settlements ahead. The forest is full of orcs, so keep your eyes open. Follow the stream to the lake and turn northwest. Perhaps you will break through. Tresh Egrassa, may fortune smile on you."

The elf nodded.

"That's all I have to say. Move quickly and try not to stop, but don't get careless. Kli-Kli, one moment."

Glo-Glo took his granddaughter to one side and the others set about checking their weapons.

Kli-Kli came running up, and Glo-Glo addressed all of us: "May the forest spirits preserve you."

And then he added, just for me: "Take good care of yourself, Dancer, and do what must be done."

I didn't know what he meant by that "do," but I nodded, just to be on the safe side.

"Thank you for getting me out of the Labyrinth, Glo-Glo."

The old shaman just chuckled, then he nodded in farewell and disappeared into the trees.

"Forward," said Egrassa, and started running alongside the stream.

16

THE SONG OF THE FLUTE

I had no more strength to run and I collapsed and fell. What I needed now was to lie there for a while, get my breath back, recover my strength. But my dreams were not fated to come true. I was grabbed by the arms from both sides and jerked back onto my feet.

We will catch you. . . . We will kill you! the drums sang behind the wall of mist.

"Run, Harold!" Eel hissed.

"Just a little farther!" said Lamplighter, adding his plea to his comrade's. "Run, lad! You can do it!"

Gulping, I nodded. I had an unmerciful stabbing pain in my side, but I had to run, I had to.

"Take him!" Eel barked, and he and Mumr dragged me on.

I set one foot in front of the other as best as I was able. Hallas and Deler followed the example of their two comrades and grabbed the exhausted Kli-Kli. She didn't have any strength to resist. So the gobliness and I were the only two who had broken down after the two-hour chase. But the warriors were tired, too, and now we were weighing them down. I accepted the support from Eel and Lamplighter for about ten minutes and then ran on my own.

"Can you manage?" the Garrakian asked me uncertainly. "Give me the spear."

I nodded weakly.

We will catch you. . . . We will kill . . .

At noon the mist was still hanging all around us, as if Zagraba had decided to hide us forever from the eyes of the world and its own primeval thickets. But I didn't care anymore. An eternity later, when Egrassa realized he was the only one who could maintain the pace he had set and everyone else urgently needed a rest, the elf ordered a halt. I dropped where I stood.

"How d'you like dashing about like this?" Kli-Kli wheezed.

"I'm not used to such long-distance sprints," I answered. "How about you?"

"I'm all right, but Deler was carrying me piggyback for the last forty minutes, and he was suffering."

"Don't worry, my friend, I'm all right," said Deler, breathing like a punctured blacksmith's bellows—as we all were.

"The drums have stopped!" Eel said, interrupting us. He was sitting on the ground, leaning back against an old golden-leaf.

"Have they really gone?" Mumr asked in relief.

Lamplighter had had it harder than anyone else. Running through the forest with a bidenhander and looking after me at the same time was no easy job.

"Either the Firstborn have decided to pursue us in silence, which isn't like them at all, or the goblin has managed to put them off our trail," Egrassa mused thoughtfully. "How much time do you need to rest, milord?"

"How much time do we have?"

"A little more than ten minutes, then we'll have to set out again if we don't want the orc patrols to find us. We'll go along the stream—it flows northward. The orcs aren't gods, they could quite easily lose our trail, and if we hurry, we'll be out of the Golden Forest in a week."

"And then it will take us another week to get out of Zagraba. We've stirred up the Firstborn, Egrassa; they probably won't stop following us at the edge of the Golden Forest," Eel objected.

"Maybe you're right, and maybe you're not," the dark elf told the Garrakian. "If we don't make any noise and attract attention to ourselves, I'm quite capable of leading us out of Zagraba. Only in the name of all the gods—move quietly. The mist is thick, the orcs are very close, and I'd prefer it if we noticed them before they know we're here."

I'd have said the eight orcs were moving very quietly, but to Egrassa's keen hearing they sounded very noisy, so we had no trouble concealing ourselves and falling on the enemy en masse. We couldn't afford to let the Firstborn go—they might come across our tracks and realize we'd duped them and then come after us again or, even worse, warn their friends. In that case the element of surprise would be completely lost, and we'd find ourselves back in the role of foxes running from a pack of hounds.

It was all over before it even started. The orcs hadn't been expecting our ambush, and the element of surprise was decisive—and fatal. Kli-Kli and Eel threw knives at the same instant, and Egrassa used his bow. Before the orcs realized what was happening, four of them were dead. The other four drew their yataghans and one dashed toward Egrassa, as the most dangerous of our group. But the Firstborn's way was blocked by Mumr, who had been ordered to protect our only bowman at any cost. Lamplighter met the Firstborn, struck him in the groin with a rapid jab, immediately dodged aside so that he was behind his opponent, and sliced off the Firstborn's leg with a single smooth stroke.

The skirmish was so brief, I didn't have time to join in. Alistan, holding his sword with both hands, clashed with another orc, but the two enemies had only exchanged one blow apiece when Egrassa put an arrow in the orc's back. The same fate overtook the orc who went for Deler.

The last of the four was felled by Hallas. The Firstborn tried to hit the gnome with an ax, but Lucky grabbed hold of the handle and struck the orc on the leg with his mattock. When the Firstborn let go of his ax and fell over on his back, the gnome brought his mattock down on his enemy's head. The whole battle lasted just over twenty seconds.

"Kli-Kli, pull out your knives and my arrows; everyone else grab these orcs by the arms and drag them well away from the stream," the elf ordered. "I'll risk using a little bit of magic, perhaps it will put them off our trail."

We hid the bodies among the roots of two old oaks that were almost intertwined with each other and then piled a heap of moldy leaves over them. Eel and Hallas went back over the site of the battle and tried to eliminate all traces of blood. Meanwhile Egrassa put some kind of spell on the improvised grave.

"It's a waste of time," Mumr sighed, wiping off the blade of his sword with a bundle of leaves. "It looks like it's been trampled by a herd of mammoths. You can't put the soil back in place or spread the leaves out again. If only Lady Miralissa was here. . . ."

The gods were kind, and for the rest of that day nobody found us. Once Egrassa thought he could hear a distant rumble of drums, but it was only the wind wandering through the branches of the trees that had lost most of their leaves. The stream that had been our escort for the last two days had grown to the size of a small river and the river flowed into a large lake, which we reached in the twilight. The mist and the advancing darkness made it impossible to see the opposite shore.

We settled in for the night beside the lake, making our resting place among the dense growth of tall reeds. It was a restless and very chilly night. Cold gusts of wind swirled through the rustling sea of reeds, chilling me to the marrow of my bones. I woke up several times, shuddering from the cold, and then went back to sleep, but the moment I did, I started dreaming there were orcs creeping through the tall reeds, about to attack us. I woke up again and stared for a long time at the swaying wall of dry grass.

Milord Alistan got us all up when it was still dark and, still shrouded in thick mist, we moved on toward the north.

By the time it grew light we'd covered quite a distance. The lake was far behind us now, but the cursed mist showed no signs of dissolving in the first rays of the sun, and Zagraba looked like a forest out of some ghost story.

The dark forms of tree trunks loomed up out of the thick mantle of white. Everything around us seemed to be dead or hiding, waiting for the mist to clear out of the forest. The only time I'd heard silence like this in Zagraba was when we were crossing the Red Spinney. And the moment I thought about what had happened there, I seemed to feel a blunt needle jab into my heart. I pulled myself up short and tried not to think about bad things. The last thing I wanted to do was call down the disaster of a h'san'kor on our heads. But the harder I tried not to think about anything frightening, the faster all sorts of unpleasant thoughts came crowding into my head. That blunt needle was still there, and I winced and gasped whenever it jabbed me really hard. Eventually I stopped trying to ignore it and turned to Kli-Kli, who was the first to sense something the last time.

"Kli-Kli, isn't there anything bothering you?" I asked in a whisper.

She stopped, sniffed at the air, thought for a moment, and replied, "A cold in the nose."

"That's not what I mean!" I protested, just a little bit annoyed by her slow-wittedness. "You sensed something was wrong in the Red Spinney, didn't you?"

"I did," she agreed. "There was real danger there. But I don't feel anything like that here. If there's danger here, it's perfectly ordinary, and I can't sense that kind. But you . . . you're the Dancer in the Shadows, maybe that's why. . . . Deler, go and tell Egrassa that our Harold's feeling uneasy."

Deler didn't argue, in fact he wasn't even surprised, he just gave me a quick, sharp glance from under his ginger eyebrows and went off to the elf at the front of our group.

But the dwarf didn't have time to warn anyone. It all happened quickly and very unexpectedly. Shadows with naked yataghans came diving at us out of the mist, another two or three jumped down out of the trees beside our track, and, to top it all, in two places the ground exploded into fountains of leaves as raging beasts emerged from concealed pits. They looked like a cross between a monkey and a wolf. The ambush had been planned brilliantly. They must have been waiting for us for a long time, and this time we were the ones taken by surprise.

"Orcs!" yelled Mumr, swinging his bidenhander down off his shoulder.

"Didre draast! Pu'i edron!" [Take them alive! Apart from the elf!] yelled one of the enemy.

One of the Firstborn blew a small hunting horn and the surprisingly loud sound resounded through the forest, startling the mist. Egrassa's bow was already in his hands, and the orc dropped his horn and clutched at the arrow sticking out of his chest. But it was too late. Another horn sounded somewhere far away, at the very limit of hearing. Before the battle swept me into its deadly vortex, I had time to see Eel holding off two orcs who were trying to reach Egrassa. Then I had my hands full myself.

Kli-Kli and I were closest to the pits, and the wolf-monkeys came dashing at us, growling. They moved very nimbly, but almost sideways, like crabs. They had gaunt bodies, covered with dirty-yellow fur with reddish patches, an impressive set of wolfish teeth, and heavy collars with metal studs.

"Gruns!" Kli-Kli squeaked, and flung one of her throwing knives at the nearest creature. The knife stuck neatly in the side of the orcs' beast, which turned a somersault over its head and started twitching, scraping at the soil and the leaves with its paws. The others kept coming at us, not bothered at all by their comrade's death.

Bang! The loud noise came from behind my back.

Hallas had used his last pistol shot. The sudden sound made one of the gruns stop dead in its tracks, and Deler, who had just polished off his orc, took his small throwing ax out from behind his back and flung it at the beast. The weapon shattered the grun's head with a dull crunch. But it didn't kill it. In its pain and fury, the beast fastened its teeth in the leg of the nearest orc.

"Look out!" yelled Kli-Kli.

Purely by instinct, I held the krasta out in front of me, and the grun impaled itself on the sharp blade at full speed. Kli-Kli threw another knife, but not so neatly this time, and it stuck in a beast's thigh. While it was whining and spinning round on the spot, the ones that were still alive came at me from both sides at once. In desperation I jerked the krasta toward me, freeing the weapon from the heavy body that was stuck on it. One of the gruns leapt through the air, aiming for my throat, and got an arrow in its side. My thanks to Egrassa. The beast crashed into me at full speed and we fell to the ground. I rolled aside smartly, almost losing my spear, and the last of the gruns landed with all four paws on the spot where I had just been lying.

But I hadn't moved far enough, and the beast just caught me with its front paw. Its claws easily ripped through the jacket, and the only thing that saved me was the chain mail I disliked so much—I was wearing it under the jacket. Ignoring the pain from the blow, I kicked the grun in the face with both feet. The beast whined and went flying off, but somehow it managed to land on its paws and jumped at me again. I was already up on my feet and I had time to prepare myself. The spear met the grun in midair and the Smoky Steel easily sliced the monkey in half. I didn't even feel any resistance.

Meanwhile Kli-Kli had finished off the wounded grun and was hastily extracting her knives from the bodies. I could hear Milord Alistan's sword whining somewhere over on the right. Egrassa had swapped his bow for a s'kash and he and Eel were standing back to back, fighting off attacks from orcs who were pressing them hard.

"Behind you, Harold," they barked at me.

I leapt to one side with no delay. The orc who had been about to slice my head off was obviously terribly upset by this, and he came blundering straight at me. One of Kli-Kli's throwing knives whistled through the air, but it hit the center of the Firstborn's shield, which had a picture of some weird and wonderful bird on it. A spear is longer than a yataghan, and I had a slight advantage—I held the orc off until Kli-Kli threw another knife.

This one hit him in the shoulder. Hit him and bounced off. The orc obviously had armor concealed under his yellow jacket. I slashed at him with the krasta and the orc nimbly covered himself with his round shield, but the Gray One's spear sliced straight through this obstacle, and the orc's arm as well. I spun round, and the orc lost his other arm.

"*Karade tig su'in tar!*"[Dispatch them to the darkness!] someone barked in orcish.

Right, so much for that, but how were the others getting on? Eel and

Egrassa were still holding out. I couldn't see Deler. Mumr was managing to hold three orcs at bay with his wagon shaft of a sword. Hallas had just finished off a Firstborn by smashing his mattock into his face. Kli-Kli was dashing to help Lamplighter. . . . But Milord Alistan was in trouble. That lad with the spear creeping up behind him was about to skewer our count like a chicken on a spit.

I yelled to attract the orc's attention and started running with the krasta to help Alistan Markauz. The orc accepted the challenge, grasped his spear with two hands like a staff, and stepped toward me. He struck with the sharp blade on the butt of the shaft, and I was barely fast enough to parry his blows. Trying to counterattack was out of the question. It was a matter of survival. The Firstborn was incredibly agile and he almost caught me in the face with the butt of the spear. I just barely managed to jerk back in time. But in the process I lost my balance and the orc attacked, pushing me away with the center of the shaft between his hands.

I almost fell, and smacked the orc on his fingers with the krasta as hard as I could. The orc howled in pain and let go of the spear with his left hand. I struck at his knees with the shaft of the krasta. My enemy collapsed and I pinned him to the ground without a second thought. Then I pulled the krasta out and hastily looked around.

Milord Alistan was finishing off the last of his opponents. The orc was fending off the blows of the sword with a well-battered shield, but his minutes were already numbered. Kli-Kli seemed to be unhurt. Egrassa and Eel were already hurrying across to help us, after finishing off their opponents. Hallas, who was farthest away from me, was harrying an orc.

The gnome had smashed the yataghan out of the Firstborn's hand, and now the orc had only a dagger to defend himself. The gnome took a step forward to put paid to his enemy, but stumbled over the body of a grun and lost his balance for a moment. The Firstborn immediately took advantage of the gnome's blunder. Moving in close to Lucky, he grabbed hold of his beard, pulled the gnome toward himself, and struck at his unprotected face with the dagger.

Lucky fell, bleeding heavily, and the orc raised his dagger for the final blow. I went dashing to help him, although I knew I'd be too late, but Deler beat me to it. With a mighty roar, he flung his terrible poleax at the orc with both hands. The weapon flashed through the air in a glittering circle and crashed into the orc, slicing through his head and upper body.

"Deler, behind you!" Eel shouted, but it was too late.

An orc who was behind Deler struck the dwarf with a short, broad sword that was quite different from the orcs' usual yataghans. The blow was so powerful that the tip of the sword emerged from the warrior's chest. The Wild Heart swayed and collapsed to his knees. Before the orc could free his sword, Egrassa took up his bow again and turned him into a pin cushion.

It was all over.

The orc who had stabbed Deler with his sword was the last one. We all rushed to Hallas or Deler. The grun that Egrassa had shot in the side was still alive and whimpering as it tried to reach the arrow with its teeth. I paused for a moment to finish the vicious beast off. The orcs' hunting horns gave voice again, but this time much closer.

"Oh, light!" Kli-Kli groaned, falling on her knees beside Hallas. "Oh, light! So much blood! So much blood!"

She kept on repeating those words, and there was panic fluttering in her eyes. It was the first time I'd ever seen our jester in such a state.

"Oh, light! How can this be?" the gobliness wailed. There was an orcish dagger with a notched blade lying beside her.

The moment I saw the gnome, I realized he was in a bad way. The blow had struck his right cheek and the notched blade had made an irregular wound. In fact, the whole right side of Hallas's face was one ragged wound. The orc had struck upward with his weapon and now there was a gaping bloody hole where Lucky's eye used to be.

And there was blood everywhere. Lots of blood. The gnome was still alive, but he seemed to be unconscious.

Egrassa unceremoniously pushed Kli-Kli aside and started trying to do something, whispering some mumbo-jumbo in orcic and sprinkling yellow powder straight onto the wound.

"Eel! How's Deler?" croaked Lamplighter, who was fussing over Hallas.

"He's dying," was the answer.

"Ah, darkness! Darkness! The darkness take them all!" Mumr howled. "Harold, run over to Eel, maybe there's still something . . ."

Without waiting for him to finish, I dashed across to help Eel. Milord Alistan was there, too. The Garrakian hadn't taken the risk of pulling the sword out of the dwarf's back—that would have increased the already powerful loss of blood. Deler was conscious and he was trying to say something, but he could only move his lips without making a sound.

"How can we help him?" I asked.

"Only a miracle can help," Alistan Markauz muttered darkly.

But no miracle happened. A minute later the ginger-haired dwarf died, without having said anything.

"May you dwell in the light," Eel murmured as he carefully closed Deler's eyes.

How had we managed to get caught out so badly? Deler was dead, Hallas was at death's door.

"Harold, we'll mourn later!" said Eel, thumping me fiercely on the shoulder. "Wake up!"

The Garrakian was right. Mumr had found some clean rags somewhere and he was bandaging the gnome's wound. The rags were immediately soaked in blood, but after Egrassa's magical first aid at least the bleeding had slowed down.

Orcish horns on the left warned us that the Firstborn were coming as fast as they could, and they were answered by other horns on the right.

"We haven't got much time, Mumr," said Egrassa.

"I know," the warrior growled as he bound up the gnome's head. "I'm almost finished!"

"How's Deler?" the elf asked.

"Dead."

Kli-Kli gasped and lowered her face into her hands. I patted her on the shoulder, trying to comfort her a little.

"Time to be going! They'll be here soon!"

"I'm done!" said Lamplighter, with his hands covered with blood. "But he won't hold on for long. We've only postponed the end."

"We have to hope for the best. There's no time to make a stretcher, the gnome will have to be carried," said Alistan.

"Kli-Kli," I said to the sniffling gobliness. "You take the krasta."

I had to carry the gnome, because if the orcs caught up with us, the warriors would have to be ready to fight them off.

"You won't manage on your own," Lamplighter said. "Eel, you carry my sword."

The Garrakian nodded and put the bidenhander over his shoulder.

"Here we go, Harold. But in the name of all the gods, be careful!"

We lifted the wounded man cautiously.

"What about Deler?" Kli-Kli sobbed. "Aren't we going to bury him?"

"We don't have time for that, goblin. The forest spirits will take care of his body," Egrassa replied.

Kli-Kli nodded reluctantly and she seemed to shrink somehow. The orcs' horns called to each other through the mist.

"Let's go!"

As we left the battlefield, I cast a final glance at Deler. Eel had attended to the dead man while we were trying to save Hallas. He had pulled out the orc's sword, set the dwarf's poleax on his chest, and folded his hands over it. As he walked along, Mumr whispered the words of the funeral song of the Wild Hearts. When we had gone about twenty yards, Kli-Kli suddenly turned round and went dashing back.

"Stop, Kli-Kli," I barked, but she completely ignored me. "Stop, you fool."

She came back a minute later, carrying the dwarf's bowler hat in her hand.

You can't run all that fast carrying a wounded gnome, but we were managing pretty well . . . so far. When my arms were just about ready to fall off, Mumr and I were replaced by Eel and Alistan Markauz. As we moved on, we swapped round again twice, and stopped twice to check on the gnome's condition. Hallas was still holding on by some miracle, but Egrassa only shook his head in disappointment: "It's only a matter of hours. Hallas won't make it through the night."

"We'll see about that!" growled Eel, furious with the whole wide world.

"We can't carry him forever. That way we only make it worse for him."

"Are you suggesting we abandon him?"

Egrassa's yellow eyes glinted in fury and he put his hand on the hilt of his crooked knife.

"You forget yourself." The elf's tone was very cold.

"The last thing we need now is a duel!" Milord Alistan roared furiously. "Eel!"

Eel worked the muscles in his jaw, but he said, "I'm sorry, Egrassa, I spoke hastily."

The dark elf gave a slight nod. "I understand. But we can't go on running forever. The Firstborn are only ten minutes away. We won't survive another battle like the last one, and they might have bowmen."

"We'll have to give battle," the Garrakian agreed. "Better do it now, before we collapse from exhaustion."

"This battle will be the last."

"So be it, elf. So be it. But I'm not just going to wait to be slaughtered, I'm going to put a few holes in some Firstborn."

Egrassa turned to Alistan Markauz.

"Milord?"

"Give me one minute, I'm thinking," said the count, knitting his brows together.

"Very well. Harold, Kli-Kli, stay beside Hallas. Eel, take the right. Mumr, take the left. Try to hold out for as long as possible and not let them through until I run out of arrows. Do you see that golden-leaf?"

The elf carried on giving instructions, but I wasn't listening any longer. May the Nameless One take me! Could this really be the end?

"We just have to hope there aren't any bowmen," Kli-Kli said in a quiet voice.

Her fingers were flickering desperately as she wove some complicated sign.

"Are you sure of what you're doing?" I asked her cautiously.

"I've never been so sure of anything, Dancer. Of course, it's not the Hornets of Vengeance, but I don't think they'll like the Hammer of Dust much better."

"How many of them are there?"

"The same number as attacked us. Only seventeen."

"We were attacked by seventeen orcs?"

"And five of their grun dogs. Didn't you notice? If not for Egrassa and his bow, they'd have us given a far worse mauling."

"Listen to me," said Alistan Markauz, suddenly breaking his silence. "We don't need to give battle now. Kli-Kli, catch!"

He threw something small to the gobliness and she caught it deftly. It turned out to be a silver ring with the count's personal crest.

"Milord, don't!" she cried out in fright.

"I must, jester, it's your only chance. If you get back, give it to my son."

"What's going on?" asked Mumr, not understanding a thing.

He wasn't the only one who didn't understand. Not everyone's as bright as Kli-Kli and Eel.

"Are you sure?" the Garrakian asked. "Perhaps I should go?"

"I'm sure," replied the captain of the royal guard. "The shaman knew, that's why he gave the thing to me. I'll try to lead them as far away from you as I can. Egrassa, lead the unit on!"

"Don't worry, milord, I'll lead them all the way to Avendoom," the dark elf said with a solemn nod. "Will you take the krasta? You'll be able to hold out longer with it."

"No, I'm used to a sword. Harold!"

"Yes, milord?" For some reason my mouth had gone dry.

"Give the Horn to Artsivus so that he can drive that snake back into the snow. If you don't, be sure I'll get you, even from the next world!"

I just nodded. The count took Glo-Glo's gift and squeezed the lump of earth in his fist. Our phantom doubles appeared out of thin air. Milord Alistan swung round and ran off to the west without looking back. Our doubles followed him, leaving perfectly real tracks on the ground.

"Egrassa, we have to hurry. Glo-Glo's spell won't last forever; we'll soon start leaving tracks again."

"You're right, Kli-Kli. Harold. Mumr! Pick up the gnome!"

The sound of the horns had faded away a long time ago, but we kept on running and running. I had a terrible empty feeling—we were only alive because Milord Alistan had led the orcs away from us. I realized in my mind that none of us would ever see the count again, at least, not in this life . . . but hope was still glimmering somewhere in my heart. Maybe he'd manage to outwit the orcs and then catch up with us?

"Until I see his body, I shall believe milord is still alive," said Kli-Kli in a quiet voice as she ran beside me. She might have been reading my thoughts. "What am I going to say to the king?"

Her question was left unanswered.

"We have to stop," Mumr panted. "His wound's started bleeding again."

I squinted at Hallas. Yes, blood was oozing from under the bandage.

"Egrassa! Eel!" Kli-Kli called to the warriors ahead of us. "Stop."

"This isn't the time."

"If we don't stop the bleeding, Hallas will die!"

"All right, but do it quickly. The hunting units have lost our trail, but that's only a brief respite."

We put Hallas down on the carpet of autumn leaves and Kli-Kli and Eel started attending to the wounded gnome.

"Harold, Mumr, one moment," the elf called to us. "I'll stand guard, and you get two long, strong poles. While we have time, we'll try to make a stretcher."

"We need more than just two poles, Tresh Egrassa."

"I know. We'll tie drokr cloaks between them. The material should take the weight. Don't waste any time, we have almost none left."

Mumr took Hallas's mattock off his belt, put it beside the krasta, and picked up his two-handed sword. It didn't take long to find what the elf wanted. Lamplighter cut down two young trees with his bidenhander, then chopped off their branches, and we were left holding two poles that we carried back to the spot where Kli-Kli was still looking after the gnome. With the elfin cloaks and the two poles we made a pretty good stretcher and then put Hallas on it.

"How is he?" I asked Kli-Kli.

"In a bad way. If only Miralissa was here. . . ."

"Miralissa's gone," Egrassa snapped ruthlessly. "Put your hope in the gods, not the dead. The gnome's life is in the hands of the gods. Eel, let's go."

And now the gnome was carried by the elf and the Garrakian. Kli-Kli led the way and Lamplighter and I followed the stretcher. An hour later I took Eel's place and Mumr replaced Egrassa. It was a lot more convenient carrying Hallas this way than in our arms. We moved faster, especially when Kli-Kli led us out onto a wide animal track that ran due north.

During the afternoon a dank autumn drizzle started to fall, and I had to cover Hallas with my cloak—I still had the jacket, and that was fine. Now our substantially reduced group was led on by Egrassa. Kli-Kli, freed from her honorable duties as guide, kept getting under our feet and checking on Lucky's condition. Sometimes the gnome groaned, and the gobliness took hold of his hand and started whispering quietly to herself.

When the wounded gnome quieted down, Kli-Kli walked along beside him, occasionally glancing back. She was clearly hoping Milord Alistan would come back, just as I was. Kli-Kli noticed my fleeting glance.

"The mist's thinning out."

"Yes, a bit," I agreed. "Probably because of the rain."

The gobliness snorted quietly at that, but she didn't say anything.

"How long will it take us to walk through the Golden Forest?"

"If Hallas lives, a week and a half, or maybe even longer. If . . ." She paused. "If he doesn't live, a week."

Such were the facts of life—the wounded gnome was slowing us down. Of course, abandoning Hallas was out of the question, but . . . Egrassa could decide to do it if we were really up against it. If he had to choose between his duty as a comrade and his duty to all the rest of the world, I was sure the elf would choose what he saw as the lesser evil, and Eel might not like that at all. I tried not to think what would happen then.

We walked on through the cold rainy forest for two hours. I thanked the gods that this was the south of Valiostr. In the north of the kingdom the first ground frosts should have started some time ago, and in the morning the puddles were probably covered with a thin crust of ice. I hoped we could get out of Zagraba before the start of November, when it would be really cold and uncomfortable.

Hallas wasn't groaning any longer. His face was almost the same color as the snow in the barren wastes of the Lonely Giant. Neither Kli-Kli nor Egrassa could do anything to help the gnome. We had all known for a long time that Hallas wouldn't survive the night, but we stubbornly carried the stretcher, as if we were trying to overtake death itself.

Bo-oom! Boo-oom! Boo-oom! Boo-oom! Boo-oom!

"Orcs! Very close," Kli-Kli gasped, snatching out her knives.

Ah, darkness! The rumble of the orcs' drums seemed to be coming from behind those golden-leafs over there. Close. Very close. Egrassa did his familiar trick of listening to the ground. When the elf got to his feet, the expression on his face promised nothing good.

"The Firstborn are no more than a fifteen-minute run away. And there are many of them."

"How many?" I said, asking the question that was on everybody's minds.

"More than forty. We are on the land of the Grun Ear-Cutters now."

Lamplighter uttered a picturesque description of the mothers of all orcs. Nobody needed to be told that we couldn't hold out against that many of them. Fifteen would have been enough to dispatch us into the light. We were too tired after all this running through Zagraba without a break.

"We need a clearing!" Kli-Kli said suddenly. "Egrassa, I need a large clearing!"

"What have you got in mind?"

"I've prepared the Hammer of Dust, all I still have to do is draw the activating rune. The spell is our only chance of holding out now. For it to work properly, there shouldn't be any trees around. We need a clearing, a big one if possible."

"Are you sure of your spell?"

"May the forest spirits take me, I am! This time you'll have to trust me. It's the spell or your swords! I'd put my money on the spell."

"We'll do it your way. A clearing, you say?"

The drums were rumbling like demons' hearts. Kli-Kli ran on ahead, and the four of us carried the stretcher.

"Stop!" Egrassa barked. "Off the path! To the left!"

I didn't know what the elf had sensed there, but the gobliness immediately did as he said and dashed into a dense fir thicket.

"Set him down!" Egrassa ordered.

We put the stretcher on the ground and the Garrakian grunted as he picked the gnome up in his arms.

"Forward! Get the branches out of the way!"

Egrassa reached for his s'kash, but I handed him the krasta. The Gray One's magical spear cleared the branches away as if they were blades of grass, and the elf easily cut us a path through the thick fir grove, without bothering at all about the orcs finding our trail. They'd find us in any case.

Boo-oom! Boo-oom! Boo-om!

The fir grove came to an end, and we emerged into a large black clearing veiled in trembling mist.

"How did you know?" Lamplighter blurted out.

"I smelt it," said the elf, and suddenly smiled. "I think Kli-Kli did, too. There's been a fire here. Look, the trees are scorched."

Black mud born from the meeting of rain, ash, and soil squelched under my boots. It was slippery, which meant that fighting would be difficult. When we stopped in the middle of the clearing, the trees surrounding it seemed like black phantoms hiding in the mist. We couldn't see a thing. Mumr put a cloak on the ground and Eel laid Hallas on it.

"When it starts, stand behind me and don't move forward, until I say so. All right?" Kli-Kli asked us as she hastily used her finger to draw something in the mud that looked like a fat caterpillar with little wings.

"All right. When you finish, go over to Hallas and stay there," said Egrassa, changing the string on his terrible bow. "Eel, you cover me as well as you can. Mumr, Harold, take the flanks. Don't move forward, thief."

"I wouldn't think of it," I answered him hoarsely.

Boo-oom! Boo-oom! Boo-oom! Boo-oom!

"They're close. Now's the time to start praying."

"This isn't a very good time that you've chosen. Especially for magic like that."

The clear young voice from behind our backs came as a complete surprise. For a moment it even seemed to drown out the rumbling of the drums. Egrassa swung round sharply, with an arrow poised to go flying from the string of his bow. Eel's "brother" and "sister" rustled out of their scabbards, the bidenhander circled round above Lamplighter's head. Kli-Kli looked up from her drawing and gave a quiet gasp. We had been taken by surprise in the most blatant manner possible, and the sensitive goblin and experienced elf hadn't sensed a thing.

When I saw the speaker, I was amazed. I was expecting anything at all, up to and including a h'san'kor riding a bubblebelly, but not four young girls, not in this place. . . . This was absolutely absurd!

There were four of them and they all looked very much like each other. Like sisters. A thought flashed through my mind: How could four twelve-year-old girls have come so far into the forest, and what were their parents thinking of?

They were just children. Not very tall, with short black hair soaked by the rain. Their eyes were large and round, almost black. The strangers had a zigzag line painted in red on their left cheeks—it looked very much like a bolt of lightning. In fact, only three of the girls had a single lightning bolt. The fourth, who had spoken to us, had lightning bolts on both cheeks and two thin red lines drawn under her eyes.

The little girls were dressed in jackets of leather, wool, and fur. Short skirts made out of long strips of leather. No shoes. They clearly weren't bothered in the slightest by the autumnal chill or the rain. But I would certainly have thought twice before wandering about barefoot in this weather.

The only jewelry they had were strings of carnelian beads and bracelets. And their only weapons were straight daggers with broad blades narrowing to a fine point.

Egrassa lowered his bow and unexpectedly went down on one knee. Kli-Kli bowed very respectfully indeed. Eel, Lamplighter, and I looked rather surprised. Well, never mind Kli-Kli, but for an elf of a royal family to bow the knee before a bunch of little girls! This really was amazing!

"The son of the House of the Black Rose greets the Daughters of the Forest!" Egrassa declared.

I gaped wide-eyed, unable to believe it.

The Daughters of the Forest! That was what the elves and the orcs called the dryads. Was this really yet another legend of Zagraba standing right here in front of me?

All sorts of things were said about the dryads, but very few men had ever met the Daughters of the Forest, and not even the elves, orcs, and goblins were very far ahead of us when it came to that. Those who had the blood of

Zagraba flowing in their veins were never quick to reveal themselves to others' eyes.

The elves and orcs regard themselves as pretty much the masters of Zagraba, but there are many other inhabitants of the forest kingdom. The dryads are really part of the forest, and they are the ones who rule it. They merely tolerate the presence of others in their forest, and the young races understand this and try not to annoy them. Even the proud and intolerant orcs bow their heads to the Daughters of the Forest.

At least, that's what they say. The dryads weren't interested in squabbles between the orcs and the elves until they started to cause damage to the forest. And they were even less interested in men. Dryads were concerned with the life of Zagraba itself. They took care of the forest and helped it, from the moths and the broods of mice to the families of oburs and the groves of golden-leafs.

And I had imagined all sorts of things, but not that they would look so much like ordinary human girls.

"The Black Moon . . . ," said the dryad standing in front of the others, and laughed. "Proud as the flame and passionate as the water." This was a reference to the House of the Black Flame and the House of Black Water. "What is your name, elf?"

"Egrassa, madam. I am at your service."

"At our service? We have no need of anyone's services. The forest helps us. But I am forgetting my manners, forgive me. My name is Babbling Brook," said the little girl, looking at the elf with a serious expression.

He bowed his head even lower.

"We are pleased to meet the Mistress," Kli-Kli squeaked in a shrill voice.

The drums were rumbling behind us, and Mumr couldn't help looking round. Babbling Brook noticed this and said, "Do not be afraid, man. We have a little time before what has been predestined happens. Arise, elf. It is not fitting for a king to kneel, even before the Mistress."

"Madam is mistaken, I am no king," Egrassa said guardedly, rising from his knees.

"Madam is merely running ahead of events," the dryad replied, imitating the elf's tone. "I am looking into the future, although I cannot see very much. Everything is covered in ripples because that man carries a blizzard within him."

Babbling Brook looked at me. "You took something from the cradle of the dead that should not have been taken, and now it is in my forest. Before, when the elves had it, I closed my eyes to the matter, but now, when its power is failing, I do not wish to see Zagraba destroyed. You must leave the forest, and go as quickly as possible."

"Believe me, my lady," Kli-Kli replied meekly. "That is what we wish. We have not the slightest desire to harm the forest."

"As is clear from the fact that you were about to work a battle spell capable of reducing a grove of golden-leafs to splinters," said Babbling Brook, shaking her head, but, fortunately for Kli-Kli, none of our group paid any attention to the Mistress's words. "I see your comrade is injured."

"Orcs."

"Orcs." She shook her head sadly. "A flinny told me what was happening, but I was not able to come any sooner. Sunpatch will attend to your friend."

One of her three companions went to the injured man and leaned down over him.

I thought about the flinny. The little lad had promised to warn those who should be warned, but how could I have guessed that he meant the dryads?

The drums kept rumbling.

"The orcs are proud and stubborn," Babbling Brook sighed. "The Horn has blinded them. They refused to listen to me and leave the artifact to its fate."

"The orcs dared to disobey?" Kli-Kli whispered in horror. "But—"

"And they are coming here to take what you have in your possession," the Mistress declared in a severe tone.

"But surely madam will not allow the Firstborn to take possession of the Horn?" Kli-Kli squealed plaintively.

"I will not allow it, although I would have preferred if it had never left the dark depths of the Cradle of the Dead. The Firstborn have made their choice, and I have made mine. The forest stands above all other things, and I shall help you leave Zagraba."

"Please pardon me for interrupting. I mean no harm by it, I'm only a simple man," Lamplighter said slowly. "But how can four little girls stop the Firstborn?"

Kli-Kli hissed at this sacrilege, but the dryad only smiled sadly. "Where steel cannot help, the forest will, man."

There was a deafening smashing and cracking sound from behind the trees, and Eel snatched his two blades out again.

"Put away your weapons!" one of the dryads told the Garrakian in a cold voice.

Eel cast a questioning glance at the elf. Egrassa nodded gently, keeping his eyes fixed on the trees. Something big was crashing its way through the forest toward us. Babbling Brook's lips were set in a mysterious smile. The bushes at the edge of the clearing swayed and collapsed with a crack. Immense shadows loomed up out of the mist.

"Sagra, save us!" Eel gasped. "They're . . ."

"They are Thunder, Whirlwind, Hail, Hurricane, Blizzard, and Boomer," said Babbling Brook, and I thought I heard a note of pride in her voice. "They have agreed to help me."

I hadn't noticed when Kli-Kli took hold of my hand. She seemed to be every bit as frightened as I was. And there was certainly something to be frightened of!

When our group first entered Zagraba, we came across a wild boar. He was a large, mature tusker, and I thought he was the king of boars, that no beast could possibly be any larger.

But I was clearly mistaken. And very badly mistaken. There was absolutely no comparison between that boar and the six standing there in front of us. They were gods of the forest. Boar kings. Each of them stood four and a half yards tall, and I couldn't even begin to imagine how much they weighed. They were monstrously huge, so huge that next to them, we were no more than pitiful bugs. Long knobbly snouts, immense dark yellow tusks that could have ripped a mammoth's stomach open with a single thrust, reddish gleaming fur, cunning little black eyes. I'm sure I'll remember the magnificence of those beautiful animals until the day I die. They surrounded us in a semicircle and waited for the Mistress of the Dryads to utter her command.

"We do not command, man," said Babbling Brook, looking into my eyes. "We cannot command the forest. We can only ask for its help. Lead on your warriors, Boomer!"

One of the boars opened its terrible jaws, roared so loudly that I was almost deafened, and went dashing toward the sound of the orcs' drums. The other five boars followed their leader, screeching belligerently. The six forest gods ran to the trees, smashed their way into the dense undergrowth, and disappeared.

"Boomer and his warriors will stop the Firstborn. It is not likely that any will escape their fangs and hooves, so now you have several days."

"My thanks, Mistress," said Egrassa, pressing his hand to his heart. "My house is irredeemably in your debt."

"I shall remember your words, elf, and I shall ask you to return the favor when the time comes," the dryad said with a serious nod.

"Madam, if the orcs find the bodies of their comrades, they will realize what has happened and pursue us once again."

"They will not find the bodies," said Sunpatch, walking away from Hallas. "Boomer's warriors always eat their enemies."

The thought of those giants devouring the bodies of the orcs sent cold shivers running down my spine. Just at that moment the orcs' drums fell silent and a second later the plaintive song of a horn rang out. But the sound broke off when it had barely begun, and silence returned to the forest.

"That is done, now it is time for you to leave," the little girl said to the elf. "Sunpatch?"

"A serious wound, Mistress. I have done everything that I could."

"Will he live?" Lamplighter blurted out.

"Yes. He has a fever now, but in two days he will be able to stand. Unfortunately I was not able to save his eye."

"The forest is not all-powerful," sighed Babbling Brook. "But the important thing is that your friend will live."

The forest is not all-powerful? Somehow I doubted that very much. At least, the most skillful of healers could not have done what the dryad had done. Not every member of the Order could have healed a wound like that and plucked the gnome out of the tenacious embrace of that beauty, Death. But this dryad, who looked so much like a twelve-year-old girl, had done it.

"Harold, take Mumr and fetch the stretcher," Egrassa said in a quiet voice.

"No need," Babbling Brook interrupted. "I do not intend to tolerate the Horn in my forest any longer than is absolutely necessary. On foot it will take you too long to find your way out. That does not suit the forest. If the power abandons the Horn close to the Cradle of the Dead, something terrible will happen. The farther you are from the place called Hrad Spein, the better for the forest. And I shall not be obliged to meddle even more in the affairs of men, elves, and orcs."

"Are you going to give us horses?" I asked in surprise.

"No. They would not move through the forest very quickly. I have something else for you. Fluffy Cloud?"

The dryad standing beside Sunpatch nodded and gave a loud whistle. Four elk walked out into the clearing.

"Thank you for answering my request, Runner in the Moonlight," Babbling Brook said with a smile. "These strangers must be taken to the lands of men as quickly as possible."

The brown eyes of one of the elk looked us over. Then the beautiful animal lowered its horned head and snorted in agreement.

"Thank you, friend. There is no time to be lost, Egrassa of the House of the Black Moon. It is time for you and your men to set out."

"How shall we sit on them and guide them?"

"There is no need for you to guide them. Fluffy Cloud and Sunpatch will go with you."

Mumr peered once again at the motionless elk in front of him and gulped, but he didn't say anything.

We mounted the elk in total silence. The first to leap up onto the back of the nearest beast was Eel. He held out his hand to Mumr and helped his friend settle behind him. My elk was a match for the size of Runner in the Moonlight and I was just trying to figure out how I was going to clamber up on it, when the animal went down on its knees. I quickly settled on its back, which was wet from the rain. Kli-Kli, determined not to let me get away, sat behind me and grabbed hold of my jacket.

The elk straightened its legs out smoothly, and to avoid falling off, I grabbed hold of one of its horns with my hand (the other hand was holding the krasta). The beast didn't seem to object to this familiar treatment. With the elf's help, the dryads loaded Hallas onto a third elk. Sunpatch stayed with the wounded gnome, holding him tightly round the waist. Egrassa and Fluffy Cloud were on Runner in the Moonlight.

"I thank you once again, Mistress, for the help that you have given us," Egrassa said in farewell. "The doors of my house are always open to the Daughters of the Forest, and no malice will be found in it. This I swear on the honor of my clan."

"Do not thank me, king. Thank the forest," said the little girl with wise eyes, looking up at the elf towering over her. "Perhaps I shall find the time to come to your house when there is peace and nothing threatens the balance. I hope so. But enough, I can already hear Boomer and his warriors on their way here. You should leave. After battle they are always hungry, and there were too few orcs to satisfy the Children of the Forest. If they decide to dine on you, not even I will be able to stop them. You had better go."

Waving her hand in farewell, Babbling Brook turned away from us. Taking this gesture as a command, Runner in the Moonlight set off at a fast trot toward the trees shrouded in mist.

Babbling Brook was right—the elk were much better than the finest of horses. The four animals raced through Zagraba, without stopping, until nightfall. In places where horses would have fallen, broken their legs, or simply not been able to get through, the elk just kept going.

Runner in the Moonlight forged straight ahead, smashing through the bushes and undergrowth with his mighty hooves. Swampy hollows, swollen by the continuous rain, and stretches of fallen trees were crossed at a run, or in mighty bounding leaps. The elk were tireless, and in half a day we covered a distance that would have taken horses at least three days, or even four.

At first I was afraid of falling off, but my misgivings proved groundless. Even in the densest thickets, the beast moved so smoothly that the king's horses would have died of envy if they could have seen it.

When twilight started drawing in, Fluffy Cloud asked Runner in the Moonlight to stop, and jumped down lightly to the ground. We followed her example and then took Hallas down off the elk. The gnome had still not recovered consciousness, but now at least he was not as pale as in the morning. The wounded warrior was groaning quietly.

"He has a fever," said Sunpatch. "The wound has almost healed over, but he is still weak."

"Light a fire," Egrassa told Eel.

The Garrakian glanced at the dryad, but the elf shook his head.

"She has nothing against fire."

The elk disappeared into the forest, and Fluffy Cloud said they would come back at dawn. Sunpatch attended to the gnome, with Kli-Kli hanging around nearby. Fluffy Cloud handed out fresh flapjacks, so we didn't go hungry. Then the dryad went up to the golden-leaf, laid her hand on its trunk, and asked the tree to protect us from the rain. I swear on my first Commission that the tree did as she asked! It seemed to lean down over us, and its branches wove themselves into something very much like a huge awning.

"You have a heavy day tomorrow," Fluffy Cloud said. "You need a good night's sleep, if you do not wish to fall off your mounts."

Egrassa tried to appoint sentries for the night, but the dryad made a disdainful face at that.

"You can sleep easy. You are in no danger while we are here."

"What about the Firstborn?"

"They would not dare to attack Daughters of the Forest. Have no fear."

Egrassa seemed perfectly satisfied with what the dryad had said, and he lay down to sleep without wasting any more time. Eel followed his example. Mumr sat beside the fire for a little while, sighing to himself, and then also settled down for the night.

"What's the matter, Harold?" Kli-Kli asked me.

"I'm not sleepy," I lied. "You go ahead, it's all right. I'll sit here for a while."

"I'm not sleepy, either," the gobliness replied.

Sunpatch sat opposite us and stared without blinking into the flames of the fire. Fluffy Cloud disappeared into the darkness of the forest. We didn't speak, and Kli-Kli's head gradually began nodding. Then Glo-Glo's granddaughter was completely overcome and she dropped off, snuggled up against my shoulder. She even started snoring. She was tired, and no wonder—we were all very tired after that day.

A hard day. An appalling day. A black day. Like so many others in recent months. Our group had suffered grievous, irreparable losses. I still couldn't believe that the ginger-headed dwarf was dead and had been abandoned to the mercy of the forest spirits.

Deler had paid for Hallas's life with his own, and if not for the dryads, that terrible price would have been paid in vain. Deler was gone now, like so many other members of the small band of brothers that had set out with me to retrieve the Rainbow Horn. Alistan had walked away into the mist, leading the orcs after him, and disappeared. And the most terrible thing was that now we would never know what had happened to the count, how he had died.

Died?

I was burying the captain of the royal guard too soon. I hadn't seen his body, so for me he would always be alive. Perhaps Milord Alistan had managed to get away from the Firstborn. Sensing someone's glance on me, I looked at the Daughter of the Forest.

"He will not come, man."

"How do you know . . . madam?"

"The forest and the forest spirits told me. You do not hear them. Believe me, I am very sorry that we could not come sooner."

"How . . ." I suddenly felt a lump in my throat. "How did he die?"

"Do you really wish to know?" she asked, with the flames of the campfire reflected in her big black eyes. "Why do you need that pain? He is dead, is that not enough?"

"No, not for me."

"Very well, look. And do not tell me afterward that I did not warn you."

Her black eyes suddenly blazed up in a flash of intense green light and, before I realized what was happening, the world was plunged into darkness.

The hunting horns called triumphantly to each other behind his back, but he ran on and on, leading the orcs farther away from the group. He hoped very much that Egrassa would be able to lead them out of this accursed forest, and then there would be some hope for Valiostr. The phantoms created by the old shaman's spell glided silently along at his back, leaving clear tracks on the earth and the leaves.

He ran quickly, but tried to husband his strength, so that he would not be winded for the battle ahead. Count Alistan Markauz had no illusions that he might escape. He knew that sooner or later the Firstborn would catch him, and there was little chance that he would survive the encounter.

The forest went on and on, with no gaps between the close-growing maples. There was mist on all sides and the long run that had brought him to the limit of his strength was no longer important. It was time to find a place to die. He had never thought he would die like this, out in the rain and mist of the bleak autumn forest.

The captain was not afraid of death; he had seen more than his share of it in his time. But he regretted that no one would know how he had died. In his young days he had seen himself dying as a hero on the battlefield, defending the banner or shielding the young king with his body. A beautiful death, worthy to be celebrated in song. But Death was not to be chosen; she decided for herself when to come to a man and take him to the light. Or the darkness. The end was the same for all, and what difference did it make where you died—at the heart of a raging battle, or in a misty forest?

He would sell his life dearly—for him the most important thing was that the orcs must not use their bows, but engage him in combat. Of course, the captain need not have drawn the pursuit after him, he could have given that task to Eel or Lamplighter, but then how would he have been able to sleep at night, knowing he had sent another into the embrace of death instead of himself? Alistan was used to being the first into a battle, the first to ride his horse against the ranks of pikemen. Always the first, always at the cutting edge of the thrust. That was why the soldiers respected him.

The horns sounded again, and the count swore by the darkness. The pursuers had cut down his lead, and he would have to hurry, unless of course he wished to give battle with his back against a maple tree. Alistan Markauz had never appealed to the gods in prayer, believing that it was not worth troubling them over trifles. He had saved his only prayer for the occasion when it was right to call on Sagra. And he called on her with all his heart and soul, asking the fearful goddess to grant him a place for combat so that she might rejoice in the sight of the most important battle of his life.

And the goddess heard him.

After he left the maples behind, the forest opened up and Milord Alistan Markauz found himself beside a deep ravine with its bottom hidden under thick mist. There was a bridge across the ravine, and it reminded him of the one in the Red Spinney. It was just as narrow, and just as convenient to defend.

Built of stone, ten yards long and two yards across. If they wished to do so, two men could walk across it together side by side, but there was only enough space for one to launch an effective attack. Along the sides, taking the place of railings, there were tall rectangular barriers half the height of a man. Every two yards, tall columns rose up out of them to twice the height of a man.

Ten yards is no distance at all, and despite the mist, he had a clear view of the opposite bank, where there was an ancient city, almost entirely untouched by time. The walls ran right along the edge of the ravine, and the bridge ended at stone gates that were, unfortunately, closed.

Now he had several minutes to take a rest and draw breath. He had to stand on the bridge, and then the battle would take place one-to-one; the orcs would not have any room to attack in numbers or outflank him, and the gates would protect his back.

Markauz slowly walked across the bridge, and when he turned to face the maples, the shamanic phantoms disappeared. Glo-Glo's spell had stopped working. Well, it had done its job, now the count had to do his.

Just for a moment the captain of the guard regretted that he was only wearing light armor, not his heavy battle plate. No helmet, no shield that would have allowed him to hold out for a very, very long time. Only a sword and a dagger for weapons. Despite the rain, the count took off his cloak and dropped it at his feet. Then he threw his scabbard away and took his sword in both hands.

The sword was somewhat longer than ordinary blades, and there was room on the hilt for the second hand. He was ready. All he had to do now was wait.

A horn sounded very close, and then the orcs emerged from the shroud of mist. Six, ten, fifteen, seventeen. Alistan Markauz's enemies spotted him, and one of them raised a clenched fist in the air. His pursuers slowed from a run to a walk, looking around suspiciously, clearly fearing an ambush.

"Where are your companions, man?" one of them shouted.

"Far away," the count said in a quiet voice, but they heard him.

"Surrender, or you will die!"

Milord Rat shook his head very slightly. Two bowmen stepped forward.

"Are you scared?" Alistan Markauz roared at the top of his lungs, and the sound of his voice carried across the ravine and the abandoned city. "Or are you not really orcs? You consider yourselves the superior race, and yet you are afraid of a man? Oh, come now, Firstborn! Do you not have the courage to face me with a yataghan, is that why you pick up the weapon of children, cowards, and elves? There are seventeen of you, and I am alone! Prove to me that you really are the Firstborn! All you have to do is bare your blades and cross the bridge!"

One of the orcs halted the bowmen and started conferring with the other warriors. The count waited and prayed. Then he suddenly felt someone's insistent gaze on his back, and swung round sharply.

She was standing behind him. A woman wearing a simple sleeveless dress, with a luxuriant mane of white hair scattered across her naked shoulders. The stranger's face was hidden behind a half-mask in the form of a skull. She was holding a bouquet of pale narcissi and gazing at Alistan Markauz out of her empty eye sockets.

"No!" he said, shaking his head in furious anger. "No! Not like that! Not with an arrow!"

She said nothing.

"I need time! Just a little bit! And then I will go with you. Grant me just a few minutes in the name of Sagra! I will take as many with me as I can!"

For a second he thought that Death would refuse him, but she thoughtfully tore the petals off the narcissi and silently walked away, back toward the gates.

"I shall wait, but not for long."

He did not really hear her words; he felt them. Gripping the hilt of his sword even more tightly, he roared in anticipation of the battle to come. The orcs finished conferring and one of them called the bowmen back.

"We offer you one last chance to surrender, rat!"

Rat? Well now. He really was the Rat; he had been granted the honor of bearing a rat in his coat of arms. "Never drive a rat into a corner"—that was his family motto. Then it has nothing to lose, and it sells its life dearly.

"Forward, Firstborn! I'll show you what rats are capable of!"

Those words decided the matter. His enemies stepped onto the bridge and moved toward him, taking their time.

At the front was a tall orc with a yataghan and a round shield. Good weapons, but the orc didn't even have chain mail, just a jacket of thick, coarse leather and a light half-helmet. Alistan Markauz walked toward him. It was better to meet in the middle of the bridge; he would have room to fall back.

At that moment Milord Alistan remembered his childhood. The count had first picked up a sword at the age of five, but found the art of swordsmanship hard to master. He could not sense the rhythm, the music, the dance of the blade. Things had gone on like that until his teacher had the idea of bringing a flute to the Armory.

The old warrior played well, the flute sang in his hands, and the music flowing through the Armory helped the boy get a feel for his weapon. The music of the flute led him and his sword after it, prompting him when to strike, when to change his stance, or defend himself against a thrust. And the old master was pleased with his sovereign's son.

The years passed, and the grave of Alistan Markauz's first teacher had long been overgrown with flowers, but the song of the flute remained in the count's heart forever. The moment he took the hilt of his sword in his hand, it awoke and sang in his ears, helping him in battle and in tournament duels. It must have been the song that eventually made him one of the finest swordsmen in Valiostr.

And now the flute was singing to him for the last time. The jolly, swaggering melody picked Alistan Markauz up and flung him into battle.

Sing, flute! Sing!

He met the first orc and struck first, without waiting for an attack. His opponent, unfortunately for him, was in a left-sided stance, holding the shield out in front of him. His left leg was exposed, a dainty morsel, and the battery sword swooped downward in a flash of pink, slicing through flesh and bone. The orc cried out and fell. Milord Alistan struck several rapid and powerful blows at his opponent's helmet.

Sing, flute! Sing!

Although his comrade had been killed, the second orc came dashing forward. A "right-sided bull" and a rapid thrust, the orc covered himself with his shield and immediately struck a rapid counterblow. The yataghan cleaved through the air with a repulsive hiss and struck against a "crown." The count's blade accepted the blow on the flat, pushed the yataghan away, struck for the face, changed direction, and smashed into the shield.

Sing, flute! Sing!

The orc staggered back, stumbled over the body of his comrade, and immediately parted with his yataghan and his right forearm.

Sing, flute! Sing!

He had no chance to finish off the Firstborn. The next orc jumped over his wounded comrade and threw himself into a furious attack. He had a yataghan and a long dagger in his hands. Other Firstborn carried the orc who had lost his arm away from the raging skirmish. This time the count was facing an experienced opponent, and the lack of a shield did not make him any more vulnerable. Yataghan and dagger danced in the air, weaving an intricate pattern of silver that was impossible to strike through.

A clash of blades. And another. Every time it met the enemy's steel, the battery sword screeched furiously and its song was echoed by the flute that the orcs could not hear.

Sing, flute! Sing!

The orc moved into the attack, the yataghan came sweeping down, encountered a "window" and tried to avoid the unexpected obstacle, and at that moment Alistan Markauz spun his enemy's blade, threw it off to the right and "entered," striking the orc a mighty blow on the chin with the pommel of his sword.

Sing, flute! Sing!

The heavy ball set on the hilt of the sword crushed the bone, and the orc collapsed limply to the ground. Alistan Markauz had no intention of sparing his opponent's life. This was no time for noble acts of chivalry; he had only one goal now—to take as many Firstborn with him as he could. The heavy battery sword twirled round the count's right wrist as lightly as if it was a feather. He shifted his grip to hold it like a staff and thrust the blade into his prone enemy with all his strength.

Sing, flute! Sing!

Not time to die yet! A little more dancing and singing!

His left cheek was damp for some reason, and something was dripping off his chin. He brought his eyes together in a squint—the entire front of his jacket was soaked in blood. Ah, darkness! That orc had been quick with the dagger. The count had not even noticed when his opponent managed to reach him. It was strange, but he did not feel any pain at all now. Even though the left side of his face was quite definitely sliced open. Sagra be praised that the blow had caught him below the eye, or the blood gushing from his forehead would have hindered him in the fight.

Sing, flute! Sing!

The flute sang, and the sword sang in harmony with it. The yataghan sliced through the air; the shield took the mighty vertical blows. When the battery sword came down again, the orc didn't stand there stupidly, he drew the shield back toward himself, taking the sting out of the blow. The sword stuck in the shield and the Firstborn drew his yataghan back triumphantly, opening himself up. The dagger that suddenly appeared in Alistan Markauz's left hand struck into the open gap, easily pierced the orc's jacket, and stuck in the place known to warriors as the "bloody apple." The count jumped back, freeing his sword with a sharp twist.

Sing, flute! Sing!

His cheek was burning, as if torturers had sewn a handful of blazing coals into it, but he had no time for pain now—two opponents flung themselves at him at once. The first one, with a spear, came charging at him like a wild boar. The second, with an ax, jumped up agilely onto the left shoulder of the bridge, and made to strike at him from above. Alistan Markauz skipped under the descending ax and struck the orc standing on the narrow border between his legs with all his might. The Firstborn lost his balance and tumbled into the ravine.

Sing, flute! Sing!

Holding his weapon above his head in both hands, as if it wasn't a spear, but some kind of battle gaff, the orc struck in rapid jabbing thrusts at Alistan Markauz's neck and chest. The count managed to parry the blows, but with great difficulty.

The sweat streamed off his face, mingling with the blood flowing from his wound. His ears were ringing, his legs were filled with lead, there was no air to breathe. He could not tell how long he had been backing away. The count's attention was completely focused on his opponent's golden eyes. The sharp sting of the spear described circles in the air, then came hurtling at his shoulder, changed direction to aim at his knee, darted up toward his chin. It was becoming harder and harder for him to parry the blows. All he could do was knock the spear away to his right or his left. And slicing through the orc's weapon was out of the question—the shaft of the spear was clad in iron for almost a quarter of its length.

Each of them waited for his opponent to make a mistake, to open himself up a little, lose his focus, stumble unexpectedly, or simply fail to cover himself against a blow. The sword in Alistan Markauz's hands grew heavier and heavier with every second that passed. He barely managed to push the thrusting sting of the spear away to the right, then carried through the movement of his blade into a hacking blow, trying to reach the Firstborn. . . .

The orc was quicker. He almost lay down on the ground and thrust his short spear forward with both hands. The narrow four-sided point pierced Alistan Markauz's chain mail and struck the count in his right side. And again he felt no pain.

He grabbed the spear sticking in his side with his left hand, pushed it hard away from him, and was delighted to see the sharp butt end of the spear strike the orc in the chest, taking him by surprise. Then he shifted the spear to the right, giving himself the opportunity to move close to his dumbfounded opponent.

Sing, flute! Sing!

The Firstborn parted with his head, and the count pressed his left hand to his right side. It was bad. The count knew what happens when steel pierces the liver. It is the end.

Demanding hands with slim elegant fingers were laid on his shoulders. He roared furiously and jerked his shoulders to throw them off, forcing Death to step back.

"It's not time! I can still take another one!"

The bridge came to an end. He had to hold his sword in one hand and squeeze his wounded side with the other. At least that would stop the bleeding and give him one more minute.

Sing, flute! Sing!

Make Death laugh! Gladden her with his song, so that she would remember this battle forever. How annoying that apart from her and these yellow-eyed reptiles, no one would see his finest fight of all! And the flute sang, and the Singing Steel of the sword sang its fierce and furious harmony. Step back, strike, catch on the counterstrike, step to the side. Another strike. And another. Press his back against the gates. Strike. Cover himself.

He threw his left hand out in front of himself, and the blood from his glove flew into the orc's eyes. The orc lost momentum for an instant and the count, grasping his sword with both hands and ignoring the bleeding, chopped at the orc's leg and charged him.

Sing, flute! Sing!

The song of the flute rang out over Zagraba and spread out across the world. He wondered if the group could hear it. Probably not, they were far away now. Very far away. The count smiled triumphantly.

Everything went dark. There was a roaring in his ears and for some reason he felt dizzy. He swung out blindly, acting intuitively, anticipating the next blow every time. Oh, just a little bit longer.

The blade of his sword struck something hard and halted for an instant, and the hilt was almost torn out of his hands, then he heard someone's short gurgling shriek.

Sing, flute! Sing!

Well, Death, do you see? This is much better than arrows. He was going to fight a little longer. The orcs would remember this battle, and they would tell their grandchildren about him.

Why is it so dark? Why do I feel so bad? Are those your hands again, Death? It's not time yet! It's not time! Can you hear the flute singing? Can you hear the music?

Sing, flute! Si—

17

OUT OF THE FOREST

The next morning Sunpatch didn't say a word about what I'd seen the night before, and I didn't ask her any more questions. Kli-Kli obviously suspected something, because she kept giving me suspicious glances all morning, but—Sagot be praised—she didn't try to pick my brain. The mist that had lingered in Zagraba for the last two days had disappeared overnight. Hallas was a lot better; at least he wasn't as pale as the day before and his breathing was stable. Sunpatch whispered spells over the gnome, while Fluffy Cloud handed out fresh bread, meat, and cheese (goodness only knows where all that came from!) to our somber little band. But just as we were about to start eating, the elk came back and we were forced to eat our rations on the move—Runner in the Moonlight wasn't going to wait while we satisfied our hunger sitting on the grass.

The four elk ran all day long, stopping only twice at the dryads' request. Even after all that crashing through the densest thickets in the depths of the forest, the massive beasts didn't seem to tire at all, which is more than could be said for us, although we were just sitting on their backs. The dryads hardly spoke to us, limiting themselves to brief meaningless phrases, although the little Daughters of the Forest were emphatically polite and affable with Egrassa.

The gobliness Kli-Kli had been pensive and dejected. There was no more of the tomfoolery that had become so familiar. The jester had disappeared. Kli-Kli had become herself, and I wasn't used to that. To be honest, I sometimes caught myself thinking that I rather missed the relentlessly cheerful fool.

A brief break was followed by more furious galloping through the autumn forest. The huge creatures hurtled along as if they were fleeing from a fire, and we had to hold on tight. They didn't stop until it was twilight, and I had the impression that our horned steeds could have run without stopping for a couple of days, and the darkness didn't bother them at all.

The campfire was burning. Mumr was quietly playing his reed pipe. The dryads and the elk had disappeared into the dark forest, leaving us to ourselves.

"Where do they go off to?" asked Eel.

"To talk to the forest," Egrassa replied after a short pause. "They find out the news, ask for advice, maybe something else as well. I don't know. . . . Neither we nor the orcs have ever learned to listen to the voice of the forest. So I can't really tell you. Maybe Kli-Kli knows more."

"No, I don't. I know just as much as Egrassa. The forest's daughters are the only ones who can talk to it. Well, and the flinnies . . . sometimes. Our old folks say the goblins used to be able to talk to Zagraba, but that was in the distant past. Zagraba doesn't speak to us now, the only ones we can talk to are the most gossipy forest spirits. . . . Too much was lost during the Gray Age. . . ."

Lamplighter had gone to see how the gnome was, and suddenly we heard him shout: "Hallas is awake!"

Lucky was sitting slumped against a tree, feeling at his bandage. When he spotted us, the gnome gave a crooked grin and then hissed at the pain.

"Who wrapped me up so nice and tight?"

"Lie down," said Kli-Kli, darting across to him. "You were wounded."

"Well, since I'm talking and I'm alive, it can't be too serious," the gnome chuckled, but he stopped fiddling with the bandage. "Who did this to me?"

"Don't you remember anything?"

"I do remember something," the gnome said thoughtfully. "But abyss of the depths! My head's spinning and my face is all on fire! Why don't you say something?"

"You've lost an eye," Eel said harshly, deciding not to hide anything. "You were badly hurt. If we hadn't had help, we'd have sung you the 'Fare-well' by now."

Hallas chewed on his lips and thought for a moment.

"Then I was lucky. An eye's not a head. I'll get over it somehow. . . . But where's Deler? And I don't see Milord Markauz anywhere, either. . . ."

"They weren't as lucky as you were," said Eel, telling the hard truth again. "They're dead."

"Deler . . . How did he . . . ?"

Eel told him.

"Leave me," the gnome mumbled after he heard the story, and turned away.

Lamplighter was about to say something, but Eel just shook his head gently. We all went back to the fire, but Kli-Kli stayed with the gnome, despite his request.

"They were very close. It's strange, really," Eel said unexpectedly. "When Lucky came to the Lonely Giant, he and Deler very nearly came to blows. And then during a raid Hallas's platoon was caught in an ambush set by the Cray-fish Duke. A magician of the Order led them into it. They were going to string the gnome up, but Deler saved him, almost took him down off the scaffold. After that the gnome got his nickname of Lucky, and he and the dwarf were absolutely inseparable, although never a day went by without them quarreling over something. . . ."

"Well, you please yourselves, but I'm going to bed," Mumr sighed. "We'll be galloping all day long again tomorrow."

"Egrassa!" I said, taking the Key out of my bag, "I think you'd better keep this."

The elf looked at the artifact and hung it round his neck without saying a word. Then he asked: "What are they like, Harold?"

"Who?"

"The Doors."

I thought about it.

"I can't describe them properly."

"I understand," Egrassa said, and suddenly smiled. "No one can describe them. Probably someday I'll get the chance to go down and see what the master craftsmen of my people created. It's very beautiful there, isn't it?"

"Not all the time," I replied cautiously. "I'm no great lover of beauty that can bite you, if you understand what I mean."

"They say there are many hoards of treasure. Did you pick up anything for yourself?" Eel asked, and the corners of his mouth trembled in a faint smile of mockery.

"Not very much," I muttered, remembering the emeralds that I'd lost. "The orcs took everything I brought out of Hrad Spein."

"My sympathies," said Egrassa.

I wondered if he was mocking me or being serious.

"Can I ask a question?" I asked, to change the subject.

"Go ahead."

"Which orc clan has black-and-white badges?"

"Black and white? You must have got something confused. What made you ask that?"

"I saw the bodies of orcs in the Palaces of Bone. They had black-and-white badges on their clothes."

"That clan hasn't existed for a long time. They were The Lost. We wiped them out during the Gray Age."

"The Lost?" Kli-Kli sat down beside us, caught Eel's eye, and said, "Hallas has gone to sleep. So, The Lost . . . that was what you said, wasn't it? Argad's clan?"

"Yes, goblin, Argad's clan. We went to great lengths to wipe it off the face of the earth."

"Why such determination?"

"Argad led his warriors almost as far as Greenwood and we couldn't tolerate a slap in the face like that. It took us some time, but we managed to defeat them. The last few hundred of The Lost took refuge in the Palaces of Bone, in one of the seven fortresses that served as checkpoints through which everyone who wished could pass without hindrance. It was as if the black-and-whites had gone completely insane; they started attacking everybody, even their own kinsmen. The other clans turned their backs on them, and that played into our hands. We took that fortress, and our shamans fused Argad and his generals into the central tower. Alive. Or that's what the legends say. Since then very few have been brave enough to pass through that fortress. My forebears rather overdid things, and the spirits of the dead still take their vengeance on travelers."

"I walked through it," I said casually.

"You've seen Argad?" Egrassa asked, gazing at me incredulously.

"If one of the dead orcs fused into the tower was Argad, then yes."

"Then you're lucky, if you managed to walk through that accursed place safe and sound."

"Or your legends are mistaken," Eel retorted in a quiet voice.

"It's just that Harold's a Dancer, that's all there is to it," said Kli-Kli, offering her weighty opinion. "No one else would have got through."

"Thank you, Kli-Kli," I answered her sarcastically. "You've really convinced me of just how special I am."

"But you really are special!" she protested. "You're a Dancer in the Shadows! The great book *Bruk-Gruk* never lies!"

"You're getting monotonous," I sighed.

"The dryads are coming," said Kli-Kli, and Sunpatch and Fluffy Cloud stepped out of the darkness into the circle of light.

"The forest has spoken with us," Sunpatch declared, but she didn't sit down yet. "The orcs are on the march. The war has begun."

I gasped and Kli-Kli squealed. Mumr, who hadn't managed to get to sleep yet, swore. Eel and Egrassa remained impassive, as if they'd been told we wouldn't be getting sweet buns for breakfast tomorrow, not that a war had started.

"When did it happen?"

"A few days ago."

"Is that all we're supposed to know?"

"No, but we understand nothing about war and we cannot tell you in the way you should be told. We will only bewilder and confuse you. Babbling Brook has sent a flinny to you; he will be here soon."

"How soon?"

Fluffy Cloud closed her eyes as if she was listening to the wind wandering through the naked branches of the trees.

"He will be here in a few minutes. And in the meantime, I think you ought to know that tomorrow we shall have to change direction."

"How?"

"To go west. We do not wish you to leave the forest and fall straight into the hands of the orcs."

Right. They didn't want the Rainbow Horn to fall into the orcs' hands. They couldn't care less about us.

"We shall lead you to the western bank of the Black River. You will be close to a human city. Moitsig, if I remember correctly. The orcs have passed it by. The flinny will be here soon. Tomorrow we shall get you out of the Golden Forest."

The dryads disappeared into the trees again. They obviously weren't very fond of our jolly company.

"Now, what does that tell us?" said Lamplighter, scratching his stubbly cheek thoughtfully. "If we leave the Golden Forest tomorrow . . . Then at that speed we'll get out of Zagraba in three . . . no, in two days?"

"Let's hope for exactly that," said Eel, clenching and unclenching his fists. "Things are getting hot now in the south of the kingdom."

"But if we come out on the western bank of the Iselina, then do we go straight from Zagraba into Valiostr?"

"You always were a genius, Harold," said Kli-Kli. "Yes, you're absolutely right. We'll be in the most southern part of the south—the south of Valiostr. You can't get any farther south. From Moitsig to Ranneng is only a nine-day journey. Then a little bit farther, and we're home."

"Don't, Kli-Kli," said Eel. "Don't ever try to guess the future. We don't know what's going to happen to us."

"I thought we'd leave Zagraba on the border with the Kingdom, near Cuckoo."

"Near Cuckoo? No, Harold, you're way off target there. Way, way off. We're nowhere near Cuckoo," Kli-Kli snorted, and reached her hands out to the fire.

"When you were in Hrad Spein, didn't you realize how far you walked, thief?" Egrassa asked, and his eyes glinted. "It was a distance of many leagues. You left the Palaces of Bone at a place far away from the entrance, and then how far did you walk with the Firstborn? We barely managed to reach the Labyrinth in time."

"You can say that again," Lamplighter confirmed.

"So there's no point in trying to go to Cuckoo. It would be a massive detour."

"But where's Honeycomb?"

"I don't think he's in the castle anymore. Milord Alistan—may he dwell in the light—left him a letter before we entered Zagraba. If Honeycomb recovered, then he should have galloped to Avendoom long ago with a message for the king."

"But what about horses? I don't expect the elk are going to rush us all the way to the capital."

"We have enough money to buy new horses."

Yes, there was gold enough, but I would miss Little Bee; I'd grown used to my own mount, and now I'd have to switch to a new one. And apart from that, Little Bee was a present from the king.

First we heard the buzzing, and then the dragoatfly came darting toward us like a tiny shadow. The flinny mounted on it was my old acquaintance, the one who had been given the elfin ring as his reward. The one who, basically, had hauled my backside out of the Labyrinth.

"Iirroo z'maa Olok of the Branch of the Lake Butterfly is glad to greet Tresh Egrassa and his traveling companions!" the flinny chanted, and the dragoatfly circled above our heads.

"I am glad to greet my brother of the little people at my campfire. What has brought you here, Iirroo z'maa Olok of the Branch of the Lake Butterfly?"

"News," said the crystal-clear little voice, like the jingling of a bell. "Unpaid."

It was clear from Iirroo's tone that this last fact was not a good thing. Flinnies were used to being paid handsomely for their labors.

"Would you care to try of our food and sup of our wine?" Egrassa inquired, employing the ritual phrase.

"Hah!" the black-haired flinny responded. "The food of dryads, and not a drop of wine anywhere in sight. Thank you for asking, but no. On this occasion the business is too urgent and too important. Food can wait. But I certainly wouldn't object to a space where I could land Lozirel. We've spent half a day on the wing."

Without waiting for permission, the dragoatfly glided down to the ground, stuck out its tongue, and bleated in relief.

"I'm glad to see that you escaped from the filthy paws of the orcs, beanpole!" said the flinny, addressing me. "Would you object, Tresh Egrassa, if I were to speak from the ground? I am afraid that Lozirel needs to rest for the next ten minutes."

No one had any objections.

The news that Iirroo recited to us didn't make very good hearing. This time the Firstborn had prepared well—they had learned the lesson of their defeat in the Spring War. The Hand had gathered absolutely everyone he could, and, when everything was ready, struck rapidly and to good effect. There were so many orcs that the military leader of the Firstborn had even taken the risk of dividing up his army of many thousands into three strike forces, or "fists."

The first fist had hammered at the Border Kingdom, the second had struck at Valiostr and was now advancing on Ranneng at a forced march, encountering almost no resistance along the way. The third fist had come crashing down on the southwestern provinces of Valiostr—but the main force of the blow had been taken by the Black Forest.

"Your compatriots, Tresh Egrassa, were not expecting anything of the kind. Before the houses were able to offer an adequate response . . ." The flinny hesitated, unwilling to convey bad news.

"Continue." Egrassa's face seemed to be carved out of stone.

"They flooded through the Black Forest. The House of Black Water gave battle while the others gathered their warriors. No members of the House of Black Water survived; the entire house was annihilated. The orcs advanced as far as Greenwood and the ancient city was totally destroyed. The Black Flame was almost extinguished. Almost all kin of the great Elodssa the Law Breaker fell in the battle. This house is now ruled by Melessana the Night Fox. The Black Moon arrived in time and closed the breach, bearing the brunt of the blow from the Firstborn. Then other houses joined them, I do not know who had the best of it."

"I see," said Egrassa, stroking the handle of his s'kash.

"That is not yet all the bad news, Tresh Egrassa."

"What could possibly be worse?"

"The Black Moon protected the Black Flame. Now all members of the House of the Black Flame have become your k'lissangs. The Flame said it was a point of honor for them to be loyal to those who had saved them."

"That is impossible," Egrassa snapped. "The Black Flame is the predominant house. They cannot serve us. The Night Fox must have gone completely insane in her grief!"

"Melessana is too young, but the words have been spoken, and the Council of the Black Flame has approved them."

"My uncle will never accept such a blatant transgression of the law!"

"Tresh Eddanrassa, the head of the House of the Black Moon, was killed while defending the Flame. His daughter—Tresh Melessana—died beside her father. I am deeply sorry."

Egrassa ground his teeth. "And what of Epilorssa?"

"Tresh Epilorssa should now assume the leafy crown, but he left for Avendoom with a detachment of bowmen more than a month ago."

"Who rules the house now?"

"Your younger brother, Tresh Egrassa. He is awaiting your return."

"The crown will be mine only after Epilorssa!" Egrassa retorted furiously. "I have business entrusted to me by the United Council of the Houses! I cannot return now. Will you give my message to my brother?"

"Yes, I will convey it without payment."

I raised one eyebrow sharply. Could this really be a flinny we saw before us? He spotted my dubious expression and announced to everyone: "These are dark times. If we do not help the elves, and the orcs are victorious, we shall have no one to tell our news to. We may be greedy, but we are not stupid. Your message, Tresh Egrassa?"

"Tell my younger brother to rely on the council and await the return of Epilorssa. I shall return as soon as I can. And something must be done about the Black Flame."

"You know what must be done, elf, you know it and you fear it," said Fluffy Cloud, emerging quietly from the gloom. "This has happened once before."

"In any case, this decision will have to be taken by Epilorssa when he returns," Egrassa snapped. "Only the head of the house—"

"But are you certain that your brother will return from the north? Are you certain that he will want the leafy crown? You know his attitude to power. Babbling Brook saw you as the king. Better hurry home, elf. We will take your friends to the lands of men. The marriage of the King of the Moon and the Queen of the Flame will resolve all difficulties and they will not be k'lissangs."

"It is a point of honor for the Flame. If an entire house has decided to serve us for eight years, that is their right. If one house is stronger than all the others, sooner or later that will lead us to one king for all. And sooner or later unitary power in the Black Forest will end in secession. I have no right to return at the moment.

"These are questions of politics. In any case, you have spoken as you see fit. Make haste, flinny!"

"Wait!" Eel called to Iirroo, who was already mounting his dragoatfly.

"You have spoken of the elves. But what of men?"

"I regret that this is not known to me. I do know that the Border Kingdom is standing firm to the death, I know that the second fist, the largest, is advancing toward Ranneng, I know that a part of the third fist is bogged down at Maiding. The Firstborn have skirted round Moitsig. These lands have not yet been touched by war, and if you hurry, you will have time to slip through. This is yesterday's news, perhaps there is more already, but I do not know. I am sorry. Farewell!"

The dragoatfly buzzed strenuously, performed a farewell circle in the air, and slipped into the darkness of the forest. And then Eel, Mumr, and Egrassa started arguing about what might happen in Valiostr and the way the orcs had stirred things up there. Their military leader had shown just what a cunning lad he was. He had tied the Border Kingdom and the elves hand and foot, while his main forces advanced on Valiostr. We couldn't expect any help from anyone. The Border Kingdom might manage with its own forces, but the garrisons on the southern border were weak and there were few troops. Most of the forces had been pulled back to the north and the border with Miranueh. The soft underbelly of the south was exposed and there for the taking.

No had one expected that the Firstborn would decide to repeat the Spring War. Sagot grant that the army would at least reach Ranneng in time. The Borderland and the whole of the south would have to be won back in battle—assuming, that is, that we stood firm at Ranneng, and the Borderlanders and the elves could contain the orcs. If the Borderland and the Black Forest fell and fresh hordes of orcs came surging at us, then all was lost. If things went really badly, we could be pushed back to the Cold Sea. A truly encouraging prospect! No Nameless One would be required. And no Horn, either. Everything would be over long before the sorcerer arrived from the Needles of Ice.

The next morning Hallas was quite steady on his feet, but he didn't react at all to the presence of the dryads and the elk. Lucky was gloomy and sullen and he hardly spoke. When he heard the news from Kli-Kli that the war had begun, the gnome just nodded. The only words Hallas spoke were when Lamplighter handed him his mattock. The gnome said, "Thank you" and slung the weapon over his shoulder. After a moment's hesitation, Kli-Kli handed Deler's hat to Lucky. The gnome twirled it in his hands, cleared his throat, and then put it on his head.

"When will they take these bandages off me?"

"When the time comes," Sunpatch answered, stroking the neck of one of the elk.

"And when will that be?"

"Soon."

Hallas snorted, but he didn't try to argue with the dryad. And the gnome didn't say anything when it turned out that he would have to ride behind the Daughter of the Forest.

We spent all that cold autumn day traveling. The elk speeded up even more, and the world around me fused into one long blur of brown and gold.

After lunchtime the Golden Forest came to an end and Lamplighter thanked Sagra. Now there was ordinary autumn forest ahead, with no leaves left on the trees, which was only natural in the final days of October. Soon the genuinely cold weather would begin, and the snow would not be far behind. Then we'd really start to freeze. How could the dryads go around barefoot in weather like this?

The presence of the Daughters of the Forest guaranteed our safety, and at night we lit huge campfires without feeling afraid that orcs might find us. The flames roared and we felt a lot warmer. Kli-Kli had caught a cold and kept sneezing all the time, so the heat of the fire was certainly good for her. We didn't talk about Glo-Glo and his apprentice's mission any longer, having come to an unspoken agreement to pretend nothing of the sort had ever happened. If Kli-Kli was supposed to take care of me, then let her. I was used to it in any case, and she was much better than anyone else. Egrassa was absorbed in his own thoughts, torn between us and his duty to his own house. Lamplighter took care of Hallas. The gnome had completely recovered from his wound, but he was still as gloomy as the autumn sky above our heads.

On the second day after we left the Golden Forest, Fluffy Cloud said we weren't going to stop for the night. Hallas said sarcastically that a full day and night of riding on a huge shaggy beast was more than even a gnome could bear, and he was against the idea. He also inquired in the most impolite fashion possible (the gnome couldn't care less that he was talking to a dryad—gnomes had never seen dryads, and he had no idea why they should be spoken to politely) when they would be pleased to remove the bandage that was pressing on his face. Sunpatch sighed and said that she would remove the bandage straightaway, but if Hallas didn't shut up after that, she would tell Runner in the Moonlight to trample the gnome with his hooves. Lucky agreed that it was fair deal.

He examined his face for a long time in Kli-Kli's mirror, and then asked Mumr for a rag to cover the empty eye socket. Lamplighter gave him a broad strip of black cloth, and it made the gnome look like a pirate or Jolly Gallows-Bird.

We galloped all night long, and this time I even managed to fall asleep, and I was woken by the elk stopping. It was early morning, and the black silhouettes of the trees stood out against the sky that was beginning to grow light. There was a fresh smell of frost and water in the air. I got down off the beast, shuddering, and helped Kli-Kli to get down as well.

"The Iselina," she explained.

It was so cold that clouds of steam erupted from our mouths as we spoke. If the Black River ran nearby, I certainly couldn't see it. The water was as black as the forest all around us.

"And now what?" Hallas blurted out, wrapping himself in his cloak.

"Thank you, Runner in the Moonlight," Fluffy Cloud said to the elk.

The beast's snorting surrounded the dryad in steam, then he turned and disappeared into the forest. Our other mounts followed him. The group of elk disappeared in an instant, and the bushes didn't even crack, as if we had been carried by intangible phantoms, not animals of flesh and blood.

"Now? Now we go by river," Sunpatch answered the gnome.

"Right now?"

"Yes."

"Don't you think it's a bit too dark and cold for a swim, dear lady?"

I swear by all the gods that in her heart of hearts Sunpatch must have regretted that she ever healed the gnome. In any case, she ignored Hallas's question. But Fluffy Cloud answered him.

"Wait a little while, and you'll understand everything."

There was nothing for it, we had to wait. I spotted two little blue dots in the branches of the nearest tree.

"Look, Kli-Kli. A forest spirit."

"I saw him ages ago. He's looking after this section of the forest."

"But where are all the others?" Eel asked. "There were far more of them in Zagraba in September."

"Hibernating. They'll sleep until spring now. They've left lookouts to keep an eye on the forest."

"That's bad luck for the lad," I said, sympathizing with the forest spirit. "Now he has to hang about here all winter."

Just then a small round sphere radiating a steady golden light flew out of the forest and landed on Sunpatch's shoulder. On closer inspection, the sphere proved to be a huge firefly. But it wasn't its size that surprised me. I'd never seen fireflies in late autumn. According to all the laws of creation, the insect ought to have died long ago, or hidden itself away in some cranny; it shouldn't be flying around the forest like some holy hermit's lamp. But this one obviously cared nothing at all for the laws of creation. Or maybe it just hadn't had time to study them yet.

"Now we can go to the water. Everything's ready," Sunpatch said, setting out confidently toward the river. The firefly gave more than enough light for us to see the path.

"Just as I thought!" Hallas muttered when we reached the river's edge. "A boat! I hate boats!"

"It's not a boat, it's a raft," Kli-Kli contradicted the gnome.

"What's the difference? Boat, raft, ferry, ship, or tub? I hate everything that floats."

The raft was large, and there was plenty of space for all of us. Eel, Lamplighter, Egrassa, and I took up the poles, and the dryads, the goblin, and the gnome stayed in the center. Hallas immediately started feeling sick.

The elf untied the thick rope holding the raft by the bank, and then we had to strain a bit, heaving on our poles, to get our new means of conveyance out into the middle of the river.

"How did a raft happen to be here?" Lamplighter asked, leaning hard on his pole.

"No doubt the dryads arranged it," I answered the warrior.

"What difference does it make how it got here? The important thing is that it did. And whether the dryads arranged it or Sagra sent it to us, I couldn't care less," Eel said, pulling his pole out of the water and laying it carefully at his feet.

I lifted my pole up, too, and the raft floated on. The bottom was too deep to reach now, so there was no point in straining myself anymore.

When it was light, the firefly soared up off Sunpatch's shoulder and flew away, buzzing, toward the forest. The gloomy, morose trees towered up on both sides of the river as if some giant was trying to squeeze it in a tight embrace. The Iselina was far narrower here than it was near Boltnik. The current carried us along at a brisk rate, so fast that the water at the stern seethed furiously.

Soon the already cloudy sky was even more overcast, and after another two hours or so it started spitting rain. It wasn't a very pleasant day—stuck on a raft in the middle of a river with water pouring down from the sky, too. We huddled up under our cloaks, but that couldn't save us from the cold and the damp.

"The last rain of the year," Kli-Kli said with a sniff.

"How do you make that out?"

"We have a nose for things like that, Mumr-Bubr. If I say it's the last, then it's the last. Cold weather's already on the way."

"It's been cold for ages," Hallas objected. "I can't even straighten up in the mornings."

"That's nothing," Kli-Kli said dismissively. "But now it's really going to get cold, and if anything falls from the sky, it'll be snow."

"You're a real expert, Kli-Kli," Eel laughed.

"Of course!" the gobliness agreed, then squinted up at the leaden sky and sighed sorrowfully.

"The river trip is almost over, Hallas. We've reached the boundaries of Zagraba. We'll be in Valiostr tomorrow morning," the elf reassured the gnome.

"If we don't drown first," the gnome grumbled.

The gobliness started whining. "Can't we light a fire? We'll be traveling all night!"

"What fire?" Mumr asked in amazement. "In rain like this? And we'd have to row to the shore, there's no timber here. Or are you thinking of lighting a fire with your cloak?

18

THE MARGEND HORSESHOE

A re you certain there aren't any orcs here, Egrassa?" Lamplighter asked the elf.

"Yes," Egrassa replied, but he kept hold of his bow.

That made me feel a bit nervous—and the others, too. We were used to trusting the dark elf's instincts. And right now Egrassa was tense and focused, as if we were about to be attacked at any moment.

"What makes you so sure?" Kli-Kli asked.

"You heard the flinny say there weren't any orcs near Moitsig, didn't you?"

"But when was that? From Maiding to Moitsig is five days' riding. The orcs don't like horses, but they're quite capable of covering the distance in that time. It's a long time since we saw the flinny, so I wouldn't be surprised if everything's changed ten times over by now and these lands are teeming with Firstborn."

"Don't talk disaster," Hallas told Kli-Kli good-naturedly. The gnome was walking in front of me.

"I'm not talking disaster, I'm just feeling a bit anxious."

"Then stop whinging, or I won't hear when an orc creeps up on you," the gnome advised the gobliness.

Our group lapsed into silence. We were all too busy looking for any signs of possible danger, and the conversation petered out of its own accord.

Early that morning, our raft had landed on the left bank of the Iselina. It was no more than three hundred yards from there to the edge of Zagraba. The dryads were the first to disembark from the raft, then they waited until we were all on the bank and led the group on. Early in the night it had stopped raining, and in the middle of the night there had been a light frost, so now the ground and the tree trunks were covered with hoary rime. The rare puddles were covered with a crust of ice.

A few more minutes, and we were out of Zagraba. Ahead of us a hilly plain stretched out for as far as the eye could see, covered with open woodland. Our group was on the southern border of Valiostr.

The dryads exchanged a few words with Egrassa in orcic. Then they nodded to us without speaking, glanced for a brief moment at the bag with the Horn in it, and walked away into the forest. I thought I saw bushes and the bare, leafless trees part to let the Daughters of the Forest pass.

Egrassa straightened his silver coronet and led us out of Zagraba in silence. After we'd gone about five hundred yards, I couldn't help looking back. It wasn't likely I would ever see the legendary forest again.

Zagraba was a dark, silent wall behind us. It was quite different now from the land teeming with greenery that I'd seen from the battlements of Cuckoo, and it certainly didn't look anything like a golden kingdom of autumn any longer. Just an ordinary forest, even if it was a big one. November had devoured all its colors. No wonder the elves and the orcs called it the gray month.

We had a very real chance of running into Firstborn now. In the two hours since we left Zagraba, everything had been quiet and peaceful. There was no indication that an army of many thousands had passed this way—there weren't any tracks on the ground apart from our own. Egrassa was leading the group along the river, and by his reckoning we should soon reach Moit-sig, which stood on the left bank of the Iselina. We couldn't avoid the city, because we needed horses (I could just imagine how the prices must have soared once the war started) and news of what was happening on the borders of the kingdom.

This war had come at a bad time. Even if we stood firm and the Firstborn didn't drive us back to the Cold Sea, the losses would be too great, and the army might not recover from the blow in time for spring. Our only hope was Artsivus and the Order. Maybe they would be able to do something with the artifact and then the Nameless One wouldn't come swooping down on us.

After walking down a low hill covered with aspens, we came out onto a wide road. The frost had frozen the mud created by the previous day's rain into a whimsical pattern of bumps and hollows. It wasn't very easy to walk on, but still a lot better than the liquid slush that would have delayed us for a long time if the weather hadn't turned cold. I'd already regretted that we didn't have any horses four times at the very least. I'd had quite enough of tramping about on my own two feet. Sagot be praised that the cobbler hadn't deceived me, and my boots hadn't fallen to pieces somewhere in the Labyrinth.

"Have you noticed anything strange?" Eel suddenly inquired.

"You have the right idea," Egrassa responded. "I don't like it, either."

"What do you mean?" asked Kli-Kli, puzzled. Just in case, she snatched out one of her throwing knives.

"We've been walking along the road for an hour, but we haven't met any-body," Eel explained.

"What's so strange about that?" said Mumr, shifting the bidenhander from one shoulder to the other. "Who'd want to go to Zagraba? That's where the road leads, doesn't it?"

"Some people would," Egrassa objected. "As I recall, there are several fishing villages along the edge of Zagraba, and this is the time when the fisherman should have sold their fish and be on their way home from Moitsig."

"Maybe the fish weren't biting? Or they don't need to sell any fish?" I suggested.

"When there's a war on? The prices for grub should shoot up so far that any fisherman could make his monthly earnings in a single day! Skipping into town and selling is exactly what they need to do!" Hallas droned.

"Then I don't know . . ."

"I do! I swear on my mountain mattock, Harold, there's something not right here. We're about to get clobbered! I swear by the Fury of the Depths that we are!"

"Now you're the one who's talking disaster," Kli-Kli teased the gnome.

"We have to do something, and not just wander along the road like a flock of sheep. Any bowman could pick us off here! Egrassa, why don't I go on ahead? That way, if we run into trouble, I'll have time to warn you."

"No," said the elf after a brief moment's thought, and he shook his head. "Eel and I will go. You stay on the road for now; we'll give you a sign if anything happens. Harold, hold the spear."

The elf handed me the krasta and he and the Garrakian went running on ahead. We waited for the two warriors to disappear over the top of the next hill before we moved on. For half an hour nothing happened, and then we heard a whistle.

For a moment my heart dropped into my boots, but Lamplighter dispelled my fears.

"That's Eel. Let's get a move on. There's something interesting up there."

"And doesn't interesting mean dangerous?"

"If it was anything dangerous, he'd have whistled in a completely different way. But try to keep behind me just in case."

"I promise not to stick my neck out. And I'll keep hold of Kli-Kli so he doesn't get under your feet." Whatever anyone might say, I do have heaps of good qualities, and the most important one is common sense.

We hurried forward as the road climbed the next low hill. Eel appeared on the top and waved to us. When we got up there, we saw what had attracted our scouts' attention—there was the city of Moitsig ahead of us.

"And who was trying to tell me the Firstborn hadn't come this far?" Hallas growled.

His question went unanswered. From up on the hill there was an excellent view of the river, a huge uneven open space with scattered patches of open woodland, and the city, just a quarter league away from us. Towering up on the right, between the open space, the city, and the river, were the mighty gray walls of a small fortress. I knew there were another two fortresses on the other side of Moitsig. The reason for building them like that was to have the city at the center of a triangle of three citadels. Quite a good defensive arrangement—before you could storm the city walls, you had to deal with the outposts, otherwise you had a good chance of being hit on the flanks or from the rear by soldiers from the castles making a sortie while you were busy trying to break down the city gates.

But storming one of the bastions was risky, too. While you were dealing with one, help could arrive from another, and the soldiers in the city wouldn't let a chance to take a lunge at you pass them by. So Moitsig was a genuinely tough nut to crack. It was practically impossible to take by storming it head on, unless you launched simultaneous attacks on all three castles and the city, using a very big army. If all the orcs had gone for Moitsig and not split up into three separate armies, they would have had a chance, but this way—this way was obviously hopeless, as the scene on the open field made clear.

It was absolutely littered with corpses. The scene was too far away for me to make out the details, but a blind beaver could have seen that the orcs had tried to storm the nearest castle and then been hit with a blow on their flank by forces from Moitsig and the other two bastions. The citadel they tried to take had stood firm, but parts of its walls and three of its six towers had been destroyed. I wouldn't have been surprised if that was the work of orcish shamanism. But not even magic had helped the Firstborn, and they had been overwhelmed by the army of men. I never doubted for a single moment who had won this battle.

"How many are there?" I asked unthinkingly.

"Without counting, no more than three thousand," said Hallas, screwing up his only eye. "They got a right royal battering. It's a pity we didn't get here in time to join in the scrap."

Personally speaking, I didn't have the slightest regret that we'd arrived late for the massacre. Darkness only can understand these gnomes, always so desperate to break someone's armor open with their mattocks.

"I don't think there are three thousand," Lamplighter objected.

"What point is there in guessing? Let's go and take a look! Or, better still, ask someone!"

"Slow down, Hallas! I reckon we'd better not stick our noses in! Our own side could take us for deserters, and that would be the end of us. If this is the way things are, I suggest we ought to avoid the city. Why go sticking your own head in the noose?"

"We'll have to go in, Mumr. It will take us too long to reach the next town without horses."

"What do we need a town for, Egrassa? We can call into any village and buy horses."

"Uh-huh!" said Kli-Kli, positively radiating skepticism. "Sure, they'll sell you horses. And throw in smart bridles and saddles to go with them. You should try using your head sometimes! You won't find a single worn-out nag in any of the villages around here! All the horses have been commandeered for the army, and if they haven't, the peasants won't let you have their own plow horses."

"So Harold will have to steal the horses from them," Mumr parried coolly.

"I'm no horse thief," I exclaimed, and added hastily, "Anyway, they could regard it as looting and string us up from the nearest tree."

"We'll have to go in," said the elf. "Right now information is far more important than horses. We have to listen to what they know here before we set out for Avendoom. The Firstborn could have the whole area ringed off, and this detachment might be no more than the advance guard."

And so saying, Egrassa started walking down the hill. The rest of us followed him. Kli-Kli took hold of my sleeve just to be on the safe side, but this time I didn't try to free myself from her tenacious fingers.

"What were they hoping to achieve?" I asked out loud. "It's almost impossible to take a fortified city like this with three thousand soldiers."

"Why is it impossible?" said Eel, who had heard me. "It's quite possible. If I remember my military history and the history of the Spring War, two thousand Firstborn took Maiding at a trot when they surprised an army of men three times that size, and then they held the city until their main army arrived. These lads probably thought they could repeat the heroic feat of their ancestors."

"But they bit off more than they could chew," Hallas concluded pitilessly. "What were they thinking of? Trying to break through defenses like these! Even dwarves would have realized the city must have heard about the orcs moving down the east bank of the Iselina and had plenty of time to prepare! These Firstborn are real oafs! Only the Doralissians could be more stupid!"

"The Firstborn weren't stupid," the elf objected. "They were young, and youth tends to be overconfident."

"I don't understand."

"Egrassa's eyesight is better than yours," Kli-Kli explained to the gnome. "Wait until we reach the battlefield, then you'll understand."

"Maybe we should go round the battlefield?"

"What's the matter, Harold?" Lamplighter asked with a frown. "Since when have you been afraid of corpses?"

Ever since I took a stroll through Hrad Spein! I thought to myself, but I wisely said nothing. I just didn't understand why we had to barge straight in and walk over the dead bodies when there was a perfectly open patch of ground if we just kept a bit farther to the left.

Egrassa seemed to think the same as I did, because he turned off the road, and when we approached the battlefield we left most of the dead on our right, but what we did see was more than enough.

The elf was right. As far as I could tell, the orcs really were young. Very young. Mere boys, in fact. And they had met their death attempting to repeat the great feat of their ancestors.

"Boys . . . ," Kli-Kli whispered. "It's strange, Harold. They're our enemies, our bitter enemies. They hate everyone who's different from them, but now I feel sorry for them."

"You're right, jester. Children shouldn't be fighting where real warriors should take up the sword. What made them do it? Why make this stupid attack? They knew they had no chance of victory," said Eel, trying not to look at the faces of the dead.

"Maybe they were surrounded and forced to give battle?" I suggested.

"The signs tell a different story. No one surrounded them, and anyway, Zagraba's not far away. They could have broken out of encirclement."

"I wonder when this battle took place?"

"Slaughter, Harold, not battle," Egrassa corrected me. "This is a field of slaughter, not a battlefield. The foolish young pups weren't given a chance. Can you sense it, Kli-Kli?"

"Yes."

"What in the name of darkness are you talking about?"

"Magic, Hallas. Magic was used here."

"I'm not blind, goblin. The gods be praised, I still have one eye left! Just look at how battered the castle is!"

"Men did that."

"What?" Lamplighter and I asked in a single voice.

"There was no shamanism here. Only wizardry. And that means it was the work of men or light elves. And, as you realize, the latter is not very likely."

"Then why did they damage their own castle, smart aleck?"

"That was the backlash, Hallas, the price paid for using wizardry. They used one of the Order's most powerful spells here. I assume that some abomination descended on the orcs and immobilized them all for a while. But the spell must have been so powerful that they couldn't control the backlash, and it hit the castle. Only the orcs took most of the blow. Do you see the depressions in the ground and what happened to the bodies?"

"I thought they'd been trampled by cavalry," Eel hissed.

"There aren't any hoofprints."

"I see that now, Kli-Kli. But there are plenty of prints from metal-shod boots."

"Aha, those who weren't caught by the backlash were finished off by the defenders. The Firstborn were unable to resist in any case, and they were dispatched into the darkness. The men didn't fight a very fair battle here."

"If you ask me, that's no more than the orcs deserve," said Mumr, spitting down at his feet. "They should stay in their Zagraba and leave our kingdom alone. And as for war . . . Well, this is war, Kli-Kli, and in war any means are fair. You can demonstrate your nobility in a duel and allow your opponent to pick up the sword that he's dropped. Here, if you lose your sword, then you lose your head as well. It doesn't matter why you went to war, what age you are, and how noble you are—you either win and snatch victory, or you rot on the battlefield. In war there is no third way."

"But even so, it's not fair," Kli-Kli argued stubbornly. "They didn't even have a shaman with them. Weapons should be fought with weapons, not with magic."

"And Sagra be praised that they didn't have a shaman," Lamplighter said furiously. "If they did, three times as many of our men would have been killed. This is war, Kli-Kli. Maybe you'll understand some time. . . ."

"I do understand," the gobliness said reluctantly.

While we were talking, we came back out onto the road leading to Moitsig and moved away from the half-ruined castle—we could see that there wasn't a single soul in it—and the field of death. The city came closer and closer.

"How long ago was the battle?" I asked, breaking the heavy silence.

"Judging from the fact that they haven't burned the orcs' bodies yet, and the crows can still fly—yesterday evening at the earliest," Eel answered.

"Why, the gates of Moitsig are standing wide open!" Kli-Kli exclaimed in amazement. "Either the townspeople have stopped being afraid after the battle, or something's happened."

"Nothing's happened!" said Eel, screwing up his eyes. "Just look how many people there are up on the walls!"

Well, if those black dots running along the wall were people . . . We were still too far from the city for me to see.

"I think we've been spotted!" said Egrassa, watching a detachment of horsemen come flying out of the gates.

"Hardly surprising," Lamplighter said with a shrug. "We're in open territory here, anyone can see us. Keep back, Egrassa. You never know . . ."

Lamplighter didn't bother to finish what he was saying, the meaning was clear enough. The lads hurrying toward us might turn out to be just a bit too hot-blooded and keen to hand out punishment. At a passionate gallop it was easy to confuse an elf with an orc.

Egrassa's eyes flashed at Mumr's words but—Sagot be praised—he didn't reach for his s'kash. I don't think Lamplighter realized he had mortally insulted the elf.

"I am not used to hiding behind the backs of others!"

"Don't be angry, Egrassa!" Eel put in hastily. "The Master of the Long Sword is talking good sense. It's best for a bowman to stand in the second line."

"Do you intend to fight?" the elf asked, raising his right eyebrow mockingly.

"No."

"Then it makes no difference," said Egrassa, putting an end to the difficult conversation.

I was starting to feel a bit nervous. "Hallas!" I called. "Don't go for your mattock!"

The riders were coming closer. Four of the warriors directed their horses to the left and started going round our little group. All four of them were armed with bows. The main group came rushing straight at us, making no effort to restrain their horses. I liked the look of this less and less. Unfortunately, Egrassa had the krasta, and you can't really fight a man on horseback with a dagger, especially when he's armed with a lance. One of the riders pressed his spurs into the flank of his horse and moved up two lengths ahead of his comrades. What was this lad intending to do? And why had he lowered his lance?

The ground started to tremble under our feet.

"Stop, Harold!" Kli-Kli hissed, clinging on hard to my clothes. "If we run, he'll hit us with his lance! Stay here. . . . Stay here. . . ."

The horse—a huge black beast that could have emerged straight from the darkness—came flying at us. At the very last moment, just when it seemed that its massive carcass would crush us, the horseman reined in his mount. It reared up on its hind legs, flailing at the air with its front hooves and almost splitting Eel's head open. The Garrakian ducked to one side, keeping his eyes on the rider, but the horseman had eyes for only one target— Egrassa. As soon as the horse's front feet touched the ground, the unknown warrior thrust with his lance with all his might, aiming for Egrassa's chest. The elf would have been spitted if not for Lamplighter. In some miraculous manner the puny Wild Heart managed to get between the rider and the dark elf. The bidenhander sliced through the air with a hiss and collided with the lance, knocking it up and away to one side, and then swung into the next stroke, which should have ended with a blow to the enemy's unprotected side, but at that point the other horsemen rode up.

The first one struck hard with his lance at the shield of the man who had attacked us. The warrior hadn't been expecting anything of the kind and he lost his seat in the saddle. I caught a momentary glimpse of a white face with an expression of absolute amazement as the lad went crashing to the ground, right at Lamplighter's feet.

"Are your brains completely addled, Borrik?" one of the riders barked. "Or have you gone blind?"

The warrior lying on the ground stared wild-eyed and gulped frantically. He'd obviously taken a hard fall when he left the saddle.

"Forgive my man, Tresh Elf," the same rider said to Egrassa.

"Elf?" the one who was called Borrik finally gasped. "I thought it was one of the orcs."

"You thought! I'll send you up onto the wall to count ravens! I won't let you back in the saddle for a year! Let me apologize again most humbly for this misunderstanding, Tresh . . ."

"Egrassa. Egrassa of the House of the Black Moon," the dark elf replied, glaring at Borrik as he tried to get up off the ground.

If there hadn't been so many horsemen present, the warrior would already have tasted the elf's s'kash. But Egrassa thought it better for the moment not to put any more strain on relations, and he postponed his vengeance on the young lad for a better time.

"I am Neol Iragen, lieutenant of the Moitsig Guard," the horseman said.

Neol Iragen was over forty years old. Eyes like a cat, thick eyebrows that met on the bridge of his nose, and the despondent features of a petty nobleman that didn't fit with the piercing blue glint of those eyes and the confident pose in the saddle.

"Are these, er . . . people with you, Tresh Egrassa?" The lieutenant stumbled over the word "people," because it was hard to apply it to a goblin and a gnome.

"Yes, these are my warriors."

I don't know what Neol Iragen thought, but Kli-Kli and I certainly attracted a couple of suspicious glances. It couldn't be helped; the gobliness and I just didn't look like warriors.

"What brings an elf to our city, when the Black Forest is ablaze?" asked the lieutenant, trying to make his question sound polite.

"Orders from the king," said Egrassa, taking out Stalkon's decree, the same one that we'd shown to the two magicians in Vishki. He handed it to the horseman.

The warrior took the document and studied the royal seal carefully. I must say that Milord Neol was certainly surprised, but it hardly showed in his face at all—his thick eyebrows merely quivered.

"When the war began, we were ordered to check any unusual and unexpected travelers," the lieutenant began cautiously as he returned the document to the elf. "There are all sorts walking the roads now. Including deserters and spies. Your appearance here is very strange, and then these papers . . . You understand, Tresh Egrassa, we can't simply let you go just like that?"

"What do you suggest?"

"We need to check everything, and it would be best if we took you into the city, to the commander of the garrison."

"We have nothing against that," Egrassa said with a casual shrug.

"Well, that's marvelous!" Neol Iragen said with a sigh of relief when he realized that the elf had no intention of being stubborn. "Borrik, give Tresh Egrassa your horse!"

The lad had recovered by this time, and he led the large black beast over to Egrassa without a murmur. Another five riders dismounted to give us their horses. They didn't offer Kli-Kli a horse. The gobliness was about to take offense and make a scene, but I put her up in front of me, and she seemed quite content with that arrangement.

As we rode toward Moitsig, we found ourselves in the center of the detachment of riders, who surrounded us, seemingly by chance, just in case these strange travelers might decide that they didn't really want to visit the city and try to make a run for it.

"What's happening with the army? Is Maiding still holding out?" asked Eel, breaking the long silence.

One of the warriors opened his mouth to answer, but caught a glance of warning from Neol Iragen and swallowed the words that had been on the tip of his tongue.

"Wait for a little while, soldier," said the lieutenant. "The commandant will tell you everything."

Eel nodded and didn't ask any more questions. I couldn't understand the reason for all the secrets. Didn't he trust the royal decree? To think of us as deserters was stupid, to say the least. And we didn't fit the role of spies. Orcs would never use men as spies. Or would they? When I remembered the First Human Assault Army that had gone over to the orcs during the Spring War, the concerns of the citizens of Moitsig didn't seem so strange.

"Lamplighter!" Egrassa suddenly called to the Wild Heart.

"Yes?"

"Thank you."

Mumr hadn't been expecting any gratitude from the elf. He screwed his eyes up in satisfaction and grinned from ear to ear.

Moitsig was a seething hive of activity. It was only half the size of Ranneng, and it couldn't bear any comparison at all with Avendoom, but that didn't prevent the inhabitants of this southern city feeling for a day that they were the luckiest folk in the Universe.

The festive atmosphere that filled the squares and streets would have been the envy of any city in the world. The holiday feeling hung in the air—we heard it in the conversations of the townsfolk and the guards at the gates, it rang out in the songs of the revelers at the inns and taverns. It was as if there was no war. Today the inhabitants of the city were victorious. They, and they alone, had crushed a force of three thousand (or perhaps even more) orcs, and what difference did it make how the victory had been snatched from the jaws of fate? The victors are never judged—isn't that what they say? Today the people were rejoicing and trying to enjoy everything life had to offer, for tomorrow the bleak times would begin again and the war would continue.

We didn't ride through the streets crammed with people for very long. Neol Iragen led our group to the municipal barracks. There were as many soldiers here as there were civilians out in the streets. The warriors seemed to be preparing for a march. They were all dashing about from one corner to another. The captains and sergeants were yelling orders, some men were packing their kit, others were saddling horses.

Were the lads getting ready to give someone a good roasting? Well, it was high time.

They brought us to the barracks and left us in the company of some soldiers. Egrassa and Eel went off together with the lieutenant of the guard to see the commandant, and we passed the time at the table. The gods be praised, they didn't intend to starve us to death. Kli-Kli didn't eat anything, and the moment I let her out of my sight, she disappeared. She must have gone running off after the elf or decided to sniff out some news.

"I don't like all this," Hallas said, chomping away and at the same time fishing a particularly appetizing piece of meat out of the pot. "Celebrations are all very well, a victory should be celebrated, but it's not good to go playing the fool. What on earth, I ask you, is the point of leaving the city gates wide open? The orcs have always been famous for their rapid attacks. There'll be a real panic when they turn up, you mark my words, Harold! The guards might not even have time to close the gates, and then what do we do? It's a lot harder fighting in the streets than up on the walls."

"Don't be so nervous. Everything will be just fine," Lamplighter said philosophically, and gave a long, drawn-out belch. "This Neol doesn't seem like a fool. If the gates are open, then there's nothing to be afraid of. I'm sure the area round the city is crawling with scouts, like fleas on a mangy dog. They'll spot any orcs a league away."

"Why can't you understand, Mumr?" the gnome exclaimed indignantly. "There has to be order in everything! If the gates are open, that's gross negligence! We gnomes would never commit a stupidity like that."

"If Deler was here—may he dwell the light—he'd soon give you an answer," Lamplighter retorted.

Hallas suddenly lost interest in the conversation, started stirring the soup round with his spoon, and then pushed the pot away.

"They've been gone a long time. I hope this commandant isn't some kind of petty tyrant who wants to keep us here longer than necessary."

"Who's going to keep us here when we have papers from the king?" Mumr asked in amazement, like a little child.

"Who's going to keep us here?" the gnome echoed, mocking his comrade. "A lot of good those papers did us at Vishki! Those magicians never even looked at them properly. If they'd felt the urge, they would have wiped their backsides with them. If it wasn't for that hand monster, darkness only knows what would have happened to us. Who can guarantee that everything will be all right this time round? Nothing to say? That's right! No one can give us any guarantee. How about you, Harold? What do you think?"

"Nothing much, really."

"Nothing much?" Hallas exclaimed. "Don't you have an opinion on the matter?"

"Hallas, stop blathering," I said, trying to calm the gnome down. "What's wrong, don't you trust Egrassa and Eel?"

At that the gnome just glared at me with his one eye and tightened his grip on the spoon, preparing to use it on me.

"Look," I said soberly, drawing a line under the conversation. "There's nothing to be worried about. Egrassa and Eel will manage to persuade the commandant somehow."

Hallas glowered at me from under his bandage and pulled the pot back toward him.

"Just the same, they're all slackers here. They left us without any guards."

"Where are you going to run to, if you don't mind telling me?" asked Mumr, licking his spoon. "There are men all around; you wouldn't get away without being spotted."

"Hey!" said one of the soldiers who was walking past our table. "I know you!"

The three of us gaped at him. Just an ordinary soldier like any other. I would have sworn I'd never seen his face before. But the crest sewn on to the warrior's jacket was familiar. A black cloud on a green field—the crest of my dear old friend, Baron Oro Gabsbarg. So this lad was one of the baron's soldiers. But what wind could have blown him so far from home?

"But we don't know you," Lucky muttered rather disagreeably. "We've never met."

"You're mistaken, honorable sir! Late summer, at Mole Castle. Do you remember now?"

"No."

"I was in Milord Gabsbarg's retinue. Agh! Listen, you're the lad who pinned Meilo Trug to the ground!" said the soldier, talking to Lamplighter now.

"Well, yes," Mumr admitted reluctantly.

"Hey! Lads!" the soldier yelled, loud enough for the whole barracks to hear, attracting everybody's attention to us. "This is the master of the long sword I was telling you about. He wiped the floor with Trug in Kind Soul Castle!"

And then it began! Apparently every soldier in the kingdom had heard about Lamplighter's heroic exploits. Anyway, a dense crowd gathered round our table, and every man was trying to pat Mumr on the shoulder. Those who couldn't reach Mumr made do with me or Hallas, as if the gnome and I had also swung double-handed swords around in the courtyard of Algert Dalli's castle during that memorable duel at the Judgment of Sagra. Hallas even thawed a bit and started grinning when he found himself the center of attention.

The lad wearing Gabsbarg's crest was almost busting a gut as he told the story of the duel for the hundredth time. The men listened delightedly. A gray-haired veteran squeezed his way through the crowd besieging our table from all sides. He had a massive two-hander nestling on his shoulder, and the gold oak leaf was clearly visible on the hilt. A master of the long sword. The warrior bowed respectfully. Mumr kept up the good tone and replied with a bow of his own.

The warrior respectfully requested Mr. Lamplighter, when he had the time, of course, to give him a few lessons. Mumr agreed. Hallas grunted and hinted rather casually that it would be rather nice to have some beer, maybe. One of the young soldiers went dashing out of the barracks and less than five minutes later we had several potbellied mugs of beer standing in front of us.

Ah, darkness! In all that wandering around Zagraba I'd forgotten what beer tasted like. So I just relished it, leaving Hallas, surrounded by eager listeners, to get on with telling his tall stories. Puffed up with pride, the gnome told the whole world how he had singlehandedly dragged me out of the Labyrinth and how—with this very mattock—he had nailed ninety-eight orcs and one h'san'kor in the Golden Forest. He was just bullshitting with the number of orcs, of course, but they believed him. How could they not believe him, when as proof he showed them an absolutely genuine horn from the forest monster?

By the end of this epic tale every soldier in the barracks would have walked through fire for the gnome. I was sure that in three days' time the entire army would know Hallas's fairy tales. The gods be praised that he didn't think of throwing in a dragon and a princess just to round things off.

I was beginning to catch inquiring glances directed my way. Probably some of those present assumed that since I was traveling with highly respected daredevils like Hallas and Deler, I was a legendary hero, too, and at the very least I must have wrung the Nameless One's neck with my bare hands. If the lads had only known that I'd walked right through Hrad Spein and now I had the Rainbow Horn in my bag, they would have been absolutely convinced that we were three great heroes from the Gray Age.

The gnome was working his way into his third mug of beer and he hadn't stopped talking for a moment. I seized my chance to attract the attention of Gabsbarg's soldier.

"How did you end up here?" I asked him.

"I'm an adjutant now, and milord's personal envoy!" the lad replied proudly. "I was sent here to get help."

"Help? Has something happened to the baron?"

"Baron?" the soldier chortled. "Think again, my friend!"

But just then, as bad luck would have it, Kli-Kli showed up.

"Wind it up, Egrassa wants us!"

Everybody wished us good luck, and started thumping us on the back all over again. When I eventually followed the gobliness out through the crowd, my shoulders were aching.

"Where are you taking us?" I asked Kli-Kli.

"Somewhere a bit quieter. Where we can talk properly," she answered.

"You mean Egrassa doesn't want us?" the gnome asked with a frown.

"Of course not!"

"What did you want to talk to us about?"

"Lots of things. I've found out a thing or two that you'll find interesting. Eel's already waiting for us."

"What about Egrassa?"

"He was invited to dine with the commandant."

"Which means that everything's been settled?"

"I've always said our Dancer was an absolute genius!" Kli-Kli chuckled as she led us out into the courtyard.

"And this is what you call privacy?"

"At least here no one will take any notice of us. Will there be any more questions?"

"What's that sack you're lugging about? Are you sure you won't rupture yourself?"

"You worry about yourself," she snorted. "Anyway, we're here."

The gobliness led us over to a building, casually kicked the door open, and we walked into a spacious room. Eel was enthroned at a table, gnawing on a chicken leg. And I should say that there was certainly plenty of food.

"My, aren't you doing well! Who paid for all this?" said Hallas, asking the question closest to the heart of every gnome.

"No one. Milord Commandant was so kind as to provide us with food from his own table and give us a room, while Egrassa dines in the company of His Grace. Do join me in the feast."

"Well, actually, we already ate in the barracks," said the gnome, trying halfheartedly to decline.

"All right, that's up to you. There'll be all the more for me."

At that Hallas rubbed his hands together and walked straight to the table.

"All right, you lot eat your fill, and I'll tell you about what's happened in Valiostr while we were walking through Zagraba. Eel already knows everything. Eat, Hallas, eat. It's better than we thought."

"How much better?" I asked Kli-Kli cautiously.

"A lot. The orcs are getting their butts kicked on all fronts!" she informed us with a delighted look on her face.

"Wha-a-at?" Hallas exclaimed, gaping in amazement with his one eye.

"That's the way of it, my dear gnome. Apparently we're not such pushovers after all. Somehow we found out about the invasion two days before the war started. Most of the border garrisons had enough time to prepare and they withdrew."

"Withdrew?" I didn't quite catch the connection between the words "prepare" and "withdrew."

"Oh, yes. The Borderland Kingdom's forces weren't going to retreat anywhere, but our men pulled back, and the glorious army of Valiostr came to meet them. The Heartless Chasseurs, the Hounds of Fortune, the Unyielding Ones, the Tramps, Gimo's Clowns, the Loons of Fate, and many, many more. At Upper Otters—a familiar name that, isn't it? They went into battle at Upper Otters and gave the Firstborn such a thrashing that it took them two days to recover. And by that time our army had vanished into thin air. We fell back again, this time beyond the Iselina. The orcs seemed to lose their senses; they advanced and got another thrashing for their efforts. By this time the northern army had arrived, too. There was a full-scale engagement near Ranneng and the orc army was split into three parts. The first part, the biggest, was driven all the way back to the Border Kingdom, but we don't know what happened there yet. The remnants of the second part managed to limp back somehow to their beloved Golden Forest, and the third part was caught and surrounded in Margend County, which is only a stone's throw from here. You can't imagine how delighted I am! The central army of the orcs has been smashed to smithereens!"

"Mm, yes," I said, unable to believe my ears. "Is all this definite?"

"Of course it's definite, blockhead! The commandant himself told Egrassa! The moment he saw the papers with the royal seal, he turned as smooth as silk. If you don't believe me, ask Eel."

This time the valiant army of Valiostr really had proved itself to be valiant, and the nightmare of the Spring War had not been repeated. The enemy had been stopped and thrown back. Ha-ha! That was what you could do with timely information and the northern army of forty thousand men that the king had assembled as a welcoming committee for the Nameless One.

"And how are things with the orcs' second and third armies?"

"The Borderlanders seemed to be standing firm and they'll hold out until our forces reach them. So the Firstborn are to be pitied. Soon they'll clear off back to their Golden Forest and won't stick their noses out for another three hundred years. They'll remember a crushing defeat like this for a very long time. As for the third army, that's all quite simple. The elves have rallied, and the latest information is that the situation in the Black Forest has stabilized. And as for the orcs who attacked Maiding"—Kli-Kli laughed conspiratorially—"they were in for just as big a surprise as the ones who went for Ranneng and ran into the Wild Hearts and the Heartless Chasseurs and the border garrisons. Our lads were expecting them, and then help arrived, and—"

"Wait, Kli-Kli!" Lamplighter interrupted, speaking for the first time. "Where did help come from there?"

"Have you forgotten about our fifteen thousand men permanently stationed on the border with Miranueh?"

"I haven't forgotten, but I'm sure Miranueh didn't forget them, either. The whole of the west is under the command of the Carp now." (This was a disdainful name for the inhabitants of Miranueh.)

"Don't worry about that! Everything's just great there as well! Twenty thousand Firstborn advanced against Maiding. The King of Miranueh couldn't bear the sight of such injustice and he added ten thousand of his pikemen and four thousand cavalry to our fifteen thousand."

"Wha-a-at!" This time all three of us gaped in amazement.

"Uh-huh. The orcs had really got up His Majesty's nose one way or another, and His Majesty decided to intervene to help his neighbor to the north."

"I don't believe it! I'll believe anything, but not Miranueh! All these centuries we've been squabbling over the Disputed Lands, and then this!"

"Don't the priests say that you should be generous, Harold?" the gobliness giggled. "Darkness only knows what made the king of Miranueh act so generously at just the right moment, but our own obliging Stalkon bowed gratefully and handed Miranueh the Disputed Lands."

Hallas choked on his wine and started coughing. Eel thumped the gnome on the back.

"No great loss. All those years spent haggling over twenty leagues of swampy land that's no good to anyone . . . Only northerners would do that sort of thing. . . ."

"Well, in Garrak you've got plenty of land to spare, but it's in short supply up here," said Lamplighter, springing to the defense of his native kingdom. "But what's done is done. So the orcs were driven back from Maiding?"

"Not just driven back, but surrounded and wiped out!" the gobliness positively sang. "Victory on all fronts! And the allied army didn't stop at that, it went into the Black Forest, to help our brothers the elves. If our generals have any brains at all, they'll clear the Firstborn out of the Golden Forest completely."

"For which—three cheers," said Hallas, raising his glass.

"So the ones who attacked Moitsig were a surviving fragment of the central army?"

"No, Mumr. They were lured out of Zagraba. Our soldiers were lucky, they picked up the clan chief of the Grun Ear-Cutters himself as he and his rabble were making their way back to their native forest. And they strung him up on the city gates, as a lesson to anyone who doesn't want to stay quietly at home in the Golden Forest. And those young pups didn't understand the message and crept out under the eye of Sagra. They wanted to retrieve the body. Well, they were massacred. . . . Right, Harold. And now for you. While you were cooling your heels in the barracks, I managed to run a couple of errands and pick up a few things." And so saying, the gobliness reached into the sack and set a crossbow on the table, together with twenty short bolts. "There . . . without a decent weapon you'll soon pine away."

I picked up the crossbow. Of course, it wasn't my little beauty, the one I'd left behind in Hrad Spein, but it wasn't bad at all. I used to have one just like it before. A "wasp"—a light weapon, and very reliable.

"Where did you get it?"

"I filched it, of course. From their armory," she said, bursting with pride.

"And what if they catch me with it now?" I chuckled, amazed at Kli-Kli's sheer cheek in stealing a weapon from right under a soldier's nose.

"If they catch you, Dancer, then you'll have to deal with it. I've done my bit. All the rest is your problem."

"Thanks a lot, Kli-Kli," I said sarcastically to my "benefactress."

"Don't mention it," she answered in the same tone of voice, and grinned gleefully. "And by the way, all of you, better get those jaws working, I've still got to take you to get some warm clothes. Winter's almost here, and you're still prancing about in those rags."

"Are we all going thieving together?" Hallas inquired, rolling his one eye.

"You have a very poor opinion of goblins, Lucky," the gobliness said resentfully. "Why do we have to go thieving? Egrassa's settled everything with the commandant. All we have to do now is pick up some warm things and we can hit the road. When we reach Avendoom, the real frosts will start to bite, and then all of you will say thank you to the little goblin, yes you will, for the nice warm clothes, because, if not for me, you would all have frozen to death."

"I thought you just said that Egrassa made the arrangements for the clothes, not you," Eel remarked innocently.

"But who do you think told him?" Kli-Kli asked spitefully.

"You told me," Egrassa replied as he walked into the room. "Get ready, there's an armed detachment leaving Moitsig in an hour. We'll leave with them."

"Why with them?" Hallas asked with a scowl. "Are we likely to lose our way?"

"You're forgetting that although the orcs have been routed, the chances of running into scattered units of Firstborn are still very high. Would you like to lose your second eye, too?"

The gnome's answer to that was to brag that he'd like to see the orcs try to get anywhere near him, and that if they did, a certain mattock would smash their skulls in for them.

"Are the Moitsig warriors going to Ranneng, too?"

"No, Eel. They're in a hurry to get to Margend County. Part of the central army of the Firstborn has been surrounded only one day's journey from here. Neol Iragen's detachment is going to take part in the forthcoming battle."

"Are there many orcs?" Lucky inquired, stroking his beard.

"About five and a half thousand."

"That's enough for me," the gnome said with a decisive nod, and Deler's hat fell down over his eyes. "Why are you all sitting there? Let's get moving, or they'll finish off all the orcs without us!"

I would have liked to say that would be for the best, but I kept my mouth shut. Why upset the gnome? Hallas was as happy as a child who'd just been promised a toy.

We left Moitsig an hour and a half later to loud howls of acclamation from the townsfolk, who were seeing their warriors off on their victorious campaign (no one had any doubt that they would be victorious). The commandant had been kind enough to present us with horses as well as warm clothes.

I'd been given a dark brown stallion with a marked inclination to try to kill his masters. In any case, the beast kept attempting to break into a gallop and dispatch his unfortunate rider directly to his grave. By some cruel jest of the gods, it was a cavalry horse, whose only aim in life was to go dashing forward at breakneck speed, preferably to the sound of a bugle. After my gentle Little Bee, this example of the equine species filled me with anxiety and creeping horror. It cost me an incredible effort just to hold the hothead back and not tumble out of the saddle. Eel watched with a compassionate expression as I struggled in vain to subdue the demon of frenzied unreason that possessed the horse, until finally he couldn't stand it anymore and offered to swap horses with me. Before the Garrakian could change his mind, I slipped out of the saddle and mounted a gentle, rather shaggy, and well-fed horse of indeterminate breed.

Now this was a horse that really suited me! She would only run if I wanted her to, or if there was an ogre chasing her.

"What's she called?" I asked.

"Horse," said the Garrakian, smiling.

One of the soldiers riding behind us overheard the conversation and roared with laughter. I don't know what he found so funny.

"All right then, Horse it is," I chuckled, patting the animal on the neck. "The name really suits her."

"Look, Harold, over there? Those men over there, in the gray cloaks."

"The members of the Order, you mean?"

"Those are the ones. It was that six who stopped the orcs at Moitsig."

"Well, good for them."

I personally felt no interest at all in the magicians.

But then I wondered what they'd say if they found out about the Rainbow Horn. And for a moment I felt the urge to hand the magical artifact over to them and never have anything more to do with magic again. I had to struggle with myself not to get rid of the Horn there and then.

The road led northward and, according to that know-all Kli-Kli, it would take us directly to Ranneng, but first we had to get past the small county of Margend, which ran along the west bank of the Iselina almost as far as Boltnik.

A detachment of mounted men six hundred strong set out from Moitsig. Two days earlier one and a half thousand heavy infantry from the Cat Halberdiers and the Rollicking Rogues had left the city in the direction of Margend. The Halberdiers had arrived in the city from Maiding immediately after the orcs in that section of the front were routed and forces had to be shifted urgently to the east, toward the Iselina. The Rollickers had been quartered in Moitsig and were spoiling for a fight.

Baron Gabsbarg's soldier was riding in our unit, and he told me all the soldiers' gossip. The lad jabbered away without a break, but just when I was going to ask about the baron he was called up to the front to Neol Iragen, and I had to postpone my questions for some other time.

In the way of things, our large mounted detachment ought soon to overtake the infantry and the large transport column wending its way toward the Second Army of the South that had encircled the remnants of the Firstborn. From what the soldiers were saying, we should arrive in the afternoon of the next day, in time to help our forces drive the orcs into the river. Egrassa was riding somewhere up at the head of the detachment with Neol Iragen, so we were left to our own devices. Or, rather, the gobliness was. Deprived of the elf's oversight, Kli-Kli decided to slip back into the role of the king's favorite jester. An hour later a good two hundred of the soldiers were laughing heartily at her jokes and songs and verses and other fancy tricks.

Ten minutes after that, the entire detachment had heard about the little sharp-tongued goblin traveling in the first unit. Naturally, the other five units started vying with each other to get Kli-Kli to join them. She was the life and soul of the honorable company once again, and she amused the soldiers until twilight fell, when the detachment halted for the night at a large village completely untouched by the war.

The locals turned out to be expecting us, and although there weren't enough houses for such a great horde, the local baron, who had come dashing from the nearest castle, complete with his numerous retinue, had made everything ready to receive his victorious guests. Thanks to Egrassa, we were even given a house where we could spend the night.

While Eel and the elf and I were settling into the new place, Kli-Kli managed to slip off. Hallas and Lamplighter didn't stay around for long, either. They were almost carried off shoulder-high to the center of the village, where the festivities in honor of the arrival of the glorious warriors were due to begin. I thought how many listeners the gnome would have now. The soldiers invited us as well, but I declined and Eel thought about it for a moment, then shook his head, too. Egrassa was invited to dine at the baron's festive table and he went in order to be polite.

It was dark outside. I breathed in the cold air that felt wintry already.

"Smells like the first snow," said Eel, as if he was reading my mind.

"It's cool, all right," I agreed. "November's a cold month in the south this year."

"Is this cold? It's nothing but a light frost," he chuckled. "See how pale the stars are? In a serious frost they burn like the jewels in the royal crown."

"Our Stalkon doesn't have all that many precious stones in his crown."

"I meant the Garrakian crown."

"Oh!" I said, realizing I'd said something stupid.

We said nothing for a while, listening to the happy shouting and laughter ringing out in the night.

"They're making merry, as if there was no war at all," I murmured.

"And why not? There'll be war and a battle tomorrow, but today they have a chance to forget about everything. Is that such a bad thing?"

"Why no," I said, embarrassed. "It's probably a good thing."

"What's bothering you, Harold?"

I paused, trying to find the right words. Unfortunately, as usual, the ones I really needed didn't come to mind.

"It's not that easy to explain. What the Gray One said, the Master, the Rainbow Horn, and, of course, the balance and all the consequences that follow. It's not very nice to think that without even wanting to, I might be carrying around the deadliest snake of all in my bag."

"Just don't think about it."

"What?"

"Look here. What do you see?" He took the "sister" out of its scabbard.

"A weapon," I muttered stupidly.

"That's right, a weapon. Is it dangerous right now?"

"No," I replied after a moment's thought.

"That's right. The 'sister' is in my hands. Everything depends on who's holding the weapon and what he wants to use it for. The Rainbow Horn is a weapon just like the 'sister,' and it's in your hands. I don't believe you want to consign the world to oblivion."

"But I won't always have it."

"The Order will take care of the Horn. Or don't you trust magicians any longer?"

"I do, but what the Gray One said . . ."

"What the Gray One said is just words, that's all. My old granny, may she dwell in the light, always used to say that prophecies never come true if we don't want them to."

"That's very reassuring," I said with a bitter grin, but I don't think the warrior could make out my pitiful grimace in the dark. "Why don't we go and join the others? Maybe they'll leave some wine for us?"

"I doubt if the lieutenant will allow the soldiers to drink much. And they're no fools, anyway: There's not much pleasure in going into battle with a hangover. So you and I can't count on anything more than a mug of beer. But let's hurry, or Hallas will guzzle our share."

The cavalry detachment left the village when the horizon in the east was marked out by a pearly-crimson thread of dawn.

"It's going to be a clear day," Lamplighter said, and a cloud of steam billowed out of his mouth.

"And very, very cold," croaked Kli-Kli, who had managed to get a sore throat. "Which of you two bright sparks was it that prophesied snow? A-agh . . ."

The first snow of the year wasn't very plentiful, and it only turned the ground into a brown and white patchwork blanket. Kli-Kli was wrong; it was cold now, but by midday the sun would be strong enough to melt the snow and transform the road into a muddy quagmire.

The detachment had been traveling at a gallop or a trot since first thing in the morning. Several times we had stopped or made the horses walk, in order to give them at least some kind of rest. On our right the Iselina glinted with bright patches of light as the sun climbed higher into the sky.

According to Kli-Kli, we were in Margend County. The gobliness's assumption was soon confirmed when we came across burned houses. The war had certainly reached this village—unlike the one where we had spent the night.

We watched the slaughter of the orcs at the Margend Horseshoe—to our great surprise the army of humans and elves was commanded by none other than my old friend Oro Gabsbarg, who was now a duke—and a week after the battle, we were in Ranneng. Duke Gabsbarg had given us forty mounted men before his army started crossing the Iselina. The precaution proved to be unnecessary—on the way to the southern capital we didn't encounter the slightest sign of danger. At almost every crossroads and in every village that hadn't suffered from the war we saw soldiers wearing white and crimson tunics over their armor, and warm jackets. The Heartless Chasseurs were standing vigilant guard over public order.

Several times we came across bodies hanging beside the roadside. The Heartless Chasseurs *were* heartless—they hanged looters, deserters, rapists, speculators, and other villains without benefit of trial or investigation. It was a bit cruel, perhaps, but highly effective.

While we were on our way to Ranneng, the real winter set in, even though it was only the middle of November. A lot of snow fell, and the weather was so cold I could happily have worn a second pair of gloves. Sitting on a horse in weather like that wasn't very enjoyable—after a few hours you couldn't feel your own hands and feet anymore. Following Lamplighter's example, I wrapped a scarf round my face, and that at least gave me some protection from the cold wind. I promised myself that if I ever went traveling again, it would only be in summer. I'd rather feel the sun baking my head and neck than the frost burning my hands and feet.

Gabsbarg's horsemen escorted us as far as Ranneng and went rushing back without halting, in order to rejoin the Second Army of the South. There are crazy people like that in Siala—they just couldn't wait to go dashing into battle of their own free will.

To be quite honest, after our adventures in the summer, I didn't really feel any great affection for Ranneng. And what I saw now only confirmed my belief that the southern pearl of Valiostr had nothing to offer us.

The city was choking on an influx of refugees driven out of their habitual haunts. For some reason, everyone had decided that the city walls offered reliable protection against the orcs and it would be easier to survive here than in some remote little village. More people had come pouring in than you could squeeze into the most terrible nightmare. Naturally, the municipal guard had stopped allowing all comers in through the gates, and tents large and small, dugouts, and anything else that could pass for a home had appeared under the city walls with catastrophic speed. There were fires everywhere, and the fuel was not just timber from the local forest, which was looking significantly sparser, but anything at all that came to hand. There was filth all around, and I started worrying that despite the cold weather some particularly repulsive plague was likely to break out in Ranneng in the near future. And the Copper Plague was all we needed to make our happiness complete.

"What now, Egrassa?" Kli-Kli inquired in a skeptical voice. "Surely you aren't desperate to stay in a rubbish heap like this?"

"No, let's try to get inside the city walls."

"They won't let us in, I wager my beard on it! We won't get anywhere! The place is so crowded, it's not even worth trying. Maybe we could find an inn outside the city walls? There used to be a lot of them."

"I'm not sure they'll have any free places, Hallas. But let's try anyway."

The horses squeezed through the filthy crowd thronging the road. There was a stench of smoke from all the fires and of rotting refuse. Someone was cooking supper beside the nearest dugout. I couldn't see properly, but I thought they were roasting a rat.

As Egrassa had suspected, all the places in the inns were taken. But at the sixth one we were offered a night's lodging in the stable for only three gold pieces. Hallas almost swallowed his own beard, but Egrassa paid without thinking twice. This was no time for economy. We had to lay out the same sum for a sparse and miserable supper.

I dreamed there was a sword slowly coming down on my head. I tried to break out of this vague, hazy dream and run away, but I couldn't, and death was getting closer and closer all the time. Then the sword blade fell and I woke up. It turned out to be Eel, shaking me frantically by the shoulder. It looked like the middle of the night to me, but the others were all wide awake. Lamplighter and Egrassa were hastily saddling the horses by the meager light of the oil lamp. Kli-Kli and Hallas were packing up our things.

"Harold, get up!" said Eel, shaking me again.

"What's happened?" I asked, confused. "What's all the hurry about?"

The Garrakian's cheek twitched.

"The Lonely Giant has fallen!"

19

THE FIELD OF FAIRIES

It seemed like absolute insanity. A continuation of my nightmare that had suddenly become reality.

Even two days after we had galloped out of Ranneng and set off along the New Highway to Avendoom, my comrades and I still couldn't believe that the Lonely Giant, the most famous and impregnable fortress in all the Northern Lands, had fallen. Destroyed. Annihilated. Wiped off the face of the earth by the army of the Nameless One.

Everybody had thought that until the Horn lost its final ounce of power, the Nameless One wouldn't dare to stick his nose out from behind the Needles of Ice. They were hoping that we didn't have to give the sorcerer a serious thought until the middle of spring. Who would risk forcing his way through the Desolate Lands in winter? It was absolute insanity!

The Nameless One had taken the risk and he had struck a terrible blow. The Order had failed to foresee his attack—everyone had been too preoccupied with the orcs in the south of the country—and the sorcerer's army had reached the fortress with no difficulty. The Wild Hearts had not been expecting an attack, but they had held the enemy under the walls of the citadel for four whole days and fought to the death. Rumors had spread round the country, each one worse than the last. Some said that all the Wild Hearts had been killed. Some, that certain units had managed to escape from the fortress and retreat. Some insisted that the walls of the bastion had been destroyed by Kronk-a-Mor, others that there had been supporters of the Nameless One among the Wild Hearts, and they had opened the gates for him.

We rode full tilt for Avendoom without sparing the horses. Everything could still be put right, all we had to do was to reach Avendoom and the Council of the Order, and then they would fill the Rainbow Horn with power. Without his magic, the Nameless One was not dangerous, and we would cope with his army one way or another. We had to cope.

The sorcerer had chosen the time of his attack very cunningly. At this very moment, when our armies had been pulled back beyond the Iselina, the north was especially vulnerable. If the king decided on a general engagement . . . Would he have time to gather the number of soldiers required?

Naturally, not all the soldiers had gone south. Some must have stayed on the northern borders. At least some . . .

The New Highway was crowded with people. Following the news of the invasion by the orcs, everyone had fled north, but now the refugees were fleeing by the hundreds to the south or west. On foot, on horses, on carts, on wagons, on sleighs, and even in carriages, all the people were dreaming of only one thing—how to get as far away as possible from the war. Every face was frozen in a grimace of fright, like a death mask.

Egrassa spurred his horse on mercilessly and rode pell-mell through the crowd, disregarding the shouts and the curses. We tried to keep up with him. It was a genuine race, and the prize was victory. It was a crazy gallop that tested the stamina of riders and horses. Who would be the first to give way? Who would beg for mercy?

The first horse fell on the second day. It was Eel's mount. The Garrakian managed to leap off the falling animal in time to avoid injury, and he continued on Kli-Kli's horse, seating the gobliness behind him. But this kind of pace could not be maintained for long, and by evening our steeds could barely stand. Just a little farther, and we would have to cover the rest of the distance to Avendoom on foot.

Egrassa halted the group on the edge of a large and wealthy village.

"We'll stay here for the night. I hope there will be free places at the inn."

"I'll gladly sleep out in the street, as long as we can find fresh horses," Eel declared.

Without saying another word, we walked toward the single-story timber building. It had the badge of the guild of innkeepers, and a sheet of tinplate with the name of the inn painted on it—Y.

"An original name, there's no denying that!" Kli-Kli snorted contemptu-ously. "If the innkeeper's as good as the name, I'm afraid for my stomach."

"You can sleep in a snowdrift, and we'll wake you in the morning," I told her.

"You're such a kind lad, Harold. It just melts my heart," the gobliness retorted, giving as good as she got.

The establishment turned out to be quite decent. At least it was clean. And most important of all, there weren't too many people. I counted eleven, including the fat innkeeper. As soon as he saw us, the landlord started look-ing nervous. Now why would that be? We didn't really look like bandits, did we? The other people in the room took no notice of us at all and just sipped their beer.

"Do you have any rooms?" asked Lamplighter, taking the bull by the horns.

The innkeeper was about to lie, but he glanced at the morose-looking elf and changed his mind.

"Yes, noble gentlemen."

"Good, then we'll stay."

The owner gave us an imploring glance and started sweating for no obvi-ous reason, but he didn't say anything and led us off to show us the rooms. As usual, I shared one with Lamplighter and Kli-Kli. After we'd settled in, we were the first back to the large room.

Nothing in the inn had changed. The ten tipplers were still sitting in the same places. We took seats at the bar and while we were waiting for Hallas, Eel, and Egrassa to join us and supper to be ready, we ordered beer.

Naturally, Kli-Kli wanted milk and, surprisingly enough, she was given it straightaway. The innkeeper kept sweating copiously. That was strange. Of course, the place was heated, and right royally, too, but it wasn't that hot! When this strange man poured the beer for me and Mumr, he missed the mugs, his hands were shaking so badly.

"Can we buy horses in the village?" Mumr asked the owner casually.

"Perhaps you can, sir. To be quite honest, I don't know about that."

"How's that, you don't know? You live here!"

"I've really never taken any interest in horses. I can tell you who sells what kind of victuals. Sausage, for instance . . ."

"What would we want with your sausage?" Lamplighter retorted. "Are you selling your own horses?"

"I don't have any horses."

"Don't lie to me. When I went into the stables, I saw ten beasts with my own eyes! Or are they not yours?"

"They're not mine, sir. They belong to guests."

"I see," the warrior muttered disappointedly, and stuck his nose in his beer mug.

"Is there any news from the north?" Now it was my turn to start asking the questions.

"People are fleeing," the landlord sighed, and cast a nervous glance behind me.

"And what about the king?"

"He's gathering an army. There'll be a battle any day now. That's what they say."

"And what about the Order?"

"The magicians? They're waiting for something. The people blame them for the Nameless One coming."

And so saying, he walked away, leaving us to ourselves.

"A strange situation, don't you think, Harold?" Kli-Kli said thoughtfully, speaking through her teeth. "Our landlord is as nervous as if someone was holding a knife to his throat."

"Maybe he just doesn't like the look of your face."

"Maybe," the little gobliness said with a serious nod. "Or maybe it's something else."

"What, for instance?"

"Haven't you noticed something odd? There are ten horses in the stable. There are ten men in this room. They're sitting in twos at five tables. And sitting so that they cover the way out of the inn."

A little bell started sounding the alarm in my head.

"Coincidence," I said, but I realized I didn't like this, either.

"Uh-huh," she said, inconspicuously lowering one hand onto the handle of a throwing knife. "Precisely, coincidence. Mumr, are you listening?"

"Oh, yes!" said Lamplighter. He had his eyes screwed up and was gazing into a metal dish leaning against the wall. It was polished like a mirror and reflected the entire room very clearly.

"Well then, another strange thing is that, although they're sitting in twos, they're not saying a word. It's as silent as the grave."

"We get the idea, Kli-Kli. Why don't you sing us a little song, and sing loud," I suggested.

Kli-Kli helpfully started crooning a simple melody.

"What are we going to do?"

"Drink our beer and wait for the others to come," Lamplighter answered.

"It looks like that's what *they're* waiting for, too."

"I know. They've decided to take us all at once. Is your crossbow loaded?"

"As always. Who are *they*?"

"What does it matter who slits your throat?" asked Mumr, keeping his eyes fixed on the "mirror."

Kli-Kli sang and wove her fingers into a pattern that I couldn't make out.

"Don't even think about it!" I hissed.

She didn't seem to hear me. Loud footsteps in the corridor leading to the barroom told us and the unusual strangers that at least two guests were approaching. I recognized Hallas's shuffling step. The innkeeper ducked smartly down under the bar. And that was the signal for action.

Kli-Kli casually snapped her fingers and a bright flash lit up the room behind us for a split second. I heard howls of pain and fury. Two of the scum put their hands over their eyes and another one just howled and rolled around on the floor. The others had been shocked by the unexpected shamanic spell, but they came rushing at us just the same. They were each holding something very sharp and deadly.

Without wasting any time, Kli-Kli flung her first two knives. I fired the crossbow and started reloading it while the gobliness sent another two knives flying through the air. Mumr blocked the attackers' advance, waving his bidenhander from side to side. Afraid of being sliced to shreds, the lads halted their frontal assault, and at this point Hallas and Eel walked into the room.

The two Wild Hearts didn't bother inquiring what the dustup was all about. Seeing us pinned back against the bar by five unpleasant types who were armed to the teeth was enough to spur them into action. They piled into the brawl. Mumr was no slouch, either. Tables and benches were sent flying. I was wary of firing the crossbow, in case I hit my own side. But Kli-Kli flung my beer mug and hit one of the attackers full square on the head.

Hallas pitilessly finished the man off when he fell, and the last bandit left alive, realizing that things were looking bad, made a dash for the door. I fired, but, as bad luck would have it, I missed. The lad jumped out into the street and Eel chased after him. There was a howl, and a moment later Egrassa walked in, looking sullen and holding a bloody dagger.

"Just don't tell me that was the last one, and you didn't leave anyone alive."

"He was the last one, Egrassa. Did you climb out through the window?"

The elf didn't answer Kli-Kli's question, he just cursed.

"It was all a bit unexpected. We never even thought of taking one for questioning."

"It's my own fault. I shouldn't have finished off the one who was trying to get away. Well, what are we going to do now?"

"What did these goons want?" said Hallas, giving the bodies on the floor a fierce look. "Look what a mess we've made of the place!"

"Where's the innkeeper?" I asked, suddenly realizing I couldn't see him.

"I'm here, noble gentlemen," a frightened voice jabbered from under the bar.

Mumr reached in and hoisted the trembling owner out into the open.

"Now, you tell us what it was your friends wanted!"

"They're not my friends! Oh, no!" the terrified man bleated. If Lamp-lighter didn't stop making those terrible faces this gent was going to throw a faint.

"Not your friends? Then who are they?"

Lamenting and wringing his hands, the innkeeper told us. The lads had arrived at the inn the evening before, frightened him to death, put a knife to his throat, and advised him to be as meek as a lamb and act just as if nothing had happened. The guests of the inn, not being stupid, had all sensed the danger and cleared out, without bothering to pay. There were no guards or Chasseurs anywhere near, so all he could do was pray to the gods and hope that everything would be all right. He'd never seen these lads before, but they definitely weren't bandits. You could see right away that they were serious people.

"Serious!" Mumr snorted, releasing his grip on his prisoner. "Maybe they were serious, but they were real fools, too, letting themselves get killed that easily."

"Maybe they weren't looking for us?" I suggested.

"No, it was us they were after," said Eel, who had been going through the dead men's pockets. "It's just as I suspected."

Lying on the Garrakian's open palm was a slim golden ring with a poison ivy crest.

"Servants of the Nameless One."

I'd forgotten all about them, but they couldn't have forgotten about us.

"Servants of the Nameless One!" the innkeeper repeated in horror, instantly turning pale. "No, good gentlemen! I don't know these murderers!

What a disaster! If the local folk find out who I have lying in here, they'll set the inn on fire. The red cock will crow here, as sure as death!"

"Stop whining!" said the gnome, interrupting the poor man's lamentations. "If you want your inn to stand for another hundred years, get rid of the bodies. And tidy the place up! And then tomorrow we can forget we ever saw you and not say anything to the Heartless or the Sandmen."

Singing the praises of all the gods and all good gentlemen, the innkeeper dashed off at speed to carry out these instructions.

"How did they find us, that's what I'd like to know."

"What difference does that make? They found us, and that's what matters, Harold. The Nameless One is still hoping to get his hands on your tin whistle."

"It's not mine. What do we do now?"

"What do we do? What do we do? I don't know about you, but I'm going to bed," Hallas sighed, getting down off the bench. "It's late."

"What about supper?" Kli-Kli asked in amazement.

"Somehow I've lost my appetite."

"There's one good thing," Egrassa said with a chuckle. "We won't have to look for horses. Or pay for them."

This time I knew I was asleep; even though it seemed so real, I could stop this nightmare—all I had to do was open my eyes and it would be gone. I could, but I didn't want to wake up. Valder kept whispering quietly in my head, telling me that this dream was very important. I tried to protest, I struggled to resist his voice, but the archmagician could be very convincing.

I gave in. All I could do was just watch and listen, constantly telling myself that everything that could happen to me had happened already, even if it was a long time ago. That it wasn't happening to me . . . Not to me . . . It was just a dream. . . .

It promised to be a clear day, even though snow had fallen again yesterday and the entire sky had clouded over. Even the frost that had held the whole of the north in its cold embrace for the last week had retreated, and the soldiers had stopped worrying that their weapons would freeze to their hands.

Stalkon's army had been waiting since early morning for the Nameless

One's army to appear. Mounted scouts had reported that the enemies' advance units were no more than two hours away. They had also said that the Nameless One would confront Valiostr's army of less than twenty-eight thousand with a force of at least sixty thousand. Lieutenant of the Royal Guard Izmi Markauz took a deep breath of the fresh morning air. They were in for a tough time today. In the absence of the two Armies of the North, the king and his commanding officers had already worked a miracle by assembling eighteen thousand regulars, three thousand mercenaries, and seven thousand members of the militia. The king was also waiting for another fifteen thousand men who were on the march to Avendoom from the border with Isilia, but any fool could see that they would only get there after the battle had already been won or lost.

"What do you think, lieutenant? Will things get hot?"

"They will, Vartek."

"It's a bad spot, though."

"Nothing better could be found. Can't greet our visitors at Avendoom, can we? The walls won't save us, and the lay of the land is on our side here. How are the lads?"

"They're betting on who'll be the first to kill one of the enemy."

"But they know the royal guard won't go into action unless things get really bad. Our task is to protect the king."

"And what are the Beaver Caps for?" Vartek grumbled. "I've heard they're putting all of us in the left reserve."

"That's what I've heard, too," Izmi said with a shrug. "But we'll get a chance to swing our axes. Or are you impatient?"

"You should put your armor on, milord," the marquis said instead of answering.

"There'll be time enough for that."

"The light cavalry is already involved in skirmishes with the advance forces, just beyond that wood. Perhaps there won't be any time."

"Milord!" cried a soldier, running up to them with a piece of paper in his hand. "From the commander of the center!"

Izmi ran his eyes over the lines of writing and nodded to tell the messenger that he was free to go.

"Vartek, get over to our men. Leave a hundred, no, better a hundred and fifty guards with the king, and take all the rest over onto the left slope."

"So we are being stuck in the reserve!" Vartek said, frowning discontentedly.

"Just do it, guardsman!" Izmi's voice suddenly had a hard edge.

"Yes, lieutenant!" Vartek picked his snow-dusted helmet up off the ground and ran to carry out his orders.

Before he went to the king for his final instructions, Izmi looked round the field one last time. For some stupid reason someone had called this huge open space, almost a league in length, the Field of Fairies. The lieutenant didn't know how they had come up with this name, and he didn't want to know. So it was the Field of Fairies. Would it have been any easier to fight here if it was called the Field of Ladybugs, for instance? Or the Field of the Great Prophecy?

Of course it wouldn't.

So what difference did it make now? The military council hadn't chosen this place for the general engagement by accident. It was four days' journey from Avendoom, and the Nameless One's army had to pass through it. At the southern end of the field stood the Pimple, a tall hill with shallow slopes. The king's headquarters were on its summit. The gnomes had set up two of their long-range cannons up there, and another monstrosity that hadn't been seen before—a Crater. Unfortunately there hadn't been enough time to bring a second Crater and its crew of gnomes from Isilia.

The huge hill was the basis of the entire defense, and the core of Stalkon's army was there. Two thousand infantry of the line, five thousand cavalry, and six thousand Wind Jugglers. A powerful force, especially taking into account that the enemy would have to climb the hill under fire from the bowmen on the summit, and a cavalry charge downhill had a more shattering impact.

Izmi wasn't too concerned about the center. Six thousand bowmen could stop anybody. And there were a thousand light cavalry on each flank of the center. He and his men were on the left, and on the right there were the Moon Stallions, brave lads. If anything went wrong, the archers would help out, and they could always be moved across to the army on the right.

The transports and the healers were behind the hill.

Half a league away, directly opposite the Pimple, was the dark Rega Forest. Two roads came down from the north, skirting round the forest on the left and the right. They ran parallel to each other for the full length of the field.

The left road cut across the Wine Brook and ran between the Pimple and another forest—the Luza. The right road ran between the hill and a narrow but deep and swift-flowing little river—the Kizevka. Standing on the road right between the hill and the river was a village—Slim Bows.

The village had provided the base for the army on the right. It had been a good decision to position soldiers in Slim Bows. If the enemy came along the road on the right, he would have to pass through the village, unless he wanted to storm the hill under fire from the bowmen, or sail along the river. And there was no need to worry about the flanks of the right army—they were securely defended.

In one week the army had transformed Slim Bows into a small fortress. They dug out a moat and ran water into it from the river, built an earthen rampart and stuck enough stakes in it to make every hedgehog in Siala jealous, dismantled all the houses and used the materials to build walls and towers for bowmen.

They built two walls, and if the enemy happened to take the first one, the defenders would have time to pull back behind the second. Now there were two thousand crossbowmen and three thousand swordsmen, selected from various detachments, ensconced in Slim Bows. The gnomes had put three cannons on the first wall. About nine hundred yards behind Slim Bows stood the dark wall of the two-thousand-man reserve.

Izmi was far more concerned about the left army. Nine thousand infantry, of which four thousand were militia and guardsmen from Avendoom, standing in the road between the Pimple and the Luza Forest. The soldiers had been divided up into battalions so as to completely cover the space between the hill and the forest. The battalions were stationed about fifty yards beyond the Wine Brook.

Although it wasn't very wide—only about a yard—the brook was deep, and it was not going to freeze. There had been a bridge here, but the eager soldiers had dismantled it, and now the enemy cavalry would have its work cut out to cross the brook. In any case, they wouldn't have enough space to get up a gallop. And the enemy infantry would have to break formation crossing the obstacle and then, before they could raise their shields again, they would be treated to thousands of welcoming crossbow bolts.

The three hundred elfin bowmen had been positioned between the battalion on the left (based on Jolly Gallows-Birds taken from twelve ships) and the Luza Forest. The dark elves themselves had insisted on being placed there. Izmi hoped that their bows would help the left army to stand firm.

But Stalkon's left army was the most vulnerable spot in the forthcoming defensive action, so two thousand of the reserve had been placed here.

Izmi looked into the distance, to where he could just make out the wall of the Rega Forest. On the bank of the Kizevka, right beside the road snaking out of the forest, stood the Castle of Nuad. Its twelve-yard-high walls and four round towers rose up menacingly above the road. The castle's garrison of four hundred men had been reinforced with five hundred Wind Jugglers. The enemy would either have to take the citadel by storm and delay his attack on the right army, or cover this section of the route under constant bombardment from the defenders of Nuad. There was another unpleasant surprise waiting for the Nameless One in the form of two gnomish cannons. And if the enemy did get by, he would be hit from the rear by three hundred horsemen lying concealed within the walls of the castle. No great force, but even so it was capable of causing plenty of trouble.

Izmi's arms bearer appeared in front of him.

"Milord?"

"Prepare my armor."

The young lad nodded his hatless head, and Izmi set off for the king's tent. Stalkon's headquarters were surrounded by a formidable ring of Royal Guards and Beaver Caps. Several other warriors, holding flambergs—terrible two-handed swords with wavy blades—were guarding the royal standard.

The king was in the tent with his younger son, Stalkon of the Spring Jasmine, who was in command of the cavalry in the center, and the head of the Order of Magicians, Artsivus. There were also two magicians unfamiliar to Izmi—a man and a woman. Both of their staffs were marked with three rings. So they were powerful, even if they weren't archmagicians.

The king noticed the lieutenant, nodded in greeting, and gestured for him to wait until the conversation was over.

"It is a real solution to the problem, Your Majesty," Artsivus continued, huddling under his warm rug.

"And what if the wind blows in our direction? Blows it onto us? We'll lose the army before the battle has even started!" the king's son blurted out abruptly.

"I assure you," the unfamiliar magician droned, "this spell will not affect people and—"

"Please remind me, Mister Balshin," the king interrupted. "Are we talking about the same spell that wiped out the entire population of a village to the south of here only this summer? What was the place called, now?"

"Vishki, Your Majesty," the woman replied reluctantly.

"Thank you, Madam Klena. You are most kind. It was Vishki. The very same village where you almost captured the people who were carrying out a special Commission for me?"

"That was a regrettable misunderstanding," said the head of the Order, interceding for the two magicians. "The thief and the elves were not in any danger."

"I can well believe that," the king agreed, although there was not a trace of belief in his voice. "Of course they were in no danger, except from your experiments, which cost me an entire village. When I gave my permission for this insane experiment in spring, Your Magicship, I had no idea that there would be civilian casualties!"

"Believe me, Your Majesty, neither did we," said Klena. "The ogre's books that we used contained an error. It has now been corrected, and the tragedy at Vishki will not be repeated."

"You must give permission, Your Majesty," said the old magician, still trying to persuade the king.

"No, Artsivus. Don't you understand what a great risk it is?"

"I understand," said the magician, lowering his head like a bird. "But you know I understand these matters . . . I guarantee that the spell will work properly."

The king drummed his fingers on the table without speaking.

"The scouts report that the Nameless One has fifteen thousand ogres. Fifteen thousand! They'll simply brush aside our left flank without even stopping. After the Nameless One himself, that is the greatest danger that threatens Valiostr. It will take at least eight of our soldiers to kill one ogre. We simply don't have the numbers. We *can*"—Artsivus laid special emphasis on the last word—"we can save the kingdom if we eliminate the ogres. That is the very reason why I have spent so long studying the ancient books of that race, that is why Madam Klena and Mister Balshin have been experimenting for so long with this spell and finally been successful, through the method of trial and error."

"It was a fine error!" the prince observed. "Hundreds of people killed in a couple of seconds, and you call it an error!"

"You only have to give the order, and two minutes later there won't be a single ogre left in Valiostr. That will greatly weaken the Nameless One's army, Your Majesty," the Master of the Order continued, ignoring Stalkon Junior. "I assure you, only ogres will be killed."

"All right!" the king finally decided. "Do it, and may Sagra be with you!"

Artsivus nodded, and Balshin and Klena bowed hastily and left the tent.

"I am relying on your experience, Your Magicship. When should I expect results?"

"In two or three minutes."

"So soon?" the king asked in surprise. "But didn't you tell me that the balance between the sorcerer's powers and the powers of the Order made such potent spells impossible?"

"This is the very simplest of all the spells that I know, Your Majesty. It was difficult to assemble, but now a first-level student could manage it. And as for the balance, for better or for worse, that is true. While there is still power in the Rainbow Horn, the Council of the Order can absorb the power of the Nameless One. His free shamans are a different matter. We won't be able to spare any time for them."

"So my soldiers are going to be roasted by shamans?"

"The Order has five free battle magicians. Those who will not be required for our circle. If Your Majesty will permit it, I shall send them to the army."

"Of course."

Artsivus grunted and got up out of his chair, leaning on his staff. He called his apprentice, Roderick, and left the tent.

"I hope you know what you are doing, Father."

"I do, Artsivus has never let me down. How are your men?"

"The cavalry are spoiling for a fight."

"Order them to dismount. Send the horses to the transports."

"But . . ."

"Listen to what I'm saying. Everyone is to dismount. Cavalry in the center won't do us any good at all. When the gnomes' cannons start roaring, the horses will go hysterical and at the very least break formation. In the worst case they will wreck the entire line of defense. Better to have five thousand dismounted cavalrymen to reinforce our infantry lines and halt anyone who tries to break through to the Wind Jugglers than to trample our own comrades-in-arms. Dismount. I know what I'm talking about."

"But what if the heavy cavalry of the Crayfish Dukedom advance against us?"

"Then you will order the bowmen to fire at the horses. Not very chivalrous, but effective."

"Very well, Father, I will do that."

"Izmi, my boy, move all your men away from my tent. I'll manage well enough with the Beavers."

"The duty of the Royal Guard is to protect its king."

"In times of peace. In times of war that is what the Beaver Caps do. Remove all your men. We'll be needing every one of them soon. . . ."

"How I regret that my father is not here," Izmi exclaimed bitterly. "He would have been able to convince Your Majesty."

"I also regret that Alistan is so far away."

"My king!" exclaimed an adjutant, rushing into the tent. "Baron Togg's mounted archers have clashed with the Nameless One's advance units and, following a brief engagement, withdrawn from the Rega Forest into the cover of Nuad!"

"It's started. Send the army commanders to me!"

"Fasten it tighter! Tighter, do you hear me! Damn you, are you stroking a girl or securing a cheval de frise? It's a cheval de frise, isn't it? Then why in the name of darkness have you got it gazing up at the sky? To frighten away the sparrows? Angle it, you thickhead! That's right. And now fix it so that no bastard on a horse can come anywhere near us! Don't even think of relying on the brook, that won't save you from the cavalry, but a good horse trap and a handy pike will get our backsides out of this cesspit. Why did Sagra have to send me such witless monkeys to command?"

Jig listened as one of the unit officers in his battalion gave some men from the militia a roasting. At least it was some amusement before the battle. The guardsman held his halberd against his body with his left hand, took a clove of garlic out of his pocket, cleaned it, popped it in his mouth, and started chewing with relish.

"Are you eating that garbage again?" asked Jig's partner, Bedbug, making a sour face.

"You don't like it?"

"Who could like it, when you stink like the Garlic Stalls on Market Square? That stench of yours will drive me crazy—and the Nameless One, too."

"That would be good."

"You spend half the day eating garlic!"

"If you don't like it, you can leave. Milord Lanten needs every guardsman he can get in Avendoom right now. If we can't hold out, the baron will be responsible for all the defenses. It's not too late to go back."

"Don't talk nonsense!" Bedbug snapped irritably. "I didn't spend four days trudging all the way here just to push off back home at the last moment."

"Then stop bellyaching."

"I'm not bellyaching. I'm just beginning to get angry. We've been hang-ing around here like idiots for an hour and a half now, and no one's arrived. My feet are frozen."

"Do you know if they're going to feed us?" one of the soldiers in the first line asked.

"You'd better ask our battalion officer that," someone farther back, prob-ably a crossbowman, advised him.

"I'll feed you this, if you don't shut your mouths!" barked a unit officer who was walking along the first line, showing them his fist. "You're like little kids! Too impatient to wait!"

"You try standing here with a halberd or a battleax, like us, and we'll see how you like it! We're telling you, the frost is burning our feet!"

"Better your feet than your backsides. They'll burn for a bit and then stop! And if you're so smart, why don't you clear off home to mummy, and stop stirring up my men! The militia have gone green already and their stomachs are churning! And then you start frightening them!"

"Who's gone green?" said another voice from the rear ranks. "We haven't gone green, we've gone blue! From cold!"

Loud guffaws ran along the ranks of the central battalion of the left army.

Jig laughed, too. Maybe these militiamen would turn out all right after all. A lot of them wouldn't be needed in this battle anyway—provided the enemy didn't break the formation, of course. It was a strong battalion, as long as it remained a single united whole.

Jig's and Bedbug's luck had placed them in the third rank from the front of the central battalion. The first two ranks consisted of pikemen—the lads had been covered in metal all the way up to the tops of their heads and given pikes the size of wagon shafts: You could have skewered a mammoth on them. At the moment the pikes were pointing up at the sky, like tree trunks, but they would be put to use just as soon as the battle began. And the reason for the pikemen's heavy armor was simple—the lads needed two hands to hold the pikes, and shields were out of the question. So, since the main blow was taken by front two ranks, they had to wear all that metal.

The men in the third rank were armed with halberds. They had one very simple job to do—strike at the heads of anyone who somehow managed to get close to the front rank. Immediately behind Jig's rank there were three ranks of men with crossbows. Their role was even simpler—to fire and then withdraw as quickly as possible to the empty center of the battalion, making way for the fourth and fifth ranks, consisting of pikemen armed with seven-yard pikes.

These lads were known as "anglers." At present all the men behind the crossbows were maintaining their distance, so that the crossbowmen would have space to withdraw in after their volley.

Immediately behind the "anglers" there were several ranks consisting of a jumbled assortment of men whose main job was to press up against the front ranks if a formation of infantry of the line clashed with the battalion. And, of course, if the ranks were broken, then they would fill the breach for a while, if only with their own bodies. This was a task that could be managed even by soldiers who weren't trained to work in battalion formation and men from the militia.

Right at the center were the commander, the standard-bearer, a number of Beaver Caps, the trumpeters, and the drummers, who gave the signal to maneuver. So the battalion was actually quite a formidable force, and it was well protected against attacks on its flanks.

"Bedbug, what are you gaping at?"

"Look over there, at our neighbors," the guardsman chuckled. "Those lads have had a real stroke of luck. As safe and cozy as in Sagra's pocket. Didn't I tell you we should have gone across to them?"

There was another battalion standing to the left of Jig's, the one that was closest of all to the Luza Forest.

"Why do you think they look so cozy?" asked Jig in surprise, breathing garlic all over Bedbug.

"Because they've got so many Beaver Caps and Jolly Gallows-Birds. And three hundred elves with bows, too!"

"Well, as far as the Gallows-Birds are concerned, they're not right in the head. And the Beavers have been put in the third line, so that battalion hasn't got any halberdiers. And those lads with the fangs . . . Sagra alone can understand the elves. Into the darkness with them, I say. They're all smiles, and then suddenly they stick a knife under your ribs."

"I'd rather have their knife under my ribs then be dispatched in the darkness by the Nameless One's magic. And what's more, they have bows, and I've heard dark elves are even better with them than the Wind Jugglers."

"You don't have anything to worry about, lad," the nearest pikeman put in. "We're only three hundred paces from the yellow-eyes, so if need be they can reach our enemies with their arrows."

"I'll stop worrying when this is all over," said Bedbug, refusing to be cheered up.

"Make way! Make way, will you!"

All eyes turned toward the battalion commander. He had another man with him. Obviously not a soldier.

"This way, good sir. Stand just behind them."

A young man in a cuirass and a light helmet, armed with a short sword, stood right behind Jig.

"Hey, commander!" one of the anglers shouted. "What's all this about? Can't you see you're breaking up the formation? What do we want a swordsman here for? Is he going to jump over our heads?"

"Why don't you shut up, you ignorant oaf! He isn't a swordsman! He's a gentleman magician! I can stand him at the other side of the battalion if you like."

"No, if he's a magician . . . no . . . I'm sorry, good sir."

"Take good care of His Magicship, lads. He'll save your little souls for you if the Nameless One's shamans get uppity."

"We will!" the ranks roared all together.

A look of relief appeared on the faces of many soldiers. Nobody had said anything, but they had all been wondering what would happen if the battalion was attacked with magic. Soldiers could fight soldiers, but what could you do with shamans? Sagra had heard their prayer and sent them magicians.

"Now we'll give them a fight!" Bedbug exclaimed, tightening his grip on the halberd.

His mood was clearly beginning to improve.

"Hey, neighbors! Neigh-bors! How are you doing? Not frozen yet?" shouted one of the men standing to the right of their battalion.

"Why, do you want to come across and warm me up?" a mischievous voice replied. It sounded like one of the militiamen this time, too.

A roar of laughter ran through the ranks again.

"Down, you peasant! But if you do feel cold we can invite you to come visiting!" the answer came back.

"If it gets too hot here, that's when we'll come over! We're not cheap! Always willing to share the heat and the enemy!" Jig barked out, surprising even himself.

The ranks backed him up with a united roar.

"Listen, you," said Bedbug, nudging Jig awkwardly in the side. "Here, this might come in handy."

"What is it?" asked Jig, looking at what Bedbug was holding out to him—a bundle of pond weed or dried grass, tied round with a blue ribbon that had faded with age.

"Well . . . ," Bedbug said, and hesitated. "You remember in the guard hut I told you my granny was a witch?"

"So?"

"Well, she made this. It's an amulet. She said it wards off bad spells for anyone who carries it."

"So?"

"What do you keep saying that for?" Bedbug asked angrily. "Are you going to take it or not?"

"What about you?"

"I've got one just the same."

Jig shrugged, took the bundle of grass, and stuck it behind his belt. He didn't believe in Bedbug's fairy tales, but Sagra took care of those who took care of themselves. This piece of trash couldn't do any harm, and Bedbug would feel better.

"Hey! You up on the horse! How are things down there? Is there going to be a fight, or can we all go home now?" one of the pikemen asked a messenger who had jumped the Wine Brook and steered his horse between the two battalions toward the hill.

The rider reined back his mount.

"Not much longer to wait!" The messenger had to shout loudly, so that the rear ranks could hear him. "The mounted patrols have already left the Rega Forest, the scouts have gone into action on the right-hand road, right beside Nuad!"

"Who have they got, then?"

"Mostly men from the north! Tribes that live on the Shore of the Ogres! And the barbarians, of course!"

"No need to worry about them just yet," Bedbug growled. "A rabble."

"And who is there that's more our style?"

"Crayfish! Moving along the left road, half an hour away from you!"

"How many of them?"

"A lot! Eight thousand cavalry and about fifteen thousand infantry."

Some whistled, some swore, some appealed to Sagra.

"Did you see any shamans?" asked the magician standing behind Jig.

"What I didn't see, I didn't see, lads! Take care! Sagra willing, we'll meet again!"

"Good luck to you!"

"You take care!"

But the rider had already gone rushing off toward the hill and he didn't hear the soldiers' good wishes.

"Well, the wait's almost over, Jig. Not much longer."

"You look like you're trembling."

"That always happens to me. Nerves. It'll pass. Eight thousand cavalry!"

"We'll hold out. They won't get to us through that forest of pikes, don't be afraid. No, better to be afraid."

The priests of Sagra walked along the line of the battalion, offering the soldiers spiritual comfort before the battle. Like all the other soldiers, Jig murmured a prayer to the goddess of death.

The sound of two loud bangs came from somewhere to the north.

"Magic!" gasped one of the pikemen nearby.

"In the name of the Nameless One, what magic?" the unit officer reassured the anxious soldiers. "That's the sound of the half-pints' cannons at Nuada. The fun must have started there already!"

The soldiers craned their necks, trying to see what was happening on the far side of the Field of Fairies, but the long dark tongue of the Rega Forest prevented them from seeing the castle and anything going on close to it.

"Look!" someone shouted.

Jig shifted his gaze from the forest to the left road. The first forces of the army of the Nameless One had appeared on that side of the field.

"Does she have a name?" asked the gnome, lighting up his pipe.

"Actually, it's a he."

"All right, so what's his name?"

"Invincible."

"Well now, that certainly suits him," the cannoneer said with a nod, examining the shaggy ling, who was nestled securely on Honeycomb's shoulder. "My name's Odzan, but the lads all call me Pepper."

"Honeycomb."

"Yes, I know already. The commander told me. A Wild Heart, if I'm not mistaken?"

"Yes."

"I heard what happened to you up at the Lonely Giant. Was it really hot?"

"I wasn't there."

"Ah . . . I heard that fifty of your lads survived and managed to get away."

"Forty-seven."

"Ah . . . Are they in your unit?"

"No, they're in the center, as far as I know."

"Hmm," said the gnome, blowing out a smoke ring. "Then how come you ended up in the army on the right?"

"They said they needed a unit officer."

"So you and your lads are going to defend our beards?"

"It looks that way."

There it was again in the distance. *Boom! Boom!* The gnome stretched himself up to his full low height, took out a little spyglass that had obviously been made by a dwarf, and pointed it at the castle that stood directly in line with Slim Bows.

"They're having a hot time of it. Forty minutes they've been blasting away. And the enemy's in no hurry to come our way. Surely Lepzan's not going to do all the work for us? He used to be a real jackass, too. Couldn't even light a fuse properly. And now just look at him blaze away! I remember what happened one time in the Steel Mines . . ."

Honeycomb wasn't listening to the garrulous gnome. He leaned against the wall and closed his eyes. It had been a bit of a surprise to find himself at the Field of Fairies. It wasn't all that long since the magician at Cuckoo Castle told the Wild Heart he was well and completely cured of the aftereffects of the orcish shamanism. A month and a half at the most.

When he left the Border Kingdom, Honeycomb had made his way to Ranneng, and from there to the capital, where he had to deliver the letter left for him by Alistan Markauz. When his business had been dealt with and the Wild Heart was wondering what to do next—wait for the group to come back to Avendoom or go straight to the Lonely Giant—the Nameless One had invaded the kingdom.

Chance had brought him together with Izmi Markauz, who remembered the yellow-haired warrior from his fight with the ogre in the royal palace. The lieutenant of the Royal Guard immediately offered the Wild Heart the command of a unit of a hundred men. Honeycomb had tried to refuse at first, saying his place was with his comrades who had survived the fall of the Lonely Giant, but Milord Izmi could be quite persuasive.

So now Honeycomb found himself in command of sixty swashbuckling rogues, selected for Slim Bows from various different forces, and forty crossbowmen from Shet's detachment of northerners. The warrior had never commanded anything bigger than a platoon of ten men before, and at first he was a little frightened, but after a week with the unit he realized there was practically no difference between ten men and a hundred. Just give the orders and make sure the lads didn't do anything rash when there's no need.

And now his unit had been ordered to defend one of the three cannons located at Slim Bows.

"Will you look at that! I swear on my granddad's bugle, those lads have all the luck!"

The gnome's sudden exclamation roused Honeycomb from his reverie. The Wild Heart got to his feet, picked his ogre-hammer up off the ground, and looked to the left. There was a detachment of cavalry approaching the hill at full gallop. And another detachment the same size—a line of red and green—was heading toward the left army.

"Four thousand in a detachment!" declared Rott—the commander of the crossbowmen in Honeycomb's unit—screwing up his eyes. "It looks as if the Crayfish have put all their cavalry into the field. The left flank is in for a tough time all right."

"Rouse the lads," Honeycomb ordered as he watched the red and green wave rolling on. "If they falter going up the hill, they'll come our way."

Bang! The heavens trembled and Honeycomb ducked and pulled his head into his shoulders in surprise.

"That's the boom of the Crater on the hill," Pepper chuckled, raising his head to look up at the sky.

Honeycomb looked up, too, and he saw a column of smoke go soaring up toward the sun, hang for a moment at its highest point, as if it was wondering whether it ought to fall or not, and then come shrieking down toward the ground.

The gnomes on the hill had miscalculated—the cavalry had already ridden past the area where the ball landed—and the mighty explosion simply threw soil up into the air. The only positive outcome was that the horses in the rear line of the cavalry were terrified, and for a while there was complete chaos in the lines.

"What do you think you're firing at, you villains?" Pepper roared, shaking his fists, as if they could hear him. "Fire at the target, you lousy bunch of dwarves. You'll be reloading the thing for another half hour now! Crackhanded idiots! Who's in that team up there? Zhirgzan! Rotate our weapon. With the help of the gods, we'll hammer the cavalry in the left flank! When are we ever going to get a chance to fire?"

Izmi Markauz's horse was still nervous after the shot from the Crater, and he scratched its ear. The animals didn't like the strange noise, but there was nothing that could be done about that.

On the left flank of the center everything was still calm and the reserve had not been required. The greater part of the battle was still to come, and all the soldiers of the Royal Guard could do was watch as the Crayfish cavalry that had arrived along the left road divided into two equal sections and made for the infantry in the center and the battalions of the left army.

Bang!
  Bang!
Two explosions shook the air behind the prince's back and two cannonballs went flying over the infantry's heads and hurtled toward the advancing cavalry. The first whistled over the horsemen's heads and landed far down the field, without doing the enemy any harm. The second smashed straight into the galloping cavalrymen, knocking several men down, and exploding in the center of the attacking formation.

Even from there he could hear the screams of the men and the whinnying of the wounded and terrified horses. The Crayfish cavalry's attack formation was broken, creating a scene of total pandemonium. The riders could scarcely control their hysterical horses, and there was no way the attack could be continued.

"Well done, the gnomes!" shouted one of the bowmen standing behind the infantry.

The prince turned round. The bowmen standing only ten yards away from him had certainly not been wasting their time. Each of them had brought two sharp-pointed poles up onto the hill, and now they were surrounded by an entire forest. Before the enemy could get to the Wind Jugglers in their light armor, he would have to force his way through this barrier. Facing a barrage of arrows. And if he did manage to get through, the warriors would hang their bows on their shoulders and take up their swords.

Bang!

Stalkon thought he must be mistaken, but it really was a cannon shot. The left flank of the enemy cavalry was flung up into the air and pieces of broken human bodies and horses went flying in all directions.

"That was a shot from Slim Bows, milord," the prince's arms-bearer told him.

"So I see. The gnomes are spoiling for a fight, too."

Meanwhile something like order had been restored to the ranks of the cavalry and, to the sound of jeering from the soldiers on the hill, the Crayfish retreated to the rear of the Field of Fairies. The prince reckoned it would take the enemy at least fifteen minutes to recover from what had happened. Exactly the amount of the time the gnomes needed to cool their weapons and reload them.

A horn sounded, and the unit commanders gave the order.

"Halberdiers into the fourth rank."

"Into the fourth rank! Change places with the pikemen!"

"Crossbowmen, at the ready! Pikemen in the fifth and six ranks, stay awake!"

"Crossbowmen, make ready!"

As if the action was taking place in a training exercise, not in a real war, Jig moved into the fourth rank without any fuss or bother, and stood sideways so that the crossbowmen could get past him easily. Bedbug repeated his partner's movements like a reflection in a mirror. The only hitch was the magician, who didn't know what he was supposed to do; a sergeant who happened to be close by shoved him into a gap.

"Crossbowmen into the fourth rank!" The order rang out in the battalions on both sides of them.

All the battalion commanders had chosen the standard arrangement for defending against cavalry. When horsemen attacked, the men with halberds could make the best use of their weapons from the fourth rank, striking slashing blows from above or thrusting above the shoulders of the pikemen standing in front of them. From there the halberdiers couldn't impede the first or second ranks, and the halberds didn't catch on the pikes. The fourth and fifth rows of "anglers" became the fifth and sixth rows.

A horn sounded again, and an order rang out in the battalions.

"Front ranks down on one knee! Pikes at the ready!"

Sticking the heels of their pikes into the frozen ground and angling their weapons so that if the cavalry tried to take the battalion head on it would have to break through a forest of pikes, the soldiers went down on one knee.

"Second ranks! Pikes at the ready!"

The second row lowered its pikes, holding them at the level of their hips, above the shoulders of the kneeling front rank.

"Third rank! Pikes at the ready!"

Another forest of pikes was added to the ones already lowered. The soldiers standing in front of the crossbowmen held their weapons at the level of their chests, in order not to hinder the second row in the fight.

The cavalry were close, a hundred and fifty yards from the Wine Brook. The horsemen had lowered their lances, preparing to rip the battalion open, to shatter it like a blow from a battering ram.

Jig watched a rider in the front line who seemed to be coming straight at him. The warrior, in a horned helmet with green plumage and a scarlet and green tunic that concealed his armor, lowered his long lance decorated with numerous ribbons and little flags.

Arrows sang in the air—the detachment of elves standing beside the Luza Forest had started bombarding the cavalrymen's right flank. The dark elves might handle their bows like gods, but here were only three hundred of them against several thousand, and they wouldn't stop the cavalry.

The uproar was indescribable. The earth shook under the pounding blows of thousands of hooves. A horn gave a low growl and the unit commanders yelled fit to burst.

"First line of crossbows! Fire!"

A sklot gave a dry click right beside Jig's ear. The second line of crossbowmen had already taken the place of the first.

"Fire!"

Then another switch of ranks.

"Fire!"

The third rank of crossbowmen hastily withdrew to the center of the battalion, where their comrades were reloading their weapons.

"Fifth and sixth rank! All together! Pikes at the ready!"

The fifth and sixth ranks of anglers had already occupied the places where the crossbowmen were standing. They swung their pikes over to the left in order not to hinder the second and third rows, and froze.

Now all three battalions standing on the left road looked like very big, very angry, and very dangerous hedgehogs that were impossible to approach.

The time between salvoes from the crossbowmen and switches of rank was no more than eight seconds. The crossbows inflicted a lot of damage on the front ranks of cavalry, the elves rained arrows down on the enemy, and now the horses in the rear ranks had to advance over the bodies of the dead, which reduced their speed. And the Wine Brook had its effect, too—while the first ranks (most of them already dead) had leapt cleanly across the obstacle, the rear ranks noticed the brook too late, and dozens of horses and riders went tumbling head over heels, sowing even more confusion.

The horses had to be reined back, disrupting the rhythm of the attack formation so that the famous impact of a shattering blow from heavy cavalry was lost. But the scramble didn't extend all the way along the Wine Brook. Many horsemen hurtled toward the battalions, as if they wanted to winkle those accursed crossbowmen out of their centers.

"Hold formation, you monkeys!"

"Stand firm! Don't run! Pikes!"

"Ho-o-o-old!"

"Sta-a-a-a-a-a-and!"

The cavalry came rolling on, closer and closer, closer. . . .

"A-a-a-a-a-a-a-a-aa-aa-aa-aaa-aaa-aa!"—all the battalions uttered the same mighty roar, combining the anticipation of battle, and a curse, and fear . . . and the desire to instill fear in the horses and their riders.

The horsemen were no fools; they had no intention of running onto the pikes.

The cavalry always tries to frighten the infantry, and it always believes the infantry will run. And very often the infantry does run, although its salvation lies in holding a solid formation, not in running away.

Most of the Crayfish had swung their horses round in time, and now they were hurtling along the line of the battalions. Another section went galloping into the gaps between the bristling squares of infantry. The crossbowmen on the sides couldn't risk firing at the enemy in case they hit their own comrades in the other battalions, but the crossbows in the rear ranks didn't hesitate, and as soon as the cavalry flew out into the rear they fired a withering salvo, and then they were joined by the crossbowmen from the front section of the battalion, who had already managed to reload their weapons.

But even so, some riders among those who attacked the left army drove their armor-clad horses straight at the pikes without the slightest fear. Some of them were fools, some were recklessly brave (that is, hopeless fools), some were carried away by the dash and fury of the battle, and some simply didn't manage to halt or turn their horses in time. The front of the battalions took the impact of several hundred horsemen.

Rumbling and clattering, desperate screams, the clanging and scraping of metal on metal.

The impact of the cavalry sent the ranks staggering back. Some men fell.

"A-a-a-a-a-a!" One of the riders was unable to stay in the saddle and, like a stone from a catapult, he went flying over the heads of the cavalry to land somewhere in the rear ranks.

Jig hoped very much that the lousy rat would be welcomed with wide open arms back there.

Up at the front there was a full-scale scrimmage. The pikemen were zealously skewering anyone who came within their reach. One of the horsemen reared his mount up on its hind legs and rode it at his enemies. The horse immediately ran its belly onto four pikes and collapsed, crushing two soldiers in the front rank; the rider leapt down agilely off the poor beast and started waving his sword, hoping to hold out until help arrived, but Bedbug had his wits about him, and his heavy halberd came plunging down on the valiant man's head right between the horns of his helmet. Without hesitating, Jig added a blow of his own, thrusting his halberd in under the man's helmet.

While several soldiers in their section were pulling their pikes out of the horse's body, another horseman performed the same maneuver, and his horse crushed part of the second rank. Two more horsemen drove in through the gap, then more.

And more.

The cavalrymen were losing their horses, but they were achieving something very important—a frontal section of the formation of the central battalion had been torn open, and the Crayfish who were nearby wasted no time.

Jig went dashing forward. The halberdier's job is to deaden the momentum of the attackers but, without even knowing how, he found himself in the thick of the slashing and hacking. There were no more than fifteen Crayfish, and only three of them were still on their horses. The pikemen grasped their swords.

Jig struck one of the cavalrymen in the back with the shaft of his halberd, hacked at the leg of another with all his might, then took a good swing and thrust the spike of his halberd through the heavy cuirass of some noble warrior. Bedbug, who had somehow appeared beside him, cut off a horse's leg, and the rider fell straight onto some soldier's thoughtfully positioned pike.

Before Bedbug could straighten up, a cavalryman nearby struck downward with his lance and pinned the guardsman to the ground. Jig screamed out loud and attacked. The rider held out his shield. The guardsman struck again, caught his enemy by the neck with the hook of his halberd, and jerked, dragging him off his horse. Once again one of the pikemen was there to finish off the man, who was lying dazed and helpless on the ground after his fall out of the saddle.

"Form up!" someone shouted at Jig, and a soldier pushed him back.

He obeyed—he couldn't bring Bedbug back now. The cavalry breakthrough had been halted and the pikemen re-formed their ranks.

"Cro-men, fire!"

The crossbows sang again. The crossbowmen in the frontal ranks of the battalion were joined by those from the rear ranks, who had already shot the cavalrymen who galloped through to the rear.

The remnants of the cavalry of the Crayfish Dukedom sensibly withdrew, taking crippling casualties from the steel rain of crossbow bolts.

"First rank stand erect! Crossbowmen! Into the third rank! At ease! Pikes in the air! Horse traps out of the ground! Ten paces back! To the count of the drum, march!"

Jig tramped back willingly with all the others, leaving an area littered with the bodies of men and horses in front of them.

"Hey, friend!"

Jig didn't realize straightaway that he was being spoken to. It was a pikeman he knew.

"Glad you're still alive."

"Me, too."

"Great, the way you dragged that bastard off his horse! Good for you!"

"That was too good for him! He killed Bedbug."

"Yes, I saw. I'm sorry for the lad, but we gave them a good mauling!"

"What did they do to us?"

"About eighty gone."

"Ha-alt!" came the order, and the battalion stopped.

The right and left battalions had followed the example of the central one, moving back to maintain the line of defense.

"Rest!" The order ran along the ranks.

It was only now that Jig realized just how heavily he had been sweating during the brief battle.

Izmi sighed in relief. Despite his misgivings, the left army had withstood the impact of the cavalry, and not only withstood it, but inflicted serious losses. More than a thousand Crayfish had been left lying on the ground, most of them killed by the hail of crossbow bolts and the elves' arrows. The sections of the Nameless One's army that retreated had now reunited with the cavalry that had been testing the strength of the center a few minutes earlier, and the surviving horsemen were re-forming into a broad attack formation. Izmi reckoned there were slightly fewer than seven thousand of them.

"Am I mistaken, milord? Doesn't it look as if they've decided to break through on to the hill?" Vartek asked, screwing up his eyes. "The gnomes haven't had time to reload the cannons yet."

"Lower your visor and be prepared to lead the men out to help if the Crayfish crush the infantry."

"Work, you sons of dwarves! Work!" Pepper tongue-lashed his cannoneers. "Can't you see what's happening out on the field? The center's not the left army, they can't muster that many pikes! We've got to give them a hand!"

"We are working, Pepper! Can't you see?" red-bearded Zhirgzan panted in his deep bass voice.

"Then you're working too slowly! Load faster!"

"Wait, Pepper!" said Honeycomb, who had borrowed the gnome's spyglass to take a look at what was happening at Nuad. "Swing the cannon round."

"What? What for?"

The Wild Heart handed the spyglass to the gnome without saying a word. Pepper looked in the direction indicated and roared.

"Agh, damnation! Looks like our turn's come! Swing it round! Swing it! And stick that ball up your backside! Load it with grapeshot!"

"My prince, I'm afraid the gnomes will not have time to fire a second salvo," said the Beaver Cap standing beside Stalkon: Two of the Beavers had been attached to the Prince of the Spring Jasmine as his bodyguards.

"Sound the alert!"

He had seen the cavalry's unsuccessful attempt to break through the left army. Now the combined forces of the Crayfish would try to break the center.

"Tell the bowmen to aim at the horses!" the commander of the center ordered, keeping his eyes fixed on the approaching enemy.

"Already done!"

"Your Magicship! Is there any way you can help us?"

"I do not have any attack spells of sufficient power, Your Highness," replied the magician sent by Artsivus. "I doubt if I could eliminate even fifty at a time."

"Well, what about five times instead of one?"

"Then I'm afraid I would not be able to protect the soldiers against the magic of the shamans."

The prince pursed his lips.

"But I think I can do something that will be useful to you."

"What?"

"The Skating Rink," the magician said, and smiled.

Izmi Markauz cursed the moment when his men were sent into the reserve. The center would need help now. That massive cloud of horsemen would sweep over the hill like an avalanche and not stop until it reached Avendoom. It looked as if the king had been too hasty in dismounting the cavalry. With them, there would have been a chance. Now everything depended on the will of Sagra and luck.

The Crayfish infantry had already appeared on the left road, and their sheer numbers were appalling. They were deploying along the Rega Forest, with the clear intention of attacking all three Valiostran armies. And with numbers like that, they could pull it off. In addition, several hundred warriors from the northern tribes were already hurrying along the road from Nuad to Slim Bows. The castle was still showing its teeth and mauling anyone moving along the road on the right, and as far as Izmi could see, the enemy hadn't stopped trying to take the most northerly bulwark of Valiostr's forces. But a large part of the Nameless One's army had passed Nuad, completely ignoring the hail of arrows.

The sorcerer's army was moving straight into battle from the march, and that was the defenders' only advantage. If the enemy had arrived all at once and bided his time, the defense would have been crushed like a ripe berry. But as it was, Valiostr still had a chance. All that had to be done was beat those who were at the front, then the ones who followed, and so on to infinity, for as long as their strength held out. Sagra be praised that the enemy had been deprived of his ogres!

"Just look at that! Look at it, will you! That's a massive force moving up on us. Looks like the lads in the center will have a hard time of it!" one of the pikemen shouted.

"Don't be so quick to bury them," said Jig's neighbor, spitting on the ground. "We'll see how the horsemen handle their lances running uphill."

The cavalry advanced, and the riders set their horses to the gallop. The enemy passed the area where the bodies of the men killed by shots from the gnomes' cannons were lying, and started climbing up the hill. From the center of the Field of Fairies the uphill slope didn't look very steep. But the reality of things is usually far worse than what we expect. Weighed down by their armor and their riders, the horses found it far from easy to manage the climb.

"Three fingers of arc! Take your aim from the unit commanders! Fire!"

A throng of arrows shot up into the air from the three thousand bowmen, hurtled over the heads of the infantry, and came crashing down on the front ranks of the enemy. Then another volley followed. And another. Even in their heavy armor men were killed—with that number of arrows many found their way in through a joint.

But the horses bore the brunt of the blow. Without any effective protection, they fell, leaving their riders with no chance of escaping the bombardment. The commander of the cavalry had apparently not expected to come up against such a large number of bowmen.

A horn sounded the retreat, and then something unbelievable happened: The ground under the hooves of the horses and the feet of the men turned to ice, and the unmitigated slaughter began. The bowmen fired arrow after arrow at the enemy without pause. The unit commanders yelled commands continuously, changing the angle of fire and making adjustments for the wind. The cold-blooded execution continued. The front rows of the infantry and the dismounted cavalry became impatient and started bombarding the Crayfish from their crossbows.

"They've massacred them, milord! I swear by Sagra, massacred them!" Vartek exclaimed.

"I can see," said Izmi, watching as about six hundred dismounted enemy horsemen launched a desperate attack on the line of infantry.

The skirmish was brief and bloody. The Crayfish were not well loved, and they paid the Valiostrans in the same coin. When it was over there was nothing left of the cavalry of the Crayfish Duke, a force that he must have spent years assembling and training. Stalkon's men took no prisoners.

"Ah, may the darkness take me!" said Vartek, pounding himself on the leg in his frustration. "I'd give everything to have been in the place of the foulest louse-ridden infantry man in the center!"

"And you're not the only one, Marquis! Not the only one!"

"Wait!"

"What should we wait for!" the red-bearded gnome asked indignantly. "We have to fire!"

"I'll fire you! Wait, I'm telling you!"

"What for? They'll be trampling all over us in a minute, Pepper!"

"Then let them! If I tell you wait, then you wait!" the cannon commander roared furiously.

"Rott!" Honeycomb called to the commander of the crossbowmen.

"Yes, sir?"

"Are the lads ready?"

"Oh, yes!"

"Act as you think necessary!"

Rott nodded and readied the powerful army crossbow standing on the wall for action. Weapons like that were used for defending castles and fortresses. Six long, heavy steel bolts could be loaded into this monster at once. Naturally, this miracle of military ingenuity was heavy, and carrying it around was a good way to get a hernia, but for firing at the enemy from behind a wall, there was nothing to beat it. Apart from its formidable penetrating power, which put the sklots of the infantry of the line in the shade, the "hailstorm" also possessed another absolutely invaluable quality—its rapid rate of fire.

Honeycomb slapped his helmet, lowered the nose guard, and glanced out from behind the wall.

There was a disorganized brown and gray rabble moving toward them along the right-hand road—barbarians and northern tribesmen. He could recognize both of them from his sorties beyond the Needles of Ice.

The barbarians wore only skins of mammoths and polar bears, along with boiled leather with plates of seal bone sewn onto it, and, instead of helmets, they used the skulls of animals from the Desolate Lands, which gave them a rather terrifying appearance. They were armed with axes and clubs, because they knew almost nothing about bows and arrows. In battle they often went completely berserk. Honeycomb would never have denied that the barbarians of the Desolate Lands were good warriors, but they were no match for the warriors of the northern tribes.

Ask any Wild Heart who he'd rather fight against if he had a choice—a thousand barbarians or five hundred northern tribe warriors, and he would choose the barbarians without any hesitation. There'd be some chance of finishing that battle without too many casualties. But that could never happen with the savage northern tribes. These short men with black hair and narrow eyes were magnificent hunters, and even better warriors. They were highly skilled in using short spears to hunt seals, and to skewer their enemies. And in addition, these lads were hardy, they lived where no other people could live—on the Shore of the Ogres.

Now here they were, totally ignorant of words like "strategy" and "tactics," "reserve" and "flanking maneuver," advancing on Slim Bows with the obvious intention of taking the fortified village. And the frightening thing was they just might be able to do it.

The catapults installed inside the second wall started bombarding the attackers with crocks of incendiary mixture and rocks. The small detachment of Wind Jugglers added its efforts to those of the catapults.

"At the enemy!" Rott barked. "Fire at will!"

Slim Bows launched a hail of steel. When he had used all six bolts, Rott dragged the crossbow down off the wall, handed it to the loader, and was immediately given another one. Honeycomb was using an ordinary sklot. He aimed it at a tall barbarian with a beard and a face daubed with blue paint, held his breath, and pressed the trigger. The bolt went straight through the skull helmet with no difficulty.

"Pretty good," Pepper said with a nod of approval, and then suddenly he yelled, "They have bowmen!"

The northern tribe warriors started peppering the wall with arrows from their short-jointed bows. One of the arrows hit a gnome in the neck as he held a smoldering fuse. Another bounced off the cuirass of the soldier who was reloading Rott's "hailstorm." A third went through the leg of a swordsman standing behind the crossbowmen.

"Healer!" Honeycomb roared. "Increase the rate of fire!"

"How can we fire any faster?" asked the commander of the crossbowmen, raising his sklot. "These brutes are good shots!"

"Ugh, damnation! I'll give them what for!" Pepper picked up the fuse dropped by the dead gnome and carried it over to the cannon.

Honeycomb managed to put his hands over his ears in time. The cannon roared, and the wall was wreathed in smoke. The two other cannons farther along the wall fired immediately after the first.

"Those gnomes are always inventing some tricky gadget or other!" said one of the crossbowmen, coughing.

The blue-gray, foul-smelling smoke stung their eyes. Pepper was already tongue-lashing his team to make them get a move on and reload as quickly as possible. When the smoke cleared, it was obvious that the grapeshot had cut a broad bloody swathe through the ranks of the enemy. The northern tribe warriors were retreating in panic. But six hundred barbarians—either completely witless or delirious with battle fever—had carried on and were already swarming across the moat.

"Swordsmen! Make ready!" Honeycomb yelled so hard that his voice almost cracked and broke. "Pepper! Leave that cannon for now and you and your lads get behind shields!"

"Damned if I will!" The gnome cursed, threw aside the swab that they used to clean the cannon, and took up his battle-mattock. "You'll never see gnomes hiding behind anyone else's back! Zhirgzan! Give me my helmet!"

At Nuad the battle was raging. The enemy had obviously decided to finish off the indomitable castle, no matter what the cost. The battalions standing on the left road heard a distant cannonade.

"My nephew's over there," the pikeman suddenly said.

"What's your name, brother?"

"Bans."

"I'm Jig."

"My hands are frozen. They'll freeze to the pike even through my gloves soon," Bans complained.

"Want some garlic?"

"Will it warm me up?"

"They're the ones who'll warm you up," said Jig, nodding in the direction of the Crayfish infantry advancing on them. "In a couple of minutes it'll be hotter than in a gnome's furnace."

"How many of those lousy mongrels are there?"

"As many as there are of us. Or more."

From the hill Izmi Markauz saw the enemy infantry divide up into three unequal sections and start moving toward the positions of the army of Valiostr. The smallest detachment, which was the farthest away, advanced on Slim Bows, almost at a run. About ten thousand Crayfish, split into five sections, made for the left army. The rest of the infantry and a countless horde of barbarians moved to attack the center.

"Why are our magicians not doing anything, milord?" Vartek asked indignantly. "The entire Council of the Order is up there on the hill!"

"The entire Council, my dear Marquis, is a standing in a circle, holding each other affectionately by the hand," one of the guardsmen growled from under his helmet. "It's thanks to them that the Nameless One hasn't done anything to us yet."

"Commander!" panted a guardsman who came running up at that moment. "The king has ordered us to watch the left flank of the defense and go into action if they need help!"

"At last!" Vartek growled in delight.

"Is there anything else?" Izmi Markauz asked the messenger.

"They say all the ogres are dead!"

A rumble of joy swept through the lines of guards.

"Who says so?"

"Everyone does. I heard it myself from one of the scouts."

"Excellent. You can rejoin the ranks."

"We fought the lousy brutes off! My, but they were stubborn buggers!" said Pepper, waving his bloody mattock.

The barbarian attack had broken down. Two thousand crossbowmen along the entire front of the right army had wrought carnage in the ranks of the attackers. The few barbarians who had managed to cross the moat and the embankment had been finished off by the swordsmen. Now there were mounds of bodies lying under the walls and Honeycomb was afraid that after a few more attacks like that the enemy would be climbing up onto the wall over the corpses of his comrades, like a stairway.

"Zhirgzan! Drop that repulsive thing!" Pepper told the red-headed gnome, who was examining a captured skull helmet curiously. "Get loading! You saw the way those slanty-eyes legged it, didn't you?"

"They won't run a second time."

"What makes you think that, centurion?"

"They're good warriors, even if they are superstitious. Next time they'll realize that not everybody dies when the thunder roars, and they'll continue with the attack."

"Honeycomb!" called the company commander, walking up to them.

"Yes, commander?"

"Our losses?"

"Eight killed and seven wounded."

"Here, take this fellow into your unit," said the commander, indicating a pale, taciturn young lad. "This is His Magicship Roderick. He'll give your boys a hand if need be."

Roderick nodded rather nervously and cast a fearful glance at two swordsmen who were throwing a barbarian's body over the wall.

"Do you have chain mail, Your Magicship?"

The Wild Heart didn't really believe this lad was a magician. By his reckoning, even Kli-Kli could run rings round this pallid youth.

"Yes," said the youth, nodding hastily.

Horns sounded outside the walls. The enemy had launched another attack.

There was a loud crash behind him, the heavens echoed the sound, and the smoking comet fired from the Crater hurtled down right into the center of the front square of infantry that was advancing on the center.

It was an appalling blow. Everyone who was anywhere near the explosion was torn to pieces. The impact of the Crater's shell put Izmi in mind of a god stepping on men by accident.

The infantry was advancing in five units. Three in the first line and another two behind them, at a distance of a thousand yards.

Jig gazed with a strange indifference through the ranks of men and raised pikes at the steel tortoise moving toward them.

"They've got crossbowmen!" one of the pikemen shouted.

Jig's blood ran cold. If the enemy infantry had sklots, then even in their armor the front ranks would be hit hard. At close range a bolt would go straight through the armor as if it was paper, not glorious Isilian steel.

The elves started bombarding the detachment advancing against the left battalion.

"Let me through! Let me through, I say!"

The magician, who had stood behind Jig all this time without saying a word, was scrambling his way forward.

Jig gave a piercing whistle and yelled: "Let the magician through to the front, you damn blockheads! Quick now, or we'll all be catching steel bolts!"

That did the trick, and the pikemen moved aside to make way. The magician dashed forward, stood in front of the first rank, and held out his hands with the open palms toward the detachment of infantry that had almost reached the Wine Brook. A blinding ball of fire went darting from the magician's hands and struck the first row of shields, vaporizing them, together with the men, then moved on to the second row, and the third row, and the fourth row of the crossbowmen, until it finally exploded. . . .

That set them wailing! Jig could hear the howls of dying men as they were burned alive. Many of the soldiers in his battalion swore in satisfaction when they saw how many casualties a single man could inflict on the enemy.

Meanwhile the magician created another fireball, then another, incinerating men by the dozen. The lines of infantry faltered and broke, scattering in panic along the bank of the Wine Brook. The smell of burnt flesh even reached Jig's battalion.

Suddenly the magician swayed and collapsed in a heap on the snow. Someone from the front ranks dashed to the fallen man, picked him up, and pulled him back into the battalion.

The vigilant unit commanders roared:

"Crossbowmen make ready! First rank! Fire! Second rank! Fire! Third rank! Fire!"

When they'd done their job, the crossbowmen moved back. They were replaced by another nine ranks taken from the rear and the sides of the battalion.

"Fire! Fire! Fire! Fire!"

The confused enemy infantry were caught in a deadly steel shower.

"Agh! The magicians have gone into action!"

Izmi wasn't listening. Like everyone else, he was following the action in the left army. Some unknown magician had shattered the central detachment of attackers with ease, but the right and left detachments were still moving forward, and had already crossed the Wine Brook. And the other two detachments of the Nameless One's troops were not far behind.

"Milord!"

Izmi Markauz turned away from the battle scene and looked at the soldier with a huge two-handed sword who had approached him.

"Milord, His Majesty has put my unit at your disposal."

"How many men do you have?"

"Two hundred."

Not bad. Two hundred Beaver Caps was more than he had counted on.

"Good. Move across to that copse behind the left army. But don't get involved in the action just yet."

"Yes, milord."

Something told Izmi that help would be needed over there very soon now.

"They have crossbowmen, commander."

"Ah, the lousy bastards!" roared the commander of the six thousand Wind Jugglers, who were now standing behind the infantry and the dismounted cavalry. He raised his fist to the heavens. "How many of them?"

"I don't know."

"Then find out! And be quick about it! Or they'll pick off all our infantry! Nark!"

"Yes, commander?"

"Take your thousand men and get forward! Put the lads in with the swordsmen. Let them fire point-blank from there! If anyone in the infantry doesn't like it, tell them I ordered it! Get going!"

"About three thousand!" panted the soldier, running back. "The scouts say three thousand! Marching ahead of the infantry."

"I can see where they're marching, I'm not blind."

The cannons roared behind them and the soldiers ducked, but the commander of the Wind Jugglers took no notice.

"So there are twice as many of us as there are of them," the old warrior muttered through his teeth, watching as the balls fired from the cannons landed in the farthest ranks of the enemy infantry. "So much the better. They won't be able to touch us. Bows have a much longer range, and we know how to use them. Listen to my orders! Two fingers of arc! Correction for wind, a quarter-finger to the right! We'll keep hitting those bird-brains until they start firing! Fire!"

The northern warrior leapt the wall easily, and Honeycomb only just managed to jump aside in time. His short, black-haired enemy handled the spear with a broad notched tip masterfully. The weapon danced in circles and zigzags, and the Wild Heart had to be quick on his feet. Although the crossbowmen were firing continually, on this section of the wall the enemy had managed to break through into Slim Bows, and now the battle was raging along the wall. They had to try to hold out until reinforcements arrived.

The warrior with the narrow eyes suddenly shot up into the air, obviously intending to strike down at Honeycomb with his spear. The Wild Heart dodged to one side and swung his ogre-hammer, and the spiked ball struck the life out of his unarmored enemy.

A barbarian popped up from behind the wall, wearing a polar bear's skull on his head, and his terrible ax struck the back of the red-headed gnome, who was fighting a soldier dressed in the colors of the Crayfish Dukedom.

The ogre-hammer descended on the bear skull, shattering it into splinters and crushing the barbarian's head.

"Damnation!" yelled Pepper, thrusting a lighted torch in the face of another soldier and swinging his mattock into the man's crotch.

"Centurion! Cover my lads!" Rott called as he and twenty of the crossbowmen brought over the reloaded hailstorms.

Seven of the men started methodically picking off the enemy warriors who had climbed over the wall; the others opened fire on those who were crossing the shallow moat. Reinforcements arrived in the form of fifty swordsmen, and together they managed to throw the enemy back off the wall. The magician, who had miraculously survived the slaughter, flung a few final gouts of fire after the routed enemy.

"Stop throwing that fire!" Pepper yelled. "Stop throwing that fire! There's powder here!"

"Rott! Fire as they retreat! Pepper, get to the cannon! Your Magicship, get off the wall, or you'll catch a stray arrow!"

The first and second ranks of the left battalion parted for a few seconds to let the Beaver Caps through. Armed with double-handed swords, the warriors maintained wide spaces between them as they dashed straight at the waiting pikes of their enemies. The others followed the Beavers slowly.

Striking with wide, sweeping movements, the Beavers chopped off the pikes and sliced into the ranks of the enemy, breaking up the formation. Of course, not all of them avoided a fatal encounter with an enemy pike, but most of them managed the job well. Swinging the large swords like scythes, they cut deep into the ranks of the attackers, inflicting appalling casualties on the shocked and terrified infantry, and their comrades came crowding on behind them, crashing into the enemy, striking with their pikes and barging on like a mammoth in a china shop, slowly and inexorably following the wedge formation of the Beavers.

The right battalion had also clashed with the Crayfish infantry, but Jig couldn't see how things were going there. The order ran along the lines:

"Crossbowmen into the sixth rank!"

The battalion was preparing to deliver a thrust like a battering ram, and no crossbows were required for that, so the crossbowmen were moved back and replaced by pikemen.

"Ranks one to six! Pikes at the ready!"

"To the drums! At the double, forward!"

The drums started rumbling in the center, the battalion thrust out its spikes and swayed.

Boom . . . Boom . . . Boom . . . Boom . . . Boom . . . Boom-boom . . . Boom-boom-boom-boom!

The drums speeded up and the battalion rushed forward, moving faster and faster toward the two-thousand-strong detachment of the second line that was advancing to take the place of infantry burnt by the magician and shot down by the crossbowmen. Jig diligently pressed against the back of the pikeman in front of him and yelled, bracing himself for the impact.

———

With their line broken by the bombardment from the bowmen on the hill, the enemy's surviving crossbowmen went rushing back without having fired a single shot, and most of them were trampled by their own infantry. The men of the line were not so easily dealt with; they kept on pushing forward up the slope, trying to get past the area under bombardment as quickly as possible. Many of them raised shields to protect themselves against the arrows. One enemy detachment even managed to create a perfectly good "tortoise," but it ran into the icy patch on the hill and fell apart, and the bowmen immediately picked off the unfortunate warriors.

"Shields together! Lances! Crossbowmen fire at will!" young Stalkon ordered.

The prince realized that, despite the casualties inflicted by the bowmen, this time the enemy would reach them. The rear ranks of bowmen halted the bombardment that had ceased to be effective, took up their swords, and merged into the ranks of the infantry. The only ones who continued firing were Nark's thousand men and a few crossbowmen, but even they were soon forced to stop. A ragged volley from the Crayfish archers was neutralized by a magician, who made most of the arrows burn up in the air. The enemy infantry pushed forward several hundred men armed with double-handed swords, with the clear intention of breaking the tidy formation of the center.

"Beavers, look lively now!"

The Beavers had their wits about them. The shields parted for a moment to let the warriors of the legendary force through. When the enemy has a sledgehammer, you need a sledgehammer, too—that's an incontestable rule of war. Skirmishes sprang up along the front, men fighting with their double-handed swords one-to-one or in groups. The Crayfish fought well, but they were still no match for the Beaver Caps and the advantage was with Valiostr, but even so the king's son gave his order to the bugler:

"Sound the retreat!

The bugle gave the signal several times, and the swordsmen pulled back behind the shields before the enemy infantry, enraged by the death of their comrades, could reach them.

"You're a pretty good magician, lad," Pepper panted to Roderick. "You should make more of those balls of fire, then you'd be absolutely invaluable."

"I try my best, Mister Gnome," the young magician said with a wry smile.

The magic that had scattered a steady line of infantry advancing against Slim Bows had obviously cost him a great effort.

"Well, centurion, you're blowing hard already, but it's only just past noon," the gnome called to Honeycomb. "Are you alive?"

"Yes, I'm alive. Here, hold Invincible."

"What do I want with that crazy rat of yours? Do you think I didn't see the way he went for that barbarian's face?"

"Hold him, I tell you! I've got to go and see the commander!"

The gnome grunted discontentedly and set the ling on his shoulder.

"I hope it won't gnaw my beard off. Be quick, will you!"

"Rott, while I'm away, you're in charge!"

"Understood!" the commander of the crossbowmen replied imperturbably.

Honeycomb found his commanding officer in the center of the village, where the temporary hospital was located. Someone had slashed his face open, and the healers were working on him. Honeycomb had to wait until they finished.

"Who's this you've brought me? Who's this you've brought?" one young man, wearing the badge of the guild of healers, was yelling.

"But all his clothes were soaked in blood!" said the medical orderly, trying to make excuses.

"He's got a cut! Do you understand, you blockhead! An ordinary deep cut!"

"But he was yelling as if his throat was being slashed!"

"How many times do I have to tell you lot that the first ones to bring to the operating table are the ones who aren't talking! If he's yelling and asking for help, that means he'll survive! Nothing's going to happen to him! But if he's lying there saying nothing and as pale as a corpse, then he's in a bad way! And if you bring me any more walking wounded, I won't answer for what I'll do to you! Load them all into carts and take them to the main hospital behind the hill! They can sort them out! Bring me only the seriously wounded, the ones with abdominal injuries and lost limbs. Can you manage to hammer that into your men's heads?"

"Did you want to see me, centurion?" the commander called to attract Honeycomb's attention.

"Yes, commander. We need to put two hundred swordsmen and at least a hundred crossbowmen on the bank of the Kizevka. Do we have any reserves?"

"We can find reserves," said the bandaged commander, looking hard at the Wild Heart. "I just don't understand why we need to move the lads across there."

"I don't think the northern tribes will storm the wall again."

"Where else will they go? They won't swim down the river!"

"That's exactly what they'll do."

"I understand if it was summer, but it's perishing cold. Who's going to jump into the water when it's about to freeze over?"

"They're well used to swimming in icy water. They live in the Desolate Lands, after all."

"What a wild idea!"

"I just don't want to find them in our rear all of a sudden."

"All right. I'll give the order. Get back to your men, we're expecting another attack any minute. By the way, have you heard the Order got rid of all the ogres?"

The battle seemed to go on forever. The poleax in the prince's hands grew heavy, but he kept hacking and slashing, like one of the dwarves' magical toys. The straight line had disappeared a long time ago, and the entire front had broken up into separate skirmishes. They had managed to throw the enemy back four times, and four times he had come back at them, determined to crush the accursed infantry.

These were the finest men of the northern kingdom of Valiostr, those who had been in the heavy cavalry and served as sandmen, the kind of men that superb fighting forces were built around. Practically all the bowmen had joined in the hand-to-hand fighting, and only a small group of the most experienced Wind Jugglers, no more than six hundred of them, had moved aside from the seething action to fire selectively at the enemy.

Stalkon was guarded and protected, his back was covered, and the enemy was given no chance to fire at the king's son. But even so, despite all their subterfuges, the heir to the throne found himself on the ground twice. The first time he was knocked off his feet by a blow from a battle hammer. Fortunately, one of the two Beavers detailed to protect him had survived the bloody melee and he held off the eager enemy with broad sweeps of his sword until Spring Jasmine was back up on his feet.

The second time a crossbow bolt caught him on the helmet. Fortunately it was only a glancing blow and the bolt bounced off without wounding the prince. But Stalkon was stunned and he fell to his knees, completely disoriented for a moment. One of the barbarians was about to grasp this opportunity, and if not for Ash—the commander of the Wild Hearts who had survived from the Lonely Giant—Spring Jasmine would not have survived the battle.

The cannons and the Crater were silent. It was pointless firing now—more of their own would be killed than of the enemy. All they could do was grit their teeth and keep slashing away.

Stalkon took another heavy blow from a barbarian on his battered shield, jabbed the bearded savage in the face, and split his skin and flesh open with the poleax. It was time to finish this battle, and the sooner the better. As if he had heard this thought, the king sent the right cavalry reserve of the center to support the infantry by attacking the enemy's flank.

Nuad was holding. The position in the center had evened out and the sudden appearance of the cavalry had disconcerted the ranks of the Nameless One's army. The Moon Stallions had appeared at exactly the right time. Slim Bows was calm for the time being—the barbarians, northern tribesmen, and units of Crayfish infantry had been forced back and now they had withdrawn to regroup. But things were not going so well for the left army. The left battalion was busy completing the rout of its opponents, the central battalion had just rammed into the second line detachment of infantry, and the right battalion was barely managing to hold, but its opponents were tenacious, and the ranks could falter at any moment.

"Vartek, gallop over to those two hundred Beavers. Tell them to attack the rear of the infantry pressing the right battalion! Do it!" Izmi ordered.

"Commander! It looks as if the elves are in trouble!"

"I can see! Do as I ordered! Bugler! Sound the attack!"

Purple spheres suddenly appeared in the ranks of the right battalion and started methodically annihilating the soldiers. The men faltered.

"The right battalion is retreating, Your Highness!"

"So I see. Gallop to the reserve, let them close the gap. I wonder how our magicians managed to let the shamans get so close?"

Before Jig could understand what was happening, the front ranks had been killed. But it had all been going so well! The battalion had successfully rammed the second line detachment of infantry. Following orders, Jig was back in the third rank when the right royal scrimmage broke out. The heavy halberds were ready and waiting for anyone who managed to get close to the pikemen. Then suddenly dark purple smoke had started rising from the armor of the front ranks, and the suits of armor had fallen to the ground, empty—their owners had disappeared into thin air.

The pikeman Bans was one of the first to be killed. And then it was the turn of Jig's own line. The weapons and armor of the soldiers beside him clanked as they fell to the ground. A second later Jig was the only one left alive out of the entire line. The battalion was still pressing forward, unaware of what had happened to the front ranks.

Jig saw three men wearing black cloaks straight in front of him. No armor, no weapons. One man threw his hands up, and a silver arrow went flying into a guardsman's chest. And then it disappeared, without doing him any harm.

"Shamans!" The cry of fright from the rear ranks could be heard even above the roar of the battle.

"A-a-a-a-a," Jig yelled with his eyes closed, realizing that this was the end.

The guardsman raised his halberd and struck out at the nearest sorcerer with all his might. For a brief moment he glimpsed a pale and utterly astonished face, and then the shaman fell at the raging guardsman's feet with his head split open.

"You can kill them!" Jig barked. "You can kill the sorcerers! Kill them, lads!"

He swung his halberd again, and the men, suddenly intoxicated with their own courage, broke formation and dashed forward, each trying to get to the accursed shamans first. Jig hooked his halberd onto the leg of a shaman who had already started to work a spell and pulled, felling the man to the ground, then stabbed him in the stomach. His comrades finished off the final shaman and roared as they went dashing at the enemy infantry, which had faltered at the sight of such powerful sorcerers being dispatched so cruelly.

"The spells have stopped, Your Majesty! The sorcerers must have been killed!"

"What does it matter now?" the king asked bitterly.

The right battalion no longer existed. The enemy had struck the running men in the rear, and a few minutes later there were no more than nine hundred of them left. Fortunately the reserve of two thousand and the two hundred Beaver Caps he had given to young Markauz had got there in time.

That lad would make something of himself. His father would be proud of him. He could only hope that the guardsmen could help to save the elves. But that was unlikely. They wouldn't be in time.

Epilorssa of the House of the Black Moon cursed and reached for another arrow from his quiver. The men had got carried away in the heat of the battle and completely forgotten about the second detachment of the second line. About two thousand men were deploying at the Wine Brook with the clear intention of wiping out the small group of elves by the Luza Forest.

"Duple! Duple!"

They couldn't expect any help from anywhere. The neighboring battalion was finishing off its surviving opponents, the central battalion was still fighting on, despite the Nameless One's shamans (Epilorssa had felt the magic), and the right battalion had been completely annihilated by sorcery and panic. The elves could have taken cover in the forest, but it wasn't all that close, and it was not their way to show their backs to the enemy when they could still fight.

And they fought, firing arrow after arrow at the enemy. The enemy ranks broke into a run, shouting to urge themselves on. Many of them fell with an arrow in the face or a joint of their armor, but there were too few elves, and the distance between them and their enemies was too short. They wouldn't have time to kill them all in any case.

The elves were standing in four lines. The first line fired from one knee, while the elves standing ten paces behind them fired from a standing position. Ten paces farther back there were more elves firing from one knee, but the archers had been shifted two body-widths to the right, so that they would not accidentally fire into the backs of the comrades standing in front of them. Behind this line was the final one, in which the warriors were standing once again.

Epilorssa gave another order and the front line jumped up, dashed back, positioned itself behind the back line, and started firing again.

Then it was the second rank's turn to withdraw. Then the third rank, then the fourth. And then the first rank ran back behind its comrades again.

The elves withdrew, firing at the enemy continually. Almost every shot found its target. But the line of shields was very close now.

The crossbows clicked. The dark elves in the first and second lines fell, struck down by the metal bolts. Something hit Epilorssa in the chest and he fell, too. The elf couldn't understand why he was in so much pain, why he wasn't fighting and the snow was burning his face so fiercely.

The red snow.

"At those bastards as they run! Straight at their backsides! Fire at will!"

The bowmen standing behind the infantry of the center, which had beaten back the enemy, once again started showering arrows down on their retreating foe.

"Grapeshot, fire!" Pepper barked, and stuck his fingers in his ears.

There was a roar of cannons, the wall at Slim Bows was wreathed in blue-gray smoke once again, and a moment later the sound of the three weapons was echoed by the Crater on the hill dispatching its generous gift of fire.

A wedge formation of Jolly Gallows-Birds suddenly separated off from the left battalion, which had now disposed of its opponents completely. The men dressed in black set the entire Field of the Fairies ringing to their roar of "Wa-a-a-a-a-tch your back" and struck at the right flank of the detachment of the Nameless One's army that was preparing to crush the surviving elves.

"There they are! There they are! Oh, damnation!" shouted one of the swordsmen, pointing toward the Kizevka. "Look how many of them there are!"

"Fire!" the officer ordered, and the crossbow bolts set the river water dancing.

"One finger of arc! All together! Fire!"

Bang! Bang! The cannons replied to the archers.

———

The wedge of "marines" sliced into the unprotected side of the enemy detachment without encountering any resistance and plowed on toward the center, sowing terror and death as it went. Their Jolly Gallows-Birds battalion was hurrying across to support them, and the central battalion, which had already polished off the first detachment of the second line, hit the enemy from the rear. The enemy forgot all about the elves and started defending themselves.

"Hey, Honeycomb! You were right! Those lads really did decide to take a dip!"

"Just keep firing!" the Wild Heart growled. "Pepper! What are you doing?"

"Give me a hand!" the gnome panted. He was holding a massive cannonball in his hands. "When will those lads ever reload my cannon? How far can you throw this?"

"What's on your mind?" asked Honeycomb, taking the cannonball from the gnome.

"You're as strong as a horse, centurion. Can you toss it over the moat?"

"With a good swing."

"Go on then," the gnome said, and lit the fuse.

If not for the Gallows-Birds, the dark elves would never have seen Zagraba again. Izmi Markauz reined in his horse in front of them and yelled.

"On the horses. Behind the cavalry, lads! Quickly!"

The elves didn't waste any time, and leapt up onto the horses behind the guardsmen. Some of them even carried on firing as they did so. The enemy's crossbowmen woke up and several guardsmen fell, but most of them were already galloping off, carrying their allies away to a safe distance. Izmi was the last to leave. Now he had to offload the elves and overhaul the enemy who had attacked the right battalion.

The retreating men still hadn't crossed the Wine Brook, and the lieutenant of the royal guard was hoping to finish off the ones who were left. Vartek was galloping along, leaning down against his horse's neck. Izmi saw a crossbow bolt in his back. The armor hadn't saved him.

"Are you alive?"

The marquis nodded feebly. Izmi Markauz grabbed the bridle of the wounded man's horse. He had to get him to the healers as quickly as possible.

Despite the unrelenting mass attacks, Slim Bows was holding out magnificently. It was a good thing the king hadn't begrudged paying the gnomes properly. Fighting without the cannons would have been an awful lot harder. The left army had returned to its positions and completely restored its line of battle. But now, of course, it had no reserve, and the central battalion had been badly mauled in the fighting.

"What kind of surprise will the Nameless One have for us now, my prince?" asked Ash, slipping his beautiful blade of back steel back into its scabbard.

"What would you say about them, Wild Heart?"

Ash screwed up his eyes and looked toward the Rega Forest, where about thirty huge figures were striding across the field with clubs over their shoulders.

"Just as I thought," the commander of the Wild Hearts chuckled. "If there are no ogres, then the giants go into action."

"Get ready!" the prince ordered. "Bowmen! Into the front ranks!"

The sound was heard by everyone who was in the Field of the Fairies. It was like a string snapping in the frosty air. The gentle, melodious note rang out above the earth, and a few seconds later purple fire came crashing down on Nuad.

"D-damnation!" exclaimed Pepper, grabbing the spyglass. "Did their powder explode?"

"I'm afraid not," said Honeycomb, shaking his head, still unable to believe what had happened.

Nuad was entirely engulfed in flames.

"It's the Nameless One! It's the Nameless One!" shouted Roderick, gaping wide-eyed and white-faced at the warriors.

"Don't talk nonsense!" Rott snapped.

"It was the Nameless One who struck them! The Order has failed! Something has disrupted the balance!"

"My prince, the Order is leaving the hill!"

"What on earth is going on up there?" Stalkon Junior raged.

"Can you see anything?"

"No, first the ground shook, and then there was a billow of smoke," Jig answered.

"I can see that much myself!" growled the centurion standing beside him.

From behind the tongue of Rega Forest, from the spot where Nuad stood, a column of blue-black smoke was rising up into the sky.

Suddenly the sky above the right army, which had been restored by using the reserve, started flickering. Everybody raised their heads and marveled at this wonder. A minute later the flickering stopped and a massive gout of fire fell on the battalion, consuming several thousand men instantly.

The ground shook again and the ranks of Jig's battalion tumbled against each other. There were screams of fear.

"Easy now! Everybody on your feet! On your feet, I said!" a centurion roared.

The terrified men were already getting up. They were all staring at the spot where the right battalion had been. There was nothing there now but a gaping black hole. The ground itself seemed to be on fire.

"What was that?"

"Let's get out of here!"

"May they dwell in the light!"

Jig looked up and saw the sky above them start flickering.

"Up there!" he barked, raising his arm to point.

"Everybody back!" shouted the magician, who had recovered his composure. "We have enough time. Back! Centurions, give the order!"

"Back! To the beat of the drum! At the double! Maintain formation, you apes! Let's go!"

The central battalion sprinted away from the spot. The one that had been standing by the Luza Forest followed. The men ran as hard as they could, but not one dropped his weapon or tried to push his comrade in the back. Everyone realized that panic would lead them straight to the grave.

A minute later two gouts of fire crashed into the positions where the left army had been standing.

"The left army's running, Your Highness!"

"I know that, and . . . darkness!"

The prince saw the two fireballs go hurtling into the places where the retreating army should have been standing. Then he was almost deafened by a crash behind him. He swung round and stared at the spot that had been the top of the hill a minute ago. Now it was a smooth, smoking platform. No cannons, no Crater, no royal pavilion.

"The king's dead . . ." The word ran through the ranks of soldiers.

"Damnation!" Stalkon Junior cursed through his teeth, then he took himself in hand and roared: "Ash, stop them! If they run, all is lost! We have to retreat through Slim Bows!"

Even a fool could see that the Battle of the Field of the Fairies had been lost.

"I shall do everything necessary, my king!"

The buglers at Slim Bows almost burst their cheeks sounding the retreat. The army was withdrawing in haste, but without panic, behind the hill in the direction of Avendoom. Everybody had seen what that blow had done to the top of the hill. Everybody knew the king had been directing the battle from up there. Everybody realized that no one could have lived through that.

Honeycomb had seen the two balls of purple fire crash into the positions of the left army, but he didn't know if any of the soldiers had survived. It was too far away, and the hill was in the way.

"The men are formed up, commander!" Rott reported.

"Leave the hailstorms, lads. Or we won't be able to run if a thunderbolt comes our way."

"It won't," said Roderick, who had stopped panicking and was calm again.

"How do you know?"

"If the Nameless One could have vaporized us, he would have done it a long time ago. Not even he's all-powerful."

"In any case, we have to get going. They'll start storming us again soon. Pepper! Let's go!"

"And the cannon? What about the cannon?"

"Let's go! We haven't got time to drag it along! I'll buy you a new one later!"

"Oh no!" the gnome muttered, and started scattering powder out of a small barrel. "He'll buy me one! Well, at least the enemy won't get my precious darling! I'll blow her up!"

Honeycomb was wondering how well the army would hold up at Avendoom. It had lost a battle, but not the war.

20

THE PLAYER

My laughter woke everyone up, but I just couldn't stop. All that effort wasted, all those lives lost, and it had all been in vain! We were too late.

Kli-Kli seemed to be more frightened for me than the others. I think you'd probably be frightened, too, if some idiot suddenly started laughing in the middle of the night for no reason at all. Eel was the one who found the remedy for my laughter. He gave me a couple of hefty slaps to the face, and I calmed down.

"I'm all right," I said, catching my breath. "You can stop pummeling me now. Sorry, lads."

"What happened, Dancer? Not ill, are you?" Kli-Kli asked in concern.

"Everything's all right," I said. "It was just another bad dream."

"Somehow I don't recall bad dreams ever making you laugh before," Hallas growled. "Mostly you just yelled blue murder. Come on, let's hear what you dreamed about this time."

So I had to tell them about the battle. Not everything, naturally, but certainly the fact that we lost.

"If the king's dead, that's bad. It won't exactly inspire the army," Mumr said pensively. He believed in my dream straightaway.

Apart from not inspiring the army, it would also cancel out my Commission. If the client was dead, the deal was dissolved. So I didn't have to take the Rainbow Horn to Avendoom, where bloody war was just about to break out under the city walls. And I could forget about my pardon and the fifty thousand gold pieces that His Deceased Majesty had promised me.

"If the battle happened yesterday, then we still have a little time. It's not very far to the capital now. We can try to make it."

"We'll make it, gnome! I swear on my house, we'll make it! Eel, Mumr, saddle up the horses. Hallas, pay the innkeeper!" said Egrassa.

The Wild Hearts dashed to carry out his instructions.

"Listen, Harold, could you let me have the Horn just for a moment?"

"What do you want it for, Kli-Kli?" I asked, but I took the artifact out of my bag and handed it to her anyway.

She took hold of it, turned it this way and that, sniffed at it, muttered some gibberish over it, took some kind of powder out of her pocket and sprinkled some on it.

"Egrassa? What do you see?"

"I am not skilled in shamanism. I don't see anything."

"I didn't see anything, either," she sighed. "Take it, Harold. Now I understand your dream."

"And?"

"You said there was a sound like a string breaking. That was the Rainbow Horn losing its power."

"Do you mean to say . . . ?"

"Exactly what I said. This is just a horn now. Nothing special about it. At least, not until the Order gets to work. The artifact has lost its power and the balance has been shaken. The Nameless One is now free to use magic here in Valiostr."

"That means we have to hurry. Get your things, we're moving on!" the elf said brusquely.

"Valder!" I called. "Valder! Is this true?"

"Yes," the dead archmagician condescended to reply about a minute later. "The Rainbow Horn has lost its power."

"But that means the Fallen Ones have escaped from the Palaces of Bone!"

"It's not that simple, my friend. Yes, the Horn is useless, and the Fallen Ones are able to move up to the top levels of Hrad Spein, but not to leave it. The Horn is a Key. Until the Key is turned and the scales of the balance are destroyed, the Fallen Ones will not come pouring out into Siala. And only the Master can turn the Key. Or another Master, or . . . the Player."

"Do you know the name of the Player?"

No reply.

———

All I remember of the days that followed is the wild galloping and the cold that crept in under my clothes. On the road to Avendoom we exhausted three pairs of horses each. We had to buy new ones. The terrible catastrophe had sent prices for all sorts of goods, and especially means of transport, soaring sky-high, but Egrassa doled out the gold without any complaints.

The news got worse and worse. Unfortunately, my dream hadn't lied— the army had been defeated on the Field of Fairies. But it hadn't been routed—most of the soldiers who survived the Nameless One's attacks managed to retreat to Avendoom. The king had been killed—may he dwell in the light. Almost the entire headquarters staff of the army and at least two archmagicians had been killed along with him. The country had a new king now, the younger son of Stalkon the Ninth, Stalkon of the Spring Jasmine.

The Order was doing everything it possibly could to stop the Nameless One, but our magicians obviously weren't having much success.

Part of the population had left the capital and the surrounding area in great haste. Anyone who didn't intend to defend the walls of the capital and could run, ran. Personally speaking, I didn't blame them; as far as I was concerned, trying to fight against magic was absolute madness. If not for the Rainbow Horn, I would probably have been halfway to Isilia or the Lowlands myself. I couldn't say what it was that stopped me doing the intelligent thing and running.

"There'll be another almighty blast in a moment! Listen, Egrassa! I understand everything, but it's like an ant trying to run across a meadow where the royal cavalry's galloping up and down! They won't even notice when they flatten us!"

"Shut up, Hallas! We're thinking!" Eel said in a most impolite manner.

We'd reached Avendoom early that morning, just in time for the start of the battle. The forces of the Nameless One were preparing to storm the walls. But for the time being the magicians and the shamans were still fighting a duel. Every now and then the air was sundered by the ear-splitting whistle of flying stones, the crackle of lightning, the roar of flames, and the howls of one kind of magical beast or another. All this accompanied by the booming of the cannon installed on the city walls. So far the Nameless One hadn't joined in this game of flexing muscles. Either he hadn't got to Avendoom yet, or he'd decided to see what his army was capable of.

We did the sensible thing and crept into a small copse of trees standing between Avendoom and the road to the south. The view was wonderful. But any fool could see that we couldn't simply stroll across to those city towers that were so close and yet so impossibly far away. The Nameless One's lads were all around and they would spot us right away.

Our army was formed up along the city walls. Quite a large crowd, really, but compared with the Nameless One's forces, it was a mere drop in the ocean. The Suburb had been totally destroyed. All that was left of it was dark patch on the snow-covered ground.

As bad luck would have it, there were several hundred barbarians hanging about right in front of the copse of trees, and we had to wait until they moved on to attack our side before we could get past without being noticed.

"We're not likely to get into the city through the gates, Egrassa," the gnome objected irritably. "I can't stand magicians! Look! Another spell! May they all rot in the darkness!"

Thousands of icicles suddenly descended on the detachment of barbarians that was inconveniencing us, and in just a few seconds the men were transformed into a bloody pulp. Immediately a huge flower of flame blossomed above the city walls. The enemy's shamans hadn't wasted any time in striking back. The two sides were systematically annihilating each other's infantry. If it kept on like this, soon there wouldn't be anybody but magicians and shamans left. The commanding officers of both sides were apparently of the same opinion. Horns sounded, drums started pounding, and the dark masses shuddered and started moving toward each other.

"Right, it's time!"

"Hang on, will you, Mumr!" said Hallas, still lying on the snow and surveying the battlefield. "Let them start fighting first!"

"Harold, you used to live in the city," Egrassa said to me. "Is there any other way to get into Avendoom apart from the city gates?"

"There is," I replied after a moment's thought. "But it's no help to us."

"Why?"

"They probably won't let us climb up the walls on a rope. And anyway, we don't have a rope that long."

"Is that the only way?"

"Well, we could try going through the municipal drains, but that—"

I was forced to break off when a fiery meteorite went crashing into the next copse and incinerated a detachment of the enemy's cavalry.

"—But that's all closed off with metal grilles. And we'd still have to get to the walls somehow. But I do have one little idea. The city walls run into the Cold Sea. I expect the fishermen who live in the villages nearby have all run off ages ago or moved into the city. We could try to find a boat."

"That won't get you anywhere! There are gnomes with cannons in the Bastion that defend the entrance to the harbor. They'll smash any boat to splinters! And we'll end up as fish food!"

"No they won't, Hallas!" Kli-Kli reassured the gnome. "We'll stand you in the boat so they can see you from the Bastion and they won't fire!"

"Me? Get in a boat? I won't do it!"

"Oh, yes you will! If you want the Nameless One to go back home, you'll get in a boat! And you'll yell loud and clear in that language of yours, so your kinsmen can hear you," said Egrassa, completely ignoring the gnome's whinging. "Here, take your mattock and smash this."

The elf handed the gnome a crystal.

"What is it?" Kli-Kli asked.

"Markauz gave it to me in Zagraba. He got it from Artsivus. He said as soon as we got close, we should smash it—and the Order would know we were here."

"Well, just how much closer could we be?" Hallas muttered, swinging his mattock.

It took the gnome two attempts to break the crystal. The stone smashed like any ordinary piece of glass and . . . and nothing happened.

"Now what?" I asked obtusely.

"How should I know?" asked Egrassa, already in the saddle. "I was told to smash it when the time came. We've done that, now it's up to the Order. Is it far from here to the Cold Sea, Harold?"

"A fair distance. We have to cross the field and go through that wood over there, then it's about fifteen hundred yards to the shoreline."

"We'll get through! Everybody stick together and don't fall back! If anyone loses their horse or just falls, yell!"

The elf was right there, the battle was raging and thundering all around, and anyone who was at the back might very easily not be heard.

We went flying out of the copse and headed toward the dark wood. Sagot save us! It looked so far away!

The space ahead of us was empty, but that wouldn't last long. I dug my heels into the sides of my horse and concentrated on trying not to fall off. We rushed up a hill and down again, and found ourselves in the (relatively) empty camp of the Nameless One's army. The Crayfish seemed very surprised to see

us there. But only one of them tried to block our way. Eel ran the brave man
down with his horse and we went flying out like a whirlwind into the rear
of the enemy's pikemen.

The lads didn't notice us, they were too busy trying to dodge the emerald-
green sparks showering down on them from out of the sky. When they hit
the ground, the sparks turned into massive great serpents that spat green
spheres. We had to veer to the left, and we'd almost reached the city walls
when Hallas's horse caught an arrow in the crupper. At full gallop, Mumr
grabbed the gnome off the animal that was going insane with the pain (how
did he manage to do that?) and dumped him across his own horse.

"Our own side's firing at us! Out into the field," Eel shouted to the elf.

To the right of us a battalion smashed into the tattered ranks of the barbarians and northern tribesmen. We had to rein in our horses again and go
dashing back in the opposite direction. Eventually we reached the wood,
but that didn't bring us any relief. We immediately found ourselves surrounded by horsemen. At first I was afraid they were the Nameless One's
lads, but then I noticed they were wearing the gray and blue uniform of the
royal guard.

"Who are you?" one of the horsemen barked.

The other soldiers sensibly kept their hands on their spears.

"We're on your side!" Hallas panted, climbing down off Eel's horse.

Naturally, they didn't believe us. But, fortunately, they weren't in any
great hurry to kill us, either. The presence of an elf and a gnome in this
bunch of deserters or vagabonds or spies of the Nameless One prevented
them from jumping to any hasty conclusions. Without making any fuss,
Egrassa took out the paper with the royal seal, which was badly crumpled
after our long journey. At least that produced some effect.

"What are you doing here?" the guardsman asked.

"We need to get into the city, milord. Can you help us?"

"I doubt it. Only the gates in the northern wall can be opened. All the
others are blocked off. And fighting your way right across the battlefield to
the other side of the city is far too difficult."

"Look!" someone gasped.

There was certainly something to look at. Two immense purple spheres
were flying slowly above the men engaged in furious battle, heading toward
the city. These spheres were much larger than the one that Lafresa had thrown
at our ferry when we were crossing the Iselina. The first one touched the
wall and exploded with a tremendous rumbling blast that almost knocked

me off my feet. Flames, smoke, stones, and men were sent flying up to the heavens, and a breach about fifty yards across appeared in the wall. Then a little cloud of blue light appeared beside the second sphere and lashed out at the Nameless One's creation. The purple sphere went flying back in the direction it had come from and exploded when it crashed into a crowd of giants.

"Those magic-mongers can do it when they want to," the gnome chuckled in delight, rubbing his hands together.

"Bugler! It's time! Sound the attack!" the commander of the guards shouted. "I don't know who you are, gentlemen, but I wish you luck."

"One question, milord! Are there any boats on the seashore?"

"I don't know, elf!"

The hundred-strong unit of horsemen went tearing out of the wood and into battle to the sound of the bugle.

The wood—which wasn't really a wood, just a big copse—was quiet. We didn't run into any more surprises. But when we came out of the wood and were almost at the sea (I could already smell the salt in the air), we had the absolutely outrageous bad luck to run into two giants. Darkness only knew what these blue-skinned brutes were doing so far away from the battle, but when they saw us, they grabbed their clubs and started moving in our direction at a brisk trot.

"Get back!" Eel barked. "We can't handle them! Into the trees! Into the trees!"

I swear by Sagot that the lads who were running at us were a good eight yards tall. Their blue, hairy skin did nothing to render these wonders of nature any more charming. And a glance at their clubs was enough to dispel even the slightest desire to make these creatures' acquaintance. So our group promptly swung its horses round and went hurtling back to the wood. When I reached the trees, I looked back and saw that Kli-Kli wasn't trying to run. The gobliness's mare was fleeing in panic, but the girl was down on her knees almost under the very feet of the giants, drawing a picture in the snow. Ah, may the demons have me! What a time to take up drawing!

I swore and pulled hard on the bridle. The little green fool had to be saved! I rode my horse straight toward the gobliness, ignoring the warning shouts that rang out behind my back.

The giants had already reached Kli-Kli, and one of them raised his huge club above her head. Beside them, Glo-Glo's granddaughter looked especially small. I shouted for her to get out of there. Kli-Kli finished her picture, looked up, and pointed a finger at the giants.

Something that looked like a hammer made out of smoke appeared in the air and struck the monsters mighty blows in the chest. The blue-skinned giants were flung back more than a hundred yards, as if they weighed nothing at all. Whatever it was the gobliness had conjured up, it seemed to have knocked the life out of them.

"Have you completely lost your wits?" I yelled at her as I reined in my horse.

She gave me one of her most stupid smiles.

"There, that's the Hammer of Dust, not some silly little cheap trick!" she said in a trembling voice, and flopped over in a dead faint.

I cursed all the gods and got down off my horse.

Egrassa and company had already ridden up.

"What's wrong with him?"

"He's all right! It must be the effect of the spell."

Hallas jumped down off Lamplighter's horse and started briskly rubbing the gobliness's face with snow. She immediately came round and asked the gnome to save the sloppy stuff for some other time.

"Are you able to stay in the saddle?" Eel asked her.

"If you're willing to share your horse. Those giants frightened my nag, we'll never catch her now."

There was a bang and rumble on the other side of the wood. The magicians were up to their tricks again.

"It's not far to the sea. If we want to get into the city, we need to hurry."

The sea was very close. Like the Suburb, the fishing village had been burnt, in case the enemy tried to use the building materials to make siege engines. But there was a perfectly good fishing boat lying on the shore. The moment Hallas saw the sea and the waves, his face turned sour and he declared that this tub, which was the only thing any intelligent person could call it, would sink as soon as it put to sea.

But we never got closer than ten yards to the boat. Three figures in gray cloaks blocked our way. One was an orc, but the other two were men. They were all armed, and all wearing smoky gray crystals on silver chains round their necks. The Gray Ones had managed to turn up at just the wrong moment.

There was a rustling sound as Eel's "brother" and "sister" were drawn out of their scabbards. Egrassa gestured to the Garrakian to stop, and shook his head in warning. There was no way we could handle three Gray Ones, no matter how hard we tried. We looked at them. They looked at us. The leaden waves of the gray sea boomed beside us.

"Give us the Horn," said one of the men. "It doesn't belong to you."

"Or to you. It doesn't belong to anyone," Kli-Kli replied. "But we need it right now."

"If the artifact stays with you, the balance may be disrupted."

"What balance are we talking about here?" Eel asked furiously. "Have you seen what's happening over by the city?"

"We ask you one last time to give us the Horn."

"And what if we don't? What then, orc?" Egrassa said with a dark laugh, tightening his grip on the krasta.

"I also advise you to return our brother's crystal and weapon," the Gray One continued as imperturbably as ever.

And then it happened. There was a deafening boom and four men carrying the staffs of archmagicians of the Order appeared out of thin air. One of the Gray Ones was killed instantly. The other two leapt nimbly to one side. The orc threw himself at the nearest magician and the man who was still alive drew a pair of twin swords. The orc took the magician with him when he died.

Two of the magicians went to work on the surviving Gray One. He dashed at the nearest archmagician, waving his sword, but a staff barred his way. There was a brief flash, and the Gray One went flying back to the very edge of the sea. Egrassa fired with his bow and hit the man in the back as he was getting up off the gravel. As the Gray One turned to face this new danger, the archmagicians cast a magical net, burning with emerald green fire, over him. The spell cut him into ten separate pieces. I looked away.

"We were lucky they were soldiers, and not magicians," Kli-Kli muttered. "If the Gray Ones had known any magic, the magicians wouldn't have had it so easy."

One of the archmagicians, who was quite young and looked a bit like Valder, came running over to us.

"Did you get the Horn?"

"Yes, Your Magicship," Egrassa said, bowing.

"This is no time for etiquette, elf!" the magician snapped brusquely. "We received your message, and the entire Council is already assembled! Where is the artifact?"

I reached into my bag. We heard a series of explosions from the direction of the city.

"Another hour, and there will be nothing left to save. Quickly!"

The archmagician grabbed the Horn out of my hands. There was another boom, and the three magicians disappeared, without even bothering to take their dead comrade's body with them. Naturally, they didn't invite us along.

"And now what do we do?" Hallas asked acidly.

"Now?" said Egrassa, peering thoughtfully at the sea. "Now we wait."

We stayed there on the cold and windy seashore.

To wait.

The war against the Nameless One ended as suddenly as it had begun. The surviving members of the Council of the Order did the job right and pumped the Horn full of power right up to the brim. The sorcerer immediately lost all his ability to work magic, and without sorcery the Nameless One's army was just an army, but we had the Order on our side.

The giants sensed that their master had lost his power and fled in fear. The ogres who had come to Valiostr had been killed much earlier by the magicians' spell, so most of our enemies were men—barbarians, warriors of the northern tribes, the remains of the army of the Crayfish Dukedom, and a whole heap of other rabble. They still outnumbered our soldiers by a long way, but despite the breach in the wall, the bombardment of the city from catapults, and the terrible attacks by the sorcerer's shamans, who had not lost their powers, Avendoom stood firm.

The battle continued for another five days, quieting down and then flaring up again. On the second day the young king withdrew all his forces into the city, after deciding not to take the field for a general engagement. The gnomes took all the cannons out of the Bastion and put them on the city walls, and the defensive action began.

There were days when one section or another of the wall changed hands six or seven times. We were thrown back, we forced the attackers back outside the wall, then they came at us again. And it went on and on like that forever. We came close to losing everything when the Nameless One's supporters among the inhabitants of the city almost got their hands on the Rainbow Horn. But Artsivus was guarding the artifact like the apple of his eye, and the traitors were met with magic and stern steel. The supporters of the Nameless One who were stupid enough to surrender were quartered or hanged on the city wall as a lesson to the aggressors.

We suffered losses, but we stood firm. On one absolutely beautiful December day we heard the roar of battle horns, and the Second Army of the South arrived, together with the First Army of the West and the Third Assault Army, reinforced by the lads from Miranueh and volunteers from Isilia. Together they struck the unsuspecting enemy a mighty blow in the rear.

Stalkon gathered all his forces together and led them out from behind the walls, hitting the enemy smack between the eyes. Our opponents still had a numerical advantage but they faltered and ran. And the Nameless One didn't hang about for a little chat with the Order, either, he took off with his heels twinkling. The army drove the retreating enemy to the north and out past the Lonely Giant.

Everybody agreed about one thing: It would be a long time before the Nameless One recovered from a blow like this, and he wouldn't try to attack the kingdom again for another five or six hundred years at least. We would have to hope that if the sorcerer did get it into his head to come back and snap at Valiostr's heels again, the Order wouldn't waste any time getting the Rainbow Horn out of its old cobweb-covered trunk.

While the army was busy with the war in the north and polishing off everyone who still needed to be polished off, the capital gradually returned to normal. Every citizen walked around with a happy and contented look, as if he personally had stuffed the Rainbow Horn up that cursed sorcerer's backside.

Well, we had our victory, but life had to go on somehow. And the army had to be fed and maintained. Surprisingly enough, now when the people gave their hard-earned money to the king's tax collectors, they hardly even complained. Somehow everybody seemed to have grasped that it was better to have a strong, well-fed army than have the Nameless One on their back. I remember that For once uttered the memorable phrase: "A kingdom sometimes needs a war to buck its ideas up and dust it off." My old teacher, now living in distant Garrak, was probably right. War is a terrible thing, but afterward you see many things through different eyes.

People gradually came back to the city; they listened to the town criers in the squares telling everyone about the army's victories in the north, and the victories of the united forces of Valiostr, the Border Kingdom, and the dark elves over the orcs in the south; restored the houses that had been ruined in the war; and put their lives back together. Everything was gradually going back to the way it used to be.

But for our little group, everything went topsy-turvy. As soon as the magicians had dealt with their business (i.e., the Nameless One), they turned their attention to me. They detailed my old friend Roderick to stay with me, and he followed good old Harold around like a tail. But, to be quite serious, they stuck every member of our group in the royal palace for a month. I don't know what they did with the others, but I personally was questioned three times a day by one of the archmagicians. They were mostly interested in Hrad Spein. The archmagicians asked their questions, I gave them answers, and Roderick wrote it all down. And on and on like that forever. I was fortunate enough to see Artsivus twice.

The old man's health had deteriorated while I was on my journey. He had lost weight and his cough was even worse; he was always huddling under a warm rug and shivering. Roderick brought his teacher medicine all the time. I felt sorry for the Master of the Order, and a blind man could have seen what an effort those conversations cost him. The archmagician asked me questions, too, but they were far more ticklish than the others, and I had to prevaricate and lie a bit. I didn't want to tell the Order about the Master, the World of Chaos, and other stuff like that.

It seemed to me that I'd told the Order everything I could, but the magicians just kept on and on asking questions. I had to tell them everything a second time, then a third time, and even a fourth. They dragged everything out of me, every last little detail, and there was no end in sight.

I hardly ever saw my friends. Only Kli-Kli, who had taken the young king under her wing (that was what she told me) sometimes dropped in to see me and share the news. Hallas, Eel, and Lamplighter were with the Wild Hearts who had survived the Lonely Giant and the Field of Fairies. Sagot be praised, Honeycomb and Invincible had survived the battle of Avendoom and now they were also with their friends. For the time being the king was keeping the Wild Hearts near him.

As for Egrassa, he had unexpectedly become the head of the House of the Black Rose. Tresh Epilorssa had been killed in the battle of the Field of the Fairies, so the leafy crown had passed to Miralissa's cousin. And now Egrassa was with the dark elves who had come to fight for Valiostr but, according to Kli-Kli, he was going to return to Zagraba in a couple of weeks.

Eventually, after I'd told the magicians my story darkness only knows how many times, they gave up and said I could push off.

"Hot pies here! Get your hot pies here!"
"The valiant army of Valiostr!"

"Have you heard? Yesterday in the Port City they knocked off a carriage full of gold!"

"What would a carriage full of gold be doing in the Port City?"

"They say the ships from Isilia are going to come three times as often."

"Praise be to the king, if he hadn't—"

"Long live the king!"

"Is it true the dark elves have killed all the orcs and now they've gone to war with the dwarves?"

"You must be a real fool, brother, to go around spreading nonsense like that!"

"Hot pies here!"

Nothing changes in our world. It was only a month and a half since the end of the war, but the people were already enjoying their favorite pastime—gossiping.

Mid-January was incredibly cold and snowy, but that didn't bother the citizens at all, and the streets were full of people having a good time. They were celebrating the latest victory: The army had pushed the last of our enemies back beyond the Lonely Giant.

I had a meeting with our entire group planned for late that evening in one of the taverns of the Inner City. At last we would have a chance to get together again. But that was in the evening, and right now I had absolutely nothing to do. My little trip to distant parts had left me completely out of touch with what was going on in the city, and now I needed to catch up with things. And I had to look for a new lair, too.

When I checked to satisfy my curiosity, I found the Knife and Ax still standing in the same old place. Despite the battering it had taken during that famous fight the previous summer, the tavern looked as good as new. The holes made in the walls by the demon had been skillfully patched up, and the entire building looked as if Vukhdjaaz had never come within a hundred yards of it. Even the sign was still the same. I pushed the door of the establishment open and walked in.

I didn't know the thugs standing at the entrance, but they obviously knew me very well, and let me in without any questions, as good as saluted me, in fact. The large hall had been repaired and now it was as noisy and crowded as ever. All the tables and benches were occupied by the brotherhood of thieves and rogues of various shades and hues. Serving wenches scurried about between them, carrying food and beer.

Of course everyone pretended they didn't recognize me, although I saw surprise and even fright in some faces. I nodded to two or three of my acquaintances and headed straight for the bar.

Old Gozmo was there at his usual battle station. When the old rogue saw me, he almost had a stroke. The expression on his long face became even more miserable and the former thief turned white and crimson by turns. Finally he managed to mumble, "Harold?"

"Glad you haven't forgotten me, Gozmo."

"How the . . . Where did you come from?"

"Meaning?" It looked as if not everyone was very pleased to see me.

"Well," said Gozmo, confused, "they said you'd left Avendoom forever. Like For."

"Who said?"

"Everybody said so. I'm glad to see it's not true. . . ."

I believed that, of course.

"I see business is still the same as usual."

"No thanks to you," the innkeeper muttered. He seemed to have recovered from his surprise. "I believe you saw what Markun's lads and the Doralissians and that monster did to the place? Do you know how much money it cost me to fix everything? Aren't you afraid I might send you the bill?"

"No, I'm not," I said with a smile.

That smile made Gozmo hold his tongue.

"Surely you agree, Gozmo, that a bit of damage to the tavern is better than having your reputation ruined, Markun chasing you, or maybe even losing your life?"

"You're a plague, Harold."

"I do my best. Is my table free?"

"Uh-huh."

"Beer. Black."

I laughed as I set out for my table. To be quite honest, Gozmo had only got what he deserved that night. But I was still glad to know the sly old dog and his establishment were alive and well.

The beer was brought to me, and for the next few minutes I did nothing but enjoy it. Then suddenly someone sat down in the empty chair beside me. I looked up from my beer mug and glanced at the face of my uninvited guest. Small, with dark hair, bushy eyebrows that ran together above his nose and a stony face.

Oho! What an important personage had decided to honor me with his presence! Urgez, the head of the Guild of Hired Assassins in person!

"Beer?" I asked him.

"Thank you, some other time," he said.

I wondered what he wanted.

"The word was out that you were back in town—I decided to check."

"Rumors certainly spread fast." It was less than ten minutes since I appeared in the Knife and Ax, and the entire underworld of the city already knew about it.

"Yes, rumors, that's what I wanted to have a word with you about. If you have no objections, master thief?"

"None at all, master assassin." It's always best to be polite with people like Urgez.

"There was a rumor going round that a certain hired assassin was trying to get your head. They also say that the shrine of Sagot was attacked. A few brave young fellows tried to get to old man For. I want to tell you that those men have nothing at all to do with the guild. My lads have no reason to get on the wrong side of the thieves, and certainly not the servants of Sagra."

"I know they weren't your lads."

"Well, that's just grand. I also want to say, from myself, that the guild has a couple of questions to ask this vagrant. They say he made use of my name, and I don't like that. So we're looking for him."

"Don't bother. He won't cause you any more trouble."

"All the better." The head of the guild was not surprised in the slightest. "Keep well, Harold."

"And you, Urgez."

The head of the assassins had done what he came for, and he left. To be honest, I was glad that Urgez's lads had nothing to do with the attempts on my life that had almost dispatched me to the light last summer. Fighting with Urgez was bad for the health.

"Mind if I take a seat?"

It looked like this was my day for unexpected visitors. This time it was Sheloz standing beside the table. With six beefy young bodyguards hovering behind him.

"Please, sit down."

Sheloz sat down, the bodyguards remained standing.

"The word was out that you were back in town—I decided to check."

Were they in this together, or what? For those who don't know, Sheloz was the lad who was fighting Markun for the right to run the Guild of Thieves.

"I'm back."

"I've always respected you, Harold. . . ."

"Likewise."

Sheloz was a pretty decent man and thief. I thought the guild would be a lot better off under his management than with Markun.

"I know you've had difficulties with the guild in the past, but then, haven't we all? That fat swine Markun just stole all the money for himself. But everything's different now. So I want to tell you that if you should feel the desire to return to the bosom of the old hearth and home, we'll be glad to see you. Naturally, we'll take you without any membership fees or levies on your Commissions."

"An honorary member?" I laughed.

"Why not? Respected masters of the trade shouldn't have to pay to work. It's enough for them to be members of the guild and make its reputation."

"Why so generous all of a sudden, Sheloz?"

"Well . . ." He hesitated. "To lay my cards on the table, Harold, I'm personally obliged to you for getting rid of Markun. And so are lots of the lads, believe me. With that fat leech gone, everything's taken a turn for the better. Consider it a little token of my gratitude. I don't like being in anyone's debt. So you think about coming back."

"All right. I'll think about it."

"Excellent. See you around, master thief."

"See you around."

It was dark and there weren't so many people around now. It had started snowing. There was no wind and the snowflakes glided smoothly down onto the pavement in absolute silence. Ah, darkness! I must have sat in Gozmo's establishment a bit longer than I meant to. I had to hurry.

I set off through the side streets to take a shortcut. Although, in a rather large percentage of cases, strolling through the alleys of the Port City could lead to the loss of your purse, or even your life, if you were inexperienced. So as I threaded my way through the dark and empty spaces, I kept my wits about me and one hand on my crossbow. There's always some greedy idiot desperate to get his hands on other people's money.

But Sagot was good and I didn't meet anyone on the way. Although at one point I had the great pleasure of running into a unit of guards. The lads watched me go by with extremely uncharitable expressions on their faces, but they didn't ask any questions this time. I turned into Stinking Bedbug

Street, came out onto the Street of the Apples, cut across Little Sour Street, turned into a dark archway, and . . .

And then someone very deft took a very strong grip on my shoulders from behind. I gave a jerk and reached for my weapon, and the stranger immediately blocked my movement with one hand and squeezed my neck so tight with the other that I could hardly even breathe, let alone struggle. The lad behind me was monstrously strong.

"Your weapon probably wouldn't be any use to you, Harold," a mocking voice said, and I shuddered and stopped trying to resist.

The Messenger! May the darkness devour him!

"Mmmm? I see you've recognized me, thief. Well, that's all to the good. I'll let you go now, but don't think of doing anything stupid. You're an intelligent man, aren't you?"

I didn't answer.

"All right then," the Master's chief servant chuckled. "I see you got the Horn."

"Believe it or not," I said, desperately trying to figure out what he could want from me. "You and your lord didn't think I could manage it, did you?"

Another quiet chuckle.

"Don't flatter yourself, Harold. Do you think the Master doesn't know which way the Game is going to go? You only had the Horn because he wanted it that way."

The powerful brute released his grip and I took a step away from him and turned round. He was standing in the shade again, and all I could see was a dark shadow and two golden eyes.

"Why did you come here?"

"Aren't you glad to see me?"

I didn't answer.

"All right, Harold," the Messenger sighed, and his eyes glinted. "Time to pay your dues."

"What dues?"

"Surely you haven't forgotten our agreement?"

"I remember our agreement, Djok," I said, calling the Messenger by his real name without thinking.

"That's good." He didn't seem to have noticed my slip of the tongue. "The Master wants you to carry out his Commission."

I sighed. I really didn't want to do anything for any master, but a deal is a deal. And it wasn't that easy to get away from the Messenger; he could turn up anywhere at any time. As bad luck would have it, there was no one else in the alley but us.

"What are the conditions of the Commission?"

"Oh, it's all very simple, thief. Before midnight today you have to steal the Rainbow Horn from the Tower of the Order."

"What? Your lord has to be joking! I won't do it!"

"Why not?"

"Why not? It's impossible. Not only does he want me to break into the Tower of the Order, he wants me to steal the Rainbow Horn! There's a magician every yard in there!"

"Now you listen to me, Harold. You're going to get that artifact. And get it today, before midnight. And not just because you accepted a deal. You'll *want* to help us as soon as possible when I tell you what's happened."

"And what has happened?" As far as I was concerned, the moon could fall from the sky, and I still wouldn't go and get that Horn of my own free will.

"The Player has betrayed the Master."

"I don't get the connection."

"The Player has betrayed my Master and now he serves another. It's a great night tonight, Harold. You can't even imagine just how great. This round of the Game is being decided. If the Player follows the instructions of our opponent, the balance will collapse and a certain someone will escape from the Palaces of Bone. If that happens, Siala will go back to the start of the Dark Era. My Master really doesn't want to have to create everything all over again. The Rainbow Horn is the thing that can disrupt the balance."

"All right, all right. Start from the beginning. What have the Horn and this Player got to do with everything?"

"If the Player uses the Horn, then the Game will be lost."

"Then don't let him get hold of the Horn."

"He already has."

"Oh!" I said, trying to think. "Then kill the Player."

"Because he is the Player, the Masters have no right to kill him."

"I thought I heard you say the Master knew how the Game would go? Surely he could have foreseen that the Horn would fall into the wrong hands? Stop. Just who is the Player?"

"Good thinking, Harold. Good thinking. The Master figured everything out, but everybody makes mistakes, especially when they have to rely on people. People are weak, and the Player has proved to be no exception to the rule. The Master knew that the Horn would end up with the Player, but he didn't expect the old fox to go running off to another den. I'm talking about Artsivus."

"No. It can't be!"

"Why not? The Master knew you would definitely give the Rainbow Horn to the Order, which means to Artsivus."

"But why him?" I could believe anything at all, but not that the fine old man Artsivus was the influential figure who wanted to kill me. . . .

"Why are you so surprised? The Player has to be a magician. The Master offered him knowledge and power for his services."

"And what did the other Master offer him?"

"Youth and immortality."

"Then it all makes sense."

And the Messenger started telling me things. It was Artsivus who had suggested I should go on the expedition to get the Horn. He thought I wouldn't manage it, and the artifact would stay in Hrad Spein.

Then, when the stars told a different story, he decided to kill me. Only at this point the Master intervened and personally forbade the magician to touch me. But then Artsivus found Paleface—it was the archmagician's ring that the two master thieves showed at the Royal Library, and that was why they killed poor old Bolt.

It was Artsivus's people who stole the Shadow Horse. The archmagician needed the magical object that could control the demons for his own purposes (by this time he had already been recruited by a Master from another world), and he didn't want to share it with the Order. But then the ubiquitous Harold put in an appearance, and old Artsivus had to save the Shadow Horse in order not to arouse the suspicions of the Dancer of Siala.

When I went for a ride in the carriage of the Master of the Order after that free-for-all over the Shadow Horse, my life was hanging by a thread. Old Artsivus had no intention of taking me to the king, he was listening to my story to see if I'd guessed that the Master of the Order was mixed up in the shady business with maps of Hrad Spein and the Shadow Horse, and taking me for delivery into the caring hands of a gang of killers. What saved me was that I said I didn't have the papers with me. Artsivus let me go and set the killers on For, quite reasonably assuming that he might have the papers.

"I could go on, thief, but time is short. You have to steal the Horn."

"Even so, there are too many things in your story that don't fit," I said. "The Horn has already been in Artsivus's hands for more than a month. Why does it have to be tonight? He could have done everything as soon as he got it. While the city was under attack, when everybody was busy with other things and no one would have bothered him?"

"Yes, he could have used the Horn at the very beginning, but he wouldn't have got the result that his new Master is expecting. It is only tonight that the Shadow Horse and the Rainbow Horn can be combined together."

"I bet that your Master has known the Player was a traitor for ages. And he definitely foresaw what was going to happen tonight. Right?"

"That could be so."

"Then, in the name of Sagot, why couldn't I have stolen the artifact sooner? Why today? Why didn't you tell me about this a week ago? A month ago?"

I thought I heard him chuckle.

"Then there wouldn't have been any risk. No edge to the Game. No interest. You are the Master's trump card. He wanted to see how well you could deal with things at the very last moment."

The world was teetering on the edge of a precipice, and the Master was still playing his silly little games!

"Then why did Artsivus let me go? Take the leash off?"

"Don't flatter yourself, Harold. Yes, he knows you're a Dancer in the Shadows, but he doesn't know a thing about your deal with the Master, and he thinks you have no idea who he is. So will you get the Horn?"

"I don't really have much choice, do I?" I said with a bitter laugh.

"I'm afraid not. Either the Rainbow Horn has to be removed from the hands of the Player or . . . you simply have no idea what that magical item is capable of if it's combined with something like the Shadow Horse! The scales of the balance will collapse, the Houses of Siala will fall, and there won't be much left of your . . . that is, our world. The Game will be lost. You don't want that to happen, do you?"

"I'm not interested in your Game. But I will try to get the Horn. What's the deposit on the deal?"

"Your life. How does that suit you?"

"Just fine. And the payment?"

"Get the Horn, and you'll never see me again."

Well, nothing could have suited me better than that arrangement.

"I request Shadow Harold to accept my Commission."

"I accept the Commission."

"I have heard you, thief. Now, in conclusion, let me advise you to get it done before midnight. At midnight the Player will commence the ritual, and then you probably won't be able to steal the artifact from right under his nose."

"I doubt that I'll even be able to get into the Tower of the Order. I can hardly expect the magicians not to ask any questions when they notice me."

"None of the magicians are in the Tower. Artsivus has sent them all away."

"That doesn't change things much. I still have to get in."

"I can't help you there. I cannot enter the Tower of the Order."

"Listen, what's the point in him doing all this? Doesn't the Master of the Order realize that after he does this, it will be the end of everything?"

"Why wouldn't he understand? Of course he does. But there are many worlds, he'll have somewhere to go."

"If the Game ends, what then?"

"What then? Oh, the winner gets a prize and Game starts all over again."

"A prize? What prize?"

"You've been in the World of Chaos and the shadows, haven't you?"

"Yes."

"Whoever wins the Game will be rewarded with one of the shadows from the Primordial World. Just imagine—with that he can create an entirely new, ideal world. And put right the mistakes committed in other universes. Victory brings the chance to create perfection and enter it in the next Game."

As he said that, the Messenger finally stepped out of the shade into the moonlight. I started. He hadn't really changed much since the time of my waking dream. That is, if you disregarded the fact that now the lad was as black as tar, had a pair of wings behind his back, and his eyes were golden; to look at he was still Djok Imargo.

May the darkness take all these Masters and their idiotic Games! Worlds are no more than playing cards to them. They play, and I suffer the consequences!

"What do I do once I get the Horn?" I asked with a sigh.

"Just get it. By doing that you will disrupt the ritual, and this round of the Game will end. The Player will become vulnerable, the Master will kill him, the Horn will stay with the Order, and everything will be over."

And so saying, he flapped his wings and was gone, as if he had never been there.

———

It was more than an hour since the Messenger and I had parted. I had absolutely no idea of how to get into the Order's citadel. And I didn't know the layout of the tower. It wasn't all that big to look at, but, remembering the abandoned tower in the Forbidden Territory, I knew I could expect absolutely anything. Tricks with space and dimensions, for instance. It could easily be much bigger on the inside than from the outside.

And then—just my luck—the gods made me remember that Kli-Kli once boasted to me about how she'd been in the new Tower of the Order and she could find any room in it with her eyes closed. She was lying! I would have sworn by the eyes of the Messenger that she was lying! But right now I didn't have any other option.

I managed to grab the gobliness just as she was walking into the tavern where we were all supposed to meet. I had to take her to one side and ask her a few questions. Of course, she immediately smelled a rat and dug her claws into me, so I couldn't help telling her everything. When she learned about Artsivus, she just nodded, and when she heard what the Master wanted, she decided she had to go along with me.

I tried to change her mind. I tried to reason. I argued, I threatened. I appealed to her conscience, asked her to listen to reason—but none of it did any good. Kli-Kli declared that if she wasn't going with me, then I'd have to find my own way out of this tricky situation. What finally finished me was the claim that she knew how to get into the tower without attracting any attention. So I agreed. And really, if she wasn't concerned about my head, why should I be worried about her? We didn't bother our friends, just left them in ignorance in the tavern. There wasn't any point in risking their lives in this undertaking, and swords weren't likely to be much help anyway.

The square where the Order's massive pale blue building stood was completely deserted and covered in snow. I shivered at the memory of the dream in which I had spoken to the Gray One.

A prophetic dream. The balance really could be destroyed. By the light of the moon and the magical lanterns, the tower seemed to be carved out of blocks of ice. The only lights inside were up on the top floor.

"Well then, how do we get in without attracting any attention?" I asked the gobliness.

"I'll show you."

She strolled up to the door covered with its fancy design of whirls and volutes and stopped.

"Like that."

"Just what am I supposed to make of that?" I hissed sarcastically.

"You asked me to show you the way into the tower, and I showed you," Kli-Kli told me without batting an eyelid.

"Kli-Kli," I said, trying to control myself. "You're trying to be funny, aren't you?"

"No, I'm not being funny at all. The only way into the Tower of the Order is through that door, or did you think the magicians wouldn't bother to close off all the other entrances?"

I should have realized sooner! I'd been taken for a ride!

"Have you ever really been inside?"

"Yes. With the king. Only for some reason they wouldn't let me go any farther than the first floor."

"Then what good are you to me?"

"I can help save your neck. And I can work a bit of magic, too."

"Kli-Kli! Don't pretend to be more stupid than you really are! You know perfectly well you're no match for a magician of the Order."

"Listen, Harold, here we are hanging about like two fools outside the door into the Order's holy of holies. Get those lock picks to work before anyone notices us."

"I'm afraid the magicians didn't bother to put a lock on the door. There's probably something else instead."

"Then check it out! Are you a thief or not?"

She was right—hanging about in open view really was stupid. I could have a word with the gobliness later (if there was any later).

I reached out my hand to the metal ring of the door and pulled it cautiously toward me. The door didn't budge. I pulled harder. The same result.

"Open," Valder whispered, and the door of the tower suddenly yielded.

"Oho!" Kli-Kli gasped in delight. "How did you do that?"

"Just lucky," I muttered, thanking fate yet again for bringing me together with the dead archmagician. "Wait for me on the edge of the square. If I'm not back out in an hour, go to the king."

"Uh-huh," the gobliness said, and darted in through the door. "You don't think I'm going to leave all the honor and the glory to you, do you?"

"Kli-Kli . . ."

"Drop that tone of voice. I'm going with you."

"What if I tie you up?"

"I'm warning you! I'll bite!"

"All right! But just don't go getting under my feet!"

"When did I ever get under your feet?" she asked, and then bit her tongue.

We were in the brightly lit entrance hall on the first floor of the tower. On the far side of it there were three corridors and a stairway.

"Don't make any noise," I warned my companion, just to be on the safe side.

"The tower's a lot bigger than it looks," said Kli-Kli.

"I know," I answered, and called: "Valder?"

"Yes?"

"Do you know which way we should go?"

"I've never been here before, but they build all these towers to the same design. I think you should go up the stairs."

"And then?"

"If the Master of the Order intends to perform a ritual, then it will take place in the Council Hall. The magical mirror will intensify his spells."

"I understand."

"You know, this business with the Horn reminds me of something. I see Zemmel isn't the only one who has ever tried to play the Game of the great ones. Be careful." And then there was silence.

"How long are you going to stand there just staring into space?" Kli-Kli inquired. Naturally, she couldn't hear my conversation with the archmagician.

"We should go that way."

The stairway of dark purple marble wound its way up the tower. At first we moved cautiously, in case there was someone else here as well as Artsivus, but after the third floor we started walking more confidently.

"How long now to midnight?"

"Still more than an hour," she panted. "We're in good time. The important thing is not to run into Artsivus."

The fifth floor. The sixth. On the seventh I cast a quick glance into a brightly lit corridor and saw someone sitting slumped against the wall in the distance. My blood ran cold for a moment because I thought it was Artsivus. But no, Sagot spared us. And the way the man was sitting there was kind of strange, too.

"Kli-Kli," I said to the gobliness, who was already creeping on up the stairs.

"Yes?"

Without saying anything, I indicated the man in the corridor with my eyes.

"We have to check!"

"Have you got nothing better to do?"

"We have to check, Dancer. We can't leave any strangers in our rear."

"All right, but be careful," I said, taking out my crossbow.

As we walked along the corridor the man didn't move. Then I saw who it was and went dashing to him.

Someone had split Roderick's head open. The floor and the wall he was slumped against were covered in blood.

"Ah, darkness!" I cursed. "Who did this to him?"

"You know who. Don't make a fuss, Harold. The lad's dead. He must have guessed something and his old teacher decided to get rid of him."

"He saved my life once. I feel sorry for the lad."

"We'll all be in need of pity soon, if we don't get a move on. Come on, Harold. We can't do anything to help him now. Listen, what's that door doing open, eh?"

It was only then I realized that the door closest to us was slightly ajar. Kli-Kli immediately stuck her curious nose through it.

"Ooh! Just look what's in here, Harold!"

I looked in. The vast hall was crammed full of boxes and all sorts of weird things. I supposed it was probably a storeroom for magical doodads.

"The artifacts depository!" Kli-Kli had had the same idea as me. "Maybe the Horn's still here?"

"Let's check then," I agreed. "But quickly!"

The storeroom was full of absolutely everything, from shelves with spell scrolls on them to mysterious and incomprehensible objects that glowed. The only things missing were the Rainbow Horn and the Shadow Horse.

"Looks like we're wasting our time wandering around in here," said Kli-Kli, giving up even before I did.

"Looks like it," I sighed, gazing at a set of shelves stacked with various shining globes and spheres.

One of them caught my eye. It was gray, and I could make out a familiar silhouette inside. I took a step toward the shelves, and the tower immediately trembled slightly.

"What's that?" Kli-Kli asked, gazing around in fright.

"I don't know," I said, puzzled.

"It's begun," Valder told me. "The ritual has begun!"

"How can it have begun!" I yelled out loud. "It's not midnight yet!"

"Harold, what are you talking about?" Kli-Kli asked in amazement.

"Bad news, Kli-Kli. Artsivus is impatient!"

"So what do we do?"

Before I could answer, Valder spoke again.

"The goblin girl should leave!"

"What?"

"She should leave, Harold. She's too powerful as a shaman, and I'm already weak. When she's here, it's hard for me to do anything at all. And today I'll need all my strength."

"Harold, what's wrong with you?"

"Let me speak to her myself."

I relaxed, leaving Valder free to do whatever he wanted.

"What on earth's happen— Oh!"

She gaped at me with amazement in her eyes, obviously listening to what Valder was saying. I couldn't hear what he told her, but Kli-Kli nodded rapidly.

"Hang in there, Dancer!" the gobliness said to me at the end. "I'll bring help."

She rushed off and the tower trembled again.

"Why did she do that?"

"It's for the best. You and I have to stop the Master of the Order."

"And how do we do that?"

"I don't know yet. Take it."

"What?"

"That sphere. It will be useful."

"What if he breaks out?"

"That will distract the Player for a while."

I grabbed the sphere with the demon inside. It was cold. Well now, perhaps the Messenger was right when he said demons had a part to play in this story.

"Leave the crossbow. And the bag, too. We won't need all that," said Valder. "Good. And now forward, my friend!"

I darted out into the corridor, clutching the sphere in my hands, and ran toward the stairs.

"How do we set him free?" I asked Valder as I ran.

"It's a magical prison. I sense that the power swirling about up there is so great, we only have to take the sphere close, and it will fall to pieces! Trust me."

I did trust him. There was nothing else I could do.

The tower was trembling continually now. Fine tremors shook the stairs and the walls, and I was beginning to feel afraid that—Sagot forbid—the whole building might collapse.

The door into the Council Chamber was standing wide open, so it only took me a moment to understand what was going on. I think I was watching everything through Valder's eyes.

The mirror floor reflected constellations never seen in Siala, and there were flaming purple auroras in its depths. The Rainbow Horn and the Shadow Horse were lying five yards apart.

The Horn was already surrounded by a glow that constantly changed color. Every now and then a shower of purple sparks came flying out of the Horse, soared up toward the transparent ceiling, and faded away in the air. Thick tentacles of Power were reaching out toward the artifacts and there was a black cloud expanding inexorably between the two magical objects. Artsivus was standing absolutely still, with his hands raised toward the ceiling. The puny archmagician had his back to us, and I immediately regretted that I'd left the crossbow downstairs.

"Don't worry about that," Valder told me. "Ordinary weapons are absolutely useless now."

"And now what do we do?"

"Wait. It's not time yet."

Artsivus chanted his spells in a harsh-sounding language, and from time to time the tower shuddered. The purple flame in the mirror blazed brighter and brighter. The black cloud directly in front of the Player was already the size of a decent carriage. But it was only black round the edge; its center was transparent. And through it I could see a strange world, a completely different world.

The world of a different Master.

It looked as if Artsivus was opening up a passage for his new lord. The Rainbow Horn was shining with a brilliance that was too painful to look at, and the sparks were streaming up toward the glass dome from the Shadow Horse.

Surely the archmagicians and ordinary magicians of the capital ought to sense what was going on?

The archmagician's chanting soared even higher and I felt the Scales of the Balance tremble. Just a little longer, and Artsivus's magic would annihilate everything for tens of leagues around, not to mention the fact that the Scales of the Balance would be overturned completely.

Ah darkness! That was Valder thinking for me again!

"It's time," the dead archmagician suddenly said. "Throw it!"

I flung the gray sphere as hard as I could. It flew almost the entire length of the hall and landed behind Artsivus. The Master of the Order was too busy with his spell to notice anything.

The sphere burst without a sound and disappeared.

"Forward! Grab the Horn!" Valder ordered. "Free me!"

I hesitated before running into the hall, and the archmagician immediately took control of my body. I dashed toward the brightly glowing artifact, hoping that Artsivus wouldn't see me too soon! He mustn't see me!

Meanwhile a new character had joined the scene in the hall—a hefty demon. There was no way the Master of the Order could fail to see this lad. Artsivus broke off his incantation in mid-word, and one of his palms started glowing with a turquoise blue light.

"Vukhdjaaz is clever," the gray demon announced, and made a dash for the magician.

The turquoise flame went darting from the magician's palm and struck Vukhdjaaz in the chest.

Nothing happened. Battle magic doesn't work on demons.

Artsivus shouted out a few hasty words. The Shadow Horse flared up and the monstrous demon howled as it was flung aside. When it came to battling the denizens of the darkness, the Doralissians' artifact was obviously much more effective than any hocus-pocus.

Vukhdjaaz cursed and reached his clawed hand out toward the Shadow Horse, clearly intending to grab the bauble that he desired so badly. My sheep-headed friend must have forgotten that a demon could only take the Shadow Horse if a human being or a Doralissian put it in his hands of their own free will. The Shadow Horse spat sparks at the impertinent demon and Vukhdjaaz howled like a thousand sinners and staggered back, shaking his burnt hand, which was charred black in places.

All of the above took no longer than three seconds, just long enough for me to cover most of the distance to the Horn. I think Artsivus had noticed me, but he didn't allow himself to be distracted, and he pointed one finger at Vukhdjaaz and started reciting a spell.

The demon didn't seem at all keen on the idea. He cursed again, dodged to one side, smashed his head through the glass of one of the tall pointed windows, and left in a hurry.

Artsivus turned all his attention to me. The Rainbow Horn was close enough now for me to reach out and touch it. So I reached out.

The glow scorched my skin even through my gloves, and when I touched the Horn I felt like I'd been struck by lightning.

"I'm free!" Valder gasped.

Artsivus babbled something, and I was tossed away. I tried to get up, but I was too dizzy, and I had to lie there on the floor and watch as the entirely real Valder fought a duel of magic with the Player.

My friend showered down magical blows on the Master of the Order, giving Artsivus no time to wonder how this stranger who was so skilled in the art of magic could have appeared in the Council Chamber.

The Player struck, Valder parried, and then the old magician had to defend himself. The tower shuddered and I spat out the blood in my mouth, thinking that this was the end. It was going to collapse.

But the duel continued. Valder just barely managed to fend off a crimson sphere, sending it soaring up toward the ceiling, and the glass dome of the Tower of the Order burst with a deafening crash. Myriads of sharp fragments came showering down on us. Both magicians immediately protected themselves against the deadly rain with glowing canopies. And Valder had to protect me, too.

The duel was renewed and the magicians whirled round the Council Chamber, exchanging magical blows. Every one of them set the tower shaking like an earthquake. The very air seemed to be wailing with magic, but neither opponent could get the upper hand.

With an immense effort, I got up on my hands and knees and started gently creeping toward the Rainbow Horn. I wondered what it was that Artsivus had hit me with, and how I'd managed to survive. They didn't seem to be taking any notice of me. I spat blood yet again and starting crawling a bit faster.

At that moment Valder shouted out some phrase and pushed Artsivus away from him as hard as he could. The old magician staggered backward, his back touched the black cloud, and he disappeared with a scream.

"Close the portal, Harold!" Valder yelled. "Take the Horn and close the portal! Close it before it's too late!"

He flung himself after Artsivus.

I kept crawling.

The tower was shuddering. The Scales of the Balance were swaying. The world held its breath in anticipation.

I kept crawling.

The tower was shaking violently now. I even thought the magical mirror had cracked. The Horn was very close.

This time the effect of the rainbow radiance was pain. I screamed out loud and tears spurted from my eyes, but I grabbed hold of the artifact and flung it as far away as I could. The Rainbow Horn flew beyond the edge of the magical mirror and its glow instantly disappeared. The portal snapped shut with a deafening crash.

There was a rumble and a flash. Cold flooded through my entire body. I opened my mouth in a silent scream and the night swallowed me up.

Epilogue

ittle Bee recognized me and snorted happily, reaching her muzzle forward for a treat. I gave her the apple I had ready and patted her on the neck. I was glad to see her, too. It turned out that when Honeycomb left Cuckoo to come to Avendoom, he had taken my horse, and there was no way I could thank the Wild Heart enough. The groom had already saddled Little Bee and all I had to do was put the saddlebags on and set off.

After what happened in the Tower of the Order, I'd been confined to bed until the middle of spring. I didn't know what it was that saved me on that terrible night, Valder's power or good luck, but the magicians who came dashing to the "fire" were rather surprised to find a man lying beside the ruined tower, clutching the Rainbow Horn in his hands.

I was surrounded with care and attention all the time I lay unconscious. And then when I came round in early spring, the magicians who were there beside the bed asked me what had happened and how I was feeling. In that order.

Sagot be praised, Kli-Kli had told the members of the Order almost everything she knew, and they didn't pester me too much. The magicians were too busy trying to restore the reputation of the Order and restore the tower to waste time on interrogating a thief. So they almost believed my suggestion that the magical explosion happened because Artsivus made a mistake in one of his spells. As for the Horn, I really had no idea how I happened to be holding it in my hands. I definitely remembered throwing it away before I blacked out.

So they left me alone. For the time being, at least.

Lying in bed was incredibly boring. And I wasn't exactly spoiled for visitors. At first Kli-Kli never left my bedside, but then she almost completely stopped coming to see me, because of some commotion at court. And when she did come, she just dropped in for a minute and went away again, without even telling me all the news.

"So you've definitely decided?"

I swung round. Kli-Kli had somehow appeared in the stable, and she was leaning against the wall, nibbling on a carrot. Invincible was ensconced on her shoulder.

"Yeah," I said, embarrassed. "It's time. I can't put it off any longer."

"So you were going to clear out of town without even saying good-bye?" she asked with a frown.

"I did try to find you."

It was true. I had tried, but they wouldn't let me into the palace, and I hadn't been able to get any news to the gobliness for a week. It was as if she'd vanished into thin air.

"I know," she sighed. "I'm sorry, I was snowed under. We have a new king, have you heard?"

"The whole city's talking about it," I laughed.

Stalkon Deprived of the Crown had suddenly recovered his reason, and since he was the elder son of Stalkon the Ninth, he had more right to the throne than Stalkon of the Spring Jasmine.

"What does Spring Jasmine think about it all?"

"He's never clung to power. He'd have been quite glad to let his elder brother have the crown. But his brother refused to take it. The elder son has been completely out of touch with the state of the kingdom for far too long in order to take power. You know, I think Artsivus was to blame for the prince losing his wits."

"The same idea occurred to me, Kli-Kli. The question is: Why did the Master of the Order do it?"

"Who can understand the Player? But I think that somehow or other, the prince found out that Artsivus wasn't really such a benign old gentleman after all. So the magician had to . . . He didn't dare kill a prince of the royal blood, so he turned him into an idiot. And when Artsivus died, the spell was broken."

We said nothing for a while. I checked the bags, Kli-Kli gnawed on her carrot. Invincible twitched his little pink nose.

"I see you've made friends with the ling."

"Uh-huh. Honeycomb decided the mouse would be better off dining at the king's table. I don't have anything against the little beast."

"Are you going to stay in Avendoom for long?"

"I don't know. For as long as I'm needed. In any case, I'll stay until everything settles down. Then I'll go back home. I have to help my grandfather."

"With his shamanism?" I chuckled.

"Yes, with his shamanism," she chuckled in reply. "Maybe you shouldn't go away?"

"Yes, I should," I sighed. "There's nothing to keep me in Avendoom. I've already put all my affairs in order, and the magicians . . . I should leave before they remember about me and the Rainbow Horn. The Master won this round of the Game, in spite of everything."

"There'll be more rounds to come. If the magicians lose the Horn, Valiostr's in for trouble in three hundred years' time."

"I shan't live that long. They can find some other fool to get the Horn for them," I laughed.

"You will live that long," she said, giving me a serious look. "You're a Dancer."

"And how are all our friends?"

To my great regret, I hadn't managed to see any of them.

"Egrassa's in Zagraba. He's the head of the house now. I think our elf friend's really got his hands full—the orcs gave the dark ones a really bad mauling. There's talk of uniting all the dark houses. Egrassa could be top elf in the Black Forest before you know it!" She grunted delightedly. "The Wild Hearts have gone back to the Lonely Giant. They told me to say good-bye, they couldn't just hang about here any longer. Before he left, Hallas palmed the h'san'kor horns off on the Order for a mountain of gold pieces. He bought an entire trade caravan of wine and a heap of other stuff, just like he was going to do with Deler. They're already restoring the Lonely Giant, have you heard?"

"Yes. It's a pity I didn't get to say good-bye to them," I said sadly.

"It is. By the way, Eel asked me to give you this," she said, holding out a long bundle.

"What is it?"

"How should I know? You don't think I'd go rummaging in other people's things, do you?"

I politely ignored that and unwrapped the bundle. Just as I thought—it was Eel's "brother" and "sister."

"The Garrakian told me you knew what to do with these."

"I do. How will he manage without them?"

"The king gave them all new weapons. Much more beautiful than the old ones."

I wrapped the two blades in the cloth and set them beside the saddlebags.

"If you see Eel, tell him I'll do everything he asked."

"All right. Listen, about the Commission . . ."

"Yes?"

"You realize they're not going to pay you fifty thousand gold pieces? The Commission was annulled."

"Don't worry, Kli-Kli, I understand."

"But when the king found out what happened, he decided that wasn't very fair."

"And?"

"Well, here's a royal pardon for you," she said, handing me a charter rolled up into a tube. "The king pardons all your wrongdoings. Frago Lanten will be absolutely raging. And here's some money for you. As much as they could manage . . ."

"And how much could they manage?" I asked, taking the heavy bag from the gobliness.

"You understand, after the war the treasury's completely empty," Kli-Kli began cautiously.

"Listen, just tell me, will you?"

"A hundred fifty gold pieces. It will be enough for a start."

"Well, now," I said with a nod. "That's not bad at all."

As I put the money away, I thought about the other two hundred gold pieces I'd taken from For's secret hiding place. My old teacher had left the nest egg for me specially. So now I had quite a tidy sum.

"And there's something else. Egrassa asked me to give you this."

Kli-Kli laid a string of smoky yellow topazes in my hand. The same ones that Miralissa had worn at Balistan Pargaid's reception. I breathed in sharply. These stones were valuable. Very valuable. But they had belonged to Miralissa . . . and that made them more valuable than any amount of gold.

"I'm afraid I'll never bring myself to sell them, Kli-Kli."

"I know," she said with a smile. "I think Egrassa knew, too. And by the way, he said the doors of the House of the Black Moon will always be open to you."

"It's not likely I'll ever be in Zagraba again. But thanks for the offer."

We stopped talking. We both realized it was time for me to leave.

"Where will you go now?"

"First to Isilia, then by ship to Garrak. I'll visit For—he's in Hozg now—and I have to deal with Eel's business. And after that . . . We'll see. Maybe to the Lowlands."

She gave a little nod.

"Is it time?"

"Yes."

"Lean down."

"What?"

"Lean down, you blockhead!"

I obediently leaned down and she kissed me on the cheek.

"You can go now."

I climbed into the saddle.

"Be seeing you, Kli-Kli."

"No," she said, shaking her head sadly. "We'll probably never meet again; I think you understand that as well as I do."

"Well, maybe sometime," I said awkwardly.

"'Sometime' and 'never' are very similar. The world's too big for us to meet, and some day you'll go to join the shadows. I know that. So good-bye forever, Dancer in the Shadows."

"Good-bye," I sighed. "I'm going to miss you."

"Likewise." She cleared her throat. "Only when you go, don't look back until you reach the city gates. That's a bad sign for goblins."

I nodded, looked at her one last time, and touched my heels to Little Bee's sides. I kept my word and didn't look back once. Although I wanted to very badly.

Although it was early morning, the Chicken Gates leading out of the city to the west were standing wide open. The guards were playing dice, and they took no notice of the solitary traveler leaving Avendoom at such an early hour. But then, our glorious servants of the law weren't taking any notice of the beggar who was sitting right beside the gates with his clay cup for alms.

The vagrant was wearing dirty boots and a hooded cloak that had seen better days. He was sitting on the ground with his legs crossed, and when he spotted me, he held out the empty cup. I stopped Little Bee, reached into my purse, and tossed him a full gold piece. The beggar took the money and gave me a dignified nod. I nodded back to him and rode on.

When I'd ridden a quarter of a league from Avendoom, I threw the charter with the royal pardon into the ditch at the side of the road. I'd lived all this time without it and I could manage without it for the same number of years. I looked back. The walls of Avendoom were shrouded in light morning mist. I took a deep breath of the cool air.

Sagot take me, but that felt good! It was spring, after all.

"Forward, Little Bee," I said, and didn't look back again.

Glossary

Annals of the Crown - the most ancient and detailed of the historical chronicles, maintained by the elves since they first appeared in the world of Siala.

Avendoom - the capital of the northern kingdom of Valiostr. The largest and richest city of the Northern Lands.

battery sword - a variety of sword with a midsized blade that can be wielded either with one hand or both.

Beaver Caps, or Beavers - soldiers of Valiostr, armed with heavy two-handed swords. Each soldier bears the title of "Master of the Long Sword" and wears a beaver-fur cap as an emblem to distinguish him from the soldiers of other units. These forces are used as a reserve striking force, to recover all kinds of difficult situations in battle. During military action the Beavers are also accorded the honor of guarding the banner and the king, taking the place of the royal guard.

bidenhander - a two-handed sword with a blade that can be a yard and a half long. They usually are designed with a massive handle, a heavy counterweight that is usually round, and a broad crosspiece. Sometimes the armorers would add massive metal spurs to prevent the blade running right through the opponent.

Border Kingdom, or Borderland - the kingdom beside the northern outcrops of the Mountains of the Dwarves and the Forests of Zagraba.

Borg's link - named after a general of ancient times who invented the chain formation, in which every single soldier plays an indispensable part in repelling an attack.

brother and sister swords - the names of the two swords in the special school of swordsmanship that is widespread among the nobility of Garrak. During combat the weapons are held at different heights in relationship to each other. The "brother," a narrow, double-sided blade held in the right hand, is used both for slashing and for thrusting. The "sister," a shorter blade with no cutting edge, is only used for thrusting blows. The weapons are either carried behind the back or in a double scabbard.

Canian forge work - weapons made from the steel mined in the Steel Mines of Isilia. The steel is worked in the famous smithies of the kingdom's capital, Cania. Following special processing and forging it acquires a ruby color and a unique quality—on encountering steel of a different type it emits a melodic ringing sound like small bells, or a shriek of fury. For this reason Canian-forged steel is also known as Singing Steel, Shrieking Steel, or Ruby Blood.

Chapel of the Hands - the assembly of the supreme priests of Sagot.

Cold Sea - the northern sea of the Western Ocean. It washes the shores of Valiostr and the Desolate Lands.

Commission - the agreement that is concluded between a master thief and his client. The thief undertakes to supply the item required or, in case of failure, to return the client's pledge and a percentage of the total value of the deal. The client undertakes to make payment in full on receiving the article in which he is interested. A Commission can only be abrogated by the mutual consent of both parties.

Crayfish Dukedom - the only state in the Desolate Lands.

crayfish grip (coll.) - a grip from which it is impossible to escape. The expression derives from the common saying that the men of the Crayfish Dukedom have a strong grip, and once they take you prisoner, you will never get away alive.

crayfish sleigh - in the Crayfish Dukedom, men who had been executed were transported to their graves on sleighs. Hence the meaning of this phrase—if the crayfish sleigh has come for you, death is at the door.

Crest of the World - the highest mountain chain in Siala. It runs from north to south across almost the entire continent. The crest is very difficult to cross and the lands beyond it are almost entirely unexplored.

Defender of the Hands - one of the highest positions in the hierarchy of the priests of Sagot.

Desolate Lands - the forests, stretches of open tundra, and ice fields in the far north. They have been settled by beings of various kinds, several of which constantly attempt to gain entry to the Northern Lands of Siala, and only the unassailable Mountains of Despair, the Lonely Giant fortress, and the Wild Hearts hold back their invasion of the world of men. Ogres, giants, svens, h'varrs, winter orcs, and dozens of other races and varieties of creatures inhabit these vast territories. People also live here, savages and barbarians who are subjects of the Nameless One. In all the Desolate Lands there is only one human state, the Crayfish Dukedom on the Crayfish Claw peninsula.

In the far north of the Desolate Lands, beyond the Needles of Ice, lies the dwelling of the Nameless One, whom savages captured by the Wild Hearts' scouts mention only in reverential whispers.

Disputed Lands - the lands lying alongside the Forests of Zagraba, between Miranueh and Valiostr.

djanga - a rapid, rhythmical dance, very popular in Zagorie.

Djashla - the kingdom of the mountain people that lies alongside the Crest of the World.

Djok Imargo, or "Djok the bringer of winter" - the man who supposedly killed the prince of the House of the Black Rose. The Long Winter began as a result of this murder.

Doralissians - a race of goat-people who live in the Steppes of Ungava.

Doralissian horses - a type of horse bred in the Steppes of Ungava and valued throughout the Northern Lands for their beauty, speed, and stamina.

dralan - a commoner who has been granted a title by a duke; the title is not hereditary.

drokr - an elfin fabric that is proof against water and odors and does not burn in fire.

D'san-dor (orcish), **or the Slumbering Forest** - a forest that lies in the Desolate Lands, close to the spurs of the Mountains of Despair.

dwarves - the race of short beings living in the Mountains of the Dwarves. They are quite different from their near cousins, the gnomes. It is astonishing how their short, thick-fingered hands can create the most wonderful items, which are valued highly in every corner of Siala, whether they are weapons, tools, or works of art.

E.D. - the Era of Dreams, the final age of Siala. The events described in this book take place in the final year of the Era of Dreams. This age was preceded by the Era of Accomplishments (the age during which men appeared in Siala, about seven thousand years ago), the Gray Era (the age deemed to have begun with the appearance of orcs and elves in Siala), and the Dark Era (it is not known who, apart from ogres, lived in Siala in these distant times and what happened then).

elves - the second young race of Siala. The elves appeared almost immediately after their relatives, the orcs. After living in the Forests of Zagraba for several thousand years, the elves became divided into light and dark.

The light elves were dissatisfied with what they could achieve using shamanism and set about studying wizardry, basing their approach on the magic of men.

The dark elves, however, felt the light elves had betrayed the memory of their ancestors. They continued to make use of the primordial magic of their race, shamanism.

The names of all dark elfin women begin with *M* and the names of the men begin with *E*. If an elf is a member of the ruling family of the Dark House, then *ssa* is added to the name.

Empire - following the birth in the imperial family of twin boys, the Empire split into two states—the Near Lakeside Empire and the Far Lakeside

Empire. These two kingdoms are constantly warring with each other to unite the Empire under the power of one of the two dynasties that trace their descent from the twin brothers.

Eyes of Death - when dice are cast and they show two "ones."

Field of Sorna - the field on which the battle between the gnomes and the dwarves took place in 1100 E.D. Cannons and battle-mattocks clashed with poleaxes and swords. In this battle there were no victors.

Filand - a kingdom lying along the southern spurs of the Mountains of the Dwarves.

Forests of Zagraba - these evergreen forests cover an immense area. In some places beautiful, in others terrifying, they conceal within themselves a host of secrets and mysterious creatures. The Forests of Zagraba are home to dark elves, orcs, goblins, and dryads.

Garrak - a kingdom in the southern region of Siala's Northern Lands, powerful and thoroughly militarized. The Garrak nobility are regarded as extremely quick-tempered, dangerous, and unpredictable.

Garrak's "Dragon" - King Garrak's guard.

garrinch (gnomish, lit. "guardian of the chests") - a creature that lives in the Steppes of Ungava. A trained garrinch makes an excellent guard for stores of treasure.

giants - one of the races that live in the Desolate Lands.

gkhols - carrion-eating scavengers. These creatures are usually to be found on battlefields or in old graveyards. If their source of food fails for some reason, gkhols are capable of hibernating for several years.

gnomes - like their larger cousins, the dwarves, gnomes appeared in the world of Siala immediately after the orcs and elves. Both gnomes and dwarves settled in the Mountains of the Dwarves, burrowing deep into their heart. Gnomes are stunted, quarrelsome creatures with beards. In the Mountains of the Dwarves their position was that of younger brothers. Gnomes are poor craftsmen, and they have never been able to produce such beautiful and delicate wares as the dwarves. However, gnomes are magnificent at working with steel and mining ore and other riches of the earth. They are good builders and diggers.

After living in the Mountains of the Dwarves for several thousand years, the gnomes finally left their old home following a decisive falling-out with their relatives the dwarves.

The race of gnomes found itself a new haven in the Steel Mines of Isilia. For the right to live in the mines they pay the kingdom an annual tribute and also supply it with steel. The gnomes invented the printing press, and then discovered how to make gunpowder (the dwarves claim that the gnomes stole the secret from a dwarf who was on his way home from a journey beyond the Crest of the World). The fierce battle that broke out between the estranged relatives on the Field of Sorna (1100 E.D.) was inconclusive. Both sides returned home having suffered immense losses.

The gnomes jealously guard the secret of gunpowder and sell cannons.

They have no magic of their own, since their last magician was killed on the Field of Sorna, and the gnomes' books are hidden deep in the Mountains of the Dwarves, in a safe hiding place that they cannot reach because of their enmity with the dwarves.

goblins - small creatures who live in the very depths of the Forests of Zagraba. The shamanism of the goblins is regarded as the most powerful after that of the ogres, but it includes almost no common attack spells.

Gray Stones - the most terrible and impregnable prison fortress in Valiostr. In all the time that it has existed, no one has ever managed to escape.

Green Leaf - one of the dark elves' most terrible tortures, which they only use on orcs (the one exception being Djok Imargo). Almost nothing is known about it, but rumors speak of the infernal torment of the victim. The torture can continue for years without interruption.

Grok - 1) the legendary general of Valiostr who held back the army of the orcs at Avendoom until the dark elves arrived to help in the final year of the Quiet Times (640 E.D.). A statue in his honor was erected in one of the central squares of the city; 2) the younger twin brother of the general Grok, who bore the same name, i.e., the magician who was dubbed the Nameless One.

hand - an orcish military leader.

Heartless Chasseurs - units of the army of Valiostr. In times of peace they perform the functions of the police. They are employed in military actions, and also assist in suppressing revolts and conspiracies, and in capturing and exterminating dangerous gangs and individual criminals.

Hospital of the Ten Martyrs - the Avendoom municipal hospital, founded by order of Grok on the precise spot where a detachment of orcs that had broken through the defenses of the human army was halted by ten warriors from the Avendoom garrison (640 E.D.).

Hrad Spein (ogric), **or Palaces of Bone** - immense underground palaces and catacombs, where ogres, orcs, elves, and, later, men have all buried fallen warriors.

h'san'kor (orcish), **or fearsome flute** - a man-eating monster that lives in the Forests of Zagraba.

I'alyala Forests - these forests lie in the Northern Lands of Siala, beside the Crest of the World. The light elves moved here from the Forests of Zagraba following the schism between the elfin houses.

imperial dog - a type of guard dog bred in the Empire.

"Innocent as Djok the Winter-Bringer" – a common saying. Djok Imargo was the man accused of the murder of the prince of the House of the Black Rose. He was handed over to the elves, who executed him. After that, from 501 to 640 E.D., the dark elfin houses of Zagraba had no contacts with Valiostr. It subsequently emerged that Djok was innocent.

irilla (orcish), **or mist spider** - an emanation generated by the shamanism of the ogres. To this day no one knows for certain if it is an immaterial substance or a living creature.

Iselina (orcish), **or Black River** - this river starts in the Mountains of the Dwarves, runs through the eastern section of the Forests of Zagraba, crosses Valiostr, then forks into a left branch and a right branch, which both flow into the Eastern Ocean.

Isilia (orcish) - a kingdom bordering on Valiostr and Miranueh.

Isilian marble - is mined in the southern spurs of the Steel Mines. Walking across this stone generates a powerful echo. It is generally used for protection against thieves, or to prevent the approach of assassins, or even simply for its beauty, despite the unpleasant sounds that have to be tolerated.

Jolly Gallows-Birds - former convicts, criminals, and pirates who have been recruited to serve as soldiers. On joining the ranks of the army of Valiostr they are pardoned for all previous transgressions. They perform the military functions of marines.

k'lissang (orcish, lit. "ever faithful") - an elf who has sworn an oath of fealty and engaged himself as a bodyguard to an elf of a more noble line for nine years. If the ever-faithful elf is killed during his period of service, his entire family is accepted into the clan of the elf whom the k'lissang was protecting.

Kronk-a-Mor - the shamanism of the ogres.

Labyrinth - an ancient structure erected by the orcs, located in the Forests of Zagraba. The orcs release prisoners into the Labyrinth and place bets on which of the unfortunates will survive longest.

languages of Siala - there are three main groups of languages in Siala. The first group is the orcish languages, spoken by orcs and elves. The second group is the gnomish languages, spoken by gnomes and dwarves. The third group includes all the human languages. There are also other languages and dialects, for instance, the languages of the ogres and goblins.

"Like looking for a smoking dwarf" - Dwarves do not smoke and they regard smokers with a certain degree of disdain, since the first beings to take up smoking were the gnomes. Following the gnomes, men also became addicted to the habit.

ling - a small animal that lives in the tundra of the Desolate Lands. Very like a shaggy-haired rat, but with much larger teeth and claws.

Lonely Giant - the fortress that closes off the only pass leading from the Desolate Lands through the Mountains of Despair to Valiostr.

Long Winter - the name given by the elves to a period of 140 years from 500 to 640 E.D. The Long Winter set in following the grotesque death of the elfin prince of the House of the Black Rose in Ranneng during festivities in the town. It came to an end in the final year of the Quiet Times (640 E.D.), during the Spring War, when the elves came to the aid of Grok and his men in the battle against the army of the orcs. Grok was presented with the Rainbow Horn to confirm that the Long Winter was over.

Lowland - the kingdom lying beside the I'alyala Forests.

Lowland masters - master craftsmen from the Lowland, famous throughout Siala for the dishes and tableware they make from a special lilac-colored porcelain.

Market Square - a famous Avendoom square where theatrical performances constantly take place.

Master of the Long Sword - a title that is given to soldiers who have completely mastered the three techniques for using the two-handed sword (classical grip, single-fang grip, staff grip). The hilt of the sword is decorated with an embossed gold image of an oak leaf.

mattockmen - a name sometimes used for the gnomes. Their favorite weapon is the so-called battle-mattock, which combines a large cutting blade with a war hammer.

Mirangrad - the capital of Miranueh, a kingdom located beside Valiostr.

Miranueh - a kingdom bordering on Garrak, Isilia, and Valiostr. Constantly at war with Valiostr over the Disputed Lands.

Mountains of Despair - the low but unassailable mountains that separate Valiostr from the Desolate Lands. There is only one pass through them, and the Lonely Giant fortress is located on it.

Mountains of the Dwarves - an immense mountain chain, so high that only the Crest of the World compares with it. It runs from east to west through the Northern Lands, dividing them in two. Zam-da-Mort, or the Castle of Death, is the tallest and most majestic peak in the Mountains of the Dwarves.

Nameless One - the title given to a Valiostran magician after he committed treason in the final year of the Quiet Times (640 E.D.).

Needles of Ice - icebound mountains far away in the Desolate Lands.

obur - a gigantic bear from the Forests of Zagraba.

ogres - a race from the Desolate Lands. The only old race of Siala still remaining in this world. From the very beginning the ogres were granted a very powerful and destructive magic, the Kronk-a-Mor. They are regarded as distant relatives of the orcs and elves. The elves say the gods took away the ogres' intelligence. If the ogres had remained as clever as they once were, they would have captured and destroyed the entire world of Siala.

Ol's Diggings - stone quarries lying at a distance of six days' journey from Avendoom. They were named after their first owner. The stone for the city's legendary walls was quarried here. Nowadays, Ol's Diggings are abandoned.

orcs - the first new race of Siala. The elves regard them as their archenemies, although they are directly related to each other. The orcs say that they were here first and should rule the entire world, and all the other races are an unfortunate mistake made by the gods. In addition to the Forests of Zagraba, orcs also live in the Desolate Lands (the winter orcs).

Order of Magicians - there is an Order in every kingdom, the only exceptions being Zagorie and Djashla. Each Order has a council of archmagicians and is headed by a Master. Within the Order there is a strict division according to rank, and ranks are marked on the magicians' staffs: magician of the Order—one ring; elemental magician (master of the specific skills of several schools)—two rings; magician with right of access to the council—three rings; archmagician—four rings; master—four rings and a small black figure of a raven on the top of the staff.

Purple Years - a period of time during which the dwarves and the gnomes waged a series of bloody wars against each other, and as a result the gnomes withdrew from the Mountains of the Dwarves.

Quiet Times - the period from 423 E.D. to 640 E.D., during which Valiostr did not wage a single war. These were times of prosperity when the kingdom flourished. They came to an end when an immense army of orcs from the Forests of Zagraba invaded Valiostr.

Rainbow Horn - a legendary artifact created by the ogres to counterbalance their own magic, the Kronk-a-Mor, if it should ever get out of control. The Horn was captured by the dark elves, who later gave it to men (in the person of Grok) as a token of their good intentions and the conclusion of an eternal alliance between the dark elves and Valiostr. Every two or three hundred years the Horn has to be saturated with magic in order not to lose its powers. Following the creation of the Secret Territory, the Horn was buried with Grok in Hrad Spein. It is the Horn's magic that keeps the Nameless One in the Desolate Lands.

River of the Crystal Dream - a narrow little river in Avendoom. It runs through the Port City and falls into the Cold Sea.

Royal Guard of Valiostr - the king's personal guard. Only nobles are recruited to serve in it. The guardsmen wear the king's colors of gray and blue. The guard is commanded by a captain.

Royal Sandmen - the king's secret police, who defend the interests of the state and the sovereign. Their nickname is derived from their emblem, an hourglass.

Sagot - one of the twelve deities of the world of Siala. Patron of thieves, swindlers, rogues, and spies.

Sagra - one the twelve deities of the world of Siala. Goddess of war, justice, and death, and also patroness of soldiers.

Secret (Forbidden) Territory, or "the Stain" - a district of Avendoom created as the result of an attempt to use the Rainbow Horn to neutralize

Kronk-a-Mor in 872 E.D. The Secret Territory is surrounded by a magical wall, through which almost no one dares to pass. Evil is said to dwell there.

shamanism - the primordial magic of Siala. It was first used by the ogres, then the orcs, the dark elves, and the goblins. The magic of men and the light elves is derived from shamanism.

Shamar - the capital of the Border Kingdom.

Siala - the world in which the events of this book take place.

Silna - the goddess of love, beauty, and nature.

s'kash (orcish) - a sword with curved blade. It is sharpened on its inner, concave edge and usually has teeth like a saw.

sklot (gnomic), or "corkscrew" - a heavy military crossbow designed to puncture the heavy armor of warriors walking the front ranks of an army.

Spring War - the war that began in the final year of the Quiet Times (640 E.D.). Men and dark elves fought on one side, and the orcs of Zagraba on the other. The War of Shame is the name that orcs use for the Spring War.

Stalkons - the royal dynasty of Valiostr.

Steel Brows - the heavy infantry of the Wild Hearts.

Steel Mines - the mountains and mines in Isilia that produce the finest steel in the Northern Lands. The race of gnomes lives here.

Steppes of Ungava - the steppes on the very southern edge of the Northern Lands.

S'u-dar (ogric), or the Icy Pass - the only route through the Needles of Ice from the Desolate Lands to the citadel of the Nameless One.

Sultanate - a state located far beyond the Steppes of Ungava.

svens, or chanters - creatures of the Desolate Lands that resemble shaggy flying spheres. When the freezing conditions in the open expanses of the Desolate Lands are at their fiercest they appear, chanting a song that kills all living things.

Thorns - the soldiers of this detachment carry out reconnaissance work and raids deep into the territory of the Desolate Lands. The Thorns have a reputation as daredevils and swashbuckling desperadoes.

tresh (orcish) - a polite term of address used by elves to an elf of noble birth. Sometimes used by other races when addressing highborn elves.

vampire - a creature of legend. Even today it is still not known if it exists in reality or only in the tales told by drunken peasants. According to the legend, only human beings and dark elves can become vampires. Vampires are credited with magical powers, such as the ability to transform themselves into a bat or mist. The Order of Magicians regards the existence of vampires as doubtful.

Vastar's Bargain - in 223 E.D. Vastar, the king of Garrak, concluded an alliance with a dragon so that the creature would assist him in attacking neighboring kingdoms. The agreement, however, proved worthless to the king: The dragon failed to engage the humans in battle and Vastar's army was routed. The term "a Vastar's bargain" signifies any similarly disadvantageous agreement.

Wild Hearts - the detachment of soldiers who serve at the Lonely Giant.

Wind Jugglers - the name given in the army to experienced bowmen, no matter to what detachment they belonged. Even when there was a strong wind interfering with the flight of the arrow, the "jugglers" almost always hit their mark.

wizardry - a higher magic possessed by the magicians of men and the light elves, based on the earlier magic, or shamanism, of the orcs and dark elves.

Zagorie, or the Free Lands - the lands beside the southern spurs of the Mountains of the Dwarves. All who are discontented with the rule of the authorities or the laws of the kingdom flee here—peasants, younger sons, courtiers in disgrace, adventurers, and criminals. Such people can always find land and work in the Free Lands.

Zam-da-Mort (gnomish), **or the Castle of Death** - the highest and most majestic peak of the Mountains of the Dwarves.